THE INHERITANCE GAMES

JENNIFER LYNN BARNES

Little, Brov
New Y

This book is a work of fiction. Names, characters, places, and incidents are the product of the author's imagination or are used fictitiously. Any resemblance to actual events, locales, or persons, living or dead, is coincidental.

Little, Brown and Company
Hachette Book Group
1290 Avenue of the Americas, New York, NY 10104
Visit us at LBYR.com

Originally published in hardcover and ebook by
Little, Brown and Company in September 2020
First Trade Paperback Edition: July 2021

Little, Brown and Company is a division of Hachette Book Group, Inc.
The Little, Brown name and logo are trademarks of Hachette Book Group, Inc.

The publisher is not responsible for websites (or their content) that are not owned by the publisher.

The Library of Congress has cataloged the hardcover edition as follows:
Names: Barnes, Jennifer (Jennifer Lynn), author.
Title: The inheritance games / Jennifer Lynn Barnes.
Description: First edition. | New York: Little, Brown and Company, 2020. | Audience: Ages 12+ | Summary: "When a teen inherits vast wealth and an eccentric estate from the richest man in Texas, she must also live with his surviving family—a family hellbent on discovering just how she earned her inheritance" —Provided by publisher.
Identifiers: LCCN 2019054648 | ISBN 9781368052405 (hardcover) | ISBN 9781368053242 (ebook)
Subjects: CYAC: Inheritance and succession—Fiction. | Wealth—Fiction. | Puzzles—Fiction.
Classification: LCC PZ7.B26225 In 2020 | DDC [Fic]—dc23
LC record available at https://lccn.loc.gov/2019054648

ISBNs: 978-0-7595-5540-2 (pbk.), 978-1-368-05324-2 (ebook)

Printed in the United States of America

LSC-C

Printing 14, 2022

PRAISE FOR

THE INHERITANCE GAMES

A *New York Times* and IndieBound Bestseller
A Goodreads Choice Awards Finalist
An Edgar Award Nominee for Best Young Adult Mystery
A *Kirkus Reviews* Best Young Adult Book of the Year
A *Publishers Weekly* Best Book of the Year
A New York Public Library Best Book for Teens
A YALSA Best Fiction for Young Adults Book
A YALSA Quick Pick for Reluctant Young Adult Readers

"Barnes is a master of puzzles and plot twists. *The Inheritance Games* was the most fun I've had all year." —E. Lockhart, #1 *New York Times* bestselling author of *We Were Liars* and *Again Again*

"A thrilling blend of family secrets, illicit romance, and a high-stakes treasure hunt, set in the mysterious world of Texas billionaires. The nonstop twists kept me guessing until the very last page!" —Katharine McGee, *New York Times* bestselling author of *American Royals*

"Impossible to put down." —Buzzfeed

★ "Part *The Westing Game*, part *We Were Liars*, completely entertaining." —*Kirkus Reviews*, starred review

★ "This strong, *Knives Out*–esque series opener…provides ample enjoyment." —*Publishers Weekly*, starred review

"Perfect for any reader seeking suspense, romance, and glamour…. Fun and fast-paced, fans of Karen M. McManus's *One of Us Is Lying* and Maureen Johnson's *Truly Devious* will find a new home at Hawthorne House." —*SLJ*

"[A] well-characterized mystery that's packed to the brim with twists and tricks." —*Booklist*

ALSO BY JENNIFER LYNN BARNES

THE INHERITANCE GAMES

The Inheritance Games

The Hawthorne Legacy

THE NATURALS

The Naturals

Killer Instinct

All In

Bad Blood

Twelve: An E-novella

THE DEBUTANTES

Little White Lies

Deadly Little Scandals

The Lovely and the Lost

For Samuel

CHAPTER 1

When I was a kid, my mom constantly invented games. The Quiet Game. The Who Can Make Their Cookie Last Longer? Game. A perennial favorite, The Marshmallow Game involved eating marshmallows while wearing puffy Goodwill jackets indoors, to avoid turning on the heat. The Flashlight Game was what we played when the electricity went out. We never walked anywhere—we raced. The floor was nearly always lava. The primary purpose of pillows was building forts.

Our longest-lasting game was called I Have A Secret, because my mom said that everyone should always have at least one. Some days she guessed mine. Some days she didn't. We played every week, right up until I was fifteen and one of her secrets landed her in the hospital.

The next thing I knew, she was gone.

"Your move, princess." A gravelly voice dragged me back to the present. "I don't have all day."

"Not a princess," I retorted, sliding one of my knights into place. "Your move, *old man*."

Harry scowled at me. I didn't know how old he was, really, and

I had no idea how he'd come to be homeless and living in the park where we played chess each morning. I did know that he was a formidable opponent.

"You," he grumbled, eyeing the board, "are a horrible person."

Three moves later, I had him. "Checkmate. You know what that means, Harry."

He gave me a dirty look. "I have to let you buy me breakfast." Those were the terms of our long-standing bet. When I won, he couldn't turn down the free meal.

To my credit, I only gloated a little. "It's good to be queen."

I made it to school on time but barely. I had a habit of cutting things close. I walked the same tightrope with my grades: How little effort could I put in and still get an A? I wasn't lazy. I was practical. Picking up an extra shift was worth trading a 98 for a 92.

I was in the middle of drafting an English paper in Spanish class when I was called to the office. Girls like me were supposed to be invisible. We didn't get summoned for sit-downs with the principal. We made exactly as much trouble as we could afford to make, which in my case was none.

"Avery." Principal Altman's greeting was not what one would call warm. "Have a seat."

I sat.

He folded his hands on the desk between us. "I assume you know why you're here."

Unless this was about the weekly poker game I'd been running in the parking lot to finance Harry's breakfasts—and sometimes my own—I had no idea what I'd done to draw the administration's attention. "Sorry," I said, trying to sound sufficiently meek, "but I don't."

Principal Altman let me sit with my response for a moment,

then presented me with a stapled packet of paper. "This is the physics test you took yesterday."

"Okay," I said. That wasn't the response he was looking for, but it was all I had. For once, I'd actually studied. I couldn't imagine I'd done badly enough to merit intervention.

"Mr. Yates graded the tests, Avery. Yours was the only perfect score."

"Great," I said, in a deliberate effort to keep myself from saying *okay* again.

"Not great, young lady. Mr. Yates intentionally creates exams that challenge the abilities of his students. In twenty years, he's never given a perfect score. Do you see the problem?"

I couldn't quite bite back my instinctive reply. "A teacher who designs tests most of his students can't pass?"

Mr. Altman narrowed his eyes. "You're a good student, Avery. Quite good, given your circumstances. But you don't exactly have a history of setting the curve."

That was fair, so why did I feel like he'd gut-punched me?

"I am not without sympathy for your situation," Principal Altman continued, "but I need you to be straight with me here." He locked his eyes onto mine. "Were you aware that Mr. Yates keeps copies of all his exams on the cloud?" He thought I'd cheated. He was sitting there, staring me down, and I'd never felt less seen. "I'd like to help you, Avery. You've done extremely well, given the hand life has dealt you. I would hate to see any plans you might have for the future derailed."

"Any plans I *might* have?" I repeated. If I'd had a different last name, if I'd had a dad who was a dentist and a mom who stayed home, he wouldn't have acted like the future was something I *might* have thought about. "I'm a junior," I gritted out. "I'll graduate next year with at least two semesters' worth of college credit. My test scores should put me in scholarship contention at UConn, which has one of the top actuarial science programs in the country."

Mr. Altman frowned. "Actuarial science?"

"Statistical risk assessment." It was the closest I could come to double-majoring in poker and math. Besides, it was one of the most employable majors on the planet.

"Are you a fan of calculated risks, Ms. Grambs?"

Like cheating? I couldn't let myself get any angrier. Instead, I pictured myself playing chess. I marked out the moves in my mind. Girls like me didn't get to explode. "I didn't cheat." I said calmly. "I studied."

I'd scraped together time—in other classes, between shifts, later at night than I should have stayed up. Knowing that Mr. Yates was infamous for giving impossible tests had made me want to redefine *possible*. For once, instead of seeing how close I could cut it, I'd wanted to see how far I could go.

And *this* was what I got for my effort, because girls like me didn't ace impossible exams.

"I'll take the test again," I said, trying not to sound furious, or worse, wounded. "I'll get the same grade again."

"And what would you say if I told you that Mr. Yates had prepared a new exam? All new questions, every bit as difficult as the first."

I didn't even hesitate. "I'll take it."

"That can be arranged tomorrow during third period, but I have to warn you that this will go significantly better for you if—"

"*Now.*"

Mr. Altman stared at me. "Excuse me?"

Forget sounding meek. Forget being invisible. "I want to take the new exam right here, in your office, right now."

CHAPTER 2

Rough day?" Libby asked. My sister was seven years older than me and way too empathetic for her own good—or mine.

"I'm fine," I replied. Recounting my trip to Altman's office would only have worried her, and until Mr. Yates graded my second test there was nothing anyone could do. I changed the subject. "Tips were good tonight."

"How good?" Libby's sense of style resided somewhere between punk and goth, but personality-wise, she was the kind of eternal optimist who believed a hundred-dollar-tip was always just around the corner at a hole-in-the-wall diner where most entrees cost $6.99.

I pressed a wad of crumpled singles into her hand. "Good enough to help make rent."

Libby tried to hand the money back, but I moved out of reach before she could. "I will throw this cash at you," she warned sternly.

I shrugged. "I'd dodge."

"You're impossible." Libby grudgingly put the money away, produced a muffin tin out of nowhere, and fixed me with a look. "You *will* accept this muffin to make it up to me."

"Yes, ma'am." I went to take it from her outstretched hand, but then I looked past her to the counter and realized she'd baked more than muffins. There were also cupcakes. I felt my stomach plummet. "Oh no, Lib."

"It's not what you think," Libby promised. She was an apology cupcake baker. A guilty cupcake baker. A please-don't-be-mad-at-me cupcake baker.

"Not what I think?" I repeated softly. "So he's not moving back in?"

"It's going to be different this time," Libby promised. "And the cupcakes are chocolate!"

My favorite.

"It's never going to be different," I said, but if I'd been capable of making her believe that, she'd have believed it already.

Right on cue, Libby's on-again, off-again boyfriend—who had a fondness for punching walls and extolling his own virtues for not punching Libby—strolled in. He snagged a cupcake off the counter and let his gaze rake over me. "Hey, jailbait."

"Drake," Libby said.

"I'm kidding." Drake smiled. "You know I'm kidding, Libby-mine. You and your sister just need to learn how to take a joke."

One minute in, and he was already making us the problem. "This is not healthy," I told Libby. He hadn't wanted her to take me in—and he'd never stopped punishing her for it.

"This is not your apartment," Drake shot back.

"Avery's my sister," Libby insisted.

"Half sister," Drake corrected, and then he smiled again. "Joking."

He wasn't, but he also wasn't wrong. Libby and I shared an absent father, but had different moms. We'd only seen each other once or twice a year growing up. No one had expected her to take custody of me two years earlier. She was young. She was barely scraping by. But she was *Libby*. Loving people was what she did.

"If Drake's staying here," I told her quietly, "then I'm not."

Libby picked up a cupcake and cradled it in her hands. "I'm doing the best I can, Avery."

She was a people pleaser. Drake liked putting her in the middle. He used me to hurt her.

I couldn't just wait around for the day he stopped punching *walls*.

"If you need me," I told Libby, "I'll be living in my car."

CHAPTER 3

My ancient Pontiac was a piece of junk, but at least the heater worked. Mostly. I parked at the diner, around the back, where no one would see me. Libby texted, but I couldn't bring myself to text back, so I ended up just staring at my phone instead. The screen was cracked. My data plan was practically nonexistent, so I couldn't go online, but I did have unlimited texts.

Besides Libby, there was exactly one person in my life worth texting. I kept my message to Max short and sweet: *You-know-who is back.*

There was no immediate response. Max's parents were big on "phone-free" time and confiscated hers frequently. They were also infamous for intermittently monitoring her messages, which was why I hadn't named Drake and wouldn't type a word about where I was spending the night. Neither the Liu family nor my social worker needed to know that I wasn't where I was supposed to be.

Setting my phone down, I glanced at my backpack in the passenger seat, but decided that the rest of my homework could wait for morning. I laid my seat back and closed my eyes but couldn't sleep, so I reached into the glove box and retrieved the only thing of value that my mother had left me: a stack of postcards. Dozens of them. Dozens of places we'd planned to go together.

Hawaii. New Zealand. Machu Picchu. Staring at each of the pictures in turn, I imagined myself anywhere but here. Tokyo. Bali. Greece. I wasn't sure how long I'd been lost in thought when my phone beeped. I picked it up and was greeted by Max's response to my message about Drake.

That mother-faxer. And then, a moment later: *Are you okay?*

Max had moved away the summer after eighth grade. Most of our communication was written, and she refused to write curse words, lest her parents see them.

So she got creative.

I'm fine, I wrote back, and that was all the impetus she needed to unleash her righteous fury on my behalf.

THAT FAXING CHIPHEAD CAN GO STRAIGHT TO ELF AND EAT A BAG OF DUCKS!!!

A second later, my phone rang. "Are you really okay?" Max asked when I answered.

I looked back down at the postcards in my lap, and the muscles in my throat tightened. I would make it through high school. I'd apply for every scholarship I qualified for. I'd get a marketable degree that allowed me to work remotely and paid me well.

I'd travel the world.

I let out a long, jagged breath, and then answered Max's question. "You know me, Maxine. I always land on my feet."

CHAPTER 4

The next day, I paid a price for sleeping in my car. My whole body ached, and I had to shower after gym, because paper towels in the bathroom at the diner could only go so far. I didn't have time to dry my hair, so I arrived at my next class sopping wet. It wasn't my best look, but I'd gone to school with the same kids my whole life. I was wallpaper.

No one was looking.

"*Romeo and Juliet* is littered with proverbs—small, pithy bits of wisdom that make a statement about the way the world and human nature work." My English teacher was young and earnest, and I deeply suspected she'd had too much coffee. "Let's take a step back from Shakespeare. Who can give me an example of an everyday proverb?"

Beggars can't be choosers, I thought, my head pounding and water droplets dripping down my back. *Necessity is the mother of invention. If wishes were horses, beggars would ride.*

The door to the classroom opened. An office aide waited for the teacher to look at her, then announced loudly enough for the whole class to hear, "Avery Grambs is wanted in the office."

I took that to mean that someone had graded my test.

I knew better than to expect an apology, but I also wasn't expecting Mr. Altman to meet me at his secretary's desk, beaming like he'd just had a visit from the Pope. "Avery!"

An alarm went off in the back of my head, because no one was ever that glad to see me.

"Right this way." He opened the door to his office, and I caught sight of a familiar neon-blue ponytail inside.

"Libby?" I said. She was wearing skull-print scrubs and no makeup, both of which suggested she'd come straight from work. In the middle of a shift. Orderlies at assisted living facilities couldn't just walk out in the middle of shifts.

Not unless something was wrong.

"Is Dad…" I couldn't make myself finish the question.

"Your father is fine." The voice that issued that statement didn't belong to Libby or Principal Altman. My head whipped up, and I looked past my sister. The chair behind the principal's desk was occupied—by a guy not much older than me. *What is going on here?*

He was wearing a suit. He looked like the kind of person who should have had an entourage.

"As of yesterday," he continued, his low, rich voice measured and precise, "Ricky Grambs was alive, well, and safely passed out in a motel room in Michigan, an hour outside of Detroit."

I tried not to stare at him—and failed. *Light hair. Pale eyes. Features sharp enough to cut rocks.*

"How could you possibly know that?" I demanded. *I* didn't even know where my deadbeat father was. How could he?

The boy in the suit didn't answer my question. Instead, he

arched an eyebrow. "Principal Altman?" he said. "If you could give us a moment?"

The principal opened his mouth, presumably to object to being removed from his own office, but the boy's eyebrow lifted higher.

"I believe we had an agreement."

Altman cleared his throat. "Of course." And just like that, he turned and walked out the door. It closed behind him, and I resumed openly staring at the boy who'd banished him.

"You asked how I know where you father is." His eyes were the same color as his suit—gray, bordering on silver. "It would be best, for the moment, for you to just assume that I know everything."

His voice would have been pleasant to listen to if it weren't for the words. "A guy who thinks he knows everything," I muttered. "That's new."

"A girl with a razor-sharp tongue," he returned, silver eyes focused on mine, the ends of his lips ticking upward.

"Who are you?" I asked. "And what do you want?" *With me*, something inside me added. *What do you want with me?*

"All I want," he said, "is to deliver a message." For reasons I couldn't quite pinpoint, my heart started beating faster. "One that has proven rather difficult to send via traditional means."

"That might be my fault," Libby volunteered sheepishly beside me.

"What might be your fault?" I turned to look at her, grateful for an excuse to look away from Gray Eyes and fighting the urge to glance back.

"The first thing you need to know," Libby said, as earnestly as anyone wearing skull-print scrubs had ever said anything, "is that I had *no* idea the letters were real."

"What letters?" I asked. I was the only person in this room who didn't know what was going on here, and I couldn't shake the feeling that not knowing was a liability, like standing on train tracks but not knowing which direction the train was coming from.

"The letters," the boy in the suit said, his voice wrapping around me, "that my grandfather's attorneys have been sending, certified mail, to your residence for the better part of three weeks."

"I thought they were a scam," Libby told me.

"I assure you," the boy replied silkily, "they are not."

I knew better than to put any confidence in the assurances of good-looking guys.

"Let me start again." He folded his hands on the desk between us, the thumb of his right hand lightly circling the cuff link on his left wrist. "My name is Grayson Hawthorne. I'm here on behalf of McNamara, Ortega, and Jones, a Dallas-based law firm representing my grandfather's estate." Grayson's pale eyes met mine. "My grandfather passed away earlier this month." A weighty pause. "His name was Tobias Hawthorne." Grayson studied my reaction—or, more accurately, the lack thereof. "Does that name mean anything to you?"

The sensation of standing on train tracks was back. "No," I said. "Should it?"

"My grandfather was a very wealthy man, Ms. Grambs. And it appears that, along with our family and people who worked for him for years, you have been named in his will."

I heard the words but couldn't process them. "His *what*?"

"His will," Grayson repeated, a slight smile crossing his lips. "I don't know what he left you, exactly, but your presence is required at the will's reading. We've been postponing it for weeks."

I was an intelligent person, but Grayson Hawthorne might as well have been speaking Swedish.

"Why would your grandfather leave anything to me?" I asked.

Grayson stood. "That's the question of the hour, isn't it?" He stepped out from behind the desk, and suddenly I knew *exactly* what direction the train was coming from.

His.

"I've taken the liberty of making travel arrangements on your behalf."

This wasn't an invitation. It was a *summons*. "What makes you think—" I started to say, but Libby cut me off. "Great!" she said, giving me a healthy side-eye.

Grayson smirked. "I'll give you two a moment." His eyes lingered on mine too long for comfort, and then, without another word, he strode out the door.

Libby and I were silent for a full five seconds after he was gone. "Don't take this the wrong way," she whispered finally, "but I think he might be God."

I snorted. "He certainly thinks so." It was easier to ignore the effect he'd had on me now that he was gone. What kind of person had self-assurance that absolute? It was there in every aspect of his posture and word choice, in every interaction. Power was as much a fact of life for this guy as gravity. The world bent to the will of Grayson Hawthorne. What money couldn't buy him, those eyes probably did.

"Start from the beginning," I told Libby. "And don't leave anything out."

She fidgeted with the inky-black tips of her blue ponytail. "A couple of weeks ago, we started getting these letters—addressed to you, care of me. They said that you'd inherited money, gave us a number to call. I thought they were a scam. Like one of those emails that claims to be from a foreign prince."

"Why would this Tobias Hawthorne—a man I've never met, never even heard of—put me in his will?" I asked.

"I don't know," Libby said, "but *that*"—she gestured in the direction Grayson had gone—"is not a scam. Did you *see* the way he dealt with Principal Altman? What do you think their agreement was? A bribe... or a threat?"

Both. Pushing down that response, I pulled out my phone and connected to the school's Wi-Fi. One internet search for Tobias Hawthorne later, the two of us were reading a news headline: *Noted Philanthropist Dies at 78.*

"Do you know what *philanthropist* means?" Libby asked me seriously. "It means *rich.*"

"It means someone who gives to charity," I corrected her.

"So... *rich.*" Libby gave me a look. "What if *you* are charity? They wouldn't send this guy's grandson to get you if he'd just left you a few hundred dollars. We must be talking thousands. You could travel, Avery, or put it toward college, or buy a better car."

I could feel my heart starting to beat faster again. "Why would a total stranger leave me anything?" I reiterated, resisting the urge to daydream, even for a second, because if I started, I wasn't sure I could stop.

"Maybe he knew your mom?" Libby suggested. "I don't know, but I do know that you need to go to the reading of that will."

"I can't just take off," I told her. "Neither can you." We'd both miss work. I'd miss class. And yet... if nothing else, a trip would get Libby away from Drake, at least temporarily.

And if this is real... It was already getting harder *not* to think about the possibilities.

"My shifts are covered for the next two days," Libby informed me. "I made some calls, and so are yours." She reached for my hand. "Come on, Ave. Wouldn't it be nice to take a trip, just you and me?"

She squeezed my hand. After a moment, I squeezed back. "Where exactly is the reading of the will?"

"Texas!" Libby grinned. "And they didn't just book our tickets. They booked them *first class*."

CHAPTER 5

I'd never flown before. Looking down from ten thousand feet, I could imagine myself going farther than Texas. Paris. Bali. Machu Picchu. Those had always been *someday* dreams.

But now…

Beside me, Libby was in heaven, sipping on a complimentary cocktail. "Picture time," she declared. "Smoosh in and hold up your warm nuts."

On the other side of the aisle, a lady shot Libby a disapproving look. I wasn't sure whether the target of her disapproval was Libby's hair, the camo-print jacket she'd changed into when she'd ditched her scrubs, her metal-studded choker, the selfie she was attempting to take, or the volume with which she'd just said the phrase *warm nuts*.

Adopting my haughtiest look, I leaned toward my sister and raised my warm nuts high.

Libby laid her head on my shoulder and snapped the pic. She turned the phone to show me. "I'll send it to you when we land." The smile on her face wavered, just for a second. "Don't put it online, okay?"

Drake doesn't know where you are, does he? I bit back the

urge to remind her that she was allowed to have a life. I didn't want to argue. "I won't." That wasn't any big sacrifice on my part. I had social media accounts, but I mostly used them to DM Max.

And speaking of... I pulled my phone out. I'd put it in airplane mode, which meant no texting, but first class offered free Wi-Fi. I sent Max a quick update on what had happened, then spent the rest of the flight obsessively reading up on Tobias Hawthorne.

He'd made his money in oil, then diversified. I'd expected, based on the way Grayson had said his grandfather was a "wealthy" man and the newspaper's use of the word *philanthropist*, that he was some kind of millionaire.

I was wrong.

Tobias Hawthorne wasn't just "wealthy" or "well-off." There weren't any polite terms for what Tobias Hawthorne was, other than really insert-expletive-of-your-choice-here filthy rich. Billions, with a *b* and plural. He was the ninth-richest person in the United States and the richest man in the state of Texas.

Forty-six point two billion dollars. That was his net worth. As far as numbers went, it didn't even sound real. Eventually, I stopped wondering why a man I'd never met would have left me something—and started wondering how much.

Max messaged back right before landing: *Are you foxing with me, beach?*

I grinned. *No. I am legit on a plane to Texas right now. Getting ready to land.*

Max's only response was: *Holy ship.*

A dark-haired woman in an all-white power suit met Libby and me the second we stepped past security. "Ms. Grambs." She nodded to me, then to Libby, as she added on a second identical greeting. "Ms. Grambs." She turned, expecting us to follow. To my chagrin, we both did. "I'm Alisa Ortega," she said, "from McNamara, Ortega, and Jones." Another pause, then she cast a sideways glance at me. "You are a very hard young woman to get ahold of."

I shrugged. "I live in my car."

"She doesn't *live* there," Libby said quickly. "Tell her you don't."

"We're so glad you could make it." Alisa Ortega, from McNamara, Ortega, and Jones, didn't wait for me to tell her anything. I had the sense that my half of this conversation was perfunctory. "During your time in Texas, you're to consider yourselves guests of the Hawthorne family. I'll be your liaison to the firm. Anything you need while you're here, come to me."

Don't lawyers bill by the hour? I thought. How much was this personal pickup costing the Hawthorne family? I didn't even consider the option that this woman might not be a lawyer. She looked to be in her late twenties. Talking to her gave me the same feeling as talking to Grayson Hawthorne. She was *someone.*

"*Is* there anything I can do for you?" Alisa Ortega asked, striding toward an automatic door, her pace not slowing at all when it seemed like the door might not open in time.

I waited until I'd made sure she wasn't going to run smack into the glass before I replied. "How about some information?"

"You'll have to be a bit more specific."

"Do you know what's in the will?" I asked.

"I do not." She gestured to a black sedan idling near the curb. She opened the back door for me. I slid in, and Libby followed suit. Alisa sat in the front passenger seat. The driver's seat was already occupied. I tried to see the driver but couldn't make out much of his face.

"You'll find out what's in the will soon enough," Alisa said, the words as crisp and neat as that dare-the-devil-to-ruin-it white suit. "We all will. The reading is scheduled for shortly after your arrival at Hawthorne House."

Not *the Hawthornes' house.* Just *Hawthorne House,* like it was some kind of English manor, complete with a name.

"Is that where we'll be staying?" Libby asked. "Hawthorne House?"

Our return tickets had been booked for tomorrow. We'd packed for an overnight.

"You'll have your pick of bedrooms," Alisa assured us. "Mr. Hawthorne bought the land the House is built on more than fifty years ago and spent every one of those years adding onto the architectural marvel he built there. I've lost track of the total number of bedrooms, but it's upward of thirty. Hawthorne House is... quite something."

That was the most information we'd gotten out of her yet. I pressed my luck. "I'm guessing Mr. Hawthorne was *quite something,* too?"

"Good guess," Alisa said. She glanced back at me. "Mr. Hawthorne was fond of good guessers."

An eerie feeling washed over me then, almost like a premonition. *Is that why he chose me?*

"How well did you know him?" Libby asked beside me.

"My father has been Tobias Hawthorne's attorney since before I was born." Alisa Ortega wasn't power-talking now. Her voice was soft. "I spent a lot of time at Hawthorne House growing up."

He wasn't just a client to her, I thought. "Do you have any idea why I'm here?" I asked. "Why he'd leave me anything at all?"

"Are you the world-saving type?" Alisa asked, like that was a perfectly ordinary question.

"No?" I guessed.

"Ever had your life ruined by someone with the last name Hawthorne?" Alisa continued.

I stared at her, then managed to answer more confidently this time. "No."

Alisa smiled, but it didn't quite reach her eyes. "Lucky you."

CHAPTER 6

Hawthorne House sat on a hill. Massive. Sprawling. It looked like a castle—more suited to royalty than ranch country. There were a half dozen cars parked out front and one beat-up motorcycle that looked like it should be dismantled and sold for parts.

Alisa eyed the bike. "Looks like Nash made it home."

"Nash?" Libby asked.

"The oldest Hawthorne grandson," Alisa replied, tearing her gaze from the motorcycle and staring up at the castle. "There are four of them total."

Four grandsons. I couldn't keep my mind from going back to the one Hawthorne I'd already met. *Grayson.* The perfectly tailored suit. The silvery gray eyes. The arrogance in the way he'd told me to assume he knew everything.

Alisa gave me a knowing look. "Take it from someone who's both been there and done that—never lose your heart to a Hawthorne."

"Don't worry," I told her, as annoyed with her assumption as I was with the fact that she'd been able to see any trace of my thoughts on my face. "I keep mine under lock and key."

The foyer was bigger than some houses—easily a thousand square feet, like the person who had built it was afraid that the entryway might have to double as a place to host balls. Stone archways lined the foyer on either side, and the room stretched up two stories to an ornate ceiling, elaborately carved from wood. Even just looking up took my breath away.

"You've arrived." A familiar voice drew my attention back down to earth. "And right on time. I trust there were no problems with your flight?"

Grayson Hawthorne was wearing a different suit now. This one was black—and so were his shirt and his tie.

"You." Alisa greeted him with a steely-eyed look.

"I take it I'm not forgiven for interfering?" Grayson asked.

"You're nineteen," Alisa retorted. "Would it kill you to act like it?"

"It might." Grayson flashed his teeth in a smile. "And you're welcome." It took me a second to realize that by *interfering*, Grayson meant coming to fetch me. "Ladies," he said, "may I take your coats?"

"I'll keep mine," I replied, feeling contrary—and like an extra layer between me and the rest of the world couldn't hurt.

"And yours?" Grayson asked Libby smoothly.

Still agog at the foyer, Libby shed her coat and handed it to him. Grayson walked underneath one of the stone arches. On the other side, there was a corridor. Small square panels lined the wall. Grayson laid a hand on one panel and pushed. He turned his hand ninety degrees, pushed in the next panel, and then, in a motion too fast for me to decode, hit at least two others. I heard a *pop*, and a door appeared, separating itself from the rest of the wall as it swung open.

"What the..." I started to say.

Grayson reached in and pulled out a hanger. "Coat closet." That wasn't an explanation. It was a label, like this was any old coat closet in any old house.

Alisa took that as her cue to leave us in Grayson's capable hands, and I tried to summon up a response that wasn't just standing there with my mouth open like a fish. Grayson went to close the closet, but a sound from deep within stopped him.

I heard a *creak*, then a *bam*. There was a shuffling sound back behind the coats, and then a figure in shadow pushed through them and stepped out into the light. A boy, maybe my age, maybe a little younger. He was wearing a suit, but that was where the similarities with Grayson ended. This boy's suit was rumpled, like he'd taken a nap in it—or twenty. The jacket wasn't buttoned. The tie lying around his neck wasn't tied. He was tall but had a baby face—and a mop of dark, curly hair. His eyes were light brown and so was his skin.

"Am I late?" he asked Grayson.

"One might suggest that you direct that query toward your watch."

"Is Jameson here yet?" the dark-haired boy amended his question.

Grayson stiffened. "No."

The other boy grinned. "Then I'm not late!" He looked past Grayson, to Libby and me. "And these must be our guests! How rude of Grayson not to introduce us."

A muscle in Grayson's jaw twitched. "Avery Grambs," he said formally, "and her sister, Libby. Ladies, this is my brother, Alexander." For a moment, it seemed like Grayson might leave it there, but then came the eyebrow arch. "Xander is the baby of the family."

"I'm the handsome one," Xander corrected. "I know what you're thinking. This serious bugger beside me can really fill out an

Armani suit. But, I ask you, can he jolt the universe on and up to ten with his smile, like a young Mary Tyler Moore incarnate in the body of a multiracial James Dean?" Xander seemed to have only one mode of speaking: fast. "No," he answered his own question. "No, he cannot."

He finally stopped talking long enough for someone else to speak. "It's nice to meet you," Libby managed.

"Spend a lot of time in coat closets?" I asked.

Xander dusted his hands off on his pants. "Secret passage," he said, then attempted to dust off his pant legs with his hands. "This place is full of them."

CHAPTER 7

My fingers itched to pull out my phone and start taking pictures, but I resisted. Libby had no such compunctions.

"Mademoiselle..." Xander side-stepped to block one of Libby's shots. "May I ask: What are your feelings on roller coasters?"

I thought Libby's eyes might actually pop out of her head. "This place has a roller coaster?"

Xander grinned. "Not exactly." The next thing I knew, the "baby" of the Hawthorne family—who was six foot three if he was an inch—was pulling my sister toward the back of the foyer.

I was dumbfounded. *How can a house "not exactly" have a roller coaster?* Beside me, Grayson snorted. I caught him looking at me and narrowed my eyes. "What?"

"Nothing," Grayson said, the tilt of his lips suggesting otherwise. "It's just...you have a very expressive face."

No. I didn't. Libby was always saying that I was hard to read. My poker face had single-handedly been funding Harry's breakfasts for months. I wasn't expressive.

There was nothing remarkable about my face.

"I apologize for Xander," Grayson commented. "He tends not to buy into such antiquated notions as thinking before one speaks and sitting still for more than three consecutive seconds." He looked down. "He's the best of us, even on his worst days."

"Ms. Ortega said there were four of you." I couldn't help myself. I wanted to know more about this family. About *him*. "Four grandsons, I mean."

"I have three brothers," Grayson told me. "Same mother, different fathers. Our aunt Zara doesn't have any children." He looked past me. "And on the topic of my relations, I feel as though I should issue a second apology, in advance."

"Gray, darling!" A woman swept up to us in a swirl of fabric and motion. Once her flowy shirt had settled around her, I tried to peg her age. Older than thirty, younger than fifty. Beyond that, I couldn't tell. "They're ready for us in the Great Room," she told Grayson. "Or they will be shortly. Where's your brother?"

"Specificity, Mother."

The woman rolled her eyes. "Don't you 'Mother' me, Grayson Hawthorne." She turned to me. "You'd think he was born wearing that suit," she said with the air of someone confiding a great secret, "but Gray was my little streaker. A real free spirit. We couldn't keep clothes on him at all, really, until he was four. Frankly, I didn't even try." She paused and assessed me without bothering to hide what she was doing. "You must be Ava."

"Avery," Grayson corrected. If he felt any embarrassment about his purported past as a toddler nudist, he didn't show it. "Her name is Avery, Mother."

The woman sighed but also smiled, like it was impossible for her to look at her son and not find herself utterly delighted in his presence. "I always swore my children would call me by my first name," she told me. "I'd raise them as my equals, you know? But then, I always imagined having girls. Four boys later…" She gave the world's most elegant shrug.

Objectively, Grayson's mother was over the top. But subjectively? She was infectious.

"Do you mind if I ask, dear, when is your birthday?"

The question took me by surprise. I had a mouth. It was fully functioning. But I couldn't keep up with her enough to reply. She put a hand on my cheek. "Scorpio? Or Capricorn? Not a Pisces, clearly—"

"Mother," Grayson said, and then he corrected himself. "*Skye.*"

It took me a moment to realize that must be her first name, and that he'd used it to humor her in an attempt to get her to stop astrologically cross-examining me.

"Grayson's a good boy," Skye told me. "Too good." Then she winked at me. "We'll talk."

"I doubt Ms. Grambs plans to stay long enough for a fireside chat—or a tarot reading." A second woman, Skye's age or a little older, inserted herself into our conversation. If Skye was flowy fabric and oversharing, this woman was pencil-skirts and pearls.

"I'm Zara Hawthorne-Calligaris." She eyed me, the expression on her face as austere as her name. "Do you mind if I ask—how did you know my father?"

Silence descended on the cavernous foyer. I swallowed. "I didn't."

Beside me, I could feel Grayson staring again. After a small eternity, Zara offered me a tight smile. "Well, we appreciate your presence. It's been a trying time these past few weeks, as I'm sure you can imagine."

These past few weeks, I filled in, *when no one could get ahold of me.*

"Zara?" A man with slicked-back hair interrupted us, slipping an arm around her waist. "Mr. Ortega would like a word." The man, who I took to be Zara's husband, didn't spare so much as a glance for me.

Skye made up for it—and then some. "My sister 'has words' with people," she commented. "I have conversations. Lovely conversations. Quite frankly, that's how I ended up with four sons. Wonderful, *intimate* conversations with four fascinating men..."

"I will pay you to stop right there," Grayson said, a pained expression on his face.

Skye patted her son's cheek. "Bribe. Threaten. Buy out. You couldn't be more Hawthorne, darling, if you tried." She gave me a knowing smile. "That's why we call him the heir apparent."

There was something in Skye's voice, something about Grayson's expression when his mother said the phrase *heir apparent*, that made me think I had greatly underestimated just how much the Hawthorne family wanted that will read.

They don't know what's in the will, either. I suddenly felt like I'd stepped into an arena, utterly unaware of the rules of the game.

"Now," Skye said, looping one arm around me and one around Grayson, "why don't we make our way to the Great Room?"

CHAPTER 8

The Great Room was two-thirds the size of the foyer. An enormous stone fireplace stood at the front. There were gargoyles carved into the sides of the fireplace. Literal gargoyles.

Grayson deposited Libby and me into wingback chairs and then excused himself to the front of the room, where three older gentlemen in suits stood, talking to Zara and her husband.

The lawyers, I realized. After another few minutes, Alisa joined them, and I took stock of the other occupants of the room. A White couple, older, in their sixties at least. A Black man, forties, with a military bearing, who stood with his back to a wall and maintained a clear line of sight to both exits. Xander, with what was clearly another Hawthorne brother by his side. This one was older—midtwenties. He needed a haircut and had paired his suit with cowboy boots that, like the motorcycle outside, had seen better days.

Nash, I thought, recalling the name that Alisa had provided.

Finally, an ancient woman joined the fray. Nash offered her an arm, but she took Xander's instead. He led her straight to Libby and me. "This is Nan," he told us. "The woman. The legend."

"Get on with you." She swatted his arm. "I'm this rascal's great-grandmother." Nan settled, with no small difficulty, into the open seat beside me. "Older than dirt and twice as mean."

"She's a softy," Xander assured me cheerfully. "And I'm her favorite."

"You are *not* my favorite," Nan grumbled.

"I'm everyone's favorite!" Xander grinned.

"Far too much like that incorrigible grandfather of yours," Nan grunted. She closed her eyes, and I saw her hands shake slightly. "Awful man." There was a tenderness there.

"Was Mr. Hawthorne your son?" Libby asked gently. She worked with the elderly, and she was a good listener.

Nan welcomed the opportunity to snort again. "Son-in-law."

"He was also her favorite," Xander clarified. There was something poignant in the way he said it. This wasn't a funeral. They must have laid the man to rest weeks earlier, but I knew grief, could feel it—could practically *smell* it.

"Are you all right, Ave?" Libby asked beside me. I thought back to Grayson telling me how expressive my face was.

Better to think about Grayson Hawthorne than funerals and grieving.

"I'm fine," I told Libby. But I wasn't. Even after two years, missing my mom could hit me like a tsunami. "I'm going to step outside," I said, forcing a smile. "I just need some air."

Zara's husband stopped me on my way out. "Where are you going? We're about to start." He locked a hand over my elbow.

I wrenched my arm out of his grasp. I didn't care who these people were. No one got to lay hands on me. "I was told there are four Hawthorne grandsons," I said, my voice steely. "By my count, you're still down by one. I'll be back in a minute. You won't even notice I'm gone."

I ended up in the backyard instead of the front—if you could even call it a yard. The grounds were immaculately kept. There was a fountain. A statue garden. A greenhouse. And stretching into the distance, as far as I could see, *land*. Some of it was treed. Some was open. But it was easy enough, standing there and looking out, to imagine that a person who walked off to the horizon might never make their way back.

"If *yes* is *no* and *once* is *never*, then how may sides does a triangle have?" The question came from above me. I looked up and saw a boy sitting on the edge of a balcony overhead, balanced precariously on a wrought-iron railing. *Drunk*.

"You're going to fall," I told him.

He smirked. "An interesting proposition."

"That wasn't a proposition," I said.

He offered me a lazy grin. "There's no shame in propositioning a Hawthorne." He had hair darker than Grayson's and lighter than Xander's. He wasn't wearing shirt.

Always a good decision in the middle of winter, I thought acerbically, but I couldn't keep my gaze from traveling downward from his face. His torso was lean, his stomach defined. He had a long, thin scar that ran from collarbone to hip.

"You must be Mystery Girl," he said.

"I'm Avery," I corrected. I'd come out here to get away from the Hawthornes and their grief. There wasn't a trace of a care on this boy's face, like life was one grand lark. Like he wasn't grieving just as much as the people inside were.

"Whatever you say, M.G.," he retorted. "Can I call you M.G., Mystery Girl?"

I crossed my arms. "No."

He brought his feet up to the railing and stood. He wobbled, and I had a moment of chilling prescience. *He's grieving, and he's too high up.* I hadn't allowed myself to self-destruct when my mom died. That didn't mean I hadn't felt the call.

He shifted his weight to one foot and held the other out.

"Don't!" Before I could say anything else, the boy twisted and grabbed the railing with his hands, holding himself vertical, feet in the air. I could see the muscles in his back tensing, rippling over his shoulder blades, as he lowered himself...and dropped.

He landed right beside me. "You shouldn't be out here, M.G."

I wasn't the shirtless one who'd just jumped off a balcony. "Neither should you."

I wondered if he could tell how fast my heart was beating. I wondered if his was racing at all.

"If I do what I should no more often than I say what I shouldn't"—his lips twisted—"then what does that make me?"

Jameson Hawthorne, I thought. Up close, I could make out the color of his eyes: a dark, fathomless green.

"What," he repeated intently, "does that make me?"

I stopped looking at his eyes. And his abs. And his haphazardly gelled hair. "Drunk," I said, and then, because I could sense an annoying comeback coming, I added two more words. "And two."

"What?" Jameson Hawthorne said.

"The answer to your first riddle," I told him. "If *yes* is *no* and *once* is *never*, then the number of sides a triangle has...is...*two*." I drew out my reply, not bothering to explain how I'd arrived at my answer.

"Touché, M.G." Jameson ambled past me, brushing his bare arm lightly over mine as he did. "Touché."

CHAPTER 9

I stayed out back a few minutes longer. Nothing about this day felt real. And tomorrow, I'd go back to Connecticut, a little richer, hopefully, and with a story to tell, and I'd probably never see any of the Hawthornes again.

I'd never have a view like *this* again.

By the time I returned to the Great Room, Jameson Hawthorne had miraculously managed to find a shirt—and a suit jacket. He smiled in my direction and gave a little salute. Beside him, Grayson stiffened, his jaw muscles tensing.

"Now that everyone is here," one of the lawyers said, "let's get started."

The three lawyers stood in triangle formation. The one who'd spoken shared Alisa's dark hair, brown skin, and self-assured expression. I assumed he was the Ortega in McNamara, Ortega, and Jones. The other two—presumably Jones and McNamara—stood to either side.

Since when does it take four lawyers to read a will? I thought.

"You are here," Mr. Ortega said, projecting his voice to the corners of the room, "to hear the last will and testament of Tobias

Tattersall Hawthorne. Per Mr. Hawthorne's instructions, my colleagues will now distribute letters he has left for each of you."

The other men began to make the rounds of the room, handing out envelopes one by one.

"You may open these letters when the reading is concluded."

I was handed an envelope. My full name was written in calligraphy on the front. Beside me, Libby looked up at the lawyer, but he passed over her and went on delivering envelopes to the other occupants of the room.

"Mr. Hawthorne stipulated that all of the following individuals must be physically present for the reading of this will: Skye Hawthorne, Zara Hawthorne-Calligaris, Nash Hawthorne, Grayson Hawthorne, Jameson Hawthorne, Alexander Hawthorne, and Ms. Avery Kylie Grambs of New Castle, Connecticut."

I felt about as conspicuous as I would have if I'd looked down and discovered that I wasn't wearing clothes.

"Since you are all here," Mr. Ortega continued, "we may begin."

Beside me, Libby slipped her hand into mine.

"I, Tobias Tattersall Hawthorne," Mr. Ortega read, "being of sound body and mind, decree that my worldly possessions, including all monetary and physical assets, be disposed of as follows.

"To Andrew and Lottie Laughlin, for years of loyal service, I bequeath a sum of one hundred thousand dollars apiece, with lifelong, rent-free tenancy granted in Wayback Cottage, located on the western border of my Texas estate."

The older couple I'd seen earlier leaned into each other. All I could think was: *ONE HUNDRED THOUSAND DOLLARS*. The Laughlins' presence wasn't mandatory for the reading of the will, and they'd just been given one hundred thousand dollars. Apiece!

I tried very hard to remember how to breathe.

"To John Oren, head of my security detail, who has saved my life more times and in more ways than I can count, I leave the contents of my toolbox, held currently in the offices of McNamara, Ortega, and Jones, as well as a sum of three hundred thousand dollars."

Tobias Hawthorne knew these people, I told myself, heart thumping. *They worked for him. They* mattered *to him. I'm nothing.*

"To my mother-in-law, Pearl O'Day, I leave an annuity of one hundred thousand dollars a year, plus a trust for medical expenses as set forth in the appendix. All jewelry belonging to my late wife, Alice O'Day Hawthorne, shall pass to her mother upon my death, to be distributed as she sees fit upon hers."

Nan harrumphed. "Don't you go getting any ideas," she ordered the room at large. "I'm going to outlive you all."

Mr. Ortega smiled, but then that smile faltered. "To..." He paused and then tried again. "To my daughters, Zara Hawthorne-Calligaris and Skye Hawthorne, I leave the funds necessary to pay off all debts accrued as of the date and time of my death." Mr. Ortega paused again, his lips pushing themselves together. The other two lawyers stared straight ahead, avoiding looking at any member of the Hawthorne family directly.

"Additionally, I leave to Skye my compass, may she always know true north, and to Zara, I leave my wedding ring, may she love as wholly and steadfastly as I loved her mother."

Another pause, more painful than the last.

"Go on." That came from Zara's husband.

"To each of my daughters," Mr. Ortega read slowly, "beyond that already stated, I leave a one-time inheritance of fifty thousand dollars."

Fifty thousand dollars? I'd no sooner thought those words than Zara's husband echoed them out loud, irate. *Tobias Hawthorne left his daughters less than he left his security detail.*

Suddenly, Skye's reference to Grayson as the *heir apparent* took on a whole new meaning.

"You did this." Zara turned toward Skye. She didn't raise her voice, but it was deadly all the same.

"Me?" Skye said, indignant.

"Daddy was never the same after Toby died," Zara continued.

"Disappeared," Skye corrected.

"God, listen to you!" Zara lost her hold on her tone. "You got in his head, didn't you, Skye? Batted your eyelashes and convinced him to bypass us and leave everything to your—"

"*Sons.*" Skye's voice was crisp. "The word you're looking for is *sons*."

"The word she's looking for is *bastards.*" Nash Hawthorne had the thickest Texas accent of anyone in the room. "Not like we haven't heard it before."

"If I'd had a son..." Zara's voice caught.

"But you didn't." Skye let that sink in. "Did you, Zara?"

"*Enough.*" Zara's husband stepped in. "We will sort this out."

"I'm afraid there's nothing to be sorted." Mr. Ortega reentered the fray. "You will find the will is ironclad, with significant disincentives to any who might be tempted to challenge it."

I translated that to mean, roughly, *shut up and sit down.*

"Now, if I may continue..." Mr. Ortega looked back down at the will in his hands. "To my grandsons, Nash Westbrook Hawthorne, Grayson Davenport Hawthorne, Jameson Winchester Hawthorne, and Alexander Blackwood Hawthorne, I leave..."

"Everything," Zara muttered bitterly.

Mr. Ortega spoke over her. "Two hundred and fifty thousand dollars apiece, payable on their twenty-fifth birthdays, until such time to be managed by Alisa Ortega, trustee."

"What?" Alisa sounded shocked. "I mean...*what*?"

"The hell," Nash told her pleasantly. "The phrase you're looking for, darlin', is *what the hell*?"

Tobias Hawthorne hadn't left everything to his grandsons. Given the scope of his fortune, he'd left them a pittance.

"What is going on here?" Grayson asked, each word deadly and precise.

Tobias Hawthorne didn't leave everything to his grandsons. He didn't leave everything to his daughters. My brain ground to a halt right there. My ears rang.

"Please, everyone," Mr. Ortega held up a hand. "Allow me to finish."

Forty-six point two billion dollars, I thought, my heart attacking my rib cage and my mouth sandpaper-dry. *Tobias Hawthorne was worth forty-six point two billion dollars, and he left his grandsons a million dollars, combined. A hundred thousand total to his daughters. Another half million to his servants, an annuity for Nan...*

The math in this equation did not add up. It *couldn't* add up.

One by one, the other occupants of the room turned to stare at me.

"The remainder of my estate," Mr. Ortega read, "including all properties, monetary assets, and worldly possessions not otherwise specified, I leave to Avery Kylie Grambs."

CHAPTER 10

This is not happening.

This cannot be happening.

I'm dreaming.

I'm delusional.

"He left everything to *her*?" Skye's voice was shrill enough to break through my stupor. "Why?" Gone was the woman who'd mused about my astrological sign and regaled me with tales of her sons and lovers. This Skye looked like she could kill someone. Literally.

"Who the hell is she?" Zara's voice was knife-edged and clear as a bell.

"There must be some mistake." Grayson spoke like a person used to dealing with mistakes. *Bribe, threaten, buy out,* I thought. What would the "heir apparent" do to me? *This is not happening.* I felt that with every beat of my heart, every breath in, every breath out. *This cannot be happening.*

"He's right." My words came out in a whisper, lost to voices being raised all around me. I tried again, louder. "Grayson's right." Heads started turning in my direction. "There must be some mistake." My voice was hoarse. I felt like I'd just jumped out of a plane. Like I was skydiving and waiting for my chute to open.

This is not real. It can't be.

"Avery." Libby nudged me in the ribs, clearly telegraphing that I should shut up and stop talking about *mistakes.*

But there was no way. There had to have been some kind of mix-up. A man I'd never met hadn't just left me a multi-billion-dollar fortune. Things like that didn't happen, period.

"You see?" Skye latched on to what I'd said. "Even Ava agrees this is ridiculous."

This time, I was pretty sure she'd gotten my name wrong on purpose. *The remainder of my estate, including all properties, monetary assets, and worldly possessions not otherwise specified, I leave to Avery Kylie Grambs.* Skye Hawthorne knew my name now.

They all did.

"I assure you, there is no mistake." Mr. Ortega met my gaze, then turned his attention to the others. "And I assure the rest of you, Tobias Hawthorne's last will and testament is utterly unbreakable. Since the majority of the remaining details concern only Avery, we'll cease with the dramatics. But let me make one thing very clear: Per the terms of the will, any heir who challenges Avery's inheritance will forfeit their share of the estate entirely."

Avery's inheritance. I felt dizzy, almost nauseous. It was like someone had snapped their fingers and rewritten the laws of physics, like the coefficient of gravity had changed, and my body was ill-suited to coping. The world was spinning off its axis.

"No will is that ironclad," Zara's husband said, his voice acidic. "Not when there's this kind of money at stake."

"Spoken," Nash Hawthorne interjected, "like someone who didn't really know the old man."

"Traps upon traps," Jameson murmured. "And riddles upon riddles." I could feel his dark green eyes on mine.

"I think you should leave," Grayson told me curtly. Not a request. An order.

"Technically..." Alisa Ortega sounded like she'd just swallowed arsenic. "It's her house."

Clearly, she really hadn't known what was in the will. She'd been kept in the dark, just like the family. *How could Tobias Hawthorne blindside them like this? What kind of person does that to their own flesh and blood?*

"I don't understand," I said out loud, dizzy and numb, because none of this made any kind of sense.

"My daughter is correct." Mr. Ortega kept his tone neutral. "You own it all, Ms. Grambs. Not just the fortune, but all of Mr. Hawthorne's properties, including Hawthorne House. Per the terms of your inheritance, which I will gladly go over with you, the current occupants have been granted tenancy unless—and until—they give you cause for removal." He let those words hang in the air. "Under no circumstances," he continued gravely, his words rife with warning, "can those tenants attempt to remove you."

The room was suddenly silent and still. *They're going to kill me. Someone in this room is actually going to kill me.* The man I'd pegged as former military strode to stand between me and Tobias Hawthorne's family. He said nothing, crossing his arms over his chest, keeping me behind him and the rest of them in his sight.

"Oren!" Zara sounded shocked. "You work for this family."

"I worked for Mr. Hawthorne." John Oren paused and held up a piece of paper. It took me a moment to realize that it was his letter. "It was his last request that I continue in the employment of Ms. Avery Kylie Grambs." He glanced at me. "Security. You'll need it."

"And not just to protect you from us!" Xander added to my left.

"Take a step back, please," Oren ordered.

Xander held his hands up. "Peace," he declared. "I make dire predictions in peace!"

"Xan's right." Jameson smiled, like this was all a game. "The entire world's going to want a piece of you, Mystery Girl. This has *story of the century* written all over it."

Story of the century. My brain kicked back into gear because there was every indication that this wasn't a joke. I wasn't delusional. I wasn't dreaming.

I was an heiress.

CHAPTER 11

I bolted. The next thing I knew, I was outside. The front door of Hawthorne House slammed behind me. Cool air hit my face. I was almost sure I was breathing, but my entire body felt distant and numb. Was this what shock felt like?

"Avery!" Libby burst out of the house after me. "Are you okay?" She studied me, concerned. "Also: Are you insane? When someone gives you money, you don't try to give it back!"

"*You* do," I pointed out, the roar in my brain so loud that I couldn't hear myself think. "Every time I try to give you my tips."

"We're not talking tips here!" Libby's blue hair was falling out of her ponytail. "We're talking *millions*."

Billions, I corrected silently, but my mouth flat-out refused to say the word.

"Ave." Libby put a hand on my shoulder. "Think about what this means. You'll never have to worry about money again. You can buy whatever you want, do whatever you want. Those postcards you kept of your mom's?" She leaned forward, touching her forehead against mine. "You can go anywhere. Imagine the possibilities."

I did, even though this felt like a cruel joke, like the universe's way of tricking me into wanting things that girls like me were never meant to—

The massive front door of Hawthorne House slammed open. I jumped back, and Nash Hawthorne stepped out. Even wearing a suit, he looked every inch the cowboy, ready to meet a rival at high noon.

I braced myself. *Billions.* Wars had been fought over less.

"Relax, kid." Nash's Texas drawl was slow and smooth, like whiskey. "I don't want the money. Never have. Far as I'm concerned, this is the universe having a bit of fun with folks who probably deserve it."

The oldest Hawthorne brother's gaze drifted from me to Libby. He was tall, muscular, and suntanned. She was tiny and slight, her pale skin standing in stark contrast to her dark lipstick and neon hair. The two of them looked like they didn't belong within ten feet of each other, and yet, there he was, slow-smiling at her.

"You take care, darlin'," Nash told my sister. He ambled toward his motorcycle, then put on his helmet, and a moment later, he was gone.

Libby stared after the motorcycle. "I take back what I said about Grayson. Maybe *he*'s God."

Right now, we had bigger issues than which of the Hawthorne brothers was divine. "We can't stay here, Libby. I doubt the rest of the family is as blasé about the will as Nash is. We need to go."

"I'm going with you," a deep voice said. I turned. John Oren stood next to the front door. I hadn't heard him open it.

"I don't need security," I told him. "I just need to get out of here."

"You'll need security for the rest of your life." He was so matter-of-fact, I couldn't even begin to argue. "But look on the bright side. . . ." He nodded to the car that had picked us up at the airport. "I also drive."

I asked Oren to take us to a motel. Instead, he drove us to the fanciest hotel I'd ever seen, and he must have taken the scenic route, because Alisa Ortega was waiting for us in the lobby.

"I've had a chance to read the will in full." Apparently, that was her version of *hello*. "I brought a copy for you. I suggest we retire to your rooms and go over the details."

"Our rooms?" I repeated. The doormen were wearing tuxedos. There were *six* chandeliers in the lobby. Nearby, a woman was playing a five-foot-tall harp. "We can't afford rooms here."

Alisa gave me an almost pitying look. "Oh, honey," she said, then recovered her professionalism. "You own this hotel."

I... what? Libby and I were getting "who let the rabble in?" looks from other patrons just standing in the lobby. I could not possibly *own this hotel.*

"Besides which," Alisa continued, "the will is now in probate. It may be some time before the money and properties are out of escrow, but in the meantime, McNamara, Ortega, and Jones will be picking up the tab for anything you need."

Libby frowned, crinkling her brow. "Is that a thing that law firms do?"

"You have probably gathered that Mr. Hawthorne was one of our most important clients," Alisa said delicately. "It would be more precise to say that he was our *only* client. And now..."

"Now," I said, the truth sinking in, "that client is me."

It took me almost an hour to read and reread and re-reread the will. Tobias Hawthorne had put only one condition on my inheritance.

"You're to live in Hawthorne House for one year, commencing

no more than three days from now." Alisa had made that point at least twice already, but I couldn't get my brain to accept it.

"The only string attached to my inheriting billions of dollars is that I *must* move into a mansion."

"Correct."

"A mansion where a large number of the people who were expecting to inherit this money still live. And I can't kick them out."

"Barring extraordinary circumstances, also correct. If it's any consolation, it *is* a very large house."

"And if I refuse?" I asked. "Or if the Hawthorne family has me killed?"

"No one is going to have you killed," Alisa said calmly.

"I know you grew up around these people and everything," Libby told Alisa, trying to be diplomatic, "but they are totally, one hundred percent going to go all Lizzie Borden on my sister."

"Really would prefer not to be ax-murdered," I emphasized.

"Risk assessment: low," Oren rumbled. "At least insofar as axes are concerned."

It took me a second to figure out that he was joking. "This is serious!"

"Believe me," he returned, "I know. But I also know the Hawthorne family. The boys would never harm a woman, and the women will come for you in the courtroom, no axes involved."

"Besides," Alisa added, "in the state of Texas, if an heir dies while a will is in probate, the inheritance doesn't revert to the original estate—it becomes part of the *heir*'s estate."

I have an estate? I thought dully. "And if I refuse to move in with them?" I asked again, a giant ball in my throat.

"She's not going to refuse." Libby shot laser eyes in my direction.

"If you fail to move into Hawthorne House in three days' time," Alisa told me, "your portion of the estate will be dispersed to charity."

"Not to Tobias Hawthorne's family?" I asked.

"No." Alisa's neutral mask slipped slightly. She'd known the Hawthornes for years. She might work for me now, but she couldn't be happy about that.

Could she?

"Your father wrote the will, right?" I said, trying to wrap my head around the insane situation I was in.

"In consultation with the other partners at the firm," Alisa confirmed.

"Did he tell you..." I tried to find a better way to phrase what I wanted to ask, then gave up. "Did he tell you *why*?"

Why had Tobias Hawthorne disinherited his family? Why leave everything to *me*?

"I don't think my father knows why," Alisa said. She peered at me, the neutral mask slipping once more. "Do you?"

CHAPTER 12

M*other-faxing elf,*" Max breathed. "*Goat-dram, mother-faxing elf.*" She lowered her voice to a whisper and let out an actual expletive. It was past midnight for me, and two hours earlier for her. I half expected Mrs. Liu to sweep in and snatch the phone away, but nothing happened.

"How?" Max demanded. "Why?"

I looked down at the letter in my lap. Tobias Hawthorne had left me an explanation, but in the hours since the will was read, I hadn't been able to bring myself to open the envelope. I was alone, sitting in the dark on the balcony of the penthouse suite of a *hotel that I owned*, wearing a plush, floor-length robe that probably cost more than my car—and I was frozen.

"Maybe," Max said thoughtfully, "you were switched at birth." Max watched a lot of television and had what could probably have been classified as a book addiction. "Maybe your mother saved his life, years ago. Maybe he owes his entire fortune to your great-great-grandfather. *Maybe you were selected via an advanced computer algorithm that is poised to develop artificial intelligence any day!*"

"Maxine." I snorted. Somehow, that was enough to allow me to say the exact words I'd been trying not to think. "Maybe my father isn't really my father."

That was the most rational explanation, wasn't it? Maybe Tobias Hawthorne *hadn't* disinherited his family for a stranger. Maybe I *was* family.

I have a secret.... I pictured my mom in my mind. How many times had I heard her say those exact words?

"You okay?" Max asked on the other end of the line.

I looked down at the envelope, at my name in calligraphy on the front. I swallowed. "Tobias Hawthorne left me a letter."

"And you haven't opened it yet?" Max said. "Avery, for fox sakes—"

"Maxine!" Even over the phone, I could hear Max's mom in the background.

"Fox, Mama. I said *fox.* As in 'for the sake of foxes and their furry little tails...'" There was a brief pause and then: "Avery? I have to go."

My stomach muscles tightened. "Talk soon?"

"Very soon," Max promised. "And in the meantime: Open. The. Letter."

She hung up. I hung up. I put my thumb underneath the lip of the envelope—but a knock at the door saved me from following through.

Back in the suite, I found Oren positioned at the door. "Who is it?" I asked him.

"Grayson Hawthorne," Oren replied. I stared at the door, and Oren elaborated. "If my men considered him a threat, he never would have made it to our floor. I trust Grayson. But if you don't want to see him..."

"No," I said. *What am I doing?* It was late, and I doubted

American royalty took kindly to being dethroned. But there was something about the way Grayson had looked at me, from the first time we'd met. . . .

"Open the door," I told Oren. He did, and then he stepped back.

"Aren't you going to invite me in?" Grayson wasn't the *heir* anymore, but you wouldn't have known it from his tone.

"You shouldn't be here," I told him, pulling my robe tighter around me.

"I've spent the past hour telling myself much the same thing, and yet, here I am." His eyes were pools of gray, his hair unkempt, like I wasn't the only one who hadn't been able to sleep. He'd lost everything today.

"Grayson—" I said.

"I don't know how you did this." He cut me off, his voice dangerous and soft. "I don't know what hold you had over my grandfather, or what kind of con you're running here."

"I'm not—"

"I'm talking right now, Ms. Grambs." He placed his hand flat on the door. I'd been wrong about his eyes. They weren't pools. They were ice. "I haven't a clue how you pulled this off, but I will find out. I see you now. I know what you are and what you're capable of, and there is *nothing* I wouldn't do to protect my family. Whatever game you're playing here, no matter how long this con—I will find the truth, and God help you when I do."

Oren stepped into my peripheral vision, but I didn't wait for him to act. I pushed the door forward, hard enough to send Grayson back, then slammed it closed. Heart pounding, I waited for him to knock again, to shout through the door. *Nothing.* Slowly, my head bowed, my eyes drawn like magnet to metal by the envelope in my hands.

With one last glance at Oren, I retreated to my bedroom. *Open.*

The. Letter. This time, I did it, removing a card from the envelope. The body of the message was only two words long. I stared at the page, reading the salutation, the message, and the signature, over and over again.

Dearest Avery,
I'm sorry.
—T. T. H.

CHAPTER 13

Sorry? Sorry for what? The question was still ringing in my mind the next morning. For once in my life, I'd slept late. I found Oren and Alisa in our suite's kitchen talking softly.

Too softly for me to hear.

"Avery." Oren noticed me first. I wondered if he'd told Alisa about Grayson. "There are some security protocols I'd like to go over with you."

Like not opening doors to Grayson Hawthorne?

"You're a target now," Alisa told me crisply.

Given that she'd been so insistent that the Hawthornes weren't a threat, I had to ask: "A target for what?"

"Paparazzi, of course. The firm is keeping a lid on the story for the time being, but that won't last, and there are other concerns."

"Kidnapping." Oren didn't put any particular emphasis on that word. "Stalking. People will make threats—they always do. You're young, and you're female, and that will make it worse. With your sister's permission, I'll arrange a detail for her as well, as soon as she gets back."

Kidnapping. Stalking. Threats. I couldn't even wrap my mind around the words. "Where is Libby?" I asked, since he'd made reference to her coming *back*.

"On a plane," Alisa answered. "Specifically, your plane."

"I have a plane?" I was *never* going to get used to this.

"You have several," Alisa told me. "And a helicopter, I believe, but that's neither here nor there. Your sister is en route to retrieve your things, as well as her own. Given the deadline for your move into Hawthorne House—and the stakes—we thought it best that you remain here. Ideally, we'll have you moved in no later than tonight."

"The second this news gets out," Oren said seriously, "you will be on the cover of every newspaper. You'll be the leading story on every newscast, the number one trending topic on all social media. To some people, you'll be Cinderella. To others, Marie Antoinette."

Some people would want to be me. Some people would hate me to the depths of their souls. For the first time, I noticed the gun holstered to Oren's side.

"It's best you sit tight," Oren said evenly. "Your sister should be back tonight."

For the rest of the morning, Alisa and I played what I had mentally termed The Uprooting Avery's Life In An Instant game. I quit my job. Alisa took care of withdrawing me from school.

"What about my car?" I asked.

"Oren will be driving you for the foreseeable future, but we can have your vehicle shipped, if you would like," Alisa offered. "Or you can pick out a new car for personal use."

For all the emphasis she put on that, you would have thought she was talking about buying gum at the supermarket.

"Do you prefer sedans or SUVs?" she queried, holding her phone in a way that suggested she was fully capable of ordering a car with a mere click of a button. "Any color preference?"

"You're going to have to excuse me for a second," I told her. I ducked back into my bedroom. The bed was piled ridiculously high with pillows. I climbed up on the bed, let myself fall back on the mountain of pillows, and pulled out my phone.

Texting, calling, and DM-ing Max all led to the same result: nothing. She had *definitely* had her phone confiscated—and possibly her laptop, which meant that she couldn't advise me on the appropriate response when one's lawyer started talking about ordering a car like it was a *foxing* pizza.

This is unreal. Less that twenty-four hours earlier, I'd been sleeping in a parking lot. The closest I'd come to splurging was the occasional breakfast sandwich.

Breakfast sandwich, I thought. *Harry.* I sat up in bed. "Alisa?" I called. "If I didn't want a new car, if I wanted to spend that money on something else—could I?"

Bankrolling a place for Harry to stay—and getting him to accept it—wouldn't be easy, but Alisa told me to consider it handled. That was the world I lived in now. All I had to do was speak, and it was *handled.*

This wouldn't last. It couldn't. Sooner or later, someone would figure out that this was some kind of screwup. *So I might as well enjoy it while it lasts.*

That was the number one thought on my mind when we went to pick up Libby. As my sister stepped out of *my* private jet. I wondered if Alisa could get her into the Sorbonne. Or buy her a little cupcake shop. Or—

"Libby." Every thought in my head came screeching to a halt

the moment I saw her face. Her right eye was bruised and swollen nearly shut.

Libby swallowed but didn't avert her eyes. "If you say 'I told you so,' I will make butterscotch cupcakes and guilt you into eating them every day."

"Is there a problem I should know about?" Alisa asked Libby, her voice deceptively calm as she eyed the bruise.

"Avery hates butterscotch," Libby said, like that was the problem.

"Alisa," I gritted out, "does your law firm have a hit man on retainer?"

"No." Alisa kept her tone strictly professional. "But I'm very resourceful. I could make some inquiries."

"I legitimately cannot tell if you are joking," Libby said, and then she turned to me. "I don't want to talk about it. And I'm fine."

"But—"

"I'm fine."

I managed to keep my mouth shut, and all of us managed to make it back to the hotel. The plan was to finish up a few final arrangements and leave immediately for Hawthorne House.

Things did not go exactly according to plan.

"We have a problem." Oren didn't sound overly bothered, but Alisa immediately put down her phone. Oren nodded to our suite's balcony. Alisa stepped outside, looked down, and swore.

I pushed past Oren and went out on the balcony to see what was going on. Down below, outside the hotel's entrance, hotel security guards were struggling with what appeared to be a mob. It wasn't until a flash went off that I realized what that mob was.

Paparazzi.

And just like that, every camera was pointed up at the balcony. At me.

CHAPTER 14

"I thought you said your firm had this locked down." Oren gave Alisa a look. She scowled back at him, made three phone calls in quick succession—two of them in Spanish—and then turned back to my head of security. "The leak didn't come from us." Her eyes darted toward Libby. "It came from your boyfriend."

Libby's answer was barely more than a whisper. "My ex."

"I'm sorry." Libby had apologized at least a dozen times. She'd told Drake everything—about the will, the conditions on my inheritance, where we were staying. *Everything.* I knew her well enough to know why. He would have been angry that she'd taken off. She would have tried to pacify him. And the moment she'd told him about the money, he would have demanded to tag along. He would have started making plans to spend the Hawthorne money. And Libby, God bless her, would have told him that it wasn't theirs to spend, that it wasn't *his.*

He hit her. She left him. He went to the press. And now they were here. A horde descended on us as Oren led me out a side door.

"There she is!" a voice yelled.

"Avery!"

"Avery, over here!"

"Avery, how does it feel to be the richest teenager in America?"

"How does it feel to be the world's youngest billionaire?"

"How did you know Tobias Hawthorne?"

"Is it true that you're Tobias Hawthorne's illegitimate daughter?"

I was shuffled into an SUV. The door closed, dulling the roar of the reporters' questions. Exactly halfway through our drive, I got a text—not from Max. From an unknown number.

I opened it and saw a screenshot of a news headline. *Avery Grambs: Who Is the Hawthorne Heiress?*

A short message accompanied the picture.

Hey, Mystery Girl. You're officially famous.

There were more paparazzi outside the gates of Hawthorne House, but once we pulled past them, the rest of the world faded away. There was no welcome party. No Jameson. No Grayson. No Hawthornes of any kind. I reached for the massive front door—locked. Alisa disappeared around the back of the house. When she finally reappeared, there was a pained expression on her face. She handed me a large envelope.

"Legally," she said, "the Hawthorne family is required to provide you with keys. Practically speaking..." She narrowed her eyes. "The Hawthorne family is a pain in the ass."

"That a legal term?" Oren asked dryly.

I ripped open the envelope and found that the Hawthorne family had indeed provided me with keys—somewhere in the neighborhood of a hundred of them.

"Any idea which one of these goes to the front door?" I asked. They weren't normal keys. They were oversized and ornately made. They all looked like antiques, and each key was distinct—different designs, different metals, different lengths and sizes.

"You'll figure it out," someone said.

My gaze jerked upward, and I found myself staring at an intercom.

"Cut the games, Jameson," Alisa ordered. "This isn't nearly as cute as you all think it is."

No reply.

"Jameson?" Alisa tried again.

Silence, and then: "I have faith in you, M.G."

The intercom cut off, and Alisa blew out a long, frustrated breath. "God save me from Hawthornes."

"M.G.?" Libby asked, bewildered.

"Mystery Girl," I clarified. "From what I've gathered, that's Jameson Hawthorne's idea of a nickname." I turned my attention to the ring of keys in my hand. The obvious solution was to try them all. Assuming one of these keys opened the front door, I'd get lucky eventually. But luck didn't feel like enough. I was already the luckiest girl in the world.

Some part of me wanted to deserve it.

I flipped through the keys, inspecting the designs on the handles. *An apple. A snake. A pattern of swirls reminiscent of water.* There were keys for each letter of the alphabet, in fancy, old-fashioned script. There were keys with numbers and keys with shapes, one with a mermaid and four different keys featuring eyes.

"Well?" Alisa said abruptly. "Do you want me to make a phone call?"

"No." I turned my attention from the keys to the door. The design was simple, geometric—not a match for anything on any of the keys I'd looked at so far. *That would be too easy,* I thought. *Too simple.* A second later, a parallel thought followed. *Not simple enough.*

I'd learned this much playing chess: The more complicated a

person's strategy seemed, the less likely an opponent was to look for simple answers. If you could keep someone looking at your knight, you could take them with a pawn. *Look past the details. Past the complications.* I shifted my focus from the handles of the keys to the part that actually went into the lock. Though the keys differed in size overall, the lock end was sized similarly from key to key.

Not just sized *similarly,* I realized, looking at two of the keys side by side. The pattern—the mechanism that actually turned the lock—was identical between the two. I moved on to a third key. *The same.* I began working my way through the ring, comparing each key to the next, one by one. *Same. Same. Same.*

There weren't a hundred keys on this ring. The faster I flipped through them, the surer I was. There were two—dozens of copies of the wrong key, dressed up to look different from each other, and then…

"This one." I finally hit a key with a different pattern from the others. The intercom crackled, but if Jameson was still on the other side, he didn't say a word. I moved to put the key in the lock, and adrenaline jolted through my veins when it turned.

Eureka.

"How did you know which key to use?" Libby asked me.

The answer came from the intercom. "Sometimes," Jameson Hawthorne said, sounding strangely contemplative, "things that appear very different on the surface are actually exactly the same at their core."

CHAPTER 15

"Welcome home, Avery." Alisa stepped into the foyer and spun to face me. I stopped breathing, just for an instant, as I crossed the threshold. It was like stepping into Buckingham Palace or Hogwarts and being told that it was *yours*.

"Down that corridor," Alisa said, "we have the theater, the music room, conservatory, solarium...." I didn't even know what half of those rooms *were*. "You've seen the Great Room, of course," Alisa continued. "The formal dining is farther down, then the kitchen, the chef's kitchen...."

"There's a chef?" I blurted out.

"There are sushi, Italian, Taiwanese, vegetarian, and pastry chefs on retainer." The voice that said those words was male. I turned to see the older couple from the will's reading standing by the entry to the Great Room. *The Laughlins*, I remembered. "But my wife handles the cooking day-to-day," Mr. Laughlin continued gruffly.

"Mr. Hawthorne was a very private man." Mrs. Laughlin eyed me. "He made do with my cooking most days because he didn't like having any more outsiders poking around in the House than necessary."

There was no doubt in my mind that she was saying *House* with a capital *H*—and even less that she considered me an *outsider.*

"There are dozens of staff on retainer," Alisa explained. "They all receive a full-time wage but work on call."

"If something needs doing, there's someone to do it," Mr. Laughlin said plainly, "and I see that it's done in the most discreet fashion possible. More often than not, you won't even know they're here."

"But I will," Oren stated. "Movement on and off the estate is strictly tracked, and no one makes it past the gates without a deep background check. Construction crews, the housekeeping and gardening staff, every masseuse, chef, stylist, or sommelier—they are all cleared through my team."

Sommelier. Stylist. Chef. Masseuse. My brain worked backward through that list. It was dizzying.

"The gym facilities are down this hall," Alisa said, returning to her tour guide role. "There are full-sized basketball and racquetball courts, a rock climbing wall, bowling alley—"

"*A bowling alley?*" I repeated.

"Only four lanes," Alisa assured me, as if it was perfectly reasonable to have a *small* bowling alley in one's house.

I was still trying to formulate an appropriate response when the front door opened behind me. The day before, Nash Hawthorne had given the impression of someone who was out of here—yet there he was.

"*Motorcycle cowboy,*" Libby whispered in my ear.

Beside me, Alisa stiffened. "If everything's in order here, I should check in with the firm." She reached into her suit pocket and handed me a new phone. "I programmed in my number, Mr. Laughlin's, and Oren's. If you need anything, call."

She left without saying a single word to Nash, and he watched her go.

"You be careful with that one," Mrs. Laughlin advised the eldest Hawthorne brother, once the door had closed. "Hell hath no fury like a woman scorned."

That cemented something for me. *Alisa and Nash.* My lawyer had advised me against losing my heart to a Hawthorne, and when she'd asked me if I'd ever had my life ruined by one of them, and I'd said no, her response had been *lucky you.*

"Don't go convincing yourself Lee-Lee is consortin' with the enemy," Nash told Mrs. Laughlin. "Avery isn't anyone's enemy. There are no enemies here. This is what he wanted."

He. Tobias Hawthorne. Even dead, he was larger than life.

"None of this is Avery's fault," Libby said beside me. "She's just a kid."

Nash swung his attention to my sister, and I could feel her trying to fade into oblivion. Nash peered through her hair to the black eye underneath. "What happened here?" he murmured.

"I'm fine," Libby said, sticking her chin out.

"I can see that," Nash replied softly. "But if you decide you'd like to give me a name? I'd take it."

I could see the effect those words had on Libby. She wasn't used to having anyone but me in her corner.

"Libby." Oren got her attention. "If you've got a moment, I'd like to introduce you to Hector, who will be running point on your detail. Avery, I can personally guarantee that Nash will not ax-murder you or allow you to be ax-murdered by anyone else while I'm gone."

That got a snort from Nash, and I glared at Oren. He didn't have to advertise how little I trusted them! As Libby followed Oren into the bowels of the house, I became keenly aware of the way that the oldest Hawthorne brother watched her go.

"Leave her alone," I told Nash.

"You're protective," Nash commented, "and you seem like you'd fight dirty, and if there's one thing I respect, it's those particular traits in combination."

There was a *crash*, then a *thud* in the distance.

"That," Nash said meditatively, "would be the reason I came back and am not living a pleasantly nomadic existence as we speak."

Another *thud*.

Nash rolled his eyes. "This should be fun." He began striding toward a nearby hall. He looked back over his shoulder. "You might as well tag along, kid. You know what they say about baptisms and fire."

CHAPTER 16

Nash had long legs, so a lazy amble on his part required me to jog to keep up. I looked in each room as we passed, but they were all a blur of art and architecture and natural light. At the end of a long hall, Nash threw open a door. I prepared myself to see evidence of a brawl. Instead, I saw Grayson and Jameson standing on opposite sides of a library that took my breath away.

The room was circular. Shelves stretched up fifteen or twenty feet overhead, and every single one was lined completely with hard-cover books. The shelves were made of a deep, rich wood. Spread across the room, four wrought-iron staircases spiraled toward the upper shelves, like the points on a compass. In the library's center, there was a massive tree stump, easily ten feet across. Even from a distance, I could see the rings marking the tree's age.

It took me a moment to realize that it was meant to be used as a desk.

I could stay here forever, I thought. *I could stay in this room forever and never leave.*

"So," Nash said beside me, casually eyeing his brothers. "Whose ass do I need to kick first?"

Grayson looked up from the book he was holding. "Must we always resort to fisticuffs?"

"Looks like I have a volunteer for the first ass-kicking," Nash said, then shot a measuring look at Jameson, who was leaning against one of the wrought-iron staircases. "Do I have a second?"

Jameson smirked. "Couldn't stay away, could you, big brother?"

"And leave Avery here with you knuckleheads?" Until Nash mentioned my name, neither of the other two seemed to have registered my presence behind him, but I felt my invisibility slip away, just like that.

"I wouldn't worry too much about Ms. Grambs," Grayson said, silver eyes sharp. "She's clearly capable of taking care of herself."

Translation: I'm a soulless, gold-digging con artist, and he sees straight through me.

"Don't pay any attention to Gray," Jameson told me lazily. "None of us do."

"Jamie," Nash said. "Zip it."

Jameson ignored him. "Grayson is in training for the Insufferable Olympics, and we really think he can go all the way if he can just jam that stick a little farther up his—"

Asterisk, I thought, channeling Max.

"Enough," Nash grunted.

"What did I miss?" Xander bounded through the doorway. He was wearing a private school uniform, complete with a blazer that he shed in one liquid motion.

"You haven't missed anything at all," Grayson told him. "And Ms. Grambs was just leaving." He flicked his gaze toward me. "I'm sure you want to get settled."

I was the billionaire now, and he was still giving orders.

"Wait a second." Xander frowned suddenly, taking in the state of the room. "Were you guys brawling in here without me?" I still saw no visible signs of a fight or destruction, but obviously, Xander had picked up on something I hadn't. "This is what I get for being the one who doesn't skip school," he said mournfully.

At the mention of *school*, Nash looked from Xander to Jameson. "No uniform," he noted. "Playing hooky, Jamie? Two ass-kickings it is."

Xander heard the phrase *ass-kicking*, grinned, bounced to the balls of his feet, and pounced with no warning, tackling Nash to the ground. *Just some friendly impromptu wrestling between brothers.*

"Pinned you!" Xander declared triumphantly.

Nash hooked his ankle around Xander's leg and flipped him, pinning him to the ground. "Not today, little brother." Nash grinned, then flashed a much darker look at the other two brothers. *"Not today."*

They were—the four of them—a unit. They were *Hawthornes*. I wasn't. I felt that now, in a physical way. They shared a bond that was impervious to outsiders.

"I should go," I said. I didn't belong here, and if I stayed, all I would do was stare.

"You shouldn't *be* here at all," Grayson replied tersely.

"Stuff a sock in it, Gray," Nash said. "What's done is done, and you know as well as I do that if the old man did it, there's no undoing it." Nash swiveled his head toward Jameson. "And as for you: Self-destructive tendencies aren't nearly as adorable as you think they are."

"Avery solved the keys," Jameson said casually. "Faster than any of us."

For the first time since I'd walked into the room, all four brothers fell into an extended silence. *What is going on here?* I wondered. The moment felt tense, electric, borderline unbearable, and then—

"You gave her the keys?" Grayson broke the silence.

I was still holding the key ring in my hand. It suddenly felt very heavy. *Jameson wasn't supposed to give me these.*

"We were legally obligated to hand over—"

"A key." Grayson interrupted Jameson and started stalking slowly toward him, snapping the book in his hand closed. "We were legally obligated to give her *a* key, Jameson, not *the* keys."

I'd assumed that I was being messed with. At best, I'd thought it was a test. But from the way they were talking, it seemed more like a tradition. An invitation.

A rite of passage.

"I was curious how she'd do." Jameson arched an eyebrow. "Do you want to hear her time?"

"No," Nash boomed. I wasn't sure if he was answering Jameson's question or telling Grayson to stop advancing on their brother.

"Can I get up now?" Xander interjected, still pinned beneath Nash and seemingly in a better humor than the other three combined.

"Nope," Nash replied.

"I told you she was special," Jameson murmured as Grayson continued closing in on him.

"And I told you to stay away from her." Grayson stopped, just out of Jameson's reach.

"So I see that you two are talking again!" Xander commented jollily. "Excellent."

Not excellent, I thought, unable to draw my eyes away from the storm brewing just feet away. Jameson was taller, Grayson broader through the shoulders. The smirk on the former's face was matched by steel on the latter's.

"Welcome to Hawthorne House, Mystery Girl." Jameson's welcome seemed to be more for Grayson's benefit than for mine. Whatever this fight was about, it wasn't just a difference of opinion on recent events.

It wasn't just about me.

"Stop calling me Mystery Girl." I'd barely spoken since the moment the library door had swung inward, but I was getting sick of playing spectator. "My name is Avery."

"I'd also be willing to call you Heiress," Jameson offered. He stepped forward into a beam of light shining down from a skylight above. He was toe-to-toe with Grayson now. "What do you think, Gray? Got a nickname preference for our new landlord?"

Landlord. Jameson was rubbing it in, like he could handle being disinherited if it meant that the heir apparent had lost everything, too.

"I'm trying to protect you," Grayson said lowly.

"I think we both know," Jameson replied, "that the only person you've ever protected is yourself."

Grayson went completely, deathly still.

"Xander." Nash stood, pulling the youngest brother to his feet. "Why don't you show Avery to her wing?"

That was either Nash's attempt to prevent a line from being crossed or an indication that one already had been.

"Come on." Xander bumped his shoulder lightly against mine. "We'll stop for cookies on the way."

If that statement was meant to dissipate the tension in the room, it didn't work, but it did draw Grayson's attention away from Jameson—for the moment.

"No cookies." Grayson's voice was strangled, like his throat was closing down around the words—like Jameson's last shot had cut off his air completely.

"Fine," Xander replied cheerily. "You drive a hard bargain, Grayson Hawthorne. No cookies." Xander winked at me. "We'll stop for scones."

CHAPTER 17

"The first scone is what I like to call the *practice* scone." Xander stuffed an entire scone in his mouth, handed one to me, then swallowed and continued lecturing. "It is not until the third—nay, *fourth*—scone that you develop any kind of scone-eating expertise."

"Scone-eating expertise," I repeated in a deadpan.

"Your nature is skeptical," Xander noted. "That will serve you well in these halls, but if there is one universal truth in the human experience, it is that a finely honed scone-eating palate does not just develop overnight."

Out of the corner of my eye, I caught sight of Oren and wondered how long he had been tailing us. "Why are we standing here talking about scones?" I asked Xander. Oren had insisted that the Hawthorne brothers weren't a physical threat, but still! At the very least, Xander should have been trying to make my life miserable. "Aren't you supposed to hate me?" I asked.

"I do hate you," Xander replied, happily devouring his third scone. "If you notice, I have kept the blueberry confections for myself and gave you"—he shuddered—"the *lemon*-flavored scones. Such is the depth of my loathing for you personally and on principle."

"This isn't a joke." I felt like I'd fallen into Wonderland—and then fallen again, rabbit hole after rabbit hole, in a vicious cycle.

Traps upon traps, I could hear Jameson saying. *And riddles upon riddles.*

"Why would I hate you, Avery?" Xander asked finally. There were layers of emotion in his tone that hadn't been there before. "You aren't the one who did this."

Tobias Hawthorne had.

"Maybe you're blameless." Xander shrugged. "Maybe you're the evil genius that Gray seems to think you are, but at the end of the day, even if you *thought* that you'd manipulated our grandfather into this, I guarantee that he'd be the one manipulating you."

I thought of the letter that Tobias Hawthorne had left me—two words, no explanation.

"Your grandfather was a piece of work," I told Xander.

He picked up a fourth scone. "I agree. In his honor, I eat this scone." He did just that. "Want me to show you to your rooms now?"

There's got to be a catch here. Xander Hawthorne had to be more than he appeared. "Just point me in the right direction," I told him.

"About that..." The youngest Hawthorne brother made a face. "There's a chance that Hawthorne House is just a tiny bit hard to navigate. Imagine, if you will, that a labyrinth had a baby with Where's Waldo?, only Waldo is your rooms."

I attempted to translate that ridiculous sentence. "Hawthorne House has an unconventional layout."

Xander did away with a fifth and final scone. "Has anyone ever told you that you have a way with words?"

"Hawthorne House is the largest privately owned residential home in the state of Texas." Xander led me up a staircase. "I could give you a number for square footage, but it would only be an estimate. The thing that truly separates Hawthorne House from other obscenely large, castle-like structures isn't so much its size as its nature. My grandfather added at least one new room or wing every year. Imagine, if you will, that an M. C. Escher drawing conceived a child with Leonardo da Vinci's most masterful designs. . . ."

"Stop," I ordered. "New rule: You're no longer allowed to use any terminology for baby-making when describing this house or its occupants—including yourself."

Xander brought a hand melodramatically to his chest. "Harsh."

I shrugged. "My house, my rules."

He gawked at me. I couldn't believe I'd said it, either, but there was something about Xander Hawthorne that made me feel like I didn't have to apologize for my own existence.

"Too soon?" I asked.

"I'm a Hawthorne." Xander gave me his most dignified look. "It's never too soon to start trash-talking." He resumed playing the tour guide. "Now, as I was saying, the East Wing is actually the Northeast Wing, located on the second floor. If you get lost, just look for the old man." Xander nodded toward a portrait on the wall. "This was his wing, these last few months."

I'd seen pictures of Tobias Hawthorne online, but once I looked at the portrait, I couldn't look away. He had silver-gray hair and a face more weather-worn than I'd realized. His eyes were Grayson's, almost exactly, his build Jameson's, his chin Nash's. If I hadn't seen Xander in motion, I might not have recognized a resemblance between him and the old man at all, but it was there in the way Tobias Hawthorne's features pulled together—not the eyes or nose or mouth, but something about the shape in between.

"I never even met him." I tore my eyes from the portrait and looked at Xander. "I'd remember if I had."

"Are you sure?" Xander asked me.

I found myself looking back at the portrait. *Had* I ever met the billionaire? Had our paths crossed, even for a moment? My mind was blank, except for one phrase, looping through over and over again. *I'm sorry.*

CHAPTER 18

Xander left me to explore my wing.

My wing. I felt ridiculous even thinking the words. *In my mansion.* The first four doors led to suites, each of them sized to make a king bed look tiny. The closets could have doubled as bedrooms. And the *bathrooms*! Showers with built-in seats and a *minimum* of three different showerheads apiece. Gargantuan bathtubs that came with control panels. Televisions inlaid in every mirror.

Dazed, I made my way to the fifth and final door on my hall. *Not a bedroom,* I realized when I opened it. *An office.* Enormous leather chairs—six of them—sat in a horseshoe shape, facing a balcony. Glass display shelves lined the walls. Evenly spaced on the shelves were items that looked like they belonged in a museum—geodes, antique weaponry, statues of onyx and stone. Opposite the balcony, at the back of the room, was a desk. As I got closer, I saw a large bronze compass built into its surface. I trailed my fingers over the compass. It turned—*northwest*—and a compartment in the desk popped open.

This wing was where Tobias Hawthorne spent his last few

months, I thought. Suddenly, I didn't just want to look in the open compartment—I wanted to rifle through every drawer in Tobias Hawthorne's desk. There had to be something, somewhere, that could tell me what he was thinking—why I was here, why he'd pushed his family aside for me. Had I done something to impress him? Did he see something in me?

Or Mom?

I got a closer look at the opened compartment. Inside, there were deep grooves, carved in the shape of the letter *T*. I ran my fingers across the grooves. Nothing happened. I tested the rest of the drawers. Locked.

Behind the desk, there were shelves filled with plaques and trophies. I walked toward them. The first plaque had the words *United States of America* engraved on a gold background; underneath them, there was a seal. It took a little more reading of the smaller print for me to realize that it was a patent—and not one issued to Tobias Hawthorne.

This patent was held by Xander.

There were at least a half dozen other patents on the wall, several world records, and trophies in every shape imaginable. A bronze bull rider. A surfboard. A sword. There were medals. Multiple black belts. Championship cups—some of them *national* championships—for everything from motocross to swimming to pinball. There was a series of four framed comic books—superheroes I recognized, the kind they made movies about—authored by the four Hawthorne grandsons. A coffee table book of photographs bore Grayson's name on the spine.

This wasn't just a display. It was practically a *shrine*—Tobias Hawthorne's ode to his four extraordinary grandsons. This made no sense. It didn't make sense that any four people—three of them teenagers—could have achieved this much, and it definitely didn't make sense that the man who'd kept this display in his office had decided that *none* of them deserved to inherit his fortune.

Even if you thought *that you'd manipulated our grandfather into this*, I could hear Xander saying, *I guarantee that he'd be the one manipulating you.*

"Avery?"

The second I heard my name, I stepped back from the trophies. Hastily, I closed the compartment I'd released on the desk.

"In here," I called back.

Libby appeared in the doorway. "This is unreal," she said. "This entire place is *unreal.*"

"That's one word for it." I tried to focus on the marvel that was Hawthorne House and not on my sister's black eye, but I failed. If possible, the bruising looked worse now.

Libby wrapped her arms around her torso. "I'm fine," she said when she noticed my stare. "It doesn't even hurt that much."

"Please tell me you're done with him." The words escaped before I could stop them. Libby needed support right now—not judgment. But I couldn't help thinking that Drake had been her *ex* before.

"I'm here, aren't I?" Libby said. "I chose *you.*"

I wanted her to choose *herself,* and I said as much. Libby let her hair fall into her face and turned toward the balcony. She was silent for a full minute before she spoke again.

"My mom used to hit me. Only when she was really stressed, you know? She was a single mom, and things were hard. I could understand that. I tried to make everything easier."

I could picture her as a kid, getting hit and trying to make it up to the person who hit her. "Libby…"

"Drake loved me, Avery. I know he did, and I tried so hard to understand…" She was hugging herself harder now. The black polish on her nails looked fresh. *Perfect.* "But you were right."

My heart broke a little. "I didn't want to be."

Libby stood there for a few more seconds, then walked over to the balcony and tested the door. I followed, and the two of us stepped out into the night air. Down below, there was a swimming pool. It must have been heated, because someone was swimming laps.

Grayson. My body recognized him before my mind did. His arms beat against the water in a brutally efficient butterfly stroke. And his back muscles…

"I have to tell you something," Libby said beside me.

That let me tear my eyes away from the pool—and the swimmer. "About Drake?" I asked.

"No. I heard something." Libby swallowed. "When Oren introduced me to my security detail, I overheard Zara's husband talking. They're running a test—a DNA test. On *you*."

I had no idea where Zara and her husband had gotten a sample of my DNA, but I wasn't entirely surprised. I'd thought it myself: The simplest explanation for including a total stranger in your will was that she *wasn't* a total stranger. The simplest explanation was that I *was* a Hawthorne.

I had no business watching Grayson at all.

"If Tobias Hawthorne was your father," Libby managed, "then our dad—*my* dad—isn't. And if we don't share a dad, and we barely even saw each other growing up—"

"Don't you dare say we're not sisters," I told her.

"Would you still want me here?" Libby asked me, her fingers rubbing at her choker. "If we're not—"

"I want you here," I promised. "No matter what."

CHAPTER 19

That night, I took the longest shower of my life. The hot-water supply was endless. The glass doors on the shower held in the steam. It was like having my own personal sauna. After drying off with plush, oversized towels, I put on my ratty pajamas and flopped down on what I was pretty sure were Egyptian cotton sheets.

I wasn't sure how long I'd been lying there when I heard it. A voice. "Pull the candlestick."

I was on my feet in an instant, whirling to put my back to the wall. On instinct, I grabbed the keys I'd left on the nightstand, in case I needed a weapon. My eyes scanned the room for the person who'd spoken, and came up empty.

"Pull the candlestick on the fireplace, Heiress. Unless you *want* me stuck back here?"

Annoyance replaced my initial fight-or-flight response. I narrowed my eyes at the stone fireplace at the back of my room. Sure enough, there was a candelabra on the mantel.

"Pretty sure this qualifies as stalking," I told the fireplace—or, more accurately, the boy on the other side of it. Still, I couldn't *not* pull the candlestick. Who could resist something like that? I wrapped my hand around the base of the candelabra. I was met with resistance, and another suggestion came from behind the fireplace.

"Don't just pull forward. Angle it down."

I did as I was instructed. The candelabra rotated, and then I heard a *click*, and the back of the fireplace separated from its floor, just by an inch. A moment later, I saw fingertips in the gap, and I watched as the back of the fireplace was lifted up and disappeared behind the mantel. Now at the back of the fireplace there was an opening. Jameson Hawthorne stepped through. He straightened, then returned the candle to its upright position, and the entry he'd just used was slowly covered once more.

"Secret passage," he explained unnecessarily. "The house is full of them."

"Am I supposed to find that comforting?" I asked him. "Or terrifying?"

"You tell me, Mystery Girl. Are you comforted or terrified?" He let me sit with that for a moment. "Or is it possible that you're intrigued?"

The first time I'd met Jameson Hawthorne, he was drunk. This time, I didn't smell alcohol on his breath, but I wondered how much he'd slept since the reading of the will. His hair was behaving itself, but there was something wild in his glinting green eyes.

"You're not asking about the keys." Jameson offered me a crooked little smile. "I expected you to ask about the keys."

I held them up. "This was your doing."

Not a question—and he didn't treat it like one. "It's a little bit of a family tradition."

"I'm not family."

He tilted his head to one side. "Do you believe that?"

I thought about Tobias Hawthorne—about the DNA test that Zara's husband was already running. "I don't know."

"It would be a shame," Jameson commented, "if we were related." He spared another smile for me, slow and sharp-edged. "Don't you think?"

What was it with me and Hawthorne boys? *Stop thinking about his smile. Stop looking at his lips. Just—stop.*

"I think that you already have more family than you can deal with." I crossed my arms. "I also think you're a lot less smooth than you think are. You want something."

I'd always been good at math. I'd always been logical. He was here, in my room, flirting for a reason.

"Everyone is going to want something from you soon, Heiress." Jameson smiled. "The question is: How many of us want something you're willing to give?"

Even just the sound of his voice, the way he phrased things—I could feel myself wanting to lean toward him. This was *ridiculous.*

"Stop calling me Heiress," I shot back. "And if you turn answering my question into some kind of riddle, I'm calling security."

"That's the thing, Mystery Girl. I don't think I'm turning anything into a riddle. I don't think I have to. You are a riddle, a puzzle, a game—my grandfather's last."

He was looking at me so intently now, I didn't dare look away.

"Why do you think this house has so many secret passages? Why are there so many keys that don't work in any of the locks? Every desk my grandfather ever bought has secret compartments. There's an organ in the theater, and if you play a specific sequence of notes, it unlocks a hidden drawer. Every Saturday morning, from the time I was a kid until the night my grandfather died, he sat my brothers and me down and gave us a riddle, a puzzle, an impossible challenge—something to solve. And then he died. And then…" Jameson took a step toward me. "There was you."

Me.

"Grayson thinks you're some master manipulator. My aunt is convinced you must have Hawthorne blood. But I think you're the old man's final riddle—one last puzzle to be solved." He took another step, bringing the two of us that much closer. "He chose you for a reason, Avery. You're special, and I think he wanted us—wanted *me*—to figure out why."

"I'm not a puzzle." I could feel my heart beating in my neck. He was close enough now to see my pulse.

"Sure you are," Jameson replied. "We all are. Don't tell me that some part of you hasn't been trying to figure us out. Grayson. Me. Maybe even Xander."

"Is this all just a game to you?" I put my hand out to stop him from advancing farther. He took one last step, forcing my palm to his chest.

"Everything's a game, Avery Grambs. The only thing we get to decide in this life is if we play to win." He reached up to brush the hair from my face, and I jerked back.

"Get out," I said lowly. "Use the normal door this time." My entire life, no one had touched me as gently as he had a moment before.

"You're angry," Jameson said.

"I told you—if you want something, ask. Don't come in here talking about how I'm special. Don't touch my face."

"You *are* special." Jameson kept his hands to himself, but the heady expression in his eyes never shifted. "And what I *want* is to figure out why. Why you, Avery?" He took a step back, giving me space. "Don't tell me you don't want to know, too."

I did. Of course I did.

"I'm going to leave this here." Jameson held up an envelope. He laid it carefully on the mantel. "Read it, and then tell me this isn't a game to be won. Tell me this isn't a riddle." Jameson reached for the candelabra, and as the fireplace passage opened once more, he offered a targeted, parting shot. "He left you the fortune, Avery, and all he left us is *you*."

CHAPTER 20

Long after Jameson had disappeared into darkness and the fireplace door had closed, I stood there, staring. Was this the only secret passage into my room? In a house like this one, how could I ever really know that I was alone?

Eventually, I moved to take the envelope Jameson had left on the mantel, even though everything in me rebelled against what he had said. I wasn't a puzzle. I was just a girl.

I turned the envelope over and saw Jameson's name scrawled across the front. *This is his letter,* I realized. *The one he was given at the reading of the will.* I still had no idea what to make of my own letter, no idea what Tobias Hawthorne was apologizing *for.* Maybe Jameson's letter would clarify something.

I opened it and read. The message was longer than mine—and made even less sense.

Jameson,

Better the devil you know than the one you don't—or is it? Power corrupts. Absolute power corrupts absolutely. All that glitters is not gold. Nothing is certain but death and taxes. There but for the grace of God go I.

Don't judge.

—Tobias Tattersall Hawthorne

By the next morning, I'd memorized Jameson's letter. It sounded like it had been written by someone who hadn't slept in days—manic, rattling off one platitude after another. But the longer the words marinated in the back of my brain, the more I began to consider the possibility that Jameson might be right.

There's something there, in the letters. In Jameson's. In mine. An answer—or at least a clue.

Rolling out of my massive bed, I went to unplug my phones, plural, from their chargers and discovered that my old phone had powered down. With some hefty pushes on the power button and a little bit of luck, I managed to cajole it back on. I didn't know how I could even begin to explain the past twenty-four hours to Max, but I needed to talk to someone.

I needed a reality check.

What I got was more than a hundred missed calls and texts. Suddenly, the reason Alisa had given me a new phone was clear. People I hadn't spoken to in years were messaging me. People who had spent their lives ignoring me clamored for my attention. Coworkers. Classmates. Even *teachers*. I had no idea how half of them had gotten my number. I grabbed my new phone, went online, and discovered that my email and social media accounts were even worse.

I had *thousands* of messages—most of them from strangers. *To some people, you'll be Cinderella. To others, Marie Antoinette.* My stomach muscles tightened. I set both phones down and stood up, my hand going over my mouth. I should have seen this coming. It shouldn't have been a shock to my system at all. But I wasn't ready.

How could a person be ready for this?

"Avery?" A voice called into my room—female and not Libby.

"Alisa?" I double-checked before opening my bedroom door.

"You missed breakfast," came the reply. Brisk, businesslike—definitely Alisa.

I opened the door.

"Mrs. Laughlin wasn't sure what you like, so she made a bit of everything," Alisa told me. A woman I didn't recognize—early twenties, maybe—followed her into the room carrying a tray. She deposited it on my nightstand, cut a narrowed-eyed glance my way, then left without a word.

"I thought the staff only came in as needed," I said, turning to Alisa once the door was closed.

Alisa blew out a long breath. "The staff," she said, "is very, very loyal and extremely concerned right now. That"—Alisa nodded to the door—"was one of the newer hires. She's one of Nash's."

I narrowed my eyes. "What do you mean, she's one of Nash's?"

Alisa's composure never faltered. "Nash is a bit of a nomad. He leaves. He wanders. He finds some hole-in-the-wall place to bartend for a while, and then, like a moth to the flame, he comes back—usually with one or two hopeless souls in tow. As I'm sure you can imagine, there's plenty of work to be had at Hawthorne House, and Mr. Hawthorne had a habit of putting Nash's lost souls to work."

"And the girl who was just in here?" I asked.

"She's been here about a year." Alisa's tone gave nothing away. "She'd die for Nash. Most of them would."

"Are she and Nash..." I wasn't sure how to phrase this. "Involved?"

"No!" Alisa said sharply. She took a deep breath and continued. "Nash would never let anything happen with someone he had any kind of power over. He has his flaws—a savior complex among them—but he's not like that."

I couldn't take the elephant in the room any longer, so I dragged it into the light. "He's your ex."

Alisa's chin rose. "We were engaged for a time," she allowed. "We were young. There were issues. But I assure you, I have no conflict of interest when it comes to your representation."

Engaged? I had to actively try to keep my jaw from dropping. My lawyer had planned to *marry* a Hawthorne, and she hadn't thought that merited a mention?

"If you'd prefer," Alisa said stiffly, "I can arrange for someone else from the firm to work as your liaison."

I forced myself to stop gawking at her and tried to process the situation. Alisa had been nothing but professional and seemed almost frighteningly good at her job. Plus, given the whole broken engagement thing, she had a reason *not* to be loyal to the Hawthornes.

"It's okay," I said. "I don't need a new liaison."

That got a very small smile out of her. "I've taken the liberty of enrolling you at Heights Country Day." Alisa moved to the next item on her to-do list with merciless efficiency. "It's the school that Xander and Jameson attend. Grayson graduated last year. I'd hoped to have you enrolled and at least partially acclimated before news of your inheritance broke in the press, but we'll deal with the hand we've been dealt." She gave me a look. "You're the Hawthorne heiress, and you're not a Hawthorne. That's going to draw attention, even at a place like Country Day, where you will be far from the only one with means."

Means, I thought. How many ways did rich people have of not saying the word *rich*?

"I'm pretty sure I can handle a bunch of prep school kids," I said, even though I wasn't sure of that. At all.

Alisa caught sight of my phones. She squatted down and plucked my old phone from the ground. "I'll dispose of this for you."

She didn't even have to look at the screen to realize what had happened. What was *still* happening, if the constant, muted buzzing of the phone was any indication.

"Wait," I told her. I grabbed the phone, ignored the messages, and went for Max's number. I transferred it to my new phone.

"I suggest you strictly regulate who has access to your new number," Alisa told me. "This isn't going to die down anytime soon."

"This," I repeated. The media attention. Strangers sending me messages. People who'd never cared about me deciding we were best friends.

"The students at Country Day will have a bit more discretion," Alisa told me, "but you need to be prepared. As awful as it sounds, money *is* power, and power is magnetic. You're not the person you were two days ago."

I wanted to argue that point, but instead, my mind cycled back to Tobias Hawthorne's letter to Jameson, his words echoing in my mind. *Power corrupts. Absolute power corrupts absolutely.*

CHAPTER 21

"You read my letter." Jameson Hawthorne slid into the back seat of the SUV beside me. Oren had already given me the rundown on the security features of the car. The windows were bulletproof and heavily tinted, and Tobias Hawthorne had owned multiple identical SUVs for times when decoys were needed.

Going to Heights Country Day School apparently wasn't one of them.

"Xander need a ride?" Oren asked from the driver's seat, catching Jameson's eyes in the mirror.

"Xan goes to school early on Fridays," Jameson said. "Extracurricular activity."

In the mirror, Oren's gaze shifted to me. "You okay having company?"

Was I okay in close quarters with Jameson Hawthorne, who'd stepped out of a fireplace and into my bedroom the night before? *He touched my face—*

"It's fine," I told Oren, squelching the memory.

Oren turned the key in the ignition and then cast a glance back over his shoulder. "She's the package," he told Jameson. "If there's an incident..."

"You save her first," Jameson finished. He kicked a foot up on the center console and reclined against the door. "Grandfather always said Hawthorne males have nine lives. I can't possibly have burned through more than five of mine."

Oren turned back to the front and put the car in drive, and then we were off. Even through the bulletproof windows, I could hear the minor roar that went up when we passed outside the gates. Paparazzi. There'd been at least a dozen before. Now there were twice that number—maybe more.

I didn't let myself dwell on that for long. I looked away from the reporters—and toward Jameson. "Here." I reached into my bag and handed him my letter.

"I showed you mine," Jameson said, playing the double entendre for all it was worth. "You show me yours."

"Shut up and read."

He did. "That's it?" he asked when he was done.

I nodded.

"Any idea what he's apologizing for?" Jameson asked. "Any great and anonymous wrongs in your past?"

"One." I swallowed and broke eye contact. "But unless you think your grandfather is responsible for my mom having an extremely rare blood type and ending up way too low on the transplant list, he's probably in the clear."

I'd meant that to sound sarcastic, not raw.

"We'll come back to your letter." Jameson did me the courtesy of ignoring every hint of emotion in my tone. "And turn our attention to mine. I'm curious, Mystery Girl, what do you make of it?"

I got the feeling that this was another test. A chance to show my worth. *Challenge accepted.*

"Your letter is written in proverbs," I said, starting with the obvious. "*All that glitters is not gold. Absolute power corrupts absolutely.*

He's saying that money and power are dangerous. And the first line—*better the devil you know than the one you don't—or is it?*—that's obvious, right?"

His family was the devil that Tobias Hawthorne had known—and I was the devil he hadn't. *But if that's true—why me?* If I was a stranger, how had he chosen me? A dart on a map? Max's imaginary computer algorithm?

And if I was a stranger—why was he sorry?

"Keep going," Jameson prompted.

I focused. "*Nothing is certain but death and taxes.* It sounds to me like he knew he was going to die."

"We didn't even know he was sick," Jameson murmured. That hit close to home. Tobias Hawthorne had apparently been a champion at keeping secrets—like my mother. *I could be the devil he doesn't know, even if he knew her. I would still be a stranger, even if she wasn't.*

I could feel Jameson beside me, watching me in a way that made me wonder if he could see straight inside my head.

"*There but for the grace of God go I,*" I said, returning to the letter's contents, intent on following this to the end. "With different circumstances, any of us could have ended up in anyone else's position," I translated.

"The rich boy can become a pauper." Jameson took his feet down from the center console and turned his head wholly toward me, his green eyes catching mine in a way that made my entire body go to high alert. "And the girl from the wrong side of the tracks can become..."

A princess. A riddle. An heiress. A game.

Jameson smiled. If this was a test, I'd passed. "On the surface," he told me, "it appears that the letter outlines what we already know: My grandfather died and left everything to the devil he didn't know, thereby reversing the fortune of many. Why? Because power corrupts. Absolute power corrupts absolutely."

I couldn't have looked away from him if I'd tried.

"And what about you, Heiress?" Jameson continued. "Are you incorruptible? Is that why he left the fortune in your hands?" The expression playing at the corners of his lips wasn't a smile. I wasn't sure what it was, exactly, other than magnetic. "I know my grandfather." Jameson stared at me intently. "There's more here. A play on words. A code. A hidden message. *Something*."

He handed my letter back. I took it and looked down. "Your grandfather signed my letter with initials." I offered up one last observation. "And yours with his full name."

"And what," Jameson said lightly, "do we make of that?"

We. How had a Hawthorne and I become a *we*? I should have been wary. Even with Oren's assurances—and Alisa's—I should have been keeping my distance. But there was something about this family. Something about these boys.

"Almost there." Oren spoke from the front seat. If he'd been following our conversation, he gave no sign of it. "The Country Day administration has been briefed on the situation. I signed off on the school's security years ago, when the boys enrolled. You should be fine here, Avery, but do not, under any circumstances, leave the campus." Our car pulled past a guarded gate. "I won't be far."

I turned my mind from the letters—Jameson's and mine—to what awaited me outside this car. *This is a high school?* I thought, taking in the sight outside my window. It looked more like a college or a museum, like something out of a catalog where all the students were beautiful and smiling. Suddenly, the uniform I'd been given felt like it didn't belong on my body. I was a kid playing dress-up, pretending that wearing a kitchen pot on her head could turn her into an astronaut, that smudging lipstick all over her face made her a star.

To the rest of the world, I was a sudden celebrity. I was a fascination—and a target. But here? How could people who'd grown up with this kind of money see a girl like me as anything but a fraud?

"I hate to puzzle and run, Mystery Girl...." Jameson's hand was already on the door handle as the SUV pulled to a stop. "But the last thing you need on your first day at this school is for anyone to see you getting cozy with me."

CHAPTER 22

Jameson was gone in a blink. He disappeared into a crowd of burgundy blazers and shiny hair, and I was left still buckled into my seat, unable to move.

"It's just a school," Oren told me. "They're just kids."

Rich kids. Kids whose baseline for normal was probably "just" being the child of a brain surgeon or hotshot lawyer. When they thought *college*, they were probably talking about Harvard or Yale. And there I was, wearing a pleated plaid skirt and a burgundy blazer, complete with a navy crest embossed with Latin words I didn't know how to read.

I grabbed my new phone and sent a message to Max. *This is Avery. New number. Call me.*

Glancing at the front seat again, I forced my hand to the door. It wasn't Oren's job to coddle me. It was his job to protect me—and not from the stares I fully expected the moment I stepped out of this car.

"Do I meet you back here at the end of the day?" I asked.

"I'll be here."

I waited a beat, in case Oren had any other instructions, and then I opened the door. "Thanks for the ride."

Nobody was staring at me. Nobody was whispering. In fact, as I walked toward the twin archways marking the entrance to the main building, I got the distinct feeling that the lack of response was deliberate. Not-staring. Not-talking. Just the lightest of glances, every few steps. Whenever I looked at anyone, they looked away.

I told myself that they were probably trying *not* to make a big deal of my arrival, that this was what discretion looked like—but it still felt like I'd wandered into a ballroom where everyone else was dancing a complicated waltz, twisting, spinning around me like I wasn't even there.

As I closed the distance to the archways, a girl with long black hair bucked the trend of ignoring me like a Thoroughbred shaking off an inferior rider. She watched me intently, and one by one, the girls around her did the same.

When I reached them, the black-haired girl stepped away from the group—toward me.

"I'm Thea," she said, smiling. "You must be Avery." Her voice was perfectly pleasant—borderline musical, like a siren who knew with the least bit of effort she could sing sailors into the sea. "Why don't I show you to the office?"

"The headmaster is Dr. McGowan. She's got a PhD from Princeton. She'll keep you in her office for at least a half hour, talking about *opportunities* and *traditions*. If she offers you coffee, take it—her own personal roast, to die for." Thea seemed well aware of the fact that we were both getting plenty of stares now. She also seemed to be enjoying it. "When Dr. Mac gives you your schedule, make sure you have time for lunch every day. Country Day uses what they call modular scheduling, which means we operate on a six-day cycle, even though we only have school five days a week. Classes meet anywhere from three to five times a cycle, so if you're not careful, you can end up in class straight through lunch on A day and B day but have practically no classes on C or F."

"Okay." My head was spinning, but I forced out one more word. "Thanks."

"People at this school are like fairies in Celtic mythology," Thea said lightly. "You shouldn't thank us unless you want to owe us a boon."

I wasn't sure how to reply to that, so I said nothing. Thea didn't seem to take offense. As she led me down a long hallway with old class portraits lining the walls, she filled the silence. "We're not so bad, really. Most of us anyway. As long as you're with me, you'll be fine."

That rankled. "I'll be fine regardless," I told her.

"Clearly," Thea said emphatically. That was a reference to the money. It had to be. Didn't it? Thea's dark eyes roved over mine. "It must be hard," she said, studying my response with an intensity that her smile did absolutely nothing to hide, "living in that house with those boys."

"It's fine," I said.

"Oh, honey." Thea shook her head. "If there's one thing the Hawthorne family isn't, it's fine. They were a twisted, broken mess before you got here, and they'll be a twisted, broken mess once you're gone."

Gone. Where exactly did Thea think I was going?

We'd reached the end of the hallway now and the door to the headmaster's office. It opened, and four boys poured out in single file. All four of them were bleeding. All four were smiling. Xander was the fourth. He saw me—and then he saw who I was with.

"Thea," he said.

She gave him a too-sweet smile, then lifted a hand to his face—or more specifically, to his bloodied lip. "Xander. Looks like you lost."

"There are no losers in Robot Battle Death Match Fight Club," Xander said stoically. "There are only winners and people whose robots sort of explode."

I thought about Tobias Hawthorne's office—about the patents I'd seen on the walls. What kind of genius *was* Xander Hawthorne? And was he missing an *eyebrow*?

Thea proceeded as if that was exactly nothing to remark upon. "I was just showing Avery to the office and giving her some insider tips on surviving Country Day."

"Charming!" Xander declared. "Avery, did the ever-delightful Thea Calligaris happen to mention that her uncle is married to my aunt?"

Zara's last name was Hawthorne-Calligaris.

"I hear Zara and your uncle are looking for ways to challenge the will." Xander gave every appearance of talking to Thea, but I got the distinct feeling that he was really issuing a warning to me.

Don't trust Thea.

Thea gave an elegant little shrug, undaunted. "I wouldn't know."

CHAPTER 23

I've slotted you into American Studies and Philosophy of Mindfulness. In science and math, you should be able to continue on with your current course of study, assuming our course load doesn't prove to be too much." Dr. McGowan took a sip of her coffee. I did the same. It was just as good as Thea had promised it would be, and that made me wonder how much truth there was to the rest of what she'd said.

It must be hard living in that house with those boys.

They were a twisted, broken mess before you got here, and they'll be a twisted, broken mess once you're gone.

"Now," Dr. Mac—as she'd insisted on being called—continued, "in terms of electives, I would suggest Making Meaning, which focuses on the study of how meaning is conveyed through the arts and includes a strong component of civic engagement with local museums, artists, theater productions, the ballet company, the opera, and so on. Given the support the Hawthorne Foundation has traditionally provided to these endeavors, I believe you will find the course... useful."

The Hawthorne Foundation? I managed—just barely—to avoid repeating the words.

"Now, for the rest of your schedule, I will need you to tell me a bit about your plans for the future. What are you passionate about, Avery?"

It was on the tip of my tongue to tell her what I'd told Principal Altman. I was a girl with a plan—but that plan had always been driven by practicalities. I'd picked a college major that would get me a solid job. The practical thing to do now was stay the course. This school *had* to have more resources than my old one. They could help me game standardized tests, maximize the college credit I received in high school, put me in the perfect position to finish college in three years instead of four. If I played my cards right, even if Zara and her husband somehow ended up undoing what Tobias Hawthorne had done, I could come out ahead.

But Dr. Mac hadn't just asked about my plans. She'd asked what I was passionate about, and even if the Hawthorne family did manage to successfully challenge the will, I'd probably still get a payout. How many millions of dollars might they be willing to pay me just to go away? Worse came to worst, I could probably sell my story for more than enough to pay for college.

"Travel," I blurted out. "I've always wanted to travel."

"Why?" Dr. Mac peered at me. "What is it that attracts you to other places? The art? The history? The peoples and their cultures? Or are you drawn to the marvels of the natural world? Do you want to see mountains and cliffs, oceans and giant sequoia trees, the rain forest—"

"Yes," I said fiercely. I could feel tears stinging in my eyes, and I wasn't entirely sure why. "To all of it. *Yes.*"

Dr. Mac reached out and took my hand. "I'll get you a list of electives to look at," she said softly. "I understand that study abroad won't be an option for the next year, due to your rather unique circumstances, but we have some marvelous programs you might consider thereafter. You might even entertain the idea of delaying graduation a bit."

If someone had told me a week earlier that there was *anything* that could tempt me to stay in high school even a minute longer than necessary, I would have thought they were delusional. But this wasn't a normal school.

Nothing about my life was normal anymore.

CHAPTER 24

Max called me back around noon. At Heights Country Day, modular scheduling meant that there were gaps in my schedule during which I wasn't expected to be anywhere in particular. I could wander the halls. I could spend time in a dance studio, a darkroom, or *one* of the gymnasiums. When, precisely, I ate lunch was up to me. So when Max called and I ducked into an empty classroom, no one stopped me, and no one cared.

"This place is heaven," I told Max. *"Actual. Heaven."*

"The mansion?" Max asked.

"The school," I breathed. "You should see my schedule. And the classes!"

"Avery," Max said sternly. "It is my understanding that you have inherited roughly a bazillion dollars, and you want to talk about your new *school*?"

There was so much I wanted to talk to her about. I had to think to remember what she knew and what she didn't. "Jameson Hawthorne showed me the letter his grandfather left him, and it's this insane, twisty puzzle-riddle thing. Jameson's convinced that's what I am—a puzzle to be solved."

"I am currently looking at a picture of Jameson Hawthorne," Max announced. I heard a flush in the background and realized she must have been in the bathroom—at a school that wasn't as lax about student free time as this one. "Gotta say. He's faxable."

It took me a second to catch on. "Max!"

"I'm just saying, he looks like he knows his way around a fax machine. He's probably really great at dialing the numbers. I bet he's even faxed long-distance."

"I have no idea what you're even talking about anymore," I told her.

I could practically hear her grinning. "Neither do I! And I'm going to stop now because we don't have much time. My parents are freaking out about all of this. Now is not the time for me to be skipping class."

"Your parents are freaking out?" I frowned. "Why?"

"Avery, do you know how many calls I've gotten? A reporter showed up at our house. My mom's threatening to lock down my social media, my email—everything."

I'd never thought of my friendship with Max as particularly public, but it definitely wasn't a secret, either.

"Reporters want to interview you," I said, trying to wrap my mind around it. "About me."

"Have you *seen* the news?" Max asked me.

I swallowed. "No."

There was a pause. "Maybe... don't." That piece of advice spoke volumes. "This is a lot, Ave. Are you okay?"

I blew a hair out of my face. "I'm fine. I've been assured by my lawyer and my head of security that a murder attempt is highly unlikely."

"You have a bodyguard," Max said, awed. "Son of a beach, your life is cool now."

"I have a staff, servants—who hate me, by the way. The house is like nothing I've ever seen. And the family! These boys, Max. They have patents and world records and—"

"I'm looking at pictures of *all* of them now," Max said. "Come to mama, you delicious mustards."

"Mustards?" I echoed.

"Bastions?" she tried.

I let out a snort of laughter. I hadn't realized how badly I'd needed this until she was there.

"I'm sorry, Ave. I have to go. Text me but—"

"Watch what I say," I filled in.

"And in the meantime, buy yourself something nice."

"Like what?" I asked.

"I'll make you a list," she promised. "Love you, beach."

"Love you, too, Max." I kept the phone up to my ear for a second or two after she was gone. *I wish you were here.*

Eventually, I managed to find the cafeteria. There were maybe two dozen people eating. One of them was Thea. She nudged a chair out from her table with her foot.

She's Zara's niece, I reminded myself. *And Zara wants me gone.* Still, I sat.

"I'm sorry if I came on a little strong this morning." Thea glanced at the other girls at her table, all of whom were just as impossibly polished and beautiful as she was. "It's just that, in your position, I'd want to know."

I recognized the bait for exactly what it was, but I couldn't keep myself from asking. "Know what?"

"About the Hawthorne brothers. For the longest time, every boy wanted to be them, and everyone who likes boys wanted to date them. The way they look. The way they act." Thea paused. "Even just being Hawthorne-adjacent changed the way that people looked at you."

"I used to study with Xander sometimes," one of the other girls said. "Before..." She trailed off.

Before what? I was missing something here—something big.

"They were magic." Thea had the oddest expression on her face. "And when you were in their orbit, you felt like magic, too."

"Invincible," someone else chimed in.

I thought about Jameson, dropping down from a second-story balcony the day we'd met, Grayson sitting behind Principal Altman's desk and banishing him from the room with an arch of his brow. And then there was Xander: six foot three, grinning, bleeding, and talking about robots exploding.

"They aren't what you think they are," Thea told me. "I wouldn't want to live in a house with the Hawthornes."

Was this an attempt to get under my skin? If I left Hawthorne House—if I moved out—I'd lose my inheritance. Did she know that? Had her uncle put her up to this?

Coming into today, I'd expected to be treated like trash. I wouldn't have been surprised if the girls at this school had been possessive over the Hawthorne boys, or if everyone, male and female, had resented me on the boys' behalf. But this...

This was something else.

"I should go." I stood, but Thea stood with me.

"Think what you want to about me," she said. "But the last girl at this school who got tangled up with the Hawthorne brothers? The last girl who spent hour after hour in that house? She *died*."

CHAPTER 25

I left the cafeteria as soon as I'd choked down my food, unsure where I was going to hide until my next class and equally uncertain that Thea had been lying. *The last girl who spent hour after hour in that house?* My brain kept replaying the words. *She died.*

I made it down one hallway and was turning toward another when Xander Hawthorne popped out of a nearby lab, holding what appeared to be a mechanical dragon.

All I could think about was what Thea had just said.

"You look like you could use a robotic dragon," Xander told me. "Here." He thrust it into my hands.

"What am I supposed to do with this?" I asked.

"That depends on how attached you are to your eyebrows." Xander raised his one remaining eyebrow very high.

I tried to summon up a reply, but I had nothing. *The last girl who spent hour after hour in that house? She died.*

"Are you hungry?" Xander asked me. "The refectory is back that way."

As much as I hated letting Thea win, I was wary—of him, of all things Hawthorne. "Refectory?" I repeated, trying to sound normal.

Xander grinned. "It's prep school for *cafeteria*."

"Prep school isn't a language," I pointed out.

"Next you'll be telling me that French isn't one, either." Xander patted the robotic dragon on its head. It burped. A wisp of smoke rose up from its mouth.

They aren't what you think they are, I could hear Thea warning me.

"Are you okay?" Xander asked, and then he snapped his fingers. "Thea got to you, didn't she?"

I handed the dragon back to him before it could explode. "I don't want to talk about Thea."

"As it so happens," Xander said, "I hate talking about Thea. Shall we discuss your little tête-à-tête with Jameson last night instead?"

He knew that his brother had been to my room. "It wasn't a tête-à-tête."

"You and your grudge against French." Xander peered at me. "Jameson showed you his letter, didn't he?"

I had no idea whether or not that was supposed to be a secret. "Jameson thinks it's a clue," I said.

Xander was quiet for a moment, then nodded in the opposite direction from the refectory. "Come on."

I followed him because it was either that or find myself another random empty classroom.

"I used to lose," Xander said suddenly as we rounded a corner. "On Saturday mornings, when my grandfather set us to a challenge, I always lost." I had no idea why he was telling me this. "I was the youngest. The least competitive. The most apt to be distracted by scones or complex machinery."

"But...," I prompted. I could hear in his tone that there was one.

"But," Xander replied, "while my brothers were trying to take one another down in the race to the finish line, I was generously sharing my scones with the old man. He was awfully chatty, full of stories and facts and contradictions. Would you like to hear one?"

"A contradiction?" I asked.

"A fact." Xander wiggled his eyebrows—*eyebrow.* "He didn't have a middle name."

"What?" I said.

"My grandfather was born Tobias Hawthorne," Xander told me. "No middle name."

I wondered if the old man had signed Xander's letter the same way he had signed Jameson's. *Tobias Tattersall Hawthorne.* He'd signed mine with initials—three of them.

"If I asked you to show me your letter, would you?" I asked Xander. He'd said that he usually came in last in their grandfather's games. That didn't mean he wasn't playing this one.

"Now, where would the fun be in that?" Xander deposited me in front of a thick wooden door. "You'll be safe from Thea in there. There are some places even she dares not tread."

I glanced through the clear pane on the door. "The library?"

"The archive," Xander corrected archly. "It's prep school for *library*—not a bad place to hang out during free mods if you're looking to get some time alone."

Hesitantly, I pushed the door open. "You coming?" I asked him.

He closed his eyes. "I can't." He didn't offer any more explanation than that. As he walked away, I couldn't shake the feeling that I was missing something.

Maybe multiple somethings.

The last girl who spent hour after hour in that house? She died.

CHAPTER 26

The archive looked more like a university library than one that belonged in a high school. The room was full of archways and stained glass. Countless shelves were brimming with books of every kind, and at the center of the room, there were a dozen rectangular tables—state of the art, with lights built into the tables and enormous magnifying glasses attached to the sides.

All the tables were empty except for one. A girl sat with her back to me. She had auburn hair, a darker red than I'd ever seen on a person. I sat down several tables away from her, facing the door. The room was silent except for the sound of the other girl turning the pages of the book she was reading.

I withdrew Jameson's letter and my own from my bag. *Tattersall.* I dragged my finger over the middle name with which Tobias Hawthorne had signed Jameson's missive, then looked at the initials scrawled on mine. The handwriting matched. Something nagged at me, and it took me a moment to realize what it was. *He used the middle name in the will, too.* What if that was the catch here? What if that was all it took to invalidate the terms?

I texted Alisa. The reply came immediately: *Legal name change, years ago. We're good.*

Xander had said that his grandfather was *born* Tobias Hawthorne, no middle name. Why tell me that at all? Deeply doubting that I would ever understand anyone with the last name Hawthorne, I reached for the magnifying glass attached to the table. It was the size of my hand. I placed the two letters side by side beneath it and turned on the lights built into the table.

Chalk one up for private schools.

The paper was thick enough that the light didn't shine through, but the magnifying glass made quick work of blowing the writing up ten times its normal size. I adjusted the glass, bringing the signature on Jameson's letter into focus. I could see details now in Tobias Hawthorne's handwriting that I hadn't been able to see before. A slight hook on his *r*'s. Asymmetry on his capital *T*'s. And there, in his middle name, was a noticeable space, twice that between any two other letters. Magnified, that space made the name appear as two words.

Tatters all. Tatters, all. "As in, he left them all in tatters?" I wondered out loud. It was a leap, but it didn't feel like much of one, not when Jameson had been so sure that there was more to this letter than met the eyes. Not when Xander had made it a point to tell me about his grandfather's lack of a middle name. If Tobias Hawthorne had legally changed his name to add in *Tattersall*, that strongly suggested he'd chosen the name himself. *To what end?*

I looked up, suddenly remembering that I wasn't alone in this room, but the girl with the dark red hair was gone. I shot off another text to Alisa: *When did TH change his name?*

Did the name change correspond to the moment he'd decided to leave his family in the billionaire version of tatters, to leave everything to me?

A text came through a moment later, but it wasn't from Alisa. It was from Jameson. I had no idea how he'd even gotten the number—for this new phone or my last.

I see it now, Mystery Girl. Do you?

I looked around, feeling like he might be watching me from the wings, but by all indications, I was alone.

The middle name? I typed back.

No. I waited, and a second text came through a full minute later. *The sign-off.*

My gaze went to the end of Jameson's letter. Right before the signature, there were two words: *Don't judge.*

Don't judge the Hawthorne patriarch for dying without ever telling his family he was sick? Don't judge the games he was playing from beyond the grave? Don't judge the way he had pulled the rug out from underneath his daughters and grandsons?

I looked back at Jameson's text, then to the letter, and read it again from the beginning. *Better the devil you know than the one you don't—or is it? Power corrupts. Absolute power corrupts absolutely. All that glitters is not gold. Nothing is certain but death and taxes. There but for the grace of God go I.*

I imagined being Jameson, getting this letter—wanting answers and being given platitudes instead. *Proverbs.* My brain supplied the alternate term, and my eyes darted back down to the sign-off. Jameson had thought we were looking for a wordplay or a code. Every line in this letter, barring the proper names, was a proverb or a slight variation thereon.

Every line except one.

Don't judge. I'd missed most of my old English teacher's lecture on proverbs, but there was only one I could think of that started with those two words.

Does "Don't judge a book by its cover" mean anything to you? I asked Jameson.

His reply was immediate. *Very good, Heiress.* Then, a moment later: *It sure as hell does.*

CHAPTER 27

"We could be making something out of nothing," I said hours later. Jameson and I stood in the Hawthorne House library, looking up at the shelves circling the room, filled with books from eighteen-foot ceiling to floor.

"Hawthorne-born or Hawthorne-made, there's always something to be played." Jameson spoke with a singsong rhythm, like a child skipping rope. But when he brought his gaze down from the shelves to me, there was nothing childlike in his expression. "Everything is something in Hawthorne House."

Everything, I thought. *And everyone.*

"Do you know how many times in my life one of my grandfather's puzzles has sent me to this room?" Jameson turned slowly in a circle. "He's probably rolling in his grave that it took me this long to see it."

"What do you think we're looking for?" I asked.

"What do *you* think we're looking for, Heiress?" Jameson had a way of making everything sound like it was either a challenge or an invitation.

Or both.

Focus, I told myself. I was here because I wanted answers at least as much as the boy beside me did. "If the clue is *a book by its cover*," I said, turning the riddle over in my mind "then I'd guess that we're looking for either a book or a cover—or maybe a mismatch between the two?"

"A book that doesn't match its cover?" Jameson's expression gave no hint of what he thought of that suggestion.

"I could be wrong."

Jameson's lips twisted—not quite a smile, not quite a smirk. "Everyone is a little wrong sometimes, Heiress."

An invitation—and a challenge. I had no intention of being *a little wrong*—not with him. The sooner my body remembered that, the better. I physically turned away from Jameson to do a three-sixty, slowly taking in the scope of the room. Just looking up at the shelves felt like standing at the edge of the Grand Canyon. We were completely encircled by books, going up two stories. "There must be thousands of books in here." Given how big the library was, given how high the shelves went up, if we *were* looking for a book mismatched to its cover sleeve…

"This could take hours," I said.

Jameson smiled—with teeth this time. "Don't be ridiculous, Heiress. It could take days."

We worked in silence. Neither one of us left for dinner. A thrill ran through my body each time I realized that I was holding a first edition. Every once in a while, I'd flip a book open to find it signed. Stephen King. J. K. Rowling. Toni Morrison. Eventually, I managed to stop pausing in awe at what I held in my hands. I lost track of time, lost track of everything except the rhythm of pulling books off shelves and covers off books, replacing the cover, replacing the book. I could hear Jameson working. I could feel him in the room, as we moved through our respective shelves, closer and closer to each other. He'd taken the upper level. I was working down below. Finally, I glanced up to see him right on top of me.

"What if we're wasting our time?" I asked. My question echoed through the room.

"Time is money, Heiress. You have plenty to waste."

"Stop calling me that."

"I have to call you something, and you didn't seem to appreciate Mystery Girl or the abbreviation thereof."

It was on the tip of my tongue to point out that I didn't call him anything. I hadn't said his name once since entering this room. But somehow, instead of offering that retort, I looked up at him, and a different question came out of my mouth instead.

"What did you mean in the car today, when you said that the last thing I needed was for anyone to see us together?"

I could hear him taking books off shelves and covers off books and replacing them both—again and again—before I got a response. "You spent the day at the fine institution that is Heights Country Day," he said. "What do you think I meant?"

He always had to be the one asking questions, always had to turn everything around.

"Don't tell me," Jameson murmured up above, "that you didn't hear any whispers."

I froze, thinking about what I had heard. "I met a girl." I made myself continue working my way through the shelf—book off, cover off, cover on, book reshelved. "Thea."

Jameson snorted. "Thea isn't a girl. She's a whirlwind wrapped in a hurricane wrapped in steel—and every girl in that school follows her lead, which means I'm persona non grata and have been for a year." He paused. "What did Thea say to you?" Jameson's attempt to sound casual might have fooled me if I'd been looking at his face, but without the expression to sell it, I heard a telltale note underneath. *He cares.*

Suddenly, I wished I hadn't brought Thea up. Sowing discord was probably her goal.

"Avery?"

Jameson's use of my given name confirmed for me that he didn't just want a response; he needed one.

"Thea kept talking about this house," I said carefully. "About what it must be like for me to live here." That was true—or true enough. "About all of you."

"Is it still a lie," Jameson asked loftily, "if you're masking what matters, but what you're saying is technically true?"

He wanted the truth.

"Thea said there was a girl and that she died." I spoke like I was ripping off a bandage, too fast to second-guess what I was saying.

Overhead, the rhythm of Jameson's work slowed. I counted five seconds of utter silence before he spoke. "Her name was Emily."

I knew, though I couldn't pinpoint how, that he wouldn't have said it if I'd been able to see his face.

"Her name was Emily," he repeated. "And she wasn't just a girl."

A breath caught in my throat. I forced it out and kept checking books, because I didn't want him to know how much I'd heard in his tone. *Emily mattered to him. She still matters to him.*

"I'm sorry," I said—sorry for bringing it up and sorry she was gone. "We should call it a night." It was late, and I didn't trust myself not to say something else I might regret.

Jameson's working rhythm stopped overhead and was replaced with the sound of footsteps as he made his way to and down the wrought-iron spiral stairs. He positioned himself between me and the exit. "Same time tomorrow?"

It suddenly felt imperative that I not let myself look at his deep green eyes. "We're making good progress," I said, forcing myself to head for the door. "Even if we don't find a way to shortcut the process, we should be able to make it through all the shelves within the week."

Jameson leaned toward me as I passed. "Don't hate me," he said softly.

Why would I hate you? I felt my pulse jump in my throat. Because of what he'd just said, or because of how close he was to me?

"There's a slight chance that we might not be done within the week."

"Why not?" I asked, forgetting to avoid looking at him.

He brought his lips right next to my ear. "This isn't the only library in Hawthorne House."

CHAPTER 28

How many libraries did this place have? That was what I focused on as I walked away from Jameson—not the feel of his body too close to mine, not the fact that Thea hadn't been lying when she'd said that there was a girl or that she'd died.

Emily. I tried and failed to banish the whisper in my mind. *Her name was Emily.* I reached the main staircase and hesitated. If I went back to my wing now, if I tried to sleep, all I would do was replay my conversation with Jameson, again and again. I glanced back over my shoulder to see if he'd followed me—and saw Oren instead.

My head of security had told me I was safe here. He seemed to believe it. But still, he trailed me—invisible until he wanted to be seen.

"Turning in for the night?" Oren asked me.

"No." There was no way I could sleep, no way I could even close my eyes—so I explored. Down one long hall, I found a theater. Not a movie theater, but something closer to an opera house. The walls were golden. A red velvet curtain obscured what had to be a stage. The seats were on an incline. The ceiling arced, and when I flipped a switch, hundreds of tiny lights came to life along that arc.

I remembered Dr. Mac telling me about the Hawthorne Foundation's support of the arts.

The next room over was filled with musical instruments—dozens of them. I bent to look at a violin with an *S* carved to one side of the strings, its mirror image on the other.

"That's a Stradivarius." Those words were issued like a threat.

I turned to see Grayson standing in the doorway. I wondered if he'd been following us—and for how long. He stared at me, his pupils black and fathomless, the irises around them ice gray. "You should be careful, Ms. Grambs."

"I'm not going to break anything," I said, stepping back from the violin.

"You should be careful," Grayson reiterated, his voice soft but deadly, "with Jameson. The last thing my brother needs is you and whatever this is."

I glanced at Oren, but his face was impassive, like he couldn't hear anything that passed between us. *It's not his job to eavesdrop. It's his job to protect me—and he doesn't see Grayson as a threat.*

"*This* being me?" I shot back. "Or the terms of your grandfather's will?" I wasn't the one who'd upended their lives. But I was here, and Tobias Hawthorne wasn't. Logically, I knew that my best option was to avoid confrontation, avoid *him* altogether. This was a big house.

Standing this close to Grayson, it didn't feel nearly big enough.

"My mother hasn't left her room in days." Grayson stared at and into me. "Xander nearly blew himself up today. Jameson is one bad idea away from ruining his life, and none of us can leave the estate without being hounded by the press. The property damage they've caused alone..."

Say nothing. Turn away. Don't engage. "Do you think this is easy for me?" I asked instead. "Do you think I want to be stalked by the paparazzi?"

"You want the money." Grayson Hawthorne looked down at me from on high. "How could you not, growing up the way you did?"

That was just dripping with condescension. "Like you *don't* want the money?" I retorted. "Growing up the way *you* did? Maybe I haven't had everything handed to me my entire life, but—"

"You have no idea," Grayson said lowly, "how ill prepared you are. A girl like you?"

"You don't know me." A rush of fury surged through my veins as I cut him off.

"I will," Grayson promised. "I'll know everything about you soon enough." Every bone in my body said that he was a person who kept his promises. "My access to funds might be somewhat limited currently, but the Hawthorne name still means something. There will always be people tripping over themselves to do favors for any one of us." He didn't move, didn't blink, wasn't physically aggressive in any way, but he bled power, and he knew it. "Whatever you're hiding, I'll find it. Every last secret. Within days, I'll have a detailed dossier on every person in your life. Your sister. Your father. Your mother—"

"Don't talk about my mother." My chest was tight. Breathing was a challenge.

"Stay away from my family, Ms. Grambs." Grayson pushed past me. I'd been dismissed.

"Or what?" I called after him, and then, possessed by something I couldn't quite name, I continued. "Or what happened to Emily will happen to me?"

Grayson jerked to a halt, every muscle in his body taut. "Don't you say her name." His posture was angry, but his voice sounded like it was about to crumble. Like I'd *gutted* him.

Not just Jameson. My mouth went dry. *Emily didn't just matter to Jameson.*

I felt a hand on my shoulder. *Oren.* His expression was gentle, but clearly, he wanted me to leave it alone.

"You won't last a month in this house." Grayson managed to pull himself together long enough to issue that prediction like a royal issuing a decree. "In fact, I'd lay money that you're gone within the week."

CHAPTER 29

Libby found me shortly after I made my way back to my room. She was holding a stack of electronics. "Alisa said I should buy some things for you. She said you haven't bought anything for yourself."

"I haven't had time." I was exhausted, overwhelmed, and past the point of being able to wrap my mind around *anything* that had happened since I'd moved into Hawthorne House.

Including Emily.

"Lucky for you," Libby replied, "I have nothing *but* time." She didn't sound entirely happy about that, but before I could probe further, she began setting things down on my desk. "New laptop. A tablet. An e-reader, loaded with romance novels, in case you need some escapism."

"Look around at this place," I said. "My life *is* escapism at the moment."

That got a grin out of Libby. "Have you seen the gym?" she asked me, the awe in her voice making it clear that she had. "Or the chef's kitchen?"

"Not yet." My gaze caught suddenly on the fireplace, and I found myself listening, wondering: Was anyone back there? *You won't last a month in this house.* I didn't think Grayson had meant that as a physical threat—and Oren certainly hadn't reacted as if my life were being threatened. Still, I shivered.

"Ave? There's something I have to show you." Libby flipped open my new tablet's cover. "Just for the record, it's okay if you want to yell."

"Why would I—" I cut off when I saw what she'd pulled up. It was a video of Drake.

He was standing next to a reporter. The fact that his hair was combed told me that the interview hadn't been a total surprise. The caption across the screen read: *Friend of the Grambs family.*

"Avery was always a loner," Drake said on-screen. "She didn't have friends."

I had Max—and that was all I'd needed.

"I'm not saying she was a bad person. I think she was just kind of desperate for attention. She wanted to matter. A girl like that, a rich old man..." He trailed off. "Let's just say that there were definite daddy issues."

Libby cut the video off there.

"Can I see that?" I asked, gesturing toward the tablet with murder in my heart—and probably my eyes.

"That's the worst of it," Libby assured me. "Would you like to yell now?"

Not at you. I took the tablet and scrolled through the related videos—all of them interviews or think pieces, all about me. Former classmates. Coworkers. Libby's mom. I ignored the interviews until I got to one that I couldn't ignore. It was labeled simply: *Skye Hawthorne and Zara Hawthorne-Calligaris.*

The two of them stood behind a podium at what appeared to be some kind of press conference—so much for Grayson's assertion that his mother hadn't left her room in days.

"Our father was a great man." Zara's hair whipped in a subtle wind. The expression on her face was stoic. "He was a revolutionary entrepreneur, a once-in-a-generation philanthropist, and a man who valued family above all else." She took Skye's hand. "As we grieve his passing, rest assured that we will not see his life's work die with him. The Hawthorne Foundation will continue operations. My father's numerous investments will undergo no immediate changes. While we cannot comment on the complex legalities of the current situation, I can assure you that we are working with the authorities, elder-abuse specialists, and a team of medical and legal professionals to get to the bottom of this situation." She turned to Skye, whose eyes brimmed with unshed tears—perfect, picturesque, dramatic.

"Our father was our hero," Zara declared. "We will not allow him, in death, to become a victim. To that end, we are providing the press with the results of a genetic test that proves conclusively that, contrary to the libelous reports and speculation circulating in the tabloids, Avery Grambs is not the result of infidelity on the part of our father, who was faithful to his beloved wife, our mother, for the entirety of their marriage. We as a family are as bewildered at recent events as all of you, but genes don't lie. Whatever else this girl may be, she is not a Hawthorne."

The video cut off. Dumbfounded, I thought back to Grayson's parting shot. *I'd lay money that you're gone within the week.*

"Elder-abuse specialists?" Libby was agog and aghast beside me.

"And the authorities," I added. "Plus a team of medical specialists. She might not have come right out and said that I'm under investigation for defrauding a dementia-ridden old man, but she sure as hell implied it."

"She doesn't get to do that." Libby was pissed—a blue-haired, ponytailed, gothic ball of fury. "She can't just say whatever she wants. Call Alisa. You have lawyers!"

What I had was a headache. This wasn't unexpected. Given the size of the fortune at stake, it was inevitable. Oren had warned me that the women would come after me in the courtroom.

"I'll call Alisa tomorrow," I told Libby. "Right now, I'm going to bed."

CHAPTER 30

"They don't have a legal leg to stand on."

I didn't have to call Alisa in the morning. She showed up and found me.

"Rest assured, we will shut this down. My father will be meeting with Zara and Constantine later today."

"Constantine?" I asked.

"Zara's husband."

Thea's uncle, I thought.

"They know, of course, that they stand to lose a great deal by challenging the will. Zara's debts are substantial, and they won't be cleared if she files a suit. What Zara and Constantine don't know, and what my father will make very clear to them, is that even if a judge were to rule Mr. Hawthorne's latest will to be null and void, the distribution of his estate would then be governed by his prior will, and *that* will left the Hawthorne family even less than this one."

Traps upon traps. I thought about what Jameson said after the will had been read, and then I thought about the conversation I'd had with Xander over scones. *Even if you* thought *that you'd manipulated our grandfather into this, I guarantee that he'd be the one manipulating you.*

"How long ago did Tobias write his prior will?" I asked, wondering if its only purpose had been to reinforce this one.

"Twenty years ago in August." Alisa ruled out that possibility. "The entire estate was to go to charity."

"Twenty years?" I repeated. That was longer than any of the Hawthorne grandsons except Nash had been alive. "He disinherited his daughters twenty years ago and never told them?"

"Apparently so. And in answer to your query yesterday"—Alisa was nothing if not efficient—"the firm's records show that Mr. Hawthorne legally changed his name twenty years ago last August. Prior to that, he had no middle name."

Tobias Hawthorne had given himself a middle name at the same time he'd disinherited his family. *Tattersall. Tatters, all.* Given everything that Jameson and Xander had told me about their grandfather, that seemed like a message. Leaving the money to me—and before me, to charity—wasn't the point.

Disinheriting his family was.

"What the hell happened twenty years ago in August?" I asked.

Alisa seemed to be weighing her response. My eyes narrowed, and I wondered if any part of her was still loyal to Nash. To his family.

"Mr. Hawthorne and his wife lost their son that summer. Toby. He was nineteen, the youngest of their children." Alisa paused, then forged on. "Toby had taken several friends to one of his parents' vacation homes. There was a fire. Toby and three other young people perished."

I tried to wrap my mind around what she was saying: Tobias Hawthorne had written his daughters out of his will after the death of his son. *He was never the same after Toby died.* Zara had said that when she'd thought she'd been passed over for her sister's sons. I searched my mind for Skye's reply.

Disappeared, Skye had insisted, and Zara had lost it.

"Why would Skye say that Toby disappeared?"

Alisa was caught off guard by my question—clearly, she didn't remember the exchange at the reading of the will.

"Between the fire and a storm that night," Alisa said, once she'd recovered, "Toby's remains were never definitively found."

My brain worked overtime trying to integrate this information. "Couldn't Zara and Skye have their lawyer argue that the old will was invalid, too?" I asked. "Written under duress, or he was mad with grief, or something like that?"

"Mr. Hawthorne signed a document reaffirming his will yearly," Alisa told me. "He never changed it, until you."

Until me. My entire body tingled, just thinking about it. "How long ago was that?" I asked.

"Last year."

What could have happened to make Tobias Hawthorne decide that instead of leaving his entire fortune to charity, he was going to leave it to me?

Maybe he knew my mother. Maybe he knew she died. Maybe he was sorry.

"Now, if your curiosity has been sated," Alisa said, "I would like to return to more pressing issues. I believe my father can get a handle on Zara and Constantine. Our biggest remaining PR issue is…" Alisa steeled herself. "Your sister."

"Libby?" That hadn't been what I was expecting.

"It's to everyone's benefit if she lies low."

"How could she possibly lie low?" I asked. This was the biggest story on the planet.

"For the immediate future, I've advised her to stay on the estate," Alisa said, and I thought about Libby's comment that she had nothing *but* time. "Eventually, she can think about charity work, if she would like, but for the time being, we need to be able to control the narrative, and your sister has a way of... drawing attention."

I wasn't sure if that was a reference to Libby's fashion choices or her black eye. Anger bubbled up inside me. "My sister can wear whatever she wants," I said flatly. "She can do whatever she wants. If Texas high society and the tabloids don't like it, that's too damn bad."

"This is a delicate situation," Alisa replied calmly. "Especially with the press. And Libby..."

"She hasn't talked to the press," I said, as sure of that as I was of my own name.

"Her ex-boyfriend has. Her mother has. Both are looking for ways to cash in." Alisa gave me a look. "I don't need to tell you that most lottery winners find their existence made miserable as they drown in requests and demands from family and friends. You are blessedly short on both. Libby, however, is another matter."

If Libby had been the one to inherit, instead of me, she would have been incapable of saying no. She would have given and given, to everyone who managed to get their hooks in her.

"We might consider a one-time payment to the mother," Alisa said, all business. "Along with a nondisclosure agreement preventing her from talking about you or Libby to the press."

My stomach rebelled at the idea of giving money to Libby's mom. The woman didn't deserve a penny. But Libby didn't deserve to have to see her mother regularly trying to sell her out on the nightly news.

"Fine," I said, clenching my teeth, "but I'm not giving *anything* to Drake."

Alisa smiled, a flash of teeth. "Him, I'll muzzle for fun." She held out a thick binder. "In the meantime, I've assembled some key information for you, and I have someone coming in this afternoon to work on your wardrobe and appearance."

"My *what*?"

"Libby, as you said, can wear whatever she wants, but you don't have that luxury." Alisa shrugged. "You're the real story here. Looking the part is always step one."

I had no idea how this conversation had started with legal and PR issues, detoured through Hawthorne family tragedy, and ended with me being told by my lawyer that I needed a makeover.

I took the binder from Alisa's outstretched hand, tossed it on the desk, then headed for the door.

"Where are you going?" Alisa called after me.

I almost said *the library*, but Grayson's warning from the day before was still fresh in my mind. "Doesn't this place have a bowling alley?"

CHAPTER 31

It really was a bowling alley. In my house. There was a bowling alley *in my house.* As promised, there were "only" four lanes, but otherwise, it had everything you'd expect a bowling alley to have. There was a ball return. Pin-setters on each lane. A touch screen to set up the games, and fifty-five-inch monitors overhead to keep track of the score. Emblazoned on all of it—the balls, the lanes, the touch screen, the monitors—was an elaborate letter *H.*

I tried not to take that as a reminder that none of this was supposed to be mine.

Instead, I focused on choosing the right ball. The right shoes—because there were at least forty pairs of bowling shoes on a rack to the side. *Who needs forty pairs of bowling shoes?*

Tapping my finger against the touch screen, I entered my initials. *AKG.* An instant later, a welcome flashed across the monitor.

WELCOME TO HAWTHORNE HOUSE, AVERY KYLIE GRAMBS!

The hairs on my arms stood up. I doubted programming my name into this unit had been a top priority for anyone the last couple of days. *And that means…*

"Was it you?" I asked out loud, addressing the words to Tobias Hawthorne. Had one of his last acts on earth been to program this welcome?

I pushed down the urge to shiver. At the end of the second lane, pins were waiting for me. I picked up my ball—ten pounds, with a silver *H* on a dark green background. Back home, the bowling alley had offered ninety-nine-cent bowling once a month. My mom and I had gone, every time.

I wished that she were here, and then I wondered: If she *were* alive, would I even be here? I wasn't a Hawthorne. Unless the old man had chosen me randomly, unless I had somehow done something to catch his attention, his decision to leave everything to me had to have something to do with her.

If she'd been alive, would you have left the money to her? At least this time, I wasn't addressing Tobias Hawthorne out loud. *What were you sorry for? Did you do something to her? Not do something to her—or for her?*

I have a secret.... I heard my mom saying. I threw the ball harder than I should have and hit only two pins. If my mom had been here, she would have mocked me. I concentrated then and bowled. Five games later, I was covered in sweat, and my arms were aching. I felt good—good enough to venture back out into the House and go hunting for the gym.

Athletic complex might have been a more accurate term. I stepped out onto the basketball court. The room jutted out in an L shape, with two weight benches and a half dozen workout machines in the smaller part of the L. There was a door on the back wall.

As long as I'm playing Dorothy in Oz...

I opened it and found myself looking up. A rock climbing wall stretched out two stories overhead. A figure grappled with a near-vertical section on the wall, at least twenty feet up, with no harness. *Jameson.*

He must have sensed me somehow. "Ever climbed one of these before?" he called down.

Again, I thought of Grayson's warning, but this time, I told myself that I didn't give a damn about what Grayson Hawthorne had to say to me. I walked over to the climbing wall, planted my feet at the base, and did a quick survey of the available hand- and footholds.

"First time," I called back to Jameson, reaching for one of them. "But I'm a quick learner."

I made it until my feet were about six feet off the ground before the wall jutted out at an angle designed to make things difficult. I braced one leg against a foothold and the other against the wall and stretched my right arm for a handhold a fraction of an inch too far away.

I missed.

From the ledge above me, a hand snaked down and grabbed mine. Jameson smirked as I dangled midair. "You can drop," he told me, "or I can try to swing you up."

Do it. I bit back the words. Oren was nowhere to be seen, and the last thing I needed to do, alone with a Hawthorne, was go higher. Instead, I let go of his arm and braced for impact.

After I landed, I stood, watching Jameson work his way back up the wall, muscles tensing against his thin white T-shirt. *This is a bad idea,* I told myself, my heart thumping. *Jameson Winchester Hawthorne is a very bad idea.* I hadn't even realized I remembered his middle name until it popped into my head, a last name, just like his first. *Stop looking at him. Stop thinking about him. The next year is going to be complicated enough without... complications.*

Feeling suddenly like I was being watched, I turned to the

door—and found Grayson staring straight at me. His light eyes were narrowed and focused.

You don't scare me, Grayson Hawthorne. I forced myself to turn away from him, swallowed, and called up to Jameson. "I'll see you in the library."

CHAPTER 32

The library was empty when I stepped through the door at nine fifteen, but it didn't stay empty for long. Jameson arrived at half past nine, and Grayson let himself in at nine thirty-one.

"What are we doing today?" Grayson asked his brother.

"We?" Jameson shot back.

Grayson meticulously cuffed his sleeves. He'd changed after his workout, donning a stiff collared shirt like armor. "Can't an older brother spend time with his younger brother and an interloper of dubious intentions without getting the third degree?"

"He doesn't trust me with you," I translated.

"I'm such a delicate flower." Jameson's tone was light, but his eyes told a different story. "In need of protection and constant supervision."

Grayson was undaunted by sarcasm. "So it would seem." He smiled, the expression razor sharp. "What are we doing today?" he repeated.

I had no idea what it was about his voice that made him so impossible to ignore.

"Heiress and I," Jameson replied pointedly, "are following a hunch, doubtlessly wasting sinful amounts of time on what I'm sure you would consider to be nonsensical flapdoodle."

Grayson frowned. "I don't talk like that."

Jameson let the arch of an eyebrow speak for itself.

Grayson narrowed his eyes. "And what hunch are the two of you following?"

When it became clear that Jameson wasn't going to answer, I did—not because I owed Grayson Hawthorne a single damn thing. Because part of any winning strategy, long-term, was knowing when to play to your opponent's expectations and when to subvert them. Grayson Hawthorne expected nothing from me. *Nothing good.*

"We think your grandfather's letter to Jameson included a clue about what he was thinking."

"What he was thinking," Grayson repeated, sharp eyes making a casual study of my features, "and why he left everything to *you*."

Jameson leaned back against the doorframe. "It sounds like him, doesn't it?" he asked Grayson. "One last game?"

I could hear in Jameson's tone that he wanted Grayson to say yes. He wanted his brother's agreement, or possibly approval. Maybe some part of him wanted for them to do this together. For a split second, I saw a spark of *something* in Grayson's eyes, too, but it was extinguished so quickly I was left wondering if the light and my mind were playing tricks on me.

"Frankly, Jamie," Grayson commented, "I'm surprised you still feel you know the old man at all."

"I am just full of surprises." Jameson must have caught himself wanting something from Grayson, because the light in his own eyes went out, too. "And you can leave any time, Gray."

"I think not," Grayson replied. "Better the devil you know than the devil you don't." He let those words hang in the air. "Or is it? Power corrupts. Absolute power corrupts absolutely."

My eyes darted toward Jameson, who stood eerily, absolutely still.

"He left you the same message," Jameson said finally, pushing off the doorway and pacing the room. "The same clue."

"Not a clue," Grayson countered. "An indication that he wasn't in his right mind."

Jameson whirled on him. "You don't believe that." He assessed Grayson's expression, his posture. "But a judge might." Jameson shot me a look. "He'll use his letter against you if he can."

He might have given his letter to Zara and Constantine already, I thought. But according to what Alisa had told me, that wouldn't matter.

"There was another will before this one," I said, looking from brother to brother. "Your grandfather left your family even less in that one. He didn't disinherit you *for* me." I was looking at Grayson when I said those words. "He disinherited the entire Hawthorne family before you were even born—right after your uncle died."

Jameson stopped pacing. "You're lying." His entire body was tense.

Grayson held my gaze. "She's not."

If I'd been guessing how this would go, I would have guessed that Jameson would believe me and that Grayson would be the skeptic. Regardless, both of them were staring at me now.

Grayson broke eye contact first. "You may as well tell me what you think that godforsaken letter means, Jamie."

"And why," Jameson said through gritted teeth, "would I give away the game like that?"

They were used to competing with each other, to pushing to the finish line. I couldn't shake the feeling that I didn't belong here—between them—at all.

"You do realize, Jamie, that I am capable of staying here with the two of you in this room indefinitely?" Grayson said. "As soon as I see what you're up to, you know I'll reason it out. I was raised to play, same as you."

Jameson stared hard at his brother, then smiled. "It's up to the interloper of dubious intentions." His smile turned to a smirk.

He expects me to send Grayson packing. I probably should have, but it was entirely possible that we were wasting our time here, and I had no particular objection to wasting Grayson Hawthorne's.

"He can stay."

You could have cut the tension in the room with a knife.

"All right, Heiress." Jameson flashed me another wild smile. "As you wish."

CHAPTER 33

I'd known that things would go faster with an extra set of hands, but I hadn't anticipated what it would feel like to be shut in a room with *two* Hawthornes—particularly these two. As we worked, Grayson behind me and Jameson above, I wondered if they'd always been like oil and water, if Grayson had always taken himself too seriously, if Jameson had always made a game of taking *nothing* seriously at all. I wondered if the two of them had grown up slotted into the roles of heir and spare once Nash had made it clear he would abdicate the Hawthorne throne.

I wondered if they'd gotten along before Emily.

"There's nothing here." Grayson punctuated that statement by placing a book back on the shelf a little too hard.

"Coincidentally," Jameson commented up above, "*you* also don't have to be here."

"If she's here, I'm here."

"Avery doesn't bite." For once, Jameson referred to me by my actual name. "Frankly, now that the issue of relatedness has been settled in the negative, I'd be game if she did."

I choked on my own spit and seriously considered throttling him. He was baiting Grayson—and using me to do it.

"Jamie?" Grayson sounded almost too calm. "Shut up and keep looking."

I did exactly that. Book off, cover off, cover on, book reshelved. The hours ticked by. Grayson and I worked our way toward each other. When he was close enough that I could see him out of the corner of my eye, he spoke, his voice barely audible to me—and not audible to Jameson at all.

"My brother's grieving for our grandfather. Surely, you can understand that."

I could, and I did. I said nothing.

"He's a sensation seeker. Pain. Fear. Joy. It doesn't matter." Grayson had my full attention now, and he knew it. "He's hurting, and he needs the rush of the game. He needs for this to mean something."

This as in his grandfather's letter? The will? Me?

"And you don't think it does," I said, keeping my own voice low. Grayson didn't think I was special, didn't believe this was the kind of puzzle worth solving.

"I don't think that you have to be the villain of this story to be a threat to this family."

If I hadn't already met Nash, I would have pegged Grayson as the oldest brother.

"You keep talking about the rest of the family," I said. "But this isn't just about them. I'm a threat to you."

I'd inherited *his* fortune. I was living in *his* house. His grandfather had chosen me.

Grayson was right beside me now. "I am not threatened." He wasn't imposing physically. I had never seen him lose control. But the closer he came to me, the more my body threw itself into high alert.

"Heiress?"

I startled when Jameson spoke. Reflexively, I stepped away from his brother. "Yes?"

"I think I found something."

I pushed past Grayson to make my way to the stairs. Jameson had found something. *A book that doesn't match its cover.* That was an assumption on my part, but the instant I hit the second story and saw the smile on Jameson Hawthorne's lips, I knew that I was right.

He held up a hardcover book.

I read the title. "*Sail Away.*"

"And on the inside..." Jameson was a showman at heart. He removed the cover with a flourish and tossed me the book. *The Tragical History of Doctor Faustus.*

"*Faust,*" I said.

"The devil you know," Jameson replied. "Or the devil you don't."

It could have been a coincidence. We could have been reading meaning where there was none, like people trying to intuit the future in the shape of clouds. But that didn't stop the hairs on my arms from rising. It didn't stop my heart from racing.

Everything is something in Hawthorne House.

That thought beat in my pulse as I opened the copy of *Faust* in my hands. There, taped to the inside cover, was a translucent red square.

"Jameson." I jerked my eyes up from the book. "There's something here."

Grayson must have been listening to us down below, but he said nothing. Jameson was beside me in an instant. He brought his fingers to the red square. It was thin, made of some kind of plastic film, maybe four inches long on each side.

"What's this?" I asked.

Jameson took the book gingerly from my hands and carefully removed the square from the book. He held it up to the light.

"Filter paper." That came from down below. Grayson stood in the center of the room, looking up at us. "Red acetate. A favorite of our grandfather's, particularly useful for revealing hidden messages. I don't suppose the text of that book is written in red?"

I flipped to the first page. "Black ink," I said. I kept flipping. The color of the ink never changed, but a few pages in, I found a word that had been circled in pencil. A rush of adrenaline shot through my veins. "Did your grandfather have a habit of writing in books?" I asked.

"In a first edition of *Faust*?" Jameson snorted. I had no idea how much money this book was worth, or how much of its value had been squandered with that one little circle on the page—but I knew in my bones that we were onto something.

"Where," I read the word out loud. Neither brother provided any commentary, so I flipped another page and then another. It was fifty or more before I hit another circled word.

"A..." I kept turning the pages. The circled words were coming quicker now, sometimes in pairs. *"There is..."*

Jameson grabbed a pen off a nearby shelf. He didn't have any paper, so he started writing the words on the back of his left hand. "Keep going."

I did. "A again..." I said. *"There is* again." I was almost to the end of the book. *"Way,"* I said finally. I turned the pages more slowly now. *Nothing. Nothing. Nothing.* Finally, I looked up "That's it."

I closed the book. Jameson held his hand up in front of his body, and I stepped closer to get a better look. I brought my hand to his, reading the words he'd written there. *Where. A. There is. A. There is. Way.*

What were we supposed to do with that?

"Change the order of the words?" I asked. It was a common enough type of word puzzle.

Jameson's eyes lit up. *"Where there is a..."*

I picked up where he'd left off. *"There is a way."*

Jameson's lips curved upward. "We're missing a word," he murmured. "*Will.* Another proverb. Where there's a *will*, there's a way." He flicked the red acetate in his hand, back and forth, as he thought out loud. "When you look through a colored filter, lines of that color disappear. It's one way of writing hidden messages. You layer the text in different colors. The book is written in black ink, so the acetate isn't meant to be used on the book." Jameson was talking faster now, the energy in his voice contagious.

Grayson spoke up from the room's epicenter. "Hence the message *in* the book, directing us where to make use of the film."

They were used to playing their grandfather's games. They'd been trained to from the time they were young. I hadn't, but their back-and-forth had given me just enough to connect the dots. The acetate was meant to reveal secret writing, but not in the book. Instead, the book, like the letter before it, contained a clue—in this case, a phrase with a single missing word.

Where there's a will, *there's a way.*

"What do you think the chances are," I said slowly, turning the puzzle over in my mind, "that somewhere, there's a copy of your grandfather's will written in red ink?"

CHAPTER 34

I asked Alisa about the will. I half expected her to look at me like I'd lost my marbles, but the second I said the word *red*, her expression shifted. She informed me that a viewing of the Red Will could be arranged, but first I had to do something for her. That *something* ended up involving a brother-sister stylist team carting what appeared to be the entire inventory of Saks Fifth Avenue into my bedroom. The female stylist was tiny and said next to nothing.

The man was six foot six and kept up a steady stream of observations. "You can't wear yellow, and I would encourage you to banish the words *orange* and *cream* from your vocabulary, but most every other color is an option." The three of us were in my room now, along with Libby, thirteen racks of clothing, dozens of trays of jewelry, and what appeared to be an entire salon set up in the bathroom. "Brights, pastels, earth tones in moderation. You gravitate toward solids?"

I looked down at my current outfit: a gray T-shirt and my second-most-comfortable pair of jeans. "I like simple."

"Simple is a lie," the woman murmured. "But a beautiful one sometimes."

Beside me, Libby snorted and bit back a grin. I glared at her. "You're enjoying this, aren't you?" I asked darkly. Then I took in the outfit she was wearing. The dress was black, which was Libby enough, but the style would have fit right in at a country club.

I'd *told* Alisa not to pressure her. "You don't have to change how you—" I started to say, but Libby cut me off.

"They bribed me. With boots." She gestured toward the back wall, which was lined with boots, all of them leather, in shades of purple, black, and blue. Ankle-length, calf-length, even one pair of thigh-highs.

"Also," Libby added serenely, "creepy lockets." If a piece of jewelry looked like it might be haunted, Libby was *there*.

"You let them make you over in exchange for fifteen pairs of boots and some creepy lockets?" I said, feeling mildly betrayed.

"And some incredibly soft leather pants," Libby added. "Totally worth it. I'm still me, just...fancy." Her hair was still blue. Her nail polish was still black. And *she* wasn't the one the style team was focused on now.

"We should start with the hair," the male stylist declared beside me, eyeing my offending tresses. "Don't you think?" he asked his sister.

There was no reply as the woman disappeared behind one of the racks. I could hear her thumbing through another, rearranging the order of the clothing.

"Thick. Not quite wavy, not quite straight. You could go either way." This giant man looked and sounded like he should be playing tight end, not advising me on hairstyles. "No shorter than two inches below your chin, no longer than mid-back. Gentle layers wouldn't hurt." He glanced over at Libby. "I suggest you disown her if she opts for bangs."

"I'll take that under consideration," Libby said solemnly. "You'd be miserable if it wasn't long enough for a ponytail," she told me.

"Ponytail." That got me a censuring look from the linebacker. "Do you hate your hair and want it to suffer?"

"I don't hate it." I shrugged. "I just don't care."

"That is also a lie." The woman reappeared from behind the clothing rack. She had a half dozen hangers' worth of clothes in her hands, and as I watched, she hung them up, face out, on the closest rack. The result was three different outfits.

"Classic." She nodded to an ice-blue skirt, paired with a long-sleeved T-shirt. "Natural." The stylist moved on to the second option—a loose and flowing floral dress combining at least a dozen shades of red and pink. "Preppy with an edge." The final option included a brown leather skirt, shorter than any of the others—and probably tighter, too. She'd matched it with a white collared shirt and a heather-gray cardigan.

"Which calls to you?" the male stylist asked. That got another snort out of Libby. She was definitely enjoying this *way* too much.

"They're all fine." I eyed the floral dress. "That one looks like it might be itchy."

The stylists seemed to be developing a migraine. "Casual options?" he asked his sister, pained. She disappeared and reappeared with three more outfits, which she added to the first three. Black leggings, a red blouse, and a knee-length white cardigan were paired with the *classic* combo. A lacy sea-green shirt and darker green pants joined the floral monstrosity, and an oversized cashmere sweater and torn jeans were hung beside the leather skirt.

"Classic. Natural. Preppy with an edge." The woman reiterated my options.

"I have philosophical objections to colored pants," I said. "So that one's out."

"Don't just look at the clothes," the man instructed. "Take in the *look*."

Rolling my eyes at someone twice my size probably wasn't the wisest course of action.

The female stylist crossed to me. She walked lightly on her feet, like she could tiptoe across a bed of flowers without breaking a single one. "The way you dress, the way you do your hair—it's not silly. It's not shallow. This..." She gestured to the rack behind her. "It's not just clothing. It's a message. You're not deciding what to wear. You're deciding what story you want your image to tell. Are you the ingenue, young and sweet? Do you dress to this world of wealth and wonders like you were born to it, or do you want to walk the line: the same but different, young but full of steel?"

"Why do I have to tell a story?" I asked.

"Because if you don't tell the story, someone else will tell it for you." I turned to see Xander Hawthorne standing in the doorway, holding a plate of scones. "Makeovers," he told me, "like the recreational building of Rube Goldberg machines, are hungry work."

I wanted to narrow my eyes, but Xander and his scones were glare-proof.

"What do you know about makeovers?" I grumbled. "If I were a guy, there'd be two racks of clothing in this room, max."

"And if I were White," Xander returned loftily, "people wouldn't look at me like I'm half a Hawthorne. Scone?"

That took the wind out of my sails. It was ridiculous of me to think that Xander didn't know what it was like to be judged, or to have to play life by different rules. I wondered, suddenly, what it was like for him, growing up in this house. Growing up Hawthorne.

"Can I have one of the blueberry scones?" I asked—my version of a peace offering.

Xander handed me a lemon scone. "Let's not get ahead of ourselves."

With only a moderate amount of teeth-gnashing, I ended up picking option three. I hated the word *preppy* almost as much as I disliked any claims to having an *edge*, but at the end of the day, I couldn't pretend to be wide-eyed and innocent, and I deeply suspected that any attempts to act like this world was a natural fit would itch—not physically, but under my skin.

The team kept my hair long but worked in layers and cajoled it into a bed-head wave. I'd expected them to suggest highlights, but they'd gone the opposite route: subtle streaks a shade darker and richer than my normal ashy brown. They cleaned my eyebrows up but left them thick. I was instructed on the finer points of an elaborate facial regimen and found myself on the receiving end of a spray tan via airbrush, but they kept my makeup minimal: eyes and lips, nothing more. Looking at myself in the mirror, I could almost believe that the girl staring back belonged in this house.

"What do you think?" I asked, turning to Libby.

She was standing near the window, backlit. Her hand was clutching her phone, her eyes glued to the screen.

"Lib?"

She looked up and gave me a deer-in-headlights look that I recognized all too well.

Drake. He was texting her. Was she texting back?

"You look great!" Libby sounded sincere, because she was sincere. Always. Sincere and earnest and way, way too optimistic.

He hit her, I told myself. *He sold us out. She won't take him back.*

"You look fantastic," Xander declared grandly. "You also don't look like someone who might have seduced an old man out of billions, so that's good."

"Really, Alexander?" Zara announced her presence with next to no fanfare. "No one believes that Avery seduced your grandfather."

Her story—her image—was somewhere between *oozing class* and *no-nonsense.* But I'd seen her press conference. I knew that while she might care about her father's reputation, she didn't have any particular attachment to mine. The worse I looked, the better for her. *Unless the game has changed.*

"Avery." Zara gave me a smile as cool as the winter colors she wore. "Might I have a word?"

CHAPTER 35

Zara didn't speak immediately once the two of us were alone. I decided that if she wasn't going to break the silence, I would. "You talked to the lawyers." That was the obvious explanation for why she was here.

"I did." Zara offered no apologies. "And now I'm talking to you. I'm sure you can forgive me for not doing so sooner. As you can imagine, this has all come as a bit of a shock."

A bit? I snorted and cut through the niceties. "You held a press conference strongly suggesting that your father was senile and that I'm under investigation by the authorities for elder abuse."

Zara perched at the end of an antique desk—one of the few surfaces in the room *not* covered with accessories or clothes. "Yes, well, you can thank your legal team for not making certain realities apparent sooner."

"If I get nothing, you get nothing." I wasn't going to let her come in here and dance around the truth.

"You look…nice." Zara changed the subject and eyed my new outfit. "Not what I would have chosen for you, but you're presentable."

Presentable, with an edge. "Thanks," I grunted.

"You can thank me once I've done what I can to ease you through this transition."

I wasn't naive enough to believe that she'd had a sudden change of heart. If she'd despised me before, she despised me now. The difference was that now she needed something. I figured that if I waited long enough, she'd tell me exactly what that something was.

"I'm not sure how much Alisa has told you, but in addition to my father's personal assets, you have also inherited control of the family's foundation." Zara took measure of my expression before continuing. "It's one of the largest private charitable foundations in the country. We give away upward of a hundred million dollars a year."

A hundred million dollars. I was never going to get used to this. Numbers like that were never going to seem real. "Every year?" I asked, stunned.

Zara smiled placidly. "Compound interest is a lovely thing."

A hundred million dollars *a year* in interest—and she was just talking about the foundation, not Tobias Hawthorne's personal fortune. For the first time, I actually ran the math in my head. Even if taxes took half of the estate, and I only averaged a four-percent yield—I'd still be making nearly a billion dollars a year. *Doing nothing.* That was just wrong.

"Who does the foundation give its money to?" I asked quietly.

Zara pushed off the desk and began pacing the length of the room. "The Hawthorne Foundation invests in children and families, health initiatives, scientific advancement, community building, and the arts."

Under those headings, you could support nearly anything. *I* could support nearly anything.

I could change the world.

"I've spent my entire adult life running the foundation." Zara's lips pulled tight across her teeth. "There are organizations that rely on our support. If you intend to exert yourself, there's a right way and a wrong way to do that." She stopped right in front of me. "You need me, Avery. As much as I'd like to wash my hands of all of this, I've worked too long and too hard to see that work undone."

I listened to what she was saying—and what she wasn't. "Does the foundation pay you?" I asked. I ticked off the seconds until her reply.

"I draw a salary commensurate with the skills I bring."

As satisfying as it would have been to tell her that her services would no longer be needed, I wasn't that impulsive, and I wasn't cruel. "I want to be involved," I told her. "And not just for show. I want to make decisions."

Homelessness. Poverty. Domestic violence. Access to preventative care. What could I do with a hundred million dollars a year?

"You're young enough," Zara said, her voice almost wistful, "to believe that money solves all ills."

Spoken like a person so rich she can't imagine the weight of problems money can *solve.*

"If you're serious about taking a role at the foundation..." Zara sounded like she was enjoying saying that about as much as she would have enjoyed dumpster diving or a root canal. "I can teach you what you need to know. Monday. After school. At the foundation." She issued each part of that order as its own separate sentence.

The door opened before I could ask where exactly the foundation was. Oren took up position beside me. *The women will come after you in the courtroom,* he'd told me. But now Zara knew that she couldn't come after me legally.

And my head of security didn't want me in this room with her alone.

CHAPTER 36

The next day—Sunday—Oren drove me to Ortega, McNamara, and Jones to see the Red Will.

"Avery." Alisa met Oren and me in the firm's lobby. The place was modern: minimalist and full of chrome. The building looked big enough to host a hundred lawyers, but as Alisa walked us past a receptionist and security guard to an elevator bank, I didn't see another soul.

"You said I was the firm's only client," I commented as the elevator began to climb. "Exactly how big is the firm?"

"There are a few different divisions," Alisa replied crisply. "Mr. Hawthorne's assets were quite diversified. That requires a diverse array of lawyers."

"And the will I asked about, it's here?" My pocket held a gift from Jameson: the square of red film we'd discovered taped to the inside cover of *Faust*. I'd told him I was coming here, and he'd handed it over, no questions asked, like he trusted me more than he trusted any of his brothers.

"The Red Will is here," Alisa confirmed. She turned to Oren. "How much company did we have today?" she asked. By *company*, she meant *paparazzi*. And by *we*, she meant *me*.

"It's tapered off a little," Oren reported. "But odds are good that they'll be piled outside the door by the time we leave."

If we ended the day without at least one headline that said something along the lines of *World's Richest Teenager Lawyers Up*, I'd eat a pair of Libby's new boots.

On the third floor, we passed through another security checkpoint, and then, finally, Alisa led me to a corner office. The room was furnished but otherwise empty, with one exception. Sitting in the middle of a heavy mahogany desk was the will. By the time I saw it, Oren had taken up position outside the door. Alisa made no move to follow me when I approached the desk. As I got closer, the type jumped out at me.

Red.

"My father was instructed to keep this copy here and show it to you—or the boys—if one of you came looking," Alisa said.

I looked back at her. "Instructed," I repeated. "By Tobias Hawthorne?"

"Naturally."

"Did you tell Nash?" I asked.

A cool mask settled over her face. "I don't tell Nash anything anymore." She gave me her most austere look. "If that's all, I'll leave you to it."

Alisa never even asked what *it* was. I waited until I heard the door close behind her before I went to sit at the desk. I retrieved the film from my pocket. "Where there's a will...," I murmured, laying the square flat on the will's first page. "There's a way."

I moved the red acetate over the paper, and the words beneath it disappeared. *Red text. Red film.* It worked exactly as Jameson and Grayson had described. If the entire will was written in red, all this was going to do was make everything disappear. But if, layered underneath the red text, there was another color, then anything written in that color would remain visible.

I made it past Tobias Hawthorne's initial bequests to the Laughlins, to Oren, to his mother-in-law. *Nothing.* I got to the bit about Zara and Skye, and as I skimmed the red film over the words, they disappeared. I glanced down at the next sentence.

To my grandsons, Nash Westbrook Hawthorne, Grayson Davenport Hawthorne, Jameson Winchester Hawthorne, and Alexander Blackwood Hawthorne…

As I ran the film over the page, the words disappeared—but not all of them. Four remained.

Westbrook.

Davenport.

Winchester.

Blackwood.

For the first time, I thought about the fact that all four of Skye's sons bore her last name, their grandfather's last name. *Hawthorne.* Each of the boys' middle names was also a surname. *Their fathers' last names?* I wondered. As my brain wrapped itself around that, I made my way through the rest of the document. Part of me expected to see something when I hit my own name, but it disappeared, just like the rest of the text—everything except for the Hawthorne grandsons' middle names.

"Westbrook. Winchester. Davenport. Blackwood." I said them out loud, committed them to memory.

And then I texted Jameson—and wondered if he would text Grayson.

CHAPTER 37

"Whoa there, kid. Where's the fire?"

I was back at Hawthorne House and headed to meet Jameson when another Hawthorne brother stopped me in my tracks. *Nash.*

"Avery just came from reading a special copy of the will," Alisa said behind me. *So much for her not telling her ex anything anymore.*

"A special copy of the will." Nash slid his gaze to me. "Would I be correct in assuming this has something to do with the gobbledygook in my letter from the old man?"

"Your letter," I repeated, my brain whirring. It shouldn't have come as a surprise. Tobias Hawthorne had left Grayson and Jameson with identical clues. *Nash, too—and probably Xander.*

"Don't worry," Nash drawled. "I'm sitting this one out. I told you, I don't want the money."

"The money is not at stake here," Alisa said firmly. "The will—"

"—is ironclad," Nash finished for her. "I believe I've heard that a time or two."

Alisa's eyes narrowed. "You never were very good at listening."

"*Listen* doesn't always mean *agree*, Lee-Lee." Nash's use of the nickname—his amiable smile and equally amiable tone—sucked every ounce of oxygen out of the room.

"I should go." Alisa turned, whip-fast, to me. "If you need anything—"

"Call," I finished, wondering just how high my eyebrows had risen at their exchange.

When Alisa closed the front door behind her, she slammed it.

"You gonna tell me where you're headed in such a hurry?" Nash asked me again, once she was gone.

"Jameson asked me to meet him in the solarium."

Nash cocked an eyebrow at me. "Got any idea where the solarium is?"

I realized belatedly that I didn't. "I don't even know *what* a solarium is," I admitted.

"Solariums are overrated." Nash shrugged and gave me an assessing look. "Tell me, kid, what do you usually do on your birthday?"

That came out of nowhere. I felt like that had to be a trick question, but I answered anyway. "Eat cake?"

"Every year on our birthdays..." Nash stared off into the distance. "The old man would call us into his study and say the same three words. *Invest. Cultivate. Create.* He gave us ten thousand dollars to invest. Can you imagine letting an eight-year-old choose stocks?" Nash snorted. "Then we got to pick a talent or interest to cultivate for the year—a language, a hobby, an art, a sport. No expenses were spared. If you picked piano, a grand piano showed up the next day, private lessons started immediately, and by midway through the year, you'd be backstage at Carnegie Hall, getting tips from the greats."

"That's amazing," I said, thinking about all the trophies I'd seen in Tobias Hawthorne's office.

Nash didn't exactly look amazed. "The old man also laid out a challenge every year," he continued, his voice hardening. "An assignment, something we were expected to create by the next birthday. An invention, a solution, a work of museum-quality art. *Something.*"

I thought about the comic books I'd seen framed on the wall. "That doesn't sound horrible."

"It doesn't, does it?" Nash said, ruminating on those words. "C'mon." He jerked his head toward a nearby corridor. "I'll show you to the solarium."

He started walking, and I had to jog to keep up.

"Did Jameson tell you about the old man's weekly riddles?" Nash asked as we walked.

"Yeah," I said. "He did."

"Sometimes," Nash told me, "at the beginning of the game, the old man would lay out a collection of objects. A fishing hook, a price tag, a glass ballerina, a knife." He shook his head in memory. "And by the time the puzzle was solved, damned if we hadn't used all four." He smiled, but it didn't reach his eyes. "I was so much older. I had an advantage. Jamie and Gray, they'd team up against me, then double-cross each other right at the end."

"Why are you telling me this?" I asked as his pace finally slowed to a near standstill. "Why tell me any of this?" About their birthdays, the presents, the expectations.

Nash didn't answer right away. Instead, he nodded down a nearby hall. "Solarium's the last door on the right."

"Thanks," I said. I walked toward the door Nash had indicated, and right before I reached my destination, he spoke up behind me.

"You might think you're playing the game, darlin', but that's not how Jamie sees it." Nash's voice was gentle enough, but for the words. "We aren't normal. This place isn't normal, and you're not a player, kid. You're the glass ballerina—or the knife."

CHAPTER 38

The solarium was an enormous room with a domed glass ceiling and glass walls. Jameson stood in the center, bathed in light and staring up at the dome overhead. Like the first time I'd met him, he was shirtless. Also like the first time I'd met him, he was drunk.

Grayson was nowhere to be seen.

"What's the occasion?" I asked, nodding to a nearby bottle of bourbon.

"Westbrook, Davenport, Winchester, Blackwood." Jameson rattled the names off, one by one. "Tell me, Heiress, what do you make of that?"

"They're all last names," I said cautiously. I paused and then decided *why the hell not.* "Your fathers'?"

"Skye doesn't talk about our fathers," Jameson replied, his voice a little hoarse. "As far as she's concerned, it's an Athena-Zeus type of situation. We're hers and hers alone."

I bit my lip. "She told me that she had four lovely conversations..."

"With four lovely men," Jameson finished. "But lovely enough for her to ever see them again? To tell us the first thing about them?"

His voice was harder now. "She's never so much as answered a question about our damned middle names, and *that*"—he picked the bourbon up off the ground and took a swig—"is why I'm drinking." He set the bottle back down, then closed his eyes, standing in the sun a moment longer, his arms spread wide. For the second time, I noticed the scar that ran the length of his torso.

Noticed each breath he took.

"Shall we go?" His eyes opened. His arms dropped.

"Go where?" I asked, so physically aware of his presence it almost hurt.

"Come now, Heiress," Jameson said, stepping toward me. "You're better than that."

I swallowed and answered my own question. "We're going to see your mother."

He took me through the coat closet in the foyer. This time, I paid close attention to the sequence of panels on the wall that released the door. Following Jameson to the back of the closet, pushing past the coats that hung there, I willed my eyes to adjust to the dark so that I could see what he did next.

He touched something. *Pulled it?* I couldn't make out what. The next thing I knew, I heard the sound of gears turning, and the back wall of the closet slid sideways. If the closet was dark, what lay beyond was even darker.

"Step where I step, Mystery Girl. And watch your head."

Jameson used his cell phone to light the way. I got the distinct feeling that was for my benefit. He knew the twists and turns of these hidden hallways. We walked in silence for five minutes before he stopped and peeked through what I could only assume was a peephole.

"Coast is clear." Jameson didn't specify what it was clear of. "Do you trust me?"

I was standing in a phone-lit passageway, close enough to feel his body's heat on mine. "Absolutely not."

"Good." He reached out, grabbed my hand, and pulled me close. "Hold on."

My arms curved around him, and the ground beneath our feet began to move. The wall beside us was rotating, and we were rotating with it, my body pressed flat against his. *Jameson Winchester Hawthorne's.* The motion stopped, and I stepped back.

We were here for a reason—and that reason had exactly nothing to do with the way my body fit against his.

They were a twisted, broken mess before you got here, and they'll be a twisted, broken mess once you're gone. The reminder echoed in my head as we stepped out into a long hallway with plush red carpet and gold moldings on the walls. Jameson strode toward a door at the end of the hall. He lifted his hand to knock.

I stopped him. "You don't need me for this," I said. "You didn't need me for the will, either. Alisa had instructions to let you see it if you asked."

"I need you." Jameson knew exactly what he was doing—the way he was looking at me, the tilt of his lips. "I don't know why yet, but I do."

Nash's warning rang in my head. "I'm the knife." I swallowed. "The fishing hook, the glass ballerina, whatever."

That *almost* took Jameson by surprise. "You've been talking to one of my brothers." He paused. "Not Grayson." His eyes roved over mine. "Xander?" His gaze flicked down to my lips and up again. "Nash," he said, certain of it.

"Is he wrong?" I asked. I thought about Tobias Hawthorne's

grandsons going to see him on their birthdays. They'd been expected to be extraordinary. They'd been expected to win. "Am I just a means to an end, worth keeping around until you know how I fit into the puzzle?"

"You *are* the puzzle, Mystery Girl." Jameson believed that. "You could tap out," he told me, "decide you can live without answers, or you could get them—with me."

An invitation. A challenge. I told myself that I was doing this because I needed to know—not because of him. "Let's get some answers," I said.

When Jameson knocked on the door, it swung inward. "Mom?" he called, and then he amended the salutation. "Skye?"

The answer came, like the tinkling of bells. "In here, darling."

Here, it became quickly apparent, was the bathroom in Skye's suite.

"Got a second?" Jameson stopped right outside the double doors to the bathroom.

"Thousands of them." Skye seemed to relish the reply. "Millions. Come in."

Jameson stayed outside the doors. "Are you decent?"

"I like to think so," his mother called back. "At least a good fifty percent of the time."

Jameson pushed the bathroom door inward, and I was greeted by the sight of the biggest bathtub I'd ever seen in my life, sitting up on a dais. I focused on the tub's claw-feet—gold, to match the moldings in the hallway—and not the woman currently in the bathtub.

"You said you were decent." Jameson did not sound surprised.

"I'm covered in bubbles," Skye replied airily. "It doesn't get any more decent than that. Now, tell your mother what you need."

Jameson glanced back at me, as if to say *and you asked why I needed the bourbon.*

"I'll stay out here," I said, turning around before I caught sight of more than bubbles.

"Oh, don't be a prude, Abigail," Skye admonished from inside the bathroom. "We're all friends here, aren't we? I make it a policy to befriend everyone who steals my birthright."

I'd never seen passive aggression quite like this.

"If you're done messing with *Avery,*" Jameson interjected, "I'd like to have a little chat."

"So serious, Jamie?" Skye sighed audibly. "Well, go on, then."

"My middle name. I've asked you before if I was named after my father."

Skye was quiet for a moment. "Hand me my champagne, would you?"

I heard Jameson moving around in the bathroom behind me—presumably, fetching her champagne. "Well?" he asked.

"If you'd been a girl," Skye said, with the air of a bard, "I would have named you after myself. Skylar, perhaps. Or Skyla." She took what I could only assume was a sip of champagne. "Toby was named for my father, you know."

The mention of her long-gone brother caught my attention. I didn't know how or why, but Toby's death had somehow started this all.

"My middle name," Jameson reminded her. "Where did you get it?"

"I'd be happy to answer your question, darling." Skye paused. "Just as soon as you give me a moment alone with your delightful little friend."

CHAPTER 39

If I'd known I was going to end up in a one-on-one conversation with a naked, bubble-covered Skye Hawthorne, I probably would have had some bourbon myself.

"Negative emotions age you." Skye shifted her position in the tub, causing water to slosh against the sides. "There's only so much one can do with Mercury in retrograde, but..." She let out a long, theatrical breath. "I forgive you, Avery Grambs."

"I didn't ask you to," I responded.

She proceeded as if she had not heard me. "You will, of course, continue to provide me a modest amount of financial support."

I was starting to wonder if this woman was legitimately living on a different planet.

"Why would I give you anything?"

I expected a sharp comeback, but all I got was an indulgent little hum, like *I* was the one being ridiculous here.

"If you're not going to answer Jameson's question," I said, "then I'm leaving."

She let me get halfway to the door. "You'll support me," she said lightly, "because I'm their mother. And I will answer your question as soon as you answer mine. What are your intentions toward my son?"

"Excuse me?" I turned to face her before I remembered, a second too late, why I'd been trying *not* to look at her the entire time I'd been in the room.

The bubbles obscured what I didn't want to see—but just barely.

"You waltzed into my suite with my shirtless, grieving son by your side. A mother has concerns, and Jameson is special. Brilliant, the way my father was. The way Toby was."

"Your brother," I said, and suddenly, I had no interest in leaving this room. "What happened to him?" Alisa had given me the gist but very few details.

"My father ruined Toby." Skye addressed her answer to the rim of her champagne glass. "Spoiled him. He was always meant to be the heir, you know. And once he was gone... well, it was Zara and me." Her expression darkened, but then she smiled. "And then..."

"You had the boys," I filled in. I wondered, then, if she'd had them *because* Toby was gone.

"Do you know why Jameson was Daddy's favorite when, by all rights, it should have been perfect, dutiful Grayson?" Skye asked. "It wasn't because my Jamie is brilliant or beautiful or charismatic. It was because Jameson Winchester Hawthorne is *hungry*. He's looking for something. He's been looking for it since the day he was born." She downed the rest of the champagne in one gulp. "Grayson is everything Toby wasn't, and Jameson is just like him."

"There's no one like Jameson." In no way had I meant to utter those words out loud.

"You see?" Skye gave me a knowing look—the same one Alisa had given me my first day at Hawthorne House. "You're already his." Skye closed her eyes and lay back in the tub. "We used to lose him when he was little, you know. For hours, occasionally for a day. We'd look away for a second, and he'd disappear into the walls. And every time we found him, I'd pick him up and cuddle him tight and know, to the depths of my soul, that all he wanted was to get lost again." She opened her eyes. "That's all you are." Skye stood up and grabbed a robe. I averted my eyes as she put it on. "Just another way to get lost. That's what she was, too."

She. "Emily," I said out loud.

"She was a beautiful girl," Skye mused, "but she could have been ugly, and they would have loved her just the same. There was just something about her."

"Why are you telling me this?" I asked.

"You," Skye Hawthorne stated emphatically, "are no Emily." She bent to pick up the champagne bottle and refilled her glass. She padded toward me, barefoot and dripping, and held it out. "I've found bubbles to be a bit of a cure-all myself." Her stare was intense. "Go on. Drink."

Was she serious? I took a step back. "I don't like champagne."

"And *I*"—Skye took a long drink—"didn't choose my sons' middle names." She held the glass up, as if she were toasting me—or toasting to my demise.

"If you didn't choose them," I said, "then who did?"

Skye finished off the champagne. "My father."

CHAPTER 40

I told Jameson what his mother had told me.

He stared at me. "The old man chose our names." I could see the gears in Jameson's head turning, and then—*nothing*. "He picked our names," Jameson repeated, pacing the long hall like an animal caged. "He picked them, and then he highlighted them in the Red Will." Jameson stopped again. "He disinherited the family twenty years ago and chose our middle names—all of them but Nash's—shortly thereafter. Grayson's nineteen. I'm eighteen. Xan will be seventeen next month."

I could *feel* him trying to make this make sense. Trying to see what we were missing.

"The old man was playing a long game," Jameson said, every muscle in his body tightening. "Our whole lives."

"The names have to mean something," I stated.

"He might have known who our fathers were." Jameson considered that possibility. "Even if Skye thought she'd kept it a secret—there were no secrets from him." I heard an undertone in Jameson's voice when he said those words—something deep and cutting and awful.

Which of your secrets did he know?

"We can do a search," I said, trying to focus on the riddle and not the boy. "Or have Alisa hire a private investigator on my behalf to look for men with those last names."

"Or," Jameson countered, "you can give me about six hours to utterly sober up, and I'll show you what I do when I'm working a puzzle and I hit a wall."

Seven hours later, Jameson snuck me out through the fireplace passageway and led me to the far wing of the house—past the kitchen, past the Great Room, into what turned out to be the largest garage I'd ever seen. It was closer to a showroom, really. There were a dozen motorcycles stacked on a mammoth shelf on the wall, and twice that many cars parked in a semicircle. Jameson paced by them, one by one. He stopped in front of a car that looked like something straight out of science fiction.

"The Aston Martin Valkyrie," Jameson said. "A hybrid hypercar with a top speed of more than two hundred miles per hour." He gestured down the line. "Those three are Bugattis. The Chiron's my favorite. Nearly fifteen hundred horsepower and not bad on the track."

"Track," I repeated. "As in *racetrack*?"

"They were my grandfather's babies," Jameson said. "And now . . ." A slow smile spread across his face. "They're yours."

That smile was devilish. It was dangerous.

"No way," I told Jameson. "I'm not even allowed to leave the estate without Oren. And I can't drive a car like these!"

"Luckily," Jameson replied, ambling toward a box on the wall, "I can." There was a puzzle built into the box, like a Rubik's Cube, but silver, with strange shapes carved onto the squares. Jameson immediately began spinning the tiles, twisting them, arranging them just so. The box popped open. He ran his fingers over a plethora of keys, then selected one. "There's nothing like speed for getting out of your own head—and out of your own way." He started walking toward the Aston Martin. "Some puzzles make more sense at two hundred miles an hour."

"Is there even room for two people in that?" I asked.

"Why, Heiress," Jameson murmured, "I thought you'd never ask."

Jameson drove the car onto a pad that lowered us down below the ground level of the House. We shot through a tunnel, and before I knew it, we were going out a back exit that I hadn't even known existed.

Jameson didn't speed. He didn't take his eyes off the road. He just drove, silently. In the seat next to him, every nerve ending in my body was alive with anticipation.

This is a very bad idea.

He must have called ahead, because the track was ready for us when we got there.

"The Martin's not technically a race car," Jameson told me. "Technically, it wasn't even for sale when my grandfather bought it."

And technically, I shouldn't have left the estate. We shouldn't have taken the car. We shouldn't have been here.

But somewhere around a hundred and fifty miles an hour, I stopped thinking about *should*.

Adrenaline. Euphoria. Fear. There wasn't room in my head for anything else. Speed was the only thing that mattered.

That, and the boy beside me.

I didn't want him to slow down. I didn't want the car to stop. For the first time since the reading of the will, I felt *free*. No questions. No suspicions. No one staring or not staring. Nothing except this moment, right here, right now.

Nothing except Jameson Winchester Hawthorne and me.

CHAPTER 41

Eventually, the car slowed to a stop. Eventually, reality crashed down around us. Oren was there, with a team in tow. *Uh-oh.*

"You and I," my head of security told Jameson the second we exited the car, "are going to be having a little talk."

"I'm a big girl," I said, eyeing the backup Oren had brought with him. "If you want to yell at someone, yell at me."

Oren didn't yell. He did personally deposit me back in my room and indicate that we would "talk" in the morning. Based on his tone, I wasn't entirely sure that I would survive a *talk* with Oren unscathed.

I barely slept that night, my brain a mess of electrical impulses that wouldn't—couldn't—stop firing. I still had no idea what to make of the names highlighted in the Red Will, if they really were a reference to the boys' fathers, or if Tobias Hawthorne had chosen his grandsons' middle names for a different reason altogether.

All I knew was that Skye had been right. Jameson was hungry. *And so am I.* But I could also hear Skye telling me that I didn't matter, that I was no Emily.

When I did fall asleep that night, I dreamed of a teenage girl.

She was a shadow, a silhouette, a ghost, a queen. And no matter how fast I ran, down one corridor after another, I could never catch up to her.

My phone rang before dawn. Groggy and in a mood, I grabbed for it with every intention of launching it through the closest window, then realized who was calling.

"Max, it's five thirty in the morning."

"Three thirty my time. Where did you get that car?" Max didn't sound even remotely sleepy.

"A room full of cars?" I replied apologetically, and then sleep cleared from my brain enough for me to process the implications of her question. "How did you know about the car?"

"Aerial photo," Max replied. "Taken from a helicopter, and what do you mean *a room full of cars*? Exactly how big is this room?"

"I don't know." I groaned and rolled over in bed. Of course the paparazzi had caught me out with Jameson. I didn't even want to know what the gossip rags were saying.

"Equally important," Max continued, "are you having a torrid affair with Jameson Hawthorne and should I plan for a spring wedding?"

"No." I sat up in bed. "It's not like that."

"Bull fox-faxing ship."

"I have to live with these people," I told Max. "For a year. They already have enough reasons to hate me." I wasn't thinking about Skye or Zara or Xander or Nash when I said that. I was thinking about Grayson. Silver-eyed, suit-wearing, threat-issuing Grayson. "Getting involved with Jameson would just be throwing gasoline on the fire."

"And what a lovely fire it would be," Max murmured.

She was, without question, a bad influence. "I can't," I reiterated. "And besides… there was a girl." I thought back to my dream and wondered if Jameson had taken Emily driving, if she had ever played one of Tobias Hawthorne's games. "She died."

"Back the fax up there. What do you mean, she *died*? How?"

"I don't know."

"How can you not know?"

I pulled my comforter tight around me. "Her name was Emily. Do you know how many people named Emily there are in the world?"

"Is he still hung up on her?" Max asked. She was talking about Jameson, but my brain went back to that moment when I'd said Emily's name to Grayson. It had gutted him. Destroyed him.

There was a rap at my door. "Max, I have to go."

Oren spent more than an hour going over security protocols with me. He indicated that he would be happy to do the same thing, every morning at dawn, until it stuck.

"Point taken," I told him. "I'll be good."

"No you won't." He gave me a look. "But I'll be better."

My second day—and the start of my first full week—at private school shaped up much like the week before. People did their best not to stare at me. Jameson avoided me. I avoided Thea. I wondered what gossip Jameson thought we would provoke if we were seen together, wondered if there had been whispers when Emily died.

I wondered *how* she'd died.

You're not a player. Nash's words of caution came back to me, again and again, every time I caught sight of Jameson in the halls. *You're the glass ballerina—or the knife.*

"I heard that you have a need for speed." Xander pounced on me outside the physics lab. He was clearly in high spirits. "God bless the paparazzi, am I right? I also heard that you had a very special chat with my mother."

I wasn't sure if he was pumping me for information or commiserating. "Your mother is something else," I said.

"Skye is a complicated woman." Xander nodded sagely. "But she taught me how to read tarot and moisturize my cuticles, so who am I to complain?"

Skye wasn't the one who'd forged them, pushed them, set them to challenges, expected the impossible. She wasn't the one who'd made them *magic*.

"Your brothers all got the same letter from your grandfather," I told Xander, examining his reaction.

"Did they now?"

I narrowed my eyes slightly. "I know that you got it, too."

"Maybe I did," Xander admitted cheerily. "But hypothetically, if I had, and if I hypothetically were playing this game and wanted, just this once—and just hypothetically—to win..." He shrugged. "I'd want to do it my way."

"Does your way involve robots and scones?"

"What doesn't?" Grinning, Xander nudged me into the lab. Like everything at Country Day, it looked like a million dollars—figuratively. Probably more than a million dollars, literally. Curved lab tables circled the room. Floor-to-ceiling windows had replaced three of the four walls. There was colored writing on the windows—calculations in different handwritings, like scratch paper was just so passé. Each lab table came complete with a large monitor and a digital whiteboard. And that wasn't even touching on the size of the microscopes.

I felt like I'd just walked into NASA.

There were only two free seats. One was next to Thea. The

other was as far away from Thea as you could get, next to the girl I'd seen in the archive. Her dark red hair was pulled into a loose ponytail at the nape of her neck. Her coloring was stop-and-stare striking—hair *that* red, skin *that* pale—but her eyes were downcast.

Thea met my gaze and gestured imperiously toward the seat next to her. I glanced back toward the red-haired girl.

"What's her story?" I asked Xander. No one was talking to her. No one was looking at her. She was one of the most beautiful people I'd ever seen, and she might as well have been invisible.

Wallpaper.

"Her story"—Xander sighed—"involves star-crossed love, fake dating, heartbreak, tragedy, twisted familial relationships, penance, and a hero for the ages."

I gave him a look. "Are you serious?"

"You should know by now," Xander replied lightly, "I'm not the serious Hawthorne."

He plopped down in the seat next to Thea, leaving me to make my way toward the red-haired girl. She proved to be a decent lab partner: quiet, focused, and able to calculate almost anything in her head. The entire time we worked in tandem, she didn't say a single word to me.

"I'm Avery," I said, once we'd finished and it became clear that she still wasn't going to introduce herself.

"Rebecca." Her voice was soft. "Laughlin." She saw the shift in my expression when she said her last name and confirmed what I was thinking. "My grandparents work at Hawthorne House."

Her grandparents *ran* Hawthorne House, and neither one of them had seemed overly enthused about the prospect of working for me. I wondered if that was why I'd gotten the silent treatment from Rebecca.

She's not talking to anyone else, either.

"Has someone shown you how to turn in assignments on your tablet?" Rebecca asked beside me. The question was tentative, like she fully expected to be slapped down. I tried to wrap my mind around the fact that someone that beautiful could be tentative about anything.

Everything.

"No," I said. "Could you?"

Rebecca demonstrated, uploading her results with a few clicks on the touch screen. A moment later, her tablet returned to its main screen. She had a photo as her wallpaper. In it, Rebecca looked off to the side, while another, amber-haired girl laughed directly into the camera. They both had wreaths of flowers on their heads, and they had the same eyes.

The other girl wasn't any more beautiful than Rebecca—and probably less—but somehow, it was impossible to look away from her.

"Is that your sister?" I asked.

"Was." Rebecca closed the cover on her tablet. "She died."

My ears roared, and I knew, then, exactly who I was looking at. I felt, on some level, like I'd known it from the moment I'd seen her. "Emily?"

Rebecca's emerald eyes caught on mine. I panicked, thinking that I should have said something else. *I'm sorry for your loss*—or something.

But Rebecca didn't seem to find my response odd or off-putting. All she said, pulling her tablet into her lap, was "She would have been very interested to meet you."

CHAPTER 42

I couldn't get Emily's face out of my mind, but I hadn't looked at the picture closely enough to recall every detail of her features. Her eyes had been green. Her hair was strawberry blonde, like sunlight through amber. I remembered the wreath of flowers on her head but not her hair's length. No matter how hard I tried to visualize her face, the only other things I could remember were that she'd been laughing and that she'd looked right at the camera, head-on.

"Avery." Oren spoke from the front seat. "We're here."

Here was the Hawthorne Foundation. It felt like it had been an eternity since Zara had offered to show me the ropes. As Oren exited the car and opened my door, I registered the fact that, for once, there wasn't a reporter or photographer in sight.

Maybe it's dying down, I thought as I stepped into the lobby of the Hawthorne Foundation. The walls were a light silvery-gray, and dozens of massive black-and-white photographs hung on them, seemingly suspended midair. Hundreds of smaller prints surrounded the larger ones. *People.* From all over the world, captured in motion and moments, from all angles, all perspectives, diverse along every dimension imaginable—age and gender and race and culture. *People*. Laughing, crying, praying, playing, eating, dancing, sleeping, sweeping, embracing—everything.

I thought about Dr. Mac asking me why I wanted to travel. *This. This is why.*

"Ms. Grambs."

I looked up to see Grayson. I wondered how long he'd watched me taking in this room. I wondered what he'd seen on my face.

"I'm supposed to meet Zara," I said, fending off his inevitable attack.

"Zara isn't coming." Grayson walked slowly toward me. "She's convinced that you are in need of…*guidance*." There was something about the way he said that word that slid past every defense mechanism I had and straight under my skin. "For some reason, my aunt seems to believe that guidance would be best received coming from me."

He looked exactly as he had the day I'd met him, down to the color of his Armani suit. It was the same light, liquid gray as his eyes—the same color as this room. Suddenly, I remembered the coffee table book I'd seen in Tobias Hawthorne's study—a book of photographs, with Grayson's name on the side.

"You took these?" I breathed, staring at the photos all around me. It was a guess—but I'd always been a good guesser.

"My grandfather believed that you have to see the world to change it." Grayson looked at me, then caught himself staring. "He always said that I was the one with the eye."

Invest. Create. Cultivate. Nash's explanation of their childhood came back to me, and I wondered how old Grayson was the first time he held a camera, how old he was when he started traveling the world, seeing it, capturing it on film.

I wouldn't have pegged him as the artist.

Irritated that I'd been tricked into thinking about him at all, I narrowed my eyes. "Your aunt must not have noticed your tendency to make threats. I'm betting she also didn't know about the background check on my dead mother. Otherwise, there is no way she could have come to the conclusion that I'd prefer working with *you*."

Grayson's lips twitched. "Zara doesn't miss much. And as for the background checks…" He disappeared behind the front desk and reappeared holding two folders. I glared at him, and he arched a brow. "Would you prefer I kept the results of my searches from you?"

He held out one folder, and I took it. He'd had no right to do this—to pry into my life or my mom's. But as I looked down at the folder in my hand, I heard my mother's voice, clear as a bell, in my head. *I have a secret….*

I flipped open the folder. Employment records, death certificate, credit report, no criminal background, a photograph…

I pressed my lips together, trying desperately to stop looking at it. She was young in the picture, and she was holding me.

I forced my eyes to Grayson's, ready to unleash on him, but he calmly handed me the second folder. I wondered what he'd found out about me—if there was anything in this folder that could possibly explain what his grandfather had seen in me. I opened it.

Inside, there was a single sheet of paper, and it was blank.

"That's a list of every purchase you've made since inheriting. Things have been purchased for you but…" Grayson dipped his eyes toward the page. "Nothing."

"Is that what passes for an apology where you're from?" I asked him. I'd surprised him. I wasn't acting like a gold digger.

"I won't apologize for being protective. This family has suffered enough, Ms. Grambs. If I were choosing between you and any one of them, I would choose them, always and every time. However…" His eyes made their way back to mine. "I may have misjudged you."

There was something intense in those words, in the expression on his face—like the boy who'd learned to see the world *saw* me.

"You're wrong." I flipped the folder closed, turning away from him. "I did try to spend some money. A big chunk. I asked Alisa to find a way to get it to a friend of mine."

"What kind of friend?" Grayson asked. His expression shifted. "A boyfriend?"

"No." I answered. What did he care if I had a boyfriend? "A guy I play chess with in the park. He lives there. In the park."

"Homeless?" Grayson was looking at me differently now, like in all his travels, he'd never encountered anything quite like this. Like me. After a second or two, he snapped out of it. "My aunt is right. You're in desperate need of an education."

He started walking, and I had no choice except to follow, but I refused to stay in his wake, like a duckling toddling after its mother. He stopped at a conference room and held the door open for me. I brushed past him, and even that split second of contact made me feel like I was going two hundred miles an hour.

Absolutely not. That was what I would have told Max if she were on the phone. What was wrong with me? Grayson had spent most of our acquaintance threatening me. *Hating* me.

He let the conference room door close behind him, then continued walking to the back wall. It was lined with maps: first a world map, then each continent, then broken down by countries, all the way down to states and towns.

"Look at them," he instructed, nodding toward the maps, "because that is what's at stake here. Everything. Not a single person. Giving money to individuals does little."

"It does a lot," I said quietly, "for those people."

"With the resources you have now, you can no longer afford to concern yourself with the individual." Grayson spoke like this was a lesson he'd had beaten into him. *By whom? His grandfather?* "You, Ms. Grambs," he continued, "are responsible for the world."

I felt those words like a lit match, a spark, a flame.

Grayson turned to the wall of maps. "I deferred college for a year to learn the ropes at the foundation. My grandfather assigned me to make a study of modes of charitable giving, with an eye to improving ours. I was to make my pitch in the coming months." Grayson stared hard at the map that hung even with his eyes. "Now I suppose that I will be making my pitch to you." He seemed to be measuring the pace of his words. "The foundation conservatorship has its own paperwork. When you turn twenty-one, it's yours, just like everything else."

That hurt him, more than any of the terms of the will. I thought about Skye referring to him as the heir apparent, even though she insisted that Jameson had been Tobias Hawthorne's favorite. Grayson had spent his gap year dedicated to the foundation. His photographs hung in the lobby.

But his grandfather chose me. "I'm—"

"Don't say that you are sorry." Grayson stared at the wall a moment longer, then turned to face me. "Don't be sorry, Ms. Grambs. Be worthy of it."

He might as well have ordered me to be fire or earth or air. A person couldn't be worthy of billions. It wasn't possible—not for anyone, and definitely not for me.

"How?" I asked him. *How am I supposed to be worthy of anything?*

He took his time replying, and I found myself wishing that I were the kind of girl who could fill silences. The kind who laughed with abandon, flowers in her hair.

"I can't teach you how to *be* anything, Ms. Grambs. But if you're willing, I can teach you a way of thinking."

I pushed back the memory of Emily's face. "I'm here, aren't I?"

Grayson began to walk down the length of the room, passing map after map. "It might *feel* better to give to someone you know than a stranger, or to donate to an organization whose story brings a tear to your eye, but that's your brain playing tricks on you. The morality of an action depends, ultimately and only, on its outcomes."

There was an intensity in the way he spoke, the way he moved. I couldn't have looked away or stopped listening, even if I'd tried.

"We shouldn't give because we feel one way or another," Grayson told me. "We should direct our resources to wherever objective analysis says we can have the largest impact."

He probably thought he was talking over my head, but the moment he said *objective analysis*, I smiled. "You're talking to a future actuarial science major, Hawthorne. Show me your graphs."

By the time Grayson finished, my head was spinning with numbers and projections. I could see exactly how his mind worked—and it was disturbingly like my own.

"I get why a scattershot approach won't work," I said. "Big problems require big thinking and big interventions—"

"Comprehensive interventions," Grayson corrected. "Strategic."

"But we also have to spread our risk."

"With empirically driven cost-benefits analyses."

Everyone had things they found inexplicably attractive. Apparently, for me it was suit-wearing, silver-eyed guys using the word *empirically* and taking for granted that I knew what it meant.

Get your mind out of the gutter, Avery. Grayson Hawthorne is not for you.

His phone rang, and he glanced down at the screen. "Nash," he informed me.

"Go ahead," I told him. "Take it." At this point, I needed a breather—from him, but also from *this*. Math, I understood. Projections, I could wrap my mind around. But this?

This was real. This was power. *One hundred million dollars a year.*

Grayson answered his phone and left the room. I walked the perimeter, looking at the maps on the walls, memorizing the names of every country, every city, every town. I could help all of them—or none. There were people out there who might live or die because of me, futures good or bad that might be realized because of my choices.

What right did I even have to be the one making them?

Overwhelmed, I came to a stop in front of the very last map on the wall. Unlike the others, this one had been hand-drawn. It took me a moment to realize that the map was of Hawthorne House and the surrounding estate. My eyes went first to Wayback Cottage, a small building tucked in the back corner of the estate. I remembered, from the reading of the will, that Tobias Hawthorne had given lifetime occupancy of this building to the Laughlins.

Rebecca's grandparents, I thought. *Emily's*. I wondered if the girls had come to visit them when they were small, how much time they'd spent on the estate—at Hawthorne House. *How old was Emily the first time Jameson and Grayson laid their eyes on her?*

How long ago did she die?

The door to the conference room opened behind me. I was glad that Grayson couldn't see my face. I didn't want him to know that I'd been thinking about *her*. I made a show of studying the map in front of me, the geography of the estate, from the northern forest called the Black Wood to a small creek that ran along the western edge of the estate.

The Black Wood. I read the label again, the rush of blood through my veins was suddenly deafening. *Blackwood.* And there, in smaller letters, the winding body of water was labeled, too. Not a creek. The Brook.

A brook, on the west side of the property. Westbrook.

Blackwood. Westbrook.

"Avery." Grayson spoke behind me.

"What?" I said, unable to fully tear my mind from the map—and the implications.

"That was Nash."

"I know," I said. He'd told me who was on the other end of the line before he'd answered.

Grayson laid a hand gently on my shoulder. Alarm bells rang in the back of my head. Why was he being so gentle? "What did Nash want?"

"It's about your sister."

CHAPTER 43

"I thought you said you'd take care of Drake." My fingers tightened around my cell phone, and my free hand wound itself into a fist at my side. "For fun."

I'd called Alisa the moment I'd made it to the car. Grayson had followed and buckled himself into the back seat beside me. I didn't have the time or mental space to dwell on his presence beside me. Oren was driving. I was pissed.

"I *did* take care of him," Alisa assured me. "You and your sister are both in possession of temporary restraining orders. If Drake attempts to contact or comes within a thousand feet of either of you for any reason, he's facing arrest."

I forced my fingers out of the fist but couldn't manage to loosen my grip on the phone. "Then why is he at the gates of Hawthorne House right now?"

Drake was here. In Texas. When Nash had called, Libby was safely inside, but Drake was spamming her phone with texts and calls, demanding a face-to-face.

"I'll handle this, Avery." Alisa recovered almost instantly. "The firm has some contacts on the local police force who know how to be discreet."

Right now, being *discreet* wasn't my priority. My priority was Libby. "Does my sister know about this restraining order?"

"She signed the paperwork." That was a hedge if I'd ever heard one. "I'll handle it, Avery. You just lie low." She hung up, and I let the hand holding my phone drop into my lap.

"Can you drive any faster?" I asked Oren.

Libby had her own security detail. Drake wouldn't get a chance to hurt her—physically.

"Nash is with your sister." Grayson spoke for the first time since we'd entered the car. "If the gentleman so much as tries to lay a finger on her, I assure you, my brother would take pleasure in removing that finger."

I wasn't sure if Grayson was referring to separating said finger from Libby's body—or from Drake's.

"Drake isn't a gentleman," I told Grayson. "And I'm not just worried about him getting violent." I was worried about him being sweet, worried that, instead of losing his temper, he'd be so kind and tender that she'd start to question the fading bruise ringing her eye.

"If it would make you feel better, I can have him removed from the property," Oren offered. "But that might cause a bit of a scene for the press."

The press? My brain clicked into gear. "There weren't any paparazzi at the foundation." I'd noted that when we'd arrived. "They're back at the house?"

The wall around the estate could keep the press off the property, but there was nothing stopping them from congregating, legally, on a public street.

"If I were a betting man," Oren commented, "I would guess that Drake placed a few calls to reporters to ensure an audience."

There was nothing discreet about the scene that greeted us when Oren pulled up to the drive, past a verifiable horde of press. Up ahead, I could see Drake's form outside the wrought-iron gates. There were two other men standing near him. Even from a distance, I could make out their police uniforms.

And so could the paparazzi.

So much for Alisa's friends on the police force being discreet. I gritted my teeth and thought about the way Drake would guilt Libby if there was footage of him being dragged down the drive.

"Stop the car," I snapped.

Oren stopped, then turned around in his seat to face me. "I would advise you to stay in this vehicle." That wasn't advice. That was an order.

I reached for the door handle.

"Avery." Oren's tone stopped me dead in my tracks. "If you're getting out, I'm getting out first."

Remembering our little one-on-one that morning, I decided not to test him.

Beside me, Grayson unbuckled his seat belt. He reached for my wrist, his touch gentle. "Oren's right. You shouldn't go out there."

I looked down at his hand on mine, and after a heartbeat, I looked back up. "And what would you do," I said, "what lengths would you go to in order to protect *your* family?"

I had him there, and he damn well knew it. He drew his hand back from mine, slowly enough that I felt the pads of his fingers skim my knuckles. My breath coming quickly now, I opened the car door and braced myself. Drake was the biggest story the press had on the Hawthorne Heiress front because we hadn't given them anything bigger. Yet.

Chin held high, I stepped out of the car. *Look at me. I'm the story here.* I walked down the drive, back toward the street. I was wearing boots with heels and my Country Day pleated skirt. My uniform blazer pulled against my body as I walked. The new hair. The makeup. The attitude.

I'm the story here. The chatter tonight wasn't going to be about Drake. The eyes of the world weren't going to be on him. I'd keep them on me.

"Impromptu press conference?" Oren asked under his breath. "As your bodyguard, I feel compelled to warn you that Alisa is going to *kill* you."

That was Future Avery's problem. I tossed my wave-perfect hair and squared my shoulders. The roar of reporters yelling my name was louder the closer we got.

"Avery!"

"Avery, look over here!"

"Avery, what do you have to say about rumors that—"

"Smile, Avery!"

I was standing right in front of them now. I had their attention. Beside me, Oren raised a hand, and just like that, the crowd went silent.

Say something. I'm supposed to say something.

"I... ummm..." I cleared my throat. "This has been a big change."

There were a few small laughs. *I can do this.* The instant I thought those words, the universe made me pay for them. A fight broke out behind me, between Drake and the cops. I saw cameras starting to angle away from me, saw the long-distance lenses zooming in on the gates.

Don't just talk. Tell the story. Make them listen.

"I know why Tobias Hawthorne changed his will," I said loudly.

The response to that announcement was electric. There was a reason this was the story of the decade, one thing that everyone wanted to know. "I know why he chose me." I made them look at me and only me. "I'm the only one who does. I know the truth." I sold that lie for all I was worth. "And if you run a word about that pathetic excuse for a human being behind me—any of you—I will make it my mission in life to ensure that you never, ever find out."

CHAPTER 44

I didn't process the magnitude of what I'd done until I was safely inside Hawthorne House. *I told the press that I have the answers they want.* It was the first time I'd spoken to them, the first real footage anyone had of me, and I'd lied through my teeth.

Oren was right. Alisa was going to kill me.

I found Libby in the kitchen, surrounded by cupcakes. Literally hundreds of them. If she'd been an apology baker back home, the addition of an industrial-grade kitchen with triple ovens had basically taken her nuclear.

"Libby?" I approached her cautiously.

"Do you think I should go for red velvet or salted caramel next?" Libby was holding an icing bag with both hands. Blue hair had escaped her ponytail and was matted to her face. She wouldn't meet my eyes.

"She's been at it for hours," Nash told me. He stood leaning back against a stainless-steel refrigerator, his thumbs hooked through the belt loops of his well-worn jeans. "Her phone's been going off for just as long."

"Don't talk about me like I'm not here." Libby looked up from the cupcakes she was icing to narrow her eyes at Nash.

"Yes, ma'am." Nash smiled, wide and slow. I wondered how long he'd been with her—*why* he'd been with her.

"Drake is gone," I told Libby, hoping Nash would take that as his cue that he wasn't needed here. "I took care of it."

"I'm supposed to take care of you." Libby shoved her hair out of her face. "Stop looking at me like that, Avery. I'm not going to break."

"'Course not, darlin'," Nash said, from his spot leaning against the fridge.

"You..." Libby looked at him, a spark of annoyance lighting up her eyes. "You shut up."

I'd never heard Libby tell someone to shut up in her life, but at least she didn't sound fragile or hurt or in any danger of texting Drake back. I thought about Alisa saying that Nash Hawthorne had a savior complex.

"Shutting up now." Nash picked up a cupcake and took a bite out of it like it was an apple. "For what it's worth, I vote for red velvet next."

Libby turned back to me. "Salted caramel it is."

CHAPTER 45

That night, when Alisa called to read me the I-can't-do-my-job-if-you-won't-let-me riot act, she didn't allow me to get a word in edgewise. After she'd said a terse good-bye, which seemed to promise more retribution to come, I sat down at my computer.

"How bad is it?" I said out loud. The answer, it turned out, was leading-story-on-every-news-site bad.

Hawthorne Heiress Keeping Secrets.

What Does Avery Grambs Know?

I barely recognized myself in the pictures the paparazzi had taken. The girl in the photos was pretty and full of righteous fury. She looked as arrogant and dangerous as a Hawthorne.

I didn't feel like that girl.

I fully expected to get a text from Max, demanding to know what was going on, but even when I messaged her, she didn't message back. I went to close my laptop but then stopped, because I remembered telling Max that the reason I had no idea what had happened to Emily was that *Emily* was such a common name. I hadn't been able to search for her before.

But I knew her last name now. "Emily Laughlin," I said out loud. I typed her name into the search field, then added *Heights Country*

Day School to narrow the results. My finger hovered over the return key. After a long moment, I pulled the trigger.

I hit Enter.

An obituary came up, but that was it. No news coverage. No articles suggesting that a local golden girl had died by suspicious cause. No mention of Grayson or Jameson Hawthorne.

There was a picture with the obituary. Emily was smiling this time instead of laughing, and my brain soaked up all the details I'd missed before. Her hair was layered, and she wore it long. The ends curved this way and that, but the rest was silky straight. Her eyes were too big for her face. The shape of her upper lip made me think of a heart. She had a scattering of freckles.

Thump. Thump. Thump.

My head shot up at the noise, and I slammed my laptop closed. The last thing I wanted was anyone knowing what I'd just looked up.

Thump. This time, I did more than just register the sound. I flipped my bedside lamp on, swung my feet to the floor, and walked toward it. By the time I ended up at the fireplace, I was fairly certain who was on the other side.

"Do you ever use doors?" I asked Jameson, once I'd utilized the candlestick to open the passage.

Jameson cocked an eyebrow and cocked his head. "Do you *want* me to use the door?"

I felt like what he was really asking was if I wanted him to be normal. I remembered sitting beside him at high speed and thought about the climbing wall—and his hand reaching out to catch mine.

"I saw your press conference." Jameson had that expression on his face again, the one that made me feel like we were playing chess and he'd just made a move designed to be seen as a challenge.

"It wasn't so much a press conference as a very bad idea," I admitted wryly.

"Have I ever told you," Jameson murmured, staring at me in a way that had to be intentional, "that I'm a sucker for bad ideas?"

When he'd shown up here, I'd felt like I'd summoned him by searching for Emily's name, but now I saw this midnight visit for exactly what it was. Jameson Hawthorne was here, in my bedroom, at night. I was wearing my pajamas, and his body was listing toward mine.

None of this was an accident.

You're not a player, kid. You're the glass ballerina—or the knife.

"What do you want, Jameson?" My body wanted to lean toward him. The rational part of me wanted to step back.

"You lied to the press." Jameson didn't look away. He didn't blink, and neither did I. "What you told them . . . it *was* a lie, wasn't it?"

"Of course it was." If I'd known why Tobias Hawthorne left me his fortune, I wouldn't have been working side by side with Jameson to figure it out.

I wouldn't have lost my breath when I'd seen that map at the foundation.

"It's hard to tell with you sometimes," Jameson commented. "You're not exactly an open book." He fixed his gaze somewhere in the vicinity of my lips. His face inched toward mine.

Never lose your heart to a Hawthorne.

"Don't touch me," I said, but even as I stepped back, I could feel something—the same something I'd felt when I brushed up against Grayson back at the foundation.

A thing I had no business feeling—for either of them.

"Our thrill ride last night paid off," Jameson told me. "Getting out of my own head let me look at the puzzle with new eyes. Ask me what I figured out about our middle names."

"I don't have to," I told him. "I solved it, too. Blackwood. Westbrook. Davenport. Winchester. They're not just names. They're places—or at least, the first two are. The Black Wood. The West Brook." I let myself focus on the puzzle and not the fact that this room was lit only by lamplight and we were standing too close. "I'm not sure about the other two yet, but..."

"But..." Jameson's lips curved upward, his teeth flashing. "You'll figure it out." He brought his lips near my ear. "*We* will, Heiress."

There is no we. *Not really. I'm a means to an end for you.* I believed that. I did, but somehow what I found myself saying was "Feel like a walk?"

CHAPTER 46

This wasn't just a walk, and we both knew it.

"The Black Wood is enormous. Finding anything there will be impossible if we don't know what we're looking for." Jameson matched his stride, slow and steady, to mine. "The brook is easier. It runs most of the length of the property, but if I know my grandfather, we're not looking for something in the water. We're looking for something on—or under—the bridge."

"What bridge?" I asked. I caught sight of movement out of the corner of my eye. *Oren.* He stayed in the shadows, but he was there.

"The bridge," Jameson replied, "where my grandfather proposed to my grandmother. It's near Wayback Cottage. Back in the day, that was all my grandfather owned. As his empire grew, he bought up the surrounding land. He built the House but always kept up the cottage."

"The Laughlins live there now," I said, picturing the cottage on the map. "Emily's grandparents." I felt guilty even saying her name, but that didn't stop me from watching his response. *Did you love her? How did she die? Why does Thea blame your family?*

Jameson's mouth twisted. "Xander said you'd had a little chat with Rebecca," he said finally.

"No one at school talks to her," I murmured.

"Correction," Jameson replied. "Rebecca doesn't talk to anyone at school. She hasn't for months." He was quiet for a moment, the sound of our footsteps drowning out all else. "Rebecca was always the shy one. The responsible one. The one their parents expected to make good decisions."

"Not Emily." I filled in the blank.

"Emily..." Jameson sounded different when he said her name. "Emily just wanted to have fun. She had a heart condition, congenital. Her parents were ridiculously overprotective. They never let her do anything as a kid. She got a transplant when she was thirteen, and after that, she just wanted to *live*."

Not survive. Not just make it through. *Live*. I thought of the way she'd laughed into the camera, wild and free and a little too canny, like she'd known when that picture was taken that we'd all be looking at it later. At her.

I thought about the way that Skye had described Jameson. *Hungry*.

"Did you take her driving?" I asked. If I could have taken the question back, I would have, but it hung in the air between us.

"There is *nothing* that Emily and I didn't do." Jameson spoke like the words had been ripped out of him. "We were the same," he told me, and then he corrected himself. "I thought that we were the same."

I thought about Grayson, telling me that Jameson was a sensation seeker. Fear. Pain. Joy. Which of those had Emily been—for him?

"What happened to her?" I asked. My internet search hadn't yielded any answers. Thea had made it sound like the Hawthornes were somehow to blame, like Emily had died *because* she spent time at Hawthorne House. "Did she live at the cottage?"

Jameson ignored my second question and answered the first. "Grayson happened to her."

I'd known, from the moment I'd said Emily's name in Grayson's presence, that she had mattered to him. But Jameson seemed pretty clear on the fact that he'd been the one involved with her. *There is* nothing *that Emily and I didn't do.*

"What do you mean, Grayson happened to her?" I asked Jameson. I glanced back, but I couldn't see Oren anymore.

"Let's play a game," Jameson said darkly, his pace ticking up a notch as we hit a hill. "I'll give you one truth about my life and two lies, and it's up to you to decide which is which."

"Isn't it supposed to be two truths and one lie?" I asked. I may not have gone to many parties back home, but I hadn't grown up under a rock.

"What fun is it," Jameson returned, "playing by other people's rules?" He was looking at me like he expected me to understand that.

Understand him.

"Fact the first," he rattled off. "I knew what was in my grandfather's will long before you showed up here. Fact the second: I'm the one who sent Grayson to fetch you."

We reached the top of the hill, and I could see a building in the distance. A cottage—and between us and it, a bridge.

"Fact the third," Jameson said, standing statue-still for the span of a heartbeat. "I watched Emily Laughlin die."

CHAPTER 47

I didn't play Jameson's game. I didn't guess which of the things he'd just said was true, but there was no mistaking the way his throat had tightened when he'd said those last words.

I watched Emily Laughlin die.

That didn't tell me what had happened to her. It didn't explain why he'd told me that *Grayson* had happened to her.

"Shall we turn our attention to the bridge, Heiress?" Jameson didn't make me guess. I wasn't sure he really wanted me to.

I forced my focus to the scene in front of us. It was picturesque. There were fewer trees here to block the moonlight. I could make out the way the bridge arched the creek, but not the water below. The bridge was wooden, with railings and balusters that looked like they'd been painstakingly handmade. "Did your grandfather build this himself?"

I'd never met Tobias Hawthorne, but I was starting to feel like I knew him. He was everywhere—in this puzzle, in the House, in the boys.

"I don't know if he built it." Jameson flashed a Cheshire Cat grin, his teeth glinting in the moonlight. "But if we're right about this, he almost certainly built something *into* it."

Jameson excelled at pretense—pretending that I'd never asked him about Emily, pretending he hadn't just told me that he'd watched her die.

Pretending that what happened after midnight stayed in the dark.

He walked the length of the bridge. Behind him, I did the same. It was old and a little creaky but solid as a rock. When Jameson reached the end, he backtracked, his hands stretched out to the sides, fingertips lightly trailing the railings.

"Any idea what we're looking for?" I asked him.

"I'll know it when I see it." He might as well have said *when I see it, I'll let you know.* He'd said that he and Emily were alike, and I couldn't shake the feeling that he wouldn't have expected her to be a passive participant. He wouldn't have treated her as just another part of the game, laid out in the beginning to be useful by the end.

I'm a person. I'm capable. I'm here. I'm playing. I took my phone from the pocket of my coat and turned on its flashlight. I made my way back over the bridge, shining the beam on the railing, looking for indentations or a carving—something. My eyes tracked the nails in the wood, counting them out, mentally measuring the distance between every one.

When I finished with the railing, I squatted, inspecting each baluster. Opposite me, Jameson did the same. It felt almost like we were dancing—a strange midnight dance for two.

I'm here.

"I'll know it when I see it," Jameson said again, somewhere between a mantra and a promise.

"Or maybe I will." I straightened.

Jameson looked up at me. "Sometimes, Heiress," he said, "you just need a different point of view."

He jumped, and the next thing I knew, he was standing on

the railing. I couldn't make out the water down below, but I could hear it. The night air was otherwise silent, until Jameson started walking.

It was like watching him teeter on the balcony, all over again.

The bridge isn't that high. The water probably isn't that deep. I turned my flashlight toward him, rising from my crouched position. The bridge creaked beneath me.

"We need to look below," Jameson said. He climbed to the far side of the railing, balancing on the bridge's edge. "Grab my legs," he told me, but before I could figure out where to grab them or what he was planning to do, he changed his mind. "No. I'm too big. You'll drop me." He was back over the railing in a flash. "I'll have to hold you."

There were a lot of firsts I'd never gotten around to after my mother's death. First dates. First kisses. First times. But this particular first—being dangled off a bridge by a boy who'd *just* confessed to watching his last girlfriend die—wasn't exactly on the to-do list.

If she was with you, why did you say that Grayson *happened to her?*

"Don't drop your phone," Jameson told me. "And I won't drop you."

His hands were braced against my hips. I was facedown, my legs between the balusters, my torso hanging off the bridge's edge. If he let go, I was in trouble.

The Dangling Game, I could almost hear my mom declaring.

Jameson adjusted his weight, serving as an anchor for mine. *His knee is touching mine. His hands are on me.* I felt more aware of my own body, my own skin, than I could ever remember feeling.

Don't feel. Just look. I flashed my light at the underside of the bridge. Jameson didn't let go.

"Do you see anything?"

"Shadows," I replied. "Some algae." I twisted, arching my back slightly. The blood was rushing to my head. "The boards on the bottom aren't the same boards we can see up top," I noted. "There's at least two layers of wood." I counted the boards. *Twenty-one.* I took another few seconds to examine the way the boards met up with the shore, and then I called back, "There's nothing here, Jameson. Pull me up."

There were twenty-one boards beneath the bridge and, based on the count I'd just completed, twenty-one on the surface. Everything added up. Nothing was amiss. Jameson paced, but I thought better standing still.

Or I would have thought better standing still if I hadn't been watching him pace. He had a way of moving—unspeakable energy, uncanny grace. "It's getting late," I said, averting my gaze.

"It was always late," Jameson told me. "If you were going to turn into a pumpkin, it would have happened by now, Cinderella."

Another day, another nickname. I didn't want to read into that—I wasn't even sure *what* to read into that. "We have school tomorrow," I reminded him.

"Maybe we do." Jameson hit the end of the bridge, turned, and walked back. "Maybe we don't. You can play by the rules—or you can make them. I know which I prefer, Heiress."

Which Emily preferred. I couldn't keep myself from going there. I tried to focus on the moment, the puzzle at hand. The bridge creaked. Jameson kept pacing. I cleared my mind. And the bridge creaked again.

"Wait." I cocked my head to the side. "Stop." Shockingly, Jameson did as I'd commanded. "Back up. Slowly." I waited, and I listened—and then I heard the creak again.

"It's the same board." Jameson arrived at that conclusion at the same time I did. "Every time." He squatted down to get a better look at it. I knelt, too. The board didn't look different from any of the others. I ran my fingers over it, feeling for something—I wasn't sure what.

Beside me, Jameson was doing the same. He brushed against me. I tried not to feel anything and expected him to pull back, but instead, his fingers slid between mine, weaving our hands together, flat on the board.

He pressed down.

I did the same.

The board creaked. I leaned into it, and Jameson began rotating our hands, slowly, from one side of the board to the other.

"It moves." My eyes darted up toward him. "Just a little."

"A little isn't enough." He pulled his fingers slowly back from mine, feather-light and warm. "We're looking for a latch—something keeping the board from rotating all the way around."

Eventually, we found it, small knots in the wood where the board met up with the balusters. Jameson took the one on the left. I took the one on the right. Moving in synchrony, we pressed. There was a popping sound. When we met back in the middle and tested the board once more, it moved more freely. Together, we rotated it until the bottom of the board faced upward.

I shined my flashlight on the wood. Jameson did the same with his. Carved into the surface of the wood was a symbol.

"Infinity," Jameson said, tracing his thumb over the carving.

I tilted my head to the side and took a more pragmatic view. "Or eight."

CHAPTER 48

Morning came way too early. Somehow, I dragged myself out of bed and got dressed. I debated if I could get away with skipping hair and makeup but remembered what Xander had said about telling the story so no one else tells it for you.

After what I'd pulled with the press the day before, I couldn't afford to show weakness.

As I finished donning what I mentally called my battle face, there was a knock at my door. I answered it and saw the maid who Alisa had told me was "one of Nash's." She was carrying a breakfast tray. Mrs. Laughlin hadn't sent one up since my first morning at Hawthorne House.

I wondered what I'd done to deserve this one.

"Our crew deep-cleans the house from top to bottom on Tuesdays," the maid informed me, once she'd set up the tray. "If it's all right with you, I'll start in your bathroom."

"Just let me hang up my towel," I said, and the woman stared at me like I'd announced an intention to do naked yoga right there in front of her.

"You can leave your towel on the floor. We'll be laundering them anyway."

That just felt wrong. "I'm Avery." I introduced myself, even though she almost certainly knew my name. "What's your name?"

"Mellie." She didn't volunteer more than that.

"Thank you, Mellie." She stared at me blankly. "For your help." I thought about the fact that Tobias Hawthorne had kept outsiders out of Hawthorne House as much as possible. And still, there was an entire crew in to clean on Tuesdays. I shouldn't have found that surprising. It should have been more surprising that the entire crew wasn't here cleaning every day. *And yet*...

I went across the hall to Libby's room because I knew she would get exactly how surreal and uncomfortable this felt. I knocked lightly, in case she was still sleeping, and the door drifted inward, just far enough for me to catch sight of a chair and ottoman—and the man currently occupying them.

Nash Hawthorne's long legs were stretched out on the ottoman, his boots still on. A cowboy hat covered his face. He was sleeping.

In my sister's room.

Nash Hawthorne was sleeping in my sister's room.

I made an involuntary sound and stepped back. Nash stirred, then saw me. Hat in hand, he slipped out of the chair and joined me in the hallway.

"What are you doing in Libby's room?" I asked him. He hadn't been in her bed, but still. What the hell was the oldest Hawthorne brother doing keeping vigil over my sister?

"She's going through something," Nash said, like that was news to me. Like I hadn't been the one to handle Drake the day before.

"Libby isn't one of your projects," I told him. I had no idea how much time they'd spent together these past few days. In the kitchen, she'd seemed to find him irritating. *Libby doesn't get irritated. She's a gothic beam of sunshine.*

"My projects?" Nash repeated, eyes narrowing. "What exactly has Lee-Lee been telling you?"

His continual use of a nickname for my lawyer only served to remind me that they had been engaged. *He's Alisa's ex. He's "saved" who knows how many members of the staff. And he spent the night in my sister's room.*

This could not possibly end well. But before I could say that, Mellie stepped out of my room. She couldn't be done with the bathroom yet, so she must have heard us. Heard Nash.

"Mornin'," he told her.

"Good morning," she said with a smile—and then she looked at me, looked at Libby's room, looked at the open door—and stopped smiling.

CHAPTER 49

Oren met me at the car with a cup of coffee. He didn't say a word about my little adventure with Jameson the night before, and I didn't ask how much he'd observed. As he opened the car door, Oren leaned toward me. "Don't say I didn't warn you."

I had no idea what he was talking about, until I realized that Alisa was sitting in the front seat. "You're looking sedate this morning," she commented.

I took *sedate* to mean *moderately less rash and therefore less likely to evoke a tabloid scandal*. I wondered how she would have described the scene I'd stumbled across in Libby's room.

This is so not good.

"I hope you don't have plans for this weekend, Avery," Alisa said as Oren put the car in drive. "Or the next weekend." Neither Jameson nor Xander had joined us, which meant that I had absolutely no buffer, and clearly, Alisa was royally pissed.

My lawyer can't ground me, can she? I thought.

"I was hoping to keep you out of the limelight a bit longer," Alisa continued pointedly, "but since that plan has gone by the wayside, you'll be attending a pink ribbon fund raiser this Saturday night and a game next Sunday."

"A game?" I repeated.

"NFL," she said curtly. "You own the team. My hope is that scheduling some high-profile social outings will provide enough grist for the gossip mill that we can delay setting up your first sit-down interview until after we've gotten you some real media training."

I was still trying to absorb the NFL bombshell when the words *media training* put a knot of dread in my throat.

"Do I have to—"

"Yes," Alisa told me. "Yes to the gala this weekend, yes to the game next weekend, yes to the media training."

I didn't say another word in complaint. I'd stoked this fire—and protected Libby—knowing that, sooner or later, I'd have to pay the piper.

I got so many stares when we arrived at school that I found myself questioning whether I'd dreamed my last two days at Heights Country Day. This was what I'd expected, back on day one. Just like then, Thea was the first to make a move toward me.

"You did a thing," she said in a tone that highly suggested what I'd done was both naughty and delicious. Inexplicably, my mind went to Jameson, to the moment on the bridge when his fingers had woven their way between mine.

"Do you really know why Tobias Hawthorne left you everything?" Thea asked, her eyes alight. "The whole school's talking about it."

"The whole school can talk about whatever they want."

"You don't like me much," Thea noted. "That's okay. I'm a

hypercompetitive, bisexual perfectionist who likes to win and looks like *this*. I'm no stranger to being hated."

I rolled my eyes. "I don't hate you." I didn't know her well enough to hate her yet.

"That's good," Thea replied with a self-satisfied smile, "because we're going to be spending a lot more time with each other. My parents are going out of town. They seem to believe that, left to my own devices, I might do something ill-advised, so I'll be staying with my uncle, and I understand that he and Zara have taken up residence at Hawthorne House. I guess they're not quite ready to cede the family homestead to a stranger."

Zara had been playing nice—or at least *nicer*. But I'd had no idea that she'd moved in. Then again, Hawthorne House was so gargantuan that an entire professional baseball team could be living there and I might have no idea.

For all I knew, I might *own* a professional baseball team.

"Why would you want to stay at Hawthorne House?" I asked Thea. She was the one who'd warned me away.

"Contrary to popular belief, I don't always do what I want." Thea tossed her dark hair over her shoulder. "And besides, Emily was my best friend. After everything that happened last year, when it comes to the charms of Hawthorne brothers, I'm immune."

CHAPTER 50

When I finally got ahold of Max, she wasn't feeling chatty. I could tell that something was wrong, but not what. She didn't have a single fake expletive to share on the topic of Thea moving in, and she cut our back-and-forth short without any commentary whatsoever on the Hawthorne brothers' physiques. I asked if everything was okay. She said that she had to go.

Xander, in contrast, was more than willing to discuss the Thea development. "If Thea's here," he told me that afternoon, lowering his voice like the walls of Hawthorne House might have ears, "she's up to something."

"*She* as in Thea?" I asked pointedly. "Or your aunt?"

Zara had thrown me together with Grayson at the foundation, and now she was moving Thea into the House. I recognized someone stacking the board, even if I couldn't see the play underneath.

"You're right," Xander said. "I seriously doubt Thea *volunteered* to spend time with our family. It is possible that she fervently wishes for vultures to dine upon my entrails."

"You?" I said. Thea's issues with the Hawthorne brothers had seemed to revolve around Emily—and that meant, I had assumed, around Jameson and Grayson. "What did you do?"

"It is a story," Xander said with a sigh, "involving star-crossed love, fake dating, tragedy, penance...and possibly vultures."

I thought back to asking Xander about Rebecca Laughlin. He hadn't said anything to indicate she was Emily's sister. He'd murmured almost exactly what he'd just said about Thea.

Xander didn't let me ruminate for long. Instead, he dragged me off to what he declared to be his fourth-favorite room in the House. "If you're going to be going head-to-head with Thea," he told me, "you need to be prepared."

"I'm not going head-to-head with anyone," I said firmly.

"It is adorable that you believe that." Xander stopped where one corridor met another. He reached up—all six foot three of him—to touch a molding that ran up the corner. He must have hit some kind of release, because the next thing I knew, he was pulling the molding toward us, revealing a gap behind it. He stuck his hand into the gap behind the molding, and a moment later, a portion of the wall swung out toward us like a door.

I was *never* going to get used to this.

"Welcome to...my lair!" Xander sounded overjoyed to be saying those words.

I stepped into his "lair" and saw...a machine? *Contraption* probably would have been the more accurate term. There were dozens of gears, pulleys, and chains, a complicated series of connected ramps, several buckets, two conveyor belts, a slingshot, a birdcage, four pinwheels, and at least four balloons.

"Is that an anvil?" I asked, frowning and leaning forward for a better look.

"That," Xander said proudly, "is a Rube Goldberg machine. As it so happens, I am a three-time world champion at building machines that do simple things in overly complicated ways." He handed me a marble. "Place this in the pinwheel."

I did. The pinwheel spun, blowing a balloon, that tipped a bucket...

As I watched each mechanism set off the next, I glanced at the youngest Hawthorne brother out of the corner of my eye. "What does this have to do with Thea moving in?"

He'd told me that I needed to be prepared, then brought me here. Was this supposed to be some kind of metaphor? A warning that Zara's actions might appear complicated, even when the goal was simple? An insight into Thea's charge?

Xander cast a sideways look at me and grinned. "Who said this had anything to do with Thea?"

CHAPTER 51

That night, in honor of Thea's visit, Mrs. Laughlin made a melt-in-your-mouth roast beef. Orgasmic garlic mashed potatoes. Roasted asparagus, broccoli florets, and three different kinds of crème brûlée.

I couldn't help feeling like it was pretty revealing that Mrs. Laughlin had pulled out all the stops for Thea—but not for me.

Trying not to seem petty, I sat down to a formal dinner in the "dining room," which probably should have been called a banquet hall instead. The massive table was set for eleven. I cataloged the participants in this little family dinner: four Hawthorne brothers. Skye. Zara and Constantine. Thea. Libby. Nan. And me.

"Thea," Zara said, her voice almost too pleasant, "how is field hockey?"

"We're undefeated this season." Thea turned toward me. "Have you decided which sport you'll be playing, Avery?"

I managed to resist the urge to snort, but barely. "I don't do sports."

"Everyone at Country Day does a sport," Xander informed me, before stuffing his mouth with roast beef. His eyes rolled upward with pleasure as he chewed. "It is an actual, real requirement and not a figment of Thea's delightfully vindictive imagination."

"Xander," Nash said in warning.

"I said she was *delightfully* vindictive," Xander replied innocently.

"If I were a boy," Thea told him with a Southern belle smile, "people would just call me driven."

"Thea." Constantine frowned at her.

"Right." Thea dabbed at her lips with her napkin. "No feminism at the dinner table."

This time, I couldn't bite back the snort. *Point, Thea.*

"A toast," Skye declared out of nowhere, holding up her wineglass and slurring the words enough that it was clear she'd already been imbibing.

"Skye, dear," Nan said firmly, "have you considered sleeping it off?"

"A toast," Skye reiterated, glass still held high. "To Avery."

For once, she'd gotten my name right. I waited for the guillotine to drop, but Skye said nothing else. Zara raised her glass. One by one, every other glass went up.

Every person in this room had probably gotten the message: No good could come of challenging the will. I might have been the enemy—but I was also the one with the money.

Is that why Zara brought Thea here? To get close to me? Is that why she left me alone at the foundation with Grayson?

"To you, Heiress," Jameson murmured to my left. I turned to look at him. I hadn't seen him since the night before. I was fairly certain he'd skipped school. I wondered if he'd spent the day in the Black Wood, looking for the next clue. *Without me.*

"To Emily," Thea added suddenly, her glass still raised, her eyes on Jameson. "May she rest in peace."

Jameson's glass came down. His chair was pushed roughly back from the table. Farther down, Grayson's fingers tightened around the stem of his own glass, his knuckles going white.

"Theadora," Constantine hissed.

Thea took a drink and adopted the world's most innocent expression. "What?"

Everything in me wanted to follow Jameson, but I waited a few minutes before excusing myself. Like that would keep any of them from knowing exactly where I was going.

In the foyer, I pressed my hand flat against the wall panels, hitting the sequence designed to reveal the coat closet door. I needed my coat if I was going to venture off into the Black Wood. I was sure that was where Jameson had gone.

As my hand hooked around the hanger, a voice spoke from behind me. "I'm not going to ask you what Jameson is up to. What you're up to."

I turned to face Grayson. "You're not going to ask me," I repeated, taking in the set of his jaw and those canny silver eyes, "because you already know."

"I was there last night. At the bridge." There were edges in Grayson's tone—not rough, but sharp. "This morning, I went to see the Red Will."

"I still have the decoder," I pointed out, trying not to read anything into the fact that he'd seen his brother and me at the bridge—and didn't sound happy about it.

Grayson shrugged, his shoulders pulling against the confines of his suit. "Red acetate is easy enough to come by."

If he'd seen the Red Will, he knew that their middle names were clues. I wondered if his mind had gone immediately to their fathers. I wondered if that hurt him, the way it hurt Jameson.

"You were there last night," I said, echoing back what he'd told me. "At the bridge." How much had he seen? How much did he know?

What had he thought when Jameson and I had touched?

"Westbrook. Davenport. Winchester. Blackwood." Grayson took a step toward me. "They're last names—but they are also locations. I found the clue on the bridge after you and my brother had gone."

He'd followed us there. He'd found what we'd found.

"What do you want, Grayson?"

"If you were smart," he warned softly, "you'd stay away from Jameson. From the game." He looked down. "From me." Emotion slashed across his features, but he masked it before I could tell what, exactly, he was feeling. "Thea's right," he said sharply, turning away from me—*walking* away from me. "This family—we destroy everything we touch."

CHAPTER 52

I knew from the map roughly where the Black Wood was. I found Jameson on the outskirts, standing eerily still, like he *couldn't* move. Without warning, he broke that stillness, punching furiously at a nearby tree, hard and fast, the bark tearing at his hands.

Thea brought up Emily. This is what even the mention of her name does to him.

"Jameson!" I was almost to him now. He jerked his head toward me, and I stopped, overwhelmed with the feeling that I shouldn't have been there, that I had no right to witness any of the Hawthorne boys hurting that much.

The only thing I could think to do was try to make what I'd just seen matter less. "Broken any fingers lately?" I asked lightly. *The Pretending It Doesn't Matter Game.*

Jameson was ready and willing to play. He held his hands up, grunting as he bent them at the knuckles. "Still intact."

I dragged my eyes from him and took in our surroundings. The perimeter was so densely wooded that if the trees hadn't already shed their leaves, no light would have been able to make it to the forest floor.

"What are we looking for?" I asked. Maybe he didn't consider me a real partner in this hunt. Maybe there was no real *we*—but he answered.

"Your guess is as good as mine, Heiress."

All around us, bare branches stretched up overhead, skeletal and crooked.

"You skipped school today to do *something*," I pointed out. "You have a guess."

Jameson smiled like he couldn't feel the blood welling up on his hands. "Four middle names. Four locations. Four clues—carvings, most likely. Symbols, if the clue on the bridge was infinity; numbers, if it was an eight."

I wondered what, if anything, he'd done to clear his mind between last night and entering the Black Wood. *Climbing. Racing. Jumping.*

Disappearing into the walls.

"Do you know how many trees four acres can hold, Heiress?" Jameson asked jauntily. "Two hundred, in a healthy forest."

"And in the Black Wood?" I prompted, taking first one step toward him, then another.

"At least twice that."

It was like the library all over again. Like the keys. There had to be a shortcut, a trick we weren't seeing.

"Here." Jameson bent down, then placed a roll of glow-in-the-dark duct tape in my hand, letting his fingers brush mine as he did. "I've been marking off trees as I check them."

I concentrated on his words—not his touch. Mostly. "There has got to be a better way," I said, turning the duct tape over in my hands, my eyes finding their way to his once more.

Jameson's lips twisted into a lazy, devil-may-care smirk. "Got any suggestions, Mystery Girl?"

Two days later, Jameson and I were still doing things the hard way, and we still hadn't found anything. I could see him becoming more and more single-minded. Jameson Winchester Hawthorne would push until he hit a wall. I wasn't sure what he would do to break through it this time, but every once in a while, I caught him looking at me in a way that made me think he had some ideas.

That was how he was looking at me now. "We aren't the only ones searching for the next clue," he said as dusk began to give way to darkness. "I saw Grayson with a map of the woods."

"Thea's tailing me," I said, ripping off a piece of tape, hyper-aware of the silence all around us. "The only way I can shake her is when she sees an opportunity to mess with Xander."

Jameson brushed gently past me and marked off the next tree over. "Thea holds a grudge, and when she and Xander broke up, it was ugly."

"They dated?" I slid past Jameson and searched the next tree, running my fingers over the bark. "Thea is practically your cousin."

"Constantine is Zara's second husband. The marriage is recent, and Xander's always been a fan of loopholes."

Nothing with the Hawthorne brothers was ever simple—including what Jameson and I were doing now. Since we'd worked our way to the center of the forest, the trees were spread farther apart. Up ahead, I could see a large open space—the only place in the Black Wood where grass was able to grow on the forest floor.

My back to Jameson, I moved to a new tree and began running my hands over the bark. Almost immediately, my fingers hit a groove.

"Jameson." It wasn't pitch-dark yet, but there was little enough light in the woods that I couldn't entirely make out what I'd found until Jameson appeared beside me, shining an extra light. I ran my fingers slowly over the letters carved into the tree.

TOBIAS HAWTHORNE II

Unlike the first symbol we'd found, these letters weren't smooth. The carving hadn't been done with an even hand. The name looked like it had been carved by a child.

"The I's at the end are a Roman numeral," Jameson said, his voice going electric. "Tobias Hawthorne the Second."

Toby, I thought, and then I heard a *crack*. A deafening echo followed, and the world exploded. Bark flying. My body thrown backward.

"Get down!" Jameson yelled.

I barely heard him. My brain couldn't process what I was hearing, what had just happened. *I'm bleeding.*

Pain.

Jameson grabbed me and pulled me toward the ground. The next thing I knew, his body was over mine and the sound of a second gunshot rang out.

Gun. Someone's shooting at us. There was a stabbing pain in my chest. *I've been shot.*

I heard footsteps beating against the forest floor, and then Oren yelled, "Stay down!" Weapon drawn, my bodyguard put himself between us and the shooter. A small eternity passed. Oren took off running in the direction the shots had come from, but I knew, with a prescience I couldn't explain, that the shooter was gone.

"Are you okay, Avery?" Oren doubled back. "Jameson, is she okay?"

"She's bleeding." That was Jameson. He'd pulled back from my body and was looking down at me.

My chest throbbed, just below my collarbone, where I'd been hit.

"Your face." Jameson's touch was light against my skin. The moment his fingertips skimmed lightly over my cheekbone, the nerves in my face were jarred alive. *Hurts.*

"Did they shoot me twice?" I asked, dazed.

"The assailant didn't shoot you at all." Oren made quick work of displacing Jameson and ran his hands expertly over my body, checking for damage. "You got hit by a couple of pieces of bark." He probed at the wound below my collarbone. "The other cut's just a scratch, but the bark's lodged deep in this one. We'll leave it until we're ready to stitch you up."

My ears rang. "Stitch me up." I didn't want to just repeat what he was saying back to him, but it was literally all my mouth would do.

"You're lucky." Oren stood, then did a quick check of the tree, where the bullet had hit. "A couple of inches to the right, and we'd be looking at removing a bullet, not bark." My bodyguard stalked past the place where the tree had been hit to another tree behind us. In one smooth motion, he produced a knife from his belt and jammed it into the tree.

It took me a moment to realize that he was digging out a bullet.

"Whoever fired this is long gone now," he said, wrapping the bullet in what appeared to be some kind of handkerchief. "But we might be able to trace this."

This, as in a bullet. Someone had just tried to shoot us. *Me.* My brain was finally catching up now. *They weren't aiming for Jameson.*

"What just happened here?" For once, Jameson didn't sound like he was playing. He sounded like his heart was beating as rapidly and viciously as mine.

"What happened," Oren replied, glancing back into the distance, "is that someone saw the two of you out here, decided you were easy targets, and pulled their trigger. Twice."

CHAPTER 53

Someone shot at me. I felt...*numb* wasn't the right word. My mouth was too dry. My heart was beating too fast. I hurt, but it felt like I was hurting from a distance.

Shock.

"I need a team in the northeast quadrant." Oren was on the phone. I tried to focus on what he was saying but couldn't seem to focus on anything, not even my arm. "We have a shooter. Gone now, almost certainly, but we'll sweep the woods just in case. Bring a med kit."

Oren hung up, then turned his attention back to Jameson and me. "Follow me. We'll stay where we have cover until the support team gets here." He led us back toward the south end of the forest, where the trees were denser.

It didn't take the team long to arrive. They came in ATVs—two of them. *Two men, two vehicles.* As soon as they pulled up, Oren rattled off coordinates: where we'd been when we were shot, the direction the bullets had come from, the trajectory.

The men didn't say anything in response. They drew their weapons. Oren climbed into the four-seat ATV and waited for Jameson and me to do the same.

"You headed back to the House?" one of the men asked.

Oren met his subordinate's eyes. "The cottage."

Halfway to Wayback Cottage, my brain started working again. My chest hurt. I'd been given a compress to hold on the wound, but Oren hadn't treated it yet. His first priority had been getting us to safer ground. *He's taking us to Wayback Cottage. Not Hawthorne House.* The cottage was closer, but I couldn't shake the feeling that what Oren had really been saying to his men was that he didn't trust the people at the House.

So much for the way he'd assured me—repeatedly—that I was safe. That the Hawthorne family wasn't a threat. The entire estate, including the Black Wood, was walled in. No one was allowed past the gate without a thorough background check.

Oren doesn't think we're dealing with an outside threat. I let that sink in, a heaviness in my stomach as I processed the limited number of suspects. *The Hawthornes—and the staff.*

Going to Wayback Cottage felt like a risk. I hadn't interacted with the Laughlins much, but they hadn't ever given me the impression that they were glad I was here. *Exactly how loyal are they to the Hawthorne family?* I thought about Alisa saying that Nash's people would die for him.

Would they kill for him, too?

Mrs. Laughlin was at home when we arrived at Wayback. *She's not the shooter,* I thought. *She couldn't have made it back here in time. Could she?*

The older woman took one look at Oren, Jameson, and me and ushered us inside. If a bleeding person being stitched up at her kitchen table was an unusual occurrence, she gave no sign of it. I wasn't sure if the way she was taking this in stride was comforting—or suspicious.

"I'll put on some tea," she said. My heart pounding, I wondered if it was safe to drink anything she gave me.

"You okay with me playing medic?" Oren asked, settling me in a chair. "I'm sure Alisa could arrange for some fancy plastic surgeon."

I wasn't okay with any of this. Everyone had been so sure that I wasn't going to get ax-murdered that I'd let my guard down. I'd pushed back the thought that people had killed over far less than what I'd inherited. I'd let every single one of the Hawthorne brothers past my defenses.

This wasn't Xander. I couldn't get my body to calm down, no matter how hard I tried. *Jameson was right next to me. Nash doesn't want the money, and Grayson wouldn't...*

He wouldn't.

"Avery?" Oren prompted, a note of concern working its way into his deep voice.

I tried to stop my mind from racing. I felt sick—physically sick. *Stop panicking.* I had a piece of wood in my flesh. I would have preferred *not* having a piece of wood in my flesh. *Pull it together.*

"Do what you need to do to stop the bleeding," I told Oren. My voice only shook a little.

Removing the bark hurt. The disinfectant hurt a hell of a lot more. The med kit included a shot of local anesthetic, but there was no amount of anesthetic that could alter my brain's awareness of the needle when Oren began stitching my skin back together.

Focus on that. Let it hurt. After a moment, I looked away from Oren and tracked Mrs. Laughlin's movements. Before handing me my tea, she laced it—heavily—with whiskey.

"Done." Oren nodded to my cup. "Drink that."

He'd brought me here because he trusted the Laughlins more than he trusted the Hawthornes. He was telling me that it was safe to drink. But he'd told me a lot of things.

Someone shot at me. They tried to kill me. I could be dead. My hands were shaking. Oren steadied them. His eyes knowing, he lifted my teacup to his own mouth and took a drink.

It's fine. He's showing me that it's fine. Unsure if I'd ever be able to kick myself out of fight-or-flight mode, I forced myself to drink. The tea was hot. The whiskey was strong.

It burned all the way down.

Mrs. Laughlin gave me an almost maternal look, then scowled at Oren. "Mr. Laughlin will want to know what happened," she said, as if she herself were not at all curious about why I was bleeding at her kitchen table. "And someone needs to clean up the poor girl's face." She gave me a sympathetic look and clucked her tongue.

Before, I'd been an outsider. Now she was hovering like a mother hen. *All it took was a few bullets.*

"Where is Mr. Laughlin?" Oren asked, his tone conversational, but I heard the question—and the implication underneath. *He's not here. Is he a good shot? Would he—*

As if summoned, Mr. Laughlin walked through the front door and let it slam behind him. There was mud on his boots.

From the woods?

"Something's happened," Mrs. Laughlin told her husband calmly.

Mr. Laughlin looked at Oren, Jameson, and me—in that order, the same order in which his wife had taken in our presence—and then poured himself a glass of whiskey. "Security protocols?" he asked Oren gruffly.

Oren gave a brisk nod. "In full force."

He turned back to his wife. "Where's Rebecca?" he asked.

Jameson looked up from his own cup of tea. "Rebecca's here?"

"She's a good girl," Mr. Laughlin grunted. "Comes to visit, the way she should."

So where is she? I thought.

Mrs. Laughlin rested a hand on my shoulder. "There's a bathroom through there, dear," she told me quietly, "if you want to clean up."

CHAPTER 54

The door Mrs. Laughlin had sent me through didn't lead directly to a bathroom. It led to a bedroom that held two twin beds and little else. The walls were painted a light purple; the twin comforters were quilted from squares of fabric in lavender and violet.

The bathroom door was slightly ajar.

I walked toward it, so painfully aware of my surroundings that I felt like I could have heard a pin drop a mile away. *There's no one here. I'm safe. It's okay. I'm okay.*

Inside the bathroom, I checked behind the shower curtain. *There's no one here*, I told myself again. *I'm okay.* I managed to get my cell phone out of my pocket and called Max. I needed her to answer. I needed not to be alone with this. What I got was voicemail.

I called seven times, and she didn't pick up.

Maybe she couldn't. *Or maybe she doesn't want to.* That hit me almost as hard as looking in the mirror and seeing my blood-streaked, dirt-smeared face. I stared at myself.

I could hear the echo of gunfire.

Stop. I needed to wash—my hands, my face, the streaks of

blood on my chest. *Turn on the water*, I told myself sternly. *Pick up the washcloth.* I willed my body to move.

I couldn't.

Hands reached past me to turn on the faucet. I should have jumped. I should have panicked. But somehow, my body relaxed into the person behind me.

"It's okay, Heiress," Jameson murmured. "I've got you."

I hadn't heard Jameson come in. I wasn't entirely sure how long I'd been standing there, frozen.

Jameson reached for a pale purple washcloth and held it under the water.

"I'm fine," I insisted, as much to myself as to him.

Jameson lifted the washcloth to my face. "You're a horrible liar." He ran the cloth over my cheek, working his way down toward the scratch. A breath caught in my throat. He rinsed the washcloth, blood and dirt coloring the sink, as he lifted the cloth back to my skin.

Again.

And again.

He washed my face, took my hands in his and held them under the water, his fingers working the dirt from mine. My skin responded to his touch. For the first time, no part of me said to pull away. He was so gentle. He wasn't acting like this was just a game to him—like I was just a game.

He picked the washcloth back up and ran it down my neck to my shoulder, over my collarbone and across. The water was warm. I leaned into his touch. *This is a bad idea.* I knew that. I'd always known that, but I let myself concentrate on the feel of Jameson Hawthorne's touch, the stroke of the cloth.

"I'm okay," I said, and I could almost believe that.

"You're better than okay."

I closed my eyes. He'd been there with me in the forest. I could feel his body over mine. Protecting me. I needed this. I needed *something.*

I opened my eyes, looked at him. Focused on him. I thought about going two hundred miles an hour, about the climbing wall, about the moment I'd first seen him up on that balcony. Was being a sensation seeker so bad? Was wanting to feel something other than *awful* really so wrong?

Everyone is a little wrong sometimes, Heiress.

Something gave inside of me, and I pushed him gently back against the bathroom wall. *I need this.* His deep green eyes met mine. *He needs it, too.* "Yes?" I asked him hoarsely.

"Yes, Heiress."

My lips closed over his. He kissed me back, gentle at first, then not gently at all. Maybe it was the aftereffects of shock, but as I drove my hands into his hair, as he grabbed my ponytail and angled my face upward, I could see a thousand versions of him in my mind: *Balanced on the balcony's railing. Shirtless and sunlit in the solarium. Smiling. Smirking. Our hands touching on the bridge. His body protecting mine in the Black Wood. Trailing a washcloth down my neck—*

Kissing him felt like fire. He wasn't soft and sweet, the way he had been while washing away the blood and dirt. I didn't need soft or sweet. *This* was exactly what I needed.

Maybe I could be what he needed, too. Maybe this didn't have to be a bad idea. Maybe the complications were worth it.

He pulled back from the kiss, his lips only an inch away from mine. "I always knew you were special."

I felt his breath on my face. I felt every last one of those words. I'd never thought of myself as special. I'd been invisible for so long. *Wallpaper.* Even after I'd become the biggest story in the world, it had never really felt like anyone was paying attention to *me*. The real me.

"We're so close now," Jameson murmured. "I can feel it." There was an energy in his voice, like the buzzing of a neon light. "Someone obviously didn't want us looking at that tree."

What?

He went to kiss me again, and, my heart sinking, I turned my head to the side. I'd thought... I wasn't sure what I'd thought. *That when he told me I was special, he wasn't talking about the money—or the puzzle.*

"You think someone shot at us because of a tree?" I said, the words getting caught in my throat. "Not, say, the fortune I inherited that your family would like to get their hands on? Not the billions of reasons that anyone with the last name Hawthorne has to hate me?"

"Don't think about that," Jameson whispered, cupping my cheeks. "Think about Toby's name carved into that tree. Infinity carved into the bridge." His face was close enough to mine that I could still feel his breath. "What if what the puzzle is trying to tell us is that my uncle isn't dead?"

Was *that* what he'd been thinking when someone was shooting at us? In the kitchen, as Oren took a needle to my wound? As he'd brought his lips to mine? Because if the only thing he'd been able to think about was the mystery...

You're not a player, kid. You're the glass ballerina—or the knife.

"Will you listen to yourself?" I demanded. My chest was tight—tighter now than it had been in the forest, in the thick of it all. Nothing about Jameson's reaction should have surprised me, so why did it hurt?

Why was I letting it hurt?

"Oren just pulled a chunk of wood out of my chest," I said, my voice low, "and if things had worked out a little differently, he could have been pulling out a bullet." I gave Jameson a second to reply—just one. *Nothing.* "What happens to the money if I die while the will is in probate?" I asked flatly. Alisa had told me the Hawthorne family didn't stand to benefit, but did *they* know that? "What happens if whoever fired that gun scares me off, and I leave before the year is up?" Did they know that if I left, it all went to charity? "Not everything is a game, Jameson."

I saw something flicker in his eyes. He closed them, just for an instant, then opened them and leaned in, bringing his lips painfully close to mine. "That's the thing, Heiress. If Emily taught me anything, it's that everything *is* a game. Even this. *Especially* this."

CHAPTER 55

Jameson left, and I didn't follow him.

Thea's right, Grayson whispered in the recesses of my mind. *This family—we destroy everything we touch.* I choked back tears. I'd been shot at, I'd been injured, and I'd been kissed—but I sure as hell wasn't destroyed.

"I'm stronger than that." I angled my face toward the mirror and looked myself in the eye. If it came down to a choice between being scared, being hurt, and being pissed, I knew which one I preferred.

I tried calling Max one more time, then texted her: *Someone tried to kill me, and I made out with Jameson Hawthorne.*

If that didn't garner a response, nothing would.

I made my way back into the bedroom. Even though I'd calmed down a little, I still scanned for threats, and I saw one: Rebecca Laughlin, standing in the doorway. Her face looked even paler than usual, her hair as red as blood. She looked shell-shocked.

Because she overheard Jameson and me? Because her grandparents told her about the shooting? I wasn't sure. She was wearing thick hiking boots and cargo pants, both of them spattered with mud. Staring at her, all I could think was that if Emily had been even half as beautiful as her sister was, it was no wonder Jameson could look at me and think only about his grandfather's game.

Everything is *a game. Even this.* Especially *this.*

"My grandmother sent me to check on you." Rebecca's voice was soft and hesitant.

"I'm okay," I said, and I almost meant it. I *had* to be okay.

"Gran said you were shot." Rebecca stayed in the doorway, like she was afraid to come any closer.

"Shot at," I clarified.

"I'm glad," Rebecca said, and then she looked mortified. "I mean, that you weren't shot. It's good, right, getting shot at instead of shot?" Her gaze darted nervously from me toward the twin beds, the quilts. "Emily would have told you to simplify and say that you were shot." Rebecca sounded more sure of herself telling me what Emily would have said than trying to summon an appropriate response herself. "There was a bullet. You were wounded. Emily would have said you were entitled to a little melodrama."

I was entitled to look at everyone like they were a suspect. I was entitled to an adrenaline-fueled lapse in judgment. And maybe I was entitled, just this once, to push for answers.

"You and Emily shared this room?" I said. That was obvious now, when I looked at the twin beds. *When Rebecca and Emily came to visit their grandparents, they stayed here.* "Was purple your favorite color as a kid or hers?"

"Hers," Rebecca said. She gave me a very small shrug. "She used to tell me that my favorite color was purple, too."

In the picture I'd seen of the two of them, Emily had been looking directly at the camera, dead center; Rebecca had been on the fringes, looking away.

"I feel like I should warn you." Rebecca wasn't even facing me anymore. She walked over to one of the beds.

“Warn me about what?” I asked, and somewhere in the back of my mind, I registered the mud on her boots—and the fact that she’d been on the premises, but not with her grandparents, when I’d been shot at.

Just because she doesn’t feel like a threat doesn’t mean she isn’t one.

But when Rebecca started talking again, it wasn’t about the shooting. “I’m supposed to say that my sister was wonderful.” She acted like that wasn’t a change of subject, like Emily *was* what she was warning me about. “And she was, when she wanted to be. Her smile was contagious. Her laugh was worse, and when she said something was a good idea, people believed her. She was good to me, almost all the time.” Rebecca met my gaze, head-on. “But she wasn’t nearly as good to those boys.”

Boys, plural. “What did she do?” I asked. I should have been more focused on who shot me, but part of me couldn’t shake the way Jameson had invoked Emily, right before walking away from me.

“Em didn’t like to choose.” Rebecca seemed to be picking her words carefully. “She wanted *everything* more than I wanted anything. And the one time I wanted something…” She shook her head and aborted that sentence. “My job was to keep my sister happy. It’s something my parents used to tell me when we were little—that Emily was sick, and I wasn’t, so I should do what I could to make her smile.”

“And the boys?” I asked.

“They made her smile.”

I read into what Rebecca was saying—what she’d been saying. *Em didn’t like to choose.* “She dated both of them?” I tried to get a handle on that. “Did they know?”

“Not at first,” Rebecca whispered, like some part of her thought Emily might hear us talking.

“What happened when Grayson and Jameson found out she was dating both of them?”

"You're only asking that because you didn't know Emily," Rebecca said. "She didn't want to choose, and neither one of them wanted to let her go. She turned it into a competition. A little game."

And then she died.

"How did Emily die?" I asked, because I might never get another opening like this one—not with Rebecca, not with the boys.

Rebecca was looking at me, but I got the general sense that she wasn't seeing me. That she was somewhere else. "Grayson told me that it was her heart," she whispered.

Grayson. I couldn't think beyond that. It wasn't until Rebecca had left that I had realized she'd never gotten around to telling me what, specifically, she *ought* to have been warning me about.

CHAPTER 56

It was another three hours before Oren and his team cleared me to go back to Hawthorne House. I rode back in the ATV with *three* bodyguards.

Oren was the only one who spoke. "Due in part to Hawthorne House's extensive network of security cameras, my team was able to track and verify locations and alibis for all members of the Hawthorne family, as well as Ms. Thea Calligaris."

They have alibis. Grayson has an alibi. I felt a rush of relief, but a moment later, my chest tightened. "What about Constantine?" I asked. Technically, he wasn't a Hawthorne.

"Clear," Oren told me. "He did not personally wield that gun."

Personally. Reading between those lines shook me. "But he might have hired someone?" *Any of them might have,* I realized. I could hear Grayson telling me that there would always be people tripping over themselves to do favors for his family.

"I know a forensic investigator," Oren said evenly. "He works alongside an equally skilled hacker. They'll take a deep dive into everyone's finances and cell phone records. In the meantime, my team is going to focus on the staff."

I swallowed. I hadn't even met most of the staff. I didn't know exactly how many of them there were, or who might have had opportunity—or motive. "The entire staff?" I asked Oren. "Including the Laughlins?" They'd been kind to me after I'd emerged from washing up, but right now I couldn't afford to trust my gut—or Oren's.

"They're clear," Oren told me. "Mr. Laughlin was at the House during the shooting, and security footage confirms Mrs. Laughlin was at the cottage."

"What about Rebecca?" I asked. She'd left the estate right after talking to me.

I could see Oren wanting to say that Rebecca wasn't a threat, but he didn't. "No stone will be left unturned," he promised. "But I do know that the Laughlin girls never learned to shoot. Mr. Laughlin wasn't even allowed to keep a gun at the cottage when they were present."

"Who else was on the premises today?" I asked.

"Pool maintenance, a sound technician working on upgrades in the theater, a massage therapist, and one of the cleaning staff."

I committed that list to memory, then my mouth went dry. "Which cleaning staff?"

"Melissa Vincent."

The name meant nothing to me—until it did. "Mellie?"

Oren's eyes narrowed. "You know her?"

I thought of the moment she'd seen Nash outside Libby's room.

"Something I should know?" Oren asked—and it wasn't really a question. I told him what Alisa had said about Mellie and Nash, what I'd seen in Libby's room, what *Mellie* had seen. And then we pulled up to Hawthorne House, and I saw Alisa.

"She's the only person I've let past the gates," Oren assured me. "Frankly, she's the only one I intend to let past those gates for the foreseeable future."

I probably should have found that more comforting than I did.

"How is she?" Alisa asked Oren as soon as we exited the SUV.

"Pissed," I answered, before Oren could reply on my behalf. "Sore. A little terrified." Seeing her—and seeing Oren standing next to her—broke the dam, and an accusation burst out of me. "You both told me I would be fine! You swore that I was not in danger. You acted like I was being ridiculous when I mentioned murder."

"Technically," my lawyer replied, "you specified *ax*-murder. And technically," she continued through gritted teeth, "it is possible that there was an oversight, legally speaking."

"What kind of oversight? You told me that if I died, the Hawthornes wouldn't get a penny!"

"And I stand by that conclusion," Alisa said emphatically. "However..." She clearly found any admission of fault distasteful. "I also told you that if you died while the will was in probate, your inheritance would pass through to your estate. And typically, it would."

"Typically," I repeated. If there was one thing I'd learned in the past week, it was that there was nothing *typical* about Tobias Hawthorne—or his heirs.

"However," Alisa continued, her voice tight, "in the state of Texas, it is possible for the deceased to add a stipulation to the will that requires heirs to survive him by a certain amount of time in order to inherit."

I'd read the will multiple times. "Pretty sure I'd remember if there was something in there about how long I had to avoid *dying* to inherit. The only stipulation—"

"Was that you must live in Hawthorne House for one year," Alisa finished. "Which, I will admit, would be quite the difficult stipulation to fulfill if you were dead."

That was her oversight? The fact that I couldn't *live* in Hawthorne House if I wasn't alive?

"So if I die..." I swallowed, wetting my tongue. "The money goes to charity?"

"Possibly. But it's also possible that *your* heirs could challenge that interpretation on the basis of Mr. Hawthorne's intent."

"I don't have heirs," I said. "I don't even have a will."

"You don't need a will to have heirs." Alisa glanced at Oren. "Has her sister been cleared?"

"Libby?" I was incredulous. Had they *met* my sister?

"The sister's clear," Oren told Alisa. "She was with Nash during the shooting."

He might as well have detonated a bomb for how well *that* went over.

Eventually, Alisa gathered her composure and turned back to me. "You won't legally be able to sign a will until you turn eighteen. Ditto for the paperwork regarding the foundation conservatorship. And *that* is the other oversight here. Originally, I was focused only on the will, but if you are unable or unwilling to fulfill your role as conservator, the conservatorship passes." She paused heavily. "To the boys."

If I died, the foundation—all the money, all the power, all that potential—went to Tobias Hawthorne's grandsons. A hundred million dollars a year to give away. You could buy a lot of favors for money like that.

"Who knows about the terms of the foundation's conservatorship?" Oren asked, deadly serious.

"Zara and Constantine, certainly," Alisa said immediately.

"Grayson," I added hoarsely, my wounds throbbing. I knew him well enough to know that he would have demanded to see the conservatorship papers himself. *He wouldn't hurt me.* I wanted to believe that. *All he does is warn me away.*

"How soon can you have documents drawn up leaving control of the foundation to Avery's sister in the event of her death?" Oren demanded. If this was about control of the foundation, that would protect me—or else it would put Libby in danger, too.

"Is anyone going to ask me what I want to do?" I asked.

"I can have the documents drawn up tomorrow," Alisa told Oren, ignoring me. "But Avery can't legally sign them until she's eighteen, and even then, it's unclear if she's authorized to make that kind of decision prior to assuming full control of the foundation at the age of twenty-one. Until then..."

I had a target on my forehead.

"What would it take to evoke the protection clause in the will?" Oren changed tactics. "There *are* circumstances under which Avery could remove the Hawthornes as tenants, correct?"

"We'd need evidence," Alisa replied. "Something that ties a specific individual or individuals to acts of harassment, intimidation, or violence, and even then, Avery can only kick out the perpetrator—not the whole family."

"And she can't live somewhere else for the time being?"

"No."

Oren didn't like that, but he didn't waste time on unnecessary commentary. "You'll go nowhere without me," Oren told me, steel in his voice. "Not on the estate, not in the House. Nowhere, you understand? I was always close by. Now I get to play visible deterrent."

Beside me, Alisa narrowed her eyes at Oren. "What do you know that I don't?"

There was a single moment's pause, then my bodyguard

answered the question. "I had my people check the armory. Nothing is missing. In all likelihood, the weapon fired at Avery wasn't a Hawthorne gun, but I had my men pull the security footage from the past few days anyway."

I was too busy trying to wrap my mind around the fact that Hawthorne House had an *armory* to process the rest.

"The armory had a visitor?" Alisa asked, her voice almost too calm.

"Two of them." Oren seemed like he might stop there, for my benefit, but he pressed on. "Jameson and Grayson. Both have alibis—but both were looking at rifles."

"Hawthorne House has an *armory*?" That was all I could manage to say.

"This is Texas," Oren replied. "The whole family grew up shooting, and Mr. Hawthorne was a collector."

"A *gun* collector," I clarified. I hadn't been a fan of firearms *before* I'd almost been shot.

"If you'd read the binder I left you detailing your assets," Alisa interjected, "you'd know that Mr. Hawthorne had the world's largest collection of late nineteenth- and early twentieth-century Winchester rifles, several of which are valued at upward of four hundred thousand dollars."

The idea that anyone would pay that much for a rifle was mind-boggling, but I barely batted an eye at the price tag, because I was too busy thinking that there was a reason Jameson and Grayson had both made visits to the armory to look at rifles—one that had nothing to do with shooting me.

Jameson's middle name was *Winchester.*

CHAPTER 57

Even though it was the dead of night, I made Oren take me to the armory. Following him through twisting hallway after hallway, all I could think was that someone could hide forever in this house.

And that wasn't counting the secret passages.

Eventually, Oren came to a stop in a long corridor. "This is it." He stood in front of an ornate gold mirror. As I watched, he ran his hand along the side of the frame. I heard a *click*, and then the mirror swung out into the hallway, like a door. Behind it, there was steel.

Oren stepped up, and I saw a line of red go down over his face. "Facial recognition," he informed me. "It's really only meant as a backup security measure. The best way to keep intruders from breaking into a safe is to make sure they don't even know it's there."

Hence, the mirror. He pushed the door inward. "The entire armory is lined with reinforced steel." He stepped through, and I followed.

When I'd heard the word *armory*, I'd pictured something out of a movie: copious amounts of black and Rambo-style cartridges on the walls. What I got looked more like a country club. The walls were lined with cabinets of a deep cherry–colored wood. There was an intricately carved table in the center of the room, complete with a marble top.

"*This* is the armory?" I said. There was a rug on the floor. A plush, expensive rug that looked like it belonged in a dining room.

"Not what you were expecting?" Oren closed the door behind us. It clicked into place, and then he flipped three additional dead bolts in quick succession. "There are safe rooms scattered throughout the house. This doubles as one—a tornado shelter, too. I'll show you the locations of the others later, just in case."

In case someone tries to kill me. Rather than dwelling on that, I focused on the reason I'd come here. "Where are the Winchesters?" I asked.

"There are at least thirty Winchester rifles in the collection." Oren nodded toward a wall of display cases. "Any particular reason you wanted to see them?"

A day earlier, I might have kept this secret, but Jameson hadn't told me that he'd looked for—possibly found—the clue corresponding to his own middle name. I didn't owe him any secrecy now.

"I'm looking for something," I told Oren. "A message from Tobias Hawthorne—a clue. A carving, most likely of a number or symbol."

The etching on the tree in the Black Wood had been neither. Mid-kiss, Jameson had seemed convinced that Toby's name was the next clue—but I wasn't so sure. The writing hadn't been a match for the carving at the bridge. It had been uneven, childlike. What if Toby had carved it himself, as a kid? What if the real clue was still out there in the woods?

I can't go back. Not until we know who the shooter is. Oren could clear a room and tell me it was safe. He couldn't clear a whole forest.

Pushing back against the echo of gunshots—and everything that had come after—I opened one of the cabinets. "Any thoughts on where your former employer might have hidden a message?" I asked Oren, my focus intense. "Which gun? Which part of the gun?"

"Mr. Hawthorne rarely took me into his confidence," Oren told me. "I didn't always know how his mind worked, but I respected him, and that respect was mutual." Oren removed a cloth from a drawer and unfolded it, spreading it across the table's marble top. Then he walked over to the cabinet I'd opened and lifted out one of the rifles.

"None of them are loaded," he said intently. "But you treat them like they are. Always."

He laid the gun down on the cloth and then ran his fingers lightly over the barrel. "This was one of his favorites. He was one hell of a shot."

I got the sense that there was a story there—one he'd probably never tell me.

Oren stepped back, and I took that as my cue to approach. Everything in me wanted to shrink back from the rifle. The bullets that had been fired at me were too fresh in my own memory. My wounds still throbbed, but I made myself examine each part of the weapon, looking for something, anything, that might be a clue. Finally, I turned back to Oren. "Where do you load the bullets?"

I found what I was looking for on the fourth gun. To load a bullet into a Winchester rifle, you cocked a lever away from the stock. On the underside of that lever, on the fourth gun I looked at, were three letters: *O. N. E.* The way it had been etched into the metal made the letters look like initials, but I read it as number, to go with the one we'd found on the bridge.

Not infinity, I thought. *Eight. And now: One.*

Eight. One.

CHAPTER 58

Oren escorted me back to my wing. I thought about knocking on Libby's door, but it was late—too late—and it wasn't like I could just pop in and say, *There's murder afoot, sleep tight!*

Oren did a sweep of my quarters and then took up position outside my door, feet spread shoulder-width apart, hands dangling by his side. He had to sleep sometime, but as the door closed between us, I knew it wouldn't be tonight.

I pulled my phone out of my pocket and stared at it. Nothing from Max. She was a night owl and two hours behind me time zone–wise. There was no way she was asleep. I DM-ed the same message I'd texted her earlier to every social media account she had.

Please respond, I thought desperately. *Please, Max.*

"Nothing." I hadn't meant to say that out loud. Trying not to feel utterly alone, I made my way to the bathroom, laid my phone on the counter, and slipped off my clothes. Naked, I looked in the mirror. Except for my face and the bandage over my stitches, my skin looked untouched. I peeled the bandage back. The wound was angry and red, the stitches even and small. I stared at it.

Someone—almost certainly someone in the Hawthorne family—wanted me dead. *I could be dead right now.* I pictured their faces, one by one. Jameson had been there with me when the shots rang out. Nash had claimed from the beginning that he didn't want the money. Xander had been nothing but welcoming. But Grayson…

If you were smart, you'd stay away from Jameson. From the game. From me. He'd warned me. He'd told me that their family destroyed everything they touched. When I'd asked Rebecca how Emily had died, it hadn't been Jameson's name she'd mentioned.

Grayson told me that it was her heart.

I flipped the shower on as hot as it would go and stepped in, turning my chest from the stream and letting the hot water beat against my back. It hurt, but all I wanted was to scrub this entire night off me. What had happened in the Black Wood. What had happened with Jameson. *All of it.*

I broke down. Crying in the shower didn't count.

After a minute or two, I got ahold of myself and turned the water off, just in time to hear my phone ringing. Wet and dripping, I lunged for it.

"Hello?"

"You had better not be lying about the assassination attempt. Or the making out."

My body sagged in relief. "Max."

She must have heard in my tone that I wasn't lying. "What the elf, Avery? What the everlasting mothing-foxing elf is going on there?"

I told her—all of it, every detail, every moment, everything I'd been trying not to feel.

"You have to get out of there." For once, Max was deadly serious.

"What?" I said. I shivered and finally managed to grab a towel.

"Someone tried to kill you," Max said with exaggerated patience, "so you need to get out of Murderland. Like, now."

"I can't leave," I said. "I have to live here for a year, or I lose everything."

"So your life goes back to the way it was a week ago. Is that so bad?"

"Yes," I said incredulously. "I was living in my car, Max, with no guarantee of a future."

"Key word: *living*."

I pulled the towel tighter around me. "Are you saying you would give up billions?"

"Well, my other suggestion involves preemptively whacking the entire Hawthorne family, and I was afraid you'd take that as a euphemism."

"Max!"

"Hey, I'm not the one who made out with Jameson Hawthorne."

I wanted to explain to her exactly how I'd let that happen, but all that came out of my mouth was "Where were you?"

"Excuse me?"

"I called you, right after it happened, before the thing with Jameson. I needed you, Max."

There was a long, pregnant silence on the other end of the phone line. "I'm doing just fine," she said. "Everything here is just peachy. Thanks for asking."

"Asking about what?"

"Exactly." Max lowered her voice. "Did you even notice that I'm not calling from my phone? This is my brother's. I'm on lockdown. Total lockdown—because of you."

I'd known the last time we'd talked that something wasn't right. "What do you mean, because of me?"

"Do you really want to know?"

What kind of question was that? "Of course I do."

"Because you haven't asked about me at all since any of this happened." She blew out a long breath. "Let's be honest, Ave, you barely asked about me before."

My stomach tightened. "That's not true."

"Your mom died, and you needed me. And with everything with Libby and that bob-forsaken shipstain, you really needed me. And then you inherited billions and billions of dollars, so of course, you needed me! And I was happy to be there, Avery, but do you even know my boyfriend's name?"

I racked my mind, trying to remember. "Jared?"

"Wrong," Max said after a moment. "The correct answer is that I don't have a boyfriend anymore, because I caught *Jaxon* on my phone, trying to send himself screenshots of your texts to me. A reporter offered to pay him for them." Her pause was painful this time. "Do you want to know how much?"

My heart sank. "I'm so sorry, Max."

"Me too," Max said bitterly. "But I'm especially sorry that I ever let him take pictures of me. *Personal* pictures. Because when I broke up with him, he sent those pictures to my parents." Max was like me. She only cried in the shower. But her voice was hitching now. "I'm not even allowed to date, Avery. How well do you think that went down?"

I couldn't even imagine. "What do you need?" I asked her.

"I need my life back." She went quiet, just for a minute. "You know what the worst part is? I can't even be mad at you, because *someone tried to shoot you.*" Her voice got very soft. "And you need me."

That hurt, because it was true. I needed her. I'd always needed her more than she had needed me, because she was my friend, singular, and I was one of many for her. "I'm sorry, Max."

She made a dismissive sound. "Yeah, well, the next time someone tries to shoot you, you're going to have buy me something really nice to make it up to me. Like Australia."

"You want me to buy you a trip to Australia?" I asked, thinking that could probably be arranged.

"No." Her reply was pert. "I want you to buy me Australia. You can afford it."

I snorted. "I don't think it's for sale."

"Then I guess that you have no choice but to *avoid getting shot at.*"

"I'll be careful," I promised. "Whoever tried to kill me isn't going to get another chance."

"Good." Max was quiet for a few seconds. "Ave, I have to go. And I don't know when I'm going to be able to borrow another phone. Or get online. Or *anything.*"

My fault. I tried to tell myself this wasn't good-bye—not forever. "Love you, Max."

"Love you, too, beach."

After we hung up, I sat there in my towel, feeling like something inside of me had been carved out. Eventually, I made my way back into my bedroom and threw on some pajamas. I was in bed, thinking about everything Max had said, wondering if I was a fundamentally selfish or needy person, when I heard a sound like scratching in the walls.

I stopped breathing and listened. There it was again. *The passageway.*

"Jameson?" I called. He was the only one who'd used this passage into my room—or at least the only one I knew of. "Jameson, this isn't funny."

There was no response, but when I got up and walked toward the passageway, then stood very still, I could have sworn I heard someone breathing, right on the other side of the wall. I gripped the candlestick, prepared to pull it and face down whoever or whatever stood beyond, but then my common sense—and my promise to Max—caught up to me, and I opened the door to the hallway instead.

"Oren?" I said. "There's something you should know."

* * *

Oren searched the passageway, then disabled its entrance into my room. He also "suggested" I spend the night in Libby's room, which didn't have passageway access.

It wasn't really a suggestion.

My sister was asleep when I knocked. She roused, but barely. I crawled into bed with her, and she didn't ask why. After my conversation with Max, I was fairly certain I didn't want to tell her. Libby's entire life had already been turned upside down because of me. Twice. First when my mom had died, then all of this. She'd already given me everything. She had her own issues to deal with. She didn't need mine.

Under the covers, I hugged a pillow tight to my body and rolled toward Libby. I needed to be close to her, even if I couldn't tell her why. Libby's eyes fluttered, and she snuggled up next to me. I willed myself not to think about anything else—not the Black Wood, not the Hawthornes, nothing. I let darkness overcome me, and I slept.

I dreamed that I was back at the diner. I was young—five or six—and happy.

I place two sugar packets vertically on the table and bring their ends together, forming a triangle capable of standing on its own. "There," I say. I do the same with the next pair of packets, then set a fifth across them horizontal, connecting the two triangles I built.

"Avery Kylie Grambs!" My mom appears at the end of the table, smiling. "What have I told you about building castles out of sugar?"

I beam back at her. "It's only worth it if you can go five stories tall!"

I woke with a start. I turned over, expecting to see Libby, but her side of the bed was empty. Morning light was streaming in through the windows. I made my way to Libby's bathroom, but she wasn't there, either. I was getting ready to go back to my room—and my bathroom—when I saw something on the counter: Libby's phone. She'd missed texts, dozens of them, all from Drake. There were only three—the most recent—that I could read without a password.

I love you.

You know I love you, Libby-mine.

I know that you love me.

CHAPTER 59

Oren met me in the hall the second I left Libby's suite. If he'd been up all night, he didn't look it.

"A police report has been filed," he reported. "Discreetly. The detectives assigned to the case are coordinating with my team. We're all in agreement that it would be to our advantage, at least for the moment, if the Hawthorne family does not realize there *is* an investigation. Jameson and Rebecca have been made to understand the importance of discretion. As much as you can, I'd like you to proceed as though nothing has happened."

Pretend I hadn't had a brush with death the night before. Pretend everything was fine. "Have you seen Libby?" I asked. *Libby isn't fine.*

"She went down for breakfast about half an hour ago." Oren's tone gave away nothing.

I thought back to those texts, and my stomach tightened. "Did she seem okay?"

"No injuries. All limbs and appendages fully intact."

That wasn't what I'd been asking, but given the circumstances, maybe it should have been. "If she's downstairs in full view of Hawthornes, is she safe?"

"Her security detail is aware of the situation. They do not currently believe she is at risk."

Libby wasn't the heiress. She wasn't the target. I was.

I got dressed and went downstairs. I'd gone with a high-necked top to hide my stitches, and I'd covered the scratch on my cheek with makeup, as much as I could.

In the dining room, a selection of pastries had been set out on the sideboard. Libby was curled up in a large accent chair in the corner of the room. Nash was sitting in the chair beside her, his legs sticking straight out, his cowboy boots crossed at the ankles. Keeping watch.

Between them and me were four members of the Hawthorne family. *All with reason to want me dead*, I thought as I walked past them. Zara and Constantine sat at one end of the dining room table. She was reading a newspaper. He was reading a tablet. Neither paid the least bit of attention to me. Nan and Xander were at the far end of the table.

I felt movement behind me and whirled.

"Somebody's jumpy this morning," Thea declared, hooking an arm through mine and leading me toward the sideboard. Oren followed, like a shadow. "You've been a busy girl," Thea murmured, directly into my ear.

I knew that she had been watching me, that she'd probably been ordered to stick close and report back. *How close was she last night? What does she know?* Based on what Oren had said, Thea hadn't shot me herself, but the timing of her move into Hawthorne House didn't seem like a coincidence.

Zara had brought her niece here for a reason.

"Don't play the innocent," Thea advised, picking up a croissant and bringing it to her lips. "Rebecca called me."

I fought the urge to glance back at Oren. He'd indicated that Rebecca would keep her mouth shut about the shooting. What else was he wrong about?

"You and Jameson," Thea continued, like she was chiding a child. "In Emily's old room, no less. A bit uncouth, don't you think?"

She doesn't know about the attack. The realization shot through me. *Rebecca must have seen Jameson come out of the bathroom. She must have heard us. Must have realized that we...*

"Are people being uncouth without me again?" Xander asked, popping up between Thea and me and breaking Thea's hold. "How rude."

I didn't want to suspect him of anything, but at this rate, the stress of suspecting and not-suspecting was going to kill me before anyone else could do me in.

"Rebecca stayed the night in the cottage," Thea told Xander, relishing the words. "She finally broke her yearlong silence and texted me *all* about it." Thea acted like a person playing a trump card—but I wasn't sure what, exactly, that card was.

Rebecca?

"Bex texted me, too," Xander told Thea. Then he glanced apologetically at me. "Word of Hawthorne hookups travels fast."

Rebecca might have kept her mouth shut about the shooting, but she might as well have taken out a billboard about that kiss.

The kiss meant nothing. The kiss isn't the problem here.

"You, there. Girl!" Nan jabbed her cane imperiously at me and then at the tray of pastries. "Don't make an old woman get up."

If anyone else had spoken to me like that, I would have ignored them, but Nan was both ancient and terrifying, so I went to pick up the tray. I remembered too late that I was injured. Pain flashed like a lightning bolt through my flesh, and I sucked a breath in through my teeth.

Nan stared, just for a moment, then prodded Xander with her cane. "Help her, you lout."

Xander took the tray. I let my arm drop back to my side. *Who saw me flinch?* I tried not to stare at any of them. *Who already knew I was injured?*

"You're hurt." Xander angled his body between mine and Thea's.

"I'm fine," I said.

"You most decidedly are not."

I hadn't realized Grayson had slipped into the banquet hall, but now he was standing directly beside me.

"A moment, Ms. Grambs?" His stare was intense. "In the hall."

CHAPTER 60

I probably shouldn't have gone anywhere with Grayson Hawthorne, but I knew that Oren would follow, and I wanted something from Grayson. I wanted to look him in the eye. I wanted to know if he'd done this to me—or had any idea who had.

"You're injured." Grayson didn't phrase that as a question. "You will tell me what happened."

"Oh, I will, will I?" I gave him a look.

"Please." Grayson seemed to find the word painful or distasteful—or both.

I owed him nothing. Oren had asked me not to mention the shooting. The last time I'd talked to Grayson, he'd issued a terse warning. He stood to gain the foundation if I died.

"I was shot." I let the truth out because for reasons I couldn't even explain, I needed to see how he would react. "Shot at," I clarified after a beat.

Every muscle in Grayson's jawline went taut. *He didn't know.* Before I could summon up even an ounce of relief, Grayson turned from me to my guard. "When?" he spat out.

"Last night," Oren replied curtly.

"And where," Grayson demanded of my bodyguard, "were you?"

"Not nearly as close as I'll be from now on," Oren promised, staring him down.

"Remember me?" I raised a hand, then paid for it. "Subject of your conversation and capable individual in her own right?"

Grayson must have seen the pain the movement caused me, because he turned and used his hands to gently lower mine. "You'll let Oren do his job," he ordered softly.

I didn't dwell on his tone—or his touch. "And who do you think he's protecting me from?" I glanced pointedly toward the banquet hall. I waited for Grayson to snap at me for daring to suspect anyone he loved, to reiterate again that he would choose each and every one of them over me.

Instead, Grayson turned back to Oren. "If anything happens to her, I will hold you personally responsible."

"Mr. Personal Responsibility." Jameson announced his presence and ambled toward his brother. "Charming."

Grayson gritted his teeth, then realized something. "You were both in the Black Wood last night." He stared at his brother. "Whoever shot at her could have hit you."

"And what a travesty it would be," Jameson replied, circling his brother, "if anything happened to me."

The tension between them was palpable. Explosive. I could see how this would play out—Grayson calling Jameson reckless, Jameson risking himself further to prove the point. How long would it be before Jameson mentioned me? *The kiss.*

"Hope I'm not interrupting." Nash joined the party. He flashed a lazy, dangerous smile at his brothers. "Jamie, you're not skipping school today. You have five minutes to put on your uniform and get in my truck, or there will be a hog-tying in your future." He waited for Jameson to get a move on, then turned. "Gray, our mother has requested an audience."

Having dealt with his siblings, the oldest Hawthorne brother shifted his attention to me. "I don't suppose you need a ride to Country Day?"

"She does not," Oren replied, arms crossed over his chest. Nash noted both his posture and his tone, but before he could reply, I interjected.

"I'm not going to school." That was news to Oren, but he didn't object.

Nash, on the other hand, shot me the exact same look he'd given Jameson when he'd made the threat about hog-tying. "Your sister know you're playing hooky on this fine Friday afternoon?"

"My sister is none of your concern," I told him, but thinking about Libby brought my mind back to Drake's texts. There were worse things than the idea that Libby might get involved with a Hawthorne. *Assuming Nash doesn't want me dead.*

"Everyone who lives or works in this house is my concern," Nash told me. "No matter how many times I leave or how long I'm gone for—people still need looking after. So..." He gave me that same lazy grin. "Your sister know you're playing hooky?"

"I'll talk to her," I said, trying to see past the cowboy in him to what lay underneath.

Nash returned my assessing look. "You do that, sweetheart."

CHAPTER 61

I told Libby I was staying home. I tried to form the words to ask her about Drake's texts and came up dry. *What if Drake's not just texting?* That thought snaked its way through my consciousness. *What if she's seen him? What if he talked her into sneaking him onto the estate?*

I shut down that line of thinking. There was no "sneaking" onto the estate. Security was airtight, and Oren would have told me if Drake had been on the premises during the shooting. He would have been the top suspect—or close to it.

If I die, there's at least a chance that everything passes to my closest blood relatives. That's Libby—and our father.

"Are you sick?" Libby asked, placing the back of her hand on my forehead. She was wearing her new purple boots and a black dress with long, lacy sleeves. She looked like she was going somewhere.

To see Drake? Dread settled in the pit of my stomach. *Or with Nash?*

"Mental health day," I managed. Libby accepted that and declared it Sister Time. If she'd had plans, she didn't think twice before ditching them for me.

"Want to hit the spa?" Libby asked earnestly. "I got a massage yesterday, and it was to die for."

I almost died yesterday. I didn't say that, and I didn't tell her that the massage therapist wouldn't be coming back today—or anytime soon. Instead, I offered up the only distraction I could think of that might also distract me from all of the secrets I was keeping from her.

"How would you like to help me find a Davenport?"

According to the internet search results Libby and I pulled up, the term *Davenport* was used separately to refer to two kinds of furniture: a sofa and a desk. The sofa usage was a generic term, like Kleenex for a tissue or dumpster for a garbage bin, but a Davenport desk referred to a specific kind of desk, one that was notable for compartments and hidey-holes, with a slanted desktop that could be lifted to reveal a storage compartment underneath.

Everything I knew about Tobias Hawthorne told me that we probably weren't looking for a sofa.

"This could take a while," Libby told me. "Do you have any idea how big this place is?"

I'd seen the music rooms, the gymnasium, the bowling alley, the showroom for Tobias Hawthorne's cars, the *solarium*... and that wasn't even a quarter of what there was to see. "Enormous."

"Palatial," Libby chirped. "And since I'm such bad publicity, I haven't had anything to do for the past week *except* explore." That publicity comment had to have come from Alisa, and I wondered how many chats she'd had with Libby without me there. "There's a literal ballroom," Libby continued. "Two theaters—one for movies and one with box seats and a stage."

"I've seen that one," I offered. "And the bowling alley."

Libby's kohl-rimmed eyes grew round. "Did you bowl?"

Her awe was contagious. "I bowled."

Libby shook her head. "It is never going to stop being bizarre that this house has a *bowling alley*."

"There's also a driving range," Oren added behind me. "And racquetball."

If Libby noticed how close he was sticking to us, she gave no indication of it. "How in the world are we supposed to find one little desk?" she asked.

I turned back to Oren. If he was here, he might as well be useful. "I've seen the office in our wing. Did Tobias Hawthorne have any others?"

The desk in Tobias Hawthorne's other office wasn't a Davenport, either. There were three rooms off the office. *The Cigar Room. The Billiards Room.* Oren provided explanations as needed. The third room was small, with no windows. In the middle of it, there was what appeared to be a giant white pod.

"Sensory deprivation chamber," Oren told me. "Every once in a while, Mr. Hawthorne liked to cut off the world."

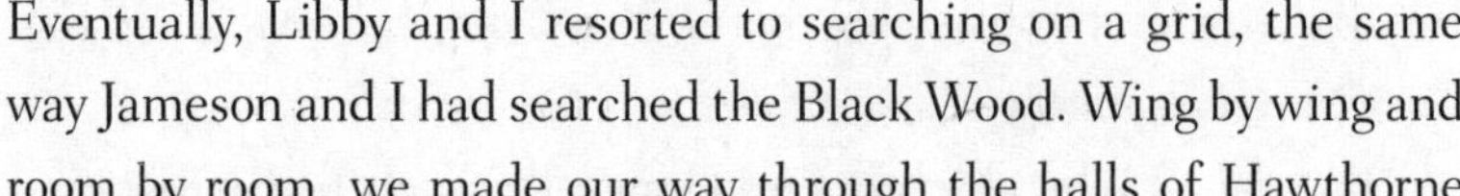

Eventually, Libby and I resorted to searching on a grid, the same way Jameson and I had searched the Black Wood. Wing by wing and room by room, we made our way through the halls of Hawthorne House. Oren was never more than a few feet behind.

"And now . . . *the spa*." Libby flung the door open. She seemed upbeat. Either that, or she was covering for something.

Pushing that thought down, I looked around the spa. We clearly weren't going to find the desk here, but that didn't stop me from taking it all in. The room was L-shaped. In the long part of the L, the floor was wooden; in the short part, it was made of stone. In the middle of the stone section, there was a small square pool built into the ground. Steam rose from its surface. Behind it, there was a glass shower as big as a small bedroom, with faucets attached to the ceiling instead of the wall.

"Hot tub. Steam room." Someone spoke up behind us. I turned to see Skye Hawthorne. She was wearing a floor-length robe, a black one this time. She strode to the larger section of the room, dropped the robe, and lay down on a gray velvet cot. "Massage table," she said, yawning, barely covering herself with a sheet. "I ordered a masseuse."

"Hawthorne House is closed to visitors for the moment," Oren said flatly, completely unimpressed with her display.

"Well, then." Skye closed her eyes. "You'll need to buzz Magnus past the gates."

Magnus. I wondered if he was the one who'd been here yesterday. If he was the one who'd shot at me—at her request.

"Hawthorne House is closed to visitors," Oren repeated. "It's a matter of security. Until further notice, my men have instructions to allow only essential personnel past the gates."

Skye yawned like a cat. "I assure you, John Oren, this massage is *essential.*"

On a nearby shelf, a row of candles was burning. Light shone through sheer curtains, and low and pleasant music played.

"What matter of security?" Libby asked suddenly. "Did something happen?"

I gave Oren a look that I hoped would keep him from answering that question, but it turned out that I was aiming that request in the wrong direction.

"According to my Grayson," Skye told Libby, "there was some nasty business in the Black Wood."

CHAPTER 62

Libby waited until we were back in the hallway to ask, "What happened in the woods?"

I cursed Grayson for telling his mother—and myself for telling Grayson.

"Why do you need extra security?" Libby demanded. After a second and a half, she turned to Oren. "Why does she need extra security?"

"There was an incident yesterday," Oren said, "with a bullet and a tree."

"A bullet?" Libby repeated. "Like, from a gun?"

"I'm fine," I told her.

Libby ignored me. "What kind of incident with a bullet and a tree?" she asked Oren, her blue ponytail bouncing with righteous indignation.

My head of security couldn't—or wouldn't—obfuscate more than he already had. "It's unclear if the shots were meant to scare Avery, or if she was a genuine target. The shooter missed, but she was injured by debris."

"Libby," I said emphatically, "*I'm fine.*"

"Shots, plural?" Libby didn't even seem like she'd heard me.

Oren cleared his throat. "I'll give you two a moment." He retreated down the hall—still in sight, still close enough to hear but far enough away to pretend he couldn't.

Coward.

"Someone shot at you, and you didn't tell me?" Libby didn't get mad often, but when she did, it was epic. "Maybe Nash is right. Damn him! I said you pretty much took care of yourself. He said he'd never met a billionaire teenager who didn't need the occasional kick in the pants."

"Oren and Alisa are taking care of the situation," I told Libby. "I didn't want you to worry."

Libby lifted her hand to my cheek, her eyes falling on the scratch I'd covered up. "And who's taking care of you?"

I couldn't help thinking about Max saying *and you needed me* again and again. I looked down. "You have enough on your plate right now."

"What are you talking about?" Libby asked. I heard her suck in a quick breath, then exhale. "Is this about Drake?"

She'd said his name. The floodgates were officially open, and there was no holding it back now. "He's been texting you."

"I don't text him back," Libby said defensively.

"You also haven't blocked him."

She didn't have a reply for that.

"You could have blocked him," I said hoarsely. "Or asked Alisa for a new phone. You could report him for violating the restraining order."

"I didn't ask for a restraining order!" Libby seemed to regret those words the second she'd said them. She swallowed. "And I don't want a new phone. All my friends have the number for this one. *Dad* has the number for this one."

I stared at her. "Dad?" I hadn't seen Ricky Grambs in two years.

My caseworker had been in touch with him, but he hadn't so much as placed a phone call to me. He hadn't even come to my mother's funeral. "Did Dad call you?" I asked Libby.

"He just... wanted to check on us, you know?"

I knew that he'd probably seen the news. I knew that he didn't have *my* new number. I knew that he had billions of reasons to want me now, when he'd never cared enough to stick around for either of us before.

"He wants money," I told Libby, my voice flat. "Just like Drake. Just like your mom."

Mentioning her mother was a low blow.

"Who does Oren think shot you?" Libby was grappling for calm.

I made an attempt at the same. "The shots were fired from inside the walls of the estate," I said, repeating what I'd been told. "Whoever shot me had access."

"That's why Oren is tightening security," Libby said, the gears in her head turning behind her kohl-lined eyes. "Essential personnel only." Her dark lips fixed themselves into a thin line. "You should have told me."

I thought about the things she hadn't told me. "Tell me that you haven't seen Drake. That he hasn't come here. That you wouldn't let him onto the estate."

"Of course I didn't." Libby went silent. I wasn't sure if she was trying not to yell at me—or not to cry. "I'm going to go." Her voice was steady—and fierce. "But for the record, *little sis*, you're a minor, and I'm still your legal guardian. The next time someone tries to shoot you, I damn well want to know."

CHAPTER 63

I knew Oren had to have heard every word of my fight with Libby, but I was also fairly certain he wouldn't comment on it.

"I'm still looking for the Davenport," I said tersely. If I'd needed the distraction before, it was downright mandatory now. Without Libby to explore with me, I couldn't bring myself to just keep wandering from room to room. *We already checked the old man's office. Where else would someone keep a Davenport desk?*

I concentrated on that question, not my fight with Libby. Not what I'd said—and what she hadn't.

"I have it on good authority," I told Oren after a moment, "that Hawthorne House has multiple libraries." I let out a long, slow breath. "Got any idea where they are?"

Two hours and four libraries later, I was standing in the middle of number five. It was on the second floor. The ceiling was slanted. The walls were lined with built-in shelves, each shelf exactly tall enough for a row of paperback books. The books on the shelves were well-worn, and they covered every inch of the walls, except for a large stained-glass window on the east side. Light shone through, painting colors on the wood floor.

No Davenport. This was starting to feel useless. This trail hadn't been laid for me. Tobias Hawthorne's puzzle hadn't been designed with me in mind.

I need Jameson.

I cut that thought off at the knees, exited the library, and retreated downstairs. I'd counted at least five different staircases in this house. This one spiraled, and as I walked down it, the sound of piano music beckoned from a distance. I followed it, and Oren followed me. I came to the entryway of a large, open room. The far wall was filled with arches. Beneath each arch was a massive window.

Every window was open.

There were paintings on the walls, and positioned between them was the biggest grand piano I'd ever seen. Nan sat on the piano's bench, her eyes closed. I thought the old woman was playing, until I walked closer and realized that the piano was playing itself.

My shoes made a sound against the floor, and her eyes flew open.

"I'm sorry," I said. "I—"

"Hush," Nan commanded. Her eyes closed again. The playing continued, building to a crashing crescendo, and then—silence. "Did you know that you can listen to concerts on this thing?" Nan opened her eyes and reached for her cane. With no small amount of effort, she stood. "Somewhere in the world, a master plays, and with the push of a button, the keys move here."

Her eyes lingered on the piano, an almost wistful expression on her face.

"Do you play?" I asked.

Nan harrumphed. "I did when I was young. Got a bit too much attention for it, and my husband broke my fingers, put an end to that."

The way she said it—no muss, no fuss—was almost as jarring as the words. "That's horrible," I said fiercely.

Nan looked at the piano, then at her gnarled, bird-boned hand. She lifted her chin and stared out the massive windows. "He met with a tragic accident not long after that."

It sounded an awful lot like Nan had arranged for that "accident." *She killed her husband?*

"Nan," a voice scolded from the doorway. "You're scaring the kid."

Nan sniffed. "She scares that easy, she won't last here." With that, Nan made her way from the room.

The oldest Hawthorne brother turned his attention to me. "You tell your sister you're playing delinquent today?"

The mention of Libby had me flashing back to our argument. *She's talking to Dad. She didn't want a restraining order against Drake. She won't block him.* I wondered how much of that Nash already knew.

"Libby knows where I am," I told him stiffly.

He gave me a look. "This ain't easy for her, kid. You're at the eye of the storm, where things are calm. She's taking the brunt of it, from all sides."

I wouldn't call getting shot at "calm."

"What are your intentions toward my sister?" I asked Nash.

He clearly found my line of questioning amusing. "What are your intentions toward Jameson?"

Was there *no one* in this house who didn't know about that kiss?

"You were right about your grandfather's game," I told Nash. He'd tried to warn me. He'd told me exactly why Jameson had been keeping me close.

"Usually am." Nash hooked his thumbs through his belt loops. "The closer to the end you come, the worse it'll get."

The logical thing to do was stop playing. Step back. But I wanted answers, and some part of me—the part that had grown up with a mom who'd turned everything into a challenge, the part who'd played my first game of chess when I was six years old—wanted to *win*.

"Any chance you know where your grandfather might have stashed a Davenport desk?" I asked Nash.

He snorted. "You don't learn easy, do you, kid?"

I shrugged.

Nash considered my question, then cocked his head to the side. "You check the libraries?"

"The circular library, the onyx one, the one with the stained-glass window, the one with the globes, the maze..." I glanced over at my bodyguard. "That's it?"

Oren nodded.

Nash cocked his head to the side. "Not quite."

CHAPTER 64

Nash led me up two sets of stairs, down three hallways, and past a doorway that had been bricked shut.

"What's that?" I asked.

He slowed momentarily. "That was my uncle's wing. The old man had it walled off when Toby died."

Because that's normal, I thought. *About as normal as disinheriting your whole family for twenty years and never saying a word.*

Nash picked up the pace again, and finally, we came to a steel door that looked like it belonged on a safe. There was a combination dial, and below it, a five-pronged lever. Nash casually twirled the dial—left, right, left—too quick for me to catch the numbers. There was a loud clicking sound, and then he turned the lever. The steel door opened out into the hall.

What kind of library needs that kind of securit—

My brain was in the process of finishing that thought when Nash stepped through the doorway, and I realized that what lay beyond wasn't a single room. It was a whole other wing.

"The old man started construction on this part of the house when I was born," Nash informed me. The hallway around us was papered with dials, keypads, locks, and keys, all affixed to the walls like art. "Hawthornes learn how to wield a lockpick young," Nash told me as we walked down the hall. I looked in a room to my left, and there was a small airplane—not a toy. An *actual* single-person airplane.

"*This* was your playroom?" I asked, eyeing the doors lining the rest of the hall and wondering what surprises those rooms held.

"Skye was seventeen when I was born." Nash shrugged. "She made an attempt at playing parent. Didn't stick. The old man tried to compensate."

By building you . . . this.

"C'mon." Nash led me toward the end of the hall and opened another door. "Arcade," he told me, the explanation completely unnecessary. There was a foosball table, a bar, three pinball machines, and an entire wall of arcade-style consoles.

I walked over to one of the pinball machines, pressed a button, and it surged to life.

I glanced back at Nash. "I can wait," he said.

I should have stayed focused. He was leading me to the final library—and possibly the location of the Davenport and the next clue. But one game wouldn't kill me. I gave a preliminary flip of the flipper, then launched the ball.

I didn't come anywhere near the top score, but when the game was over, it prompted me for my initials anyway, and when I entered them, a familiar message flashed across the screen.

WELCOME TO HAWTHORNE HOUSE, AVERY KYLIE GRAMBS!

It was the same message I'd gotten at the bowling alley, and just as I had then, I felt the ghost of Tobias Hawthorne all around me. *Even if you* thought *that you'd manipulated our grandfather into this, I guarantee that he'd be the one manipulating you.*

Nash walked behind the bar. "Refrigerator is full of sugary drinks. What's your poison?"

I came closer and saw that he wasn't kidding when he said *full*. Glass bottles lined every shelf of the fridge, with soda in every imaginable flavor. "Cotton candy?" I wrinkled my nose. "Prickly pear? *Bacon and jalepeno?*"

"I was six when Gray was born," Nash said, like that was an explanation. "The old man unveiled this room the day my new little brother came home." He twisted the top off a suspiciously green soda and took a swig. "I was seven for Jamie, eight and a half for Xander." He paused, as if weighing my worth as his audience. "Aunt Zara and her first husband were having trouble conceiving. Skye would leave for a few months, come back pregnant. Wash, rinse, and repeat."

That might have been the most messed up thing I'd ever heard.

"You want one?" Nash asked, nodding toward the fridge.

I wanted to take about ten of them but settled for Cookies and Cream. I glanced back at Oren, who'd been playing my silent shadow this whole time. He gave no indication that I should avoid drinking, so I twisted off the cap and took a swig.

"The library?" I reminded Nash.

"Almost there." Nash pushed through to the next room. "Game room," he said.

At the center of the room, there were four tables. One table was rectangular, one square, one oval, one circular. The tables were black. The rest of the room—walls, floor, and shelves—was white. The shelves were built into three of the room's four walls.

Not bookshelves, I realized. They held games. Hundreds, maybe thousands, of board games. Unable to resist, I went up to the closest shelf and ran my fingers along the boxes. I'd never even heard of most of these games.

"The old man," Nash said softly, "was a bit of a collector."

I was in awe. How many afternoons had my mom and I spent playing garage-sale board games? Our rainy-day tradition had involved setting up three or four and turning them all into one massive game. But *this*? There were games from all over the world. Half of them didn't have English writing on the boxes. I suddenly pictured all four Hawthorne brothers sitting around one of those tables. Grinning. Trash-talking. Outmaneuvering each other. Wrestling for control—possibly literally.

I pushed that thought back. I'd come here looking for the Davenport—the next clue. *That* was the current game—not anything held in these boxes. "The library?" I asked Nash, tearing my eyes away from the games.

He nodded toward the end of the room—the one wall that wasn't covered in board games. There was no door. Instead, there was a fire pole and what appeared to be the bottom of some kind of chute. A slide?

"Where's the library?" I asked.

Nash came to stand beside the fire pole and tilted his head toward the ceiling. "Up there."

CHAPTER 65

Oren went up first, then returned—via pole, not slide. "Room's clear," he told me. "But if you try to climb up, you might pull a stitch."

The fact that he'd mentioned my injury in front of Nash told me something. Either Oren wanted to see how he would respond, or he trusted Nash Hawthorne.

"What injury?" Nash asked, taking the bait.

"Someone shot at Avery," Oren said carefully. "You wouldn't happen to know anything about that, would you, Nash?"

"If I did," Nash replied, his voice low and deadly, "it would already be handled."

"Nash." Oren gave him a look that probably meant *stay out of it*. But from what I'd been able to tell, "staying out of it" wasn't really a Hawthorne trait.

"I'll be going now," Nash said casually. "I have some questions to ask my people."

His people—including Mellie. I watched Nash saunter off, then turned back to Oren. "You knew he would go talk to the staff."

"I know they'll talk to him," Oren corrected. "And besides, you blew the element of surprise this morning."

I'd told Grayson. He'd told his mother. Libby knew. "Sorry about that," I said, then I turned to the room overhead. "I'm going up."

"I didn't see a desk up there," Oren told me.

I walked over to the pole and grabbed hold. "I'm going up anyway." I started to pull myself up, but the pain stopped me. Oren was right. I couldn't climb. I stepped back from the pole, then glanced to my left.

If I couldn't make it up the pole, it would have to be the slide.

The last library in Hawthorne House was small. The ceiling sloped to form a pyramid overhead. The shelves were plain and only came up to my waist. They were full of children's books. Well-worn, well-loved, some of them familiar in a way that made me ache to sit and read.

But I didn't, because as I stood there, I felt a breeze. It wasn't coming from the window, which was closed. It came from the shelves on the back wall—*no.* As I walked closer, I discovered that it was coming from a crack between the two shelves.

There's something back there. My heart caught like a breath stuck in my throat. Starting with the shelf on the right, I latched my fingers around the top of the shelf and pulled. I didn't have to pull hard. The shelf was on a hinge. As I pulled, it rotated outward, revealing a small opening.

This was the first secret passage I'd discovered on my own. It was strangely exhilarating, like standing on the edge of the Grand Canyon or holding a priceless work of art in your hands. Heart pounding, I ducked through the opening and found a staircase.

Traps upon traps, I thought, *and riddles upon riddles.*

Gingerly, I walked down the steps. As I got farther from the light above, I had to pull out my phone and turn on the flashlight so I could see where I was going. *I should go back for Oren.* I knew that, but I was going faster now—down the steps, twisting, turning, until I reached the bottom.

There, holding a flashlight of his own, was Grayson Hawthorne.

He turned toward me. My heart beat viciously, but I didn't step back. I looked past Grayson and saw the only piece of furniture on the landing of the hidden stairs.

A Davenport.

"Ms. Grambs." Grayson greeted me, then turned back to the desk.

"Have you found it yet?" I asked him. "The Davenport clue?"

"I was waiting."

I couldn't quite read his tone. "For what?"

Grayson looked up from the desk, silver eyes catching mine in the dark. "Jameson, I suppose."

It had been hours since Jameson had left for school, hours since I'd seen Grayson last. How long had he been here, waiting?

"It's not like Jamie to miss the obvious. Whatever this game is, it's about us. The four of us. Our names were the clues. Of course we would find something here."

"At the bottom of this staircase?" I asked.

"In our wing," Grayson replied. "We grew up here—Jameson, Xander, and me. Nash, too, I suppose, but he was older."

I remembered Xander telling me that Jameson and Grayson used to team up to beat Nash to the finish line, then double-cross each other at the end of the game.

"Nash knows about the shooting," I told Grayson. "I told him." Grayson gave me a look I couldn't quite discern. "What?" I said.

Grayson shook his head. "He'll want to save you now."

"Is that such a bad thing?" I asked.

Another look—and more emotion, heavily masked. "Will you

show me where you were hurt?" Grayson asked, his voice not quite strained—but *something.*

He probably just wanted to see how bad it is, I told myself, but still, the request hit me like an electric shock. My limbs felt inexplicably heavy. I was keenly aware of every breath I took. This was a small space. We stood close to each other, close to the desk.

I'd learned my lesson with Jameson, but this felt different. Like Grayson wanted to be the one to save me. Like he *needed* to be the one.

I lifted my hand to the collar of my shirt. I pulled it downward—below my collarbone, exposing my wound.

Grayson lifted his hand toward my shoulder. "I am sorry that this happened to you."

"Do you know who shot at me?" I had to ask, because he'd apologized—and Grayson Hawthorne was not the type to apologize. *If he knew*...

"No," Grayson swore.

I believed him—or at least I wanted to. "If I leave Hawthorne House before the year is up, the money goes to charity. If I die, it goes to charity or my heirs." I paused. "If I die, the foundation goes to the four of you."

He had to know how that looked.

"My grandfather should have left it to us all along." Grayson turned his head, forcefully pulling his gaze from my skin. "Or to Zara. We were raised to make a difference, and you..."

"I'm nobody," I finished, the words hurting me to say.

Grayson shook his head. "I don't know what you are." Even in the minimal light of our flashlights, I could see his chest rising and falling with every breath.

"Do you think Jameson's right?" I asked him. "Does this puzzle of your grandfather's end with answers?"

"It ends with *something*. The old man's games always do." Grayson paused. "How many of the numbers do you have?"

"Two," I replied.

"Same," he told me. "I'm missing this one and Xander's."

I frowned. "Xander's?"

"Blackwood. It's Xander's middle name. The West Brook was Nash's clue. The Winchester was Jameson's."

I looked back toward the desk. "And the Davenport is yours."

He closed his eyes. "After you, Heiress."

His use of Jameson's nickname for me felt like it meant something, but I wasn't sure what. I turned my attention to the task at hand. The desk was made of a bronze-colored wood. Four drawers ran perpendicular to the desktop. I tested them one at a time. Empty. I ran my right hand along the inside of the drawers, looking for anything out of the ordinary. Nothing.

Feeling Grayson's presence beside me, knowing that I was being watched and judged, I moved on to the top of the desk, raising it up to reveal the compartment underneath. Empty again. As I had with drawers, I ran my fingers along the bottom and sides of the compartment. I felt a slight ridge along the right side. Eyeballing the desk, I estimated the width of the border to be an inch and a half, maybe two inches.

Just wide enough for a hidden compartment.

Unsure how to trigger its release, I ran my hand back over the place where I'd felt the ridge. Maybe it was just a seam, where two pieces of wood met. *Or maybe*... I pressed the wood in, hard, and it popped outward. I closed my fingers around the block that had just released and pulled it away from the desk, revealing a small opening. Inside was a keychain, with no key.

The keychain was plastic, in the shape of the number one.

CHAPTER 66

Eight. One. One.

I slept in Libby's room again that night. She didn't. I asked Oren to confirm with her security team that she was okay and on the premises.

She was—but he didn't tell me where.

No Libby. No Max. I was alone—more alone than I'd been since I got here. *No Jameson.* I hadn't seen him since he'd left that morning. *No Grayson.* He hadn't lingered with me for long after we'd discovered the clue.

One. One. Eight. That was all I had to concentrate on. Three numbers, which confirmed for me that Toby's tree in the Black Wood had just been a tree. If there was a fourth number, it was still out there. Based on the keychain, the clue in the Black Wood could appear in any format, not just a carving.

Late into the night and nearly asleep, I heard something like footsteps. *Behind me? Below?* The wind whistled outside my window. Gunshots lurked in my memory. I had no idea what was lurking in the walls.

I didn't fall asleep until dawn. When I did, I dreamed about sleeping.

"I have a secret," my mom says, cheerfully bouncing onto my bed, jarring me awake. "Care to make a guess, my newly fifteen-year-old daughter?"

"I'm not playing," I grumble, pulling the covers back over my head. "I never guess right."

"I'll give you a hint," my mom wheedles. "For your birthday." She pulls the covers back and flops down beside me on my pillow. Her smile is contagious.

I finally break and smile back. "Fine. Give me a hint."

"I have a secret... about the day you were born."

I woke with a headache to my lawyer throwing open the plantation shutters. "Rise and shine," Alisa said, with the force and surety of a person making an argument in court.

"Go away." Channeling my younger self, I pulled the covers over my head.

"My apologies," Alisa said, not sounding apologetic in the least. "But you really do have to get up now."

"I don't have to do anything," I muttered. "I'm a billionaire."

That worked about as well as I expected it to. "If you'll recall," Alisa replied pleasantly, "in an attempt to do damage control after your impromptu press conference earlier this week, I arranged for your debut in Texas society to take place this weekend. There is a charity benefit that you will be attending this evening."

"I barely slept last night." I tried for pity. "Someone tried to shoot me!"

"We'll get you some vitamin C and a pain pill." Alisa was without mercy. "I'm taking you dress shopping in half an hour. You have media training at one, hair and makeup at four."

"Maybe we should reschedule," I said. "Due to someone wanting to kill me."

"Oren signed off on us leaving the estate." Alisa gave me a look. "You have twenty-nine minutes." She eyed my hair. "Make sure you're looking your best. I'll meet you at the car."

CHAPTER 67

Oren escorted me to the SUV. Alisa and two of his men were waiting inside it—and they weren't the only ones.

"I know you weren't planning on going shopping without me," Thea said, by way of greeting. "Where there are high-fashion boutiques, so there is Thea."

I looked toward Oren, hoping he'd kick her out of the car. He didn't.

"Besides," Thea told me in a haughty little whisper as she buckled her seat belt, "we need to talk about Rebecca."

The SUV had three rows of seats. Oren and a second bodyguard sat in the front. Alisa and the third sat in the back. Thea and I were in the middle.

"What did you do to Rebecca?" Thea waited until she was satisfied that the other occupants of the car weren't listening too closely before she asked the question, low and under her breath.

"I didn't do anything to Rebecca."

"I will accept that you didn't fall into the Jameson Hawthorne trap for the *purpose* of dredging up memories of Jameson and

Emily." Thea clearly thought she was being magnanimous. "But that's where my generosity ends. Rebecca's painfully beautiful, but the girl cries ugly. I know what she looks like when she's spent all night crying. Whatever her deal is—this isn't just about Jameson. What happened at the cottage?"

Rebecca knows about the shooting. She was forbidden from telling anyone. I tried to wrap my mind around the implications. *Why was she crying?*

"Speaking of Jameson," Thea changed tactics. "He is oh so clearly miserable, and I can only assume that I owe that to you."

He's miserable? I felt something flicker in my chest—a *what-if*—but quelled it. "Why do you hate him so much?" I asked Thea.

"Why don't you?"

"Why are you even here?" I narrowed my eyes. "Not in this car," I amended, before she could mention high-fashion boutiques, "at Hawthorne House. What did Zara and your uncle ask you to come here to do?"

Why stick so close to me? What did they want?

"What makes you think they asked me to do anything?" It was obvious in Thea's tone and in her manner that she was a person who'd been born with the upper hand and never lost it.

There's a first time for everything, I thought, but before I could lay out my case, the car pulled up to the boutique, and the paparazzi circled us in a deafening, claustrophobic crunch.

I slumped back in my seat. "I have an entire mall in my closet." I shot Alisa an aggrieved look. "If I just wore something I already have, we wouldn't have to deal with this."

"This," Alisa echoed as Oren got out of the car and the roar of the reporters' questions grew louder, "is the point."

I was here to be seen, to control the narrative.

"Smile pretty," Thea murmured directly into my ear.

The boutique Alisa had chosen for this carefully choreographed outing was the kind of store that had only one copy of each dress. They'd closed the entire shop down for me.

"Green." Thea pulled an evening gown from the rack. "Emerald, to match your eyes."

"My eyes are hazel," I said flatly. I turned from the dress she was holding up to the sales attendant. "Do you have anything less low-cut?"

"You prefer higher cuts?" The sales attendant's tone was so carefully nonjudgmental that I was almost certain she was judging me.

"Something that covers my collarbone," I said, and then I shot a look at Alisa. *And my stitches.*

"You heard Ms. Grambs," Alisa said firmly. "And Thea is right—bring us something green."

CHAPTER 68

We found a dress. The paparazzi snapped their pictures as Oren ushered the lot of us back into the SUV. As we pulled away from the curb, he glanced in the rearview mirror. "Seat belts buckled?"

Mine was. Beside me, Thea fastened hers. "Have you thought about hair and makeup?" she asked.

"Constantly," I replied in a deadpan. "These days, I think of literally nothing else. A girl has to have her priorities in order."

Thea smiled. "And here I was thinking your priorities all had the last name Hawthorne."

"That's not true," I said. *But isn't it?* How much time had I spent thinking about them? How badly had I wanted Jameson to mean it when he'd told me I was special?

How clearly could I still feel Grayson checking my wound?

"Your bodyguard didn't want me to come today," Thea murmured as we turned onto a long and winding road. "Neither did your lawyer. I persevered, and do you know why?"

"Not a clue."

"This has nothing to do with my uncle or Zara." Thea played with the tips of her dark hair. "I'm just doing what Emily would want me to do. Remember that, would you?"

Without warning, the car swerved. My body kicked into panic mode—fight or flight, and neither one of them was an option, strapped into the back seat. I whipped my head toward Oren, who was driving—and noticed that the guard in the passenger seat had his hand on his gun, vigilant, ready.

Something's wrong. We shouldn't have come. I shouldn't have trusted, even for a moment, that I was safe. *Alisa pushed this. She wanted me out here.*

"Hold tight," Oren yelled.

"What's going on?" I asked. The words lodged themselves in my throat and came out as a whisper. I saw a flash of movement out of my window: a car, jerking toward us, high speed. I screamed.

My subconscious was screaming at me to *run*.

Oren swerved again, enough to prevent full-scale impact, but I heard the screech of metal on metal.

Someone is trying to run us off the road. Oren laid on the gas. The sound of sirens—police sirens—barely broke through the cacophony of panic in my head.

This can't be happening. Please don't let this be happening.

Please, no.

Oren roared into the left lane, ahead of the car that had attacked us. He swung the SUV around, up and over the median, sending us racing in the opposite direction.

I tried to scream, but it wasn't loud or shrill. I was keening, and I couldn't make it stop.

There was more than one siren now. I turned toward the back of the car, expecting the worst, preparing for impact—and I saw the car that had hit us spinning out. Within seconds, the vehicle was surrounded by cops.

"We're okay," I whispered. I didn't believe it. My body was still telling me that I would never be okay again.

Oren eased off the gas, but he didn't stop, and he didn't turn around.

"What the hell was that?" I asked, my voice high enough in pitch and volume to crack glass.

"That," Oren replied calmly, "was someone taking the bait."

The bait? I swung my gaze toward Alisa. "What is he talking about?"

In the heat of the moment, I'd thought that it was Alisa's fault that we were here. I'd doubted her—but Oren's response suggested that maybe I should have blamed them both.

"This," Alisa said, her trademark calm dented but not destroyed, "was the point." That was the same thing she'd said when we'd seen the paparazzi outside the boutique.

The paparazzi. Making sure we were seen. The absolute need to come dress shopping, despite everything that had happened.

Because *of everything that had happened.*

"You used me as *bait*?" I wasn't a yeller, but I was yelling now.

Beside me, Thea recovered her voice—and then some. "What the hell is going on here?"

Oren exited the highway and slowed to a stop at a red light. "Yes," he told me apologetically, "we used you—and ourselves—as bait." He glanced toward Thea and answered her question. "There was an attack on Avery two days ago. Our friends at the police station agreed to play this my way."

"Your way could have killed us!" I couldn't make my heart stop pounding. I could barely breathe.

"We had backup," Oren assured me. "My people, as well as the police. I won't tell you that you weren't in danger, but the situation being what it was, danger was not a possibility that could be eliminated. There were no good options. You had to continue living in that house. Instead of waiting for another attack, Alisa and I engineered what looked like a prime opportunity. Now, maybe we can get some answers."

First, they'd told me that the Hawthornes weren't a threat. Then they'd used me to flush out the threat. "You could have told me," I said roughly.

"It was better," Alisa told me, "that you didn't know. That *no one* knew."

Better for whom? Before I could say that, Oren got a call.

"Did Rebecca know about the attack?" Thea asked beside me. "Is that why she's been so upset?"

"Oren." Alisa ignored Thea and me. "Did they apprehend the driver?"

"They did." Oren paused, and I caught him looking at me in the rearview mirror, his eyes softening in a way that made my stomach twist. "Avery, it was your sister's boyfriend."

Drake. "Ex-boyfriend," I corrected, my voice getting caught in my throat.

Oren didn't respond to my assertion. "They found a rifle in his trunk that, at least preliminarily, matches the bullets. The police will be wanting to talk to your sister."

"What?" I said, my heart still banging mercilessly at my rib cage. "Why?" On some level, I knew—I knew the answer to that question, but I couldn't accept it.

I wouldn't.

"If Drake was the shooter, someone would have had to sneak

him onto the estate," Alisa said, her voice uncharacteristically gentle.

Not Libby, I thought. "Libby *wouldn't—*"

"Avery." Alisa put a hand on my shoulder. "If something happens to you—even without a will—your sister and your father are your heirs."

CHAPTER 69

These were the facts: Drake had tried to run my car off the road. He had a weapon that was a likely match for the bullets Oren had recovered. He had a felony record.

The police took my statement. They asked questions about the shooting. About Drake. About Libby. Eventually, I was escorted back to Hawthorne House.

The front door flew open before Alisa and I had even made it to the porch.

Nash stormed out of the house, then slowed when he saw us. "You want to tell me why I'm just now getting word that the police hauled Libby out of here?" he asked Alisa.

I'd never heard a Southern drawl sound quite like that.

Alisa lifted her chin. "If she's not under arrest, she had no obligation to go with them."

"She doesn't know that!" Nash boomed. Then he lowered his voice and looked her in the eye. "If you'd wanted to protect her, you could have."

There were so many layers to that sentence, I couldn't begin to untangle them, not with my brain focused on other things. *Libby. The police have Libby.*

"I'm not in the business of protecting every sad story that comes along," Alisa told Nash.

I knew she wasn't *just* talking about Libby, but that didn't matter. "She's not a sad story," I gritted out. "She's my sister!"

"And, more likely than not, an accessory to attempted murder." Alisa reached out to touch my shoulder. I stepped back.

Libby wouldn't hurt me. She wouldn't let anyone hurt me. I believed that, but I couldn't say it. Why couldn't I say it?

"That bastard's been texting her," Nash said beside me. "I've been trying to get her to block him, but she feels so damn guilty—"

"For what?" Alisa pushed. "What does she feel guilty for? If she's got nothing to hide from the police, then why are you so concerned about her talking to them?"

Nash's eyes flashed. "You're really going to stand there and act like we weren't both raised to treat 'never talk to the authorities without a lawyer present' like a Commandment?"

I thought about Libby, alone in a cell. She probably wasn't even *in* a cell, but I couldn't shake the image. "Send someone," I told Alisa shakily. "From the firm." She opened her mouth to object, and I cut her off. *"Do it."*

I might not hold the purse strings now, but I would someday. She worked for me.

"Consider it done," Alisa said.

"And leave me alone," I told her fiercely. She and Oren had kept me in the dark. They'd moved me around like a chess piece on a board. "All of you," I said, turning back toward Oren.

I needed to be alone. I needed to do everything in my power to keep them from planting even a seed of doubt, because if I couldn't trust Libby…

I had no one.

Nash cleared his throat. "You want to tell her about the media consultant waiting in the sitting room, Lee-Lee, or should I?"

CHAPTER 70

I agreed to sit down with Alisa's high-priced media consultant. Not because I had any intention of going through with tonight's charity gala, but because it was the one way I knew of to make sure that everyone else left me alone.

"There are three things we're going to work on today, Avery." The consultant, an elegant Black woman with a posh British accent, had introduced herself as Landon. I had no idea if that was her first name or her last. "After the attack this morning, there will be more interest in your story—and your sister's—than ever."

Libby wouldn't hurt me, I thought desperately. *She wouldn't let Drake hurt me.* And then: *She didn't block his number.*

"The three things we will be practicing today are what to say, how to say it, and how to identify things you shouldn't say and demur." Landon was poised, precise, and more stylish than either of my stylists. "Now, obviously, there is going to be some interest in the unfortunate incident that took place this morning, but your legal team would prefer you say as little on that front as possible."

That front being the second attempt on my life in three days. *Libby isn't involved. She can't be.*

"Repeat after me," Landon instructed, *"I'm grateful to be alive, and I'm grateful to be here tonight."*

I blocked out the thoughts dogging me, as much as I could. "I'm grateful to be alive," I repeated stonily, "and I'm grateful to be here tonight."

Landon gave me a look. "How do you think you sound?"

"Pissed?" I guessed dourly.

Landon offered me a gentle suggestion. "Perhaps try sounding less pissed." She waited a moment, and then assessed the way I was sitting. "Open up your shoulders. Loosen those muscles. Your posture is the first thing the audience's brain is going to latch on to. If you look like you're trying to fold in on yourself, if you make yourself small, that sends a message."

With a roll of my eyes, I tried to sit up a little straighter and let my hands fall to my sides. "I'm grateful to be alive, and I'm grateful to be here tonight."

"No." Landon gave a shake of her head. "You want to sound like a real person."

"I am a real person."

"Not to the rest of the world. Not yet. Right now you're a spectacle." There was nothing unkind in Landon's tone. "Pretend you're back home. You're in your comfort zone."

What was my comfort zone? Talking to Max, who was MIA for the foreseeable future? Crawling into bed with Libby?

"Think of someone you trust."

That hurt in a way that should have hollowed me out but left me feeling like I might throw up instead. I swallowed. "I'm grateful to be alive, and I'm grateful to be here tonight."

"It seems forced, Avery."

I ground my teeth. "It *is* forced."

"Does it have to be?" Landon let me marinate in that question for a moment. "Is no part of you grateful to have been given this opportunity? To live in this house? To know that no matter what happens, you and the people you love will always be taken care of?"

Money was security. It was safety. It was knowing that you could screw up without screwing up your life. *If Libby did let Drake onto the estate, if he's the one who shot at me—she couldn't have known that's what was going to happen.*

"Aren't you grateful to be alive, after everything that's happened? Did you *want* to die today?"

No. I wanted to live. Really live.

"I'm grateful to be here," I said, feeling the words a little more this time, "and I'm grateful to be alive."

"Better, but this time . . . let it hurt."

"Excuse me?"

"Show them that you're vulnerable."

I wrinkled my nose at her.

"Show them that you're just an ordinary girl. Just like them. That's the trick of my trade: How real, how vulnerable, can you seem without letting yourself actually be vulnerable at all?"

Vulnerable wasn't the story I'd chosen to tell when they'd been designing my wardrobe. I was supposed to have an edge. But sharp-edged girls had feelings, too.

"I'm grateful to be alive," I said, "and I'm grateful to be here tonight."

"Good." Landon gave a little nod. "Now we're going to play a little game. I'm going to ask you questions, and you're going to do the one thing you absolutely must master before I let you out of here to go to the gala tonight."

"What's that?" I asked.

"You're *not* going to answer the questions." Landon's expression was intent. "Not with words. Not with your face. Not at all—unless and until you get a question that you can, in some way, answer with the key message we've already practiced."

"Gratitude," I said. "Et cetera, et cetera." I shrugged. "Doesn't sound hard."

"Avery, is it true that your mother had a long-standing sexual liaison with Tobias Hawthorne?"

She almost got me. I almost spat out the word *no*. But somehow, I refrained.

"Did you stage today's attack?"

What?

"Watch your face," she told me, and then, without losing a beat: "How is your relationship with the Hawthorne family?"

I sat, passive, not allowing myself to so much as think their names.

"What are you going to do with the money? How do you respond to the people calling you a con woman and a thief? Were you injured today?"

That last question gave me an opening. "I'm fine," I said. "I'm grateful to be alive, and I'm grateful to be here tonight."

I expected accolades but got none.

"Is it true that your sister is in a relationship with the man who tried to kill you? Is she involved with the attempt on your life?"

I wasn't sure if it was the way she'd snuck the questions in, right after my previous answer, or how close to the quick the question cut, but I snapped.

"*No.*" The word burst from my mouth. "My sister had *nothing* to do with this."

Landon gave me a look. "From the top," she said steadily. "Let's try again."

CHAPTER 71

After my session with Landon, she dropped me off in my bedroom, where my style team awaited. I could have told them that I wasn't going to the gala, but Landon had gotten me thinking: What kind of message would that send?

That I was afraid? That I was hiding away—or hiding something? That Libby was guilty?

She's not. That was what I kept telling myself, over and over again. I was halfway through hair and makeup when Libby let herself into my bedroom. My stomach muscles clenched, my heart jumping into my throat. Her face was streaked with running makeup. She'd been crying.

She didn't do anything wrong. She didn't. Libby hesitated for three or four seconds, then threw herself at me, catching me up in the biggest, tightest hug of my life. "I'm sorry. I am so, so sorry."

I had a moment—exactly one—where my blood ran cold.

"I should have blocked him," Libby continued. "But for what it's worth, I just put my phone in the blender. And then I turned the blender on."

She wasn't apologizing for aiding and abetting Drake. She was apologizing for not blocking his number. For fighting with me when I'd wanted her to.

I bowed my head, and a set of hands immediately lifted my chin back up as the stylists continued their work.

"Say something," Libby told me.

I wanted to tell her that I believed her, but even saying the words felt disloyal, like an acknowledgment that I really hadn't been sure until now. "You're going to need a new phone," I said.

Libby gave a strangled little laugh. "We're also going to need a new blender." She swiped the heel of her right hand across her eyes.

"No tears!" the man making me up barked. That was aimed at me, not Libby, but she straightened, too. "You want to look like the picture we were given, correct?" the man asked me, aggressively working some mousse through my hair.

"Sure," I replied. "Whatever." If Alisa had given them a picture, that was one less decision for me to make, one less thing to think about.

Like the current billion-dollar question: If Drake had shot at me, and Libby hadn't let him onto the estate—who had?

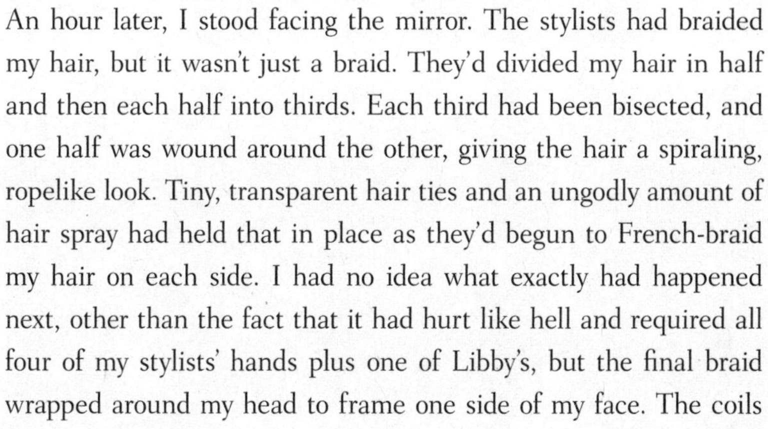

An hour later, I stood facing the mirror. The stylists had braided my hair, but it wasn't just a braid. They'd divided my hair in half and then each half into thirds. Each third had been bisected, and one half was wound around the other, giving the hair a spiraling, ropelike look. Tiny, transparent hair ties and an ungodly amount of hair spray had held that in place as they'd begun to French-braid my hair on each side. I had no idea what exactly had happened next, other than the fact that it had hurt like hell and required all four of my stylists' hands plus one of Libby's, but the final braid wrapped around my head to frame one side of my face. The coils were multicolored, showing off my lowlights and the natural blonde streaks in my ashy-brown hair. The effect was hypnotizing, like nothing I'd ever seen.

The makeup was less dramatic—natural, fresh, understated everywhere but the eyes. I had no idea what witchcraft they'd invoked, but my charcoal-lined eyes looked twice their normal size, and *green*—a true green, with flecks that looked more gold than brown.

"And the pièce de résistance..." One of the stylists slipped a necklace around my neck. "White gold and three emeralds."

The jewels were the size of my thumbnail.

"You look beautiful," Libby told me.

I looked nothing like myself. I looked like someone who belonged at a ball, and still, I almost backed out of going to the gala. The one thing that kept me from throwing in the towel was Libby.

If there was ever a time for me to control the narrative, it was now.

CHAPTER 72

Oren met me at the top of the stairs.

"Have the police gotten anything out of Drake?" I asked. "Has he admitted to the shooting? Who is he working with?"

"Deep breath," Oren told me. "Drake has more than implicated himself, but he's trying to paint Libby as the mastermind. That story doesn't add up. There is no security footage of him entering the estate, and there would be if, as he claims, Libby had let him through the gate. Our best guess at the moment is that he came in through the tunnels."

"The tunnels?" I repeated.

"They're like the secret passages in the house, except they run under the estate. I know of two entrances, and they're both secure."

I heard what Oren left unsaid. "There are two that you know of—but this is Hawthorne House. There could be more."

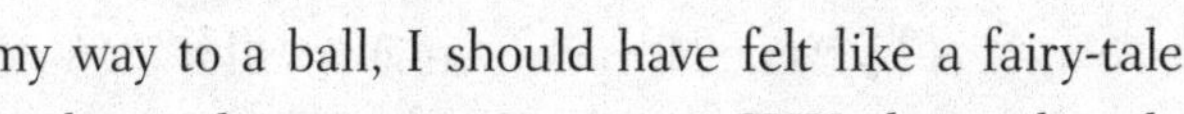

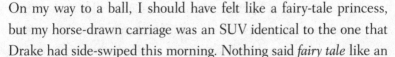

On my way to a ball, I should have felt like a fairy-tale princess, but my horse-drawn carriage was an SUV identical to the one that Drake had side-swiped this morning. Nothing said *fairy tale* like an attempted assassination.

Who knows the location of the tunnels? That was the question of the hour. If there were tunnels that Hawthorne House's head of security didn't even know about, I seriously doubted that Drake had come across them on his own. Libby wouldn't have known about them, either.

So who? Someone very, very familiar with Hawthorne House. *Did they reach out to Drake? Why?* That last question was less of a mystery. After all, why commit murder yourself when there was someone else out there willing and ready to do it for you? All someone would have had to know was that Drake existed, that he'd already gotten violent once, that he had every reason to hate me.

Within the walls of Hawthorne House, none of that was a secret.

Maybe his accomplice had sweetened the pie by telling him that if anything happened to me, Libby stood to inherit.

They let a felon do the dirty work—and take the fall. I sat in my bulletproof SUV in a five-thousand-dollar dress and a necklace that probably could have paid for at least a year of college, wondering if Drake's capture meant that the danger was over—or if whoever had given him tunnel access had other plans for me.

"The foundation purchased two tables for tonight's event," Alisa told me from the front seat. "Zara was loath to part with any seats, but since it's technically *your* foundation, she didn't have much of a choice."

Alisa was acting like nothing had happened. Like I had every reason to trust her, when it felt like reasons not to were stacking up.

"So I'll be sitting with them," I said without expression. "The Hawthornes."

One of whom—at *least* one of whom—might still want me dead.

"It's to your advantage if everything appears friendly between you." Alisa had to realize how ridiculous that sounded, given the context. "If the Hawthorne family accepts you, that will go a long way toward squelching some of the less seemly theories as to why you inherited."

"And what about the unseemly theories that one of them—*at least* one—wants me dead?" I asked.

Maybe it was Zara, or her husband, or Skye, or even Nan, who'd more or less told me that she'd killed her husband.

"We're still on high alert," Oren assured me. "But it would be to our benefit if the Hawthornes didn't realize that. If the conspirator's hope was to pin things on Drake—and Libby—let them think they've succeeded."

Last time around, I'd blown the element of surprise. This time, things would be different.

CHAPTER 73

"Avery, look over here!"

"Any comment about the arrest of Drake Sanders?"

"Can you comment on the future of the Hawthorne Foundation?"

"Is it true that your mother was once arrested for solicitation?"

If it hadn't been for the *seven* rounds of practice questions I'd been put through earlier, that last one would have gotten me. I would have answered, and my answer would have contained expletives, plural. Instead, I stood near the car and waited.

And then the question I'd been waiting for came. "With everything that's happened, how do you feel?"

I looked directly at the reporter who'd asked that question. "I'm grateful to be alive," I said. "And I'm grateful to be here tonight."

The event was held in an art museum. We entered on the upper floor and descended a massive marble staircase into the exhibit hall. By the time I was halfway down, everyone in the room was either staring at me or not-staring in a way that was worse.

At the bottom of the stairs, I saw Grayson. He wore a tuxedo exactly the way he wore a suit. He was holding a glass—clear, with clear liquid inside. The moment he saw me, he froze in place, as suddenly and fully as if someone had stopped time. I thought back to standing with him at the bottom of the hidden staircase, to the way he'd looked at me, and on some level, I thought that was the way he was looking at me now.

I thought I'd taken his breath away.

Then he dropped the glass in his hand. It hit the floor and shattered, shards of crystal spraying everywhere.

What happened? What did I do?

Alisa nudged me to keep moving. I finished descending the stairs as the waitstaff hurried over to clean up the glass.

Grayson stared at me. "What are you doing?" His voice was guttural.

"I don't understand," I said.

"Your hair," Grayson choked out. He lifted his free hand to my braid, his fingers nearly touching it before he pulled them into a fist. "That necklace. That dress…"

"What?" I said.

The only word he managed in reply was a name.

Emily. It was always Emily. Somehow, I made my way to the bathroom without looking too much like I was running away. I fumbled to tear my phone out of the black satin handbag I'd been given, unsure what I was planning to do with the phone once I got it out. Someone stepped up to the mirror beside me.

"You look nice," Thea said, casting a glance sidelong at me. "In fact, you look *perfect*."

I stared at her, and comprehension dawned. "What did you do, Thea?"

She glanced down at her own phone, hit a few buttons, and a moment later, I had a text. I hadn't even realized she had my number.

I opened the text and the picture attached, and all of the blood drained from my face. In this photo, Emily Laughlin wasn't laughing. She was smiling at the camera—a wicked little smile, like she was on the verge of a wink. Her makeup was natural, but her eyes looked unnaturally large, and her hair…

Was exactly like mine.

"What did you do?" I asked Thea again, more accusation this time than question. She'd invited herself along on my shopping trip. She was the one who'd suggested I wear green—just like Emily wore in this photo.

Even my necklace was eerily like hers.

I'd assumed, when the stylist had asked if I wanted to look like the picture, that Alisa was the one who'd supplied it. I'd assumed it was a photo of a model. *Not a dead girl.*

"Why would you do this?" I asked Thea, amending my question.

"It's what Emily would have wanted." Thea pulled a tube of lipstick out of her purse. "If it's any consolation," she said, once she was finished turning her lips a sparkling ruby red, "I didn't do this to *you*."

She'd done it to *them*.

"The Hawthornes didn't kill Emily," I spat. "Rebecca said that it was her heart."

Technically, she'd said that *Grayson* had said it was her heart.

"How sure are you that the Hawthorne family isn't trying to kill *you*?" Thea smiled. She had been there this morning. She'd been shaken. And now she was acting like this was all a joke.

“There is something fundamentally wrong with you,” I said.

My fury didn’t seem to penetrate. “I told you the day we met that the Hawthorne family was a twisted, broken mess.” She stared at the mirror a moment longer. “I never said that I wasn’t one, too.”

CHAPTER 74

I took off the necklace and stood holding it in front of the mirror. The hair was a bigger problem. It had taken two people to put it up. It would take an act of God for me to get it down.

"Avery?" Alisa stuck her head into the bathroom.

"Help me," I told her.

"With what?"

"My hair."

I reached back and started pulling at it, and Alisa caught my hands in hers. She transferred my wrists to her right hand and flipped a lock on the bathroom door with her left. "I shouldn't have pushed you," she said, her voice low. "This is too much, too soon, isn't it?"

"Do you know who I look like?" I asked her. I shoved the necklace in her face. She took it from my hands.

She frowned. "Who you look like?" That seemed like an honest question from a person who didn't like asking questions she didn't already know the answers to.

"Emily Laughlin." I couldn't keep from cutting a glance back to the mirror. "Thea dressed me up just like her."

It took Alisa a moment to process that. "I didn't know." She paused, considering. "The press won't, either. Emily was just an ordinary girl."

There was nothing ordinary about Emily Laughlin. I didn't know when I'd come to believe that. The moment I'd seen her picture? My conversation with Rebecca? The very first time Jameson had said her name, or the first time I'd said it to Grayson?

"If you stay in this bathroom much longer, people will take note," Alisa warned me. "They already have. For better or worse, you need to get out there."

I'd come tonight because in some twisted way I'd thought that putting on a happy face would protect Libby. I'd hardly be here if my own sister had tried to have me killed, would I?

"Fine," I told Alisa through gritted teeth. "But if I do this for you, I want your word that you'll protect my sister in any way you can. I don't care what your deal is with Nash, or what Nash's is with Libby. You don't just work for me anymore. You work for her, too."

I saw Alisa swallowing back whatever it was she really wanted to say. All that exited her mouth was: "You have my word."

I just had to make it through dinner. A dance or two. The live auction. Easier said than done. Alisa led me to the pair of tables that the Hawthorne Foundation had purchased. At the table on the left, Nan was holding court among the white-haired set. The table on the right was half-filled with Hawthornes: Zara and Constantine, Nash, Grayson, and Xander.

I made a beeline for Nan's table, but Alisa sidestepped and gently steered me to the seat directly next to Grayson. Alisa took the next chair over, leaving only three open seats—at least one of which I assumed was for Jameson.

Beside me, Grayson said nothing. I lost the battle not to flick my eyes in his direction and found him staring straight ahead, not looking at me—or anyone else at the table.

"I didn't do this on purpose," I told him under my breath, trying to keep the expression on my face normal for the benefit of our audience, partygoers and photographers alike.

"Of course not," Grayson replied, his tone stiff, the words rote.

"I'd take the braid out if I could," I murmured. "But I can't do it myself."

His head tilted down slightly, his eyes closing, just for a moment. "I know."

I was overcome then by the mental image of Grayson helping Emily take down her hair, his fingers working the braid out, bit by bit.

My arm bumped Alisa's wineglass. She tried to catch it but didn't move fast enough. As the wine stained the white tablecloth red, I realized what should have been obvious right from the beginning, from the moment the will had been read.

I didn't belong here in this world—not at a party like this, not sitting beside Grayson Hawthorne. And I never would.

CHAPTER 75

I made it through dinner without anyone trying to kill me, and Jameson never showed. I told Alisa that I needed some air, but I didn't go outside. I couldn't face the press again this soon, so I ended up in another wing of the museum instead, Oren playing shadow behind me.

The wing was closed. The lights were dim, and the exhibit rooms were blocked off, but the corridor was open. I walked down the long hall, Oren's footsteps trailing mine. Up ahead, there was a light shining, bright against all its surroundings. The cord blocking off this exhibit room had been moved to one side. Stepping past it felt like stepping out of a dark theater and into the sun. The room was bright. Even the frames on the paintings were white. There was only one person in the room, wearing a tuxedo without the jacket.

"Jameson." I said his name, but he didn't turn. He was standing in front of a small painting, looking at it intently from three or four feet away. He glanced at me as I walked toward him, then turned back to the painting.

You saw me, I thought. *You saw the way they did my hair.* The room was quiet enough that I could hear the beating of my own heart. *Say something.*

He nodded toward the painting. "Cézanne's *Four Brothers,*" he said as I came to stand beside him. "A Hawthorne family favorite, for obvious reasons."

I made myself look at the painting, not at him. There were four figures on the canvas, their features blurred. I could make out the lines of their muscles. I could practically *see* them in motion, but the artist hadn't been aiming for realism. My eyes went to the gold tag under the painting.

Four Brothers. Paul Cézanne. 1898. On loan from the collection of Tobias Hawthorne.

Jameson angled his face back toward mine. "I know you found the Davenport." He arched an eyebrow. "You beat me to it."

"So did Grayson," I said.

Jameson's expression darkened. "You were right. The tree in the Black Wood was just a tree. The clue we're looking for is a number. *Eight. One. One.* There's just one more."

"There is no *we,*" I said. "Do you even see me as a person, Jameson? Or am I just a tool?"

"I might have deserved that." He held my gaze a moment longer, then looked back at the painting. "The old man used to say that I have laser focus. I'm not built to care about more than one thing at a time."

I wondered if that thing was the game—or *her.*

"I'm done, Jameson." My words echoed in the white room. "With you. With whatever this was." I turned to walk away.

"I don't care that you're wearing Emily's braid." Jameson knew exactly what to say to make me stop. "I don't care," he repeated, "because *I don't care about Emily.*" He let out a ragged breath. "I broke up with her that night. I got tired of her little games. I told her I was done, and a few hours later, she died."

I turned back, and green eyes, a little bloodshot, settled on mine. "I'm sorry," I said, wondering how many times he'd replayed their last conversation.

"Come with me to the Black Wood," Jameson pleaded. He was right. He had laser focus. "You don't have to kiss me. You don't even have to like me, Heiress, but please don't make me do this alone."

He sounded raw, real in a way that he never had before. *You don't have to kiss me.* He'd said that like he wanted me to.

"I hope I'm not interrupting."

In unison, Jameson and I looked toward the doorway. Grayson stood there, and I realized that from his vantage point, all he would have seen of me when he'd walked into the room was the braid.

For a moment, Grayson and Jameson stared at each other.

"You know where I'll be, Heiress," Jameson told me. "If there's any part of you that wants to find me."

He brushed past Grayson on his way out the door. Grayson watched him go for the longest time before he turned back to me. "What did he say, when he saw you?"

When he saw my hair. I swallowed. "He told me that he broke up with Emily the night she died."

Silence.

I turned back to look at Grayson.

His eyes were closed, every muscle in his body taut. "Did Jameson tell you that I killed her?"

CHAPTER 76

After Grayson left, I spent another fifteen minutes in the gallery—alone—staring at Cézanne's *Four Brothers* before Alisa sent someone to find me.

"I agree," Xander told me, even though I hadn't said anything for him to agree with. "This party sucks. The socialite-to-scone ratio is pretty much unforgivable."

I wasn't in the mood for scone jokes. *Jameson says he broke up with Emily. Grayson claims that he killed her. Thea is using me to punish them both.* "I'm out of here," I told Xander.

"You can't leave yet!"

I gave him a look. "Why not?"

"Because..." Xander waggled his lone eyebrow. "They just opened up the dance floor. You want to give the press something to talk about, don't you?"

One dance. That was all I was giving Alisa—and the photographers—before I got the hell out of here.

"Pretend I'm the most fascinating person you've ever met," Xander advised as he escorted me onto the dance floor for a waltz.

He held a hand out for mine, then curved his other arm around my back. "Here, I'll help: Every year on my birthday, from the time I was seven until I was twelve, my grandfather gave me money to invest, and I spent it all on cryptocurrency because I am a genius and not at all because I thought *cryptocurrency* sounded kind of cool." He spun me once. "I sold my holdings before my grandfather died for almost a hundred million dollars."

I stared at him. "You what?"

"See?" he told me. "Fascinating." Xander kept right on dancing, but he looked down. "Not even my brothers know."

"What did your brothers invest in?" I asked. All this time, I'd been assuming that they'd been cut off with *nothing*. Nash had told me about Tobias Hawthorne's birthday tradition, but I hadn't thought twice about their "investments."

"No idea," Xander said jauntily. "We weren't allowed to discuss it."

We danced on, the photographers snapping their shots. Xander brought his face very close to mine.

"The press is going to think we're dating," I told him, my mind still spinning at his revelation.

"As it so happens," Xander replied archly, "I excel at fake dating."

"Who exactly did you fake date?" I asked.

Xander looked past me to Thea. "I am a human Rube Goldberg machine," he said. "I do simple things in complicated ways." He paused. "It was Emily's idea for Thea and me to date. Em was, shall we say, *persistent*. She didn't know that Thea was already with someone."

"And you agreed to put on a show?" I asked incredulously.

"I repeat: I am a human Rube Goldberg machine." His voice softened. "And I didn't do it for Thea."

Then for who? It took me a moment to put it together. Xander had mentioned fake dating *twice* before: once with respect to Thea, and once when I'd asked him about Rebecca.

"Thea and Rebecca?" I said.

"Deeply in love," Xander confirmed. *Thea called her painfully beautiful.* "The best friend and the younger sister. What was I supposed to do? They didn't think Emily would understand. She was possessive of the people she loved, and I knew how hard it was for Rebecca to go against her. Just once, Bex wanted something for herself."

I wondered if Xander had feelings for her—if fake dating Thea had been his twisted, Rube Goldberg way of saying that. "Were Thea and Rebecca right?" I asked. "About Emily not understanding?"

"And then some." Xander paused. "Em found out about them that night. She saw it as a betrayal."

That night—the night she died.

The music came to an end, and Xander dropped my hand, keeping his other arm around my waist. "Smile for the press," he murmured. "Give them a story. Look deep into my eyes. Feel the weight of my charm. Think of your favorite baked goods."

The edges of my lips turned up, and Xander Hawthorne escorted me off the dance floor to Alisa. "You can go now," she told me, pleased. "If you'd like."

Hell yes. "You coming?" I asked Xander.

The invitation seemed to surprise him. "I can't." He paused. "I solved the Black Wood." That got my full attention. "I could win this." Xander looked down at his fancy shoes. "But Jameson and Grayson need it more. Head back to Hawthorne House. There'll be a helicopter waiting for you when get there. Have the pilot fly you over the Black Wood."

A helicopter?

"Where you go," Xander told me, "they'll follow."

They, as in his brothers. "I thought you wanted to win," I said to Xander.

He swallowed. Hard. "I do."

CHAPTER 77

I'd only halfway believed Xander when he'd promised me a helicopter, but there it was, on the front lawn of Hawthorne House, blades still. Oren wouldn't let me step foot aboard until he'd checked it over. Even then, he insisted on taking the pilot's spot. I climbed in the back and discovered Jameson already there.

"Order a helicopter?" he asked me, like that was a perfectly normal thing to do.

I buckled myself into the seat next to him. "I'm surprised you waited for liftoff."

"I told you, Heiress." He gave me a crooked smile. "I don't want to do this alone." For a split second, it was like the two of us were back at the racetrack, barreling toward the finish line, then outside the helicopter, a flash of black caught my eye.

A tuxedo. Grayson's expression was impossible to read as he climbed on board.

Did Jameson tell you that I killed her? The echo of the question was deafening in my mind. As if he'd heard it, Jameson's head whipped toward Grayson. "What are you doing here?"

Xander had said that where I went, both of them would follow. *Jameson didn't follow me*, I reminded myself, every nerve in my body alive. *He got here first.*

"May I?" Grayson asked me, nodding toward an empty seat. I could feel Jameson staring at me, feel him willing me to say no.

I nodded.

Grayson sat behind me. Oren checked to make sure we were secure, then turned on the rotor. Within a minute, the sound of the blades was deafening. My heart jumped into my throat as we took to the air.

I'd enjoyed my first time on an airplane, but this was different—it was more. The noise, the vibration, the heightened sense that almost nothing separated me from the air—or the ground. My heart was beating, but I couldn't hear it. I couldn't hear myself think—not about the way Grayson's voice had broken as he'd asked that question, not about the way Jameson had told me that I didn't *have* to kiss him or like him.

All I could think about was looking down.

As we flew over the edge of the Black Wood, I could make out the twisted tangle of trees down below—too dense for sunlight to shine through. But when my gaze shifted toward the center of the forest, the trees thinned out, opening to a clearing in the very center. Jameson and I had been nearing the clearing when Drake had started taking shots. I'd noted the grass, but I hadn't *seen* it, not the way I was seeing it now.

From overhead, the clearing, the lighter ring of trees surrounding it, and the dense outer forest formed what looked like a long, skinny letter O.

Or a zero.

By the time the copter touched down, I felt like I was getting ready to burst out of my skin. I hopped out before the blades had fully stopped, adrenaline-fueled and giddy.

Eight. One. One. Zero.

Jameson bounded toward me. "We did it, Heiress." He stopped right in front of me, lifting his hands, palm up. Drunk on the high of the helicopter, I did the same, and his fingers locked through mine. "Four middle names. Four numbers."

Kissing him had been a mistake. Holding his hands now was a mistake—but I didn't care.

"Eight, one, one, zero," I said. "That's the order we discovered the numbers in—and the order of the clues in the will." Westbrook, Davenport, Winchester, and Blackwood, in that order. "A combination, maybe?"

"There are at least a dozen safes in the House," Jameson mused. "But there are other possibilities. An address . . . coordinates . . . and there's no guarantee that the clue isn't scrambled. To solve it, we may have to reorder the numbers."

An address. Coordinates. A combination. I closed my eyes, just for a second, just long enough for my brain to put another possibility into words. "A date?" All four clues were numbers; they were also single digits. For a combination lock or coordinates, I would have expected some two-digit entries. But a date . . .

The one or the zero would have to go at the front. 1-1-0-8 would be 11/08. "November eighth," I said, and then I ran through the rest of the possibilities. *08/11.* "August eleventh." *01/18.* "January eighteenth."

Then I hit the last possibility—the last date.

I stopped breathing. This was too big of a coincidence to be a coincidence at all.

"Ten-eighteen—October eighteenth." I sucked in a breath. Every nerve in my body felt like it was alive. "That's my birthday."

I have a secret, my mother had told me on my fifteenth birthday, two years ago, days before she'd died, *about the day you were born*. . . .

"No." Jameson dropped my hands.

"Yes," I replied. "I was born on October eighteenth. And my mother—"

"This isn't about your mother." Jameson balled his fingers into fists and stepped back.

"Jameson?" I had no idea what was going on here. If Tobias Hawthorne had chosen me because of something that had happened the day I was born, that was big. *Huge*. "This could be it. Maybe his path crossed my mom's while she was in labor? Maybe she did something for him while she was pregnant with me?"

"Stop." The word cracked like a whip. Jameson was looking at me like I was unnatural, like I was broken, like the sight of me could turn stomachs, including and especially his.

"What are you—"

"The numbers are not a date."

Yes, I thought fiercely. *They are*.

"This can't be the answer," he said.

I stepped forward, but he jerked back. I felt a light touch on my arm. *Grayson*. As gentle as his touch was, I got the distinct sense that he was holding me back.

Why? What had I done?

"Emily died," Grayson told me, his voice tight, "on October eighteenth, a year ago."

"That sick *son of a bitch*," Jameson cursed. "All of this—the clues, the will, her—all of it for *this*? He just found a random person born on that day to send a message? *This* message?"

"Jamie—"

"Don't talk to me." Jameson swung his gaze from Grayson to me. "Screw this. I'm done."

As he stalked away into the night, I called after him. "Where are you going?"

"Congratulations, Heiress," Jameson called back, his voice dripping with everything but felicitations. "I guess you had the good fortune of being born on the right day. Mystery solved."

CHAPTER 78

There had to be more to the puzzle than this. There *had* to be. I couldn't just be a random person born on the right calendar date. *That can't be it.* What about my mother? What about her secret—a secret she'd mentioned on my fifteenth birthday, a full year before Emily had died? And what about the letter Tobias Hawthorne had left me?

I'm sorry.

What had Tobias Hawthorne had to apologize for? *He didn't just randomly select a person with the right birthday. There has to be more to it than that.*

But I could still hear Nash telling me: *You're the glass ballerina—or the knife.*

"I'm sorry." Grayson spoke again beside me. "It's not Jameson's fault that he's like this. It's not Jameson's fault..." The invincible Grayson Hawthorne seemed to be having trouble talking. "...that this is how the game ends."

I was still wearing my clothes from the gala. My hair was still in Emily's braid.

"I should have known." Grayson's voice was swollen with

emotion. "I *did* know. The day that the will was read, I knew that all of this was because of me."

I thought of the way Grayson had shown up at my hotel room that night. He'd been angry, determined to figure out what *I* had done.

"What are you talking about?" I searched his face and eyes for answers. "How is this because of you? And don't tell me you killed Emily."

No one—not even Thea—had called Emily's death a murder.

"I did," Grayson insisted, his voice low and vibrating with intensity. "If it weren't for me, she wouldn't have been there. She wouldn't have jumped."

Jumped. My throat went dry. "Been where?" I asked quietly. "And what does any of this have to do with your grandfather's will?"

Grayson shuddered. "Maybe I was meant to tell you," he said after a long while. "Maybe that was always the point. Maybe you were always meant to be equal parts puzzle…and penance." He bowed his head.

I'm not your penance, Grayson Hawthorne. I didn't get the chance to say that out loud before he was talking again—and once he started, it would have taken an act of God to stop him.

"We'd always known her. Mr. and Mrs. Laughlin have been at Hawthorne House for decades. Their daughter and granddaughters used to live in California. The girls came to visit twice a year—once with their parents at Christmastime, and again in the summer, for three weeks, alone. We didn't see much of them at Christmas, but in the summers, we all played together. It was a bit like summer camp, really. You have camp friends, who you see once a year, who have no place in your ordinary life. That was Emily—and Rebecca. They were so different from the four of us. Skye said it was because they were girls, but I always thought it was because there were only two of them, and Emily came first. She was a force of nature, and their parents were always so worried she'd overexert herself. She was allowed to play cards with us, and other quiet, indoor games—but she wasn't allowed to roam outside the way we did, or to run.

"She'd get us to bring her things. It became a bit of a tradition. Emily would set us on a hunt, and whoever found what she'd requested—the more unusual and hard to find, the better—won."

"What did you win?" I asked.

Grayson shrugged. "We're brothers. We didn't have to win anything in particular—just *win*."

That tracked. "And then Emily got a heart transplant," I said. Jameson had told me that much. He'd said that afterward, she wanted to *live*.

"Her parents were still protective, but Emily had lived in glass cages long enough. She and Jameson were thirteen. I was fourteen. She'd breeze in for the summers, the consummate daredevil. Rebecca was always after us to be careful, but Emily insisted that her doctors had said that her activity level was only limited by her physical stamina. If she *could* do it, there was no reason she *shouldn't*. The family moved here permanently when Emily was sixteen. She and Rebecca didn't live on the estate, the way they had during visits, but my grandfather paid for them to attend private school."

I saw where this was going. "She wasn't just a summer camp friend anymore."

"She was everything," Grayson said—and he didn't exactly say it like it was a compliment. "Emily had the entire school eating out of the palm of her hand. Maybe that was our fault."

Even just being Hawthorne-adjacent changed the way that people looked at you. Thea's statement came back to me.

"Or maybe," Grayson continued, "it was just because she was

Em. Too smart, too beautiful, too good at getting what she wanted. She had no fear."

"She wanted you," I said. "And Jameson, and she didn't want to choose."

"She turned it into a game." Grayson shook his head. "And God help us, we played. I want to say that it was because we loved her—that it was because of *her*, but I don't even know how much of that was true. There's nothing more Hawthorne than *winning*."

Had Emily known that? Used it to her advantage? Had it ever hurt her?

"The thing was..." Grayson choked. "She didn't just want us. She wanted what we could give her."

"Money?"

"Experiences," Grayson replied. "Thrills. Race cars and motorcycles and handling exotic snakes. Parties and clubs and places we weren't supposed to be. It was a rush—for her and for us." He paused. "For me," he corrected. "I don't know what it was, exactly, for Jamie."

Jameson broke up with her the night she died.

"One night, I got a call from Emily, late. She said that she was done with Jameson, that all she wanted was me." Grayson swallowed. "She wanted to celebrate. There's this place called Devil's Gate. It's a cliff overlooking the Gulf—one of the most famous cliff-diving locations in the world." Grayson angled his head down. "I knew it was a bad idea."

I tried to form words—any words. "How bad?"

He was breathing heavily now. "When we got there, I headed for one of the lower cliffs. Emily headed for the top. Past the danger signs. Past the warnings. It was the middle of the night. We shouldn't have been there at all. I didn't know why she wouldn't let me wait until morning—not until later, when I realized she'd lied about *choosing* me."

Jameson had broken up with her. She'd called Grayson, and she hadn't been in the mood to *wait*.

"Cliff diving killed her?" I asked.

"No," Grayson said. "She was fine. *We* were fine. I went to grab our towels, but when I came back... Emily wasn't even in the water anymore. She was just lying on the shoreline. Dead." He closed his eyes. "Her heart."

"You didn't kill her," I said.

"The adrenaline did. Or the altitude, the change in pressure. *I don't know.* Jameson wouldn't take her. I shouldn't have, either."

She made decisions. She had agency. It wasn't your job to tell her no. I knew instinctively that no good could come of saying any of that, even if it was true.

"You know what my grandfather told me, after Emily's funeral? *Family first.* He said that what happened to Emily wouldn't have happened if I'd put my family first. If I'd refused to play along, if I'd chosen my brother over her." Grayson's vocal cords tensed against his throat, as if he wanted to say something else but couldn't. Finally, it came. "That's what this is about. One-zero-one-eight. October eighteenth. The day Emily died. Your birthday. It's my grandfather's way of confirming what I already knew, deep down.

"All of this—all of it—is because of me."

CHAPTER 79

When Grayson left, Oren escorted me back to the house.

"How much did you hear?" I asked him, my mind tangled with thoughts and emotions I wasn't sure I was ready to handle.

Oren gave me a look. "How much do you want me to have heard?"

I bit at the inside of my lip. "You knew Tobias Hawthorne. Would he have picked me to inherit just because Emily Laughlin died on my birthday? Did he decide to leave his fortune to a random person born on October eighteenth? Hold a lottery?"

"I don't know, Avery." Oren shook his head. "The only person who ever really knew what Tobias Hawthorne was thinking was Mr. Hawthorne himself."

I made my way back through the halls of Hawthorne House, back toward the wing I shared with my sister. I wasn't certain that either Grayson or Jameson would ever speak a word to me again. I didn't know what the future held, or why the idea that I might have been chosen for a completely trivial reason felt like such a punch to the gut.

How many people on this planet shared my birthday?

I stopped on the stairs, in front of the portrait of Tobias Hawthorne that Xander had shown me what felt like a lifetime ago. I racked my mind now, as I'd done then, for any memory, any moment in time when my path had crossed with the billionaire's. I looked Tobias Hawthorne in the eye—Grayson's silver eyes—and silently asked him *why*.

Why me?

Why were you sorry?

I pictured my mother playing I Have A Secret. *Did something happen the day I was born?*

I stared at the portrait, taking in every wrinkle on the old man's face, every hint to personality in his posture, even the muted color in the background. *No answers.* My eyes caught on the artist's signature.

Tobias Hawthorne X. X. VIII

I looked back at the old man's silver eyes. *The only one who ever really knew what Tobias Hawthorne was thinking was Mr. Hawthorne himself.* This was a self-portrait. And the letters next to the name?

"Roman numerals," I whispered.

"Avery?" Oren said beside me. "Everything okay?"

In Roman numerals, *X* was ten, *V* was five, and *I* was one.

"Ten." I put my finger under the first X, then moved it to the rest of the letters, reading them as a single unit. "Eighteen."

Remembering the mirror that had hidden the armory, I reached behind the portrait's frame. I wasn't sure what I was feeling for until I found it. A button. *A release.* I pushed it, and the portrait swung outward.

Behind it, on the wall, was a keypad.

"Avery?" Oren said again, but I was already bringing my fingers up to the keypad. *What if the numbers aren't the final answer?* The possibility caught me in its jaws and wouldn't let go. *What if they're meant to lead to the next clue?*

I brought my index finger to the keypad and tried the obvious combination. "One. Zero. One. Eight."

There was a beep, and then the top of the step below me began to rise, revealing a compartment underneath. I ducked down and reached inside. There was only one thing in the hollowed stair: a piece of stained glass. It was purple, in the shape of an octagon, with a tiny hole in the top, through which a sheer, shimmering ribbon had been threaded. It looked almost like a Christmas ornament.

As I held the stained glass up by the string, my eyes caught on the underside of the panel. Etched into the wood was the following verse.

Top of the clock
Meet me at high
Tell the late day hello
Wish the morning good-bye
A twist and a flip
What do you see?
Take them two at a time
And come find me

CHAPTER 80

I didn't know what I was supposed to do with the stained-glass ornament or what to make of the words written under the stair, but as Libby helped me let my hair down that night, one thing was perfectly clear.

The game wasn't over.

The next morning, with Oren in my wake, I went in search of Jameson and Grayson. I found the former in the solarium, shirtless and standing in the sun.

"Go away," he said when I opened the door, without even looking to see who it was.

"I found something," I told him. "I don't think the date is the answer—at least, not all of it."

He didn't reply.

"Jameson, are you listening to me? I *found something.*" For what little time I'd known him, he'd been driven, obsessed. What I held in my hand should have engendered at least a glimmer of curiosity, but when he turned to face me, his eyes dull, all he said was "Toss it over with the rest."

I looked, and in a nearby trash can, I saw at least half a dozen stained-glass octagons, identical to the one that I held, right down to the ribbon.

"The numbers ten and eighteen are everywhere in this godforsaken house." Jameson's voice was muted, his manner contained. "I found them scratched onto a panel on my closet floor. That little purple bugger was underneath."

He didn't bother gesturing to the trash can or specifying which piece of stained glass he was referring to.

"And the others?" I asked.

"Once I started looking for the numbers, I couldn't stop, and once you see it," Jameson said, his voice low, "you can't unsee it. The old man thought he was so smart. He must have hidden hundreds of those things, all over the house. I found a chandelier with eighteen crystals in the outer circle and ten in the middle—and a hidden compartment down below. There are eighteen stone leaves on the fountain outside, and ten finely drawn roses in its bowl. The paintings in the music room..." Jameson looked down. "Everywhere I look, everywhere I go, another reminder."

"Don't you see," I told him fiercely. "Your grandfather couldn't have done this all after Emily died. You would have noticed—"

"Workmen in the house?" Jameson said, finishing my sentence. "The great Tobias Hawthorne added a room or wing to this place every year, and in a house this size, something is always needing to be replaced or repaired. My mother was always buying new paintings, new fountains, new chandeliers. We wouldn't have noticed a thing."

"Ten-eighteen isn't the answer," I insisted, willing his eyes to mine. "You have to see that. It's a clue—one he didn't want us to miss."

Us. I'd said *us*—and I meant it. But that didn't matter.

"Ten-eighteen is answer enough," Jameson said, turning his back on me. "I told you, Avery: I'm not playing anymore."

Grayson was harder to find. Eventually, I tried the kitchen and found Nash instead.

"Have you seen Grayson?" I asked him.

Nash's expression was guarded. "I don't think he wants to see you, kid."

The night before, Grayson hadn't blamed me. He hadn't lashed out. But after he'd told me about Emily, he'd walked away.

He'd left me alone.

"I need to see him," I said.

"Give it some time," Nash advised. "Sometimes, you gotta excise a wound before it can heal."

I ended up back on the staircase to the East Wing, back in front of the portrait. Oren got a call, and he must have decided the threat to me was contained enough now that he didn't need to watch me mope around Hawthorne House all day. He excused himself, and I went back to staring at Tobias Hawthorne.

It had seemed like fate when I'd found the clue in this portrait, but after talking to Jameson, I knew that it wasn't a sign—or even a coincidence. The clue I'd found had been one of many. *You didn't want them to miss this*, I addressed the billionaire silently. If he really had done all of this after Emily's death, his persistence seemed cruel. *Did you want to make sure that they wouldn't forget what happened?*

Is this whole twisted game just a reminder—an incessant reminder—to put family first?

Is that all I am?

Jameson had said, right from the beginning, that I was special. I hadn't realized until now how badly I'd wanted to believe that he was right, that I wasn't invisible, wasn't wallpaper. I wanted to believe that Tobias Hawthorne had seen something in me that had told him I could do this, that I could handle the stares and the limelight, the responsibility, the riddles, the threats—all of it. I wanted to matter.

I didn't want to be the glass ballerina or the knife. I wanted to prove, at least to myself, that I was *something.*

Jameson may have been done with the game, but I wanted to win.

CHAPTER 81

Top of the clock
Meet me at high
Tell the late day hello
Wish the morning good-bye
A twist and a flip
What do you see?
Take them two at a time
And come find me

I sat on the steps, staring at the words, then worked through the rhyme line by line, turning the piece of stained glass over in my hands. *Top of the clock.* I pictured a clock's face in my head. *What's at the top?*

"Twelve." I rolled that over in my mind. *The number at the top of a clock is twelve.* Like dominos, that set off a chain reaction in my mind. *Meet me at high*...

High what?

"Noon." That was a guess, but the next two lines seemed to confirm it. Noon happened in the middle of the day, when you said good-bye to the morning and hello to what came after.

I moved on to the second half of the riddle... and I got nothing.

A twist and a flip
What do you see?
Take them two at a time
And come find me

I focused on the stained glass. Was I supposed to twist it? Flip it? Did we need to assemble *all* of the pieces somehow?

"You look like you swallowed a squirrel." Xander plopped down on the stairs next to me.

I definitely did *not* look like I'd swallowed a squirrel, but I was guessing that was Xander's way of asking if I was okay, so I let it go. "Your brothers don't want anything to do with me," I said quietly.

"I guess my kind gesture of sending you all to the Black Wood together exploded." Xander made a face. "To be fair, most of my gestures end up exploding."

That startled a laugh out of me. I tilted the step in his direction. "The game's not over," I told him. He read the inscription. "I found it last night, after the Black Wood." I held up the stained glass. "What do you make of this?"

"Now, where," Xander said thoughtfully, "have I seen something that looks like that?"

CHAPTER 82

I hadn't been back in the Great Room since the reading of the will. Its stained-glass window was tall—eight feet high to only three feet wide—and the lowest point was even with the top of my head. The design was simple and geometric. In the topmost corners were two octagons, the exact size, shade, color, and cut as the one in my hand.

I craned my neck to get a better look. *A twist and a flip*...

"What do you think?" Xander asked me.

I cocked my head to the side. "I think we're going to need a ladder."

Perched high on the ladder, with Xander holding it down below, I pressed my hand against one of the stained-glass octagons. At first, nothing happened, but when I pushed on the left side, the octagon rotated—seventy degrees, and then something stopped it.

Does that qualify as a twist?

I turned the second octagon. Pressing left and right didn't do anything, but pushing at the bottom did. The glass flipped a hundred and eighty degrees and then some, before locking into place.

I made my way back down to Xander, who was holding the

ladder, unsure what I'd accomplished. "*A twist and a flip,*" I recited. "*What do you see?*"

We stepped back, taking in the wide view. Sun shone through the window, causing diffused colored lights to appear on the Great Room Floor. The two panels I'd turned, in contrast, cast purple beams. Eventually, those beams crossed.

What do you see?

Xander squatted at the spot where the beams of light met on the floor. "Nothing." He tested the floorboard. "I was expecting it to pop out, or to give..."

I went back to the riddle. *What do you see?* I saw the light. I saw the beams crossing.... When that didn't go anywhere, I went farther back in the poem—all the way to the top.

"Noon," I remembered. "The first half of the riddle described noon." The gears in my brain turned faster. "The angle of the beams must depend at least a little on the angle of the sun. Maybe the *twist* and the *flip* only show you what you need to see at noon?"

Xander chewed on that for a second. "We could wait," he said. "Or..." He dragged out the word. "We could cheat."

We spread out, testing the surrounding floorboards. It wasn't that long until noon. The angles couldn't change that much. I tapped the heel of my hand against board after board. *Secure. Secure. Secure.*

"Find anything?" Xander asked me.

Secure. Secure. Loose. The board beneath my hand wasn't wiggling, but it had more give than the others. "Xander—over here!"

He joined me, placed his hands on the board, and pressed. The board popped up. Xander removed it, revealing a small dial underneath. I turned the knob, not sure what to expect. The next thing I knew, Xander and I were sinking. The floor around us was sinking.

When it stopped, Xander and I weren't in the Great Room

anymore. We were underneath it, and directly in front of us was a set of stairs. I was going to go out on a limb and guess that this was one of the entrances to the tunnels that Oren *didn't* know about.

"Take the stairs two at a time," I told Xander. "That's the next line." *Take them two at a time and come find me.*

CHAPTER 83

I had no idea what would have happened if we hadn't descended the stairs two at a time, but I was glad we hadn't found out.

"Have you ever been in the tunnels?" I asked Xander, once we'd made it uneventfully down.

Xander was silent long enough to make the question feel loaded. "No."

Concentrating, I took in my surroundings. The tunnels were metal, like a giant pipe or something out of a sewer system, but they were surprisingly well lit. *Gaslights?* I wondered. I'd lost any sense of how far down we were. Up ahead, the tunnels spread out in three directions.

"Which way?" I asked Xander.

Solemnly, he pointed straight ahead.

I frowned. "How do you know?"

"Because," Xander replied jauntily, "that's what he said." He gestured near my feet. I looked down and yelped.

It took me a moment to realize that there were gargoyles at the bottom of the stairs, a match for the ones in the Great Room, except that the gargoyle on the left had one hand—and one finger—extended, pointing the way.

Come find me.

I started walking. Xander followed. I wondered if he had any idea what we were walking toward.

Come find me.

I remembered Xander telling me that even if I'd thought that I had manipulated Tobias Hawthorne, the old man would have been the one manipulating me.

He's dead, I told myself. *Isn't he?* That thought hit me hard. The press certainly thought Tobias Hawthorne had died. His family seemed to believe it. But had they actually seen his body?

What else could it mean? *Come find me.*

Five minutes later, we hit a wall. There was nowhere else to go, nothing to see, no turns we could have taken since we'd started down this path.

"Maybe the gargoyle *lied.*" Xander sounded like he was enjoying that statement a little too much.

I pushed against the wall. *Nothing.* I turned back. "Did we miss something?"

"Perhaps," Xander said thoughtfully, "the gargoyle lied!"

I looked back way we'd come. I walked the path back slowly, taking in every detail of the tunnel. *Bit. By bit. By bit.*

"Look!" I told Xander. "There."

It was a metal grate, built into the tunnel floor. I ducked down. There was a brand name engraved on the metal, but time had worn away most of the letters. The only ones that were left were *M* . . .

And *E.*

"Come find *me,*" I whispered. Squatting down, I grabbed the grate with my fingers and pulled. Nothing. I pulled again, and this time the grate popped up. I fell backward, but Xander caught me.

The two of us stared down into the hole below.

"It is possible," Xander whispered, "that the gargoyle was telling the truth." Without waiting for me, he lowered himself into the hole—and dropped. "You coming?"

If Oren knew I was doing this, he would kill me. I dropped down and found myself in a small room. *How far underground are we now?* The room had four walls, three of them identical. The fourth was made of concrete. Three letters had been carved into the cement.

A. K. G.

My initials.

I walked toward the letters, mesmerized, and then I saw a red laser-like light pass over my face. There was a beep, and then the concrete wall split in two, like an elevator opening. Behind it was a door.

"Facial recognition," Xander said. "It didn't matter which one of us found this place. Without you, we wouldn't have been able to get past the wall."

Poor Jameson. He'd gone to all that effort to keep me close, then ditched me before I could play my part. *The glass ballerina. The knife. The girl with the face that unlocks the wall that reveals the door that…*

"That what?" I stepped forward to examine the door. There were four touch pads, one in each corner of the door. Xander hit one to wake it up, and an image of a fluorescent hand appeared.

"Uh-oh," Xander said.

"What *uh-oh*?" I asked.

"This one has Jameson's initials on it." Xander moved on to the next one. "Grayson's. Nash's." At the last one, he paused. "Mine."

He placed his hand flat on the screen. It made a beeping sound, and then I heard what sounded like a deadbolt being thrown.

I tried the door's handle. "Still locked."

"Four locks." Xander winced. "Four brothers."

My face had been needed to get this far. Their hands were required to go farther.

CHAPTER 84

Xander left me to guard the room. He said that he would be back—with his brothers.

Easier said than done. Jameson had made his feelings clear. Grayson had made himself very hard to find. Nash had never gotten sucked in to their grandfather's game in the first place. *What if they don't come?* Whatever was behind this door, it was what Tobias Hawthorne had wanted us to find. *October eighteenth* wasn't the answer—not in its entirety.

Out of all the people in the world with my birthday, why me? What was the billionaire sorry for? *There are too many pieces*, I thought. *I can't fit it together—any of it.* I needed help.

Overhead, there were footsteps. Abruptly, the sound stopped.

"Xander?" I called. No response. "Xander, is that you?"

More footsteps—coming closer. *Who else knows about this tunnel?* I'd been so intent on finding answers and following this to its end that I'd almost forgotten: Someone in Hawthorne House had given Drake access to the tunnels.

These tunnels.

I pressed my back against the wall. I could hear someone moving directly overhead. The footsteps stopped. A figure appeared above me, backlit and looming over my only exit from this space. *Female. Pale.*

"Rebecca?"

CHAPTER 85

Avery." Rebecca stared down at me. "What are you doing down there?" She sounded perfectly normal, but all I could think was that Rebecca Laughlin had been on the estate the night Drake had shot at me. She didn't have an alibi, because when we'd arrived at Wayback Cottage, she wasn't there, and neither of her grandparents knew where she was. She'd said something about *warning* me.

The next day, Rebecca had looked—according to Thea—like she'd been crying. *Why?*

"Where were you," I asked her, my mouth going dry, "the night of the shooting?"

Rebecca closed her eyes. "You don't know what it's like," she said softly, "to have your entire life revolve around one person, and then you wake up one day, and that person is gone."

That wasn't an answer to my question. I thought about Thea telling me that she was only doing what Emily would have wanted.

What would Emily have wanted Rebecca to do to me?

Xander needed to get back here—quick.

"It was my fault, you know," Rebecca said up above, her eyes still closed. "Emily was taking huge risks. I told our parents. They grounded her, forbade her from seeing the Hawthornes. But Em had her ways. She convinced our mom and dad that she was done acting out. They didn't lift the ban on the boys, but they did start letting her hang out with Thea again."

"Thea," I repeated, "who you were secretly dating."

Rebecca's eyelids shot open. "Emily found us together that afternoon. She was...*angry*. As soon as she got me alone, she told me that what Thea and I had wasn't love, that if Thea *really* loved me, she never would have pretended to be with Xander. Emily said..." Rebecca was caught up in memory now, fully. *Violently*. "She told me that Thea loved her more—and she would prove it. She asked Thea to cover about the cliff diving. I begged Thea not to, but she said that after everything, we owed it to Em."

Thea had covered for Emily the night she had died.

"Most of the things Emily talked the boys into, she *could* do, but even professional cliff divers don't jump from the top of Devil's Gate. It would have been dangerous for anyone, but that much adrenaline, that much cortisol, a change in altitude and pressure, with *her* heart?" Rebecca was speaking so softly now that I wasn't sure she truly remembered I was listening. "I'd tried telling my parents what she was doing, and that didn't work. I'd tried begging Thea, and she'd chosen Emily over me. So I decided to go to Jameson. He was the one who was supposed to take her to Devil's Gate."

Rebecca's head dipped, deep red hair falling into her face. Thea was right—Rebecca Laughlin was beautiful. But right now she didn't look quite right.

"I had a voice recording," she said softly, "of Emily talking. She used to tell me everything the boys did with her and for her and to her. She liked to keep score." Rebecca paused, and when she spoke again, her voice was sharper-edged. "I played the recording for Jameson. I told myself that I was doing it to protect my sister, to keep him from taking her to the cliffs. But the truth was, she'd taken Thea away from me."

So you took something away from her, I thought. "Jameson broke up with her," I said. He'd told me that much.

"If he hadn't," Rebecca replied, "maybe she wouldn't have needed to push things so much. Maybe she would have relented and jumped from one of the lower cliffs. Maybe it would have been okay." Her voice got even softer. "If Emily hadn't caught Thea and me together that afternoon, if she hadn't seen our relationship as such a betrayal—she might not have needed to jump at all."

Rebecca blamed herself. Thea blamed the boys. Grayson took the weight of all of it onto himself. *And Jameson...*

"I'm sorry." Rebecca's apology jarred me from my thoughts. Her tone told me she wasn't talking about Emily anymore. She wasn't talking about something that had happened over a year ago.

"Sorry for what?" I asked. *What are you doing down here, Rebecca?*

"It's not that I have anything against you. But it's what Emily would have wanted."

She is not well. I had to find a way out of here. I had to get away from her.

"Emily would have hated you for stealing their money. She would have hated the way they look at you."

"So you decided to get rid of me," I said, stalling for time. "For Emily."

Rebecca stared at me. "No."

"You knew about the tunnels, and somehow, you told Drake..."

"*No,*" Rebecca insisted. "Avery, I wouldn't do that."

"You said it yourself. Emily would have wanted me gone."

"I'm *not* Emily." The words were guttural.

"Then what were you apologizing for?" I asked.

Rebecca swallowed. "Mr. Hawthorne told me about the tunnels one summer when I was little. He showed me all the entrances, said I deserved something that was just mine. A secret. I come down here when I need to get away—sometimes when I'm visiting my grandparents, but since Emily died, things are pretty awful at home, so sometimes I enter from the outside."

I waited. "And?"

"The night of the shooting, I saw someone else in the tunnels. I didn't say anything, because Emily wouldn't have wanted me to. I owed her, Avery. After what I did—*I owed her.*"

"Who did you see?" I asked. She didn't answer. "Drake?"

Rebecca met my eyes. "He wasn't alone."

"Who else was there?" I waited. *Nothing.* "Rebecca, who else was in the tunnel with Drake?"

Who would Emily have wanted her to protect?

"One of the boys?" I asked, feeling like the ground was crumbling beneath me.

"No," Rebecca said quietly. "Their mother."

CHAPTER 86

"Skye?" I tried to wrap my mind around that. She'd never seemed like a threat, the way Zara had. Passive-aggressive, sure, and petty. But violent?

We're all friends here, aren't we? I could hear her declaring. *I make it a policy to befriend everyone who steals my birthright.*

I could see her holding out a glass of champagne and telling me to drink.

"Skye was down here with Drake the night of the shooting," I said, making myself confront the implications head-on. "She gave him access to the estate, probably even pointed him toward the Black Wood."

Toward me.

"I should have told someone," Rebecca said softly. "After the shooting, as soon as I realized what I'd seen—I should have spoken up."

"Yes." That word was razor sharp—and spoken by someone other than me. "You should have." Overhead, Grayson stepped into view.

Rebecca turned to face him. "It was your mother, Gray. I *couldn't*—"

"You could have told me," Grayson said quietly. "I would have taken care of it, Bex."

I doubted Grayson's method of *taking care of it* would have involved turning his mother over to the police.

"Drake tried again," I said, glaring daggers at Rebecca. "You know that, right? He tried to run us off the road. He could have killed me—and Alisa and Oren and *Thea.*"

Rebecca made a garbled sound the second I said Thea's name.

"Rebecca," Grayson said, his voice low.

"I know," Rebecca said. "But Emily wouldn't have wanted..."

"Emily's gone." Grayson's tone wasn't harsh, but his words took Rebecca's breath away. "Bex." He made her look at him. "Rebecca. I'll take care of this. I promise you: Everything is going to be fine."

"Everything is *not* fine," I told Grayson.

"Go," he murmured to Rebecca. She went, and we were alone.

Grayson lowered himself slowly into the hidden room. "Xander said you needed me."

He'd come. Maybe that would have meant more if I hadn't just had that conversation with Rebecca.

"Your mother tried to have me killed."

"My mother," Grayson said, "is a complicated woman. But she's family."

And he would choose family over me, every time.

"If I asked you to let me handle this," he continued, "would you? I can guarantee that no more harm will come to you or yours."

How exactly he could guarantee anything was unclear, but there was no doubt that he believed he could. *The world bends to the will of Grayson Hawthorne.* I thought about the day I'd met him, how sure he'd seemed of himself, how invincible.

"What if I play you for it?" Grayson asked when I didn't reply.

"You like a challenge. I know you do." He stepped toward me. "Please, Avery. Give me a chance to make this right."

There was no making this right—but all he'd asked for was a chance. *I don't owe him that. I don't owe him anything. But—*

Maybe it was the expression on his face. Or the knowledge that he'd already lost everything to me once. Maybe I just wanted him to see me and think about something other than October eighteenth.

"I'll play you for it," I said. "What's the game?"

Grayson's silver eyes held mine. "Think of a number," he told me. "One to ten. If I guess it, you let me handle the situation with my mother my way. If I don't..."

"I turn her in to the police."

Grayson took half a step toward me. "Think of a number."

The odds were in my favor here. He only had a 10 percent chance of guessing correctly. I had a 90 percent chance that he would get it wrong. I took my time choosing. There were certain numbers that people defaulted to. Seven, for instance. I could go for an extreme—one or ten, but those seemed like easy guesses, too. Eight was on my brain, from the days we'd spent solving the numerical sequence. Four was the number of Hawthorne brothers.

If I wanted to keep him from guessing, I needed to go for something unexpected. No rhyme, no reason.

Two.

"Do you want me to write the number down?" I asked.

"On what?" Grayson asked softly.

I swallowed. "How do you know that I won't lie about my number if you get it right?"

Grayson was quiet for a few seconds, then spoke. "I trust you."

I knew, with every fiber of my being, that Grayson Hawthorne didn't trust easily—or much. I swallowed. "Go ahead."

He took at least as much time generating his guess as I had choosing my number. He looked at me, and I could feel him trying to unravel my thoughts and impulses, to solve me, like one more riddle.

What do you see when you look at me, Grayson Hawthorne?

He made his guess. "Two."

I turned my head toward my shoulder, breaking eye contact. I could have lied. I could have told him that he was wrong. But I didn't. "Good guess."

Grayson let out a ragged breath, and then I felt him gently turning my face back toward his. "Avery." He almost never used my given name. He gently traced the line of my jaw. "I won't let anyone hurt you ever again. You have my word."

He thought he could protect me. He *wanted* to. He was touching me, and all I wanted was to let him. Let him protect me. Let him touch me. Let him—

Footsteps. The clattering above pushed me into taking a step back from him, and a few moments later, Xander and Nash climbed down into the room.

I managed to look at them—not Grayson "Where's Jameson?" I asked.

Xander cleared his throat. "I can report that some very colorful language was used when I requested his presence."

Nash snorted. "He'll be here."

We waited—five minutes, then ten.

"You might as well unlock yours," Xander told the others. "Your hands, if you please."

Grayson went first, then Nash. After the touch pads scanned their hands, we heard the telltale sound of deadbolts being thrown, one after the other.

"Three locks down," Xander murmured. "One to go."

Another five minutes. Eight. *He's not coming,* I thought.

"Jameson isn't coming," Grayson said, like he'd lifted the thought from my mind as easily as he'd guessed my number.

"He'll be here," Nash repeated.

"Don't I always do what I'm told?"

We looked up—and Jameson jumped. He landed between his brothers and me, going almost to the ground to absorb the shock. He straightened, then met their eyes, one at a time. *Nash. Xander. Grayson.*

Then, me. "You don't know when to stop, do you, Heiress?" That didn't exactly feel like an indictment.

"I'm tougher than I look," I told him. He stared at me for a moment longer, then turned to the door. He placed his hand flat on the pad that bore his initials. The last deadbolt was thrown, and the door was released. It creaked open—an inch, maybe two. I expected Jameson to reach for the door, but instead, he walked back to the opening and jumped, catching its sides with his hands.

"Where are you going?" I asked him. After everything it had taken to get to this point, he couldn't just walk away.

"To hell, eventually," Jameson answered. "Probably to the wine cellar, for now."

No. He couldn't just leave. He was the one who had dragged me into this, and he was going to see it through. I jumped to catch onto the opening overhead, to go after him. I felt my grip slipping. Strong hands grabbed me from beneath—*Grayson.* He pushed me upward, and I managed to climb out and to my feet.

"Don't leave," I told Jameson.

He was already walking away. When he heard my voice, he stopped but didn't turn back.

"I don't know what's on the other side of that door, Heiress, but I do know that the old man laid this trap for me."

"Just for you?" I said, an edge working its way into my voice. "That's why it required all four brothers' hands and my face to get this far?" Clearly, Tobias Hawthorne had meant for *all* of us to be here.

"He knew that any game he left, I would play. Nash might say screw it, Grayson might get bogged down in legalities, Xander might be thinking about a thousand and one other things—but *I would play.*" I could see him breathing—see him *hurting.* "So, yes, he meant this for me. Whatever is on the other side of that door..." Jameson drew in another ragged breath. "He knew. He knew what I did, and he wanted to make sure I never forgot."

"What did he know?" I asked.

Grayson appeared beside me and repeated my question. "The old man knew what, Jamie?"

Behind me, I could hear Nash and Xander climbing into the tunnel, but my mind barely registered their presence. I was focused—wholly, intensely—on Jameson and Grayson.

"Knew what, Jamie?"

Jameson turned back to face his brother. "What happened on ten-eighteen."

"It was my fault." Grayson strode forward, taking Jameson's shoulders in his hands. "I'm the one who took Emily there. I knew it was a bad idea, and I didn't care. I just wanted to win. I wanted her to love *me.*"

"I followed you that night." Jameson's statement hung in the air for several seconds. "I watched the two of you jump, Gray."

All of a sudden, I was back with Jameson, headed for the West Brook. He'd told me two lies and one truth. *I watched Emily Laughlin die.*

"You followed us?" Grayson couldn't make sense of that. "Why?"

"Masochism?" Jameson shrugged. "I was pissed." He paused. "Eventually, you ran off to get the towels, and I..."

"Jamie." Grayson dropped his hands to his sides. "What did you do?"

Grayson had told me that he'd left to get the towels, and when he'd gotten back, Emily was lying on the shore. *Dead.*

"What did you do?"

"She saw me." Jameson turned from his brother to look at me. "She saw me, and she smiled. She thought she'd won. She thought she still had me, but I turned and walked away. She called my name. I didn't stop. I heard her gasp. She was making this little strangling sound."

I brought my hand to my mouth in horror.

"I thought she was playing with me. I heard a splash, but I didn't turn around. I made it probably a hundred yards. She wasn't calling after me anymore. I glanced back." Jameson's voice broke. "Emily was hunched over, crawling out of the water. I thought she was *pretending.*"

He'd thought she was manipulating him.

"I just stood there," Jameson said dully. "I didn't do a damn thing to help her."

I watched Emily Laughlin die. I thought I was going to be sick. I could see him, standing there, trying to show her that he wasn't hers anymore, trying to resist.

"She collapsed. She went still, and she *stayed still.* And then you came back, Gray, and I left." Jameson shuddered. "I hated you for taking her there, but I hate myself more because I let her die. I stood there, and *I watched.*"

"It was her heart," I said. "What could you have—"

"I could have tried CPR. I could have done *something.*" Jameson swallowed. "But I didn't. I don't know how the old man knew, but he cornered me a few days later. He told me that he knew I'd been there and asked whether I felt culpable. He wanted me to tell you, Gray, and I wouldn't. I said that if he was so damn set on you knowing that I'd been there, he could tell you himself. But he didn't. Instead . . . he did this."

The letter. The library. The will. Their middle names. The date of my birth—and Emily's death. The numbers, scattered all over the estate. The stained glass, the riddle. The passage down into the tunnel. The grate marked M. E. The hidden room. The moving wall. The door.

"He wanted to make damn sure," Jameson said, "that I never forgot."

"No," Xander blurted out. The others turned to look at him. "That's not what this is," he swore. "He wasn't making a point. He wanted us—all four of us—together. Here."

Nash put a hand on Xander's shoulder. "The old man could be a real bastard, Xan."

"*That's not what this is,*" Xander said again, his voice more intense than I'd ever heard it—like he wasn't speculating. Like he *knew.*

Grayson, who hadn't said a word since Jameson's confession, spoke up now. "What precisely are you saying, Alexander?"

"The two of you were walking around like ghosts. You were a robot, Gray." Xander was speaking quickly now—almost too quickly for the rest of us to follow. "Jamie was a ticking time bomb. You hated each other."

"We hated ourselves more," Grayson said, his voice like sandpaper.

"The old man knew he was sick," Xander admitted. "He told me, right before he died. He asked me to do something for him."

Nash's eyes narrowed. "And what was that?"

Xander didn't answer. Grayson's eyes narrowed. "You had to make sure we played."

"It was my job to make sure you saw this to the end." Xander looked from Grayson to Jameson. "Both of you. If either of you stopped playing, it was my job to draw you back."

"You knew?" I said. "All this time, you knew where the clues led?"

Xander was the one who'd helped me find the tunnel. He was the one who'd solved the Black Wood. Even back at the very beginning…

He told me that his grandfather didn't have a middle name.

"You helped me," I said. He'd *manipulated* me. Moved me around, like a lure.

"I told you that I am a living, breathing Rube Goldberg machine." Xander looked down. "I warned you. Kind of." I thought of the moment he'd taken me to see the machine he'd built. I'd asked him what it had to do with Thea, and his response had been *Who said this had anything to do with Thea?*

I stared at Xander—the youngest, tallest, and arguably most brilliant Hawthorne. *Where you go,* he'd told me back at the gala, *they'll follow.* All this time, I'd thought that Jameson was the one who was using me. I'd thought that he'd kept me close for a reason.

It had never once occurred to me that Xander had his reasons, too.

"Do you know why your grandfather chose me?" I demanded. "Have you known the answer all this time?"

Xander held his hands up in front of his body, like he thought I might throttle him. "I only know what he wanted me to know. I have no idea what's on the other side of that door. I was only supposed to get Jamie and Gray here. *Together.*"

"All four of us," Nash corrected. "Together." I remembered what he'd said in the kitchen. *Sometimes you gotta excise a wound before it can heal.*

Was that what this was? Was that the old man's grand plan? Bring me here, spur them into action, hope that the game let the truth come out?

"Not just the four of us," Grayson told Nash. He looked back toward me. "Clearly, this was a game for five."

CHAPTER 87

We dropped back down into the room, one at a time. Jameson laid his hand flat against the door and pushed it inward. The cell beyond was empty, except for a small wooden box. On the box, there were letters—golden letters etched into golden tiles that looked like they'd come out of the world's most expensive game of Scrabble.

The letters on the box spelled out my name: AVERY KYLIE GRAMBS.

There were four blank tiles, one before my first name, one after my last, and two separating the names from each other. After everything that had just happened—Jameson's confession, then Xander's—it seemed wrong that this should come down to me.

Why me? This game might have been designed to bring Jameson and Grayson back together, to bring secrets to the surface, to bleed out poison before it turned to rot—but somehow, for some reason, it ended with me.

"Looks like it's your rodeo, kid." Nash nudged me to the box.

Swallowing, I knelt. I tried to open the box, but it was locked. There was no spot for a key, no combination pad.

Above me, Jameson spoke. "The letters, Heiress."

He just couldn't help himself. Even after everything, he couldn't stop playing the game.

I reached tentatively for the *A* in *Avery*. It came off the box. One by one, I peeled off the other letters and the blank tiles, and I realized *this* was the trigger for the lock. I stared at the pieces, nineteen of them total. *My name.* That clearly wasn't the combination to unlock the box. *So what is?*

Grayson dropped down beside me. He organized the letters, vowels first, consonants in alphabetical order.

"It's an anagram," Nash commented. "Rearrange the letters."

My gut response was that my name was just my name, not an anagram of anything, but my brain was already sifting through the possibilities.

Avery was easy to turn into words, two of them, just by adding the space that had been in front of the name to split it. I placed the tiles back on the top of the box, pushing each one into place with a click.

A very…

I put another space after *very*. That left two blank tiles and all the letters from my middle and last names.

Kylie Grambs, arranged according to Grayson's method, read: *A, E, I, B, G, K, L, M, R, S, Y.*

Big. Balm. Bale. I started pulling words out, seeing what each of them left me with, and then I saw it.

All at once, I saw it.

"You have got to be kidding me," I whispered.

"What?" Jameson was 100 percent in this now, whether he wanted to be or not. He knelt next to Grayson and me as I put the letters up, one by one.

Avery Kylie Grambs—the name I'd been given the day I was

born, the name that Tobias Hawthorne had programmed into the bowling alley and the pinball machine and who knew how many other places in the House—became, reordered, *A very risky gamble.*

"He kept saying that," Xander murmured. "That no matter what he planned, it might not work. That it was..."

"*A very risky gamble,*" Grayson finished, his gaze making its way to me.

My name? I tried to process that. *First my birthday, now my name.* Was that it? Was that *why*? How had Tobias Hawthorne even found me?

I snapped the last blank tile into place, and the box's lock disengaged. The lid popped open. Inside, there were five envelopes, one with each of our names.

I watched as the boys opened and read theirs. Nash swore under his breath. Grayson stared at his. Jameson let out a broken little laugh. Xander shoved his into his pocket.

I turned my attention from the four of them to my envelope. The last letter Tobias Hawthorne had sent to me had explained nothing. Opening this one, I expected clarity. *How did you find me? Why tell me you're sorry? What were you sorry for?*

There was no paper inside my envelope, no letter. The only thing it contained was a single packet of sugar.

CHAPTER 88

I place two sugar packets vertically on the table and bring their ends together, forming a triangle capable of standing on its own. "There," I say. I do the same with the next pair of packets, then set a fifth across them horizontal, connecting the two triangles I built.

"Avery Kylie Grambs!" My mom appears at the end of the table, smiling. "What have I told you about building castles out of sugar?"

I beam back at her. "It's only worth it if you can go five stories tall!"

In my dream, that was where the memory had ended, but this time, holding the sugar in my hand, my brain took me one step further. *A man eating in the booth behind me glances back. He asks me how old I am.*

"Six," I say.

"I have some grandsons at home who are just about your age," he says. "Tell me, Avery, can you spell your name? Your full name, like your mom said a minute ago?"

I can, and I do.

"I met him," I said quietly. "Just once, years ago—just for a moment, in passing." Tobias Hawthorne had heard my mom say my full name. He'd asked me to spell it.

"He loved anagrams more than scotch," Nash said. "And he was a man who *loved* a good scotch."

Had Tobias Hawthorne mentally rearranged the letters in my full name right in that moment? Had it amused him? I thought about Grayson, hiring someone to dig up dirt on me. On my mother. Had Tobias Hawthorne been curious about us? Had he done the same?

"He would have kept track of you," Grayson said roughly. "A little girl with a funny little name." He glanced at Jameson. "He must have known her date of birth."

"And after Emily died…" Jameson was looking at me now—only at me. "He thought of you."

"And decided to leave me his entire fortune because of *my name*?" I said. "That's insane."

"You're the one who said it, Heiress: He didn't disinherit us *for* you. We weren't getting the money anyway."

"It was going to charity," I argued. "And you're telling me that on a whim, he wiped out the will he'd had for twenty years? That's—"

"He needed something to get our attention," Grayson said. "Something so unexpected, so bewildering, that it could only be seen—"

"—as a puzzle," Jameson finished. "Something we couldn't ignore. Something to wake us up again. Something to bring us here—all four of us."

"Something to purge the poison." Nash's tone was hard to read.

They'd known the old man. I hadn't. What they were saying—it made sense to *them*. In their eyes, this hadn't been a whim. It had been a very risky gamble. *I* had been a very risky gamble. Tobias Hawthorne had bet that my presence in the House would shake things up, that old secrets would be laid bare, that somehow, someway, one last puzzle would change everything.

That, if Emily's death had torn them apart, I could bring them back together.

"I told you, kid," Nash said beside me. "You're not a player. You're the glass ballerina—or the knife."

CHAPTER 89

Oren met me the moment I stepped foot into the Great Room. That he'd been waiting made me wonder why he'd left my side in the first place. Had it really been a phone call—or had Tobias Hawthorne left him with instructions to let the five of us finish the game alone?

"Do you know what's down there?" I asked my head of security. He was more loyal to the old man than he was to me. *What else did he ask you to do?*

"Besides the tunnel?" Oren replied. "No." He made a study of me, of the boys. "Should I?"

I thought about what had happened down there while Xander was gone. About Rebecca and what she had told me down below. About Skye. I looked at Grayson. His eyes caught mine. There was a question there, and hope, and something else I couldn't name.

All I told Oren was "No."

That night, I sat at Tobias Hawthorne's desk, the one in my wing. In my hands, I held the letter he'd left me.

Dearest Avery,

I'm sorry.

—T. T. H.

I'd wondered what he was sorry for, but I was starting to think I'd had things reversed. Maybe he hadn't left me the money as an apology. Maybe he was apologizing for leaving me the money. *For using me.*

He'd brought me here for *them*.

I folded the letter in half and then in half again. This—all of it—had nothing to do with my mom. Whatever secrets she'd been keeping, they predated Emily's death. In the grand scheme of things, this entire life-changing, mind-blowing, headline-grabbing chain of events had nothing to do with *me*. I was just a little girl with a funny little name, born on the right day.

I have some grandsons at home, I could hear the old man telling me, *who are just about your age*.

"This was always about them." I said the words out loud. "What am I supposed to do now?" The game was over. The puzzle was solved. I'd served my purpose. And I'd never felt so insignificant in my life.

My eyes were drawn to the compass built into the desk's surface. As I had my first time in this office, I turned the compass, and the panel on the desk popped up, revealing the compartment underneath. I traced my finger lightly over the *T* etched into the wood.

And then I looked down at my letter—at Tobias Hawthorne's signature. *T. T. H.*

My gaze traveled back to the desk. Jameson had told me once that his grandfather had never purchased a desk without hidden compartments. Having played the game, having lived in Hawthorne House—I couldn't help seeing things differently now. I tested the wood panel on which the *T* had been etched.

Nothing.

Then I placed my fingers in the *T*, and I pushed. The wood gave. *Click*. And then it popped back up into place.

"*T*," I said out loud. And then I did the same thing again. Another *click*. "*T*." I stared at the panel for a long time before I saw it: a gap between the wood and the top of the desk, at the base of the *T*. I pushed my fingers underneath and found another groove—and above it a latch. I unhooked the latch, and the panel rotated counterclockwise.

With a ninety-degree turn, I was no longer looking at a *T*. I was looking at an *H*. I pressed all three bars of the *H* at the same time. *Click*. A motor of some kind was engaged, and the panel disappeared back into the desk, revealing another compartment underneath.

T. T. H. Tobias Hawthorne had intended for this to be my wing. He'd signed my letter with initials, not his name. And those initials had unlocked this drawer. Inside, there was a folder, much like the one that Grayson had shown me that day at the foundation. My name—my full name—was written across the top.

Avery Kylie Grambs.

Now that I'd seen the anagram, I couldn't unsee it. Unsure what I would find—or even what I was expecting—I lifted the folder out and opened it. The first thing I saw was a copy of my birth certificate. Tobias Hawthorne had highlighted my date of birth—and my father's signature. The date made sense. But the signature?

I have a secret, I could hear my mother saying. *About the day you were born.*

I had no idea what to make of that—any of it. I flipped to the next page and the next and the next. They were full of pictures, four or five a year, from the time I was six.

He would have kept track of you, I could hear Grayson saying. *A little girl with a funny little name.*

The number of pictures went up significantly after my sixteenth birthday. *After Emily died.* There were so many, like Tobias Hawthorne had sent someone to watch my every move. *You couldn't risk everything on a total stranger,* I thought. Technically, that was exactly what he'd done, but looking at these pictures, I was overwhelmed with the sense that Tobias Hawthorne had done his homework.

I wasn't just a name and a date to him.

There were shots of me running poker games in the parking lot and shots of me carrying way too many cups at once at the diner. There was a picture of me with Libby, where we were laughing, and one where I was standing with my body between hers and Drake's. There was a shot of me playing chess in the park and one of me and Harry in line for breakfast, where all you could see was the back of our heads. There was even one of me in my car, holding a stack of postcards in my hands.

The photographer had caught me dreaming.

Tobias Hawthorne hadn't known me—but he'd known *about* me. I might have been a very risky gamble. I might have been a part of the puzzle and not a player. But the billionaire had known that I could play. He hadn't entered into this blindly and hoped for the best. He'd plotted, and he'd planned, and I'd been a part of that calculation. Not just Avery Kylie Grambs, born on the day that Emily Laughlin had died—but the girl in these photos.

I thought about what Jameson had said, that first night when he'd stepped from the fireplace into my room. Tobias Hawthorne left me the fortune—and all he'd left them was *me*.

CHAPTER 90

Early the next morning, Oren informed me that Skye Hawthorne was leaving Hawthorne House. She was moving out, and Grayson had instructed security that she wasn't to be allowed back on the premises.

"Any idea why?" Oren gave me a look that strongly suggested that he knew that I knew something.

I looked at him, and I lied. "Not a clue."

I found Grayson in the hidden staircase, with the Davenport. "You kicked your mother out of the House?"

That wasn't what I'd expected him to do, when he'd won our little wager. For better or worse, Skye was his mother. *Family first.*

"Mother left of her own volition," Grayson said evenly. "She was made to understand it was the better option."

Better than being reported to the police.

"You won the bet," I told Grayson. "You didn't have to—"

He turned and took a step up so that he was standing on the same stair as me. "Yes, I did."

If I were choosing between you and any one of them, he'd told me, *I would choose them, always and every time.*

But he hadn't.

"Grayson." I was standing close to him, and the last time we'd stood together on these stairs, I'd bared my wounds—literally. This time, I found my hands rising to *his* chest. He was arrogant and awful and had spent the first week of our acquaintance dead set on making my life hell. He was still half in love with Emily Laughlin. But from the first moment I'd seen him, looking away had been nearly impossible.

And at the end of the day, he'd chosen me. *Over family. Over his mother.*

Hesitantly, I let my hand find its way from his chest to his jaw. For a single second, he let me touch him, and then he turned his head away.

"I will always protect you," he told me, his jaw tight, his eyes shadowed. "You deserve to feel safe in your own home. And I'll help you with the foundation. I'll teach you what you need to know to take to this life like you were born to it. But this . . . us . . ." He swallowed. "It can't happen, Avery. I've seen the way Jameson looks at you."

He didn't say that he wouldn't let another girl come between them. He didn't have to.

CHAPTER 91

I went to school, and when I came home, I called Max, knowing that she probably didn't even have her phone. My call got sent to voicemail. "This is Maxine Liu. I've been sequestered in the technological equivalent of a virtual convent. Have a blessed day, you rotten scoundrels."

I tried her brother's phone and got sent to voicemail again. "You have reached Isaac Liu." Max had commandeered *his* voicemail as well. "He is an entirely tolerable younger brother, and if you leave a message, he will probably call you back. Avery, if this is you, stop trying to get yourself killed. You owe me Australia!"

I didn't leave a message—but I did make plans to see what it would take for Alisa to send the entire Liu family first-class tickets to Australia. I couldn't travel until my time in Hawthorne House was up, but maybe Max could.

I owed her.

Feeling adrift and aching from what Grayson had said and the fact that Max wasn't there to process it with, I went looking for Libby. We seriously needed to get her a new phone, because a person could get lost in this place.

I didn't want to lose anyone else.

I might never have found her, but when I got close to the music room, I heard the piano playing. I followed the music and found Libby sitting on the piano bench beside Nan. They both sat with their eyes closed, listening.

Libby's black eye had finally faded away. Seeing her with Nan made me think about Libby's job back home. I couldn't ask her to just keep sitting around Hawthorne House every day, doing nothing.

I wondered what Nash Hawthorne would suggest. *I could ask her to put together a business plan. Maybe a food truck?*

Or maybe she would want to travel, too. Until the will exited probate, I was limited as to what I could do—but the fine people at McNamara, Ortega, and Jones had reason to want to stay on my good side. Eventually, the money would be mine. Eventually, it would exit the trust.

Eventually, I'd be one of the richest and most powerful women in the world.

The piano music ended, and my sister and Nan looked up and saw me. Libby did her best mother-hen impression.

"Are you sure you're okay?" she asked me. "You don't look okay."

I thought about Grayson. About Jameson. About what I'd been brought here to do. "I'm fine," I told Libby, my voice steady enough that I could almost believe it.

She wasn't fooled. "I'll make you something," she told me. "Have you ever had a quiche? I've never made a quiche."

I had no real desire to try one, but baking was Libby's way of showing love. She headed for the kitchen. I went to follow, but Nan stopped me.

"Stay," she ordered.

There was nothing to do but obey.

"I hear my granddaughter is leaving," Nan said tersely after letting me sweat it for a bit.

I considered dissembling, but she'd pretty much proven she wasn't the type for niceties. "She tried to have me killed."

Nan snorted. "Skye never did like getting her hands dirty herself. You ask me, if you're going to kill someone, you should at least have the decency to do it yourself and do it right."

This was probably the strangest conversation I'd ever had in my life—and that was saying something.

"Not that people are decent nowadays," Nan continued. "No respect. No self-respect. No grit." She sighed. "If my poor Alice could see her children now...."

I wondered what it had been like for Skye and Zara, growing up in Hawthorne House. What it had been like for Toby.

What twisted them into this?

"Your son-in-law changed his will after Toby died." I studied Nan's expression, wondering if she'd known.

"Toby was a good boy," Nan said gruffly. "Until he wasn't."

I wasn't sure quite what to make of that.

Her hands went to a locket around her neck. "He was the sweetest child, smart as a whip. Just like his daddy, they used to say, but oh, that boy had a dose of me."

"What happened?" I asked.

Nan's expression darkened. "It broke my Alice's heart. Broke all of us, really." Her fingers tightened around the locket, and her hand shook. She set her jaw, then opened the locket. "Look at him," she told me. "Look at that sweet boy. He's sixteen here."

I leaned down to get a better look, wondering if Tobias Hawthorne the Second had resembled any of his nephews. What I saw took my breath away.

No.

"That's Toby?" I couldn't breathe. I couldn't think.

"He was a good boy," Nan said gruffly.

I barely heard her. I couldn't tear my eyes away from the picture. I couldn't speak, because I knew that man. He was younger in the picture—much younger—but that face was unmistakable.

"Heiress?" A voice spoke up from the doorway. I looked to see Jameson standing there. He looked different than he had the past few days. Lighter, somehow. Marginally less angry. Capable of offering a lopsided little half smile to me. "What's got your pants in a twist?"

I looked back down at the locket and sucked in a breath that scalded my lungs. "Toby," I managed. "I know him."

"You what?" Jameson walked toward me. Beside me, Nan went very still.

"I used to play chess with him in the park," I said. "Every morning." *Harry.*

"That's impossible," Nan said, her voice shaking. "Toby's been dead for twenty years."

Twenty years ago, Tobias Hawthorne had disinherited his family. *What is this? What the hell is going on here?*

"Are you sure, Heiress?" Jameson was right beside me now. *I've seen the way Jameson looks at you,* Grayson had said. "Are you absolutely certain?"

I looked at Jameson. This didn't feel real. *I have a secret,* I could hear my mother telling me, *about the day you were born....*

I reached for Jameson's hand and squeezed hard. "I'm sure."

EPILOGUE

Xander Hawthorne stared down at the letter, the way he had every day for a week. On the surface, it said very little.

Alexander,

Well done.

Tobias Hawthorne

Well done. He'd gotten his brothers to the end of the game. He'd gotten Avery there, too. He'd done exactly as he'd promised—but the old man had made him a promise, too.

When their game is done, yours will begin.

Xander had never competed the way his brothers did—but oh, how he'd wanted to. He hadn't been lying when he'd told Avery that, just once, he wanted to win. When they'd made it to the final room, when she'd opened the box, when he'd torn open his envelope, he'd been expecting...*something.*

A riddle.

A puzzle.

A clue.

And all he'd received was this. *Well done.*

"Xander?" Rebecca said softly beside him. "What are we doing here?"

"Sighing melodramatically," Thea sniped. "Obviously."

That he'd gotten both of them here, in the same room, was a feat. He wasn't even sure why he'd done it, other than the fact that he needed a witness. *Witnesses.* If Xander was being honest with himself, he'd brought Rebecca because he wanted her there, and he'd brought Thea because if he hadn't...

He would have been alone with Rebecca.

"There are many types of invisible ink," Xander told them. In the past few days, he had held a match to the back of the page, heating its surface. He'd bought a UV light and gone to town. He'd tried every way he knew of unmasking a hidden message on a page, except for one. "But there's only one kind," he continued evenly, "that destroys the message after it's revealed."

If he was wrong about this, it was over. There would be no game, no winning. Xander didn't want to do this alone.

"What exactly do you think you're going to find?" Thea asked him.

Xander looked down at the letter one last time.

Alexander,

Well done.

Tobias Hawthorne

Perhaps the old man's promise had been a lie. Perhaps, to Tobias Hawthorne, Xander had only been an afterthought. But he had to try. He turned to the tub beside him. He filled it with water.

"Xander?" Rebecca said again, and her voice nearly undid him.

"Here goes nothing." Xander laid his letter gingerly on the surface of the water, then pressed down.

At first, he thought he'd made a horrible mistake. He thought nothing was happening. Then, slowly, writing appeared, on either side of his grandfather's signature. *Tobias Hawthorne*, he'd signed it, *no middle name*, and now the reason for that omission was clear.

The invisible ink darkened on the page. To the right of the signature, there were only two letters, equating to one Roman numeral: *II*. And to the left, there was a single word: *Find*.

Find Tobias Hawthorne II.

ACKNOWLEDGMENTS

Writing this book was a challenge and a joy, and I am so thankful to the incredible teams (plural!) that have supported me through every step of the process. I worked with two fantastic editors on this project. I am so grateful to Kieran Viola for recognizing that *this* was absolutely the book I needed to write next and for helping me bring Avery, the Hawthorne brothers, and their world to life. Lisa Yoskowitz then guided the book to publication, and her passion and vision for this project, along with her market savvy and grace, have made the process a dream. Any author would be lucky to work with either one of these editors; I am incredibly blessed to have gotten to work with both!

Huge thanks go out to the entire team at Little, Brown Books for Young Readers, especially Janelle DeLuise, Jackie Engel, Marisa Finkelstein, Shawn Foster, Bill Grace, Savannah Kennelly, Hannah Koerner, Christie Michel, Hannah Milton, Emilie Polster, Victoria Stapleton, and Megan Tingley. Special thanks go out to my publicist, Alex Kelleher-Nagorski, whose enthusiasm for this project has made my day more than once; to Michelle Campbell, for her incredible outreach to librarians and teachers; and to Karina Granda, for her work on the most beautiful cover I have ever seen! I am also in awe of and indebted to artist Katt Phatt, who created the incredible artwork on the cover. Thank you to Anthea Townsend, Phoebe Williams, and the entire team at Penguin Random House UK for their passion for and work on this project, and the team at Disney • Hyperion, who saw the potential in this book in 2018, when it was just a four-page proposal.

Elizabeth Harding has been my agent since I was in college, and I could not ask for a wiser, more incredible advocate! To my entire team at Curtis Brown—thank you, thank you, thank you. Holly Frederick championed TV rights for this book. Sarah Perillo did incredible work on foreign rights (in the midst of a pandemic, no less!). Thank you also to Nicole Eisenbraun, Sarah Gerton, Maddie Tavis, and Jazmia Young. I appreciate you all so much!

I'm immensely grateful for the family and friends who saw me through the writing of this project. Rachel Vincent sat across from me at Panera once a week, told me that I could do this, was always available for brainstorming, and made me smile even when I was stressed enough to want to cry. Ally Carter is always there through the highs and lows of publishing. My colleagues and students at the University of Oklahoma have been supportive in so many ways. Thank you, all!

Finally, thank you to my parents and husband, for endless support, and to my kids, for letting me get enough sleep to write this book.

TURN THE PAGE FOR A SNEAK PEEK AT
THE THRILLING SEQUEL TO
THE INHERITANCE GAMES

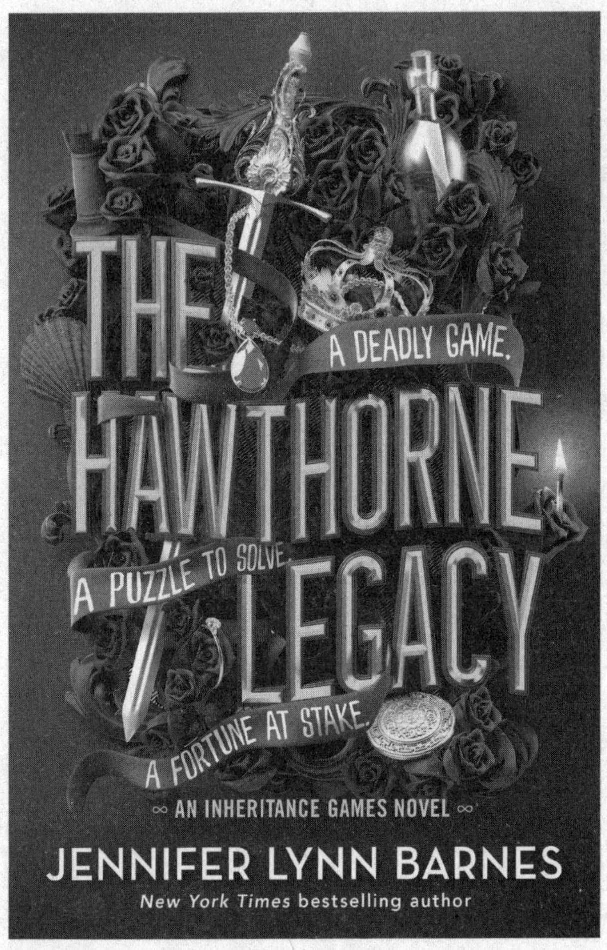

CHAPTER 1

"Tell me again about the first time the two of you played chess in the park." Jameson's face was candlelit, but even in the scant light, I could see the gleam in his dark green eyes.

There was nothing—and no one—that set Jameson Hawthorne's blood pumping like a mystery.

"It was right after my mother's funeral," I said. "A few days, maybe a week."

The two of us were in the tunnels beneath Hawthorne House—alone, where no one else could hear us. It had been less than a month since I'd first stepped into the palatial Texas mansion and a week since we'd solved the mystery of why I'd been brought there.

If we'd truly solved that mystery.

"My mom and I used to go for walks in the park." I shut my eyes so that I could concentrate on the facts and not the intensity with which Jameson locked on to my every word. "She called it the Strolling Aimlessly Game." I steeled myself against the memory, letting my eyelids open. "A few days after her funeral, I went to the park without her for the first time. When I got near the pond, I saw a crowd gathered. A man was lying on the sidewalk, eyes closed, covered in tattered blankets."

"Homeless." Jameson had heard all of this before, but his laser focus on me never wavered.

"People thought he was dead—or passed out drunk. Then he sat up. I saw a police officer making his way through the crowd."

"But you got to the man first," Jameson finished, his eyes on mine, his lips crooking upward. "And you asked him to play chess."

I hadn't expected Harry to take me up on the offer, let alone win.

"We played every week after that," I said. "Sometimes twice a week, three times. He never told me more than his name."

His name wasn't really Harry. He lied. And that was why I was in these tunnels with Jameson Hawthorne. That was why he'd started looking at me like I was a mystery again, a puzzle that he, and only he, could solve.

It couldn't be a coincidence that billionaire Tobias Hawthorne had left his fortune to a stranger who knew his "dead" son.

"You're sure that it was Toby?" Jameson asked, the air between us charged.

These days, I was sure of little else. Three weeks earlier, I'd been a normal girl, scraping by, desperately trying to survive high school, get a scholarship, and get out. Then out of the blue, I'd received word that one of the richest men in the country had died and named me in his will. Tobias Hawthorne had left me billions, very nearly his entire fortune—and I'd had no idea why. Jameson and I had spent two weeks unraveling the puzzles and clues the old man had left behind. *Why me?* Because of my name. Because of the day I was born. Because Tobias Hawthorne had bet everything on the long shot that somehow I could bring his splintered family back together.

Or at least that was what the conclusion to the old man's last game had led us to believe.

"I'm sure," I told Jameson fiercely. "Toby's alive. And if your grandfather knew that—and I know that's a big *if*—but if he did know, then we have to assume that either he chose me because I knew Toby, or he somehow masterminded bringing us together in the first place."

If there was one thing I'd learned about deceased billionaire Tobias Hawthorne, it was that he was capable of orchestrating nearly anything, manipulating nearly anyone. He'd loved puzzles and riddles and games.

Just like Jameson.

"What if that day in the park wasn't the first time you met my uncle?" Jameson took a step toward me, an unholy energy rolling off him. "Think about it, Heiress. You said that the one time my grandfather met you, you were six years old, and he saw you in the diner where your mother was a waitress. He heard your full name."

Avery Kylie Grambs, rearranged, became A Very Risky Gamble. The kind of name a man like Tobias Hawthorne would remember.

"That's right," I said. Jameson was close to me now. Too close. Every one of the Hawthorne boys was magnetic. Larger than life. They had an effect on people—and Jameson was very good at using that to get what he wanted. *He wants something from me now.*

"Why was my grandfather, a Texas billionaire with a whole host of private chefs on call, eating at a hole-in-the-wall diner in a small Connecticut town that no one's ever heard of?"

My mind raced. "You think he was looking for something?"

Jameson smiled deviously. "Or someone. What if the old man went there looking for Toby and found *you*?"

There was something about the way he said the word *you*. Like I was someone. Like I mattered. But Jameson and I had been down that road before. "And everything else is a distraction?" I asked, looking away from him. "My name. The fact that Emily died on my birthday. The puzzle your grandfather left us—it was all just a lie?"

Jameson didn't react to the sound of Emily's name. In the throes of a mystery, nothing could distract him—not even her. "A lie," Jameson repeated. "Or misdirection."

He reached to brush a strand of hair out of my face, and every nerve in my body went on high alert. I jerked back. "Stop looking at me like that," I told him sternly.

"Like what?" he countered.

I folded my arms and stared him down. "You turn on the charm when you want something."

"Heiress, you wound me." Jameson looked better smirking than anyone had a right to look. "All I want is for you to rifle through your memory banks a little. My grandfather was a person who thought in four dimensions. He might have had more than one reason for choosing you. Why kill two birds with one stone, he always said, when you could kill twelve?"

There was something about his voice, about the way he was still looking at me, that would have made it easy to get caught up in it all. The possibilities. The mystery. *Him.*

But I wasn't the kind of person who made the same mistake twice. "Maybe you've got it wrong." I turned away from him. "What if your grandfather didn't know that Toby was alive? What if *Toby* was the one who realized that the old man was watching me? Considering leaving the entire fortune to me?"

Harry, as I'd known him, had been one hell of a chess player. Maybe that day in the park wasn't a coincidence. Maybe he'd sought me out.

"We're missing something," Jameson said, coming up to stand close behind me. "Or maybe," he murmured, directly into the back of my head, "you're holding something back."

He wasn't entirely wrong. I wasn't built to lay all my cards on the table—and Jameson Winchester Hawthorne didn't even pretend to be trustworthy.

"I see how it is, Heiress." I could practically *hear* his crooked little grin. "If that's how you want to play it, why don't we make this interesting?"

I turned back to face him. Eye to eye, it was hard not to remember that when Jameson kissed a girl, it wasn't tentative. It wasn't gentle. *It wasn't real*, I reminded myself. I'd been a part of the puzzle to him, a tool to be used. I was still a part of the puzzle.

"Not everything is a game," I said.

"And maybe," Jameson countered, eyes alight, "that's the problem. Maybe that's why we're spinning our wheels in these tunnels day after day, rehashing this and getting nowhere. Because this isn't a game. *Yet.* A game has rules. A game has a winner. Maybe, Heiress, what you and I need to solve the mystery of Toby Hawthorne is a little motivation."

"What kind of motivation?" I narrowed my eyes at him.

"How about a wager?" Jameson arched an eyebrow. "If I figure all of this out first, then you have to forgive and forget my little lapse of judgment after we decoded the Black Wood."

The Black Wood was where we'd figured out that his dead ex-girlfriend had died on my birthday. That was the moment when it had first become clear that Tobias Hawthorne hadn't chosen me because I was special. He'd chosen me for what it would do to them.

Immediately afterward, Jameson had dropped me cold.

"And if I win," I countered, staring into those green eyes of his, "then you have to forget that we ever kissed—and never try to charm me into kissing you again."

I didn't trust him, but I also didn't trust myself with him.

"Well then, Heiress." Jameson stepped forward. Standing directly to my side, he brought his lips down to my ear and whispered, "Game on."

CHAPTER 2

Our wager struck, Jameson took off in one direction in the tunnels, and I went in another. Hawthorne House was massive, sprawling, big enough that, even after three weeks, I still hadn't seen it all. A person could spend years exploring this place and still not know all the ins and outs, all the secret passageways and hidden compartments—and that wasn't even counting the underground tunnels.

Lucky for me, I was a quick learner. I cut from underneath the gymnasium wing to a tunnel that went below the music room. I passed beneath the solarium, then climbed a hidden staircase into the Great Room, where I found Nash Hawthorne leaning casually against a stone fireplace. Waiting.

"Hey, kid." Nash didn't bat an eye at the fact that I'd just appeared seemingly out of nowhere. In fact, the oldest Hawthorne brother gave the impression that the whole mansion could come crashing down around him and he'd just keep leaning against that fireplace. Nash Hawthorne would probably tip his cowboy hat to Death herself.

"Hey," I replied.

"I don't suppose you've seen Grayson?" Nash asked, his Texas drawl making the question sound almost lazy.

That did nothing to soften the impact of what he'd just said. "Nope." I kept my answer short and my face blank. Grayson Hawthorne and I had been keeping our distance.

"And I don't suppose you know anything about a chat Gray had with our mother, right before she moved out?"

Skye Hawthorne, Tobias Hawthorne's younger daughter and the mother of all four Hawthorne grandsons, had tried to have me killed. The person who'd actually pulled the trigger was the one in a jail cell, but Skye had been forced to leave Hawthorne House. By Grayson. *I will always protect you*, he'd told me. *But this... us... It can't happen, Avery.*

"No clue," I said flatly.

"Didn't think so." Nash gave me a little wink. "Your sister and your lawyer are looking for you. East Wing." That was a loaded statement if I'd ever heard one. My lawyer was his ex-fiancée, and my sister was...

I didn't know what Libby and Nash Hawthorne were.

"Thanks," I told him, but when I made my way up the winding staircase to the East Wing of Hawthorne House, I didn't go looking for Libby. Or Alisa. I'd made a bet with Jameson, and I intended to win. First stop: Tobias Hawthorne's office.

In the office, there was a mahogany desk, and behind the desk was a wall of trophies and patents and books with the name *Hawthorne* on the spine—a breathtaking visual reminder that there was nothing ordinary whatsoever about the Hawthorne brothers. They had been given every opportunity, and the old man had expected them to be extraordinary. But I hadn't come here to gawk at trophies.

Instead, I took a seat behind the desk and released the hidden compartment I'd discovered not long ago. It held a folder. Inside the folder, there were pictures of me. Countless photographs, stretching back years. After that fateful meeting in the diner, Tobias Hawthorne had kept tabs on me. *All because of my name? Or did he have another motive?*

I thumbed through the photos and pulled out two. Jameson had been right, back in the tunnels. I was holding out on him. I'd been photographed with Toby twice, but both times, all the photographer had captured of the man beside me was the back of his head.

Had Tobias Hawthorne recognized Toby from behind? Had "Harry" realized we were being photographed and turned his head away from the camera on purpose?

As far as clues went, this wasn't much to go on. All the file really proved was that Tobias Hawthorne had been keeping tabs on me for years before "Harry" had shown up. I thumbed past the photographs to a copy of my birth certificate. My mother's signature was neat, my father's an odd mix of cursive and print. Tobias Hawthorne had highlighted my father's signature, as well as my date of birth.

10/18. I knew the significance there. Both Grayson and Jameson had loved a girl named Emily Laughlin. Her death—on October 18—had torn them apart. Somehow, the old man had intended for me to bring them back together. But why would Tobias Hawthorne have highlighted my father's signature? Ricky Grambs was a deadbeat. He hadn't even cared enough to pick up the phone when my mother died. If it had been left up to him, I would have gone into foster care. Staring at Ricky's signature, I willed Tobias Hawthorne's reasoning in highlighting it to become clear.

Nothing.

In the back of my mind, I heard my mother's voice. *I have a secret*, she'd told me, long before Tobias Hawthorne had written me into his will, *about the day you were born*.

Whatever she'd been referring to, I was never going to guess it now that she was gone. The one thing I knew for certain was that I wasn't a Hawthorne. If my father's name on that birth certificate weren't proof enough, a DNA test had already confirmed that I had no Hawthorne blood.

Why did Toby seek me out? Did *he seek me out?* I thought about what Jameson had said about his grandfather killing twelve birds with one stone. Going back through the folder again, I tried to find some shred of meaning. What wasn't I seeing? There had to be *something*—

A rap at the door was the only warning I got before the doorknob began to twist. Moving quickly, I gathered the photographs and slipped the file back into the hidden compartment.

"There you are." Alisa Ortega, attorney-at-law, was a model of professionalism. She arched her brows into what I had mentally termed the Alisa Look. "Would I be correct in assuming you've forgotten about the game?"

"The game," I repeated, unsure *which* game she was talking about. I felt like I'd been playing since the moment I'd first stepped through the door of Hawthorne House.

"The football game," Alisa clarified, with another Alisa Look. "Part two of your debut into Texas society. With Skye's exit from Hawthorne House, appearances are more important than ever. We need to control the narrative. This is a Cinderella story, not a scandal—and that means that *you* need to play Cinderella. In public. As frequently and convincingly as possible, starting with making use of your owner's box tonight."

Owner's box. That clicked. "The game," I repeated again, comprehension dawning. "As in, an NFL game. Because I own a football team."

That was still so absolutely mind-blowing that I almost succeeded in distracting myself from the other part of what Alisa had said—the bit about Skye. Per the deal I'd struck with Grayson, I couldn't tell anyone about his mother's part in my attempted murder. In exchange, he'd handled it.

Just like he'd promised he would.

"There are forty-eight seats in the owner's suite," Alisa said, going into lecture mode. "A general seat map is created months in advance. VIPs only. This isn't just football; it's a way of buying a seat at a dozen different tables. Invites are highly sought after by just about everyone—politicians, celebrities, CEOs. I've had Oren vet everyone on the list for tonight, and we'll have a professional photographer on hand for some strategic photo opportunities. Landon has crafted a press release that will go out an hour before the game. All that's left to worry about is..."

Alisa trailed off delicately.

I snorted. "Me?"

"This is a Cinderella story," Alisa reminded me. "What do you think Cinderella would wear to her first NFL game?"

That had to be a trick question.

"Something like this?" Libby popped into the doorway. She was wearing a Lone Stars jersey with a matching scarf, matching gloves, and matching boots. Her blue hair was tied into pigtails with a thick bunch of blue and gold ribbons.

Alisa forced a smile. "Yes," she told me. "Something like that—minus the black lipstick, the black nail polish, and the choker." Libby was pretty much the world's most cheerful goth, and Alisa was not a fan of my sister's sense of fashion. "As I was saying," Alisa continued emphatically, "tonight is important. While Avery plays Cinderella for the cameras, I'll circulate among our guests and get a better sense of where they stand."

"Where they stand on what?" I asked. I'd been told again and again that Tobias Hawthorne's will was ironclad. As far as I knew, the Hawthorne family had given up on trying to challenge it.

"It never hurts to have a few extra power players in your corner," Alisa said. "And we want our allies breathing easy."

"Hope I'm not interrupting." Nash acted like he'd just happened upon the three of us—like he wasn't the one who'd warned me that Alisa and Libby were looking for me. "Go on, Lee-Lee," he told my lawyer. "You were sayin' something about breathing easy?"

"We need people to know that Avery isn't here to shake things up." Alisa avoided looking directly at Nash, like a person avoiding looking into the sun. "Your grandfather had investments, business partners, political relationships—these things require a careful balance."

"What she means when she says that," Nash told me, "is that she needs people to think that McNamara, Ortega, and Jones has the situation entirely under control."

The situation? I thought. *Or me?* I didn't relish the idea of being anyone's puppet. In theory, at least, the firm was supposed to work for me.

That gave me an idea. "Alisa? Do you remember when I asked you to get money to a friend of mine?"

"Harry, wasn't it?" Alisa replied, but I got the distinct feeling that her attention was divided three ways: between my question, her grand plans for the night, and the way Nash's lips ticked upward on the ends when he saw Libby's outfit.

The last thing I needed my lawyer focused on was the way that her ex was looking at my sister. "Yes. Were you able to get the money to him?" I asked. The simplest way to get answers would be to track down Toby—before Jameson did.

Alisa tore her eyes away from Libby and Nash. "Unfortunately," she said briskly, "my people have been unable to find a trace of your Harry."

I rolled the implication of that over in my mind. Toby Hawthorne had appeared in the park days after my mother's death, and less than a month after I left, he was gone.

"Now," Alisa said, clasping her hands in front of her body, "about your wardrobe…"

CHAPTER 3

I had never seen a game of football in my life, but as the new owner of the Texas Lone Stars, I couldn't exactly say that to the crowd of reporters who mobbed the SUV when we pulled up to the stadium, any more than I could have admitted that the off-the-shoulder jersey and metallic-blue cowboy boots I was wearing felt about as authentic as a Halloween costume.

"Lower the window," Alisa told me, "smile, and yell, 'Go, Lone Stars!'"

I didn't want to lower the window. I didn't want to smile. I didn't want to yell anything—but I did it. Because this was a Cinderella story, and I was the star.

"Avery!"

"Avery, look over here!"

"How are you feeling about your first game as the new owner?"

"Do you have any comments about reports that you assaulted Skye Hawthorne?"

I hadn't had much media training, but I'd had enough to know the cardinal rule of having reporters shout questions at you rapid-fire: Don't answer. Pretty much the only thing I was allowed to say was that I was excited, grateful, awed, and overwhelmed in the *most incredible* possible way.

So I did my best to channel excitement, gratitude, and awe. Nearly a hundred thousand people would attend the game tonight. Millions would watch it around the world, cheering for the team. *My* team.

"Go, Lone Stars!" I yelled. I went to roll up my window, but just as my finger brushed the button, a figure pulled away from the crowd. Not a reporter.

My father.

Ricky Grambs had spent a lifetime treating me like an afterthought, if that. I hadn't seen him in more than a year. But now that I'd inherited billions?

There he was.

Turning away from him—and the paparazzi—I rolled my window up.

"Ave?" Libby's voice was hesitant as our bulletproof SUV disappeared into a private parking garage beneath the stadium. My sister was an optimist. She believed the best of people—including a man who'd never done a damn thing for either one of us.

"Did you know he'd be here?" I asked her, my voice low.

"No!" Libby said. "I swear!" She caught her bottom lip between her teeth, smudging her black lipstick. "But he just wants to talk."

I bet he does.

Up in the driver's seat, Oren, my head of security, parked the SUV and spoke calmly into his earpiece. "We have a situation near the north entrance. Eyes only, but I want a full report."

The nice thing about being a billionaire with a security team brimming with retired Special Forces was that the chances of my being ambushed again were next to none. I shoved down the feelings that seeing Ricky had dredged up and stepped out of the car into the bowels of one of the biggest stadiums in the world. "Let's do this," I said.

"For the record," Alisa told me as she exited the car, "the firm is more than capable of handling your father."

And *that* was the nice thing about being the sole client of a multi-billion-dollar law firm.

"Are you okay?" Alisa pressed. She wasn't exactly the touchy-feely type. More likely she was trying to assess whether I would be a liability tonight.

"I'm fine," I said.

"Why wouldn't she be?"

That voice—low and smooth—came from an elevator behind me. For the first time in seven days, I turned to look directly at Grayson Hawthorne. He had pale hair and ice-gray eyes and cheekbones sharp enough to count as weapons. Two weeks ago, I would have said that he was the most self-assured, self-righteous, arrogant jerk I'd ever met.

I wasn't sure what to say about Grayson Hawthorne now.

"Why," he repeated crisply, stepping out of the elevator, "would Avery be anything other than fine?"

"Deadbeat dad made an appearance outside," I muttered. "It's fine."

Grayson stared at me, his eyes piercing mine, then turned to Oren. "Is he a threat?"

I'll always protect you, he'd sworn. *But this*... *us*... *It can't happen, Avery.*

"I don't need you to protect me," I told Grayson sharply. "When it comes to Ricky, I'm an expert at protecting myself." I stalked past Grayson, into the elevator he'd stepped out of a moment earlier.

The trick to being abandoned was to never let yourself long for anyone who left.

A minute later, when the elevator doors opened into the owner's suite, I stepped out, Alisa to one side and Oren to the other, and I didn't so much as look back at Grayson. Since he'd taken the elevator down to meet me, he'd obviously already been up here, probably schmoozing. Without me.

"Avery. You made it." Zara Hawthorne-Calligaris wore a string of delicate pearls around her neck. There was something about her sharp-edged smile that made me feel like she could probably kill a man with those pearls if she were so inclined. "I wasn't sure you would be putting in an appearance tonight."

And you were ready to hold court in my absence, I concluded. I thought about what Alisa had said—about allies and power players and the influence that could be bought with a ticket to this suite.

As Jameson would say, *Game on*.

Kim Haynes Photography

JENNIFER LYNN BARNES

is the *New York Times* bestselling author of more than twenty acclaimed young-adult novels, including *Little White Lies*, *Deadly Little Scandals*, *The Lovely and the Lost*, and The Naturals series: *The Naturals*, *Killer Instinct*, *All In*, *Bad Blood*, and the e-novella *Twelve*. Jen is also a Fulbright Scholar with advanced degrees in psychology, psychiatry, and cognitive science. She received her PhD from Yale University in 2012 and is currently a professor of psychology and professional writing at the University of Oklahoma. You can find her online at jenniferlynnbarnes.com or follow her on Twitter @jenlynnbarnes.

MORE FROM JENNIFER LYNN BARNES

THE NATURALS

DEBUTANTES

A MYSTERY

THE INHERITANCE GAMES

THE HAWTHORNE LEGACY

∞ AN INHERITANCE GAMES NOVEL ∞

#1 *New York Times* bestselling author

JENNIFER LYNN BARNES

Little, Brown and Company

New York Boston

Little, Brown and Company
Hachette Book Group
1290 Avenue of the Americas, New York, NY 10104
Visit us at LBYR.com

Originally published in hardcover and ebook by Little, Brown and Company in September 2021
First Trade Paperback Edition: August 2022

The Library of Congress has cataloged the hardcover edition as follows:
Names: Barnes, Jennifer (Jennifer Lynn), author.
Title: The Hawthorne legacy / Jennifer Lynn Barnes.
Description: First edition. | New York : Little, Brown and Company, 2021. | Series: An inheritance games novel | Audience: Ages 12 & up. | Summary: Rumors spread that Tobias Hawthorne's lost son may still be alive, casting doubt on seventeen-year-old Avery's inheritance and changing the rules of the game.
Identifiers: LCCN 2020048435 | ISBN 9780759557635 (hardcover) | ISBN 9780759557642 (ebook) | ISBN 9780759557659 (ebook other)
Subjects: CYAC: Inheritance and succession—Fiction. | Wealth—Fiction. | Puzzles—Fiction. | Missing persons—Fiction. | Secrets—Fiction.
Classification: LCC PZ7.B26225 Haw 2021 | DDC [Fic]—dc23
LC record available at https://lccn.loc.gov/2020048435

ISBNs: 978-0-316-10518-7 (pbk.), 978-0-7595-5764-2 (ebook)

Printed in the United States of America

LSC-C

Printing 5, 2023

PRAISE FOR

THE INHERITANCE GAMES

A *New York Times* and IndieBound Bestseller
A Goodreads Choice Awards Finalist
An Edgar Award Nominee for Best Young Adult Mystery
A *Kirkus Reviews* Best Young Adult Book of the Year
A *Publishers Weekly* Best Book of the Year
A New York Public Library Best Book for Teens
A YALSA Teens' Top Ten Winner
A YALSA Best Fiction for Young Adults Book

"Barnes is a master of puzzles and plot twists. *The Inheritance Games* was the most fun I've had all year." —E. Lockhart, #1 *New York Times* bestselling author of *We Were Liars* and *Again Again*

"A thrilling blend of family secrets, illicit romance, and a high-stakes treasure hunt, set in the mysterious world of Texas billionaires. The nonstop twists kept me guessing until the very last page!" —Katharine McGee, *New York Times* bestselling author of *American Royals*

"Impossible to put down." —Buzzfeed

★ "Part *The Westing Game*, part *We Were Liars*, completely entertaining." —*Kirkus Reviews*, starred review

★ "This strong, *Knives Out*–esque series opener . . . provides ample enjoyment." —*Publishers Weekly*, starred review

"Perfect for any reader seeking suspense, romance, and glamour. . . . Fun and fast-paced, fans of Karen M. McManus's *One of Us Is Lying* and Maureen Johnson's *Truly Devious* will find a new home at Hawthorne House." —*SLJ*

"[A] well-characterized mystery that's packed to the brim with twists and tricks." —*Booklist*

ALSO BY JENNIFER LYNN BARNES

THE INHERITANCE GAMES

The Inheritance Games

The Hawthorne Legacy

The Final Gambit

THE NATURALS

The Naturals

Killer Instinct

All In

Bad Blood

Twelve: An E-novella

THE DEBUTANTES

Little White Lies

Deadly Little Scandals

The Lovely and the Lost

For Charlie

THE HAWTHORNE LEGACY

A DEADLY GAME.

A PUZZLE TO SOLVE.

A FORTUNE AT STAKE.

CHAPTER 1

"Tell me again about the first time the two of you played chess in the park." Jameson's face was candlelit, but even in the scant light, I could see the gleam in his dark green eyes.

There was nothing—and no one—that set Jameson Hawthorne's blood pumping like a mystery.

"It was right after my mother's funeral," I said. "A few days, maybe a week."

The two of us were in the tunnels beneath Hawthorne House—alone, where no one else could hear us. It had been less than a month since I'd first stepped into the palatial Texas mansion and a week since we'd solved the mystery of why I'd been brought there.

If we'd truly solved that mystery.

"My mom and I used to go for walks in the park." I shut my eyes so that I could concentrate on the facts and not the intensity with which Jameson locked on to my every word. "She called it the Strolling Aimlessly Game." I steeled myself against the memory, letting my eyelids open. "A few days after her funeral, I went to the park without her for the first time. When I got near the pond, I saw a crowd gathered. A man was lying on the sidewalk, eyes closed, covered in tattered blankets."

"Homeless." Jameson had heard all of this before, but his laser focus on me never wavered.

"People thought he was dead—or passed out drunk. Then he sat up. I saw a police officer making his way through the crowd."

"But you got to the man first," Jameson finished, his eyes on mine, his lips crooking upward. "And you asked him to play chess."

I hadn't expected Harry to take me up on the offer, let alone win.

"We played every week after that," I said. "Sometimes twice a week, three times. He never told me more than his name."

His name wasn't really Harry. He lied. And that was why I was in these tunnels with Jameson Hawthorne. That was why he'd started looking at me like I was a mystery again, a puzzle that he, and only he, could solve.

It couldn't be a coincidence that billionaire Tobias Hawthorne had left his fortune to a stranger who knew his "dead" son.

"You're sure that it was Toby?" Jameson asked, the air between us charged.

These days, I was sure of little else. Three weeks earlier, I'd been a normal girl, scraping by, desperately trying to survive high school, get a scholarship, and get out. Then out of the blue, I'd received word that one of the richest men in the country had died and named me in his will. Tobias Hawthorne had left me billions, very nearly his entire fortune—and I'd had no idea why. Jameson and I had spent two weeks unraveling the puzzles and clues the old man had left behind. *Why me?* Because of my name. Because of the day I was born. Because Tobias Hawthorne had bet everything on the long shot that somehow I could bring his splintered family back together.

Or at least that was what the conclusion of the old man's last game had led us to believe.

"I'm sure," I told Jameson fiercely. "Toby's alive. And if your grandfather knew that—and I know that's a big *if*—but if he did know, then we have to assume that either he chose me because I knew Toby, or he somehow masterminded bringing us together in the first place."

If there was one thing I'd learned about deceased billionaire Tobias Hawthorne, it was that he was capable of orchestrating nearly anything, manipulating nearly anyone. He'd loved puzzles and riddles and games.

Just like Jameson.

"What if that day in the park wasn't the first time you met my uncle?" Jameson took a step toward me, an unholy energy rolling off him. "Think about it, Heiress. You said that the one time my grandfather met you, you were six years old, and he saw you in the diner where your mother was a waitress. He heard your full name."

Avery Kylie Grambs, rearranged, became A Very Risky Gamble. The kind of name a man like Tobias Hawthorne would remember.

"That's right," I said. Jameson was close to me now. Too close. Every one of the Hawthorne boys was magnetic. Larger than life. They had an effect on people—and Jameson was very good at using that to get what he wanted. *He wants something from me now.*

"Why was my grandfather, a Texas billionaire with a whole host of private chefs on call, eating at a hole-in-the-wall diner in a small Connecticut town that no one's ever heard of?"

My mind raced. "You think he was looking for something?"

Jameson smiled deviously. "Or someone. What if the old man went there looking for Toby and found *you*?"

There was something about the way he said the word *you*. Like I was someone. Like I mattered. But Jameson and I had been down that road before. "And everything else is a distraction?" I asked, looking away from him. "My name. The fact that Emily died on my birthday. The puzzle your grandfather left us—it was all just a lie?"

Jameson didn't react to the sound of Emily's name. In the throes of a mystery, nothing could distract him—not even her. "A lie," Jameson repeated. "Or misdirection."

He reached to brush a strand of hair out of my face, and every nerve in my body went on high alert. I jerked back. "Stop looking at me like that," I told him sternly.

"Like what?" he countered.

I folded my arms and stared him down. "You turn on the charm when you want something."

"Heiress, you wound me." Jameson looked better smirking than anyone had a right to look. "All I want is for you to rifle through your memory banks a little. My grandfather was a person who thought in four dimensions. He might have had more than one reason for choosing you. Why kill two birds with one stone, he always said, when you could kill twelve?"

There was something about his voice, about the way he was still looking at me, that would have made it easy to get caught up in it all. The possibilities. The mystery. *Him.*

But I wasn't the kind of person who made the same mistake twice. "Maybe you've got it wrong." I turned away from him. "What if your grandfather didn't know that Toby was alive? What if *Toby* was the one who realized that the old man was watching me? Considering leaving the entire fortune to me?"

Harry, as I'd known him, had been one hell of a chess player. Maybe that day in the park wasn't a coincidence. Maybe he'd sought me out.

"We're missing something," Jameson said, coming up to stand close behind me. "Or maybe," he murmured, directly into the back of my head, "you're holding something back."

He wasn't entirely wrong. I wasn't built to lay all my cards on the table—and Jameson Winchester Hawthorne didn't even pretend to be trustworthy.

"I see how it is, Heiress." I could practically *hear* his crooked little grin. "If that's how you want to play it, why don't we make this interesting?"

I turned back to face him. Eye to eye, it was hard not to remember that when Jameson kissed a girl, it wasn't tentative. It wasn't gentle. *It wasn't real*, I reminded myself. I'd been a part of the puzzle to him, a tool to be used. I was still a part of the puzzle.

"Not everything is a game," I said.

"And maybe," Jameson countered, eyes alight, "that's the problem. Maybe that's why we're spinning our wheels in these tunnels day after day, rehashing this and getting nowhere. Because this isn't a game. *Yet.* A game has rules. A game has a winner. Maybe, Heiress, what you and I need to solve the mystery of Toby Hawthorne is a little motivation."

"What kind of motivation?" I narrowed my eyes at him.

"How about a wager?" Jameson arched an eyebrow. "If I figure all of this out first, then you have to forgive and forget my little lapse of judgment after we decoded the Black Wood."

The Black Wood was where we'd figured out that his dead ex-girlfriend had died on my birthday. That was the moment when it had first become clear that Tobias Hawthorne hadn't chosen me because I was special. He'd chosen me for what it would do to them.

Immediately afterward, Jameson had dropped me cold.

"And if I win," I countered, staring into those green eyes of his, "then you have to forget that we ever kissed—and never try to charm me into kissing you again."

I didn't trust him, but I also didn't trust myself with him.

"Well then, Heiress." Jameson stepped forward. Standing directly to my side, he brought his lips down to my ear and whispered, "Game on."

CHAPTER 2

Our wager struck, Jameson took off in one direction in the tunnels, and I went in another. Hawthorne House was massive, sprawling, big enough that, even after three weeks, I still hadn't seen it all. A person could spend years exploring this place and still not know all the ins and outs, all the secret passageways and hidden compartments—and that wasn't even counting the underground tunnels.

Lucky for me, I was a quick learner. I cut from underneath the gymnasium wing to a tunnel that went below the music room. I passed beneath the solarium, then climbed a hidden staircase into the Great Room, where I found Nash Hawthorne leaning casually against a stone fireplace. Waiting.

"Hey, kid." Nash didn't bat an eye at the fact that I'd just appeared seemingly out of nowhere. In fact, the oldest Hawthorne brother gave the impression that the whole mansion could come crashing down around him and he'd just keep leaning against that fireplace. Nash Hawthorne would probably tip his cowboy hat to Death herself.

"Hey," I replied.

“I don’t suppose you’ve seen Grayson?” Nash asked, his Texas drawl making the question sound almost lazy.

That did nothing to soften the impact of what he’d just said. “Nope.” I kept my answer short and my face blank. Grayson Hawthorne and I had been keeping our distance.

“And I don’t suppose you know anything about a chat Gray had with our mother, right before she moved out?”

Skye Hawthorne, Tobias Hawthorne’s younger daughter and the mother of all four Hawthorne grandsons, had tried to have me killed. The person who’d actually pulled the trigger was the one in a jail cell, but Skye had been forced to leave Hawthorne House. By Grayson. *I will always protect you,* he’d told me. *But this… us… It can’t happen, Avery.*

“No clue,” I said flatly.

“Didn’t think so.” Nash gave me a little wink. “Your sister and your lawyer are looking for you. East Wing.” That was a loaded statement if I’d ever heard one. My lawyer was his ex-fiancée, and my sister was…

I didn’t know what Libby and Nash Hawthorne were.

“Thanks,” I told him, but when I made my way up the winding staircase to the East Wing of Hawthorne House, I didn’t go looking for Libby. Or Alisa. I’d made a bet with Jameson, and I intended to win. First stop: Tobias Hawthorne’s office.

In the office, there was a mahogany desk, and behind the desk was a wall of trophies and patents and books with the name *Hawthorne* on the spine—a breathtaking visual reminder that there was nothing ordinary whatsoever about the Hawthorne brothers. They had been given every opportunity, and the old man had expected them to be extraordinary. But I hadn’t come here to gawk at trophies.

Instead, I took a seat behind the desk and released the hidden compartment I'd discovered not long ago. It held a folder. Inside the folder, there were pictures of me. Countless photographs, stretching back years. After that fateful meeting in the diner, Tobias Hawthorne had kept tabs on me. *All because of my name? Or did he have another motive?*

I thumbed through the photos and pulled out two. Jameson had been right, back in the tunnels. I was holding out on him. I'd been photographed with Toby twice, but both times, all the photographer had captured of the man beside me was the back of his head.

Had Tobias Hawthorne recognized Toby from behind? Had "Harry" realized we were being photographed and turned his head away from the camera on purpose?

As far as clues went, this wasn't much to go on. All the file really proved was that Tobias Hawthorne had been keeping tabs on me for years before "Harry" had shown up. I thumbed past the photographs to a copy of my birth certificate. My mother's signature was neat, my father's an odd mix of cursive and print. Tobias Hawthorne had highlighted my father's signature, as well as my date of birth.

10/18. I knew the significance there. Both Grayson and Jameson had loved a girl named Emily Laughlin. Her death—on October 18—had torn them apart. Somehow, the old man had intended for me to bring them back together. But why would Tobias Hawthorne have highlighted my father's signature? Ricky Grambs was a deadbeat. He hadn't even cared enough to pick up the phone when my mother died. If it had been left up to him, I would have gone into foster care. Staring at Ricky's signature, I willed Tobias Hawthorne's reasoning in highlighting it to become clear.

Nothing.

In the back of my mind, I heard my mother's voice. *I have a secret*, she'd told me, long before Tobias Hawthorne had written me into his will, *about the day you were born*.

Whatever she'd been referring to, I was never going to guess it now that she was gone. The one thing I knew for certain was that I wasn't a Hawthorne. If my father's name on that birth certificate weren't proof enough, a DNA test had already confirmed that I had no Hawthorne blood.

Why did Toby seek me out? Did *he seek me out?* I thought about what Jameson had said about his grandfather killing twelve birds with one stone. Going back through the folder again, I tried to find some shred of meaning. What wasn't I seeing? There had to be *something*—

A rap at the door was the only warning I got before the doorknob began to twist. Moving quickly, I gathered the photographs and slipped the file back into the hidden compartment.

"There you are." Alisa Ortega, attorney-at-law, was a model of professionalism. She arched her brows into what I had mentally termed the Alisa Look. "Would I be correct in assuming you've forgotten about the game?"

"The game," I repeated, unsure *which* game she was talking about. I felt like I'd been playing since the moment I'd first stepped through the door of Hawthorne House.

"The football game," Alisa clarified, with another Alisa Look. "Part two of your debut into Texas society. With Skye's exit from Hawthorne House, appearances are more important than ever. We need to control the narrative. This is a Cinderella story, not a scandal—and that means that *you* need to play Cinderella. In public. As frequently and convincingly as possible, starting with making use of your owner's box tonight."

Owner's box. That clicked. "The game," I repeated again, comprehension dawning. "As in, an NFL game. Because I own a football team."

That was still so absolutely mind-blowing that I almost succeeded in distracting myself from the other part of what Alisa had said—the bit about Skye. Per the deal I'd struck with Grayson, I couldn't tell anyone about his mother's part in my attempted murder. In exchange, he'd handled it.

Just like he'd promised he would.

"There are forty-eight seats in the owner's suite," Alisa said, going into lecture mode. "A general seat map is created months in advance. VIPs only. This isn't just football; it's a way of buying a seat at a dozen different tables. Invites are highly sought after by just about everyone—politicians, celebrities, CEOs. I've had Oren vet everyone on the list for tonight, and we'll have a professional photographer on hand for some strategic photo opportunities. Landon has crafted a press release that will go out an hour before the game. All that's left to worry about is..."

Alisa trailed off delicately.

I snorted. "Me?"

"This is a Cinderella story," Alisa reminded me. "What do you think Cinderella would wear to her first NFL game?"

That had to be a trick question.

"Something like this?" Libby popped into the doorway. She was wearing a Lone Stars jersey with a matching scarf, matching gloves, and matching boots. Her blue hair was tied into pigtails with a thick bunch of blue and gold ribbons.

Alisa forced a smile. "Yes," she told me. "Something like that—minus the black lipstick, the black nail polish, and the choker." Libby was pretty much the world's most cheerful goth, and Alisa was not a fan of my sister's sense of fashion. "As I was saying," Alisa continued emphatically, "tonight is important. While Avery plays Cinderella for the cameras, I'll circulate among our guests and get a better sense of where they stand."

"Where they stand on what?" I asked. I'd been told again and again that Tobias Hawthorne's will was ironclad. As far as I knew, the Hawthorne family had given up on trying to challenge it.

"It never hurts to have a few extra power players in your corner," Alisa said. "And we want our allies breathing easy."

"Hope I'm not interrupting." Nash acted like he'd just happened upon the three of us—like he wasn't the one who'd warned me that Alisa and Libby were looking for me. "Go on, Lee-Lee," he told my lawyer. "You were sayin' something about breathing easy?"

"We need people to know that Avery isn't here to shake things up." Alisa avoided looking directly at Nash, like a person avoiding looking into the sun. "Your grandfather had investments, business partners, political relationships—these things require a careful balance."

"What she means when she says that," Nash told me, "is that she needs people to think that McNamara, Ortega, and Jones has the situation entirely under control."

The situation? I thought. *Or me?* I didn't relish the idea of being anyone's puppet. In theory, at least, the firm was supposed to work for me.

That gave me an idea. "Alisa? Do you remember when I asked you to get money to a friend of mine?"

"Harry, wasn't it?" Alisa replied, but I got the distinct feeling that her attention was divided three ways: between my question, her grand plans for the night, and the way Nash's lips ticked upward on the ends when he saw Libby's outfit.

The last thing I needed my lawyer focused on was the way that her ex was looking at my sister. "Yes. Were you able to get the money to him?" I asked. The simplest way to get answers would be to track down Toby—before Jameson did.

Alisa tore her eyes away from Libby and Nash. "Unfortunately," she said briskly, "my people have been unable to find a trace of your Harry."

I rolled the implication of that over in my mind. Toby Hawthorne had appeared in the park days after my mother's death, and less than a month after I left, he was gone.

"Now," Alisa said, clasping her hands in front of her body, "about your wardrobe..."

CHAPTER 3

I had never seen a game of football in my life, but as the new owner of the Texas Lone Stars, I couldn't exactly say that to the crowd of reporters who mobbed the SUV when we pulled up to the stadium, any more than I could have admitted that the off-the-shoulder jersey and metallic-blue cowboy boots I was wearing felt about as authentic as a Halloween costume.

"Lower the window," Alisa told me, "smile, and yell, 'Go, Lone Stars!'"

I didn't want to lower the window. I didn't want to smile. I didn't want to yell anything—but I did it. Because this was a Cinderella story, and I was the star.

"Avery!"

"Avery, look over here!"

"How are you feeling about your first game as the new owner?"

"Do you have any comments about reports that you assaulted Skye Hawthorne?"

I hadn't had much media training, but I'd had enough to know the cardinal rule of having reporters shout questions at you rapid-fire: Don't answer. Pretty much the only thing I was allowed to say was that I was excited, grateful, awed, and overwhelmed in the *most incredible* possible way.

So I did my best to channel excitement, gratitude, and awe. Nearly a hundred thousand people would attend the game tonight. Millions would watch it around the world, cheering for the team. *My* team.

"Go, Lone Stars!" I yelled. I went to roll up my window, but just as my finger brushed the button, a figure pulled away from the crowd. Not a reporter.

My father.

Ricky Grambs had spent a lifetime treating me like an afterthought, if that. I hadn't seen him in more than a year. But now that I'd inherited billions?

There he was.

Turning away from him—and the paparazzi—I rolled my window up.

"Ave?" Libby's voice was hesitant as our bulletproof SUV disappeared into a private parking garage beneath the stadium. My sister was an optimist. She believed the best of people—including a man who'd never done a damn thing for either one of us.

"Did you know he'd be here?" I asked her, my voice low.

"No!" Libby said. "I swear!" She caught her bottom lip between her teeth, smudging her black lipstick. "But he just wants to talk."

I bet he does.

Up in the driver's seat, Oren, my head of security, parked the SUV and spoke calmly into his earpiece. "We have a situation near the north entrance. Eyes only, but I want a full report."

The nice thing about being a billionaire with a security team brimming with retired Special Forces was that the chances of my being ambushed again were next to none. I shoved down the feelings that seeing Ricky had dredged up and stepped out of the car into the bowels of one of the biggest stadiums in the world. "Let's do this," I said.

"For the record," Alisa told me as she exited the car, "the firm is more than capable of handling your father."

And *that* was the nice thing about being the sole client of a multi-billion-dollar law firm.

"Are you okay?" Alisa pressed. She wasn't exactly the touchy-feely type. More likely she was trying to assess whether I would be a liability tonight.

"I'm fine," I said.

"Why wouldn't she be?"

That voice—low and smooth—came from an elevator behind me. For the first time in seven days, I turned to look directly at Grayson Hawthorne. He had pale hair and ice-gray eyes and cheekbones sharp enough to count as weapons. Two weeks ago, I would have said that he was the most self-assured, self-righteous, arrogant jerk I'd ever met.

I wasn't sure what to say about Grayson Hawthorne now.

"Why," he repeated crisply, stepping out of the elevator, "would Avery be anything other than fine?"

"Deadbeat dad made an appearance outside," I muttered. "It's fine."

Grayson stared at me, his eyes piercing mine, then turned to Oren. "Is he a threat?"

I'll always protect you, he'd sworn. *But this... us... It can't happen, Avery.*

"I don't need you to protect me," I told Grayson sharply. "When it comes to Ricky, I'm an expert at protecting myself." I stalked past Grayson, into the elevator he'd stepped out of a moment earlier.

The trick to being abandoned was to never let yourself long for anyone who left.

A minute later, when the elevator doors opened into the owner's suite, I stepped out, Alisa to one side and Oren to the other, and I didn't so much as look back at Grayson. Since he'd taken the elevator down to meet me, he'd obviously already been up here, probably schmoozing. Without me.

"Avery. You made it." Zara Hawthorne-Calligaris wore a string of delicate pearls around her neck. There was something about her sharp-edged smile that made me feel like she could probably kill a man with those pearls if she were so inclined. "I wasn't sure you would be putting in an appearance tonight."

And you were ready to hold court in my absence, I concluded. I thought about what Alisa had said—about allies and power players and the influence that could be bought with a ticket to this suite.

As Jameson would say, *Game on*.

CHAPTER 4

The owner's suite had a perfect view of the fifty-yard line, but an hour before kickoff, no one was looking at the field. The suite extended back and widened, and the farther you got from the seats, the more it looked like an upscale bar or club. Tonight, I was the entertainment—an oddity, a curiosity, a paper doll dressed up just so. For what felt like an eternity, I shook hands, posed for photographers, and pretended to understand football jokes. I managed not to gawk at a pop star, a former vice president, and a tech giant who probably made more money in the time it took him to urinate than most people made in a lifetime.

My brain pretty much stopped functioning when I heard the phrase "Her Highness" and realized there was actual royalty in attendance.

Alisa must have sensed that I was reaching my limit. "It's almost time for kickoff," she said, laying one hand lightly on my shoulder—probably to keep me from fleeing. "Let's get you in your seat."

I made it until halftime, then bolted for real. Grayson intercepted me. Wordlessly, he nodded to one side and then started walking, confident that I would follow.

Despite myself, I did. What I found was a second elevator.

"This one goes up," he told me. Going anywhere with Grayson Hawthorne was probably a mistake, but given that the alternative was more mingling, I decided to take my chances.

The two of us rode the elevator up in silence. The door opened to a small room with five seats, all empty. The view of the field was even better than it was below.

"My grandfather could only mingle in the suite for so long before he got fed up and came up here," Grayson told me. "My brothers and I were the only ones allowed to join him."

I sat and stared out at the stadium. There were so many people in the crowd. The energy, the chaos, the sheer volume of it was overwhelming. But in here, it was silent.

"I thought you might come to the game with Jameson." Grayson made no move to sit, like he didn't trust himself too close to me. "The two of you have been spending a lot of time together."

That irritated me, for reasons I couldn't even explain. "Your brother and I have a bet going."

"What kind of bet?"

I had no intention of answering, but when I let my eyes travel toward his, I couldn't resist saying the one thing guaranteed to get a reaction. "Toby is alive."

To someone else, Grayson's reaction might not have been noticeable, but I saw the jolt go through him. His gray eyes were glued to me now. "Pardon me?"

"Your uncle is alive and gets his jollies by pretending to be a homeless man in New Castle, Connecticut." I probably could have been a little more delicate.

Grayson came closer. He deigned to sit next to me, tension visible in his arms as he folded his hands together between his knees. "What, precisely, are you talking about, Avery?"

I wasn't used to hearing him call me by my first name. It was too late to take back what I'd said. "I saw a picture of Toby in your nan's locket." I closed my eyes, flashing back to that moment. "I recognized him. He told me that his name was Harry. We played chess in the park every week for more than a year." I opened my eyes again. "Jameson and I aren't sure what the story is there—yet. We have a bet going about who finds out first."

"Who have you told?" Grayson's voice was deadly serious.

"About the bet?"

"About Toby."

"Nan was there when I found out. I was going to tell Alisa, but—"

"Don't," Grayson cut in. "Don't breathe a word of this to anyone. You understand?"

I stared at him. "I'm starting to get the feeling that I don't."

"My mother has no grounds on which to challenge the will. My aunt has no grounds on which to challenge the will. But Toby?" Grayson had grown up as the heir apparent. Of all the Hawthorne brothers, he had taken being disinherited the hardest. "If my uncle is alive, he is the one person on this planet who might be able to break the old man's will."

"You say that like it's a bad thing," I told him. "From my perspective, sure. But from yours..."

"My mother cannot find out. Zara cannot find out." Grayson's expression was intense, everything in him focused on me. "McNamara, Ortega, and Jones cannot find out."

In the week that Jameson and I had been discussing this turn of events, we'd been completely focused on the mystery—not on what might happen if Tobias Hawthorne's lost heir suddenly turned up alive.

"Aren't you even a little bit curious?" I asked Grayson. "About what this means?"

"I know what this means," Grayson replied tersely. "I am telling you what this means, Avery."

"If your uncle were interested in inheriting, don't you think he would have come forward by now?" I asked. "Unless there's a reason he's in hiding."

"Then let him hide. Do you have any idea how risky—" Grayson didn't get to finish that question.

"What's life without a little risk, brother?"

I turned toward the elevator. I hadn't noticed it going down or coming back up, but there Jameson was. He strolled past Grayson and settled into the seat on the other side of mine. "Made any progress on our bet, Heiress?"

I snorted. "Wouldn't you like to know?"

Jameson smirked, then opened his mouth to say something else, but his words were drowned out by an explosion. More than one. *Gunfire.* Panic shot through my veins, and the next thing I knew, I was on the ground. *Where's the shooter?* This was like Black Wood. Just like the Black Wood.

"Heiress."

I couldn't move. Couldn't breathe. And then Jameson was on the floor with me. He brought his face level with mine and cupped my head in his hands. "Fireworks," he told me. "It's just fireworks, Heiress, for halftime."

My brain registered his words, but my body was still lost in memory. Jameson had been there in the Black Wood with me. He'd thrown his body over mine.

"You're okay, Avery." Grayson knelt beside Jameson, beside me. "We won't let anything hurt you." For a long, drawn-out moment, there wasn't a sound in the room except our breathing. Grayson's. Jameson's. And mine.

"Just fireworks," I repeated back to Jameson, my chest tight.

Grayson stood, but Jameson stayed exactly where he was. He stared at me, his body against mine. There was something almost tender in his expression. I swallowed—and then his lips twisted into a wicked smile.

"For the record, Heiress, *I* have been making excellent progress on our bet." He let his thumb trace the outline of my jaw.

I shuddered, then glared at him and climbed to my feet. For the sake of my own sanity, I needed to win this bet. *Fast.*

CHAPTER 5

Monday meant school. Private school. A private school with seemingly endless resources and "modular scheduling," which left me with random pockets of free time scattered throughout the day. I used that time to dig up everything I could about Toby Hawthorne.

I already knew the basics: He was the youngest of Tobias Hawthorne's three children and, by most accounts, the favorite. At the age of nineteen, he and some friends had taken a trip to a private island the Hawthorne family owned off the coast of Oregon. There was a deadly fire and a horrible storm, and his body was never recovered.

The tragedy had made the news, and sifting through articles gave me a few more details about what had happened. Four people had gone out to Hawthorne Island. None had made it back alive. Three bodies had been recovered. Toby's was presumed lost to the ocean storm.

I found out what I could about the other victims. Two of them were basically Toby clones: prep school boys. *Heirs.* The third was a girl, Kaylie Rooney. From what I gathered, she was a local, a troubled teen from a small fishing village on the mainland. Several articles mentioned that she had a criminal record—a sealed juvenile record. It took me longer to find a source—though not necessarily a reputable one—that claimed that Kaylie Rooney's criminal record included drugs, assault, and arson.

She started the fire. That was the story the press ran with, without coming right out and saying the words. *Three promising young men, one troubled young woman. A party that spun out of control. Everything, engulfed in flames.* Kaylie was the one the press blamed—sometimes between the lines, sometimes explicitly. The boys were lionized and eulogized and held up as shining beacons in their communities. *Colin Anders Wright. David Golding. Tobias Hawthorne II.* So much brilliance, so much potential, gone too soon.

But Kaylie Rooney? She was trouble.

My phone buzzed, and I glanced down at the screen. A text—from Jameson: *I have a lead.*

Jameson was a senior at Heights Country Day. He was somewhere on this magnificent campus. *What kind of lead?* I thought, but I resisted giving him the satisfaction of texting back. Eventually, my phone informed me that he was typing.

Tell me what you know, I thought.

Then the text finally came through. *Wanna raise the stakes?*

The Heights Country Day refectory didn't look like a high school cafeteria. Long wooden tables stretched the length of the room. Portraits hung on the walls. The ceilings were high and arching, and the windows were made of stained glass. As I grabbed my food, I scanned the room reflexively for Jameson—and found another Hawthorne brother instead.

Xander Hawthorne was sitting at a dining table, staring intently at a contraption he'd set on its surface. The gizmo looked a bit like a Rubik's Cube, but elongated, with tiles that could swivel and fold out in any direction. I suspected it was a Xander Hawthorne original. He'd told me once that he was the brother most apt to be distracted by complex machinery—and scones.

That got me thinking as I watched him fidget three tiles back and forth in his fingers. When his brothers had been off playing their grandfather's games, Xander had often ended up sharing his scones with the old man. *Did they ever talk about Toby?* There was only one way to find out. I crossed the room to sit next to Xander, but he was so absorbed in thought that he didn't even notice me. Back and forth, back and forth, he twisted the tiles.

"Xander?"

He turned toward me and blinked. "Avery! What a pleasant and not objectively unexpected surprise!" His right hand meandered to the far side of the contraption and a notebook that sat there. He snapped it closed.

I took that to mean Xander Hawthorne was up to something. Then again, so was I. "Can I ask you something?"

"That depends," Xander replied. "Are you planning to share those baked goods?"

I looked down at the croissant and cookie on my tray and slid the latter his way. "What do you know about your uncle Toby?"

"Why do you want to know?" Xander took a bite of the cookie and frowned. "Does this have craisins in it? What kind of monster mixes butterscotch chips and craisins?"

"I was just curious," I said.

"You know what they say about curiosity," Xander warned me happily, taking another gargantuan bite of the cookie. "Curiosity killed the—Bex!" Xander gulped down the bite he'd just taken, his face lighting up.

I followed his gaze to Rebecca Laughlin, who was standing

behind me, holding a lunch tray and looking the way she always did: like some kind of princess, plucked from a fairy tale. Hair as red as rubies. Impossibly wide-set eyes.

Guilty as sin.

As if she could hear my thoughts, Rebecca quickly averted her eyes. I could feel her trying not to look at me. "I thought you might need help," she told Xander hesitantly, "with the—"

"The thing!" Xander leaned forward and cut her off.

I narrowed my eyes and turned my head back toward the youngest Hawthorne—and the notebook he'd flipped closed the moment he'd seen me. "What thing?" I asked suspiciously.

"I should go," Rebecca said behind me.

"You should sit and listen to me complain about craisins," Xander corrected.

After a long moment, Rebecca sat, leaving a single empty chair between us. Her clear, green eyes drifted toward mine. "Avery." She looked down again. "I owe you an apology."

The last time Rebecca and I had spoken, she'd confessed to covering for Skye Hawthorne's role in my attempted murder.

"I'm not sure I want one," I said, an edge creeping into my voice. On an intellectual level, I understood that Rebecca had spent her whole life living in her sister's shadow, that Emily's death had wrecked her, that she'd felt some kind of sick responsibility to her dead sister to say nothing about Skye's plot against me. But on a more visceral level: *I could have died.*

"You're not still holding a little grudge about all of that, are you?" Thea Calligaris asked, claiming the seat that Rebecca had left open.

"Little grudge?" I repeated. The last time I'd been this close to Thea, *she* had admitted to setting me up to attend my debut in Texas society dressed like a dead girl. "You play mind games. And Rebecca almost got me killed!"

"What can I say?" Thea let her fingertips brush Rebecca's. "We're complicated girls."

There was something deliberate about those words, that brush of skin. Rebecca looked at Thea, looked at their hands—and then curled her fingers toward her palm and placed her hand in her lap.

Thea kept her eyes on Rebecca's for three long seconds, then turned back to me. "Besides," she said pertly, "I thought this was supposed to be a *private* lunch."

Private. Just Rebecca and Thea and Xander, the three of whom—last I'd checked—were barely on speaking terms with one another for complicated reasons involving, as Xander liked to say, star-crossed love, fake dating, and tragedy.

"What am I missing here?" I asked Xander. The notebook. The way he'd dodged my question about Toby. The "thing" Rebecca had come to help him with. And now *Thea*.

Xander saved himself from having to answer by jamming the rest of the cookie into his mouth.

"Well?" I prompted as he chewed.

"Emily's birthday is on Friday," Rebecca said suddenly. Her voice was quiet, but what she'd just said sucked the oxygen from the room.

"There's a memorial fundraiser," Thea added, staring me down. "Xander, Rebecca, and I scheduled this *private* lunch to iron out some plans."

I wasn't sure I believed her, but either way, that was clearly my cue to leave.

CHAPTER 6

Trying to talk to Xander had been a bust. I'd gotten as far as I could reading about the fire. *What next?* I thought, walking down a long corridor toward my locker. *Talk to someone who knew Toby?* Skye was out, for obvious reasons. I didn't trust Zara, either. Who did that leave? *Nash, maybe? He would have been about five when Toby disappeared. Nan. Maybe the Laughlins.* Rebecca's grandparents ran the Hawthorne estate and had for years. *Who is Jameson talking to? What's his lead?*

Frustrated, I pulled out my phone and shot off a text to Max. I didn't really expect a reply, because my best friend had been on technological lockdown ever since my windfall—and the accompanying attention from the press—had ruined her life. But even with the guilt I was carrying about what my instant fame had done to Max, texting her made me feel a little less alone. I tried to imagine what she would tell me if she were here, but all I came up with was a string of fake curse words—and strict orders not to get myself killed.

"Did you see the news?" I heard a girl down the hallway ask in a hushed voice as I stopped in front of my locker. "About her father?"

Gritting my teeth, I tuned out the sounds of the gossip mill. I opened my locker—and a picture of Ricky Grambs stared back at me. It must have been cut out of an article, because there was a headline above the photograph: *I Just Want to Talk to My Daughter.*

Rage simmered in the pit of my stomach—rage that my deadbeat of a father would have dared to talk to the press, rage that someone had taped this article to the back of my locker door. I looked around to see if the perpetrator would make themselves known. Heights Country Day lockers were made of wood and didn't have locks. It was a subtle way of saying, *People like us don't steal.* What need was there for security among the elite?

As Max would say, *Bullship.* Anyone could have accessed my locker, but no one in the hallway was watching my reaction now. I turned back to tear the picture down, and that was when I noticed that whoever had taped it up had also papered the bottom of my locker with scraps of bloodred paper.

Not scraps, I realized, picking one up. *Comments.* For the past three weeks, I'd done a good job at staying offline, avoiding what internet commenters were saying about me. *To some people, you'll be Cinderella,* Oren had told me when I first inherited. *To others, Marie Antoinette.*

In all caps, the comment in my hand read, *SOMEONE NEEDS TO TEACH THAT STUCK-UP BITCH A LESSON.* I should have stopped there, but I didn't. My hand shook slightly as I picked up the next comment. *When will this SLUT die?* There were dozens more, some of them graphic.

One commenter had just posted a photo: my face, with a target photoshopped over it, like I'd been caught in the sight of a gun.

"This was almost certainly just a bored teenager pushing boundaries," Oren told me as we arrived back at Hawthorne House that afternoon.

"But the comments..." I swallowed, some of the threats still emblazoned on my brain. "They're real?"

"And nothing you need to worry about," Oren assured me. "My team keeps tabs on these things. All threats are documented and assessed. Of the hundred or so worst offenders, there are only two or three to date that merit watching."

I tried not to get hung up on the numbers. "What do you mean, *watching*?"

"Unless I'm mistaken," a cool, even voice said, "he's referring to the List."

I looked up to see Grayson standing a few feet away, wearing a dark suit, his expression impossible to read but for a line of tension in his jaw.

"What list?" I said, trying not to pay too much attention to his jawline.

"Do you want to show her?" Grayson asked Oren calmly. "Or should I?"

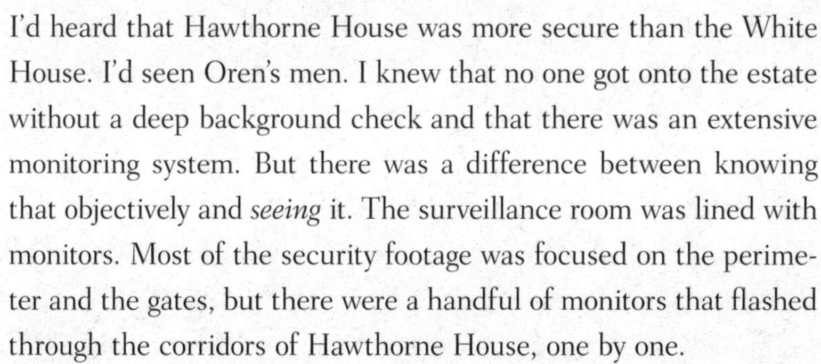

I'd heard that Hawthorne House was more secure than the White House. I'd seen Oren's men. I knew that no one got onto the estate without a deep background check and that there was an extensive monitoring system. But there was a difference between knowing that objectively and *seeing* it. The surveillance room was lined with monitors. Most of the security footage was focused on the perimeter and the gates, but there were a handful of monitors that flashed through the corridors of Hawthorne House, one by one.

"Eli." Oren spoke, and one of the guards who was monitoring the feeds stood. He looked to be in his twenties, with a military-style haircut, several scars, and vibrant blue eyes ringed with amber around the pupil. "Avery," Oren said, "meet Eli. He'll be shadowing you at school, at least until I've completed a full assessment of the locker situation. He's the youngest member of our team, so he'll blend better than the rest of us would."

Eli looked military. He looked like a bodyguard. He did not look like he would *blend* at my high school. "I thought you weren't concerned about my locker," I told Oren.

My head of security met my eyes. "I'm not." But he also wasn't taking any chances.

"What, precisely," Grayson said, coming up behind me, "happened at your locker?"

I had a brief and infuriating urge to tell him, to let him protect me, the way he'd sworn he would. But not everything was Grayson Hawthorne's business. "Where's this list?" I asked, stepping away from him and redirecting the conversation to the reason I was here.

Oren nodded to Eli, and the younger man handed me an actual, literal list. Names. The one at the top was *RICKY GRAMBS*. I scowled but managed to scan the rest of the list. There were maybe thirty names, total. "Who are these people?" I asked, my throat tightening around the words.

"Would-be stalkers," Oren answered. "People who've attempted to break onto the estate. Overly zealous fans." He narrowed his eyes. "Skye Hawthorne."

I took that to mean that my head of security knew why Skye had left Hawthorne House. I'd promised Grayson secrecy, but this was Hawthorne House. Most of the occupants were far too clever for their own good—or anyone else's.

"Could you give me a moment with Avery?" Grayson did Oren the courtesy of pretending that was a request. Unimpressed, Oren glanced toward me and arched a questioning brow. I was tempted to keep Oren there out of spite, but instead, I nodded at my head of security, and he and his men slowly filed out of the room. I half expected Grayson to cross-examine me about what I'd told

Oren about Skye, but once the two of us were alone, that cross-examination never came.

"Are you okay?" Grayson asked instead. "I can see how this would be a lot to take in."

"I'm fine," I insisted, but this time I couldn't muster the will to tell him that I didn't need his protection. I'd known, objectively, that I would need security for the rest of my life, but seeing the threats laid out on paper felt different.

"My grandfather had a List as well," Grayson said quietly. "It comes with the territory."

With being famous? With being rich?

"Regarding the situation we discussed last night," Grayson continued, his voice low, "do you understand now why you need to leave it alone?" He didn't say Toby's name. "Most of these people on the List would lose interest in you if you lost the fortune. *Most* of them."

But not all. I stared at Grayson for a moment, my eyes lingering on his face. If I were to lose the fortune, I'd lose my security team. That was what he wanted me to understand.

"I understand," I replied, ripping my eyes from Grayson's, because I also understood this: I was a survivor. I took care of myself. And I wouldn't let myself want or expect anything from him.

Turning away, I stared at the security monitors. A flash of movement on one of the feeds caught my eye. *Jameson.* I tried not to be too obvious as I watched him striding with purpose through a corridor I couldn't place. *What are you up to, Jameson Hawthorne?*

Beside me, Grayson's attention was on me, not the monitors. "Avery?" He sounded almost hesitant. I hadn't been sure that Grayson Davenport Hawthorne, former heir apparent, was capable of hesitating.

"I'm fine," I said again, keeping half an eye on the screen. A moment later, the feed flashed to another corridor, and I saw Xander, walking with just as much purpose as Jameson. He was carrying something in his hands.

A sledgehammer? Why would he have a—

The question cut off in my mind because I recognized Xander's surroundings, and suddenly I knew exactly where he was going. And I would have bet my last dollar that Jameson was on his way there, too.

CHAPTER 7

At some point after his son's disappearance and supposed death, Tobias Hawthorne had walled off Toby's wing. I'd seen it once: solid bricks laid over what I had assumed to be a door.

"Sorry," I told Grayson, "I have to go." I understood why he wanted me to leave the Toby situation alone. He probably wasn't wrong. *And yet*...

Neither Oren nor his men trailed me when I left. The threats on the List—they were external. And that meant that I could make my way to Toby's wing without a shadow. I arrived to see Xander hoisting the sledgehammer over his shoulder. He caught sight of me out of the corner of his eye. "Pay no attention to this sledgehammer!"

"I know what you're doing," I told him.

"What sledgehammers were put on God's green earth to do," Xander replied solemnly.

"*I know*," I said again, waiting for those words to sink in.

Xander lowered the business end of the sledgehammer to the ground. Brown eyes studied me intently. "What is it you think you know?"

I took my time with my reply. "I know that you didn't want to answer my question about Toby. I know that you and Rebecca and Thea were up to something at lunch today." I was building my way up to the true gambit here. "I know your uncle's alive."

Xander blinked, his incredible brain moving at what I could only assume was warp speed. "Did the old man say something in your letter?"

"No," I said. Tobias Hawthorne had left us each a letter at the end of the last puzzle. "Did he say something in yours?"

Before Xander could answer, Jameson strolled up to join us. "Looks like a party." He reached for the sledgehammer. "Shall we?"

Xander pulled it back. "Mine."

"The sledgehammer," Jameson replied loftily, "or what's behind that wall?"

"Both," Xander gritted out, and there was a note of intensity in his voice that I'd never heard from him before. Xander was the youngest Hawthorne brother. The least competitive. The one who'd been in on their grandfather's last game.

"Is that the way it is?" Jameson eyes narrowed. "Want to wrestle for it?"

That did not strike me as a rhetorical question. "Xander, your uncle and I know each other." I cut in before any actual wrestling could take place. "I met Toby right after my mother died." It took me a minute, maybe less, to lay out the rest of it, and when I'd finished, Xander stared at me, a little bit in awe.

"I should have seen it."

"Seen what?" I asked him.

"You weren't just a part of *their* game," Xander replied. "Of course you weren't. The old man's mind didn't operate that way. He didn't just choose you for *them*."

Them being Grayson and Jameson. *Their* game being the one we'd already solved. "He left you a game, too," I said slowly. It was the only thing that made sense. Nash had warned me once that their grandfather had, in all likelihood, never intended me to be a player.

I was the glass ballerina or the knife. A part of the puzzle. A *tool*. I narrowed my eyes at Xander. "Either tell us what you know, or give me that sledgehammer."

No matter the old man's intentions—I wasn't here to be *used*.

"Not much to tell!" Xander declared jollily. "The old man left me a letter congratulating me for getting my hardheaded and much less handsome brothers to the end of their game. He signed the letter as Tobias Hawthorne, no middle initial, but when submerged in water, that signature became 'Find Tobias Hawthorne the Second.'"

Find Toby. The old man had left his youngest grandson with that charge. And there was a good chance that the only real clue he'd left him . . . was me. *Twelve birds with one stone.*

"I guess that answers the question of whether the old man knew Toby was alive," Jameson murmured.

Tobias Hawthorne knew. My entire body rang with that revelation.

"If we have Toby's last known location," Xander mused, "perhaps a sledgehammering is unnecessary. My plan was to search his room and see if any clues turned up, but . . ."

I shook my head. "I have no idea how to find Toby. I asked Alisa to get money to him, right after I inherited, before I even knew who he was. He was already in the wind."

Jameson cocked his head to the side. "Interesting."

"Is Toby's wing the lead you mentioned earlier?" I asked him.

"Maybe it is," Jameson said, grinning. "Or maybe it isn't."

"Far be it from me to interrupt banter," Xander interjected. "But this is *my* lead. And my sledgehammer!" He heaved it over his shoulder.

I stared at the wall and wondered what lay beyond it. "Are you sure about this?" I asked Xander.

He took a deep breath. "As sure as anyone holding a sledgehammer has ever been."

CHAPTER 8

The wall came down easily enough that I wondered if it had been meant to come down. How long had Tobias Hawthorne waited for someone to hammer their way through the barrier he'd erected? For someone to ask questions?

For someone to find his son.

As I stepped through what remained of the bricks, I tried to imagine what the old man had been thinking. *Why didn't he find Toby himself? Why didn't he bring him home?*

I stared down a long hallway. The floor was made of white marble tiles. The walls were completely lined with mirrors. I felt like I'd stepped into a fun house. On high alert, I made my way slowly down the hall, taking stock. There was a library, a sitting room, a study, and, at the end of the hall, a bedroom every bit as large as mine. Clothes still hung in the closet.

A towel hung on a rack next to an enormous shower.

"How long has this place been bricked up?" I asked, but the boys were in another room—and I didn't need them to tell me the answer. *Twenty years.* Those clothes had been hanging in the closet since the summer Toby had "died."

Emerging from the bathroom, I found Xander's legs poking out from underneath a king-sized bed. Jameson was running his hands over the top of an armoire. He must have found some kind of latch or lever, because a second later, the top of the armoire popped up like a lid.

"Looks like Uncle Toby was a fan of contraband," Jameson commented. I climbed up on the dresser to get a better look and saw a long, thin compartment completely lined with travel-sized liquor bottles.

"Found a loose floor panel," Xander called from under the bed. When he reappeared, he was holding a small plastic bag full of pills—and another one full of powder.

Toby's wing was brimming with secret compartments: hollowed-out books, trick drawers, a false back to the closet. A secret passage in the study led back past the entryway, revealing that the mirrors that lined the hallway were two-way. From where I stood in the passage, I could see Jameson lying facedown on the marble floor, examining the tiles one by one.

I stared at him for longer than I should have, then retreated back to the library. Xander and I had screened hundreds of books for hidden compartments. Nineteen-year-old Toby's tastes had been eclectic—everything from comic books and Greek philosophy to pulp horror and law. The only shelf on the built-in bookshelves that wasn't full of books framed a clock that was about eight inches tall and affixed to the back of the shelf. I studied the clock for a moment. *No movement of the second hand.* I reached out to test how firmly the clock was attached to the shelf.

It didn't budge.

I almost left it there, but some instinct wouldn't let me. Instead, I twisted the clock, and it rotated, loosening. The face of the clock came away from the wall. There were no gears inside, no electronics. Instead, I found a flat, circular object made of cardboard. Closer inspection revealed two concentric cardboard circles attached with a brad in the center. Each one was lined with letters.

"A homemade cipher disk." Xander crowded me to get a better look. "See how the *A* on the outside disk aligns with the *A* on the smaller one? Twist either disk so that different letters align, and it generates a simple substitution code."

Clearly, Toby Hawthorne had been raised the same way his nephews had: playing the old man's games. *Were you playing with me, Harry?*

"Wait a second." Xander straightened suddenly. "Hear that?"

I listened. Silence. "Hear what?"

Xander pointed his index finger at me. *"Exactly."* The next second, he took off. I tucked the cipher disk into the band of my pleated skirt and followed. In the hallway, Jameson was silently lowering a marble tile back into place.

He'd found something—and apparently hadn't planned on sharing that with his brother or me.

"Aha!" Xander said triumphantly. "I knew you were being too quiet." He strode over to Jameson and squatted beside him, pressing on the floor tile Jameson had just lowered. I heard a popping sound, and the tile released, like it was on a spring.

Glaring at Jameson, who winked back at me, I knelt next to Xander. Beneath the tile was a metal compartment. It was empty, but I saw an inscription on the bottom, engraved into the metal.

A poem.

"*I was angry with my friend,*" I read out loud. "*I told my wrath, my wrath did end.*" I glanced up. Jameson was already standing and walking away, but Xander's eyes were locked on the inscription as I continued. "*I was angry with my foe: I told it not, my wrath did grow.*"

The words hung in the air for a few seconds after I said them.

Xander whipped out his phone. "William Blake," he said after a moment.

"Who?" I asked. I glanced back at Jameson, who pivoted and paced back toward us. I'd thought he was off and running, but really he was thinking, concentration in motion.

"William Blake," Jameson echoed, an almost chaotic energy marking the words and his stride. "Eighteenth-century poet—and a favorite of Aunt Zara's."

"And Toby's, apparently," Xander added.

I stared down at the engraving. The word *wrath* jumped out at me. I thought about the alcohol and drugs we'd found in Toby's room. I thought about the fire on Hawthorne Island and the way the press had lauded Toby as such an outstanding young man.

"He was angry about something," I said. My mind raced. "Something he couldn't say?"

"Maybe," Jameson replied pensively. "Maybe not."

Xander handed me his phone. "Here's the entire poem."

"A Poison Tree," by William Blake, I read.

"Long story short," Xander summarized, "the author's hidden wrath grows into a tree, the tree bears fruit, the fruit is poisoned, and the enemy—who doesn't know they are enemies—eats the fruit. The whole shebang ends with a dead body. Very catchy."

A dead body. My mind went, unbidden, to the three bodies that had been recovered from the fire on Hawthorne Island. Exactly how angry was Toby that summer?

Don't leap to conclusions, I told myself. I had no idea what this poem meant—no idea why a nineteen-year-old would have had these words inscribed on a hidden compartment. No idea if this *was* Toby's handiwork, rather than the old man's. For all we knew, Tobias Hawthorne had done this after his son went missing, right before bricking up the door.

"What the hell are you kids doing in here?" That question sounded like it had been ripped forcibly from someone's throat. My head whipped toward the doorway. Mr. Laughlin stood there, on the other side of the demolished bricks. He looked tired and old and almost *hurt*.

"Just putting everything back where we found it!" Xander said brightly. "Right after we—"

The groundskeeper didn't let him finish. He stepped through the opening in the brick wall and pointed his finger at us. *"Out."*

CHAPTER 9

That night, I lay in bed, thinking about the poem and staring at the cipher disk. I turned the smaller wheel, watching as it generated code after code. What exactly had Toby used this for? Answers didn't come, but eventually sleep did. I woke the next morning with "A Poison Tree" still on my mind. *I was angry with my friend: / I told my wrath, my wrath did end. / I was angry with my foe: / I told it not, my wrath did grow.*

A knock on my door interrupted that thought. It was Libby. She was still dressed in her pajamas—skull print, with bows.

"Everything okay?" I asked.

"Just making sure you're up and getting ready for school."

I gave her a look. Libby had never, in the history of her legal guardianship of me, gotten me up for school. "Really?"

She hesitated, her right index finger picking at the dark nail polish on her left, and then the floodgates broke. "You know Dad didn't mean to give that interview, right? Ave, he had *no* idea the person he was talking to was a reporter."

Ricky had gotten back in touch with Libby around the time that news of my inheritance hit the press. If she wanted to give him another chance, that was her business, but he didn't get to use her as an intermediary with me.

"He wants money," I said flatly. "And I'm not giving him any."

"I'm not an idiot, Avery. And I'm not defending him."

She was absolutely defending him, but I didn't have the heart to say that. "I should get ready for school."

My morning routine took five times longer now than it had before I had a team of stylists, a media consultant, and a "look." By the time I finished applying eight different concoctions to my face and at least half that many to my hair, sitting down to breakfast was out of the question. Running late, I rushed into the kitchen—not to be confused with the chef's kitchen—to pick up a banana and was greeted with the sound of an oven door slamming closed.

Mrs. Laughlin straightened and wiped her hands on her apron. Soft brown eyes narrowed at me. "Can I help you with something?"

"Banana?" I said. Something about the expression on her face made it difficult for me to form a full sentence. I still wasn't used to having a staff. "I mean, could I get a banana, please?"

"Too good for breakfast?" Mrs. Laughlin replied stiffly.

"No," I said quickly. "It's just, I'm running late, and—"

"No matter." Mrs. Laughlin checked the contents of another oven. From what I'd been told, the Laughlins had run the estate for decades. They hadn't been thrilled when I inherited, but everything continued to run like clockwork. "Take what you like." Mrs. Laughlin briskly nodded to a fruit bowl. "Your type always does."

My type? I bit back the urge to throw out a retort. Clearly, I'd misstepped somehow. And just as clearly, I didn't want to be on her bad side. "If this is about what happened with Mr. Laughlin yesterday…," I said, flashing back to the way her husband had thrown us out of Toby's wing.

"You stay away from Mr. Laughlin." Mrs. Laughlin wiped her hands against her apron again, harder this time. "It's bad enough, what you've done to poor Nan."

Nan? My answer came with my next breath. The boys' great-grandmother had been the one to show me a picture of Toby. She'd been there when I realized I knew him. "Nan told you," I said slowly. "About Toby." I thought about Grayson's warning, about the importance of this secret staying a secret.

Xander knew—and now Mrs. Laughlin. Quite possibly her husband, too.

"You should be ashamed of yourself," Mrs. Laughlin said fiercely. "Playing with an old woman's feelings like that. And dragging the boys into whatever you were doing in Toby's wing? It's cruel is what it is."

"Cruel?" I repeated, and that was when I realized: She thought I was lying.

"Toby's dead," Mrs. Laughlin said, her voice tight. "He's gone, and the whole House mourned him. I loved that boy like he was my own." She closed her eyes. "And the thought of you tormenting Nan, telling that poor woman that he's *alive*…defiling his things…" Mrs. Laughlin forced her eyes open. "Hasn't this family suffered enough without you making up something like this?"

"I'm not lying," I said, feeling sick to my stomach. "I wouldn't do that."

Mrs. Laughlin pursed her lips. I could see her biting back whatever she wanted to say. Instead, she stiffly handed me a banana. "You should go to school."

CHAPTER 10

True to Oren's word, Eli stuck to my side at school. Despite my head of security's promise about "blending," there was nothing discreet about being a seventeen-year-old with a bodyguard.

American Studies. Philosophy of Mindfulness. Calculus. Making Meaning. As I sat through my classes, my fellow students didn't stare. They not-stared—so conspicuously, it felt worse. By the time I made it to Physics, I was ready to take my chances with the internet commenters and locker vandals of the world on my own.

"Can you just wait in the hall?" I asked Eli.

"If I want to be out of a job," he replied gamely, "sure."

Part of me had to wonder if Oren was really going to this length because of the locker incident—or if it was because Ricky was in town and making noise.

Trying to shut out that thought, I plopped down into a seat. On a normal day, the fact that my high school physics laboratory looked like something that belonged at NASA would still have provoked some awe, but today I had other things on my mind.

Right before class began, Thea sat down at my lab table. She raked her eyes over Eli, then turned back to me. "Not bad," she murmured.

My life was literally a tabloid story, but at least Thea Calligaris thought my new bodyguard was hot.

"What do you want?" I asked her under my breath.

"Things I'm not supposed to," Thea mused. "Things I can't have. Anything that I'm told is just out of reach."

"What do you want from me?" I clarified, keeping my voice low enough to prevent anyone but Eli from overhearing.

Class started before Thea deigned to answer, and she didn't speak again until we were let loose on the lab assignment. "Rebecca and I were there when Sir Geeks-a-Lot sank that letter of his in the tub," Thea said lightly. "We know all about the new game." Her expression shifted, and for a split second Thea Calligaris looked almost vulnerable. "It's the first thing in an eternity that has gotten Bex to wake up."

"Wake up?" I repeated. I knew that Thea and Rebecca had a history. I knew that they'd split up in the wake of Emily's death, that Rebecca had withdrawn from everyone and everything.

But I had no idea why Thea expected me to care about either of them now.

"You don't know her," Thea told me, her voice low. "You don't know what Emily's death did to her. If she wants to help Xander with this? I'm going to help *her.* And I just thought that you might want to know that we know about you-know-who." *About Toby.* "We're in this. And we're not telling anyone."

"Is that a threat?" I asked, my eyes narrowing.

"Literally the opposite of a threat." Thea gave an elegant little shrug, like she really didn't care whether I trusted her or not.

"Fine," I said. Thea was Zara's niece by marriage. That Toby was alive wasn't a secret I would have trusted her with, but Xander had—which made no sense, because Xander didn't even *like* Thea.

Deciding it was useless to engage further, I focused first on my lab work, then on what we'd found in Toby's room the night before. *The cipher disk. The poem.* Was there something else in the room we were supposed to find and decode?

Beside me, Thea placed her tablet flat on the table. I glanced at it and realized that she'd done the same search that Xander had the day before, for "A Poison Tree." I took that to mean that Xander had told her—and presumably Rebecca—exactly what we'd found.

I'm going to kill him, I thought, but then my eyes caught on one of the results that Thea's search had turned up: *fruit of the poisonous tree doctrine.*

CHAPTER 11

On the way home from school, I did a search of my own. The fruit of the poisonous tree doctrine was a legal rule that said that evidence obtained illegally was inadmissible in court.

"You're thinking." Jameson was beside me in the car. Some days, he and Xander caught a ride in my bulletproof SUV. Other days, they didn't. Xander wasn't there now.

"I'm always thinking," I replied.

"That's what I love about you, Heiress." Jameson had a habit of tossing out words that should matter like they didn't at all. "Care to share those thoughts?"

"And tip my hand?" I shot back. "So you can get there first and double-cross me?"

Jameson smiled. It was his slow, dangerous, heady smile, designed to elicit a reaction. I didn't give him one.

When we got to Hawthorne House, I retreated to my wing and waited fifteen minutes before I locked my hand around a candlestick on my fireplace mantel and pulled. That motion released a latch, and the back of the stone fireplace popped up just enough that I could fit my hands underneath and lift it upward. Oren had disabled this passageway back when there was a threat on the estate, but after that threat was resolved, it hadn't stayed disabled for long.

I stepped into the secret passageway to find Jameson waiting for me. "Fancy meeting you here, Heiress."

"You," I told him, "are the most annoying person on the face of the planet."

His lips quirked upward on one side. "I try. Headed back to Toby's wing?"

I could have lied, but he would have known I was lying, and I didn't want to wait. "Just try not to get caught by the Laughlins," I told him.

"Don't you know by now, Heiress? I never get caught."

Taking a deep breath, I stepped past the brick debris and made a beeline for Toby's study. I ran my fingers along the edges of the books, going through them shelf by shelf.

We'd checked every volume in here, but only for hidden compartments.

"Care to tell me what you're looking for?" Jameson asked.

The day before, I'd noticed the variety of books Toby Hawthorne read. Comic books and pulp horror. Greek philosophy and law volumes. Without a word to Jameson, I pulled one of the legal books off the shelf.

It took Jameson less than a minute to figure out why. "Fruit of the poisonous tree," he murmured behind me. "Brilliant."

I wasn't sure if he was talking about me—or Toby.

The book's index directed me to the entry for the fruit of the poisonous tree doctrine. As I reached the page in question, my heart sped up. There it was.

Certain letters in certain words were blacked out. The notations went on for pages. Every once in a while, there would be a punctuation mark that had been struck through—a comma, a question mark. I didn't have a pen or paper, so I used my phone to record the letters, painstakingly typing them in one by one.

The result was a string of consonants and vowels with no meaning. *For now.*

"You're thinking." Jameson paused. "You know something."

I was going to deny it, but I didn't, for one simple reason. "I found a cipher disk yesterday," I admitted, "but it was set at neutral. I don't know the code."

"Numbers." Jameson's reply was immediate and electric. "We need numbers, Heiress. Where did you find the cipher?"

My breath caught in my throat. I walked over to the clock, the one I'd taken apart the day before. I turned it over and stared at its face: the hour hand frozen at twelve and the minute hand at five.

"The fifth letter of the alphabet is *E*," Jameson said behind me. "The twelfth is *L*."

Without another word to him, I ran for the cipher disk in my room.

CHAPTER 12

Jameson followed me. Of course he did. All I cared about was getting there first.

Arriving back in my suite, I pulled the cipher disk out of my desk drawer. I matched the fifth letter on the outer wheel to the twelfth letter on the inner. *E* and *L*. And then, with Jameson standing behind me, his hands on the desk on either side of me, our bodies far too close, I began decoding the message.

S-E-C-R-E-

Partially through the first word, breath whooshed out of my lungs, because this was going to work. *Secrets.* That was the first word. *Lies.*

Beside me, Jameson grabbed a pen, but I grabbed it back from him. "My room," I told him. "My pen. My cipher disk."

"If you want to get technical, Heiress, it's all yours. Not just this room or that pen."

I ignored him and transposed letter after letter, until the entire message was decoded. I went back and added spaces and line breaks, and what I was left with was another poem.

One that I could only assume was a Toby Hawthorne original.

Secrets, lies,
All I despise.
The tree is poison,
Don't you see?
It poisoned S and Z and me.
The evidence I stole
Is in the darkest hole.
Light shall reveal all
I writ upon the...

I looked up. Jameson was still leaning over me, his face so close to mine that I could feel his breath on my cheek. Pushing my chair back into him, I stood. "That's it," I told him. "It ends there."

Jameson read the poem aloud. "*Secrets, lies, all I despise. The tree is poison, don't you see? It poisoned S and Z and me.*" He paused. "S for Skye, Z for Zara."

"*The evidence I stole,*" I picked up, then paused. "Evidence of *what*?"

"*Is in the darkest hole,*" Jameson continued. "*Light shall reveal all I writ upon the...*" He trailed off, and in the back of my head, something clicked.

"There's a word missing," I said.

"And it rhymes with *all*."

An instant later, Jameson was in motion—and so was I. We ran back, through corridor after corridor, to Toby's abandoned wing. We came to a stop just outside the door. Jameson looked at me as he stepped over the threshold.

Light shall reveal all I writ upon the...

"Wall," Jameson whispered, like he'd lifted the word directly from my thoughts. He was breathing hard—hard enough to make me think that his heart was pounding even faster than mine.

"Which wall?" I asked, stepping up beside him.

Slowly, Jameson turned, three hundred and sixty degrees. He didn't answer my question, so I threw out another one.

"Invisible ink?"

"Now you're thinking like a Hawthorne." Jameson closed his eyes. I could practically feel him vibrating with energy.

My entire body was doing the same. "*Light shall reveal all.*"

Jameson's eyelids flew open, and he turned again, until we were facing each other. "Heiress, we're going to need a black light."

CHAPTER 13

As it turned out, we needed more than one black light—and the member of the Hawthorne family in possession of seven of them was Xander. The three of us lined Toby's suite with them. We turned the overhead lights off, and what I saw took me nearly to my knees.

Toby hadn't written *a* message on the wall of his bedroom. He'd written tens of thousands of words across all the walls in the suite. Toby Hawthorne had kept a diary. His whole life was documented on the walls of his wing of Hawthorne House. He couldn't have been more than seven or eight when he'd started writing.

Jameson and Xander fell silent beside me as the three of us read. The tone of Toby's writing started off completely at odds with everything else we'd found—the drugs, the message we'd decoded, "A Poison Tree." That Toby had been seething with anger. But Young Toby? He sounded more like Xander. There was an unbridled energy to everything he wrote. He talked about conducting experiments, some of them involving explosions. He adored his older sisters. He spent entire days disappearing into the walls of the House. He worshipped his father.

What changed? That was the question I asked myself as I read faster and faster, speeding through Toby's twelfth year, his thirteenth, his fourteenth, his fifteenth. Shortly after his sixteenth birthday, I came to the exact moment when everything changed.

All that entry said was: *They lied.*

It took months—maybe years—before Toby actually put into words what that lie was. What he'd discovered, why he was angry. When I got to that confession, my entire body went leaden.

"Avery?" Xander stopped what he was doing and turned to look at me. Jameson was still reading at warp speed. He must have already read the secret that had turned me to stone, but his laser focus had remained uncompromised. He was on the hunt—and my body felt like it was shutting down.

"You okay there, champ?" Xander asked me, coming to put a hand on my shoulder. I barely felt it.

I couldn't take another step. I couldn't read another word. Because the lie that Toby Hawthorne had referenced, the secrets he mentioned in his poem?

They had to do with who he was.

"Toby was adopted." I turned to look at Xander. "Nobody knew. Not Toby. Not his sisters. *No one.* Your grandmother faked a pregnancy. When Toby was sixteen, he found something. Proof. I don't know what." I couldn't stop talking. I couldn't slow down. "They adopted him in secret. He wasn't even sure it was legal."

"Why would anyone keep an adoption a secret?" Xander sounded truly baffled.

That was a good question, but I could barely process it, because all I could think, over and over again, was that if Toby Hawthorne wasn't biologically related to the Hawthorne family, then he didn't share one ounce of their DNA.

And neither would his child.

"His handwriting..." I choked out the words. It was on the

walls, all around me—and now that I was looking for it, I recognized something I should have noticed the moment the writing had changed from a childish scrawl.

From the time he was twelve or thirteen, Toby Hawthorne had started writing in an odd fashion—a very distinctive mix of print and cursive. I'd seen that handwriting before.

I have a secret, I could hear my mother telling me less than a week before she died. *About the day you were born.*

CHAPTER 14

Late into the night, I sat in the massive leather chair behind Tobias Hawthorne's desk, staring at my birth certificate, at the signature the billionaire had highlighted. The name was my father's, but the handwriting was the same as the writing on the walls of Toby's wing.

A distinctive mix of print and cursive.

Toby Hawthorne signed my birth certificate. I couldn't say those words out loud. All I could do was think about Ricky Grambs. By the age of seven, I'd been done letting him hurt me—but at six, I thought he hung the moon. He would breeze into town, pick me up, swing me around. He'd call me his girl and tell me that he'd gotten me a present. I'd fish through his pockets, and whatever I found there—a pen, loose change, a restaurant mint—I got to keep.

It took me years to realize that every piece of treasure he ever gave me was trash.

My vision blurred, and I blinked back tears, staring at that signature: Ricky's name but Toby's writing.

I have a secret about the day you were born. I could hear my mom, as clearly as if she were in the room with me. *I have a secret.*

It was a game we had played my whole life. She was wonderful at guessing my secrets. I'd never guessed hers.

Now it was right there in front of me. Highlighted. "Toby Hawthorne signed my birth certificate." It hurt to talk. It hurt to remember every game of chess I'd played with Harry.

Ricky Grambs hadn't picked up the phone when my mother died. But Toby? He'd shown up within days. And if Toby was adopted, if he wasn't biologically a Hawthorne, then the DNA test that Zara and her husband had run meant *nothing*. It no longer ruled out the simplest solution to the question of why Tobias Hawthorne had left his fortune to a stranger.

I wasn't a stranger.

Why had "Harry" sought me out right after my mother's death? Why had a Texas billionaire visited the New England diner where my mother worked when I was six years old? Why had Tobias Hawthorne left me his fortune?

Because his son is my father. Everything else—my birthday, my name, the entire puzzle the Hawthorne brothers and I had thought we'd solved—it was exactly what Jameson had called it down in the tunnel: misdirection.

I stood up, unable to stay in one place a moment longer. I hadn't needed a father in a very long time. I'd learned to expect nothing. I'd stopped letting it hurt. But now all I could think about was that, yes, Harry used to scowl when I outmaneuvered him on the chess board, but his eyes had gleamed. He'd called me *princess* and *horrible girl*, and I'd called him *old man*.

A jagged breath caught in my throat. I walked forward, toward the double doors that separated the office from its balcony. I burst through them, and they ricocheted back.

"Toby Hawthorne signed my birth certificate." My voice was rough in my throat, but I had to say the words out loud. I had to hear them to believe them. I gulped in air and tried to take what I'd just said to its logical conclusion, but I couldn't.

I physically couldn't say the words. I couldn't even think them.

Down below, I saw movement in the pool. *Grayson.* His arms cut through the water in a brutal, punishing breaststroke. Even from a distance, I could see the way his muscles pulled against his skin. No matter how long I watched him, his pace never changed.

I wondered if he was swimming to get away from something. To silence the thoughts in his mind. I wondered how it was possible that watching him made breathing easier and harder at the same time.

Finally, he pulled himself out of the pool. As if guided by some kind of sixth sense, his head angled up. *Toward me.*

I stared at him—through the night, through the space between us. He looked away first.

I was used to people walking away. I was good at not expecting anything from anyone.

But as I retreated back inside the office, I found myself staring at my birth certificate again.

I couldn't make this not matter. I couldn't make Toby—*Harry*—not matter. Even though he'd lied to me. Even though he'd let me live in my car and buy *him* breakfast, when he came from one of the richest families in the world.

He's my father. The words came. Finally. Brutally. I couldn't unthink them. Every sign pointed to the same conclusion. I forced myself to say it out loud. "Toby Hawthorne is my father."

Why didn't he tell me? Where is he now?

I wanted answers. This wasn't just a mystery that needed solving or another layer to a puzzle. It wasn't a *game*—not to me.

Not anymore.

CHAPTER 15

"We need to talk." Jameson found me hidden away in the archive (prep school for *library*) the next day. Until now, he'd kept his distance within the walls of Heights Country Day.

Not that anyone but Eli was around to see us.

"I have to finish my calculus homework." I avoided looking directly at him. I needed space. I needed to think.

"It's E-day." Jameson pulled up a seat next to mine. "You have plenty of free time."

The modular scheduling system at Heights Country Day was complicated enough that I hadn't even memorized my own schedule. But Jameson apparently had.

"I'm busy," I insisted, annoyed at the way I always felt his presence. The way he *wanted* me to.

Jameson leaned back in his chair, balancing it on two legs, then let the front legs drop down and leaned to whisper directly into my ear. "Toby Hawthorne is your father."

I followed Jameson. Eli, who couldn't possibly have heard Jameson's whisper, followed me—out of the main building, across the quad, down a stone path to the Art Center. Inside, Jameson strode past studio after studio, until we ended up in what a sign informed me was the Black Box Theater: an enormous square room with black walls, a black floor, and stage lights built into a black ceiling. Jameson flipped a series of switches, and the overhead lights turned on. Eli took up a position by the door, and I followed Jameson to the far side of the room.

"What I said in the archive," Jameson murmured. "It was just a theory." The room was built for acoustics, built for voices to carry. "Tell me I'm wrong."

I glanced back at Eli and chose my words carefully in response. "I found a hidden compartment in your grandfather's desk. There was a copy of my birth certificate."

I didn't say Toby's name. I wouldn't, not with an audience.

"And?" Jameson prompted.

"The name was my father's." I lowered my voice so much that Jameson had to step closer to hear it. "The signature wasn't."

"I knew it." Jameson started pacing, but he turned back toward me before he got too far away. "Do you realize what this means, Heiress?" he asked, his green eyes alight.

I did. I'd said it out loud once. It made sense—more sense than anything else had made since I arrived for the reading of the will. "There could be other explanations," I said hoarsely, even though I didn't really believe that. *I have a secret.* My mom hadn't invented that game out of nowhere. My whole life, she'd been telling me there was something I didn't know.

Something big.

Something about me.

"It makes perfect sense—*Hawthorne* sense." Jameson couldn't contain himself. If I would have let him, he probably would have picked me up and twirled me around. "Twelve birds, one stone, Heiress. Whatever happened twenty years ago, the old man intended to use you to pull his prodigal son back onto the board now."

"Doesn't seem like it worked," I said, the words bitter on my tongue. I was the biggest news story in the world. I had no idea where Toby was, but the same couldn't be said in reverse.

If he is my father, then where is he? Why isn't he here?

As if that thought had beckoned him toward me, Jameson came closer. "Let's call off the bet," he said softly.

I whipped my head up to look at him. I searched for a tell on his face, something to let me know what angle he was playing.

"This is big, Heiress." If he'd been anyone else, his voice might have sounded gentle—but the Jameson Hawthorne I knew wasn't gentle. "Big enough that neither of us needs extra motivation now. Neither of us is going to solve this alone."

There was something undeniable about the way he said the word *us*, but I resisted the pull of it. "I'm at the center of this." It would have been so easy to let myself get sucked back in. To let myself feel like we really were a team. "You need me."

That was what this was about. The gentle voice. *Us*.

"And you don't need anyone?" Jameson stepped forward. Despite every warning screeching in the back of my brain, when he reached out to touch me, I didn't pull back.

The past twelve hours had turned my entire world upside down. I needed…*something*. It didn't have to mean anything. There didn't have to be feelings involved. "Fine," I said, my voice rough in my throat. "Let's call off the bet."

I expected him to kiss me then—to take advantage of my moment of weakness, to push me back against the wall and wait for my head to angle up toward his, wait for a *yes*. He looked like he wanted to. *I* wanted it.

But instead, Jameson took a step back and cocked his head to the side. "How would you feel about getting some air?"

Two minutes later, Jameson Hawthorne and I were on *top* of the Art Center. This time, Eli didn't get a chance to position himself in the doorway before Jameson locked him out.

My bodyguard knocked on the door to the roof, then pounded.

"I'm fine," I yelled back, watching as Jameson walked over to stand at the very edge of the roof. The toes of his dress shoes hung over the edge. The wind picked up. "Be careful," I said, even though he didn't know the meaning of the word.

"You know something funny, Heiress? My grandfather always said that Hawthorne men have nine lives." Jameson turned back to me. "*Hawthorne men*," he repeated, "*have nine lives*. He was talking about Toby. The old man knew his son had survived. He knew that Toby was out there. But he never did more than drop hints until he left that message for Xander."

"Find Tobias Hawthorne the Second," I said quietly.

After holding my gaze for a moment longer, Jameson disappeared behind a nearby column and came back with what appeared to be a roll of Astroturf and a bucket of golf balls. He set the bucket down, then rolled out the turf. He disappeared a second time, then came back with a golf club and snatched a ball from the bucket. He laid the ball on the turf and lined up his shot.

"I come up here," he said, looking out at the picturesque woods on the back side of the campus, "to get away." His feet shoulder width apart, he swung the club back, then took his shot. The golf ball soared off the roof of the Art Center and into the woods. "I'm not saying that I think you're overwhelmed, Heiress. I'm not saying that I think you're hurting. I'm just saying"—he held the golf club out to me—"sometimes it feels good to smack the hell out of something."

I stared at him, incredulous, then smiled. "This has got to be against the rules."

"What rules?" Jameson smirked. When I didn't move to take the club, he got another ball and lined up another shot. "Allow me to let you in on a Hawthorne trade secret, Heiress: There are no rules that matter more than winning." He paused, just for a moment. "I don't know who my father is. Skye was never what one would call *maternal*. The old man raised us. He made us in his own image." Jameson swung, and the ball went soaring. "Xan has his mind. Grayson got the gravitas. Nash has a savior complex. And I..." Another ball. Another shot. "I don't know when to give up."

Jameson turned back to me and held the club out once more. I remembered Skye telling me that the word to describe Jameson was *hungry*.

I took the club from his hand. My fingers brushed his.

"I'm the one who doesn't give up," Jameson reiterated. "But Xander's the one the old man asked to find Toby."

On the other side of the door to the roof, Eli was still banging. *I should put him out of his misery.* I looked at Jameson. *I should walk away.* But I didn't. This was the closest Jameson had come to opening up to me about what it was like growing up Hawthorne.

I walked over to the bucket of golf balls and tossed one onto the turf. I'd never held a golf club before. I had no idea what I was doing, but it looked satisfying. Sometimes, it *did* feel good to smack the hell out of something.

The first time I swung, I missed the ball.

"Head down," Jameson told me. He stepped up behind me and adjusted my grip, his arms wrapping around mine, guiding them from shoulder to fingertips. Even through my uniform blazer, I could feel the heat of his body.

"Try again," he murmured.

This time, when I swung back, Jameson swung, too. Our bodies moved in sync. I felt my shoulders rotating, felt him behind me, felt every inch of contact between us. The club connected with the ball, and I watched it soar.

A rush of emotion built up inside me, and this time I didn't push it down. Jameson had brought me up here to let go.

"If Toby's my father," I said, louder than I'd meant to, "where has he been all my life?"

I turned to face Jameson, well aware that we were standing far too close. "You know the way your grandfather's mind operated," I told him fiercely. "You know his go-to tricks. What are we missing?"

We. I'd said *we.*

"Toby 'died' years before you were born." Jameson always looked at me like I had the answer. Like I *was* the answer. "It's been twenty years since the fire on Hawthorne Island."

I felt my thoughts fall in sync with his. It had been twenty years since the fire. Twenty years since Tobias Hawthorne had revised his will to disinherit his entire family. And just like that, I had an idea.

"In the last game we played," I told Jameson, my heart thudding, "there were clues embedded in the old man's will." My pulse jumped, and it had nothing—almost nothing—to do with the way he was *still* looking at me. "But that wasn't the old man's only will."

Jameson knew exactly what I was saying. He saw what I saw. "The old man changed his middle name to Tattersall right after Toby's supposed death. And right after that, he wrote a will disinheriting the family."

I swallowed. "You're always saying he had favorite tricks. What do you think the chances are that the old will is part of *this* puzzle?"

CHAPTER 16

Wind whipping in my hair, I called Alisa from the roof to ask about the will.

"I'm unaware of any special copies of Mr. Hawthorne's prior will, but McNamara, Ortega, and Jones certainly has an original on file that you could view."

I knew exactly what Alisa meant when she said "special," but just because there wasn't an equivalent to the Red Will didn't mean that this was a dead end. Not yet.

"How soon can I see it?" I asked, my eyes still on Jameson's.

"I need you to do two things for me first."

I scowled. When I'd asked to see the Red Will, Alisa had leveraged my request to put me in a room with a team of stylists. "Not another makeover," I groaned. "Because this is about as made over as I get."

"You're perfectly presentable these days," Alisa assured me. "But I will need you to clear some time in your schedule for an appointment with Landon right after school."

Landon was a media consultant. She handled PR—and prepping me to talk to the press.

"Why do I need to meet with Landon right after school?" I asked suspiciously.

"I'd like you interview-ready within the next month. We need to be sure that we're the ones controlling the story, Avery." Alisa paused. "Not your father."

I couldn't say what I wanted to say, which was that Ricky Grambs *wasn't* my father. It wasn't *his* signature on my birth certificate.

"Fine," I said sharply. "What else?" Alisa had said "two things."

"I need you to recover your senses and let your poor bodyguard onto that roof."

After school, I met with Landon in the Oval Room.

"Last time we met, I taught you how not to answer questions. The art of answering them is a bit more complicated. With a group of reporters, you can ignore questions you don't want to answer. In a one-on-one interview, that ceases to be an option."

I tried to at least look like I was paying attention to what the media consultant was saying.

"Instead of ignoring questions," Landon continued, her posh British accent pronounced, "you have to redirect them, and you must do so in a way that ensures that people are interested enough in what you're saying that they fail to notice when you take a detour directly toward one of your preordained talking points."

"My talking points," I echoed, but my thoughts were on Tobias Hawthorne's will.

Landon's deep brown eyes didn't miss much. She arched an eyebrow at me, and I forced myself to focus.

"Lovely," she declared. "The first thing you need to decide is what you want people taking away from any given interview. To do that, you will need to formulate a personal theme, exactly six talking points, and no fewer than two dozen personal anecdotes that will humanize you *and* redirect any category of question you might receive toward one of your talking points."

"Is that all?" I asked dryly.

Landon ignored my tone. "Not quite. You'll also need to learn to identify 'no' questions."

I could do this. I could be a good little heiress celebrity. I could refrain from rolling my eyes. "What are 'no' questions?"

"They're questions that you can answer in a single word, most typically *no*. If you can't spin a question around to a talking point, or if talking too much will make you look guilty, then you need to be able to look the interviewer in the eye and, without sounding the least bit defensive, give her that one-word answer. *No. Yes. Sometimes.*"

The way she said those words sounded *so* sincere—and she hadn't even been asked a question.

"I don't have anything to feel guilty about," I pointed out. "I haven't done anything wrong."

"That," she said evenly, "is exactly the kind of thing that is going to make you sound defensive."

Landon gave me homework, and I left our session determined to ensure that Alisa held up her end of the bargain. An hour later, Oren, Alisa, Jameson, and I were on the way to the law firm of McNamara, Ortega, and Jones.

To my surprise, Xander was sitting out front when we got there. "Did you tell him we were coming?" I asked Jameson as the two of us stepped out of the SUV.

"I didn't have to," Jameson murmured back, his eyes narrowing. "He's a Hawthorne." He raised his voice loud enough for Xander to hear it. "And he'd better not have me bugged."

The fact that surveillance technology was even a possibility here said a lot about their childhood.

"It's a wonderful day for looking at legal documents," Xander replied cheerfully, sidestepping the comment about having Jameson bugged.

Neither Alisa nor Oren said a word as the five of us entered the building and rode the elevator up. When the doors opened, my lawyer led me to a corner office, where a document was lying on the desk. *Déjà vu.*

Alisa gave the three of us an Alisa Look. "I'll leave the door open," she announced, taking up a position next to Oren, right outside the door.

Jameson called after her, amused. "Would you close the door if I promised very sincerely not to ravish your client?"

"Jameson!" I hissed.

Alisa glanced back and rolled her eyes. "I've literally known you since you were in diapers," she told Jameson. "And you have *always* been trouble."

The door stayed open.

Jameson cut his eyes toward me and gave a little shrug. "Guilty as charged."

Before I could reply, Xander vaulted past us to get to the will first. Jameson and I crowded in beside him. All three of us read.

> *I, Tobias Tattersall Hawthorne, being of sound body and mind, decree that my worldly possessions, including all monetary and physical assets, be disposed of as follows:*
>
> *In the event that I predecease my wife, Alice O'Day Hawthorne, all my assets and worldly possessions shall be bequeathed unto her. In the event that*

Alice O'Day Hawthorne predeceases me, the terms of my will shall be as follows:

To Andrew and Lottie Laughlin, for years of loyal service, I bequeath a sum of one hundred thousand dollars apiece, with lifelong, rent-free tenancy granted in Wayback Cottage, located on the western border of my Texas estate.

Xander tapped his finger against that sentence. "Sounds familiar."

The bit about the Laughlins had appeared in Tobias Hawthorne's more recent will as well. Going on instinct, I scanned the will in front of us for other similarities. Oren wasn't mentioned in this one, but Nan was, under the exact same terms as Tobias Hawthorne's later will. Then I came to the part about the Hawthorne daughters.

To my daughter Skye Hawthorne, I leave my compass, may she always know true north. To my daughter Zara, I leave my wedding ring, may she love as wholly and steadfastly as I loved her mother.

The wording there was familiar, too, but in his final will, Tobias Hawthorne had also left his daughters money to cover all debts accrued as of his date of death, and a onetime inheritance of fifty thousand dollars. In this version, he really *had* left them nothing except trinkets. Nash, the only Hawthorne grandson who'd been born before this will was written, wasn't mentioned at all. There was no provision allowing the Hawthorne family to continue living in Hawthorne House. Instead, the rest of the will was simple.

The remainder of my estate, including all properties, monetary assets, and worldly possessions not other-

wise specified, is to be liquefied and the proceeds split equally among the following charities…

The list that followed was long—dozens in total.

Attached to the back of Tobias Hawthorne's will was a copy of his wife's will, containing nearly identical terms. If she died first, everything went to her husband. If he predeceased her, their assets went to charity—with the same bequests to the Laughlins and Nan, and nothing left to Zara and Skye.

"Your grandmother was in on it," I told the boys.

"She died right before Grayson was born," Jameson said. "Everyone says the grief over Toby killed her."

Had the old man told his wife that their son was still alive? Had he known—or even suspected—the truth back when this will was written?

I returned my attention to the document and read it again from the top. "There are only two major differences between this will and the last one," I said when I was done.

"You aren't in this one." Xander ticked off the first. "Which, barring time travel, makes sense, given that you weren't born until three years after it was written."

"And the charities." Jameson was in laser-focus mode. He didn't so much as spare a glance for his brother—or for me. "If there's a clue in here, it's in that list."

Xander grinned. "And you know what that means, Jamie."

Jameson made a face that suggested that he did, in fact, know what that meant.

"What?" I asked.

Jameson sighed theatrically. "Don't mind me. This is what I look like when I'm preparing to be painfully bored and predictably annoyed. If we want the rundown on the charities on this list, there's an efficient way of getting it. Prepare yourself for a lecture, Heiress."

That was the exact moment when I realized what he was talking about—and who had the information we needed. The member of the Hawthorne family who knew its charitable works intimately. Someone I'd already told about Toby. "Grayson."

CHAPTER 17

The Hawthorne Foundation looked exactly as it had the last time I'd been there. The walls were still a light silver-gray—the color of Grayson's eyes. Massive black-and-white photographs still hung all around the room. Grayson's handiwork.

This place *was* Grayson—but this time Jameson and Xander were there as a buffer between us.

"If he says the phrase *effective altruism*," Xander warned me with mock solemnity, "run."

I snorted back laughter. A door opened and shut nearby, and Grayson strode into the room. His gaze settled on me for a second or two before he looked past me to his brothers.

"To what do I owe the honor, Jamie? Xan?"

Xander opened his mouth, but Jameson beat him to speaking. "I invoke the ancient rite of *On Spake*."

Xander looked startled, then delighted.

"The what?" I said.

Grayson narrowed his eyes at his brother, then answered my question. "Anagram it."

It took me less than three seconds. "No speak."

"Exactly," Jameson said. "Once I begin telling him what I have to say, my dearest, darling older brother here can't say a single word until I finish."

"At which point, if I choose, I can invoke the sacred rite of *Taeb Nwod*." Grayson dusted an imaginary speck off the cuff of his suit. "I believe those rules expired when I was ten."

"I recall no such expiration!" Xander volunteered.

I did a little mental rearranging of the words Grayson had spoken and then shook my head. "Beatdown? You've got to be kidding me."

"It's a friendly beatdown," Xander assured me. "A *brotherly* beatdown." He paused. "More or less."

"Well?" Jameson gave Grayson a look.

In reply, Grayson took off his suit jacket and laid it on a nearby desk, presumably preparing for part two of this little ritual. "Whatever you have to tell me, Jamie, I'm all ears."

"We went to see the will the old man wrote right after Toby 'died.'" Jameson took his time with what he had to say—because he could. "Yes, I know you think asking to see the will was a bad idea. No, I don't have any particular objection to bad ideas. Long story short, we found a list of charities. We need you to look through them and see what, if anything, you notice."

Grayson arched an eyebrow.

"He can't talk until I cease *On Spake*," Jameson told me. "Let's just cherish the sound of silence for another moment."

A vein in Grayson's forehead pulsed. "Come on," I told Jameson.

He blew out a long breath. "Cease *On Spake*."

Grayson began cuffing the sleeves of his dress shirt.

"You two aren't actually going to fight, are you?" I asked warily. I turned to Xander. "They're not actually going to fight, are they?"

"Who can say?" Xander replied merrily. "But perhaps you and I should wait outside in case this gets ugly."

"I'm not going anywhere," I insisted. "Jameson, this is ridiculous."

"Not my call, Heiress."

"Grayson!" I said.

He turned to look at me. "I really would prefer you wait outside."

CHAPTER 18

"Your brothers are idiots," I told Xander, pacing back and forth in front of the building. Oren, who stood a few feet away, looked somewhat amused.

"It's fine," Xander assured me. "This is just what brothers do."

I highly doubted that.

From inside the building, there was silence.

"By tradition, the first blow is Gray's," Xander offered helpfully. "He usually goes for a leg sweep. Classic! But he'll circle Jameson first. They'll circle each other, really, and Gray will go into warnings-and-orders mode, which will cause Jamie to mock him, so on and so forth, until the first blow is struck."

There was a thud from inside. "And after that?" I asked, my eyes narrowing.

Xander grinned. "We have an average of three black belts apiece, but it usually devolves into wrestling. One of them will pin the other. Argue, argue, bicker, bicker, and voilà."

Given that Grayson had made it very clear that he thought pulling at the strings of Toby's disappearance was a bad idea, I had a guess or two about what that argument might sound like.

"I'm going back in," I muttered, but before I could, the door to the building opened.

Jameson stood there, looking only slightly worse for the wear. He didn't seem injured. A little sweaty, maybe, but not bleeding or bruised. "I take it there was no beatdown?" I said.

Jameson grinned. "What would make you think that?" He glanced over at Oren. "If you wait out here, you have my word that she'll be perfectly safe inside. It's secure."

"I know." Oren stared Jameson down. "I designed the security on this building myself."

"Can you give us a minute, Oren?" I asked. My head of security shot a hard look in Jameson's direction, then Xander's, and then nodded. Xander and I followed Jameson back inside.

"Don't worry," Jameson murmured as Grayson came into view. "I took it easy on him."

Like Jameson, Grayson appeared unharmed. As I watched, he slipped his suit jacket back on. "You two are idiots," I muttered.

"Be that as it may," Grayson replied, "you want my help."

He wasn't wrong. "Yes, we do."

"I told you this was a bad idea, Avery." Grayson's focus was on me and me alone. It was intense. I wasn't used to people being protective of me. But right now, *protection* wasn't what I wanted—or needed—from him.

"While you and Jameson were playing WWF like eight-year-olds," I said, "did he happen to tell you that Toby was adopted?" I swallowed and looked down because this next part was harder to say. "Did he tell you about my birth certificate?"

"Your what?" Xander said immediately.

Grayson stared at me. He was just as capable as any Hawthorne of reading between the lines. Toby was adopted. I'd mentioned my birth certificate. Everyone in this room knew why this search mattered to me now.

"Here's a picture I took." I held my phone out to Grayson. "Those are the charities listed in the will your grandfather wrote shortly after Toby's disappearance."

Grayson managed to take the phone from me without our fingers so much as brushing. Beside me, I could feel Jameson's stare, just as palpable as his brother's.

"There are very few surprises on this list." Grayson looked up from the phone just in time to catch me watching him read. "Most of these organizations have received regular support—or, at the very least, a sizable onetime donation—from the Hawthorne Foundation."

I forced myself to pay attention to what Grayson was saying, not the way his silvery eyes settled on mine as he talked. "You said 'few surprises,'" I pointed out. "Not none."

"Off the top of my head, I see four organizations that I don't recognize. That doesn't mean we haven't given to them before...."

"But it's a start." Jameson's voice buzzed with a familiar energy—familiar to me, almost certainly familiar to his brothers.

"The Allport Institute," Grayson rattled off. "Camden House. Colin's Way. And the Rockaway Watch Society. Those are the only four organizations on this list that I haven't seen in the foundation's records."

Immediately, my brain started cataloging what Grayson had said, playing with the words and the letters, looking for a pattern. "Institute, house, way, watch," I tried out loud.

"Watch, house, institute, way." Jameson scrambled the order.

"Four words," Xander offered. "And four names. Allport, Camden, Colin, Rockaway."

Grayson stepped between the two of us and past Jameson—and

kept on walking. "I'll leave you three to it," he said. Near the doorway, he paused. "But, Jamie? You're wrong." And then Grayson said something in a language I deeply suspected was Latin.

Jameson's eyes flashed, and he responded in the same language.

I glanced at Xander. The youngest Hawthorne's eyebrows—well, eyebrow, really, since he'd burned the other one off—skyrocketed. He clearly understood what had just been said but volunteered no translation.

Instead, he tugged me toward the doorway—and the SUV parked outside. "Come on."

CHAPTER 19

On the drive back to Hawthorne House, Jameson, Xander, and I buried ourselves in our phones. I assumed that their missions were the same as mine: to research the four charities that Grayson had identified.

My intuition was that they might not actually *be* charities, that Tobias Hawthorne might have made them up as part of the puzzle, but a series of internet searches quickly dispelled that theory. The Allport Institute, Camden House, Colin's Way, and the Rockaway Watch Society were all registered nonprofits. Sorting out the details of each one took longer.

The Allport Institute was a research facility based in Switzerland, dedicated to studying the neuroscience of memory and dementia. I scrolled through the staff page, reading each of the scientists' bios. Then I clicked on some news coverage about the institute's latest clinical trials. *Short-term memory loss. Dementia. Alzheimer's. Amnesia.*

I sat with that for a moment. *Is this a clue? To what?* I glanced out the window and caught sight of Jameson's reflection in the glass. His hair could never quite decide which way to lie, and even caught up in thought, his face was always in motion.

When I finally managed to turn my attention back to my phone, the next search term I typed in wasn't one of the charities. It was my best approximation of the words that Grayson had said to Jameson back at the foundation.

Est unus ex nobis. Nos defendat eius. As I'd suspected, it was Latin. An online translator told me that it meant *It is one of us. We protect it.* Jameson's response, *Scio*, meant *I know.* It only took me one more search to realize that the same translation would hold if *it* was replaced with *she. She is one of us. We protect her.*

Maybe I should have bristled at that. Three weeks ago, I probably would have, but three weeks ago, I never would have dreamed that they would come to see me as one of them.

That I could *be* one of them, not just an outsider looking in.

Trying not to let that thought consume me, I forced myself to move on to the next charity on my list. Camden House was an in-patient rehabilitation center for substance abuse and addiction, focused on the "whole person." The website was full of testimonials. The staff was full of doctors, therapists, and other professionals. The grounds were beautiful.

But the website didn't provide any answers.

An institute for memory research in Switzerland. An addiction treatment facility in Maine. I thought about the pills and powder that we'd found in Toby's room. What if Tobias Hawthorne had used his will—and these four charities—to tell a story? *Maybe Toby was an addict. Maybe he was a patient at Camden House. As for the Allport Institute...*

I didn't get the chance to finish that thought before we pulled through the gates of the estate. As we wound our way up the long drive, I snuck a look at the boys. Xander was still fixated on his phone, but Jameson was staring straight ahead. The moment we stepped out of the car, he took off.

So much for working on this *together.*

"Oh, look," Xander said, nudging me in the side. "There's Nan. Hello, Nan!"

The boys' great-grandmother glared at Xander from the porch. "And just what have you been up to?" she asked him sharply.

"Nonsense and mischief," he replied solemnly. "Always."

She scowled, and he bounded up onto the porch and kissed the top of her head. She swatted at him. "Think you can sugar me up, do you?"

"Perish the thought," Xander replied. "I don't *have* to sugar you up. I'm your favorite!"

"Are not," Nan grunted. She poked him with her cane. "Go on with you. I want to talk to the girl."

Nan didn't ask if I wanted to talk. She just waited for me to approach, then took my arm for balance. "Walk with me," she ordered. "In the garden."

She said nothing for at least five minutes as we made our way, at a snail's pace, through a topiary garden. Dense bushes had been shaped into sculptures. Most were abstract, but I saw a topiary elephant and couldn't keep an incredulous look from settling over my face.

"Ridiculous," Nan scoffed. "All of it." After a long moment, she turned to me. "Well?"

"Well, what?" I said.

"What have you done to find my boy?" Nan's harsh expression trembled slightly, and her grip on my arm tightened.

"I'm trying," I said quietly. "But I don't think Toby wants to be found."

If Toby Hawthorne had wanted to be found, he could have returned to Hawthorne House at any time in the last twenty years. *Unless he doesn't remember.* That thought hit me out of nowhere.

The Allport Institute focused on memory research—Alzheimer's, dementia, and *memory loss*. What if *that* was the story Tobias Hawthorne was telling in the will? What if his son had lost his memory?

What if Harry didn't *know* he was Toby Hawthorne?

The thought that he might not have lied to me nearly took me to my knees. I forced myself to slow down. I was leaping to conclusions. I didn't even know for certain that the four charities had been chosen to tell a story.

"Have you ever heard of Camden House?" I asked Nan. "It's a treatment center for—"

"I know what it is." Nan cut me off, her voice gruff.

There was no easy way to ask this next question. "Did your daughter and son-in-law send Toby there?"

"He wasn't an addict," Nan spat. "I know addicts. That boy was just...confused."

I wasn't about to bicker with her about words. "But they sent him to Camden House, for his *confusion*?"

"He was angry when he left and angry when he got back." Nan shook her head. "That summer..." Her lip quivered. She didn't finish what she was saying.

"Was that the summer of the fire?" I asked softly.

Before Nan could reply, a shadow fell across the two of us. Mr. Laughlin stepped onto the garden path. He was holding a pair of shears. "Everything okay here?" He scowled, and I thought about Mrs. Laughlin calling me cruel.

"Everything's fine," I said, my voice tight.

Mr. Laughlin looked toward Nan. "We talked about this, Pearl," he said gently. "It isn't healthy." Clearly, he knew what I'd told Nan about Toby. And clearly, he didn't believe me any more than his wife did.

After a long silence, Mr. Laughlin turned back to me. "I made some repairs in the House." A muscle in his jaw tightened. "To one of the older wings. When things fall into disrepair around here..." He gave me a look. "People get hurt."

I understood then that *one of the older wings* was code for *Toby's*. I wasn't sure what the groundskeeper meant by repairs until I made my way back into Hawthorne House and went to check.

Toby's wing had been bricked up again.

CHAPTER 20

On the way from Toby's wing to mine, I found myself glancing back over my shoulder every hundred feet. As I stepped into my hall, I heard Libby's voice: "Did you know about this?"

"You're going to have to be a bit more specific, darlin'." That was Nash, obviously. I could see his silhouette in the doorway to my sister's room.

"Your lawyer girlfriend. These papers. Did you know?"

I couldn't see Libby at all, so I had no idea how she was looking at Nash or what kind of papers she was holding.

"Sweetheart, I wouldn't let Alisa hear you refer to her as my anything."

"Don't call me sweetheart."

This didn't feel like a conversation I had any business overhearing, so I crept for the door to my room, opened it, and slipped inside. Closing the door behind me, I flipped on my light. A breeze caught my hair.

I turned to see that one of the massive windows on my far wall was open. *I didn't leave that window open.* A breath caught in my throat, and I felt the drum of my heart in every inch of my body. I'd had nightmares like this before: First you notice one thing that's off, and then—

Blood. The muscles in my throat tightened like a vise. *There's blood.* Panic flooded my body like a shot of adrenaline straight to the heart. *Get out. Get out get out get—*

But I couldn't move. All I could do was stare in horror at the white bedsheet lying under my open window, drenched in blood. *Move. You have to move, Avery.* Sitting on top of the white sheet, there was a heart.

Human?

And through the heart—*a knife.* My lungs felt like they were locked. My body didn't listen no matter how many times I told it to run. *There's a knife. And a heart. And—*

I let out a low gurgling sound. I still couldn't run, but I managed to stumble backward.

I tried to scream, but no sound came out. I felt the way I had in the Black Wood, in the sights of someone who wanted me dead. *I have to get out of here. I have to—*

"Breathe, kid." Nash was there suddenly. He placed a hand on each of my shoulders. He bent down, putting his face even with mine. "In and out. That's a good girl."

"My room," I wheezed. "There's a heart in my room. A knife—"

A dangerous expression flickered across Nash's face. "Call Oren," he told Libby, who had appeared beside us. When Nash turned back to me, his expression was gentle. "In and out," he said again.

I sucked in a frantic breath and tried to look at my room, but the eldest Hawthorne brother sidestepped and blocked me from seeing a damn thing except for his face. He was suntanned and had a five o'clock shadow. He was wearing his trademark cowboy hat. His gaze was steady.

I breathed.

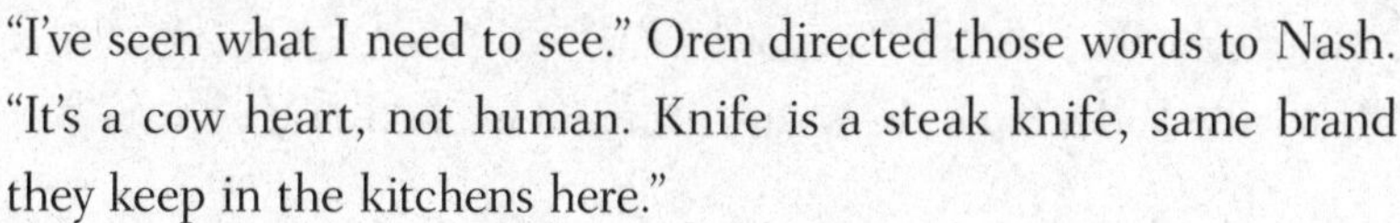

"I've seen what I need to see." Oren directed those words to Nash. "It's a cow heart, not human. Knife is a steak knife, same brand they keep in the kitchens here."

My mind went to the List. Would-be stalkers. *Threats.*

"The linens are Hawthorne linens," Oren continued.

"Inside job?" Nash asked, his jaw tightening. "One of the staff?"

"Likely," Oren confirmed. He turned to me. "Upset anyone lately?"

I managed to get ahold of myself. "I might have upset the Laughlins." I thought about Mrs. Laughlin calling me cruel. About her husband, warning me about people getting hurt.

"You think the Laughlins did this?" Libby asked, her eyes wide.

"Not a chance in the world." Nash's reply was firm. He glanced at Oren. "More likely, someone on the staff got wind that Mr. and Mrs. L are in a tizzy about something and took that to mean it's gloves off."

Oren digested that. "Can you get someone in here to clean this up?" he asked Nash.

Nash responded by making a call. "Mel? I need a favor."

I recognized the maid who showed up a few minutes later. Mellie had a habit of looking at Nash like he hung the moon.

"Can you take care of this for me, darlin'?" Nash asked, gesturing toward the mess.

Mellie nodded, her dark brown eyes fixed on his. Alisa had told me once that Mellie was "one of Nash's." I had no idea how many of the household staff the oldest Hawthorne brother had saved—or how many of "my" people saw me as a villain who'd stolen Nash's inheritance.

"I need you to talk to folks for me," Nash told Mellie. "Make it clear: This ain't open season. I don't care who's looking the other way or why. Hands off. You got me?"

Mellie laid a hand on Nash's arm and nodded. "Of course."

CHAPTER 21

"There will be some changes to your security protocol on the estate until we get this figured out," Oren told me after everyone else had left. "But before we talk about those, we need to talk about the Laughlins. More specifically, we need to talk about *how* you upset them."

I grappled for a way to respond without giving too much away. "Jameson, Xander, and I were messing around in Toby's wing."

Oren folded his arms over his chest. "I know. I also know *why*."

Oren had access to the security system—and one of his men had been in the Black Box that afternoon. *What exactly did Eli overhear?*

My head of security laid it out for me. "Tobias Hawthorne the Second. You think he's alive."

"I *know* he is."

Oren was silent for a long moment. "Have I told you how I came to be in Mr. Hawthorne's employ?"

I had no idea where that question had come from. "No."

"I was career military, ages eighteen to thirty-two. I would have stayed in until I hit twenty years, but there was an incident." The way Oren said the word *incident* sent ice down my spine. "Everyone in my unit was killed except me. By the time Mr. Hawthorne found me a year later, I was in bad shape."

I couldn't picture Oren out of control. "Why are you telling me this?"

"Because," Oren said, "I need you to understand that I owe Mr. Hawthorne my life. He gave me a purpose. He dragged me back into the light. And the last thing he asked of me was that I stay on to head *your* security team." Oren let that sink in. "Whatever I have to do to keep you safe," he continued, his voice low, "I will do it."

"Do you think there's a threat?" I asked him. "A real one? Are you worried about whoever left that heart?"

"I'm worried," Oren replied, "about what you and the boys are doing. About the ghosts you're digging up."

"Toby's alive," I said fiercely. "I knew him. I think he's—"

"Stop," Oren ordered.

My father, I finished silently. "Grayson would kill me for telling you this," I said. "He thinks that if it gets out that Toby's alive—"

Oren finished my sentence for me. "The repercussions could be deadly."

"What?" That hadn't been what I was going to say. At all.

"Avery," Oren said, his voice low, "right now the family believes that there is no effective way of challenging the will—no way of getting ahold of the fortune that Mr. Hawthorne left to you. Zara and Constantine would much rather deal with you inheriting and the law firm holding the reins than with the fortune passing to *your* heirs, and that's assuming that your death wouldn't count as defaulting on the terms of the will and revert the entire fortune to charity. Mr. Hawthorne always thought ten steps ahead. He tied their fortunes to yours. He made you as safe as he could. But if the will isn't ironclad? If there's another heir..."

Someone might decide that killing me is worth it? I didn't say that out loud.

"You need to lie low," Oren told me. "Whatever it is you and the boys are up to—stop."

I couldn't stop. That night, with security posted right outside my door, I resumed the search I'd started conducting that afternoon.

The Allport Institute was a center for memory research. Camden House was an addiction treatment facility—and, based on my conversation with Nan that afternoon, Toby had been a patient there. A new search on the Rockaway Watch Society told me that Rockaway Watch was a small coastal town directly across from Hawthorne Island. *Kaylie Rooney was from Rockaway Watch.* It took me a good fifteen minutes to put it together, but once I did, the neurons in my brain started firing painfully fast.

There was a story here—one that started with Toby angry and addicted, one that involved the fire and the young people who'd died there. *What about the Allport Institute?* Had Toby lost his memory after the fire? Was that why he'd never returned home?

With laser focus to rival Jameson's, I did a search for the last remaining charity on Grayson's list: Colin's Way. I'd verified earlier that it existed, but I hadn't dug deep. This time I did a once-over of the website. The first thing I saw on the landing page was a picture of a bunch of elementary schoolers playing basketball. I clicked on a tab labeled *Our Story* and read.

> *Colin's Way provides a safe after-school environment for kids between the ages five and twelve. Founded in memory of Colin Anders Wright (pictured at right), we are in the business of Playing, Giving, and Growing—so all children have a future.*

It took me a second to place the name. Like Kaylie Rooney, Colin Anders Wright had died on Hawthorne Island twenty years earlier. *How soon did Colin's family create a charity in his memory?* I wondered. It must have been nearly immediate, for Colin's Way to have been included in Tobias Hawthorne's twenty-year-old will. I searched for news articles within a month of the fire with the search term *Colin's Way* and found a half dozen articles.

Right after the fire, then. I toggled back to the Colin's Way website and dug through the media section—through years, then decades, until I hit the first press clipping available—a press conference of some kind.

I hit Play on the video. There was a family on-screen: a woman with two young children, standing behind a man. At first I thought they were husband and wife, but it soon became clear that they were siblings.

"This is a horrific tragedy, one from which our family will never recover. My nephew was an incredible young man. He was intelligent and driven, competitive but kind. There is no telling what good he would have done in this world had the actions of others not robbed him of that opportunity. I know that if Colin were here, he would tell me to let go of the anger. He would tell me to concentrate on what matters. And so, along with his mother, his siblings, and my wife, who could not be here today, I am proud to announce the formation of Colin's Way, a charity that will channel my nephew's competitive and giving spirit to bring the joy of athletics, teamwork, and family to underprivileged children in our communities."

There was something about the man's voice that stuck with me, something jarring. Something familiar. When the camera zoomed in closer, I noticed his eyes.

Ice blue, bordering on gray. Once he ended his speech, reporters called out for his attention. "Mr. Grayson!"

"Mr. Grayson, over here!"

A ticker bar ran across the bottom of the screen. Feeling dazed and borderline dizzy, I read the name of Colin Anders Wright's uncle: *Sheffield Grayson*.

CHAPTER 22

The next morning, Jameson called to me from the other side of my fireplace, and I pulled the candlestick on the mantel to trigger the release.

"Did you find what I found?" he asked me. "Two of the four charities have connections to victims of the fire. I'm still piecing together the rest, but I have a theory."

"Does your theory involve Toby having been a patient at Camden House and potentially losing his memory after the fire?" I asked.

Jameson leaned toward me. "We're brilliant."

I thought about the rest of what I'd discovered. He hadn't mentioned Sheffield Grayson.

"Heiress?" Jameson leaned back and assessed me. "What is it?"

It was obvious to me that he hadn't looked up anything about Colin's Way beyond the charity's namesake. Obvious that he hadn't seen the video I'd seen. Without a word, I pulled it up for him on my phone. I handed it over. As Jameson watched, I finally found my voice.

"His eyes," I said. "And his last name is Grayson. I know that Skye never told you anything about your fathers, but you all have last names as first names. Do you think…"

Jameson handed the phone back. "Only one way to find out." He came to stand right behind me. "We could go out your door, like normal people, but one of Oren's men is stationed outside, and I doubt anyone on your security team would sign off on you going to visit my mother."

Going to visit a woman who'd tried to have me killed was a bad idea. I knew that. But Grayson was nineteen, which meant that he'd been conceived twenty years ago—not long after the fire on Hawthorne Island. What were the chances that was a coincidence? There was no such thing in Hawthorne House. And right now, the only person who could answer our questions was Skye.

"Oren isn't going to be happy about this," I told Jameson.

He smiled. "We'll be back before anyone realizes we're gone."

Jameson knew the secret passageways like the back of his hand. He got us to the massive indoor garage unseen. He pulled a motorcycle off a rack on the wall and solved the puzzle box where the keys were kept. The next thing I knew, he was wearing a helmet and holding a second one out to me.

"Do you trust me, Heiress?" Jameson had donned a leather jacket. He looked like trouble. The good kind.

"Not even a little," I replied, but I took the helmet from his outstretched hand, and when he climbed onto the motorcycle, I climbed on behind him.

CHAPTER 23

Skye Hawthorne was staying at a luxury hotel—a hotel I *owned*. It was the kind of place that had caviar on the room-service menu and offered in-room spa services. I had no idea how Skye was paying for a room, or if she was paying. The idea that *this* was her punishment for an attempt on my life was infuriating.

"Easy," Jameson murmured beside me as he knocked on the door. "We need her to talk."

Talk first, I thought. *Have security remove her from the premises later.*

Skye opened the door wearing a crimson silk robe that brushed the tips of her toes and flowed around her as she moved. "Jamie." She smiled at Jameson. "Shame on you for not visiting your poor mother until now."

Jameson gave me the briefest of warning looks, a clear *Let me handle this.*

"I'm an awful son," Jameson agreed, dialing his level of charm up to meet Skye's. "Horrid, really, so preoccupied with the person you tried to have killed that I've barely spared a thought for how difficult getting caught must have been for you."

I hadn't breathed a word to Jameson about what his mother had done, but he knew Skye had moved out. It probably hadn't taken him long to figure out that Grayson had *forced* her out—and why.

"What has your brother been telling you?" Skye demanded, without specifying which brother she was talking about. "And you believe him? Believe *her*—"

"I believe," Jameson said smoothly, "that I've found Grayson's father."

That got an eyebrow arch out of Skye. "Was he lost?" The victim act melted off her like snow in the sun.

"Sheffield Grayson." I said the name, forcing Skye's gaze to flit toward me. "His nephew died in the fire on Hawthorne Island, along with your brother, Toby."

"I haven't the faintest idea what you're talking about."

"And I have no idea why you think lying to me is a good idea, when I could have you kicked out of this hotel," I shot back. I'd intended to let Jameson handle this. Really. It just hadn't worked out that way.

"You?" Skye sniffed. "This hotel has been in my family for decades. You are under quite the delusion if you think—"

"That the management will care more about the feelings of the new owner than about yours?"

"Aren't you just adorable?" Skye retreated into the room. "Don't just stand there," she called back. "You're letting in a draft."

With a glance at Jameson, I crossed the threshold—and found myself almost immediately joined by Oren and Eli. Apparently, I'd been under closer guard than I'd realized.

Skye gave every appearance of being delighted at the appearance of my security team. "It appears we have a party." She sat down on a chaise longue and stretched out her legs. "Let's get down to business, shall we? I have something you want, and I would like a few assurances, starting with how very welcome I will be to stay in this penthouse indefinitely."

Like hell, I thought.

"Counteroffer," Jameson interjected before I could reply. "If you answer our questions, I won't tell Xander what you did." He flopped down on a sofa next to Skye's chaise. "I'm sure Nash has put two and two together. I figured it out quickly enough. But Xan? For all he knows, this is just another little trip of yours. I'd hate to have to tell him about your murderous impulses."

"Jameson Winchester Hawthorne, I am your mother. I brought you into this world." Skye reached for a nearby glass of champagne, and I noticed that there was a second glass beside it.

She wasn't here alone.

"However," she continued with a heavy sigh, "because I am in such a generous mood, I suppose I will answer a question or two."

"Is Sheffield Grayson Gray's father?" Jameson wasted no time.

Skye took a sip. "Not in any way that signifies."

"Biologically," Jameson pressed.

"If you must know," Skye said, staring at him over the rim of her glass, "then, yes, technically Sheff is Grayson's father. But what does a little biology matter? I'm the one who raised you all."

Jameson snorted. "By some definitions."

"Does Sheffield Grayson know that he has a son?" I asked, my mind full of Grayson, wondering what this would mean for him.

Skye gave an elegant little shrug. "I haven't the faintest idea."

"You never told him?" Jameson asked.

"Why would I?"

I stared at her. "You got pregnant on purpose." Nash had told me as much.

"You were grieving," Jameson said softly. "So was he."

The softness seemed to get to Skye in a way that nothing else had. "Toby and I were so close. Sheff practically raised Colin. We understood each other, for a time."

"For a time," Jameson repeated. "Or for a night?"

"Honestly, Jamie, what does it matter?" Skye was getting impatient now. "You boys never wanted for anything. My father gave you the world. The staff spoiled you. You all had each other, and you had me. Why wasn't that enough?"

"Because," Jameson said, his voice rough, "we didn't really have you."

Skye set her glass down. "Don't you dare rewrite history. What do you think it was like for me? Son after son—and every single one of you preferred my father."

"They were children," I said.

"Hawthornes are never children, darling," Skye told me archly. "But let's not argue. We're family, Jamie, and family is so very important. Don't you agree, Avery?"

Something about that question and the way she'd said it was deeply unsettling.

"In fact," Skye continued, "I'm considering having another child. I'm young enough, still. Healthy. My sons have turned their backs on me. I deserve something of my own, don't I?"

Something, I thought, my heart aching for Jameson. *Not someone.*

"You never told Sheffield Grayson that he had a son." I returned to the issue at hand. The sooner I could get Jameson out of here, the better.

"Sheff knew who I was," Skye said. "If he'd wanted to follow up, he could have. It was a test of sorts: If I didn't matter enough to chase—then what use were they to me?"

They. I registered her word choice. She wasn't just talking about *Grayson*'s father.

Skye leaned back against the chaise longue. "Frankly, I suspect that Sheff knows exactly what came of our time together." She met Jameson's eyes. "This family is prominent enough that any of the men I slept with would have to live under a rock not to know that they had a son."

She was telling him that *his* father—whoever he was—knew.

"We're done here," I said, standing up. "Come on, Jameson."

He didn't move. I laid a hand on his shoulder. After a moment, he reached up to touch my fingers. I let him. Jameson Hawthorne didn't like being vulnerable. He didn't like needing people any more than I did.

"Come on," I told him again. We'd gotten what we came for: confirmation.

"Won't you stay a bit longer?" Skye asked. "I'd love to introduce you to my new friend."

"Your friend," Jameson repeated, his eyes going to the second glass of champagne.

"Your little heiress knows him," Skye said, taking a sip of champagne. She waited for that comment to land, waited for confusion to really sink in before she smiled and went for the jugular. "Your father is such a *lovely* man, Avery."

CHAPTER 24

Skye Hawthorne. And Ricky. Skye Hawthorne was sleeping with Ricky.

He's not my father. I clung to that as Oren and Eli ushered us away from Skye's suite. *Ricky Grambs is not my father.* He also wasn't a "lovely man." Skye Hawthorne was caviar and champagne, and Ricky was throwing-up-cheap-beer-in-motel-bathrooms. He didn't have two dimes to rub together. But he did have a claim—however tenuous—to me.

I felt like I was going to be sick. *In fact*, I could hear Skye saying with a billion-dollar twinkle in her eyes, *I'm considering having another child*. Was that her plan? Get pregnant with my half-sibling? *Not mine.* That thought wasn't as comforting as it should have been, because any child of Ricky's would be *Libby*'s half-sibling—and I would do anything for Libby.

"What were you thinking?" Oren snapped when we were sequestered safely in an elevator. "A woman who tried to have you killed is sleeping with a man who stands to inherit if you die—and you ditched your protection detail to *put yourself in a room with her*."

I'd never thought of Ricky as one of my heirs, but I was too young for a will. His name was on my birth certificate.

"Why didn't you know?" I shot back at Oren before I could rein in the storm of emotions churning in my gut. "They're both on your list, aren't they? How could you not know that they..." I trailed off, sucking in a breath that I couldn't bring myself to let out.

"You did know," Jameson concluded. Oren didn't deny it. The second the elevator door opened, Jameson pulled me out. "Let's get out of here, Heiress."

Eli stepped to block him. Oren broke Jameson's hold on my arm. I could feel the exact moment when the other people in the lobby noticed us. The moment they recognized me.

"She's not going anywhere but school," Oren told Jameson quietly. His expression looked perfectly pleasant. My head of security knew how not to make a scene.

Jameson crooked his head to look at me. He *excelled* at making scenes. There was an invitation in his green eyes—and a promise. If I went with him, he'd find a way to make us both forget what had just happened.

I wanted that. But girls like me didn't always get what we wanted. I looked down. "Jameson." My voice was quiet. People were staring. Out of the corner of my eye, I saw someone lift a phone and snap our picture.

"On second thought," Jameson said grandly, "Oren's right. Play it safe, Heiress." The look he gave me then was one I felt through every square inch of my body. "For now."

CHAPTER 25

Eli stuck to my side all day. Anytime I tried to get space, amber-ringed blue eyes stared me down. At one point, he informed me that Oren had tightened all security protocols—not just at Country Day but also on the estate. I wasn't going *anywhere* without an escort.

When Oren came to collect us that afternoon, Alisa was in the back seat of the SUV. The first thing she did after I buckled myself in was hand me a tablet. I looked down at the screen and saw a photograph, one that had been taken at the hotel. Jameson's eyes were dark and glittering, and I was staring at him the way a thousand other girls had probably stared at Jameson Hawthorne.

Like he mattered.

The headline read *Tensions Grow Between Heiress and Hawthorne Family.*

"This is not the message we want to be sending," Alisa told me. "I've already arranged for damage control. There's a memorial fundraiser at Country Day tomorrow evening. You and the Hawthorne brothers will be in attendance."

Some teenagers got grounded. I got sentenced to black-tie galas. "Fine," I said.

"I'll also need your signature on this." Alisa handed me a three-page form. I flashed back to the conversation I'd overheard between Libby and Nash, then read the bold print on the form: **Petition for Emancipation of Minor**.

"Emancipation?" I said.

"You're seventeen. You have permanent housing and substantial income. Your legal guardian is willing to consent, and you have the most powerful law firm in the state behind you. We're not anticipating any difficulties here."

"Libby consented?" I asked. She hadn't sounded happy about the papers to me.

"I can be very persuasive," Alisa said. "And with Ricky in the picture, this is the right move. Once you're emancipated, he has no standing to try anything in the courts."

"And," Oren added from the front seat, "you'll be able to sign a will."

Once I was emancipated, Ricky would have nothing to gain from my death.

Alisa handed me a pen. As I read through the form, I thought about Libby. Then I thought about Ricky, about Skye—and I signed.

"Excellent," Alisa declared. "Now, there's just one final matter that needs your attention." She handed me a small square of paper with a number written on it.

"What's that?" I asked.

"It's your friend Max's new phone number."

I stared at her. "What?"

Alisa laid her hand lightly on my shoulder. "I got her a phone."

"But her mother—"

"Will never know," Alisa said briskly. "That probably makes me a very bad influence, but you need someone. I understand that,

Avery. And you don't want that someone to be a Hawthorne. Whatever's going on with you and Jameson—"

"There's nothing going on between us."

That got me an Alisa Look and then some. "First the roof, then the hotel." She paused. "Call your friend Max. Let her be your person. Not one of them."

CHAPTER 26

"You glorious beach." An hour later, Max answered her new phone sounding downright upbeat.

"You got the phone."

"It is the most beautiful thing I have seen in my bobforsaken life. Hold on a second. I have to turn on the shower."

A second later, I could hear running water. "You're not actually in the shower, are you?"

"My parents don't need to overhear me talking to you on my new burner phone," Max replied. "This is some double-oh-seven-level shift right here, Ave. I'm motherfaxing James Bond, motherfaxers! And yes, I am in the shower. Stealth, thy name is Max."

I snorted. "I've missed you." I paused then, thinking of our last couple of conversations. Max had accused me of making our friendship all about me. She hadn't been wrong. "I know that I haven't been—"

"Don't," Max cut me off. "Okay?"

"Okay." I hesitated for a second or two. "Are we... okay?"

"That depends," Max replied. "Anyone try to kill you lately?"

After I'd been shot at, Max had wanted me to get out, but

leaving Hawthorne House meant giving up the inheritance. To get the money, I had to stay for a year—Alisa had made that very clear.

"Your silence on the issue of people trying to kill you is deeply disturbing."

"I'm fine," I told Max. "It's just…"

"Just?"

I tried to decide where to start. "Someone left a bloody cow heart in my bedroom. With a knife."

"Avery!" Max sighed. "Tell me everything."

"So, to summarize," Max said, "the dead uncle? Not dead, might be your father. Hot boys are also tragic, everyone wants a piece of your fine ash, and the woman who tried to have you killed is foxing your father?"

I winced. "That pretty much covers it."

"You know what I'd like for my birthday?" Max asked calmly.

Max's birthday. It's tomorrow. "A little less drama?"

"Functional life-sized re-creations of the top-three most lovable droids in the *Star Wars* universe," Max corrected. "And a little less drama."

"How are you?" I asked. That was the question I'd failed to ask way too many times before.

"Delightful," Max replied.

"Max."

"Things here have been…fine."

"That sounds like a lie," I said. Max's ex had sent compromising photos of her to her parents when she broke up with him for trying to sell information on me to the press.

Her life definitely wasn't *fine* right now.

"I'm thinking of going on a mission trip," Max told me. "Maybe a long one."

Max's parents were religious. So was Max. It wasn't just something she did for their benefit—but I'd never heard her talking about mission trips before.

How bad are things at home? At school? "Is there anything I can do?" I asked.

"Yes," Max replied seriously. "You can tell your sorry excuse for a father to stick his head up his asp and eat ship. And ducks. Ducks and ship, in that order."

There was a reason Max was my best friend. "Anything else?"

"You could tell me what Jameson Hawthorne's abs feel like," Max suggested innocently. "Because I saw that picture of the two of you, and my psychic senses are telling me that you have communed with those abs."

"No!" I said. "There has been absolutely no communing."

"And why is that?" Max pressed.

"I have a lot going on right now."

"You always have a lot going on," Max told me. "And you don't like wanting things." She sounded oddly serious. "You're really good at protecting yourself, Avery."

She wasn't telling me anything I didn't know. "So?"

"You're a billionaire now. You have an entire team of people to protect you. The world is your motherfaxing oyster. It's okay to want things." Max turned off the shower. "It's okay to go after what you want."

"Who says I want anything?" I asked.

"My psychic senses," Max replied. "And that picture."

CHAPTER 27

I wasn't surprised to find Eli positioned outside my door. After the incident with the heart, I could probably expect a personal security escort—even on the estate—for the foreseeable future. I was, however, surprised to find Grayson standing beside Eli. He was wearing a black suit with an immaculate white dress shirt and no tie, and my mind went to the way he'd looked cuffing his sleeves, preparing to fight.

Whatever hushed conversation Eli and Grayson had been having ceased the second I stepped out into the hall.

"You didn't tell me that someone left a bloody heart in your room." Grayson was Not Pleased—and no one did Not Pleased like Grayson Hawthorne "Why?"

It was clear from his tone that Grayson expected an answer. As a general rule, when Grayson Hawthorne demanded something, the world obliged.

"When would I have told you?" I asked. "I haven't seen you since it happened. With very few exceptions, you've been doing an excellent job of avoiding me all week."

"I'm not avoiding you," Grayson said, but he couldn't even say the words without looking away.

In the back of my mind, I could hear Max telling me that I didn't like wanting things. It was annoying when she was right.

"You went to see my mother." Grayson didn't phrase that sentence as a question.

I glared at Eli, who apparently had a very big mouth.

"Hey," Eli said, holding up his hands. "I didn't tell him."

"Oren?" I asked Grayson, scowling. "Or Alisa?"

"Neither," Grayson replied, and he brought his gaze back to mine. "I saw a picture of you at the hotel. I'm more than capable of making inferences myself."

I tried not to read too much into that last sentence, but I couldn't help thinking about the *inference* that Max had made about that picture of Jameson and me. Was that why Grayson was acting like this?

You're the one who stepped back, I thought. *This is what you wanted.*

"If you needed something from Skye," Grayson said, his voice strained, "all you had to do was tell me."

I remembered then *what* I'd needed from Skye. What she'd confirmed. Suddenly, nothing else mattered.

"Have you seen Jameson today?" I asked Grayson, a muscle in my stomach twisting. "He skipped school. Did he... come find you?"

"No." Grayson's jaw tightened. "Why?"

Jameson hadn't told Grayson about his father, but it didn't feel right for me to do it. "We figured something out." I looked down. "About the charities in the will."

"You don't stop." Grayson shook his head. His arms stayed by his sides, but I saw the thumb on his right hand rubbing the back of his forefinger—a small loss of control that made me think he might be on the verge of a bigger one. "And neither," he continued, "does Jameson." He turned then, tension visible in his neck and jaw, even as his voice remained deadly calm. "If you'll excuse me, I need to have a word with my brother."

CHAPTER 28

I followed Grayson. Eli followed me. To Grayson's credit, he gave up trying to lose me pretty quickly. He let me trail him all the way to the third floor, through a series of twisting hallways, up a small wrought-iron staircase, to an alcove. There was an antique sewing machine in the corner. The walls were covered with quilts. Grayson lifted one to reveal a crawl space.

"If I told you to go back to your room, would you?" he asked.

"Not a chance in this world," I said.

Grayson sighed. "About ten feet in, you'll find a ladder." He held the quilt back and waited, his chin tilted downward, his eyes on mine. The world might bend to the will of Grayson Hawthorne—but I didn't.

Leaving Eli behind, I made my way through the crawl space on all fours. I could feel and hear Grayson behind me, but he didn't say a word until I started to climb the ladder. "There's a pull-down door at the top. Be careful. It sticks."

I pushed down the urge to turn back and look at him and managed to get the door open and climb through, blinking when harsh sunlight hit my eyes. I'd expected an attic—not the roof.

Looking around, I climbed out onto a small, flat area, about five feet by five feet, nestled among the grand angles of the Hawthorne House roofline. Jameson was leaning back against the roof, his face aimed skyward, like he was sunbathing.

In his hand, he held a knife.

"You kept that?" Grayson stepped onto the roof behind me.

Jameson, eyes still closed, twirled the knife in his hand. The handle on the blade parted in two, revealing a compartment inside. "Empty." Jameson opened his eyes and pressed the compartment closed. "This time."

Grayson's mouth settled into a firm line. "I invoke—"

"Oh no," I said fiercely. "Not this again. No one is invoking anything!"

Jameson caught my gaze. His green eyes were liquid and shadowed. "Did you tell him?" he asked me.

"Tell me what?" Grayson said sharply.

"Well, that answers that." Jameson pushed himself into a standing position. "Heiress, before we start spilling secrets, I'm going to need you to promise me a plane."

"A plane?" I gave him an incredulous look.

"You have several." Jameson smiled. "I want to borrow one."

"Why do you need a plane?" Grayson asked suspiciously.

Jameson waved away the question.

"Fine," I told him. "You can take one of my planes." Yet another sentence I never thought I'd say.

"Why," Grayson repeated through gritted teeth, "do you need a plane?"

Jameson looked back at the sky. "Colin's Way was founded in memory of Colin Anders Wright." I wondered if Grayson could hear the undertone in Jameson's voice. Not quite sadness, not quite regret—but *something*. "Colin was one of the victims of the fire on Hawthorne Island. The charity was founded by his uncle."

"And?" Grayson was getting impatient.

Jameson looked suddenly toward me. *He can't say it. He can't be the one who tells him.*

I pressed my lips together and took a breath. "That uncle's name is Sheffield *Grayson*."

Absolute silence greeted that statement. Grayson Hawthorne wasn't a person who showed much emotion, but in that moment, I felt every subtle shift of his expression in the pit of my stomach.

"That's why you went to see Skye," Grayson said. His voice was tight.

"She confirmed it, Gray." Jameson ripped the bandage off. "He's your father."

Grayson went quiet again, and Jameson moved suddenly, tossing the knife at him. Grayson's hand whipped up to catch it by the handle.

"There is no way that the old man didn't know," Grayson said harshly. "For twenty years, he included Colin's Way in his will." A muscle in Grayson's throat tightened. "Was he trying to make a point to Skye?"

"Or was he leaving her a clue?" Jameson countered. "Think about it, Gray. He left a clue for us in the newer will. Maybe that was an old trick, one he'd used before."

"This isn't just a *clue*," Grayson said, his voice low and harsh. "This is my..." He couldn't say the word *father*.

"I know." Jameson crossed to stand in front of his brother, lowering his forehead until it touched Grayson's. "I know, Gray, and if you let this be a game, it doesn't have to hurt."

I was overcome with the feeling that I shouldn't be there, that I wasn't supposed to see the two of them like this.

"Nothing has to matter," Grayson replied tightly, "unless you let it."

I turned to go, but Grayson caught my movement out of the corner of his eye. He pulled away from Jameson and turned to me. "This Sheffield Grayson might know something about the fire, Avery. About Toby."

He'd just had his world shattered with a revelation about his father, and he was thinking about me. About Toby. About that signature on my birth certificate.

He knew I wasn't going to stop. "You don't have to do this," I told him.

Grayson's grip tightened over the handle of the knife. "Neither one of you is going to leave this alone. If I can't stop you, I can at least make sure that someone with a modicum of common sense oversees the process."

In a flash, Grayson tossed the blade back to Jameson, who caught it.

"I'll arrange for the plane." Jameson smiled at his brother. "We leave at dawn."

CHAPTER 29

That *we* didn't include me. To inherit, I had to live in Hawthorne House for a year. I wasn't sure I *could* travel, and even if there was a way, I couldn't insert myself into this. Grayson had a right to meet his father without me tagging along. He had Jameson, and I couldn't shake the feeling that this was something they needed to do together.

Without me there.

So I went to school the next day and kept my head down and waited. In between classes, I kept checking my phone, kept expecting an update. That they'd landed in Phoenix. That they'd made contact—or that they hadn't. *Something.*

"I could ask you where my brothers are." Xander fell in next to me in the hallway. "And what they're up to. Or..." He flashed me a ridiculous smile. "I could beckon you to the dark side through the overwhelming power of my charisma."

"The dark side?" I snorted.

"Would it help if I brooded?" Xander asked as we came to the door of my next class. "I can brood!" He scowled fiercely, then grinned. "Come on, Avery. This is *my* game. They're *my* knuckleheaded, notably less charismatic brothers. You have to deal me in."

He followed me into the classroom and helped himself to the seat next to mine.

"Mr. Hawthorne." Dr. Meghani shot him an amused look. "Unless I'm mistaken, you are not in this class."

"I'm free until lunch," Xander told her. "And I *need* to make meaning."

In any other school, that never would have flown. If he'd been anyone other than a Hawthorne, it might not have here, either, but Dr. Meghani allowed it. "Last class," she lectured at the front of the room, "we talked about white space in the visual arts. Today, I want you working in small groups to conceptualize the equivalents in other art forms. What serves the function of white space in literature? Theater? Dance? How can meaning be made—or emphasized—through purposeful gaps or blanks? When does *nothing* become *something*?"

I thought about my phone. About the lack of communication from Jameson and Grayson.

"I expect two thousand words on that topic and a plan of artistic exploration by the end of next week." Dr. Meghani clapped her hands together. "Get to work."

"You heard the woman," Xander said beside me. "Let's get to work."

I snuck another glance at my phone. "I'm waiting to hear from your brothers," I admitted, keeping my voice low and trying to look like I was deeply pondering the true meaning of art.

"About?" Xander prompted.

Dr. Meghani passed by our table, and I waited until she was out of earshot before continuing. "Does the name Sheffield Grayson mean anything to you?" I asked Xander.

"Indeed it does!" he replied jauntily. "I created a database of major donors for all the charities on our list. The name Sheffield Grayson appears on that list precisely twice."

"For Colin's Way," I said immediately. "And..."

"Camden House."

I filed that away for future reference. "Have you seen a picture of Sheffield Grayson?" I asked Xander quietly. *Do you know who he is to your brother?*

In response, Xander did an image search and then sucked in a breath. "Oh."

Xander somehow persuaded Dr. Meghani that I intended to approach my essay by comparing white space in nature to white space in the arts, and she authorized us to spend the rest of the class period outside. When we reached the perimeter of the wooded acreage just south of the baseball diamond, Xander stopped. So did I—and four feet away, so did Eli.

"What are we waiting for?" I asked.

Xander pointed, and I saw Rebecca coming toward us from about a hundred yards away.

"I'm starting to understand why you call your side the dark side," I muttered.

"The old man had a soft spot for Rebecca," Xander told me. "Bex knew him pretty well, and I don't think he expected me to do this alone."

I gestured to myself. "You're not alone."

"And you're on my team? Not Jamie's?" Xander gave me a look. "Not Gray's?"

"Why do there have to be teams?" I asked.

"It's just the way they are. Hawthornes, I mean." Rebecca came to a stop in front of me. When I turned to look at her, she looked down. "You said you have news?" she asked Xander.

"Let's wait for Thea," Xander suggested.

"Thea?" I grumbled.

"She's delightfully Machiavellian, and she hates to lose." Xander was absolutely unapologetic. "I like what that does to my odds."

"She's also Zara's niece," I couldn't help pointing out. "And she hates you and your brothers."

"*Hates* is a strong word," Xander hedged. "Thea just loves us in a somewhat negative and occasionally vitriolic way."

"Thea isn't coming," Rebecca said, interrupting the back-and-forth between Xander and me.

"She isn't?" Xander raised his lone eyebrow.

"I just…" Rebecca took a breath, and the wind caught in her dark red hair. "I can't, Xan. Not today."

What's today?

"What's the new lead?" Rebecca asked, her expression begging Xander not to press her further. "What do we know?"

Xander gave a slight nod, and then he cut to the chase. "One of our persons of interest is Grayson's father. Jamie and Gray are, I assume, making contact. Until we find out what they find out, our only option is following up on my other lead."

"What other lead?" I asked.

"Camden House," Xander said definitively. "Cross-referencing its major donors to the victims on Hawthorne Island led to two matches. David Golding's family are platinum-level supporters. Colin Anders Wright's uncle gave a onetime, but very generous, donation. And though I haven't identified any direct donations from my grandfather, I have a theory."

"Toby was a patient there," I cut in. "Nan told me as much."

"I'm almost positive that all three of the boys did a stint at Camden House," Xander said. "I think that's where they met."

I thought about the news coverage of the fire. The suggestion that there had been a wild party that had spun out of control. The way that the tragedy had been blamed, again and again, on Kaylie

Rooney, when the three upstanding young men had been partying straight out of rehab.

"If the boys met at Camden House," Rebecca said slowly, "then..."

"Exactly! Then...*what*?" Xander bounced from one foot to the other.

"This tells us something about their state of mind that summer," I said. "Leading up to the fire."

"The fire," Rebecca repeated, "and their deaths." She closed her eyes tight, and when she opened them, she shook her head and began backing away. "I'm sorry, Xan. I want to play this game. I want to help you. I want to be able to do this with you, and I will, okay? Just not today."

CHAPTER 30

It took me longer than it should have to piece together that when Rebecca had said earlier in the week that Emily's birthday was Friday—today—she hadn't been lying. Neither had Thea when she'd said that there was a memorial fundraiser.

The *same* fundraiser that Alisa was planning that I would attend.

"I booked you a session with Landon for this afternoon. She had limited availability, so we may have to double up with hair and makeup."

I buckled my seat belt and narrowed my eyes at Alisa as Eli settled into the front passenger seat. "You failed to mention that tonight's memorial was for Emily Laughlin."

"Did I?" Alisa didn't sound even the least bit guilty. "Country Day is building a new chapel in her honor."

I heard a cough from the driver's seat and realized that Oren wasn't the one driving. This man had lighter, longer hair. I'd almost gotten used to Eli shadowing me at school, but this was the first time since the will had been read that Oren had willingly let me out of his sight while I was in transit. "Where's Oren?" I asked.

"Otherwise occupied," the driver replied. "There was a situation."

"What kind of situation?" I pressed. No response. I looked at Alisa, but she just shrugged and redirected the conversation.

"You wouldn't happen to know why Jameson and Grayson took one of your jets, would you?"

Back at Hawthorne House, we found Oren waiting at the door with the *situation* he'd been dealing with.

"Max?" I was stunned to see her. We hadn't been together in person in more than a year, but there Max was, her black hair tied up in messy buns on either side of her head.

She beamed at me, then shot the world's most aggrieved look in Oren's direction. "Finally! Avery, will you tell Monsieur Bodyguard over here that I'm not a security risk?"

My shock started to wear off. "Max!" I took a step toward her, and that was all Max needed to launch herself at me. She hugged me. Hard. "What are you doing here?" I asked.

She shrugged. "I told you that I was considering a mission trip. I am here to bring the love of God to these poor, backward billionaires. It's an ugly job, but someone's got to do it."

"She's joking," I told Oren. "Probably." I studied Max a little more closely. As glad as I was to see her, I also knew her parents wouldn't have approved this trip. She was already on thin ice with them.

And that was when I realized: "Today's your birthday, too."

"Too?" For a split second, I saw raw emotion behind Max's eyes, but then she shook it off. "I'm eighteen." Max was legally an adult. Had her parents kicked her out, or had she left on her own? "Got a spare bedroom?" she asked me, all bravado.

I squeezed her hand. "I probably have forty."

Max offered me her brashest, most invincible Maxine Liu smile. "So what does a girl have to do around here to get a tour?"

Ten minutes into Max's tour, my phone rang. I looked down at the screen. "Jameson," I reported.

Max gave me a look. "Don't mind me." She beamed. "Pretend I'm not even here."

I answered the call. "What's going on? Is everything okay?"

"Other than the fact that my stick-in-the-mud brother utterly refuses to play Drink or Dare while we wait?" Jameson had a way of making everything sound like a joke—and dark humor at that. "Things are just peachy."

"Drink or Dare?" I asked. "No—don't answer that. What exactly are you waiting on?"

There was a beat of silence on the other end of the line. "Sheffield Grayson has security that rivals ours. There's no getting near the man unless he wants you to."

The muscles in my chest tightened. "And he doesn't want Grayson near him." I ached, just thinking about that. "Is he okay?"

Jameson did not answer that question. "Grayson has business cards—and yes, I mocked him mercilessly for that. He wrote our hotel information on the back of one and left it with the guard at the gate to the Grayson estate."

The less serious Jameson sounded, the more I ached for him, too. "And so you wait," I said quietly.

There was a brief silence on the other end of the line. "And so we wait."

There was a heaviness in Jameson's tone. The fact that he'd let me hear it was shocking.

"Don't worry, Heiress." Jameson fell back into banter. "I *will* prevail on the Drink or Dare front if we have to wait around much longer."

When I hung up the phone, Max practically pounced on me. "What did he say?"

"So the boys you want to fax took your private jet to Arizona in hopes that the mystery father of one of said boys knows something about a tragic and deadly fire, lo these many years ago."

"That about covers it," I told Max. "Except I don't want to fax anyone."

"Only in your mind and only with your eyes," Max said solemnly.

"Max!" I said, and then I turned the tables on her. "You want to tell me what you're doing here? We both know you're not okay."

Max looked up at the twenty-foot ceiling. "Maybe I'm not. But I *am* standing in the middle of a bowling alley *in your house*. This place is unbelievable!"

If she wanted a distraction, she'd come to the right place.

"Now, is there anything else about the Bonkers Life of Billionaire Avery that you left out?"

I knew better than to press her if she didn't want to talk. "There is one more thing," I said. "Remember Emily?"

"Died and left a thousand broken pieces in her wake?" Max said immediately. "Loss reverberates through all the players in her tragedy to this day? Yes, I remember Emily."

"Tonight, I'm going to a fundraiser in her honor."

CHAPTER 31

Where are you with developing your talking points and your theme?" Landon asked. Apparently, she had no qualms whatsoever about quizzing me while my face was being contoured and my hair aggressively moussed.

"You have a theme?" Max piped up beside me. "Is it *smash the patriarchy*? I hope it's smash the patriarchy."

"I like it," I told Max. "Why don't you come up with some talking points?"

"Hold still." Firm hands grabbed my chin.

Landon cleared her throat. "I don't think that would be prudent," she told me, glancing delicately at Max.

"Patriarchy smashing is *always* prudent," Max assured her.

"Look up," the makeup artist commanded. "I'm going to get started on your eyes."

That sounded way more ominous than it should have. Doing my best not to blink, I gritted my teeth. "Why don't you just save us all a lot of time and effort and tell me what you want me to say?" I asked Landon.

"We need to communicate that you are relatable, grateful for the tremendous opportunity you've been given, on good terms with the Hawthorne family, and exceedingly unlikely to throw multiple billion-dollar industries into chaos." She let a second pass, then continued. "But *how* you communicate those things is up to you. If I write the script, it will sound like a script, so you need to do the work here, Avery. What can you authentically say about this whole experience?"

I thought about Hawthorne House, about the boys who lived here, about the secrets built into the very walls. "It's incredible."

"Good," Landon replied. "And?"

My throat tightened. "I wish my mom were here."

I wished that she could see me. I wished that I'd had money—any money—when she'd gotten sick. I wished that I could ask her about Toby Hawthorne.

"You're on the right track," Landon told me. "Truly. But for the time being, it would be best to avoid bringing up your mother."

If I'd been able to, I would have stared at her, but instead, my chin was tilted roughly back, and I found myself staring at the ceiling.

Why doesn't she want me talking about my mom?

Two hours later, I was bedecked in a knee-length dress made of lavender silk, with an impossibly delicate black lace wrap. Instead of heels, I wore knee-high boots—black, suede, and not comfortable in the least. *Preppy with an edge*, my signature look.

I was still thinking about Landon—and my mother.

"I did some research." Max waited until the two of us were alone to share. "Looks like there's a tabloid that keeps writing stories about your mom."

"Saying what?" I asked. My heart rate ticked up. The dress I'd been told to wear was tight enough that I was almost certain you could *see* my heart beating. *Does the press suspect that she lied about who my father is?* I pushed down the thought.

"The tabloid claims your mom was living under a fake name." Max handed me her phone. "So far, no one else has picked up the story, so it's probably bullship, but..."

"But Landon doesn't want me talking about my mom," I finished. I closed my smoky eyes, just for a second. "She didn't have any family," I told Max when I opened them. "It was just her and me." I thought of every ridiculous guess I'd ever made in a game of I Have A Secret. I'd gone down the secret-agent-living-under-a-false-identity route more than once.

"It might make sense," Max said. "Wasn't Toby living under a fake name, too?"

That raised a whole sea of questions that I'd been avoiding: How exactly had my mom come to be involved with Tobias Hawthorne's son? Had she known who he really was?

A sharp knock at the door broke into my thoughts. "Are you ready?" Alisa called.

"Are we sure I can't skip this?" I called back.

"You have five minutes."

I turned back to Max. "We wear the same size," I said.

"And that is of interest why?" Max asked, her brown eyes dancing.

I led her over to my closet, and when I threw open the doors, she literally gasped at the sight beyond. "Get dressed, birthday girl. There's no way I'm going to this thing on my own."

CHAPTER 32

The biggest indoor space at Heights Country Day was called the Commons. It was part lounge, part meeting space, and tonight it had been transformed. Gold curtains lined the sides of the room. The furniture had been replaced with dozens of circular tables covered with silk tablecloths in a deep midnight purple. *Emily's favorite color.* Near the front of the room, two enormous pictures sat on golden easels. One was an architect's sketch of the new chapel. The other was a photograph of Emily Laughlin. I tried not to stare at it—and failed.

Emily's hair was strawberry blond, with just enough of a natural wave to make her look a little unpredictable. Her skin was unbearably clear, her eyes all-knowing. She wasn't as beautiful as Rebecca, but there was something about the way she smiled. . . .

I couldn't help thinking that maybe it was a good thing that Jameson and Grayson weren't here. They'd loved her, both of them. *Maybe they still do.*

Beside me, Xander bumped his shoulder into mine. Alisa had given him strict orders to stay close to me, just like she'd reluctantly assigned Nash as Libby's escort tonight. Part of the damage control we were supposed to do was conveying that I was on good terms with the Hawthorne family—easier said than done, given that Xander and Nash weren't the only Hawthornes in attendance.

On the far side of the room, I caught sight of Zara and Constantine, mingling.

"We need to work the room," Alisa murmured directly into the back of my head. She began herding Xander and me toward a string quartet, and that was the exact moment when I spotted Skye Hawthorne. She was laughing freely, surrounded by admirers—some male, some female.

"The couple on the left are Christine Terry and her husband, Michael," Alisa murmured. "Third-generation oil money. Not people you want as enemies."

I translated that to mean: *not people we want laughing with Skye*.

"I'll introduce you," Alisa told me.

"Help me," I mouthed at Max.

"I would," she whispered, "but there's a waiter who just walked by, and he's carrying shrimp!"

Ten seconds later, I was shaking hands with Christine Terry. "Skye here was telling us you're not much of a football fan," her husband declared, jovial and loud. "Any chance you feel like parting with the Lone Stars?"

"You'll have to forgive my husband," Christine told me. "I keep telling him there's a time and a place for business."

"And a time and place for football!" Michael boomed.

"Avery's not looking to part with any assets at the moment," Alisa said evenly. "I don't know what could have given anyone that idea."

By *anyone*, she meant Skye, but the boys' murderous mother was a Hawthorne to her bones—and thoroughly undaunted. "Darling Avery here is a Libra," Skye cooed. "Ambivalent, people-pleasing, and cerebral. We can all read between those lines." She paused, then extended a hand to her right. "Isn't that right, Richard?"

She couldn't have timed his appearance better if she'd tried. *Richard*—which was 100 percent not Ricky's given name—wrapped an arm around Skye's waist. She'd dressed the deadbeat in an expensive tailored suit. Looking at him, I tried to remind myself that he was nothing to me.

But when he smiled, I still felt seven years old and about three inches tall.

I tightened my grip on Xander, but he stepped away from me suddenly. About a dozen yards away, I saw the Laughlins. Mr. and Mrs. Laughlin looked distinctly uncomfortable in formal wear. Rebecca was standing beside them, and next to her was a woman in her forties or fifties who looked eerily like Emily would have if she'd lived to grow older.

As I watched, the woman—who I could only assume was the girls' mother—downed a large glass of wine in one gulp. Rebecca's eyes met Xander's, and a second later, he was gone, leaving me to his mother's mercies.

"Have I introduced you to Avery's father?" Skye asked the group, her gaze settling on Christine Terry. "I have it on good authority that he'll be filing for custody of our little heiress very soon."

Forty minutes later, when I saw Ricky heading for the bar, I tasked Max with distracting Alisa so I could corner him alone.

"Why the long face, Cricket?" Ricky Grambs smiled as I came to stand beside him. He was the kind of drunk who had effusive praise for everyone. I should have expected the charm offensive. The fact that he'd called me by a nickname shouldn't have mattered.

"Don't call me Cricket. My name is Avery."

"It was supposed to be Natasha," he declared grandly. "Did you know that?"

My throat tightened. He was a deadbeat. He'd always been a

deadbeat. Based on what I'd discovered, he probably wasn't even my father. So why did talking to him hurt?

"Your mom had a middle name all picked out, so I was going to choose your first. I've always liked the sound of the name Natasha." The bartender approached, and Ricky Grambs didn't miss a beat. "One more for me," he said, then winked. "And one for my daughter."

"I'm underage," I said stiffly.

His eyes sparkled. "You have my permission, Cricket."

Something inside me snapped. "You can shove your *permission* up your—"

"Smile," he murmured, leaning toward me "For the press."

I glanced back and saw a photographer. Alisa had dragged me to this party to tell a story, not make a scene.

"You really should smile more, pretty girl."

"I'm not that pretty," I said quietly. "And you're not my father."

Ricky Grambs accepted a bottled beer from the bartender. He lifted it to his lips, but not before I saw his bulletproof charm waver.

Does he know that I'm not his? Is that why he's never cared? Why I never mattered?

Ricky recovered. "I may not have been there as much as either of us would have liked, Ladybug, but I was never more than a phone call away, and I'm here now to make things right."

"You're here for the money." It took everything in me not to yell. Instead, I lowered my voice enough that he had to lean forward to hear it. "You're not going to get a dime. My legal team will bury you. You refused to take custody when Mom died. You think a judge won't see through your sudden interest now?"

He stuck his chin out. "You weren't alone after your mom. My Libby took good care of you." He clearly expected credit for that, when he'd never done a damn thing for Libby, either.

"You never even signed my birth certificate," I gritted out. I half expected him to deny it.

Instead, he gulped the rest of the beer and placed the empty bottle on the bar. I stared him down for a second or two, then picked up the bottle, turned, and walked toward Alisa, who was *still* trying to get around Max.

I handed my lawyer the beer bottle. "I want a DNA test," I murmured.

Alisa stared at me for a moment, then schooled her face into a perfect pleasant expression. "And I want you to go find a half dozen items to bid on in the silent auction."

I accepted the terms of her deal. "Done."

CHAPTER 33

I had no idea how a silent auction worked, but Max, high on shrimp and her victory in distracting Alisa, quickly caught me up on what she'd managed to glean. "There's a sheet beneath each item. Bidders write down their names and their bids. If you want to outbid someone, you write your name below theirs." Max strode over to what appeared to be a teddy bear and upped the high bid by two hundred and fifty dollars.

"Did you just bid eight hundred dollars for a teddy bear?" I asked her, aghast.

"A *mink* teddy bear," Max told me. "Pearl Earrings over there is stalking this auction." My best friend nodded to a woman who looked to be in her seventies. "She wants that bear and doesn't care if she has to slice a motherfaxer's neck to get it."

Sure enough, a few minutes later, the woman glided by the teddy bear and scrawled down another bid.

"I'm a philanthropist," Max declared. "So far, I've cost the people in this room ten thousand dollars!"

All things considered, she really should have been the heiress. With a shake of my head, I circled the room, looking at the items on auction. Art. Jewelry. A designated parking space. The farther I walked, the bigger ticket the items became. Designer purses. A Tiffany sculpture. A private chef dinner for ten. A yacht party for fifty.

"The real big-ticket items are in the live auction," Max told me. "From what I've gathered, you donated most of them."

This was unreal. This life was never going to stop being unreal.

"Personally," Max said, adopting a snooty accent, "I think you should bid on the tickets to the Masters at Augusta. *With housing.*"

I looked her dead in the eye. "I have no idea what that means."

She grinned. "Neither do I!"

Alisa had told me to bid, so I circled the room again. There was a basket of high-end makeup. Bottles of wine and scotch with high bids that nearly made my eyes bulge out of their sockets. Backstage passes. Vintage pearls.

None of this was me.

Eventually, I saw a grandfather clock. The description said it had been carved by a retired Country Day football coach. It was simple but perfect. Across the room, Alisa nodded at me. I gulped and upped the current high bid by what the page informed me was the minimum.

I felt nauseous.

"It's for a good cause," Max assured me. "Sort of."

This school didn't need a new chapel any more than *I* needed a bronzed sculpture of a cowboy on the back of a wild, bucking bull, but I bid on that, too. I bid on a baking lesson with a local pastry chef for Libby and doubled down on the mink teddy bear for Max. And then I saw the photograph.

I knew, before I even looked down, that it was one of Grayson's.

"He does have an eye."

I turned to find Zara standing beside me.

"Are you going to bid on it?" I asked her.

Zara Hawthorne-Calligaris arched a brow at me. Then, without a word, she went to up the bid that I had placed on the grandfather clock.

"Well, *ship*," Max whispered beside me. "I'm pretty sure she just challenged you to a rich-people duel."

"Easy there, slugger." Xander appeared beside me.

"Where have you been?" I asked him, annoyed.

"I was helping Rebecca with her mom." Xander's voice was uncharacteristically quiet. "She doesn't do well with wine."

I didn't get a chance to probe that statement further before Alisa came over to escort us to our table. "Plated dinner," she told me. "Followed by the live auction."

I managed to sit, eat my salad with the correct fork, and not spill anything on the silk tablecloth. Then things took a turn for the worse. A loud crashing sound broke through the din of polite chitchat. Everyone in the room turned to see Rebecca, beautiful and wan, trying to help her mother back to her feet. The easels holding the picture of Emily and the architect's sketch had been knocked over. Rebecca's mother yanked her arm out of her daughter's grip and stumbled again.

Suddenly, Thea was there, kneeling between Rebecca and her mom. Thea said something to the distraught woman, and even from across the room, I could see the expression on Rebecca's face, like she'd just remembered a thousand things she'd been trying desperately to forget.

Like this moment and the way Thea reached for her might destroy her in the best and worst possible way.

A moment later, Libby was there, trying to help Rebecca's mom to her feet, and the grieving woman exploded.

"You." She pointed a finger at Libby. My sister was dressed in a black cocktail dress. Her blue hair had been ironed silky straight. Instead of a necklace, she wore a black ribbon tied around her neck.

She looked about as sedate as Libby ever looked, but Rebecca's mother was sneering at her like she was monstrous. "I saw you with him. That Hawthorne boy." She managed to stand. "Never trust a Hawthorne," she slurred. "They take *everything*."

"Mom." Rebecca's whisper cut through the room. Her mother dissolved in sobs. Libby became aware of the number of people staring at her and fled. I ran after her and ignored Alisa when she tried to call me back. As I passed Rebecca, Thea, and Rebecca's mom, I heard the drunk woman whimpering the same words, over and over again.

"Why do all my babies die?"

CHAPTER 34

I made it outside to Libby and found Nash already there. "Hey now, darlin'," he murmured. "Come back inside. You didn't do anything wrong."

Libby lifted her head up and looked past him to me. "Sorry, Ave. When I saw her go down, I went on autopilot." Before our lives had gotten turned upside down, Libby had been an orderly at a nursing home. She grimaced. "This is exactly what Alisa meant when she told me not to cause a scene tonight."

"She told you what now?" Nash said, his voice low and dangerous.

Libby shrugged.

"You had no way of knowing that Rebecca's mom was going to explode like that," I told Libby, then I cut a glance toward Nash, who sighed.

"She's the Laughlins' daughter. Grew up on the estate. It was before my time—she's got about fifteen years on Skye. From what I've gathered, the relationship between Mr. and Mrs. L and their daughter has always been a bit tense. After they lost Emily..." Nash shook his head. "She blamed my family."

Both Jameson and Grayson had been there the night Emily died.

"She said all her babies die," I murmured. Belatedly, I processed the fact that she'd been looking right at Rebecca—her living daughter—when she'd said it.

"Miscarriages." Nash said quietly. "She and her husband were older when they started trying for kids. Mrs. Laughlin mentioned once that they'd lost multiple babies before they had Emily."

If I thought about any of this for too long, I was going to start feeling even sorrier for Rebecca Laughlin. "Are you okay?" I asked Libby instead.

She nodded and looked toward Nash. "Could you give us a minute?"

With one last look at my sister, Nash sauntered off, and Libby turned back to me. "Avery, what did you say to Dad earlier?"

I wasn't going to have this conversation with her. "Nothing."

"I get it," Libby told me. "You hate him, and you have every right to. And, yes, the thing with Skye is kind of weird, but—"

"Weird," I repeated. "Libby, she tried to have me killed!" It took me a full three seconds to realize what I'd done.

Libby stared at me. "What? When?" *Libby knew Skye moved out—but she didn't know why.* "Have you told the police?" she demanded.

"It's complicated," I hedged. I was trying to figure out how to explain my promise to Grayson, but Libby didn't give me more than a second.

"And I'm not," she said quietly, her chin jutting out.

At first, I wasn't sure what she was saying. "What?"

"I'm not complicated," Libby clarified. "That's what you think. It's what you've always thought. I'm too optimistic and too trusting. I never went to college. I don't think the way you think. I give people too many chances. I'm naive—"

"Where is this coming from?" I asked.

Blue hair fell into Libby's face as she looked down. "Forget it," she said. "I signed the emancipation papers. Pretty soon, you officially won't have to listen to me. Or Dad. Or anyone." Her voice caught. "That's what you want, right?"

I hadn't *asked* to be emancipated. That was all Alisa, but I recognized that it was probably the right move. "Lib, it's not like that." Before I could say anything else, my phone rang.

It was Jameson.

I looked back up from the screen to Libby. "I have to take this," I told her. "But..."

Libby just shook her head. "You do what you have to do, Ave—and I'll try not to cause any more scenes."

CHAPTER 35

"Hello?"

For a moment, there was silence on the phone. "Avery?"

I recognized that low, rich voice in a heartbeat. *Not Jameson.* "Grayson?" He'd never called me before. "Did something happen? Are you—"

"Jameson dared me to call."

Nothing—literally nothing—about that sentence made sense. "Jameson what?"

"Jameson when, Jameson where, Jameson *who*?" That was Jameson, in the background, his voice taking on a musical lilt, his tone almost philosophical.

"Am I on speakerphone?" I asked. "And is Jameson *drunk*?"

"He shouldn't be," Grayson said, sounding truly disgruntled. "He doesn't really turn down dares."

Grayson wasn't slurring his words. His speech wasn't slow. His voice coated me, surrounded me—but it occurred to me suddenly that *Grayson* might be drunk.

"Let me guess," I said. "You're playing Drink or Dare."

"You're really good at guessing things," drunk Grayson said. "Do you think the old man knew that about you?" His tone was hushed and almost confessional. "Do you think that he knew that you were...you?"

I heard a thud in the background. There was a long pause, and then one of them—I was betting on Jameson—started cracking up.

"We have to go," Grayson said with a great deal of dignity, but when he went to hang up the phone, he must have hit the wrong button, because I could still hear the two of them.

"I think we can both agree," Jameson said, "that it's time for Drink or Dare to give way to Drink or Truth."

A better person probably would have hung up right then, but I turned the volume on my phone all the way up.

"What did you say to Avery," I heard Jameson ask, "the night we solved the old man's puzzle?"

Grayson hadn't said anything to me that night. But the next day, after he'd sent Skye on her way, he'd had plenty to say. *I will always protect you. But this...us...It can't happen, Avery.*

"Because right after that," Jameson continued, "she took to the tunnels with me."

Grayson started to say something—what, I couldn't quite hear—but then he cut off. "The door," Grayson said, clear as day. He sounded dumbfounded.

Someone's at the door, I realized. And then I heard some more muffled sounds. And then I heard Grayson's father.

At first, I couldn't entirely make out the words being exchanged, but at some point, either the conversation moved closer to the phone, or the phone moved closer to the conversation, because suddenly, I hear every word.

"You obviously aren't surprised to see me." That was Grayson. He'd sobered up quickly.

"I've built three different companies from the ground up. You don't achieve what I have achieved without an eye to potential eventualities. Potential risks. Frankly, young man, I expected Skye to tell you about me years ago."

A knot in my stomach twisted. Poor Grayson. His father saw him as a *risk*.

"You were married when I was conceived." Grayson's tone was neutral—almost dangerously so. "Still are. You have children. I can't imagine that you are happy at my intrusion on your life, so let's keep this short, shall we?"

"Why don't you cut to the chase and tell me why you're really here?" That was a demand. An order. "You were recently cut out of the family fortune. Financially speaking, you may have found that you have certain... needs."

"You think we're here for money?" That was Jameson.

"I've found that the simplest explanation is most often the correct one. If you're here for a payout—"

"I am not."

My entire body felt tense. I could see Grayson in my mind's eye, every muscle in his body taut, but his expression even and cool. *Bribe. Threaten. Buyout.* Grayson had been raised to be formidable. There was a reason he'd already mentioned the man's wife.

"For reasons I won't be sharing with you," I heard him say, "I am looking into what happened twenty years ago on Hawthorne Island."

The pause that greeted those words told me that Sheffield Grayson hadn't been expecting that. "Are you, now?"

"My sources have led me to believe that the press coverage of the tragedy is, shall we say... incomplete."

"What sources?"

I could practically *hear* Grayson smile. "I'll make you a deal. You tell me what the news stories left out, and I'll tell you what my sources have said about Colin."

At the mention of his nephew's name, Sheffield Grayson's voice went too low for me to hear. Whatever he'd said, Grayson reacted defensively.

"My grandfather was the most honorable man I know."

"Tell that to Kaylie Rooney," Sheffield's voice was audible again, booming. "Who do you think spoon-fed that story to the press? Who do you think quashed anything the least bit unflattering to his family?"

Grayson's response was garbled. Had he turned away?

"Toby Hawthorne was a little punk." That was Sheffield again. "No regard for the law, for his own limitations, for anyone but himself."

"And Colin wasn't like that?" Jameson was needling the man. It worked.

"Colin was going through a rough patch, but he would have come out of it. I would have *dragged* him out of it. He had his whole life ahead of him."

Again, the response was garbled.

"The Rooney girl never even should have been there!" Sheffield exploded. "She was a criminal. Her parents? Criminals. Cousins, grandparents, aunts, and uncles? *Criminals.*"

"But the fire wasn't her fault." Grayson's voice was louder now, clearer. "You've implied as much already."

"Do you know how much I paid to private detectives to get real answers?" Sheffield snapped. "Probably only a fraction of what your grandfather paid the police to bury their report. The fire on Hawthorne Island wasn't an accident. It was arson—and the person who purchased the accelerant was your uncle Toby."

CHAPTER 36

When the line went silent, I said Grayson's name, then Jameson's. Again. And again. Nobody heard me. I hung up and called back, but nobody picked up.

No matter how many times I called, no one picked up.

I was worried—about Grayson, about the barely controlled anger I'd heard in his father's voice. Beneath that worry, my gut was churning for different reasons. *What did you do, Harry?*

If the fact that Toby Hawthorne had survived the fire had been public knowledge, would his father have been able to bury this scandal? Would the police have been so easy to buy off—assuming they *had* been bought off—if this weren't a tragedy with no survivors?

If he set that fire... I couldn't think much past that, so I thought about Tobias Hawthorne instead. Why had the billionaire disinherited his entire family after the fire on Hawthorne Island? Why use his will to point to what had happened there, when he'd apparently paid good money to cover it up?

"Avery." Alisa's heels hit the pavement with a rapid *click, click, click* as she approached me. "You need to get back inside. The live auction is about to start."

I made it through the rest of the evening. As Max had promised, most of the items in the live auction had been donated by... me. A weeklong stay in a four-bedroom house on Abaco, in the Bahamas. Two weeks in Santorini, Greece, private plane included. A castle in Scotland to be used as a wedding venue.

"How many vacation homes do you *have*?" Max asked me on the way home.

I shook my head. "I don't know."

"You could actually look at the binder I gave you," Alisa suggested from the front seat.

I barely heard her, but that night, after I'd placed another six fruitless phone calls and spent hours turning the conversation with Grayson's father over in my head, I slipped out of bed and walked to my desk. The binder in question was just sitting there. Alisa had given it to me weeks ago, as a primer on my inheritance.

I flipped through it until I found myself staring at a villa in Tuscany. A thatched cottage in Bora-Bora. A literal castle in the Scottish Highlands. This was *unreal*. Page after page, I drank in the pictures. Patagonia. Santorini. Kauai. Malta. Seychelles. A flat in London. Apartments in Tokyo and Toronto and New York. Costa Rica. San Miguel de Allende...

I felt like I was having some kind of out-of-body experience, like it was impossible to feel what I was feeling and still be flesh and blood. My mom and I had dreamed of traveling. Stashed in my enormous closet, in a ratty bag from home, was a stack of blank postcards. Mom and I had imagined going to those places. I'd wanted to see the world.

And the closest I'd ever come was postcards.

A ball of emotion rising in my throat, I flipped another page—and I stopped breathing. The cabin in this photograph looked like it had been built into the side of a mountain. The snow-covered roof was A-line, and dozens of light fixtures lit up the brown stone like lanterns. *Beautiful.*

But that wasn't what had robbed the breath from my lungs. Every muscle in my chest tightened as I lifted my fingers to the text at the top of the page, where the details of the home were written. It was in the Rocky Mountains, ski in/ski out, eight bedrooms—and the house had a name.

True North.

CHAPTER 37

"To my daughter Skye Hawthorne, I leave my compass, may she always know true north." The next morning, I paced in front of Max, unable to contain myself. "The part about the compass and true north was in both of Tobias Hawthorne's wills. The older one was written twenty years ago. The clues in that will couldn't have been meant for the Hawthorne grandsons—not originally." If there was a connection between that line in the will and the home I'd inherited in Colorado, that message had been meant explicitly for Skye. "This game was for Tobias Hawthorne's daughters."

"Daughters, plural?" Max inquired.

"The old man left Zara a bequest, too." My mind raced as I tried to recall the exact wording. *"To my daughter Zara, I leave my wedding ring, may she love as wholly and steadfastly as I loved her mother."*

What if that was a clue, too?

"One piece of the puzzle is at True North," I said. "And if there's another one, it must have something to do with that ring."

"So," Max said gamely, "first, we go to Colorado, and then we steal ourselves a ring."

It was tempting. I wanted to see True North. I wanted to go

there. I wanted to experience even a fraction of what that binder told me my new world had to offer. "I can't," I said, frustrated. "I can't go anywhere. I have to stay here for a year to inherit."

"You go to school," Max pointed out. "So, obviously, you don't have to stay holed up at Hawthorne House twenty-four hours a day." She grinned. "Avery, my billionaire friend, how long do you think it would take us to fly by private jet to Colorado?"

I called Alisa, and she arrived within the hour.

"When the will says that I have to live in Hawthorne House for a year, what does that mean exactly? What constitutes *living* at Hawthorne House?"

"Why do you ask?" Alisa replied, blinking.

"Max and I were looking at the binder you gave me. At all of those vacations homes."

"Absolutely not." Oren spoke from the doorway. "It's too risky."

"I agree," Alisa said firmly. "But since I have a professional obligation to answer your question: The will's appendix makes it clear that you may spend no more than three nights per month away from Hawthorne House."

"So we *could* go to Colorado." Max was delighted.

"Out of the question," Oren told her.

"Given what's at stake here, I concur." Alisa gave me the Alisa Look to end all Alisa Looks. "What if circumstances prevented you from returning on time?"

"I have school on Monday," I argued. "Today's Saturday. I'd only be gone for one night. That gives us plenty of leeway."

"What if there's a storm?" Alisa countered. "What if you're injured? One thing goes wrong, and you lose everything."

"So do you."

I looked back to the doorway and saw a stranger standing there.

A brown-haired woman wearing khaki slacks and a simple white blouse. Belatedly, I recognized her face. *"Libby?"* My sister had dyed her hair a sedate medium brown. I hadn't seen her with a natural human hair color since...*ever.* "Is that a French braid?" I asked, horrified. "What happened?"

Libby rolled her eyes. "You make it sound like I was kidnapped and forcibly braided."

"Were you?" I asked, only half joking.

Libby turned back to Alisa. "You were just telling my sister that you can't *allow* her to do something?"

"Go to Colorado," Max clarified. "Avery owns a house there, but her keepers here think traveling is too big a risk."

"It's not really their decision, is it?" Libby looked down at the ground, but her voice was steady. "Until Avery's emancipated, *I* am her guardian."

"And I control her assets," Alisa replied. "Including the planes."

I cut a glance at Max. "I guess we could fly commercial."

"No," Alisa and Oren responded in unison.

"Did it ever occur to you that Avery needs a break?" Libby stuck out her chin. "From..." Her voice caught in her throat. "All of this?"

I felt a stab of guilt, because I wasn't overwhelmed by *all of this.* I was doing fine here. *But Libby isn't.* I could hear it in her tone. When I'd inherited, she lost everything. Her job. Her friends. Her freedom to walk outside without a bodyguard. "Libby—"

She didn't let me get more than her name out of my mouth. "You were right about Ricky, Ave." She shook her head. "And Skye. You were right, and I was just too stupid to see it."

"You aren't stupid," I said fiercely.

Libby fingered the end of her French braid. "Skye Hawthorne asked me who I thought a judge would think is more respectable: the new and improved Ricky or me."

That was why she'd dyed her hair. That was why she was dressed the way she was. "You didn't have to do this," I said. "You don't—"

"Yes," Libby cut in softly. "I do. You're my sister. Taking care of you is *my* job." Libby turned back to Alisa, her eyes blazing. "And if *my* sister needs a break, you and that billion-dollar law firm can damn well find a way to give her one."

CHAPTER 38

Oren and Alisa agreed to a weekend at True North. Fly out this morning, fly back Sunday evening—one night away. Oren would bring a six-man team. Alisa was coming along to get some "candid shots" that Landon could slip to the press. Our itinerary gave me a little less than thirty-six hours to find whatever Tobias Hawthorne had left for his daughter at True North—without ever tipping Alisa off that I was looking.

On the way to the airport, I texted Jameson. Again. I told myself that I didn't need to worry about him and Grayson. That they were probably drunk or hungover or following a new lead without me. I told them where I was going—and why.

A few minutes later, I got a text back. Not from Jameson—from Xander. *Meet you at the plane.*

"Okay," I muttered. "He definitely has some kind of surveillance on Jameson's phone."

Max arched an eyebrow at me. "Or yours."

"I do solemnly swear that I'm not surveilling anyone who doesn't share at least twenty-five percent of my DNA." In Xander's world, that passed for a greeting. "And in other excellent news, Rebecca and Thea will both be joining us on this lovely jaunt to Colorado."

Max shot a sideways glance at me. "Are we happy 'Rebecca' and 'Thea' are coming?" She punctuated the names with air quotes, like she suspected they were aliases, even though I had definitely mentioned both of them to her.

"We're resigned," I told Max, shooting Xander a look.

He'd told me once that Grayson and Jameson had a history of teaming up during the old man's games. They'd also had a habit of double-crossing each other, but to Xander, the fact that his brothers had gone to meet Sheffield Grayson without him probably seemed like just another team-up.

I couldn't really blame him for stacking *his* team.

"Maxine." Xander offered my best friend his most charming Xander Hawthorne smile. "There's nothing I admire more than a woman who makes liberal use of air quotes. May I ask: What are your feelings on robots that sometimes explode?"

The interior of the jet—*my private jet*—had luxury seating for twenty and looked more like a high-end business lounge than a vehicle. Security sat near the front, and behind them, Alisa and Libby sat in leather chairs opposite a granite-topped table. Nash, who'd tagged along, was stretched out across two seats on the other side of that table, facing Libby and Alisa. *Awkward.* But at least the tension was likely to keep the three of them busy, which let those of us under the age of nineteen get down to business in the back of the plane.

Two extra-long suede sofas stretched out, with another granite table between them. Max and I sat on one side of the table. Xander, Rebecca, and Thea sat on the other. A platter of baked goods rested on the table between us, but I was more focused on Xander's "team." Something about the way Rebecca's body angled toward Thea's made me think about the expression I'd glimpsed on Rebecca's face the night before at the auction.

"We don't know *what* we're looking for." Xander kept his voice low enough that the adults at the front of the plane couldn't hear us. "But we know the old man left it for Skye. It will be in or very near to the cabin, and it will probably have Skye's name on it."

"Do we have anything else to go on?" Rebecca asked. "Any particular wording in the prior clue?"

"Very good, young Padawan." Xander bowed toward her.

"No *Star Wars* references," Thea shot back. "Listening to you talk geeky gives me a migraine."

"You knew I was quoting from *Star Wars.*" Xander gave her a triumphant look. "I win!"

"Sorry," Rebecca told Max and me. "They're just like this."

I got the distinct sense that I was getting a view into what all three of them had been like *before*. Rebecca's phone rang then, and she looked down. Deep-red hair covered her alabaster face. I could almost *see* her shrinking into herself.

"Everything okay?" I asked. I wondered if her mother was the one calling.

"It's fine," Rebecca said from behind a wall of hair.

She wasn't fine. That wasn't a secret. I'd known it since that night in the tunnels, when she'd confessed. I'd just been trying very hard not to care.

A determined expression on her face, Thea made a grab for the ringing phone. "Rebecca's phone," she answered, pressing it to her ear. "Thea speaking."

Rebecca's head whipped up. "Thea!"

"Everything's fine, Mr. Laughlin." Thea held out a hand to ward off Rebecca's attempts to grab the phone from her. "Bex just nodded off. You know how she gets on planes." Thea twisted to block Rebecca again. "Sure, I'll tell her. Take care. Bye."

Thea hung up the phone and angled her face toward Rebecca. "Your grandfather says to have a good trip. He'll take care of your mom. Now..." Thea tossed the phone down on the table and turned back to the rest of us. "I believe Rebecca asked about the wording of the clue."

Max poked me in the side. "When you fly private, you can talk on the phone!"

I didn't respond, because I'd just realized how quiet Xander was being. He hadn't answered Rebecca's original question, so I did. "A compass. The clue that pointed us toward True North was in the part of Tobias Hawthorne's will where he left Skye his compass."

"Oh," Thea said innocently. "Like the antique compass Xander's hiding in his pocket?"

Xander scowled at her. Max reached for the pastry platter and beaned Xander with a croissant. "Holding out on us?" she demanded.

"I see our budding friendship has reached its croissant phase," Xander told her. "I am pleased."

"You're also hiding things," I accused. "You have the compass the old man left Skye?"

Xander shrugged. "A Hawthorne always comes prepared." And this was *his* game.

"Can I see it?" I asked. Xander reluctantly handed me the compass. I opened it and stared at the face. The design was simple; it didn't look expensive.

A phone buzzed—not Rebecca's this time. Mine. Looking down, I realized that Jameson had finally texted back.

His text was exactly three words long: *Meet you there.*

CHAPTER 39

I stared out the window as the jet began its descent. From a distance, all I could see was mountains and clouds and snow, but soon I could make out the tree line. A month ago, I'd never even been on a plane. Now I was flying private. No matter how focused I tried to stay on the task at hand, I couldn't help wanting to lose myself in the vastness of the sight out that window.

I couldn't shake the feeling that this life was never meant for me.

We landed at a private airstrip. It took half an hour—and three enormous SUVs—to make the drive to True North, which was nestled higher up on the mountain, far away from the resort town below.

"The house has ski-in/ski-out access," Alisa informed Max and me on the drive. "It's private, but there's a trail that will take you to the lodge below."

As True North came into view, it hit me that the photos hadn't done it justice. The A-line roof was white with snow. The house was massive but somehow still looked like an extension of the mountain.

"I called ahead to have the caretaker open up the house," Alisa said as she, Oren, Max, and I stepped out onto the snow. "We should be stocked with food. I took the liberty of having appropriate attire delivered for you girls."

"*Fox me,*" Max whispered, awed, as she took in the sight in front of us.

"It's beautiful," I told Alisa.

A soft smile crossed my lawyer's lips, and her eyes crinkled at the edges. "This property was one of Mr. Hawthorne's favorites," Alisa told me. "He always seemed different up here."

A second, identical SUV parked next to ours, and Libby stepped out, followed by Nash and more of Oren's men. A half dozen strands of Libby's hair had fought their way free of her French braid and blew wildly in the mountain wind.

"I understand that Grayson and Jameson will be joining us," Alisa said, deliberately turning away from Nash and my sister. "Whatever you do," she cautioned, "do not let any of the Hawthornes challenge you to a Drop."

CHAPTER 40

The inside of the house matched the outside perfectly. The living room ceiling stretched up two stories, with giant beams visible in the rafters. The floors were wood, the walls wood-paneled, and everything—the furniture, the rugs, the light fixtures—was oversized. Fur throws draped the enormous leather sofa—softer than anything I'd ever felt.

A fire crackled in a stone fireplace, and I walked toward it, mesmerized.

"There are four bedrooms on this floor, two at basement level, and two up." Alisa paused. "I've put you in the biggest bedroom on this floor."

I turned away from the fire and tried to make my next question sound natural. "Actually... which bedroom was Skye's?"

The stairway to the third floor was lined with family photographs. It looked almost... *normal*. The frames weren't expensive. The photos were snapshots. There was one of a much younger Grayson, Jameson, and Xander with their heads sticking out of a tent. Another of what appeared to be a chicken fight between all four brothers. One of Nash with his arms around Alisa. And farther up the wall there were photos of Tobias Hawthorne's children.

Including Toby.

I tried not to stare at pictures of Toby Hawthorne at twelve and fourteen and sixteen, searching for some kind of resemblance to myself. I failed. There was one photo in particular—it was impossible for me to look away. Toby was standing between teenage girls I assumed to be Zara and Skye. It had obviously been taken at True North. All three of them were on skis. All three were smiling.

And I thought that maybe Toby's smile looked a bit like mine.

At the top of the stairs, Max and I deposited our bags in the room that we'd been told was once Skye's. With a glance back over my shoulder, I closed the door.

"Look for hidden compartments," I told Max as I examined a wooden chest. "Secret drawers, loose floor panels, false backs to the furniture—that kind of thing."

"Sure," Max said, drawing out the word as she watched me making quick work of the wooden chest. "Absolutely. That is a thing I know how to do."

It wasn't that I expected to hit payload immediately, but after searching Toby's wing, I knew how to look. I didn't find anything of note until I ventured into the closet. There were clothes hanging on the racks and sweaters folded on the shelves. None of them looked like things I would expect Skye to wear now. I went through the items one by one and eventually came to the ski jacket that Skye had been wearing in the picture on the stairs. How old had she been when she wore this? Fifteen? Sixteen?

Had these clothes been hanging in this closet that long?

A thump sounded on the other side of the closet wall, and then I heard a creak. Parting the clothes, I saw a crack of light at the back of the closet and found the source. There, cut directly into the wall, was a small door. I pushed, and the wall moved, allowing me to step into a narrow passageway beyond.

The passageway smelled like cedar. I felt around for the walls, then managed to locate a light switch. The moment I turned it on, I saw a pair of eyes.

Someone stepped toward me.

I scrambled back, meeting the eyes—and stifling a scream as I recognized them. "Thea!"

"What?" she said with a small smirk. "Feeling jumpy?" Beyond her, I could see Rebecca standing near a second doorway, identical to the one behind me.

"Whose room is that?" I asked.

"It used to be Zara's," Rebecca murmured. "I'm staying here tonight."

Thea turned to shoot her a meaningful look. "Good to know."

Pushing past them, I explored Zara's room and found a closet nearly identical to Skye's. The clothes on the racks tended more toward icy-blue tones, but like Skye's closet, this one looked like it had been frozen in time.

"I found something." Thea announced, back in the passageway. "And you're welcome."

I backtracked. Rebecca followed me, and Max squeezed into the passageway from the other side. It was a tight fit, but I managed to kneel next to Thea, who was holding a wooden board in her hands.

One of the floorboards, I realized as she set it aside to reach into the compartment she'd bared.

"What is it?" I said as she withdrew an object.

"A glass bottle?" Max leaned into Thea to get a better look. "With a message inside. A message in a motherfaxing bottle! Now we're cooking."

"Motherfaxing?" Thea arched a brow at Max, then stood and sauntered past me, back into Zara's room. She tipped the bottle upside down on a nearby desk, and with some jiggling, a small piece of paper fell out. As Thea attempted to unroll it, I noted that it was yellowed with age.

"I'm guessing that's pretty old," Max said.

I thought about Tobias Hawthorne's will. "Like, twenty years?" But when Thea finished unraveling the paper, the writing I saw on the missive wasn't Tobias Hawthorne's. It was cursive, with the occasional embellishment, neat enough that it could have passed for a font.

Feminine.

"I don't think this is what we came here to find," I said. Had I really thought it would be that easy? Still, I read the message. We all did.

You knew, and you did it anyway. I will never forgive you for this.

"Did what?" Thea queried. "Knew what?"

I stated the obvious out loud. "These rooms were Zara's and Skye's."

"In my experience, Zara isn't what I'd call the forgiving type." Thea looked toward Rebecca. "Bex? Any thoughts? You know the Hawthorne family as well as anyone."

Rebecca didn't reply immediately. I thought about the picture I'd seen of Zara, Skye, and Toby smiling. Had the three of them been close once?

The tree is poison, don't you see? Toby had written. *It poisoned S and Z and me.*

"Well?" I asked Rebecca. "Did you ever overhear any arguments between Zara and Skye?"

"I overheard a lot of things growing up." Rebecca gave a little shrug. "People paid attention to Emily, not me."

Thea put a hand on Rebecca's shoulder. For a moment, Rebecca leaned into Thea's touch.

"I don't know who did what to whom," Rebecca said, looking down at that hand. "But I do know..." She took a step back from Thea. "Some things are unforgivable."

Why did I get the feeling that she wasn't still talking about Zara and Skye?

"People aren't perfect," Thea told Rebecca. "No matter how hard they try. No matter how much they hate showing weakness. People make mistakes."

Rebecca's lips parted, but she didn't say anything.

Max raised her eyebrows, then turned to me. "So," she said loudly. "Mistakes."

I turned back to look out the window again and focus on the task at hand. *What "mistake" poisoned the relationship between Zara and Skye?*

CHAPTER 41

I was staring out the largest ground-floor window when a new SUV pulled up outside. Jameson stepped out first, then Grayson. Both of them were wearing sunglasses. I wondered if they were hungover.

I wondered if either one of them had slept the night before, after that conversation with Grayson's father.

It took me fifteen minutes to get one of them alone. Jameson and I ended up on a balcony. My breath visible in the air, I caught him up on what I'd found. He listened, quiet and still.

Neither one of those was an adjective I associated with Jameson Hawthorne.

When I finished, Jameson turned his back on the mountain view and leaned against the snow-covered railing. He was still dressed for Arizona. His elbows were bare, but he acted like he couldn't even feel the cold. "I have something to tell you, too, Heiress."

"I know."

"Sheffield Grayson believes that Toby set the fire on Hawthorne Island." Jameson's eyes were still hidden behind sunglasses. It made it difficult to tell what, if anything, he was feeling.

"I know," I repeated. "Grayson forgot to hang up the phone last night. I didn't hear everything, but I got the gist. The last thing I heard was that Toby had purchased accelerant. Then the phone went dead. I tried to call you both. Repeatedly. But nobody answered."

Jameson didn't say anything for a full four or five seconds. I wasn't sure he was going to reply to what I'd just said at all.

"The bastard made it clear that he wants nothing to do with Gray. He said that Colin was the closest thing he'll ever have to a son." Jameson swallowed, and even though his eyes were still masked by the sunglasses, I could feel the way those words had affected him.

I didn't want to think about the impact they might have had on Grayson.

"For once, Skye wasn't lying." Jameson's voice was low. "Grayson's father has always known about him."

I was used to Jameson flirting and rattling off riddles, balancing precariously on the edges of rooftops and throwing caution to the wind. He didn't let things matter. He didn't let them hurt.

If I took off those sunglasses, what would I see?

I stepped toward him. The door to the balcony opened. Alisa looked at me, looked at Jameson, looked at the foot of space between us, and then gave me a pointed smile. "Ready to hit the slopes?"

No. I couldn't say that. I couldn't tip my hand that the reason we were here had nothing to do with wanting a winter getaway. Whatever our plan for searching the rest of the house, we had to be subtle.

"I..." I searched for an appropriate response. "I don't know how to ski."

Grayson appeared in the doorway behind Alisa. "I'll teach you."

Jameson stared at him. So did I.

CHAPTER 42

That True North was "ski in/ski out" meant we had direct access to the slopes. All you had to do was step out the back door, pop on your skis, and *go*.

"There's an easy trail here," Grayson told me after he'd showed me the basics. "If we take it long enough, we'll hit the busier ski areas on the mountain."

I glanced back at Oren and one of his men—not Eli. This man was older. Oren had called him the team's arctic specialist. Because every Texas billionaire needed an arctic specialist on their security team.

I wobbled on my skis. Grayson reached out to steady me. For a moment, we stood there, his body bracing mine. Then, slowly, he stepped back and took my hands, pulling me forward on the very slight incline near the house, skiing backward as he did.

"Show me your stop," he said. *Always issuing orders.* But I didn't complain. I turned my toes inward and managed to stop without falling... barely.

"Good." Grayson Hawthorne actually smiled—and then he caught himself smiling, like it was forbidden for his lips to do *that* in my vicinity.

"You don't have to do this," I told him, lowering my voice to avoid being overheard. "You don't have to teach me anything. We can tell Alisa I chickened out. I'm not here to ski."

Grayson gave me a look—a know-it-all, never-wrong, do-not-question-me kind of look. "No one is going to believe *you* chickened out of anything," he said.

From the way he'd phrased that, you would have thought I was fearless.

It took me all of five minutes to lose a ski. The trail was still relatively private. Other than my bodyguards, it was like Grayson and I were alone on the mountain. He zipped to retrieve my ski with the ease of someone who'd been skiing from the time he could walk. Returning to my side, he dropped the ski in the snow, then took my elbows in his hands.

This afternoon was the most he'd touched me—ever.

Refusing to let that mean anything, I popped the ski back on and repeated what I'd told him earlier. "You don't have to do this."

He let go of my arms. "You were right." That had to be a first: Grayson Hawthorne admitting someone else was right about *anything*. "You said that I've been avoiding you, and I have. I promised I'd teach you what you need to know to live this life."

"Like skiing?" I could see myself in the reflection of his ski goggles, but I couldn't see his eyes.

"Like skiing," Grayson said. "To start."

We made it to the bottom, and Grayson taught me how to get on a ski lift. Oren went on the lift in front of us; the other guard on the one behind.

That left me alone with Grayson: two bodies, one lift, our feet dangling as we ascended the mountain. I caught myself sneaking glimpses at him. He'd pulled his goggles down, so I could make out all the lines of his face now. I could see his eyes.

After a few seconds, I decided I wasn't about to spend the entire ride in silence. "I heard your conversation with Sheffield," I told Grayson quietly. "Most of it, anyway."

Down below, I could see skiers making their way down the mountain. I looked at them instead of Grayson.

"I'm starting to understand why my grandfather disinherited his children." Grayson didn't sound quite like himself—the same way Jameson hadn't. The difference was, the night before had made Jameson more reserved, and it seemed to have had the opposite effect on his brother. "If Toby set that fire, if my grandfather had to cover it up, and then Skye—" He cut off abruptly.

"Skye what?" I said. We passed over a patch of snow-kissed trees.

"She sought Sheffield Grayson out, Avery. The man blamed our family for his nephew's death. He slept with her out of spite. God knows why Skye did it, but I was the result."

I looked at him in a way that forced him to look back at me. "You don't get to feel guilty about that," I said, my voice steady. "Pissed?" I continued. "Sure. But not guilty."

"The old man disinherited the entire family around the time I was conceived." Grayson steeled himself against that truth even as he said it. "Was Toby really the straw that broke the camel's back—or was I?"

This was Grayson Hawthorne, showing weakness. *You don't always have to bear the weight of the world—or your family—on your shoulders.* I didn't say that.

"The old man loved you," I said instead. I wasn't sure about much when it came to billionaire Tobias Hawthorne, but I was sure of that. "You and your brothers."

"We were his chance to do something right." Grayson's voice was taut. "And look how disappointed he was in the end—in Jameson, in me."

"That's not true," I said, aching for him. For *them*.

Grayson swallowed. "Do you remember the knife Jameson had up on the roof?" The question caught me by surprise.

"The one with the hidden compartment?"

Grayson inclined his head. I couldn't see the muscles in his shoulders or neck, but I could picture them beneath his ski jacket, tensing. "There was one puzzle sequence my grandfather constructed years ago. The knife was part of it."

For reasons I couldn't even pinpoint, the muscles in my own throat tightened. "And the glass ballerina?" I asked.

Grayson looked at me like I'd just said something very unexpected. Like *I* was unexpected. "Yes. To win the game, we had to shatter the ballerina. Jameson, Xander, and I got the next part wrong. We fell for the misdirection. Nash didn't. He knew the answer was the shards." There was something in the way he was looking at me. Something I didn't even have a word for. "My grandfather told us that as you amass the kind of power and money he had—things get broken. *People.* I used to think that he was talking about his children."

"The tree is poison," I quoted softly. *"Don't you see? It poisoned S and Z and me."*

"Exactly." Grayson shook his head, and when he spoke again, the words came out rough. "But I'm starting to believe we missed the point. I've been thinking about the things—and people—that *we* have broken. All of us. Toby and the victims of that fire. Jameson and me and..."

He couldn't say it, so I said it for him. "Emily. It's not the same, Grayson. You didn't kill her."

"This family breaks things." Grayson's tone never wavered. "My grandfather knew that, and he brought you here anyway. He put you on the board."

Grayson wanted me safe, and I wasn't. Having inherited the Hawthorne fortune, I might never be *safe* again.

"I'm not the glass ballerina," I said firmly. "I'm not going to shatter."

"I know you won't." Grayson's voice was almost hoarse "So I'm not going to avoid you anymore, Avery. I'm not going to keep telling you to stop doing the things that I know you can't and won't stop doing. I know what Toby is to you—what he means to you." Grayson's breath was heavy. "I know, better than anyone, why you can't stop."

Grayson had met his father. He'd looked him in the eyes and discovered what he meant to the man. And, yeah, the answer to that question was *nothing*—but he knew why I couldn't just leave the mystery of Toby alone.

"So you're in this?" I asked Grayson, my heart skipping a beat.

"Yes." He said the word like a vow. It hung in the air between us, and then he swallowed. "As your friend."

Friend. The word had edges. This was Grayson pulling back, keeping me at arm's length. Pretending that he got to make the rules.

It would have stung if I'd let it, but I didn't. "Friends," I repeated, fixing my gaze on the end of the lift, which was quickly approaching.

"Slide forward in your seat," Grayson told me. *All business*. "Tilt the tips of your skis up. Lean forward, and *go*."

The chair gave me a little push, and I zoomed forward, fighting to keep my balance. I didn't need Grayson Hawthorne to do *this*.

Through sheer force of will, I kept my skis underneath me and managed to stop.

See? I don't need you to hold me up. I turned back toward my *friend* Grayson, a smile spreading across my face, fully prepared to gloat—and that was when I saw the paparazzi.

CHAPTER 43

Oren and the arctic specialist got me back to True North in impressive time. Eli and another guard were waiting outside when we got there.

"Do a sweep of the perimeter," Oren told his men. "If anyone needs a reminder that this is private property, feel free to provide it."

"I guess that's it for skiing," I said. In theory, that was a good thing. I now had an excuse to stay at True North, to do what I'd come to do. *Less time on the mountain with Grayson.*

Pressing that thought down, I took my skis off. Grayson did the same, and we headed inside, but before we made it to the back door, a clump of snow fell down from the roof, right at our feet.

I looked up just in time to see Jameson dropping. He landed beside me on skis, no poles in sight.

"Nice entrance," Grayson told him dryly.

"I try." Jameson smiled, and then he brandished an object in his hands. It took me a second to realize that it was a picture frame.

Why is he holding a picture frame? This was Jameson Hawthorne. We'd come here for a reason. I knew why. My heart jackrabbited. "Is that...," I started to say.

Jameson shrugged. "What can I say? I really am just that good."

He lazily placed the frame in my hand, then turned to grab a pair of ski poles leaning against the side of the house. "And I challenge *you*," he told Grayson, "to a Drop."

The picture in the frame was one I'd seen on the stairs, of all three of Tobias Hawthorne's children. Jameson hadn't provided any information before taking off, but as I walked down the interior stairs toward the basement, I turned the frame over in my hands and saw the image carved into the back.

The face of a compass.

I was so engrossed in what I was looking at that I almost ran into Rebecca. And Thea. *Thea and Rebecca*, I realized, taking a step back. The former had the latter pressed up against the wall of the stairwell. Rebecca's hands were on the sides of Thea's face. Thea's hair looked like it had been torn from its ponytail.

They were kissing.

The last words I'd heard them exchange rang in my ears. *Some things are unforgivable. People aren't perfect.*

Thea noticed me but didn't pull back from the kiss until Rebecca's green eyes went almost comically wide, and even then Thea took her sweet time stepping back.

"Avery." Rebecca sounded mortified. "This isn't—"

"Any of your business," Thea finished, her lips lifting up on the ends.

I sidestepped both of them. "Agreed." This star-crossed—and probably ill-advised—make-out session was not my concern.

The frame in my hand was. So I made my way down the rest of the staircase, a woman on a mission. On the lower level, I found Max on Xander's shoulders, inspecting the blades of a fan.

"He's very tall," Max told me approvingly. "And he's only dropped me once!"

Thea and Rebecca came into the room behind me. Xander shot them a look, but I stayed on task.

"Jameson gave me this." I held up my bounty and sat down on an oversized suede chair. "A picture frame from the stairwell." I placed it facedown on my lap. "Look at the back."

Max dismounted, and everyone crowded around me.

"Take the back off the frame," Xander said immediately.

I looked up at him. "We're going to need a screwdriver."

Four minutes later, all five of us were sequestered in the third-floor room that had once belonged to Skye. I removed the final screw and lifted the back off the frame. Beneath it, behind the picture of Toby, Zara, and Skye, I found a piece of notebook paper folded in half. Inside, there was another picture.

This photo had clearly been taken around the same time as the one that had been on display in the frame. Zara and Skye were wearing the same jackets. They both looked to be teenagers. Zara had one arm around Skye and the other around a boy who looked slightly older than either of them. He had shaggy hair and a killer smile.

I turned the picture over. There was no caption on the back. Max bent to pick up the piece of paper that had been folded over the photo.

"Blank," she said.

"For now," Xander corrected.

Max didn't get the implication right away. She wasn't used to the Hawthornes and their games. "Invisible ink?" Rebecca asked, before I could. "On either the picture or the paper it was wrapped in?"

"Almost certainly," Xander replied. "But do you know how many different kinds of invisible ink there are?"

"A lot?" Thea said dryly.

Xander blew out a long breath. "My guess is that this is only half a clue. The old man left half to Skye and half to—"

"Zara," I finished. "The ring." Carefully, I took the blank page from Max. I had no idea how we were supposed to use a ring to make writing appear on this page, but I could see the logic in what Xander was saying. It was Hawthorne logic.

Tobias Tattersall Hawthorne logic.

He gave himself that middle name as a signal that he intended to leave them all in tatters. He used that name to sign a will and buried clues in the will for his daughters. I'd known that this game hadn't originally been meant for us. I'd known we were here to find Skye's clue. But now I had to wonder.

"What do you think this picture would mean to Skye?" I asked, holding up the photo that had been hiding behind Tobias Hawthorne's smiling children. Skye, Zara, and a guy. "Who is he?" I asked, and then I thought about the message we'd found in the bottle hidden under the floorboards in the passage between Skye's room and Zara's.

You knew, and you did it anyway. I will never forgive you for this.

"My psychic senses," Max announced, "are now attuned to that picture, and I'm getting some pretty clear messages about communing and abs."

They fought over a boy, I thought. The same way Jameson and Grayson had over Emily Laughlin.

"Jameson just gave you this?" Xander flopped down on the bed. "He found it and just *gave* it to you?"

I nodded. I could tell it bothered Xander that he hadn't been the one to find the clue.

"And where is Jameson now?" Xander asked, sounding a little more mutinous than I'd ever heard him.

I cleared my throat. "He challenged Grayson to something called a Drop."

"Without me?" Now Xander sounded downright offended. "He gave *you* this and challenged *Grayson* to a Drop?" Xander bounded to his feet. "That's it. The gloves are coming off. No more Mr. Nice Xander. Avery, can I see that picture?"

I handed him the photograph of Zara, Skye, and the boy with the shaggy hair. A second later, Xander was on his way out the door.

"Where are you going?" Rebecca and I called after him in unison.

Max jogged to catch up. "Where are *we* going?" she corrected.

Xander glowered at us—though it wasn't a terribly convincing glower. "To the lodge."

CHAPTER 44

Somehow I talked Alisa into okaying another little venture: one last photo op. Oren wasn't thrilled, but I got the distinct feeling this wasn't his first time securing a trip to the lodge at the base of the mountain.

"My grandfather outlawed the Drop when I was around twelve," Xander announced in the SUV on the way down. "Too many broken bones."

"Because that's not concerning or anything," Max said cheerfully.

"Hawthornes," Thea scoffed.

"Be nice." Rebecca gave her a look.

"It's just a friendly game of ski-lift chicken," Xander assured us. "You ride the lift up, until someone calls 'drop.' And then you"—Xander shrugged—"drop."

"As in jump off the lift?" I stared at him.

"The first person to call is the challenger. If the other person declines, the challenger has to drop. If the other person accepts the challenge, they drop and get a fifteen-second head start in the race."

"The race?" Max and I said in unison.

"To the bottom," Xander clarified.

"That is the single dumbest thing I've ever heard in my life," I told Xander.

"Maybe," Xander replied stubbornly. "But as soon as we've finished at the lodge, I've got winner."

At the lodge, we were escorted through the main dining room to a private alcove overlooking the slopes beyond. Two of Oren's men took position at the door while my head of security stayed glued to me.

"You sit," Alisa told me. "You sip on hot chocolate. We get a few pictures—and we get you out."

That was her plan. We had our own. Namely, identify the boy in the photo. Xander seemed to think that some of the staff at the lodge had worked here for decades. Given how tight security was on me, I wasn't holding my breath that I'd be able to do this myself, but Max and Xander were a different story.

So were Thea and Rebecca.

Oren let the four of them venture off to the bathroom with a single guard. When they came back ten minutes later, that bodyguard looked like he had developed a migraine.

"These two," Max told me, nodding toward Thea and Rebecca, "are *really* useful in getting information out of people."

"Thea's better at flirting," Rebecca murmured.

Thea met Rebecca's eyes. "And you're a very quick learner."

"What did they find out?" I asked Max and Xander.

"The guy in the photo used to work on the mountain." Max was clearly relishing this. "He was a ski instructor, early twenties. Very big with the ladies."

"Did you get a name?" I asked.

Xander was the one who provided that answer. "Jake Nash."

Jake. My brain whirred. *Nash.*

CHAPTER 45

In the wake of that bombshell, Xander went to find Jameson and Grayson. Hours later, all three brothers returned from the slopes, looking scraped up and worse for the wear. Jameson eased himself into a wingback chair.

"Don't bleed on that," Grayson ordered.

"Wouldn't dream of it," Jameson retorted. "What are your thoughts on vomiting in that vase?"

"You're an idiot," Grayson replied.

"You're all idiots," I corrected. They turned to look at me. I was wearing a pair of thick winter pajamas, part of the True North wardrobe Alisa had ordered for me. "Did Xander tell you what we found?"

"What *I* found, Heiress," Jameson corrected me, then smiled. "I know about the picture. The page with what we can assume is likely a message of some kind, written in invisible ink."

Grayson studied me for a moment, then turned to Xander. "What *else* did you find?"

"For the record," Xander said grandly, hobbling over to sit on the fireplace, "I won the Drop." He looked down at his feet. "And

I might have neglected to mention that the guy in that photo is Nash's father."

That statement had the exact effect it was supposed to—on Jameson and Grayson. But I wasn't surprised. After what we'd learned at the lodge, it was the logical conclusion. All four of the Hawthorne brothers had last names as first names. Grayson's father was Sheffield *Grayson*. The guy in the picture—the guy Zara had her arm around—was Jake *Nash*.

You knew, the note in the closet had read, *and you did it anyway*.

"Are you going to tell Nash?" I asked the boys.

"Tell me what?"

I turned to see Nash in the doorway, Libby beside him. "Tell him what?" She narrowed her eyes at the silence that followed. "Come on, Ave," Libby groaned. "No more secrets."

She was the reason I'd gotten to come here, and she had no idea why.

Across from me, Grayson stood. "Nash, might we have a moment outside?"

Alone with Libby, I had only a second or two to make a decision about what I was going to tell her. Looking at that plain brown hair, knowing everything she'd given up for me, it was a surprisingly easy decision to make.

I told her everything. About Harry and who he really was. About what we'd found in Toby's wing. About my birth certificate and the charities in the will and why I'd wanted to come to True North.

"I know this is a lot," I said.

Libby blinked four or five times. I waited for her to say something. Anything. "What are Grayson and Jameson telling Nash out there?" she asked finally.

There was no reason to hold back now, so I answered the question.

"So Nash's father…," she said.

"Is probably Jake Nash," I confirmed.

"And your father…," Libby looked at me and swallowed.

My father is Toby Hawthorne.

"It makes sense," I said quietly. Unable to look her directly in the eye, I let my gaze travel to a massive window nearby. "Toby's the one who signed my birth certificate, and we met for the first time right after Mom died. I think he was checking up on me. I think he meant for us to meet." I paused. "I think Tobias Hawthorne knew everything."

"And that's why he left you the money." Libby could read between the lines as well as I could. "If your dad isn't Ricky," she said slowly, "then you and I aren't really…"

"If you say we aren't sisters, I will flying-tackle you right here, right now." I was fully prepared to do it, too, but Libby seemed to decide not to tempt me.

"Have you tried to find him?" she asked me instead. "Toby?"

I looked down. "Before I even knew who he was. Alisa's people couldn't find a trace of him."

Libby snorted. Audibly. "Or so Alisa Ortega claims. Does *she* know who he is?"

I looked up at her. "No."

"So how much do you think your lawyer prioritized looking for a random homeless guy you used to play chess with?" Libby's hands made their way to her hips. "Have *you* tried to find him? Forget the puzzles. Forget the clues. Have you actually looked for the man?"

When she put it that way, I felt a little ridiculous. From inside Tobias Hawthorne's game, everything I'd done made perfect sense.

But from an outside perspective? We were going about all of this in the most roundabout way possible.

"You saw how hard it was to talk Oren and Alisa into letting me come here," I said. "There's no way they'll let me jet off to New Castle to pick up Toby's trail."

"Do you want me to go?" The question was tentative, but Libby got over her hesitation pretty quickly. "I could take a trip home. No one would question why I might want to. I can bring security with me."

"The paparazzi will follow you," I warned. "You're news by association."

Libby ran a hand over her French braid and grinned. "I blend now. I'm not sure the paparazzi would even recognize me."

All I could think in that moment was that I should have told her the truth days ago. What was wrong with me that I went to such lengths to keep the people who mattered most at a distance?

"It's settled, then," Libby declared. "You'll fly back to Hawthorne House, and I'll take the other plane to Connecticut."

"Correction, darlin'." Nash strolled back into the room. I couldn't get a read on his expression, on any effect of the bombshell his brothers had just dropped. "*We* will."

CHAPTER 46

That night, a little after midnight, Max nudged me awake.

"What is it?" I blinked at her, and after a few seconds' delay, my fight-or-flight instincts kicked in. "Is everything okay?"

"Everything's fine," Max told me. She smiled wickedly. "*Very* fine." She nudged me again. "Jameson Hawthorne is in the hot tub."

I narrowed my eyes at her, then rolled over in bed and pulled the covers over my head.

She pulled them back down. "Did you hear me? Jameson Hawthorne is in the hot tub. This is a DEFCON-faxing-one situation."

"What is it with you and Jameson?" I asked.

"What is it with *you* and Jameson?" Max retorted.

For reasons I couldn't begin to explain, I didn't toss her out of my bed. I answered her question. "He doesn't want me," I told Max. "Not really. He wants the mystery. He wants to keep me close until he can use me. I'm a part of the puzzle to him."

"But . . . ," Max prompted, "would you *like* to be used by him?"

I thought about Jameson: the way his eyes gleamed when he knew something I didn't, the crook of his smile, the way he'd covered my body with his when gunshots went off in the Black

Wood—and later cupped my face with his hands when the sound of fireworks sent me plunging into dark memories. The annoying way he called me Heiress. Golfing on the rooftop. My body clinging to his on the back of a motorcycle. The exact tilt of his lips when he'd told me to play it safe—*for now.*

"You like him." Max sounded way too satisfied with herself.

"I might like the way I feel when I'm with him." I chose my wording very carefully. "But it's not that simple."

"Because of Grayson."

I stared at the ceiling and flashed back to the ski lift. "We're friends."

"No," Max corrected. "You and I are friends. Grayson is the physical manifestation of your avoidant attachment style. He won't let himself want you. You don't want to want to be wanted. Everybody stays at arm's length. Nobody gets hurt, and *nobody gets any.*"

Max gave me her most aggrieved best friend look.

"Why do you care?" I asked her. "Since when are you this invested in my love life?"

"Lack of," Max corrected, and then she shrugged. "My life has exploded. My parents won't take my calls. They won't let my brother talk to me, either. You're all I have right now, Ave. I want you to be happy."

"You tried calling your parents?" I didn't want to push her too hard, but I did want to be there for her.

Max looked down. "That's not the point. The point is, *Jameson Hawthorne is in the hot tub.*" She crossed her arms over her chest. "So what are you going to do about it?"

CHAPTER 47

The clothing Alisa had ordered for me included a designer bathing suit: a black bikini trimmed in gold. Narrowing my eyes, I put it on, then quickly covered myself with a floor-length robe, the unspeakably soft kind I imagined they used in high-end spas. The hot tub was on the main level. I'd made it to the back door when I realized that Oren was shadowing me.

"You're not going to tell me to stay inside?" I asked him.

He shrugged. "I have men in the woods." Of course he did.

I put my hand on the doorknob, took a deep breath, and pushed out into the freezing night air. Once the cold hit me, there was no room for hesitation. I made a beeline for the hot tub. It was big enough for eight people, but Jameson was the only one there. His body was nearly completely submerged. All I could see was his face pointed skyward, the lines of his neck, and the barest hint of his shoulders.

"You look like you're thinking." I sat on the side of the hot tub farthest away from him, pulled up my robe, and sank my legs into the water, up to my knees. Steam rose into the air, and I shivered.

"I'm always thinking, Heiress." Jameson's green eyes stayed fixed on the sky. "That's what you love about me."

I was too cold to do anything but shed the robe and slip into the steaming water. My body objected, then relaxed into the sting of the heat. I could feel a flush rising on my face.

Jameson angled his eyes toward mine. "Any guesses what I'm thinking about?" We were separated by four or five feet, but that didn't feel like much—not with the way he was looking at me. I knew what he wanted me to think he was thinking about.

I also knew *him*. "You're thinking about the ring."

Jameson shifted position, the top of his chest rising out of the water. "The ring," he confirmed. "It's the obvious next step, but getting it from Zara could be a challenge."

"You like a challenge."

He pushed off the side and came closer to me. "I do."

This is Max's fault, I thought, my heart beating a merciless rhythm against my rib cage.

"Hawthorne House has a vault." Jameson came to a stop a foot or so away from me. "But even I don't know its location."

It took everything in me to focus on what he was saying—and not his body. "How is that possible?"

Jameson shrugged, the water lapping against his shoulders and chest. "Anything is possible."

I swallowed. "I could ask to see it." I tried my hardest to stop staring and cleared my throat. "The vault."

"You could," Jameson agreed, with one of those devastating Jameson Winchester Hawthorne smiles. "You're the boss."

I looked down. I had to, because suddenly I was very aware of just how little of my body this swimsuit covered. "We just have to find the wedding ring your grandfather left your aunt." I tried to stay detached. "Then, somehow, that ring will help us make invisible ink a little more..."

"Visible?" Jameson suggested. He bent toward me so that he could catch my eye. For three full seconds, neither one of us could look away. "Okay, Heiress," Jameson murmured. "What am I thinking *now*?"

I moved forward. Just like that, our bodies were separated by inches instead of a foot. "Not about the ring," I said. I let my hand float to the surface of the water.

"No," Jameson agreed, his voice low and inviting. "Not about the ring." He lifted one of his hands to mine. We didn't touch, not quite. He let his arm float, a hairbreadth away from my submerged skin. "The question is," Jameson said, throwing down the gauntlet, "what are you thinking about?"

I turned my hand over and it brushed his, electric. "Not the ring." I thought about Max telling me that it was okay to want things. Right now, there was only one thing I wanted.

One thing on my mind.

I moved again through the water. The rest of the space between us vanished. I brought my lips to Jameson's, and he kissed me, hard. My body remembered this. I kissed him back.

It was like the hot tub was on fire, like the two of us were burning, and all I cared about was burning more. His hands found their way to the sides of my face. Mine were buried in his hair.

"This isn't real," I murmured as his lips began to work their way down my neck, toward the surface of the water.

"Feels real to me." Jameson was smiling, but I didn't let it fool me.

"Nothing ever feels real to you," I whispered, but the magical thing was that I didn't care. This didn't have to be real to be right. "This... us..." I let my lips hover over his. "It doesn't have to be anything other than what it is. No messy feelings. No obligations. No promises. No expectations."

"Just this," Jameson whispered, and he pulled my body tight to his.

"Just this." It was better than riding on the back of a motorcycle going a thousand miles an hour or standing on a rooftop fifty stories tall. It wasn't just the rush or the thrill. I felt completely, utterly in control. I felt unstoppable.

Like *we* were unstoppable.

And then, without warning, Jameson froze. "Don't move," he whispered, his breath visible in the air between his lips and mine. "Oren?" Jameson called.

I did the one thing he'd told me not to do. I moved, whirling around to face the forest, my back to him, so that I could see what he was seeing. *A flash of movement. And eyes.*

"I've got her," Oren told Jameson, and just like that, my head of security was pulling me from the hot tub. The freezing air hit me like a truck. Adrenaline shot through me as Oren bit out an order. "Eli, go!"

The younger guard, positioned near the tree line, took off running toward the intruder. I tried to track his movements, like doing that might somehow make me safer. *I'm fine. Oren's here. I'm fine.* So why couldn't I remember how to breathe?

Oren ushered me inside.

"What was that?" I wheezed. "Who was that?" My brain clicked into gear. "Paparazzi? Did he take pictures?" The thought was horrifying.

Oren didn't reply. On some level, I became aware that Grayson had heard the commotion. Someone wrapped a towel around me. Not Jameson. Not Grayson.

It was a full five minutes before Eli came back. "I lost him." He was breathing hard.

"Paparazzi?" Oren asked.

Eli's bright blue eyes narrowed until all I could see was the amber ring around the center. "No. This was a professional."

That statement landed like a bomb. I felt like my own ears were ringing. "A professional what?" I asked.

Oren didn't answer. "Go pack," he told me. "We leave at dawn."

CHAPTER 48

I stared out the plane's window, watching the mountain get smaller and farther away until the jet hit cruising height. I'd barely slept, but I didn't feel tired.

"What did Eli mean, *a professional*?" I said out loud. "A professional *what*?" I turned my attention from the view out the jet's window to Max, who was seated beside me. I'd caught her up to speed—on the security situation *and* the hot tub. "A private detective? A spy?"

"An assassin!" Max said giddily. She read a lot of books and watched a lot of TV shows. "Sorry." She held up a hand and tried to appear a little less enthralled with this latest turn of events. "Assassins, bad. I'm sure the man in the woods wasn't a deadly assassin from an ancient league of deadly assassins. Probably."

Before inheriting, I would have told Max that she was reaching, but *Who would want me dead?* wasn't a dismissive question anymore. It was a question with answers. *Skye.* I thought about confronting Ricky at the gala. Libby had fought with him, too. If she'd told him that I was getting emancipated, if he'd told Skye that their golden ticket was disappearing...

What exactly would they do? *He's one of my heirs. If something happens to me...*

"No one is going to hurt you." Grayson sat opposite me, with Jameson beside him. "Isn't that right, Jamie?" Grayson's tone sharpened. I got the feeling that he wasn't just talking about the man in the woods.

"If I weren't so confident in our brotherly affection for each other," Jameson replied languidly, "I would find that comment a bit pointed."

"Pointed?" Xander repeated in faux horror. "Gray? *Never.*"

"So," I said, before this situation could devolve, "who's up for a friendly game of poker?"

"I call." I stared Thea down. She had a good poker face—but mine was better.

Thea laid down her hand: a full house. I laid down mine: the same. But aces were high, and I had them. I went to collect the pot, but Jameson stopped me.

"Not so fast, Heiress. I'm still in. And I have…" He shot me a wicked little smile that made me feel like I was right back in the hot tub. "Nothing." He showed his cards.

"You always did talk a big game," Thea said.

Beside her, Rebecca's phone buzzed. Rebecca looked down at it. This time, when Thea reached for it, Rebecca was faster. "No."

The phone buzzed again. And again. Thea caught a glimpse of the screen, and her expression shifted.

"It's your mom." Thea tried to catch Rebecca's gaze. "Bex?"

Rebecca turned the phone off.

"That wasn't what I meant," Thea said. "Maybe you should see what she wants."

Rebecca seemed to fold in on herself a little. "I'll be home soon enough."

"Bex, your mom—"

"Don't tell me what she needs." Rebecca's voice was soft, but her whole body seemed to vibrate with intensity. "You think I don't know she's not okay? Do you honestly think I need *you* to tell me that?"

"No, I—"

"She looks at me, and it's like I'm not even there." Rebecca stared holes in the table. "Maybe if I were more like Em, maybe if I were better at mattering—"

"You matter." Thea's voice had gone almost guttural.

"You know," Max said awkwardly, "this seems kind of like a private conversation, so maybe—"

"I don't matter enough." Rebecca's voice went brittle. "It's been fun, running around, playing detective, pretending the real world away, but it can't just be like this."

"Like what?" Thea reached for Rebecca's hand.

"Like *this*. The way you find reasons to touch me." Rebecca pulled her hand back from Thea's. "The way I let you. You were my world, and I would have done anything for you. But I begged you not to cover for Emily that night, and you—"

"Don't do this." If Thea were anyone else, she would have sounded like she was begging.

"If I were better at mattering..." Rebecca spoke louder. "If, for once in my life, I'd been enough for anyone—for the girl I *loved*—my sister might still be alive."

Thea had no response. Silence descended again. Painful, awkward, excruciating silence.

Jameson was the one who put Thea out of her misery. "So, Heiress," he said, throwing out a subject change like he was throwing a tarp over a fire. "How are we going to go about getting that ring?"

CHAPTER 49

Once we arrived back at Hawthorne House, I asked Oren to show me the elusive Hawthorne vault. He took me, and only me, to see it. We zigged and zagged through hallways until we reached an elevator. When the elevator door opened, I went to step on, but Oren stopped me. He pressed the call button a second time, holding his index finger flat against it.

"Fingerprint scan," he told me. After a moment, the back wall of the elevator began to slide, revealing a small walkway.

"What happens if someone pries the doors open while the elevator is on a different floor?" I asked.

"Nothing." Oren's lips parted in a very subtle smile. "The passage only opens if the elevator is present."

"Whose fingerprints can open it?" I asked.

"Currently?" Oren returned. "Mine and Nan's."

Not Zara's. Not Skye's. And not mine. In Tobias Hawthorne's will, he'd left all of his wife's jewelry to her mother. At the time of the will's reading, that had seemed trivial, but as we walked toward an honest-to-God vault door—the kind you'd expect to see on a bank vault—it didn't seem so trivial now.

"If everything in the Hawthorne vault belongs to Nan...," I started to say.

"Not everything," Oren cut in. "Nan owns the late Mrs. Hawthorne's jewelry, but Mr. Hawthorne also had an impressive collection of watches and rings, as well as pieces he purchased for artistic and sentimental reasons. Mrs. Hawthorne's jewelry passed to Nan, but many of the museum-quality pieces are yours."

"Museum-quality?" I swallowed. "Am I getting ready to see the crown jewels?" I was only partially joking.

"Of what country?" Oren replied—and he wasn't joking at all. "Anything valued over two million dollars is kept off the premises, in a more secure location."

The vault's lock disengaged. Oren spun the handle on the door and opened it. Holding my breath, I stepped into a steel room lined, ceiling to floor, with metallic drawers. I reached for one at random. When I pulled it out, displays popped up: three of them, each containing a set of tear-drop earrings: diamonds, bigger than any engagement ring I'd ever seen. I opened three or four more drawers and blinked. Repeatedly.

My brain refused to compute.

"Is there something in particular you were looking for?" Oren asked me.

I tore my eyes away from a ruby half the size of my fist. "Wedding ring," I managed. "Tobias Hawthorne's." Oren stared at me for a second or two, then walked over to the far wall. He pulled one drawer, then another, and I found myself staring at a dozen Rolex watches and a pair of varnished silver cuff links.

"Is the ring hidden?" I asked, my fingers wandering toward one of the watches.

"If the ring isn't in that drawer, it isn't here," Oren said. "My guess would be that Mr. Hawthorne had it placed in the envelope that was given to Zara at the reading of the will."

In other words: I was surrounded by a fortune in jewels, but the one thing I needed wasn't here.

CHAPTER 50

"You're going to need someone to run interference if you want to search Zara's wing." Grayson had apparently meant it when he promised to help me see this through to the end.

"Gray excels at distraction," Jameson said loftily. "I attribute it to his uncanny ability to be boring and long-winded on cue."

Grayson didn't rise to the bait. "We'll need to make sure Constantine stays clear, too."

"I, too, excel at the art of distraction," Max volunteered. "I attribute it to my ability to channel any or all of my favorite fictional spies on cue."

"Grayson and Max can set up a perimeter." Xander's voice was uncharacteristically muted. "Jameson, Avery, and I will do a sweep of the wing."

Rebecca had split the moment the plane landed. Thea hadn't lingered long once Rebecca was gone. Xander's team had abandoned him, but he wasn't backing down.

He wasn't about to let Jameson and me search for the ring on our own.

"This is a very bad idea." Eli didn't even pretend that he hadn't been eavesdropping.

That's why we waited until Oren was off duty to do it, I thought.

The door to Zara's wing was at least ten feet tall—and locked.

"Do you want to pick it?" Jameson asked Xander. "Or should I?"

Two minutes later, the three of us were in. Grayson and Max stayed behind and took up posts at the far ends on the hall. Eli grumbled as he followed me into the belly of the beast.

A quick inspection told me there were seven doors lining the main hall in Zara's wing. Behind three of them we found bedrooms, each one the equivalent of an entire suite. Two of the three suites were clearly in use.

"Do Zara and her husband sleep in different rooms?" I asked Jameson.

"Don't know," he replied.

"Don't want to know," Xander added cheerily.

I saw men's shoes in one room. The other was immaculate. *Zara's.* There was a marble fireplace near the back of the room. Built-in shelves lined the wall to the left. There were books on the shelves, large, leather-bound volumes. The kind of books a person *displayed*, not the kind they read.

"If I were a person whose bookshelves looked like that," I murmured, "where would I keep my jewelry?"

"A safe," Xander answered, probing a molding on the wall.

Jameson stepped past me, letting his body brush mine. "And that safe," Jameson told me, "is assuredly hidden."

It took ten minutes for our search to hit pay dirt: a remote control taped to the bookshelf, behind one of the leather-bound books. I peeled off the tape and got a better look at the remote, which had only one button.

"Well, Heiress..." Jameson flashed me a smile. "Will you do the honors?"

Looking at that smile, I flashed back to the hot tub. There was no reason for me to be thinking about it. No reason for me to be thinking about Jameson that way right now.

I pushed the button.

As the massive built-in shelves began to move, slowly disappearing into the wall, I stared at what had been hidden behind them. "More shelves," I said, dumbfounded. "And... more books?"

Rows of paperbacks were stacked two deep. Romance. Science fiction. Cozy mysteries and paranormal. I tried to picture Zara reading a romance novel, or a space opera, or the type of mystery that had a cat and a ball of yarn on the cover—and couldn't.

"If we take the books off these shelves, will we find another remote?" Xander postulated. "And *more* shelves? And another remote? And—" Xander cut off.

It took me a second to realize what he'd heard: the sound of high heels clicking against the wood floor.

Zara.

Jameson pulled me into the closet. If it had been hard not to think of the hot tub before, it was impossible now.

"So much for Gray's distraction," he murmured into my neck as he pulled me close, and we disappeared back into the seemingly endless racks of clothes. I stood still, barely breathing and all too aware that he was doing the same behind me.

Xander must have hidden, too, because for several seconds, the only sound in the bedroom was the clicking of Zara's heels. I willed my heart to stop beating so hard and tried to stay focused on tracking Zara's movements—not on the way my body fit against Jameson's.

Not on the fact that I could feel his heart beating, too.

The footsteps stopped directly outside the closet. I felt Jameson's breath on the back of my neck and pushed back the urge to shiver. *Don't move. Don't breathe. Don't think.*

"The bodyguard positioned at the door is a dead giveaway," Zara called, her voice as clear as a bell and sharp as a knife. "You might as well come out."

Jameson pressed a finger to my lips, then stepped out of our hiding place, leaving me hidden in shadow, still feeling the ghost of his touch. "I was hoping we could talk," he told his aunt.

"Of course," Zara replied smoothly. "After all, the proper way of starting a conversation often involves lurking in your conversation partner's closet." She peered past Jameson to the rack of clothes where I was still hiding. "I'm waiting."

After a long moment, I stepped out.

"Now," Zara said. "Explain."

I swallowed. "Your father left you his wedding ring."

"I am aware," Zara replied.

"Twenty years ago, when the old man first revised his will to disinherit you all, he left you the exact same thing," Jameson added.

Zara arched an eyebrow at us. "And?"

"Can we see it?" That was Xander, who had poked his head out of the bathroom. Even though he was the one who'd asked the question, I was the one who received the response.

"Allow me to get this straight," Zara said, staring past Jameson and straight to me. "You, to whom my father left virtually everything, want the one and only thing he left to me?"

"When she puts it that way," Max said, appearing in the doorway, "it does sound like kind of a deck move." Behind her, I could see Eli. He wasn't acting like Zara was a threat.

"Five minutes." Jameson flipped into negotiation mode. "Just give us five minutes with the ring. There must be something you want. Name your terms."

Again, Zara's attention stayed focused on me. "Five million dollars." Her smile didn't come even close to reaching her eyes. "I'll give you lot five minutes with my father's ring," she enunciated, "for the low, low price of five million dollars."

CHAPTER 51

"*Five million dollars?*" I said those words repeatedly as we retreated from Zara's wing to Tobias Hawthorne's study to strategize. "*Five. Million. Dollars.* Does Zara honestly think that Alisa is just going to agree to cut that kind of check?"

The will was still in probate. Even once the estate was settled, I was a minor. There were trustees. I could practically hear my lawyer throwing out terms like *fiduciary duty*.

"She's playing with us." Jameson sounded more pensive than outraged.

Grayson tilted his head to the side. "Perhaps it would be wise to—"

"I can get the money," Xander blurted out. His brothers stared at him.

"You want to pay Zara five million dollars to show us your grandfather's wedding ring?" I said, stunned.

"Wait." Grayson narrowed his eyes. "You have five million dollars?"

Each year on their birthdays, the Hawthorne grandsons had been given ten thousand dollars to invest. Xander had spent years dumping it into cryptocurrency, then sold at just the right time, and *that* money wasn't part of Tobias Hawthorne's estate. It was Xander's—and apparently, his brothers hadn't been aware of it until now.

"Look, ash-hole," Max said, pointing a finger at Xander, "nobody is giving anybody five million dollars. We'll just have to find another way to get the ring."

"You're still a minor," Grayson told Xander, his voice low. "If Skye finds out you have that kind of money..."

"It's in a trust," Xander assured him. "Nash is the trustee. Skye isn't getting near it."

"And you think Nash is going to let you write Zara a check for five million dollars?" I asked incredulously. That seemed about as likely as Alisa letting me access the funds.

"I can be very persuasive," Xander insisted.

"There's another way." Jameson had that look on his face—the one that told me he'd found a way of moving this chess game into three dimensions. "We'll set up a trade."

Grayson's eyes narrowed. "And what, precisely, do you think our aunt would trade for her father's wedding wing?"

Jameson smiled at me as he replied, like he and I were in this together. Like he expected me to anticipate his words. "Her mother's."

I didn't know much about the late Alice O'Day Hawthorne, but I did know who had inherited her jewelry. We found Nan in the music room, sitting in a small wingback chair, facing ceiling-to-floor windows that looked out on the pool and the estate beyond.

"Don't just stand there," Nan ordered without ever turning around. "Help an old lady up."

We made our way into the room. Grayson offered his great-grandmother an arm, but she looked past him to me. "You, girl."

I helped her out of the chair. Nan leaned on her cane and examined the five of us. "Who's she supposed to be?" the old woman grunted, nodding toward Max.

"That's my friend Max," Xander replied.

"*Your* friend Max?" I repeated.

"I promised to build her a droid," Xander said cheerily. "We're very close now. But that's beside the point."

"We need your help, Nan." Grayson circled back to the reason we were here.

"You do, do you?" Nan snorted in her great-grandsons' direction, then cut a glance toward me. She was scowling, but the flash of raw hope in her eyes was heartbreaking.

Without meaning to, I thought back to the Laughlins telling me how cruel I was for playing with an old woman. Nan loved Toby. She wanted us to find him.

Here's hoping she wants that badly enough to give us the ring. I took a deep breath.

"We found a message that your son-in-law left for Skye, right after Toby disappeared." *Message* was probably stretching it a little, but it was less complicated than the truth. "We think the old man left a similar message for Zara and that together they might somehow lead us to Toby."

"But to get what we need from Zara," Jameson interjected, "we need to offer her something in return."

"And what might that something be?" Nan's eyes narrowed.

Jameson looked at Grayson. Neither one of them actually wanted to say it.

"We need your daughter's wedding ring," I told her evenly. "So that we can trade it for your son-in-law's."

Nan harrumphed. "Zara always was a strange, quiet little thing."

"I feel a story coming on." Xander rubbed his hands together. "Nan tells the best stories."

Nan swiped at him with her cane. "Don't you try to butter me up, Alexander Hawthorne."

"Is that what I'm doing?" Xander asked innocently.

Nan scowled, but she couldn't resist a captive audience. "Zara was a shy, bookish child. Not like my Alice, who loved attention. I remember when Alice was pregnant with Zara, how giddy she was at the thought of having a little girl of her own to spoil." Nan shook her head. "But Zara never took much to spoiling. It drove my Alice up the wall. I used to tell her that the girl was just sensitive, that all she needed was some toughening up. I told her Skye was the one to worry about. That child came out of the womb tap-dancing."

I thought about the picture of Toby, Zara, and Skye. They'd looked so happy—before Toby had found out about the secrets and lies, before Skye had gotten pregnant with Nash, before Zara had gone from quiet and bookish to the cold, hypercontrolled force she was now.

"About that ring," Jameson said, turning on the charm. "The old man left Zara the same bequest in multiple wills: his wedding ring, *may she love as wholly and steadfastly as I loved her mother.* That ring is a clue."

"Not much of one. Steadfastly?" Nan grunted. "Wholly? Leaving his own daughter nothing but a damned wedding ring? Tobias never was as subtle as he liked to think."

It took me a second to understand what she was implying. *He left Zara his wedding ring and a message about being steadfast in love to make a point.*

"Constantine is Zara's second husband." Grayson didn't miss much. "Twenty years ago, when Toby disappeared, Zara was married to someone else."

“She was having an affair.” Xander didn’t phrase that as a question.

Nan turned back toward the window and stared out at the estate. “I’ll give you Alice’s ring,” she said abruptly. She began walking slowly toward the doorway, and I saw Eli standing just outside. “When you give it to her, you tell Zara that she’ll get no judgment from me. She’s toughened up just fine, and we all do what we have to do to survive.”

CHAPTER 52

Alice Hawthorne's wedding ring wasn't what I'd pictured. The diamond, singular, was small. The bands, which had been soldered together, were thin and made of gold. I'd been expecting platinum and a stone the size of my knuckle, but this wasn't ostentatious.

It looked like it had cost a few hundred dollars at most.

"You should take it to her." Jameson looked from the ring to my face. "Alone, Heiress. Zara clearly sees this as an issue between her and you."

I saw something inside the band then. **8-3-75.** *A date*, I thought. *August third, nineteen seventy-five. Their wedding date?*

"Avery?" Grayson must have seen something on my face. "Is everything okay?"

I took my phone out and snapped a picture of the inside of the ring. "Time to make a trade."

"Nan just...gave it to you?" Zara somehow managed not to choke on those words. "Legally. She transferred its ownership to *you*."

I got the feeling that this could go south very quickly, so I reiterated why I was here. "Nan gave me this ring to trade *you* for your father's ring."

Zara's eyes closed. I wondered what she was thinking, what she was *remembering*. Finally, Zara reached for a delicate chain around her neck and pulled a thick silver band out from underneath her lacy dress-shirt. She closed her fist over it, then opened her eyes. "My father's ring," she agreed hoarsely, "in exchange for my mother's."

Her hands shook as she undid the clasp on the chain. I handed her Alice Hawthorne's ring, and she handed me the old man's. Unable to resist the impulse, I turned the ring in my hand, looking for an inscription, and there it was—another date. **9-7-48**.

"His date of birth?" I asked, taking a stab in the dark.

Zara didn't have to glance down at the ring to know what I was talking about. This was the only thing her father had left her. I had no doubt she'd been over it with a fine-tooth comb.

"No," Zara said stiffly.

"Your mother's?"

"No." She brushed off the question in a way that distinctly discouraged follow-up questions, but I had to ask at least one.

"What about August third, nineteen-seventy-five," I said. "Was that the day they got married?"

"No, it was not," Zara replied. "Now, if you could please take that ring and see yourself out, I would greatly appreciate it."

I walked toward the door, then hesitated. "Didn't you wonder?" I asked Zara. "About the inscription?"

Silence. I started to think she had no intention of replying, but just as my hand closed around the doorknob, Zara surprised me. "I did not have to wonder," she said tersely.

I glanced back at her.

Zara shook her head, her grip on her mother's wedding ring

iron-tight. "It's a code, obviously. One of his little games. I'm supposed to decode it. Follow the clue wherever it leads."

"Why didn't you?" If she'd known that there was meaning to this bequest, why hadn't she played?

"Because I don't *want* to know what else my father had to say." Zara pressed her lips together, and something about her expression made her look decades younger. Vulnerable. "I was never enough for him. Toby was his favorite, then Skye. I was last, no matter what I did. That was never going to change. He left his fortune to a total stranger rather than leaving it to me. What else could I possibly need to know?"

Zara didn't seem so formidable now.

"Nan said to tell you something." I cleared my throat. "She said to tell you that 'we all do what we have to do to survive.'"

Zara let out a low, dry laugh. "That sounds like her." She paused. "I was never her favorite, either."

The tree is poison, Toby had written. *Don't you see? It poisoned S and Z and me.*

"Your father left Skye a clue, too." I didn't know why I was telling her this. I shouldn't have been telling her this. Grayson had been very clear in his warning: Zara and Skye couldn't find out that Toby was alive.

"At True North, I assume?" Zara really was Hawthorne. She'd seen the meaning in the will. She just hadn't cared. *No*, I thought. *She cared. She just wasn't going to give him the satisfaction of playing.*

"He left Skye a picture," I said softly. "Of you and her and a guy named Jake Nash."

Zara sucked in a breath. She looked like I'd slapped her. "Now would be a good time for you to leave," she said.

On the way out, I placed her father's wedding ring on an end table. I'd committed the date to memory. I'd gotten what I needed.

There was no reason for me to take this from her, too.

CHAPTER 53

Late into the night, the five of us dug into the Hawthorne family history, looking for meaning in those dates. *August 3, 1975. September 7, 1948.* Tobias Hawthorne had been born in 1944. Alice had been born in 1948—but in February, not September. The two of them were married in 1974. Zara was born two years later, Skye three years after that, and Toby two years later, in 1981. Tobias Hawthorne had filed his first patent in 1969. He'd founded his first company in 1971.

A little before midnight, I got a phone call from Libby. I answered the phone with a question. "Did you find something?"

We might have hit a wall, but Libby had spent hours in New Castle. She'd had time to ask about Harry. Time to look for him.

"No one at the soup kitchen has seen him for weeks." My sister's tone was hard for me to place. "So we tried the park."

"Libby?" I could hear my own heart beating in the silence that followed. "What did you find?"

"We talked to an older man. Frank. Nash tried to bribe him."

"Didn't work, did it?" I asked. More silence. "Lib?"

"He wasn't going to tell us anything, but then he looked at me for a minute, and he asked me if my name was Avery. Nash told him it was."

I should have been there myself. I should have been the one talking to Frank. "What did he say?"

"He gave me an envelope with your name on it. A message from Harry."

The world came screeching to a halt. *Toby left me a message.* I wanted to stop the thought there, but I couldn't. *My father... left me... a message.*

"Take a picture of the envelope," I told Libby, recovering my voice. "And the letter. I want to read it myself."

"Ave..." Libby's voice got very soft.

"Just do it!" I said urgently. *"Please."*

Less than a minute later, the pictures came through. My first name was written on the envelope in familiar scrawl, part print, part cursive. I scrolled through to the next picture—the message—and my heart sank all the way to my stomach.

The only words that Toby Hawthorne had for me were *STOP LOOKING*.

I couldn't sleep. The next day was Monday. I had school, and at this rate, I was going to be up staring at my ceiling all night. Rolling out of bed and walking over to my closet, I withdrew the lone, ratty bag I'd brought from home. I unzipped the pocket on the side and pulled out my mom's postcards—the only thing I had left of her.

I have a secret. I could hear her saying it. I could see her smile, like she was there with me right now.

"Why didn't you just tell me?" I whispered. Why had she

pretended my father was someone else? Why hadn't Toby been a part of my life?

Why didn't he want me looking for him now?

Something snapped inside of me, and before I knew it, I was walking. Out of my room, past Oren, who was positioned outside my door. I barely heard his objections. My pace picked up, and by the time I rounded the corner to Toby's wing, I was running.

The brick wall stared back at me. The Laughlins thought I had no business in Toby's wing. I'd been warned away. I'd walked into my bedroom to find it bloody, and right now, I didn't care if they were the ones who'd done it, or if it was another member of the staff. I didn't care who'd been the stalker in the woods at True North or who'd "decorated" my locker. I didn't care about Ricky Grambs or Skye Hawthorne or the way the skin over my knuckles split as I punched them into that wall.

Toby thought he could tell me to stop looking? He didn't want to be found?

He didn't get to tell me to stop. Nobody did. Oren moved to restrain me, and I fought him. I wanted to fight someone. Oren let me. He wasn't going to allow me to hurt myself, but he wouldn't stop me from lashing out at him. That just made me angrier.

I ducked his grip and barreled toward the bricks.

"Heiress." Suddenly, Jameson was standing between me and the wall. I tried to stop, but couldn't in time, and my fist connected with his chest. He didn't even blink.

I uncurled my fists, staring at him, realizing what had happened and horrified that I had hit him.

"I'm sorry." I had no excuse for losing it like this. So Toby had told me to stop looking? So he didn't want to be found? So what?

What was that to me?

“Tell me what you need.” Jameson wasn’t flirting. He wasn’t being cryptic. He wasn’t using me, in any way that I could tell.

I let out a long, effortful breath. “I need to take this damn wall down.”

Jameson nodded. He looked past me to Oren. “We’re going to need a sledgehammer.”

CHAPTER 54

I took that wall down, brick by brick, and when my arms couldn't hold the sledgehammer any longer, Jameson took over for me. With one last swing, he cleared enough that I could step through the rubble.

Jameson ducked in after me.

Oren let us go. He didn't even try to follow. He stayed positioned at the entrance to Toby's wing, on the lookout for anyone who might decide that we didn't belong there.

"You must think I've lost it." I snuck a look at Jameson as I walked across the marble floor of Toby's hall.

"I think," Jameson murmured, "that you finally let go."

I remembered the way his skin had felt under my hands in the hot tub. *That* was letting go. This was me, hanging on to something. I didn't even know what.

"He doesn't want me to find him." Saying the words out loud made it feel real.

"Which suggests," Jameson added, "that he thinks we might be able to."

We.

I stepped into Toby's bedroom. The black lights were still there. Jameson turned them on. The writing was still on the literal walls.

"I've been thinking," Jameson said, like it was a confession, like his mind wasn't always on the move. "The old man didn't leave Xander an impossible task. He left a game, one originally meant for Zara and Skye. And that means that if we follow this through to the end, there will be an end. This is all leading somewhere. I can feel it."

I took a step toward him. Then another. And another.

"You can feel it, too, can't you?" Jameson said as I closed the space between us.

I *could* feel it. The chase was gaining momentum. The hunt was closing in. Eventually, we'd figure out what the dates on the rings meant. We were barreling forward. *Jameson and me.*

I pushed him up against the closest wall. I could see Toby's writing all around him, but I didn't want to think about Toby, who'd told me to stop looking.

I didn't want to think about anything, so I kissed the boy. This time it wasn't rough or frantic. It was gentle and slow and terrifying and *perfect*. And for once in my life, I didn't feel alone.

CHAPTER 55

The next day at school, I didn't wait for Jameson to find me. I found him. "What if the numbers aren't dates?" I said.

That got me a slow, winding, wicked smile. "Heiress, you took the words right out of my mouth."

I half expected to end up back on the roof, but this time Jameson took me to one of the "learning pods" in the STEM Center. Basically, it was a small, square room where the walls, ceiling, and floor were all painted with whiteboard material. There were two white rolling chairs in the center of the room, and nothing else.

Eli started to follow us inside, and Jameson took that as his cue to run a hand down my back and bring his lips to the spot where my neck met my jawline. I arched my neck, and Eli went bright red and stepped out of the room.

Jameson shut the door—and went to work. There were five dry-erase markers attached to the back of each of the rolling chairs. Jameson grabbed one of the markers and began writing on the wall directly in front of the chair. "Eight, three, seven, five," he said.

I rattled off the next four numbers from memory as he continued writing. "Nine, seven, four, eight."

Writing the numbers without the dashes freed up countless possibilities. "A passcode?" I asked Jameson. "A PIN number?"

"Not enough digits in either of them for a phone number or a zip code." Jameson stepped back, sat down in one of the chairs, and pushed off. "An address. A combination."

I flashed back to the moment when he and I had stepped off a helicopter, with a different sequence of numbers. The air between us had felt electric—just like it did now. We'd been flying high—and thirty seconds later, he'd gone cold.

But this time was different, because this time we were on the same page. This time there were no expectations. I was in control. "Coordinates," I said. That had been one of Jameson's suggestions, the last time around.

He turned the chair and, with a push of his heels, came skidding back to me. "Coordinates," he repeated, eyes alight. "Nine-seven-four-eight. Assuming the numbers are already in the correct order, nine has to be the number of degrees. Ninety-seven is too big."

I thought back to my fifth-grade geography class. "Latitude and longitude run from negative ninety to ninety."

"You two don't know the valence of any of the numbers, obviously."

Jameson and I whipped our heads back toward the door of the pod. Xander was standing there. I could see Eli, still red-faced, behind him. Xander stepped into the pod, shut the door, and, with no hesitation whatsoever, leaped forward to flying-tackle Jameson to the ground.

"How many times do I have to tell you?" the youngest Hawthorne demanded. "This is my game. No one is solving this without me." He plucked the marker from Jameson's hand and stood. "That was a friendly tackle," he assured me. "Mostly."

Jameson rolled his eyes. "We don't know the valence of the numbers." He echoed the last thing Xander had said pre-tackle. "And we also don't know which is latitude and which is longitude, so nine degrees could be nine degrees north, south, west, or east."

"Eight-three-seven-five." I grabbed another marker off one of the chairs and underlined the numbers on the board in different combinations. "The degrees could be eight *or* eighty-three."

Jameson smiled. "North, south, east, or west."

"How many total possibilities?" Xander mused.

"Twenty-four," Jameson and I answered at the exact same time.

Xander gave us a look. "Is there something going on here that I should be aware of?" he asked, gesturing between the two of us.

Jameson shared a brief look with me. "Nothing of note." He said *nothing* like it was *something*.

"None of my business!" Xander declared. "But for the record: You lovebirds are incorrect. There are way more than twenty-four possible locations here."

Jameson narrowed his eyes. "I can do the math, Xan."

"And I can humbly inform you, big brother, that there are three different ways of listing coordinates." Xander grinned. "Degrees, minutes, seconds. Degrees, decimal minutes. And decimal degrees."

"With only four digits," Jameson insisted, "we're probably looking at decimal degrees."

Xander winked at me. "But *probably* is never good enough."

"Pacific Ocean," Jameson called out, and I wrote the location next to the designated coordinates. "Indian Ocean. Bay of Bengal."

Xander picked up right where his brother had left off. "Arctic Ocean. Arctic Ocean again!"

Both of them were entering coordinates into a map search. My brain kicked up a gear with each location they called out. *The*

Arctic. That couldn't be where this clue was supposed to point us, could it? And that was assuming that these numbers were coordinates at all.

"Antarctic Ice Shield," Jameson offered. "Times four."

By the time we were finished, the number of actual, non-arctic land locations on our list was much smaller than I'd expected. There were two in Nigeria, one in Liberia, one in Guinea, and one in...

"Costa Rica." I said out loud, unsure at first why that location was the one that had jumped out to me, but a moment later, I remembered the last time I'd read the words *Costa Rica*—in the binder.

"You have that look on your face," Jameson told me, his lips quirking upward. "You know something."

I closed my eyes and focused on the memory, not his lips. Skye's bequest had led to True North, one of the Hawthorne family's many vacation homes—mine, now. I tried to remember the pages I'd flipped through the night of the auction. *Patagonia. Santorini. Kauai. Malta. Seychelles*...

"Cartago, Costa Rica." I opened my eyes. "Tobias Hawthorne owned a house there." I pulled out my phone and looked up the latitude and longitude of Cartago, then turned my phone's screen toward the boys. "It's a match."

I tried to remember what the Cartago house looked like, but all I could see in my mind's eye was the surrounding vegetation and flowers, lush and bright and larger than life.

"We need to go to Costa Rica." Xander didn't exactly sound put out about that.

"I can't," I said, frustrated. I'd had to fight to go to Colorado. There was no way that Oren and Alisa would sign off on international travel—not when I could only spend two more nights away from Hawthorne House this month.

"Xander's not going anywhere, either."

For a second time, I found myself turning toward the doorway of the pod. Thea stood there.

"Are you just letting *anyone* in?" I called to Eli.

The reply I got was muffled, but I made out the words "not my job."

"Rebecca needs you," Thea told Xander. For the first time since I'd met her, she wasn't wearing any makeup. She looked almost mortal. "She didn't come to school today. It's her mom. I know it is. Rebecca won't answer my calls, so it's going to have to be you." It was clearly killing Thea to ask him, but there she was.

I expected Xander to put up a fight. How many times had he said that this was *his* game? But Xander just stared at Thea for a moment, then turned back to Jameson. "I guess you're going to Cartago."

Jameson glanced at me. I was fully prepared for him to ask me for another plane. Instead, the expression on his face shifted. "Can you call Libby and Nash?"

CHAPTER 56

"It makes no sense," I told Max that afternoon. "Jameson never lets up on a puzzle. What's his angle here?"

Nash and Libby had agreed to go to Cartago. I was sitting in my bedroom, staring at the photograph of the Cartago house. A quartet of columns held a tile roof over a large porch, but the house itself was small, less than a thousand square feet.

"Maybe he doesn't have an angle," Max said.

My eyes narrowed. "He's Jameson Hawthorne. He always has an angle."

A sharp knock at the door cut off whatever Max would have said in reply. I went to answer it, annoyed that a part of me couldn't think about Jameson without thinking about the way it felt when his lips brushed lightly against my neck.

I opened the door to find someone holding a tall stack of fluffy white towels. The towels blocked the person's face, and my mind went to the bloodied heart that someone—likely a staff member—had left in my room. I took a step back. My heart rate jumped. Then Eli stepped into view. "She's clear," he told me.

I nodded and stepped back. The person holding the towels

walked past me. *Mellie.* She didn't say a word to us and made her way into my bathroom.

"I will never get used to someone else doing my—" I didn't get to say the word *laundry* before a gut-rattling scream tore through the air. My body responded before my brain did, launching me into the bathroom just in time to see Mellie slamming closed the doors to my bathroom armoire.

"Snake," she wheezed. "There's a snake in your—"

Eli pulled me back into the bedroom. I heard him making a call, and less than two minutes later, my room was flooded with guards.

"What the elf!" Max demanded. "Did she say *snake*?"

"Rattlesnake." Oren took Max and me aside. "Dead—no actual danger."

I met his eyes and said what he wasn't saying. "Just a threat."

Someone wanted me scared. *Who—and why?* Deep down, some part of me knew the answer. An hour later, I went back to Toby's wing. Max went with me—and so did Oren.

The entire wing had been bricked up again.

I turned back to Oren. "The Laughlins did this." I wasn't sure if I was talking about the wall—or the snake. *They don't want me asking questions about Toby.*

"The threat level has been assessed," Oren told me. "It will continue to be assessed, and we will respond accordingly."

"Avery?"

I turned and saw Grayson making his way down the hall toward us. He always seemed so in control, so certain that the world would bend to his will. If he wanted me safe, I would *be* safe.

"I take it you heard about the snake," I said wryly.

"I did." Grayson arched an eyebrow at Oren. "I trust it's being handled."

Oren did not dignify that comment with a response.

"I also talked to Jameson." Grayson's tone gave away nothing. I saw myself with Jameson at school, in Toby's wing, in the hot tub, and I had to look away from Grayson's piercing silver eyes. "I understand we're in a waiting pattern."

It took me a moment to realize that when he said he'd talked to Jameson, he meant about the numbers—about Cartago. *Not us.*

"I thought perhaps," Grayson said evenly, "you could use a distraction."

"What kind of distraction?" Max asked, her tone just innocent enough to make me think the question wasn't innocent at all.

"A *friendly* one," I told her sternly. That's all Grayson and I were. *Friends.*

He straightened his suit jacket and smiled. "Either of you ladies up for a game?"

CHAPTER 57

The game room at Hawthorne House sent Max into a state of nearly apoplectic joy. The room was lines with shelves, the shelves filled with hundreds—maybe even thousands—of board games from around the world.

We started with Settlers of Catan. Grayson decimated us. We worked our way through four other games, none of which I'd even heard of before. As we were debating our next selection, Jameson strolled into the room.

"How about an old Hawthorne standard?" he suggested wickedly. "Strip bowling."

"What the shelf is strip bowling?" Max demanded, then she looked at me, eyes sparkling.

Don't you dare, I told her silently.

"Never mind!" Max grinned. "Avery and I are in."

Strip bowling was exactly what it sounded like, in that it involved both bowling and, if you were unsuccessful, stripping.

"The goal is to knock over the *least* pins," Jameson explained. "But you have to be careful, because any time your ball ends up in the gutter, you lose an article of clothing."

I could feel heat rising in my cheeks. My entire body felt warm—too warm. This was a horrible idea.

"This is a horrible idea," Grayson said. For a second or two, he and Jameson engaged in a silent standoff.

"Then why are you here?" Jameson volleyed back, waltzing over to pick out a dark green bowling ball with the Hawthorne crest on it. "No one is forcing you to play."

Grayson didn't move, and neither did I.

"So theoretically," Max said, "I want to knock over either zero pins or only one—whichever I can manage without putting the ball in the gutter?"

When Jameson answered, his green eyes locked on to mine. "Theoretically."

It became quickly apparent that excelling at strip bowling required precision and a high tolerance for risk. The first time Jameson cut things too close and his ball landed in the gutter, he took off a shoe.

Then another shoe.

A sock.

Another sock.

His shirt.

I tried not to look at the scar that ran the length of his torso, tried not to picture myself touching his chest. Instead, I focused on taking my turn. I was losing—badly. I'd even bowled a strike once, so determined was I to stay out of the gutter.

This time I cut things a little closer. When I knocked a single pin down, a breath left my chest. Grayson went next and lost his suit jacket. Max made it all the way down to her polka-dotted bra. Then it was Jameson's turn again, and the ball hung to the edge of the lane until the very end—then toppled into the gutter.

I tried—and failed—to look away as Jameson's fingers reached for the waistband of his jeans.

"Help me, Cheez-Its," Max murmured beside me.

Without warning, the door to the room burst inward, and Xander barreled into the bowling alley, then skidded to a halt. He was breathing hard enough to make me wonder how long he'd been running.

"Seriously?" Xander wheezed. "You're playing strip bowling without me? Never mind. Focus! This is me focusing."

"Focusing on what?" I asked.

"I have news," Xander blurted out.

"What kind of news?" Max asked. Xander glanced toward her. He definitely noticed the polka-dotted bra.

"Focus," Max reminded him. "What kind of news?"

"Is Rebecca okay?" Jameson asked, and I remembered Xander's conversation with Thea.

"For some values of okay," Xander said. That sentence made sense to no one except Xander, but he plowed on. "Thea was right. Rebecca's mom is having a rough day. There was vodka involved. She told Rebecca something."

"What kind of something?" Jameson took his turn trying to prompt Xander into spilling. Jameson's pants were still in place, but the top button had been undone.

Okay, now I *need to focus.*

"Avery, do you remember what Rebecca's mom said at the fundraiser, about all of her babies dying?"

"Nash said there were miscarriages," I said quietly. "Before Rebecca."

"That's what Bex thought she meant, too," Xander said quietly.

"But it wasn't?" I stared at him, having no idea whatsoever where this was going.

"She was talking about Emily," Grayson said, his voice pained.

"Emily," Xander confirmed. "And Toby."

I felt the world slow down around me. "What are you talking about?"

"Toby was a Laughlin." Xander swallowed. "Rebecca didn't know. No one did. Her parents were forty when they had Emily, but twenty-five years earlier—for the math-minded among us, that would be forty-two years ago—when Rebecca's mom was a teenager living in Wayback Cottage..."

"She got pregnant." Jameson stated the obvious.

"And Mr. and Mrs. Laughlin covered it up?" Grayson was intent on getting answers. "Why?"

Xander raised his shoulders up as high as they would go, then let them fall in the world's most elaborate shrug. "Rebecca's mom wouldn't explain—but she did rant to Bex, at length, about the fact that when one of the Hawthorne daughters got pregnant years later, she didn't have to hide her pregnancy. She got to keep *her* baby."

Skye hadn't been forced to put Nash up for adoption. I remembered what Rebecca's mother had said to Libby at the fundraiser. *Never trust a Hawthorne. They take everything.*

"Did Rebecca's mom want to keep her baby?" I asked, horrified. "Did they make her give him away? And why would they force her to hide the pregnancy?"

"I don't know the details," Xander said, "but according to Rebecca, her mother wasn't even told that the Hawthornes were the ones adopting the baby. She thought that our grandmother really was pregnant with a little boy, and that her own baby was adopted by a stranger."

That was horrifying. *That's why they kept Toby's adoption a secret? So she wouldn't know her baby was right there?*

"But as Toby grew up..." Xander shrugged again, the motion understated this time.

"She figured it out?" I imagined giving up a baby and then realizing that a child you'd seen grow up was yours.

I imagined being Toby and discovering this secret.

"Rebecca's been forbidden from seeing any of us." Xander grimaced. "Her mom said that the Hawthorne family takes and takes. She said that we don't play by any rules and don't care who we hurt. She blames our family for Toby's death."

"And Emily's," Grayson added roughly.

"For all of it." Xander sat down, right where he was standing. The room went quiet. Max and Jameson weren't wearing shirts, I was down one shoe, I knew instinctively that our game of strip bowling was over, and none of it mattered, because all I could think was that Rebecca's mom thought Toby was dead.

And so did Mr. and Mrs. Laughlin.

CHAPTER 58

The next day, before school, I went to find Mrs. Laughlin. I located her in the kitchen and asked Eli to give us a moment. The most he would give me was six or seven extra feet.

Mrs. Laughlin was kneading dough. She saw me out of the corner of her eye and kneaded harder. "What can I do for you?" she asked tersely.

I braced myself because I was almost certain this wasn't going to go well. I probably should have just kept my mouth shut, but I'd spent most of the night thinking that if Rebecca's mom was Toby's mom, then the Laughlins hadn't just watched Toby grow up. They hadn't just loved him because he was lovable.

He was their grandson. *And that makes me*...

I pressed my lips together, then decided that the best way to rip a bandage off was quickly. "I need to talk to you about Toby." I kept my voice low.

Wham. Mrs. Laughlin picked the dough up and expertly slammed it back down, then wiped her hands on her apron and whipped her head to look directly at me. "Listen to me, little miss. You may own this House. You may be richer than sin. You could own the sun for all I care, but I will not let you hurt everyone who loved that boy by dredging this up and—"

"He was your grandson." My voice shook. "Your daughter got pregnant. You hid it, and the Hawthornes adopted the baby."

Mrs. Laughlin went pale. "Hush," she ordered, her voice shaking even more than mine had. "You can't walk around here saying things like that."

"Toby was your grandson," I repeated. My throat felt like it was swelling, and my eyes were starting to sting. "And I think he's my father."

Mrs. Laughlin's mouth opened, then twisted, like she'd been on the verge of yelling at me, then run out of air. Both of her hands went to the flour-covered countertop, and she held on to it like what I'd just said was threatening to bring her to her knees.

I took a step toward her. I wanted to reach out, but I didn't press my luck. Instead, I held out the file I had retrieved from Tobias Hawthorne's study. Mrs. Laughlin didn't take it. I wasn't sure she could.

"Here," I said.

"No." She closed her eyes and shook her head. "No, I'm not going to—"

I took a single sheet of paper out of the file. "This is my birth certificate," I said quietly. "Look at the signature."

And bless her, she did. I heard a sharp intake of air, and then finally she looked back at me.

My eyes were stinging worse now, but I kept going. I didn't want to stop, because part of me was terrified about what she might say. "Here are some pictures Tobias Hawthorne had a private detective take of me, shortly before he died." I laid three photographs out on the counter. Two of me playing chess with Harry, one of the two of us in line for a breakfast sandwich. Toby wasn't facing the camera in any of them, but I willed Mrs. Laughlin to look at what she could see—his hair, his body, the way he stood. *Recognize him.*

"That man," I said, nodding to the pictures. "He showed up right after my mother died. I thought he was homeless. Maybe he was. We played chess in the park every week, sometimes every morning." I could hear the raw emotion in my own voice. "He and I had this ongoing bet that if I won, he had to let me buy him breakfast, but if he won, I couldn't even offer. I'm competitive, and I'm good at chess, so I won a lot—but he won more."

Mrs. Laughlin closed her eyes, but they didn't stay closed for long, and when she opened them, she stared right at the photographs "That could be anyone," she said roughly.

I swallowed. "Why do you think Tobias Hawthorne left me his fortune?" I asked quietly.

Mrs. Laughlin's breath grew ragged. She turned to look at me, and when she did, I saw every emotion I felt mirrored in her eyes—and then some.

"Oh, Tobias," she whispered. It was the first time I'd ever heard her call her former employer anything but *Mr. Hawthorne*. "What did you do?"

"We're still trying to figure it out," I said, a ball of emotion rising in my throat. "But—"

I never got the chance to finish that sentence, because the next thing I knew, Mrs. Laughlin was hugging me, holding on to me for dear life.

CHAPTER 59

The downside of modular scheduling was that some days, my classes were scheduled so tightly that I barely even had time for lunch. Today was one of those days. I had exactly one mod—twenty-two minutes—to make it to the refectory, buy food, eat it, and haul myself back to the physics lab, across campus.

While I was waiting in line, I got a text from Libby: a photograph, taken out the window of a plane. The ocean below was a brilliant green-blue. The land in the distance was tree-covered. And coming into view amid those trees was what I recognized as the very top of an architectural marvel. The Basílica de Nuestra Señora de los Ángeles—in Cartago.

I made it to the front of the line and paid. As I sat down to eat, all I could think was that Libby and Nash were landing in Cartago. They would make their way to the house. They would find *something.* And somehow, the puzzle that Tobias Hawthorne had left first for his daughters—and then for Xander—would start to make sense.

"May I sit?"

I looked up to see Rebecca, and for a moment, I just stared at her. She'd cut her long, dark red hair off at the chin. The ends were uneven, but something about the way it flared out around her face made her look almost otherworldly.

"Sure," I said. "Knock yourself out."

Rebecca sat. Without her long hair to hide behind, her eyes looked impossibly large. Her chest rose and fell—a deep breath. "Xander told you," she said.

"He did," I replied, and then my sense of empathy got the better of me, because as much of a mind warp as this revelation had been for me, it might have actually been worse for her. "Don't expect me to start calling you Aunt Rebecca."

That surprised a laugh out of her. "You sounded like her just then," she told me after a moment. "Emily."

That was the exact instant that I realized that if Rebecca was my aunt, then Emily had been, too. I thought about Thea, dressing me up like Emily. I'd never thought we looked anything alike, but when Grayson had seen me coming down the stairs at the charity gala, he'd looked like he'd seen a ghost.

Do I have some Emily in me?

"Was your dad...," I started to ask Rebecca, but I wasn't sure how to phrase my question. "How long have your parents been together?"

"Since high school," Rebecca said.

"So your dad was Toby's father?"

Rebecca shook her head. "I don't know. I'm not even one hundred percent sure my dad knows there *was* a baby." She looked down. "My dad loves my mom, that fairy-tale, all-encompassing, even-our-own-kids-will-never-compare kind of love. He took her name when they got married. He let her make all the decisions about Emily's medical treatment."

I took that to mean that if Rebecca's mother had doted on Emily and ignored Rebecca, her father had backed that decision, too.

"I'm sorry," Rebecca said softly.

"About what?" I asked. As messed up as the Laughlin family secrets were, I wasn't the one who'd grown up in Toby's shadow. This had affected Rebecca's life more than mine.

"I'm sorry about what I did to you," Rebecca clarified. "About what I *didn't* do."

I thought about the night Drake had tried to kill me. After a disastrous make-out session with Jameson, I'd ended up in a room alone with Rebecca. We'd talked. If she'd told me then what she knew about Drake and Skye, there would have been nothing to forgive.

"I've been trying so hard to be okay." Rebecca wasn't even looking at me anymore. "But I'm not. That poem Toby left? The William Blake one? I have a copy on my phone, and I keep reading it over and over, and all I can think is that I wish I had read it sooner, because when I was growing up, I buried all my anger. No matter what Emily wanted or what I had to give up for her—I was supposed to be okay with it. I was supposed to smile. And the one time I let myself get mad, she..."

Rebecca couldn't say it, so I said it for her. "Died."

"It messed me up, and I messed up, and I'm so, so sorry, Avery."

"Okay," I said—and to my surprise, I meant it.

"If it's any consolation," Rebecca continued, "I'm angry now, finally—at so many people."

I thought back to her fight with Thea on the plane, and then I thought about the absolutely infuriating message Toby had left me.

"I'm angry, too," I told Rebecca. "And for the record: I like your hair."

CHAPTER 60

When Oren picked Eli and me up after school, Alisa was in the passenger seat—and Landon was in the back, tapping furiously away on her phone.

"Everything is fine," Alisa assured me, which was pretty much the opposite of comforting. "We've got this under control, but—"

"But what?" I glanced over at Landon. "What's she doing here?"

There was a beat of silence. That was all it took for Alisa to craft her reply. "Skye and your father are offering themselves as an interview package to the highest bidder." Alisa expelled an aggrieved breath. "If we want to quash the story, Landon is going to have to make it worth the high bidder's while to bury it."

I'd had enough on my mind these past few days that I'd barely thought about Ricky Grambs. I tried to read between the lines of Alisa's statement. "Are you saying you're going to pay off whoever buys their interview?"

Landon finally looked up from her phone. "Yes and no," she told me before turning her attention to Alisa. "Monica thinks she can make the network pony up, but we're going to have to guarantee them Avery *and* at least one Hawthorne."

"They'll pay for exclusivity from Skye?" Alisa asked. "Complete with an NDA preventing Skye and Grambs from taking their story elsewhere?"

"They'll pay for it. They'll bury it." Landon pinched the bridge of her nose, like she could feel a migraine coming on. "But the latest they'll agree to for a sit-down with Avery is tomorrow night."

"Good lord." Alisa shook her head. "Can she handle it?"

"I'm sitting right here," I pointed out.

"She'll have to." Landon spoke over me. "But we're going to have to crunch."

"*Crunch* what, exactly?" I asked. Everyone in the car ignored the question.

"Avery's interview is nonexclusive," Alisa told Landon, "and they have a deal."

"They'll want an embargo on other interviews for at least a month." Landon's reply was automatic.

"Three weeks," Alisa countered. "And it applies only to Avery, not any of her surrogates."

Since when did I have surrogates? I wasn't running for president here.

"Which Hawthorne am I offering as part of the package?" Landon asked, all business.

My brain was struggling to keep up, but I was pretty sure that what was happening here was that we were giving my first interview to whoever bought Skye's, under the conditions that the interview with Skye and Ricky never aired and whoever bought it contractually prevented the duo from talking to anyone else.

"Why do we even care about *their* interview?" I said.

"We care," Alisa said emphatically. Then she turned back to Landon. "And you can tell Monica that we'll guarantee a sit-down Wednesday evening with Avery and... Grayson."

CHAPTER 61

"Grayson, move a little closer to Avery. Tilt your head toward her."

Landon had set us up in the tea room for a mock interview. This was take *seven*. How Alisa had gotten Grayson to agree to this, I had no idea, but there he was, sitting stiffly in the chair next to me. At Landon's instruction, he angled his legs slightly toward mine. Instinctively, I mirrored the movement, and then I was hit with self-consciousness and self-doubt, because Landon hadn't asked *me* to move.

My body had gravitated toward his all on its own.

"Good." Landon nodded at the two of us, then focused on Grayson. "Remember your core message."

"This has been a difficult time for my family," Grayson said, every inch the heir apparent he'd once been. "But some things happen for a reason."

"Good," Landon said again. "Avery?"

I was supposed to respond to what Grayson had said. The more we talked to each other, the easier it would be to sell the fact that I was on good terms with the Hawthorne family.

"Some things happen for a reason," I repeated, but the words came out flat. "I've never believed that," I admitted. I could practically hear Landon groaning internally. "I mean, yeah, things happen for a reason, but most of the time that reason isn't fate or because it was predestined. It's because the world sucks, or someone out there's being an asshole."

A muscle in Grayson's jaw tightened slightly. It was a good enough look for him that it took me a second to realize that he was trying very hard not to laugh.

"Let's try to avoid the word *asshole*, shall we?" Landon said, her British accent pronounced. "Avery, we need for you to project gratitude and awe. It's fine to be overwhelmed, but you need to be overwhelmed in the best possible way."

Gratitude. Awe. I was expected to be some kind of wide-eyed everygirl, and all Grayson had to do was sit there, with those cheekbones and that suit and be a *Hawthorne*.

"Avery's right." Grayson was still in interview mode. He projected confidence, his tone dripping power, like he was an immortal deigning to explain to humans what they should believe, think, and do. "We all make decisions, and those decisions affect other people. They ripple through the world, and the more power you have, the greater the ripple. Fate didn't choose Avery." Grayson's tone brooked no argument. "My grandfather did. We might never know his reasons, but I have no doubt that he had them. He always did."

All I could think was that we *did* know the reasons—or at least, we had theories. But that wasn't something I could say in front of Landon. It wasn't something I could admit on national television.

When you can't tell the truth, I could hear Landon lecturing me, *tell* a *truth*.

"I wish I knew what those reasons were," I said. *For sure*, I added silently. I shot Grayson a look. "Sometimes, it feels like Hawthornes always just know. Like you're all so sure of everything."

Grayson's eyes locked on to mine. "Not everything."

There was something about the way he looked at me when he said those words that made me realize I might be the one person on the planet with the ability to make Grayson Hawthorne question himself and the decisions he'd made.

Like the decision to step back from me. To be *friends*.

Landon clasped her hands together. "Avery, that's the most natural I've heard you sound. Very relatable! And, Grayson, you're perfection." Like he needed anyone else telling him that. "Just remember, both of you: short answers if they ask about the attempts on Avery's life. Grayson, don't be afraid to seem protective of her. Avery, you know the rest of your 'no' questions."

If they asked if I knew anything about my mother's past: *no*.

If they asked what I had done to work my way into Tobias Hawthorne's will: *nothing*.

"Grayson, whenever possible, talk about your grandfather. And your brothers! The audience will eat that up, and we want them walking away with the idea that your grandfather knew exactly what he was doing when he chose Avery, and no one's worried. And, Avery?"

"Gratitude," I said quickly. "Overwhelmed. Relatable. One day, I'm scrounging to pay the electric bill, and the next, I'm Cinderella. I don't know what I'll do with the money yet—I'm just seventeen. But I'd like to help people."

"And?" Landon prompted.

"Someday I'd like to travel the world." That was something we'd settled on as a talking point, something that made me sound dreamy and wide-eyed and overwhelmed. And it was true.

"Perfect," Landon said. "One more time, from the top."

CHAPTER 62

By the time Landon finally let us go, the sun was starting to set.

"You look like you want to hit something," Grayson observed. He was getting ready to go on his way, and I was getting ready to go on mine—probably to find Max.

"I don't want to hit anything," I said in a tone that did absolutely nothing to sell that statement.

Grayson tilted his head to the side, and his eyes settled directly on mine. "How would you feel about swinging a sword?"

Grayson took me through the topiary garden to a part of the estate I'd never seen before.

"Is that . . . ," I started to say.

"A hedge maze?" Grayson had a way of smiling: lips closed, slightly uneven. "I'm surprised Jamie's never brought you out here."

The moment he mentioned Jameson, I was hit with the feeling that I shouldn't be out here—not with Grayson. But we were just friends, and whatever Jameson and I were at the moment, it came with no strings attached.

That was the point.

I turned my attention to the maze. The hedges were taller than I was, and dense. *A person could get lost in there.* I stood at the entrance, Grayson beside me.

"Follow me," he said.

I did. The farther into the maze we got, the more I focused on marking our path—not on the way he moved, the shape of his body in front of me.

Right turn. Left turn. Left again. Forward. Right. Left.

Finally, we arrived at what I assumed was the center: a large, square area, surrounded by twinkling lights. Grayson knelt and spread the grass with his fingertips, revealing something metal underneath. In the twilight, I didn't see exactly what he did, but a moment later, I heard a mechanical whirring sound, and the ground started moving.

My first thought was that he'd triggered an entrance to the tunnels, but when I stepped closer, I saw a steel compartment embedded in the ground, six feet long, three feet wide, and not all that deep. Grayson reached into the compartment and removed two long objects wrapped in cloth. He nodded toward the second, and I knelt, unwinding the fabric to reveal a flash of metal.

A sword.

It was nearly three feet long, heavy, with a T-shaped hilt. I ran my fingers over the hilt, then looked up at Grayson, who was unwrapping a second sword.

"Longswords," he said, clipping the word. "Italian. Fifteenth century. They should probably be in a museum somewhere, but..." He gave a little shrug.

This was what it meant to be a Hawthorne. *This should probably be in a museum, but my brothers and I like to hit things with it instead.*

I went to pick up the sword, but Grayson stopped me. "Both

hands," he said. "A longsword is designed to be used with both hands."

I wrapped my hands around the hilt, then managed to stand up.

Grayson placed his own sword down carefully on the cloth it had been wrapped in, then came up behind me. "No," he said softly. "Like this." He moved my right hand up, directly underneath the cross on the *T*. "Quillons," he told me, nodding toward that part of the sword. He nodded toward the end of the hilt. "Pommel. Never put your hand on the pommel. It has its own job to do." He placed my left hand above it, a little below my right. "Grip the sword with the bottom fingers of both hands. Keep the upper ones looser. You move, and the sword moves. Don't fight the movement of the sword. Let it do the work for you."

He stepped back and picked up his own sword. Slowly, he demonstrated.

"Shouldn't I be using some kind of...practice sword?" I asked.

Grayson met my eyes. "Probably."

This was a bad idea. I knew it. He knew it. But I'd spent the last five hours being prepped for an interview I absolutely did not want to give, an interview I only had to give because of Ricky—who *wasn't* my father—and Skye, who had probably hired the stalker at True North.

Sometimes all a girl really needed was a very bad idea.

"Watch your posture. Let the sword lead you, not the other way around."

I corrected, and Grayson gave the slightest of nods. "I'm sorry about all of this," I said.

"You should be sorry. You're getting sloppy again. Already."

I adjusted my stance and my grip. "I'm sorry about the interview," I specified with a roll of my eyes.

Grayson slowly brought his sword to contact mine, the movement so perfectly controlled that I was overcome with the sense that he could cut a hair in half if he wanted to. "It doesn't signify," he assured me. "I'm a Hawthorne. As a general rule, we're press-ready by our seventh birthdays." He stepped back. "Your turn," he told me. "*Control.*"

I didn't talk at all until my sword had touched his—a little harder than I'd meant for it to. "I'm *still* sorry that you got dragged into *this* interview."

Grayson lowered his sword and began cuffing his sleeves. "You're sorrier about an interview than you were when I was disinherited."

"That's not true. I *was* sorry—you were just too busy being an asshole to notice."

Grayson gave me his most austere look. "Let's try to avoid using the word *asshole*, shall we?"

His Landon impression was *spot-on*. Grinning, I swung at him again, letting the sword lead me this time, aware of every muscle in my body and every inch of his. I stopped the sword a microsecond before it touched his blade. He stepped forward. Once. Twice.

Longswords weren't meant to be wielded at such close range. And still he came closer, forcing my blade vertical, until there was nothing but inches and two swords separating him from me. I could see him breathing, hear it, *feel* it.

Muscles in my shoulders and arms began to ache—but the rest of me ached more. "What are we doing?" I whispered.

His eyes closed. His body shuddered. He stepped back and lowered the sword. "Nothing."

CHAPTER 63

That night, when I couldn't sleep, I told myself that it was because we still hadn't heard anything from Libby and Nash. Every text I sent went unread and unanswered. That was what kept me up so late that I was guaranteed to wake up the next morning with dark circles under my eyes. *Not Grayson.*

The next evening, I still hadn't heard from Libby, and Grayson Hawthorne and I were sitting next to each other, under a flood of lights, with Monica Winfield smiling into the camera.

I am so not ready for this.

"Avery, let's start with you. Walk us through what happened the day Tobias Hawthorne's will was read."

That was a softball question. *Gratitude. Awe. Relatability.* I could do this—and I did. Grayson answered his first softball question just as easily.

He even managed to make eye contact with me the first time he said my name.

We got two more softballs apiece before Monica moved on to trickier territory. "Avery, let's talk about your mother."

Keep it short, I could hear Landon telling me. *And sincere.*

"She was wonderful," I said fiercely. "I would give anything for her to be here now."

That was short, and it was sincere—but it also opened me up to a follow-up. "You must have heard some of the . . . rumors."

That my mom was living under a fake name. That she was a con artist. I couldn't lose my temper. *Spin the question.* That was what I was supposed to do: Start talking about my mother but end up talking about how grateful and awed and gosh darn *normal* I was.

Beside me, Grayson leaned forward. "When the world is watching your every move, when everyone knows your name, when you're famous just by *being*—you stop following rumors pretty quickly. Last I heard, I was supposedly dating a princess, and my brother Jameson had some very questionable tattoos."

Monica's eyes lit up. "Does he?"

Grayson leaned back in his seat. "A Hawthorne never tells."

He was good at this—much better than I was—and just like that, the interviewer was redirected off the topic of my mother. "Your family has been very closemouthed about this entire situation," she told Grayson. "The last the world heard, your aunt Zara was implying there might be a legal solution to your dilemma."

The last public statement Zara had given had more or less accused me of elder abuse.

"You can say a lot of things about my grandfather," Grayson replied smoothly, "but Tobias Hawthorne wasn't known for leaving loopholes."

Something about the way he said that made it clear that the topic was closed. *How does he do that?*

"Avery." Monica zeroed back in on me. "We've talked a bit about your mother. Let's talk about your father."

That was one of my "no" questions. I shrugged. "There's not much to say."

"You're a minor, correct? And your legal guardian is your sister, Libby?"

I could tell where this was going. Just because the network wasn't airing the interview with Ricky and Skye didn't mean that Monica hadn't filed away their statements for future reference. She was going to ask me about custody.

Not if I redirect. "Libby took me in after my mom died. She didn't have to. She was twenty-three. Because our dad was never around, we hadn't spent much time together. We were practically strangers, but she took me in. She is the single most loving person I've ever met in my life."

That was one of the core truths of my existence, and I didn't have to work to sell it.

"I suppose that's one thing Avery and I have in common," Grayson added beside me. He didn't elaborate and forced Monica into asking the follow-up question.

"And what is that?"

"If you're going to come at our siblings," he told her, his smile sharp, his gaze full of warning, "you're going to have to go through us."

This was the Grayson I'd met weeks ago: dripping power and well aware that he could come out on top in any battle. He didn't make threats, because he didn't *have* to.

"Did you feel protective of your brothers after you realized your grandfather had essentially written them out of the will?" Monica asked him. I got the sense that she *wanted* Grayson to say that he resented me. She wanted to poke holes in the message he'd been delivering.

"You could say that." Grayson held her gaze, then broke it to glance deliberately at me.

"I think we're all protective of Avery now. It's not something that my brothers or I expect anyone else to understand, but the simple truth is that we're not normal. My grandfather didn't raise us to be *normal*, and this is what he wanted. This is his legacy." His gaze burned into me. "*She* is."

He sold every single word—enough that I could almost believe that he really thought I was special.

"And you have no reservations about the entire situation?" Monica pressed.

Grayson gave her a wolfish smile. "None."

"No desire to overturn the will?"

"I've already told you: That can't be done."

The trick to answering "no" questions was perfect, bulletproof confidence in your reply. Grayson was a master of the art.

"But if it could?" Monica asked.

"This is what my grandfather wanted," Grayson replied, returning to his core message. "My brothers and I are lucky—luckier than almost anyone else watching this. We've been given every opportunity, and we have a lot of the old man in us. We'll make our own way." He glanced toward me again, but this time it felt more choreographed. "Someday, what I make of myself will give *your* fortune a run for its money."

I grinned. *Take that, Monica.*

"Avery, how does it feel when Grayson says those words: *your fortune*?"

"Unreal." I shook my head. "Before the will was read, back when I knew that I'd been left something but didn't know what, I figured that Tobias Hawthorne had left me a couple thousand dollars. And even that? It would have been life-changing."

"So this?"

"Unreal," I repeated, projecting every ounce of gratitude and awe and bewilderment that I had felt in that moment.

"Do you ever feel like it might all go away?"

Beside me, Grayson shifted slightly, his body angling toward mine. But I didn't need his protection right now. I was on a roll.

"Yes."

"And what if I told you—both of you—that there might be another heir?"

I went still, my face frozen. I couldn't risk even looking at Grayson, but I wondered if he'd sensed something was off the moment before, if that was why he'd shifted. I could see now all the ways the interviewer had been leading up to this. She'd asked Grayson about overturning the will—twice. She'd asked me how I'd feel if it all went away.

"Avery, do you know what the term *pretermitted* means, in the context of inheritance law?"

My brain couldn't catch up fast enough. *Toby. She can't know about Toby. Skye doesn't. Ricky doesn't.* "I..."

"It typically refers to an heir who was not yet born at the deceased's time of death, but interpreted a bit more broadly, our experts say that it could refer to any heir who was not 'alive' at the time of death."

She *knew.* I glanced at Grayson. I couldn't help it. His gaze was focused on the interviewer's as he spoke. "I'm sure your experts told you that in the state of Texas, a pretermitted child is entitled only to a share that is equal to the deceased's other children's." Grayson's eyes were sharp—and so was his close-lipped smile. "Since my grandfather left very little to his children, even if he had somehow conceived a child before his death, it would hardly alter the distribution of his assets at all."

In that moment, Grayson didn't seem like he was nineteen years old. He hadn't just spouted off legal precedent—he'd deliberately overlooked the fact that Monica had made it clear she wasn't talking about an unborn child.

"Your family really has been looking for loopholes, haven't they?" Monica said, but she didn't mean it as a question. "Perhaps they should have a sit-down with our experts, because it's not clear, based on precedent, whether a child assumed to be dead would be entitled only to their siblings' share, or to the share left to that child in a prior will."

Grayson stared her down. "I'm afraid I don't follow."

He did. Of course he did. He was just hiding it better than I did, because all I could do was sit there silently and think one name, over and over.

Toby.

"You had an uncle." Monica was still focused on Grayson.

"He died," Grayson said sharply. "Before I was even born."

"Under tragic and suspicious circumstances." Monica swung her head to face me. "Avery." She hit a button on a remote I hadn't even been aware she was holding. A trio of pictures flashed on a large screen behind us.

The same pictures I'd shown Mrs. Laughlin the day before.

"Who is this man?"

I swallowed. "My friend. Harry." *Tell a story.* "We used to play chess in the park."

"Do you have many friends in their forties?"

When you can't tell the truth, tell a *truth. Tell a story.* "He was the only one who could take my queen. We had a running bet: If I won a game, he had to let me buy him breakfast. I knew he didn't have the money to buy it himself. I was afraid he might not eat otherwise, but he hated charity, so I had to win, fair and square."

I'd done Landon proud—but Monica wasn't deterred. "So it is your statement that this man is not Tobias Hawthorne the Second?"

"How dare you?" Grayson's voice vibrated with intensity. He stood. "Hasn't my family suffered enough? We just lost my grandfather. To dredge up this tragedy—"

"Avery." Monica knew who the weak link here was. "Is this or is this not Tobias Hawthorne's supposedly deceased son? The true heir to the Hawthorne fortune?"

"This interview is over." Grayson turned to block the camera and helped me to my feet. He met my gaze, and even though he didn't say a word, I heard him loud and clear: *We need to get out of here.*

He ushered me to the wings, where Alisa was trying to bust past a security guard. Monica followed us, a cameraman with a handheld in her wake. "What is your connection to Toby Hawthorne?" she yelled after me.

The world was falling down around me. We hadn't prepared for this. I wasn't ready. But I had an answer to that question. I had a truth, and if they knew this much, then what would the harm be in telling them the rest.

What is your connection to Toby Hawthorne?

"I'm his—"

Before I could get the word *daughter* out, Grayson leaned his head down and crushed his lips to mine. He kissed me to save me from what I'd been about to say. For a small eternity, nothing in the world existed outside of that kiss.

His lips. Mine.

For show.

CHAPTER 64

The kiss ended as the two of us were shuffled off-camera and into an elevator. My heart was thudding. My brain was a mess. My lips felt…my whole body felt…

There were no words.

"What the hell was that?" Alisa waited for the elevator door to close before she exploded.

"That was an ambush," Landon replied, her posh accent doing absolutely nothing to soften the words. "If you keep information from me, I can't keep you from being ambushed. Alisa, you know how I operate. If you won't allow me to do my job, then it is, simply put, no longer my job."

The elevator door opened, and Landon left.

As Max would say: *fax*. My eyes found their way to Grayson's, but he wouldn't even look at me. It was like he *couldn't*.

"I am going to ask one more time," Alisa said, her voice low. "What the hell was that?"

"You'll get your answer," Oren told her. "In the car. We need to move out now. I've sent two of my men to the car and deployed the decoy. We'll go out the back. *Move*."

We made it out of the parking lot before the vultures descended. Alisa let us marinate in silence for a full minute before she spoke again. This time she didn't ask what was going on. "Who knew?" she demanded instead. *"Who knew?"*

I looked down. "I did."

"Obviously." Alisa shifted her gaze to Grayson. "Are you going to lie and tell me you didn't?" Then she glanced to the driver's seat. "Oren?"

My head of security didn't reply.

"This will be easier if we start at the beginning," Grayson said, sounding calmer than he should have. *Like we never kissed at all.* "You will recall that Avery asked you to locate an acquaintance of hers, to whom she was hoping to give economic aid?"

"Harry." Alisa's memory was a sieve—and I knew in my bones that she would *never* forget what had just happened. She probably wouldn't forgive it, either.

"Toby," I corrected. I looked over at Grayson. *You can't do this for me. You can't protect me the way you did back there.* "I didn't know who he was at the time," I continued, "but then I saw a picture of him in Nan's locket."

"You should have told me. Immediately." Alisa was angry, furious enough that she let loose an impressive string of curse words of her own—some in English and some not. "And you *shouldn't* have told anyone else." She shot dagger eyes at Grayson, so it was pretty clear who she was referring to.

"Xander already knew," Grayson said quietly. "My grandfather left him a clue."

That took the wind out of Alisa's sails, but only slightly. "Of course he did." She let out a breath, then took in another, and then repeated the process two or three times. "If you had told me, Avery, I might have been able to get a handle on this. We could have hired a team to—"

"Find him?" I said. "Your team already looked."

"There are teams," Alisa told me, "and there are *teams*. I have a fiduciary duty to the estate—to you. There is no way I could license millions to find *Harry*, but to find *Toby*?"

I dug my phone out and pulled up the picture Libby had sent me of Toby's message. "He doesn't want to be found." I passed the phone into her hands.

"*Stop looking*." She read the words aloud, completely unimpressed. "Who took this? Where was it taken? Have we verified the handwriting?"

I answered the questions in the order she'd asked them. "Libby. New Castle. The handwriting is definitely Toby's."

Alisa rolled her eyes heavenward. "You sent *Libby* after him?"

I was getting ready to tell her that there was nothing wrong with Libby, when Grayson clarified the situation. "And Nash."

It took Alisa a full four or five seconds to recover from the fact that Nash had known—and that he was with Libby now. "And *you*," she told Grayson heatedly. "You had time to look up the legal precedent, but it didn't occur to you to *talk to a lawyer*?"

Grayson looked down at the cuff link on his right sleeve, considering his response. He must have decided on honesty, because when he lifted his gaze back up to Alisa, all he said was, "We couldn't be certain where your loyalties would lie."

This time Alisa didn't look angry. She looked like she might cry. "How could you say that to me, Gray?" She searched his expression for a response, and I was reminded that she'd grown up with the Hawthorne family. She'd known Grayson and Jameson and Xander their entire lives. "When did I become the enemy here? I have only *ever* done what the old man wanted me to do." She spoke like those words were being physically torn out of her. "Do you have any idea what that's cost me?"

It was clear from the tone of her voice that she wasn't just talking about the will, or me, or anything that had happened in the wake of Tobias Hawthorne's death. She'd called him "the old man," the same way they did, when I'd only ever heard her refer to him as *Mr. Hawthorne* or *Tobias Hawthorne* before. And when she spoke about what her loyalty to the old man had cost her...

She's talking about Nash.

"I am holding this empire together by a thread." Alisa swiped angrily at her face with the back of her hand, and I realized a single tear had escaped. Her expression made it damn clear that it would be the last. "Avery, I will handle this situation. I will put out this fire. I will do what needs to be done, but the next time you keep a secret from me, the next time you lie to me? I will throw you to the wolves *myself*."

I believed her. "There is one more thing." I gulped—there was no way of sugarcoating this. "Well, two more things. One: Toby was adopted, and his biological mother was the Laughlins' then-teenage daughter."

Alisa stared at me for a good three seconds. Then she arched an eyebrow, waiting for the other thing.

"And two," I continued, thinking back to the moment when Grayson had stopped me from saying this on camera—and how. "I have reason to believe that Toby is, in all likelihood, my father."

CHAPTER 65

"Well," Max said, flopping down on my bed. "That could have gone better." She'd seen the interview. The whole world had. "Are you sure you're okay?"

Grayson had warned me, from the very beginning, not to pull at this thread. He warned me against telling anyone about Toby, and how many people had I told?

When we'd arrived back at Hawthorne House, I had tried to talk to him, but my mouth had refused to say a single word.

"Grayson didn't *have* to kiss me," I told Max, the words bursting out of my mouth, like I didn't have much bigger things to think about. "He could have cut me off."

"Personally, I find this turn of events *delightful*," Max declared. "But you look like a motherfaxing deer caught in motherfaxing headlights."

I felt like one. "He shouldn't have kissed me."

Max grinned. "Did you kiss him back?"

His lips. Mine. "I don't know!" I bit out.

Max gave me her most innocent look. "Would you like me to pull up the footage?"

I'd kissed him back. Grayson Hawthorne had kissed me, and

I'd kissed him back. I thought about the night before in the hedge maze. The way he'd corrected my form. How close we'd been standing.

"What am I doing?" I asked Max, feeling like I was in a maze now. "Jameson and I are..."

"What?" Max probed.

I shook my head. "I don't know." I knew what Jameson and I were supposed to be: adrenaline and attraction and the thrill of the moment. No strings attached. No messy emotions.

So why did I feel like I'd betrayed him?

"Close your eyes," Max advised me, closing her own. "Picture yourself standing on a cliff overlooking the ocean. The wind is whipping in your hair. The sun is setting. You long, body and soul, for one thing. One person. You hear footsteps behind you. You turn." Max opened her eyes. "Who's there?"

The problem with Max's question was that it assumed I was capable of longing, body and soul, for anything. Anyone. When I pictured myself on that cliffside, I pictured myself alone.

Late into the night, long after Max had retired to her room, I pulled up news searches to see what people were saying about that disastrous interview. Most headlines were calling Toby "the lost heir." Skye was already giving interviews.

Apparently her NDA didn't cover *this*.

In the comments section of nearly every article, there was speculation that I'd slept with Grayson to get him on my side. Some people were claiming that he wasn't the only Hawthorne I'd slept with. It shouldn't have mattered that strangers were calling me a *slut*—or worse—but it did.

The first time I'd ever heard that word, another kid in elementary school had used it to describe my mom. I couldn't ever remember her even dating *anyone*, but I existed, and she'd never been married, and for some people that was enough.

I walked over to my closet and pulled out the bag with the postcards—the ones my mom had given me. *Hawaii. New Zealand. Machu Picchu. Tokyo. Bali.* I flipped through them as a reminder of who I was, who she'd been. This was what we'd daydreamed about—not being swept off our feet.

Not some kind of epic seaside love.

I wasn't sure how long I'd been sitting there when I heard a noise. *Footfalls.* My head whipped up. The last I'd checked, Oren was stationed outside my room. He'd warned me that this news getting out could put me in danger.

A voice spoke, on the other side of the fireplace. "It's me, Heiress."

Jameson. That should have been a relief. Knowing it was him, I should have felt safer. But somehow, as I locked my hand around the candlestick on the mantel, the last thing I felt was safe.

I triggered the passage. "I take it you saw the interview?"

Jameson stepped into my room. "Not your best showing."

I waited for him to say something about that kiss. "Jameson, I didn't—"

He held a finger up to my lips. He never actually touched me, but my lips burned anyway.

"If *yes* is *no*," he said, his eyes on mine, "and *once* is *never*, then how many sides does a triangle have?"

That was a riddle he'd thrown out at me, the first day we'd met. At the time, I'd solved it by converting everything to a number. If you coded *yes*—or the presence of something—as a one, and *no*—or the absence of that thing—as a zero, then the first two parts of the riddle were redundant. *If one equals zero, how many sides does a triangle have?*

"Two," I said now, just as I had then, but this time I couldn't help wondering if Jameson was talking about a different kind of triangle—about him and Grayson and me.

"A girl named Elle finds a card on her doorstep. The front of the envelope says *To*, the back says *Elle*. Between them, inside the envelope, she finds two identical letters, then spends the rest of the day underground. Why?"

I wanted to tell him to stop playing games, but I couldn't. He'd thrown out a riddle. I had to solve it. "The front of the card says *To*, the back says *Elle*." I thought as I spoke. "She spends the whole day underground."

There was a gleam in Jameson's eyes, one that reminded me of the time *we* had spent underground. I could practically see him, torch-lit and pacing. And just like that, I saw the method in Jameson's particular brand of madness. "The two letters inside the envelope were *N*," I said softly.

There were probably a thousand adjectives to describe Jameson Hawthorne's smile, but the one that felt truest to me was *devastating*. Jameson Winchester Hawthorne had a devastating smile.

I kept going. "The front of the envelope said 'to'—spelled *t-u*," I continued, resisting the urge to step forward. "The back said 'Elle,' spelled—"

"*E-l*," Jameson finished my sentence. Then *he* took a step forward. "Two *n*'s make *tunnel*, which is why she spent the day underground. You win, Heiress."

We were standing too close now, and a warning siren went off in the back of my head, because if Jameson had seen Grayson kiss me on air, if he was here now, moving toward me—then what were the chances that this wasn't about me?

What were the chances that I was just another prize to be won? Territory to be marked.

"Why are you here?" I asked Jameson, even though I knew the answer, had just *thought* the answer.

"I'm here," he said with another devastating smile, "because I'd be willing to wager five dollars that you aren't checking the messages on your phone."

He was right. "I turned it off," I replied. "I'm thinking of chucking it out that window."

"I'll bet you another five dollars that you can't hit the statue in the courtyard."

"Make it ten," I told him, "and you have a deal."

"Sadly," he replied, "if you did throw your phone out the window, you wouldn't get the message from Libby and Nash."

I stared at him. "Libby and Nash—"

"They found something," Jameson told me. "And they're on their way home."

CHAPTER 66

I woke at dawn the next morning and found Oren standing directly outside my door. "Have you been out here all night?" I asked him.

He gave me a look. "What do you think?"

He'd warned me that if the news about Toby got out, it would be a security liability. I had no idea *how* the news had gotten out, but here we were.

"Right," I said.

"Consider yourself on a six-foot leash," Oren told me. "You're not leaving my side until this dies down. *If* it dies down."

I winced. "How bad is it?"

Oren's reply was matter-of-fact. "I have Carlos and Heinrich posted at the entrance to your wing. They've already had to turn away Zara, Constantine, and both Laughlins, in some cases forcibly. And that's not even touching what Skye tried at the gates, in full view of the paparazzi."

"How many paparazzi?" I asked tentatively.

"Double what we've seen before."

"How is that even possible?" I'd already been front-page news before last night's interview had aired.

"If there's one thing the world loves more than an accidental heiress," Oren replied, "it's a lost heir." He very deliberately did not say, *I told you so,* but I knew he was thinking it.

"I am sorry about this," I said.

"So am I."

"What do *you* have to be sorry for?" I asked flippantly.

Oren's answer wasn't flippant at all. "When I said that I would be within six feet of you at all times, I meant me, personally. I never should have delegated that responsibility, under any circumstance."

"You're human," I said. "You have to sleep." He didn't reply, and I crossed my arms over my chest. "Where's Eli?"

"Eli has been removed from the premises."

"Why?" I demanded, but my brain was already whirring. Oren had apologized to me. He blamed himself for allowing someone else in on my immediate protection detail, and that someone else had been barred from Hawthorne House.

Eli had been the one guarding me when I'd gone to talk to Mrs. Laughlin about Toby.

"He leaked the pictures." I answered my own question. Eli had been on my protection detail for over a week. He'd been in a position to overhear... a lot.

"Eli isn't as good at hiding his digital footprint as my man is at uncovering digital ghosts," Oren told me, his voice like steel. "He leaked the photos. In all likelihood, he's also the one who's responsible for the heart and the snake."

I stared at Oren. "Why?"

"I assigned him to your protection detail at school. He obviously wanted that extended to the estate. I trusted Eli. That trust was clearly misplaced. For whatever reason—possibly a payout from the press—he wanted to be closer to you. I didn't see it. I should have."

I'd never felt unsafe around Eli. He hadn't harmed me, and he could have, if that had been his goal. *For whatever reason,* I replayed Oren's words in my head. *Possibly a payout from the press.*

I thought of Max's ex-boyfriend, who'd tried to access her phone, so he could sell our texts. About my "father" and Skye selling their stories. About the payout that Alisa had arranged, back at the beginning, to have Libby's mother sign an NDA.

It was starting to sink in that for the rest of my life, the people I met, the people I became close to—there would always be a chance that they saw me as a payout.

"This is the second time that my error in judgment has cost you dearly," Oren said stiffly. "If you feel the need to hire new security, I'm sure Alisa could—"

"No!" I said. If Alisa hired someone, that person's loyalty would be to her. Whatever mistakes Oren had made, I believed that his allegiance was to me. He'd do whatever he could to protect me, because Tobias Hawthorne had asked him to.

"Yes?" Oren said curtly. It took me a second to realize that he wasn't talking to me. He was wearing an earpiece and talking to one of his men. *How many of them can we trust? How many of them would sell me out for the right payout?*

"Let them through," Oren ordered, and then he turned back to me. "Your sister and Nash have arrived at the gates."

CHAPTER 67

I waited for Libby and Nash in Tobias Hawthorne's study and requested that security allow Grayson, Jameson, and Xander to come back. I texted the boys to meet me, then waited, alone but for Oren, who stood no more than six feet away. I was jittery and on edge. *Why did it take Libby so long to text me back? What did they find in Cartago?*

"Avery, get behind me." Oren stepped forward, drawing his gun. I had no idea why until I followed his line of vision to the display case on the back wall, the one that housed shelves and shelves of Hawthorne trophies. The wall was moving, rotating toward us.

I moved behind Oren. He took a step forward and called out to the person behind the wall. "Identify yourself. I have a gun."

"So do I." Zara Hawthorne-Calligaris stepped into the room, looking like she was headed to some kind of country club brunch. She was wearing a sweater-set, slacks, and classic, neutral flats.

She was holding a gun.

"Put it down." Oren trained his gun on Zara.

Her own weapon held steady, Zara gave Oren her most unimpressed look. "I think we all know that I'm the least murderous

Hawthorne of my generation," she said, her voice high and clear, "so I will happily lower my weapon once you lower yours, John."

I forgot, most of the time, that Oren had a first name.

"Don't do this," Oren told her. "I don't want to shoot you, Zara, but make no mistake that I will. Put your gun down, and we can talk."

Zara didn't waffle. "You know me, John. Intimately." Her tone never changed, but there was no mistaking what she meant by that. "Do you really believe that I'm capable of harming a child?"

The "child" in question was clearly me, but that barely even registered. My heart was pounding so hard that I felt like it might bruise my rib cage, but I still managed to speak. "Intimately?" I asked Oren.

"Not since my father's death, I assure you," Zara told me. "John has always been quite clear on where his priorities lie. First with my father, and then with you."

Twenty years ago, when Tobias Hawthorne had left Zara his wedding ring, he'd been making a point about her infidelity. Now she was married to a different man, but the text in Tobias Hawthorne's will had remained the same.

She was having another affair. With Oren.

"You shouldn't be here, Zara," Oren said, his gun's aim never wavering.

"Shouldn't I?" she asked. After a moment longer, she lowered the gun, placing it on the desk. "Had your men allowed me entrance in a more traditional fashion, I would not have had to sneak in like a thief, and were I certain you would not have me escorted out, I would have no need of a firearm now. But here are. However, as a show of good will that *none* of you deserve, so long as no one attempts to remove me, my gun will stay right where it is, on that desk."

After a long moment, Oren lowered his own weapon and Zara

turned toward me. "Young lady, you will tell me what that nonsense on the news last night was. *Now.*" Toby was her brother. I could only begin to imagine what her reaction had been to what she had heard.

"Talk," Zara told me. "You owe me that much, at least."

All things considered, I probably did, but before I could say a word, a voice spoke up from the doorway. "Wouldn't you rather hear it from us, Aunt Z?"

All three of us turned to face Jameson. Grayson and Xander stood to his sides. Thus far, Zara had managed to keep her expression schooled into a mix of disdain and calm, but the moment she saw her nephews, that mask wavered.

It was the first time since I'd stepped through the doors of Hawthorne House that it occurred to me that she loved them.

"Please," Zara said quietly. "Boys. Just tell me about Toby."

And so they did, taking turns, working their way through the entire story with brutal efficiency. When Grayson told her that Toby was adopted, she drew in a sharp breath but said nothing. She didn't react again until Xander told her what Rebecca had told him.

"The Laughlins' daughter...," Zara trailed off. "She left for college when I was still in elementary school, and she never came back, not until Emily was born, years later."

I wondered if Zara was imagining, the way I had, how painful this must have been for Rebecca's mother. I wondered if she was questioning, the way I had, what could have led the Laughlins and her own parents to be so cruel.

"It's so easy," Zara murmured, "for all the wrong people to have children."

Silence hit the room like a semitruck.

Zara was the first to overcome it. "Go on," she told the boys. "Out with the rest of it. In this family, there's always a *rest of it.*"

There was only a little more. Zara already knew about the picture that her father had left for Skye at True North. That left only the fact that, along with that picture, he'd left a blank page of paper, and the fact that the numbers inside her parents' wedding rings had pointed us to Cartago, where Libby and Nash had found *something.*

"And what, pray tell, did you find?" Zara asked, and I realized that Libby and Nash had arrived.

Without even meaning to, I took a step toward them. This was it. Everything had been building to this. I felt like I was free-falling at a thousand miles an hour.

"We found my father," Nash said. "And this." He held up a small vial filled with purple powder.

"Your father?" I repeated. *"Jake Nash?"* I thought about the picture of Zara, Skye, and the messy-haired guy.

Nash nodded to Zara. "He asked about you."

Raw vulnerability flashed across Zara's features.

"I reckon you loved him," Nash said quietly.

Zara shook her head. "You don't understand."

"You loved him," Nash repeated. "Skye went after him, and I was the result." I saw a muscle in Nash's throat tighten. "Even then," he said quietly, "you didn't hate me."

Zara shook her head. "How could I? It was easy enough to stay away when you were a baby. I got married. I was starting a life of my own. But then you were a little boy. A wonderful little boy, and the newness of it all had worn off for Skye, and you were so lonely because she was never there."

"But you were," Nash replied. "For a time. Memory's a bit hazy, but before Toby died, you used to take care of me."

"I found Jake," Zara said quietly. "For you."

Slowly, the gears in my brain started turning. At the time that Tobias Hawthorne had first rewritten his will—right after Toby had "died"—Zara had been having an affair. Tobias Hawthorne had been aware of it.

"You and Nash's father?" I said.

"I brought Jake pictures of his son," Zara replied crisply. "I was working on convincing him to go against my father, to be a part of Nash's life, but then he disappeared for parts unknown. Cartago, apparently, at what I can only assume was my father's behest."

"He's been the caretaker at the Cartago property ever since," Nash confirmed. "The old man gave him strict instructions that if you ever came to call, he was to give you this." Nash nodded again to the vial in his hands. "Took a bit for Libby and me to persuade him to give it to us."

I looked at the powder in the vial. This was what we needed to decode Skye's message. *This is it.* Twenty years ago, Tobias Hawthorne had woven a puzzle to set his daughters on the trail of the truth. That trail had led to a picture from before their relationship had splintered—and to Jake Nash, over whom they'd apparently fought.

"I have the note from True North," Xander said. "I think we all know what we're supposed to do with that powder."

"You Hawthornes and your invisible ink," I said, shaking my head. "Will we need anything except the powder?"

"A makeup brush," Zara answered immediately. Then the boys chimed in, all four of them in unison: "And a heat source."

CHAPTER 68

The blank page was unfolded and laid out. The powder was poured onto the page; the brush dusted it over the surface of the letter. And it *was* a letter. That much became clear the moment the heat source—a nearby lamp bulb—was applied.

Words appeared on the page in tiny, even scrawl—Tobias Hawthorne's. All I saw before Zara snatched the letter up was the salutation: *Dearest Zara, Dearest Skye.* Zara stalked to the corner of the room. As she read, her chest rose and fell with heavy breaths. At some point, tears overflowed and began carving paths down her face. Finally, she let the letter go. It dropped from her hand, floating gently toward the ground.

The boys were all frozen in place, like they'd never seen their aunt shed a single tear before now. Slowly, I walked forward. Zara didn't tell me to stop, so I stooped to pick up the letter, and I read.

Dearest Zara, Dearest Skye,

If you are reading this, then I am dead. I cannot express how sorry I am to leave you in this way—or how necessary I believe what I have done for you truly is. Yes, <u>*for*</u> *you, not to you.*

If you are reading this, my daughters, then you have set aside your differences long enough to follow the trail I left you. If this has happened, then everything I have done has served at least one purpose. And perhaps, my dears, you are now ready for the other.

As you might have gathered, depending on how closely you examined the charities to which I left my fortune, your brother did not perish on Hawthorne Island. Of that I am certain. He was, as far as I have been able to piece together, pulled from the ocean, severely burned, by a local fisherman. It has taken me years to piece together even this much. I have written and rewritten this letter to you countless times as my investigation into your brother's disappearance has evolved.

I have never found him. I came close once but found something else instead. I can only conclude that Toby does not want to be found. Whatever happened on the island, he has been running from it for half his life.

Or perhaps, he has been running from me.

I have made mistakes with all of you. Zara, I asked too much of you at times and gave you too little of my approval at others; Skye, of you I never asked enough. I treated both of you differently because you were female.

I hurt Toby worst of all.

I won't make the same mistakes with the next generation. I will push them, all in equal measure. They'll learn to put each other first. I will do for them everything I should have done for you, including this: Not one of you will see my fortune. There are things I have done that I am not proud of, legacies that you should not have to bear.

Know that I love you, both of you. Find your brother. Perhaps, once I am gone, he will finally stop running. Below, you will find a list of locations to which I have traced his whereabouts these past twelve years. In a safe-deposit box at Montgomery National Bank, number 21666, you will find a police report about the incident on Hawthorne Island, as well as extensive files put together by my investigators over the years.

You'll find the key to the safe-deposit box in my toolbox. There is a false bottom. Be brave, my dears. Be strong. Be true.

Yours sincerely,
Father

I looked up from the letter, and the boys came to me—Grayson, Jameson, and Xander. Nash, Libby, and Oren stayed where they stood. Zara sank to her knees behind me.

As the boys read the letter, I processed its contents. We had confirmation now that Tobias Hawthorne had known that his son was alive, that he had been searching for him, and that, just as Sheffield Grayson had claimed, the old man had buried a police report about what had happened on the island. There might be more details in the safe-deposit box, once we found the key.

"The toolbox," I said suddenly. I turned toward Oren. "Tobias Hawthorne left you his toolbox."

That had been a part of the updated will. Had the old man realized that Oren was sleeping with Zara? Was that why he'd made him a part of this? Tobias Hawthorne had written the phrase *these past twelve years* in the letter, suggesting that it hadn't been updated recently. *Eight years. He wrote this eight years ago.*

When Tobias Hawthorne had updated his will the year before, leaving me everything, he'd laid a new trail to follow. A new game. A new attempt at mending family bonds that had been torn asunder.

But he'd included the same words to Zara and Skye—the same clues.

Had he continued to add information to the safe-deposit box over the last eight years?

"What do you think he meant," Grayson said slowly, "about legacies we shouldn't have to bear?"

"I care less about that," Jameson replied, "than about the list at the bottom. What do you make of it, Heiress?"

Coming to stand between Jameson and Grayson should have been awkward. It should have been unbearable—but in this moment, it wasn't.

Slowly, I looked back down at the letter, at the list. There were dozens of locations listed, scattered all over the world, like Toby had never stayed in one place for long. But one by one, certain locations jumped out at me. *Waialua, Oahu. Waitomo, New Zealand. Cuzco, Peru. Tokyo, Japan. Bali, Indonesia.*

I literally stopped breathing.

"Heiress?" Jameson said.

Grayson stepped toward me. "Avery?"

Oahu was one of the islands of Hawaii. Cuzco, Peru, was the nearest city to Machu Picchu. My eyes roved back over the list. *Hawaii. New Zealand. Machu Picchu. Tokyo. Bali.* I stared at the page.

"Hawaii," I said out loud, my voice shaking. "New Zealand. Machu Picchu. Tokyo. Bali."

"For a guy on the run," Xander commented, "he sure made his way around."

I shook my head. Xander didn't see what I was seeing. He couldn't. "Hawaii, New Zealand, Machu Picchu, Tokyo, Bali—I know this list."

There were more. At least five or six that I recognized. Five or six places that I had imagined going. Places that I had held in my hand.

"My mother's postcards," I whispered, and took off running. Oren bolted after me, and the others weren't far behind.

I made it to my room in a matter of seconds, to my closet in less than that, and soon I was holding the postcards in my hand. There was nothing written on the back, no postage. I'd never questioned where my mother had gotten them.

Or from whom.

I looked up at Jameson and Grayson, Xander and Nash.

"You Hawthornes," I whispered hoarsely, "and your invisible ink."

CHAPTER 69

A black light revealed writing on the postcards, the same way it had on Toby's walls. *The same handwriting.* Toby had written these words. The answers we were looking for—there was a chance that they were all *here*, but it took everything in me just to read the salutation, the same on every postcard.

"*Dear Hannah*," I read, "*the same backward as forward*."

Hannah. I thought about the tabloid's accusations that my mom was living under a fake identity. I'd spent my whole life thinking she was Sarah.

The words on the postcards blurred in front of me. *Tears. In my eyes.* My thoughts were detached, like this was all happening to someone else. The room around me was still filled with the buzzing electricity of the moment, of what I'd just discovered, but all I could think was that my mom's name was *Hannah*.

I have a secret.... How many times had we played? How many chances had she had to tell me?

"Well," Xander piped up, "what do they say?"

Everyone else was standing. I was on the floor. Everyone was waiting. *I can't do this.* I couldn't look at Xander—or Jameson or Grayson.

"I'd like to be alone," I said, my voice rough against my throat. I realized now how Zara must have felt reading her father's letter. *"Please."*

There was a beat of silence and then: "Everyone out." The realization that it was Jameson who had spoken those words, Jameson who was willingly stepping back from the puzzle—for me—rocked me to my core.

What was his angle here?

Within moments, the Hawthornes were gone. Oren was a respectful six feet away. And Libby knelt beside me.

I stole a glance at her, and she squeezed my hand. "Did I ever tell you about my ninth birthday?" Libby asked.

Through a fog, I managed to shake my head.

"You were about two then. My mom hated Sarah, but sometimes she'd let her babysit. Mom always said it didn't count as charity if *that bitch* did it, because if it weren't for Sarah and for you, maybe Ricky would have come back to us. She said your mom owed her, and your mom acted like she did so she could spend time with me. So I could spend time with you."

I didn't remember anything like that. Libby and I had barely seen each other growing up—but at two, I wouldn't have remembered much.

"My mom dumped me at your place for almost a week. And it was the best week of my life, Ave. Your mom baked me cupcakes on my birthday, and she had all these cheap Mardi Gras beads, and we must have been wearing about ten apiece. She got these clip-on hair streaks in a rainbow of neon colors, and we wore them in our hair. She taught you to sing 'Happy Birthday.' My mom didn't even call, but Sarah tucked me in every night, into *her* bed, and she slept on the couch, and you would crawl into bed with me, and your mom would kiss us both. Every night."

The tears in my eyes were falling now.

"And when my mom came back and she saw how happy I was—she never let me come over to your place again." Libby's breath went ragged, but she managed to smile. "My point is that you know who your mom was, Avery. We both do. And she was *wonderful*."

I closed my eyes. I willed myself to stop crying, because Libby was right. My mom was *wonderful*. And if she'd lied to me or kept too many secrets—maybe she'd had to.

Taking a deep breath, I turned back to the postcards. There were no dates, so it was impossible to tell the order in which they'd been written; no postmarks, so they hadn't ever been mailed. I spread the postcards out on the floor and started with the one on the far left, aiming the black light at it. Slowly, I read it.

I drank up every word.

There were things in that first postcard that I didn't understand—references whose meaning was lost with my mom. But near the end, there was something that caught my eye. *I hope you read the letter I left you that night. I hope that some part of you understood. I hope you go far, far away and never look back, but if you ever need anything, I hope you do exactly what I told you to do in that letter. Go to Jackson. You know what I left there. You know what it's worth.*

"Jackson," I said, my voice coming out wispy. What had Toby left for my mother in Jackson? *Mississippi?* Had that even been on Tobias Hawthorne's list?

Setting the first postcard aside, I kept reading and realized that Toby had never meant to send these messages. He was writing to her, but for himself. The postcards made it clear that he was staying away from her on purpose. The only other thing that was clear was that they were in love. Epic, incomplete-without-the-other, once-in-a-lifetime love.

The kind of love that I'd never believed in.

The next postcard read:

Dear Hannah, the same backward as forward,

Do you remember that time on the beach? When I didn't know if I would ever walk again, and you cursed at me until I did? It sounded like you'd never cursed before in your life, but oh, how you meant it. And when I took that step and swore right back at you, do you remember what you said?

"That's one step," you spat. "What now?"

You were backlit, and the sun was sinking into the horizon, and for the first time in weeks, it felt like my heart had finally remembered how to beat.

What now?

It was hard to read Toby's words without feeling a wealth of emotion. My whole life, my mom had never been involved with anyone but Ricky. I'd never seen anyone adore her the way she deserved to be adored. It took me longer to focus on the implications of the words. Toby had been injured—badly enough that he wasn't sure if he would walk again, and my mother had *cursed* at him?

I thought about what the old man had said in his letter to Zara and Skye, about a fisherman pulling Toby from the water. How badly had he been injured? And where had my mother come in?

My mind spinning, I read on. Another postcard and then another, and I realized that, yes, my mom had been there, in Rockaway Watch, in the wake of the fire.

Dear Hannah, the same backward as forward,

Last night, I dreamed of drowning, and I woke up with your name on my lips. You were so quiet in those early days. Do you remember that? When you couldn't stand to look at me.

Wouldn't speak to me. You hated me. I felt it, and I was awful to you. I didn't know who I was or what I'd done. I remembered nothing of my life or the island. But still, I was horrid. Withdrawal was a beast, but I was worse. And you were there, and I know now that I didn't deserve a damn thing from you. But you changed my bandages. You held me down. You touched me, more gently than I could ever deserve.

Knowing what I know now, I don't know how you did it. I should have drowned. I should have burned. My lips should never have touched yours, but for the rest of my life, Hannah, O Hannah—I will feel every kiss. Feel your touch when I was halfway dead and wholly rotten and you loved me despite myself.

"He lost his memory." I looked up at Libby. "Toby. Jameson and I thought that he might have had amnesia—there was a hint to that in Tobias Hawthorne's old will. But this letter confirms it. When he met my mom, he was hurt and in withdrawal—probably from some kind of drug—and he didn't know who he was."

Or what he'd done. I thought about the fire. About Hawthorne Island and the three people who hadn't survived it. Had my mom been from Rockaway Watch? Or another nearby town?

More postcards, more messages. One after the other, without answers.

Dear Hannah, the same backward as forward,

Ever since the island, I'm terrified of water, but I keep forcing myself onto ships. I know that you would tell me that I don't need to, but I do. Fear is good for me. I remember all too well what it was like when I had none.

If I had met you then, would your touch have broken through to me? Would you have hated me until you loved me?

If we'd met in a different time, under different circumstances, would I still dream of you every night—and wonder if you dream of me?

I should let you go. When everything came crashing back, when I realized what you'd been hiding from me, I promised that I would. Promised myself. Promised you.

Promised Kaylie.

The name stopped me dead in my tracks. *Kaylie Rooney.* The local who'd died on Hawthorne Island. The girl on whom Tobias Hawthorne had pinned much of the blame in the press. I scoured the rest of the postcards, all of them, looking for something that would tell me what exactly to make of Toby's words, and finally—*finally*—I found it, near the end of a message that started off with a much dreamier tone.

I know that I will never see you again, Hannah. That I don't deserve to. I know that you will never read a word I write, and because you will never read this, I know that I can say what you forbade me to say long ago.

I'm sorry.

I'm sorry, Hannah, O Hannah. I'm sorry for leaving in the dead of night. I'm sorry for letting you love me even a fraction as much as I will, to the day I die, love you. I'm sorry for what I did. For the fire.

And I will never stop being sorry about your sister.

CHAPTER 70

Sister. That word echoed in my mind over and over again. *Sister. Sister. Sister.* "Toby told my mom—told *Hannah*—that he was sorry about her sister." Thoughts crashed into one another in my brain, like a ten-car pileup, the cacophony deafening. "And in another postcard, he mentioned Kaylie. Kaylie Rooney—she's the girl who died in the fire on Hawthorne Island. Sometime after that, my mom helped nurse Toby back to life. He didn't remember what had happened, but he said that she hated him. She must have known."

"Known what?" Libby asked, reminding me that I wasn't just talking to myself.

I thought about the fire, the buried police report, Sheffield Grayson saying that Toby had purchased accelerant. "That Toby was responsible for her sister's death."

The next thing I knew, I had my laptop out, and I was doing yet another internet search on Kaylie Rooney. At first I didn't find anything I hadn't already seen, but then I started adding search terms. I tried *sister* and got nothing. I tried *family*, and I found the one and only interview with a member of the Rooney family. It wasn't much of an interview. All the reporter had gotten out of Kaylie's mother was, and I quote, *My Kaylie was a good girl, and those rich bastards killed her.* But there was also a picture. A photograph of… *my grandmother*? I tried to wrap my mind around that possibility. Then I heard the door open behind me.

Max poked her head into the room. "I come in peace." She squeezed by the door and strolled past Oren. "For the record, I'm armed only with sarcasm." Max ended her stroll right next to me and hopped up on the desk. "What are we doing?"

"Looking at a picture of my grandmother." Saying the words made them feel just a little bit more real. "My mom's mom. Maybe."

Max stared at the picture. "Not maybe," she said. "She even *looks* like your mom."

The woman in the picture was scowling. I'd never seen my mom scowl. She had her hair pulled into a tight bun, and my mom always wore hers loose. Twenty years ago, this woman had looked decades older than my mom had when she died.

But still, Max was right. Their features were the same.

"How has no one made this connection?" Max asked incredulously. "With all the rumors about your mom, and people trying to find a connection between you and the Hawthornes, no one thought to look at the family of a girl they pretty much murdered? And what about your mom's relatives and the people who knew her growing up? Someone must have recognized her, once you made the news. Why hasn't anyone tipped off the press?"

I thought about Eli, selling me out for a payday. What kind of town was Rockaway Watch that no one would have done the same?

"I don't know," I told Max. "But I do know that whatever Tobias Hawthorne left in that safe-deposit box—that police report, his investigators' files—I want to see it all. I *need* to see it. Now."

CHAPTER 71

Oren retrieved the key from his toolbox, but he didn't give it to me. He gave it to Zara, then told me to get ready for school.

"Have you lost your mind?" I asked him. "I'm not going to school."

"It's the safest place for you right now," Oren said. "Alisa will agree with me."

"Alisa's doing damage control from the interview," I retorted. "I'm sure the last thing she wants is me out in public. No one would question why I might want to stay home."

"Country Day isn't public," Oren told me, and a few seconds later, he had Alisa on speakerphone, and she was echoing what he had said: I was to put on my private school uniform, put on my best face, and pretend that nothing had happened.

If we treated this like a crisis, it would be seen as a crisis.

Since I'd promised to keep Alisa in the loop, I told her everything, and she still didn't change her mind. "Act normal," she told me.

I hadn't been *normal* in weeks. But less than an hour later, I was dressed in a pleated skirt, a white dress shirt, and a burgundy blazer, with my hair tousled just so and my makeup minimal, except for the eyes. Preppy with an edge, for all the world to see—or at least all the denizens of Heights Country Day School.

I felt like I had on my very first day. No one looked directly at me, but the way they were not-looking at me felt far more conspicuous. Jameson and Xander slipped out of the car after me, and each of them took one of my sides. At least this time, it was me *and* the Hawthornes against the world.

⁂

I made it through the day bit by bit, and by lunch, I was done. Done with the stares. Done pretending everything was normal. Done trying to put on a happy face. I was hiding—or making an attempt at it—in the archive when Jameson found me. "You look like someone who needs a distraction," he told me.

A few feet away, Oren crossed his arms over his chest. "No."

Jameson shot my bodyguard his most innocent look.

"I know you," Oren replied. "I know your *distractions*. You're not taking her skydiving. Or parasailing off the coast. No racetracks. No motorcycles. No ax throwing—"

"Ax throwing?" I looked at Jameson, intrigued.

He turned back to Oren. "What are your feelings on roofs?"

⁂

Ten minutes later, Jameson and I were back on top of the Art Center. He rolled out the turf and teed up a ball.

"Keep away from the edge," Oren told me, and then he turned deliberately away from us both.

I waited for Jameson to ask me about the postcards. I waited for him to flirt with me, to touch me, to Jameson Hawthorne the answer out of me. But all he did was hand me a club.

I lined up the shot. Part of me wanted him to come stand behind me, wanted his arms to wrap around mine. *Jameson on the roof. Grayson in the maze.* My mind was a mess. I was a mess.

I dropped the club.

"My mother was Kaylie Rooney's sister," I said. And so it began. It was hard to put into words everything I'd learned, but I managed. The more I said, the easier it was to see Jameson thinking.

The more he thought, the closer to me he came.

"What do you think Toby left in Jackson that's worth so much?" he asked. "And where in Jackson?" Jameson studied me like my face held the answers. "How long did Toby's amnesia last? Why stay 'dead' once his memory returned?"

"Guilt." I almost choked on the word, though I couldn't have explained why. "Toby loathed himself almost as much as he loved my mom."

That was the first time I'd said that last bit out loud. *Toby Hawthorne loved my mother. She loved him.* It had been an epic, seaside kind of love. Literally. Just knowing that made me feel like I'd been lying to myself every time I'd pretended that I didn't have feelings, that things didn't have to be messy.

That I could have what I wanted without ever really longing for anything, body and soul.

"Heiress?" There was a question in Jameson's deep green eyes. I wasn't sure what he was asking, what he wanted from me.

What I wanted from him.

"Knock, knock!" Xander stuck his head out the door to the roof. "I just happened to have my ear pressed to this door. I might have overheard some things, and I have a suggestion!"

Jameson looked like he might actually throttle his brother. I glanced at Oren, who was still pointedly ignoring all three of us. I could practically hear him thinking, *Not my job.*

"Call her!" Xander tossed something at me. It wasn't until I'd caught it that I realized it was his phone—and a number had already been plugged in.

"Call who?" Jameson asked, his eyes narrowing.

"Your grandmother," Xander told me. "Like I said, I inadvertently overheard some things while my ear was casually pressed to this steel door. Kaylie Rooney's mother is your grandmother, Avery. That's a piece of the puzzle we've never had before, and *that*"—he nodded to the phone—"is her phone number."

"You don't have to call," Jameson told me, which made about as much sense as the fact that he'd willingly stepped back from the postcards.

"Yes." I swallowed. "I do." My heart jumped into my throat just thinking about it, but I hit the Call button. The line rang and rang and rang, with no one picking up and no voicemail. I couldn't bring myself to hang up, so I just let it ring, and then finally someone answered. All I got out was a hello and my name before the person who'd answered cut me off.

"I know who you are." At first I thought the gravelly voice belonged to a man, but as the words kept coming, I realized that the speaker was a woman. "If my worthless daughter had taught you the first damn thing about this family, you wouldn't dare have dialed my number."

I wasn't sure what I'd been expecting. My mom had always told me that she didn't have a family. But still, each word her mother—my *grandmother*—spoke cut into me.

"If that little bitch hadn't run, I would have put a bullet in her myself. You think I want a dime of your blood money, girl? You think you're family? You hang up that phone. You forget my name. And if you're *lucky*, I'll make sure this family—this whole town—forgets yours."

The sound on the other end of the line cut out. I stood there, the phone still pressed to my ear, frozen.

"You okay there, buddy?" Xander asked.

I couldn't reply. I couldn't say anything. *You think I want a dime of your blood money, girl? You think you're family?*

I wasn't even sure if I was breathing.

If that little bitch hadn't run—

Jameson came up beside me. He put his hands on my shoulders. For a second, I thought he might force my eyes to his, but he didn't. He walked me over to the edge of the roof. The very edge, close enough that Oren called out, but in response, all Jameson did was spread my arms to each side, until his and mine were both held out in a *T*. "Close your eyes," he whispered. "Breathe."

If that little bitch hadn't run—

I closed my eyes. I breathed. I felt him breathing. The wind picked up. And I told them everything.

CHAPTER 72

By the time the SUV passed the gates of Hawthorne House that afternoon, I was still shaken. To my surprise, Zara met Jameson, Xander, and me in the foyer. For the first time since I'd met Tobias Hawthorne's firstborn, she looked less than perfect. Her eyes were puffy. Stray hairs were stuck to her forehead. She was holding a folder. It was only an inch or so thick, but even that was enough to stop me in my tracks.

"That's what was in the safe-deposit box?" Xander asked.

"Do you want an overview?" Zara replied crisply. "Or would you prefer to read it for yourself?"

"Both," Jameson said. First, we'd take the big picture, and then we'd comb through the actual materials, looking for subtle hints, clues, anything Zara might have missed.

Where's Grayson? The question came into my mind unbidden. Some part of me had expected him to be here, waiting. Even though he'd barely spoken to me since the interview. Even though he'd barely been able to look at me.

"Overview?" I asked Zara, forcing myself to focus.

Zara gave a slight dip of her chin—assent. "Toby had been in and out of rehab for a year or two at the time of his disappearance. He was obviously angry, though at the time I didn't know why. From what my father was able to piece together, Toby met two other boys at rehab. They all went on a road trip together that summer. It very much appears that the boys partied—and slept—their way across the country. One young woman in particular, a waitress at a bar where the boys stopped, was quite informative when my father's investigator tracked her down. She told the investigator exactly what Toby had been snorting, and exactly what he had said the morning after they had intercourse."

"What did he say?" Xander asked.

Zara's tone never wavered. "He told her that he was going to burn it all down."

I stared at Zara for a moment, then shifted my gaze to Jameson. He'd been there when Sheffield Grayson had claimed that Toby was responsible for the fire. Even after reading the postcards and seeing the kind of guilt Toby carried, some part of me had still thought the fire was an accident, that Toby and his friends were drunk or high, and things got out of control.

"Did Toby happen to specify *what* he was going to burn down?" Jameson asked.

"No." Zara kept her reply curt. "But right before they got to Rockaway Watch, he purchased a great deal of accelerant."

He set the fire. He killed them all. "Was that in the police report?" I managed to ask. "What Toby said about burning it all down—did the police know?"

"No," Zara replied. "The woman Toby said that to—she had no idea who he was. Even when our private investigators tracked her down, she remained entirely in the dark. The police never found her. They never had motive. But they knew about the accelerant.

From what the arson investigators were able to tell, the house on Hawthorne Island had been thoroughly soaked. The gas had been turned on."

I felt my hand pressing to my mouth. A sound escaped around my fingers, somewhere between a horrified gasp and a mewl.

"Toby wasn't an idiot." Jameson's expression was sharp. "Unless this was some kind of suicide pact, he would have had a contingency plan to make sure that he and his friends weren't caught in the flames."

Zara closed her eyes tightly. "That's the thing," she whispered. "The house was soaked in accelerant. The gas was turned on—but no one ever lit a match. There was a lightning storm that night. Toby might well have been planning to burn down the house from a safe distance. The others might have helped him. But none of them actually set the fire."

"Lightning," Xander said, horrified. "If the gas was already on, if they'd soaked the floorboards in accelerant..."

I could see it in my mind. Had the house exploded? Had they still been inside, or had the fire spread quickly across the island?

"For months, my father believed that Toby truly had died. He convinced the police to bury the report. It wasn't arson, not technically. At best, it was *attempted* arson."

And they'd never gotten to finish the attempt.

"Why didn't the police just blame it on the lightning?" I asked. I'd read the articles in the press. They hadn't mentioned the weather. The picture they'd painted was one in which a teenage party had gotten out of hand. Three upstanding boys had died—and one not-so-upstanding girl from the wrong side of the tracks.

"The house went up like a fireball," Zara replied evenly. "They could see it from the mainland. It was obvious it wasn't just a lightning strike. And the girl who was there with them, Kaylie Rooney, she'd just gotten out of juvenile detention for *arson*. It was easier to deflect blame toward her than to try to pin it on nature."

"If she was a juvenile," Xander said slowly, "the record would have been sealed."

"The old man unsealed it." Jameson didn't phrase that as a question. "Anything to protect the family name."

I could understand why my mother's mother had called Tobias Hawthorne's fortune blood money. Had he left it to me in part out of guilt?

"I wouldn't feel too sorry for Kaylie Rooney," Zara said coldly. "What happened to her—what happened to all of them—it was a tragedy, of course, but she was far from innocent. From what the investigator was able to piece together, the Rooney family runs just about every drug that comes through Rockaway Watch. They have a reputation for being merciless, and Kaylie was almost certainly already elbow-deep in the family business."

If my worthless daughter had taught you the first damn thing about this family, you wouldn't dare have dialed my number. The conversation I'd had that afternoon came back to me.

If that little bitch hadn't run, I would have put a bullet in her myself.

If what Zara was saying about my mother's family was true, that statement probably wasn't metaphorical.

"What about the fisherman who pulled Toby from the water?" I asked, trying to concentrate on the facts of the case and not think too long or hard about where my mom had come from. "Did the file elaborate on that at all?"

"The storm was severe that night," Zara replied. "Initially, my father believed there were no boats out, but eventually the investigator talked to someone who swore that there was one boat on the water during the storm. Its owner was practically a shut-in. He lives in a shack near an old abandoned lighthouse in Rockaway Watch. The locals steer clear of him. Based on the investigator's discussions with townsfolk, most seem to think he's not quite well in the head. Hence, taking his boat out that night, in the midst of a man-killing storm."

"He finds Toby," I said, thinking out loud. "Pulls him from the water. Brings him home. And no one's the wiser."

"My father believed that Toby had lost his memory, though whether this was the result of an injury or psychological trauma is unclear. Somehow this man, this Jackson Currie, managed to nurse him back to health."

Not just the man, I thought. *My mom was there, too.* She'd helped nurse him back to life.

I was so busy thinking about my mom and reassembling that part of the story in my head that I missed the rest of what Zara had said. The *name* she'd said.

"Jackson," Jameson breathed. "Heiress, the fisherman's name was *Jackson*."

I froze, just for an instant. *I hope you go far, far away*, Toby had written, *but if you ever need anything, I hope you do exactly what I told you to do in that letter. Go to Jackson. You know what I left there. You know what it's worth.*

Not Jackson, Mississippi.

Jackson Currie. The fisherman who'd pulled Toby from the water.

"What I don't understand," Zara said, "is why Toby was so intent on running once he got his memory back—assuming he got it back. He had to have known that our security could protect him from any threat. The Rooneys may run Rockaway Watch, but it's a small town. They're small people with a small reach, and the legal situation had already been taken care of. Toby could have come home, but he fought it."

He didn't come home, because he didn't think he deserved to. Having read the postcards, I understood Toby. Wasn't that how I would have felt if I'd done what he'd done?

A ringing sound jarred me from that thought. My phone. I looked down. Grayson was calling.

I flashed back to the moment he'd kissed me. I'd kissed him back. Since then we hadn't even managed to look at each other. We hadn't really talked. So why was he calling now?

Where is he? "Hello?" I answered.

"Avery." Grayson lingered on my name, just for a moment.

"Where are you?" I asked. There was a pause at the other end of the line, and then he sent me an invite to switch over to a video chat. I accepted it, and the next thing I saw was his face. Gray eyes, sharp cheekbones, sharper jawline. In the sunlight, his light blond hair looked platinum.

"After some convincing, Max told me about what was written on your postcards," Grayson said. "About your mother. Do you remember when I told you that I was in this? That I would help you?" He turned his phone, and I saw ruins. Charred ruins. Burned trees. "That's what I'm doing."

"You went to Hawthorne Island without us?" Xander was absolutely indignant.

He did this for me. I wasn't sure how I was supposed to feel about that when, if he'd waited a few hours, we could have gone together. This didn't feel like a larger-than-life gesture. It felt like Grayson running away.

Keeping his promise as far away from me as he could.

"Hawthorne Island," Grayson confirmed in response to Xander's accusation. "And Rockaway Watch. I wouldn't call the locals friendly, but I'm optimistic that I'll find our missing piece, whatever that might be."

He was optimistic that *he* would find the answer. Had he even considered dealing me in?

"Rockaway Watch," Xander said slowly.

The town's name echoed in my mind. *Rockaway Watch. My mother's family.* Suddenly, I had much bigger concerns than what Grayson's behavior did or did not mean—and what it did or did not make me feel.

"Grayson." My voice sounded urgent, even to my own ears. "You don't understand. My mother changed her name and left that place because her family is dangerous. I don't know what they know about Toby. I don't know if that's the reason they hated her so much—but they blame the Hawthornes for their daughter's death. You have to get out of there."

Beside me, Oren cursed. Grayson turned the phone back around and those gray eyes locked on mine. "Avery, have I ever given you reason to believe that I'm particularly averse to danger?"

Grayson Hawthorne was arrogant enough to consider himself bulletproof—and honorable enough to see a promise through to its end.

"You have to get out of there," I said again, but the next thing I knew, Jameson was sticking his head over my shoulder, yelling to his brother.

"You're looking for a man named Jackson Currie. He's a recluse, living near an abandoned lighthouse. Talk to him. See what he knows."

Grayson smiled, and that smile cut into me, every bit as much as his kiss. "Got it."

CHAPTER 73

It was another hour before we heard from Grayson again, and Oren spent a good chunk of that time calling in favors on the West Coast. I wasn't the only one concerned about the safety of a Hawthorne anywhere near the town of Rockaway Watch.

When my phone did ring again, Grayson was less than happy about the security detail that had descended on him.

"Did you find him?" Jameson squeezed in beside me to talk to his brother. "Jackson Currie?"

"He has a very colorful vocabulary," Grayson reported. "And the land near his shack is booby-trapped."

"Father and his investigator ran into similar issues," Zara said behind us. "They never got a word out of the man. Grayson, you should come home. This is a fool's errand. There are other leads that we could follow."

In any other circumstances, I would have asked what those leads were, but all I could think was that Toby had told my mom to go to Jackson if she needed anything. That seemed to suggest that if my mom had shown up, he would have opened the door.

"Can you get close enough to put me on the phone with him?" I asked.

"Assuming no one tries to restrain me..." Grayson glanced pointedly back over his shoulder at what I could only assume was his security detail and then turned back to look straight into the camera—straight at me. "I can try."

Jackson Currie's shack really *was* a shack. I would have laid money that he'd built it himself. It wasn't large. There were no windows.

Grayson knocked on what appeared to be a metal door. *Then again, maybe* shack *is the wrong word,* I thought. What Jackson Currie had built was closer to a bunker.

Grayson knocked again, and all he got for his effort was a large rock chucked at him from somewhere up above.

"I don't like this," Oren said stonily.

Neither did I, but we were so close—not just to Toby but to answers. *I have a secret....*

I knew so much now that I hadn't before. Maybe I knew everything, but I couldn't help feeling like this was my chance—maybe my last chance—to know for sure, to know my mom in a way that I'd never known her before.

To understand what she and Toby had.

"See if he'll talk to me," I told Grayson. "Tell him..." My voice caught. "Tell him that Hannah's daughter is on the phone. Hannah Rooney." That was the first time I had said the name my mom had been born with. The name she'd never told me.

The image on the phone screen went blurry for a moment. Grayson must have lowered the phone. I heard him in the background, yelling something.

Talk to me, I willed Jackson Currie from a distance. *Tell me anything and everything you know. About Toby. About my mom. About whatever it is that Toby left with you.*

"I told him." Grayson's face came back into focus. "No reply. I think we—"

I never got to hear the rest of what Grayson thought, because a moment later, I heard the distinct sound of metal on metal. *Dead bolts,* I realized, *being thrown open.*

Grayson turned the camera in time for me to see the metal door creak open. All I saw at first was Jackson Currie's enormous beard—but then I saw his narrowed eyes.

"Where is she?" he grunted.

"Here," I said, my voice verging on a yell. "I'm here. I'm Hannah's daughter."

"No." He spat. "Don't trust phones." And just like that, he slammed the door.

"What does he mean, he doesn't trust phones?" Jameson demanded. "What's not to trust?"

My thoughts were elsewhere. We knew now that Jackson Currie would talk to me. He wouldn't talk to Grayson. He hadn't talked to Tobias Hawthorne's investigators. He was paranoid and pretty much a shut-in. He didn't trust phones.

But he would talk to me—in person.

"I'll call you back," I told Grayson, and then I placed another phone call—to Alisa. "I'm allowed to spend three nights per month away from Hawthorne House. So far, I've only spent one."

CHAPTER 74

Alisa didn't like the idea of my visiting Hawthorne Island. Oren liked it even less. But there was no stopping me now.

"Fine." Oren gave me a look. "I will arrange security for you." His eyes narrowed. "And *only* you."

Beside me, Xander jumped to his feet. "I object!"

"Overruled." Oren's reply was immediate. "We will be flying into a high-threat situation. I want at least an eight-person security team on the ground. We can't afford a single distraction. Avery is the package—the only package—or I will duct-tape all three of you to chairs and call it a day."

All three of us. My eyes found their way to Jameson's. I waited for him to argue with Oren. Jameson Winchester Hawthorne had never sat out a race in his life. He wasn't capable of it. So why wasn't he attempting to negotiate with Oren now?

Jameson noticed something about the way I was looking at him. "What?"

"You're not going to complain about this?" I stared at him.

"Why would I, Heiress?"

Because you play to win. Because Grayson's already there. Because this was our game—yours and mine—before it was anyone else's. I tried to stop myself there. *Because your brother kissed me. Because when you and I kiss, you feel it, the same way I do.*

I wasn't about to say a single word of that out loud. "Fine." I kept my eyes on Jameson's a moment longer, then turned to Oren. "I'll go alone."

It took a little under four hours to fly from Texas to the Oregon coast. Including travel time to and from the airport on each side, that was closer to five. I was standing on Jackson Currie's doorstep—such as it was—by dusk.

"Are you ready?" Grayson asked beside me, his voice low.

I nodded.

"Your men will have to stay back," Grayson told Oren. "They can set up a perimeter, but I'd bet a very large amount of money that Currie will not open the door if Avery shows up with her own army."

Oren nodded to his men and made some kind of hand signal, and they spread out. If this went as planned, my mother's family would never even know I was here. But if they figured it out, small-time criminals didn't hold a candle to the power of the Hawthornes.

My power, now. I tried to really believe that as I reached forward and knocked on Jackson Currie's door. My first knock was hesitant, but then I banged with my fist.

"I'm here!" I said. "For real this time." No response. "My name's Avery. I'm Hannah's daughter." If I had come all this way and he still wouldn't open the door, I didn't know what I would do. "Toby wrote my mother postcards." I kept yelling. "He said that if she ever needed anything, she should come here. I know you saved Toby's life after the fire. I know my mom helped you. I know that they were in love. I don't know if her family found out, or what happened exactly—"

The door opened. "That family always finds out," Jackson Currie grunted. Over the phone, I hadn't realized just how big he was. He had to have been at least six foot six, and he was built like one of Oren's men.

"Is that why my mom changed her name?" I asked him. "Is that why she ran?"

The fisherman stared at me for a moment, his expression hard as rocks. "You don't look much like Hannah," he grunted. For one terrifying moment, I thought he might slam the door in my face. "Except for the eyes."

With that, he let the door swing the rest of the way inward, and Oren, Grayson, and I followed him inside.

"Just the girl," Jackson Currie growled without ever turning around.

I knew Oren was going to argue. "Please," I told him. "Oren, *please*."

"I'll stay in the doorway." Oren's voice was like steel. "She stays in my sight at all times. You don't come closer than three feet to her."

I expected Jackson Currie to balk at all of that, but instead he nodded. "I like him," he told me, then he issued another order. "The boy stays outside, too."

The boy. As in Grayson. He didn't like stepping back from me, but he did it. I turned for just a moment to watch him go.

"That the way it is?" Currie asked me, like he'd seen something in that moment that I hadn't meant to show.

I turned back to him. "Please, just tell me about my mother."

"Not much to tell," he said. "She used to come check on me now and then. Always nagging at me to go to the hospital over every little scrape. She was in school to be a nurse. Wasn't half-bad at stitches."

She was in nursing school? That felt like such a mundane thing to be learning about my mother.

"She helped you nurse Toby after you pulled him from the water?" I said.

He nodded. "She did. Can't say she particularly enjoyed it, but she was always going on about some oath."

The Hippocratic oath. I dug through my memory and remembered the gist of it. "First do no harm."

"It was the damnedest thing for a Rooney to say," Currie grunted. "But Hannah always was the damnedest Rooney."

The muscles in my throat tightened. "She helped you treat Toby even though she knew who he was. Even though she blamed him for her sister's death."

"You telling this story, or am I?"

I went silent, and after a second or two, my silence was rewarded. "She loved her sister, ya know. Always said Kaylie wasn't like the rest of 'em. Hannah was going to get her out."

My mom couldn't have been more than three or four years older than me when all of this had gone down. Kaylie would have been her younger sister. I wanted to cry. At this point, I wasn't even sure what else to ask, but I pushed on. "How long did Toby stay here after the accident?"

"Three months, give or take. He mostly healed up in that time."

"And they fell in love."

There was a long silence. "Hannah always was the damnedest Rooney."

In other circumstances, it might have been harder for me to understand, but if Toby had been suffering from amnesia, he wouldn't have known what had happened on the island. He wouldn't have known about Kaylie—or who she was to my mother.

And my mom had a big heart. She might have hated him at first, but he was a Hawthorne, and I knew all too well that Hawthorne boys had a way about them.

"What happened after three months?" I asked.

"Kid's memory came back." Jackson shook his head. "They had a big fight that night. He came damn near close to killing himself, but she wouldn't let him. He wanted to turn himself in, but she wouldn't let him do that, either."

"Why not?" I asked. No matter how in love with him she'd been, Toby was responsible for three deaths. He'd planned to set a fire that night, even if he'd never lit a match.

"How long you think the person who killed Kaylie Rooney would last in any jail hereabouts?" Jackson asked me. "Hannah wanted to run away, just the two of them, but the boy said no. He couldn't do that to her."

"Do what to her?" I asked. My mom had ended up running anyway. She'd changed her name. And three years later, there was me.

"Hell if I could make sense of either of 'em," Jackson Currie muttered. "Here." He tossed something at my feet. Behind me, Oren twitched, but he didn't object when I moved forward to pick up the object on the ground. It was wrapped in linen. Unrolling it, I found two things: a letter and a small metal disk, the size of a quarter.

I read the letter. It didn't take me long to realize that it was the one Toby had mentioned in the postcards.

Dear Hannah, the same backward as forward,

Please don't hate me—or if you do, hate me for the right reasons. Hate me for being angry and selfish and stupid. Hate me for getting high and deciding that burning the dock wasn't enough—we had to burn the house to really hit my father where it hurt. Hate me for letting the others play the game with me—for treating it like a game. Hate me for being the one who survived.

But don't hate me for leaving.

You can tell me over and over again that I never would have struck the match. You can believe that. On good days, maybe I will, too. But three people are still dead because of me. I can't stay here. I can't stay with you. I don't deserve to. I won't go home, either. I won't let my father pretend this away.

Sooner or later, he'll figure this out. He always does. He'll come for me, Hannah. He'll try to make it all better. And if I let him find me, if I let him wag his silver tongue in my ear, I might start to believe him. I might be tempted to let him wash away my sins, the way that only billions can, so you and I can live happily ever after. But you deserve better than that. Your sister deserved better. And I deserve to fade away.

I won't kill myself. You extracted that promise, and I will keep it. I won't turn myself in. But we can't be together. I can't do that to you. I know you—I know that loving me must hurt you. And I won't hurt you again.

Leave Rockaway Watch, Hannah. Without Kaylie, there's nothing holding you here. Change your name. Start anew. You love fairy tales, I know, but I can't be your happily-ever-after. We can't stay here in our little castle forever. You have to find a new castle. You have to move on. You have to live, for me.

If you ever need anything, go to Jackson. You know what the circle is worth. You know why. You know everything. You might be the only person on this planet who knows the real me.

Hate me, if you can, for all the reasons I deserve it. But don't hate me for leaving while you sleep. I knew you wouldn't let me go, and I cannot bear to say good-bye.

Harry

I looked up from the letter, my ears ringing. "He signed it Harry."

Jackson tilted his head to the side. "That's what I called him 'fore I knew his name. It's what Hannah called him, too."

Something gave inside me. I closed my eyes and let my head fall, just for a moment. I had no idea what had happened between Toby leaving this shack twenty years ago and my mother's death. If he was my father, he had to have found her at some point. They had to have been together again, if only once.

"He found me after she died," I whispered. "He told me his name was Harry."

"She's dead?" Jackson Currie stared at me. "Little Hannah?"

I nodded. "Natural causes." Given the context, that seemed important to clarify. Jackson turned suddenly. A second later, he was rummaging around in the cabinets. He thrust another object at me, coming close enough for our fingertips to brush this time.

"I was supposed to give this to Harry," he grunted. "If he ever came back. Hannah sent them here, year after year. But if she's gone—only seems right to give them to you."

I looked down at the thing he'd just handed me. I was holding another bundle of postcards.

CHAPTER 75

It was one thing to read Toby's love letters to my mother. It was another entirely to read hers to him. She sounded like herself, so much that I could hear her voice with every single word I read.

She loved him. The muscles in my chest tightened. *It hurt to love him, and she loved him anyway.* I breathed—in and out. *He left her, and she loved him anyway.* That string of thoughts cycled through my head on repeat as we drove back to the airstrip where the jets awaited. What my mom and Toby had—it was tragic and messy and all-consuming, and if the postcards made one thing clear, it was that she would have done it all again.

"Are you okay?" Grayson asked beside me, like it was just the two of us in this SUV, like we weren't surrounded by Oren's men. There were two other SUVs, one in front of us and one at our rear. There were four armed men, including Oren, in this car alone.

"No," I told Grayson. "Not really." My entire life, I'd grown up knowing that I was enough for my mom. She hadn't dated. She hadn't wanted or needed a damn thing from Ricky. Her life was full of love. *She* was full of love—but romance? That wasn't something she'd needed. It wasn't something she'd wanted. It wasn't even something she was open to—and now I knew why.

Because she'd never stopped loving Toby.

Close your eyes, I could hear Max telling me. *Picture yourself standing on a cliff overlooking the ocean. The wind is whipping in your hair. The sun is setting. You long, body and soul, for one thing. One person. You hear footsteps behind you. You turn.*

Who's there?

And my answer had been: *no one.*

But after reading even just a couple of my mom's postcards? It was getting harder to ignore Grayson's presence beside me, harder not to think about Jameson. My eyes stung, even though there was zero reason for me to be crying.

I stared through my tears at the postcards my mom had written to Toby and forced myself to keep reading. Soon, the focus of my mom's writing shifted from what they'd had to a different kind of love story. From that point on, every single postcard was about me.

Avery took her first steps today.

Avery's first word is "uh-oh!"

Today, Avery invented a game that combines Candy Land, Chutes and Ladders, and checkers.

On and on it went, up until the postcards stopped. Up until she died.

My hand shook, holding the last postcard, and Grayson's hand made its way to mine.

"She wrote these," I said, my voice catching in my throat, "to Toby about me." It couldn't have been clearer reading them: He really was my father. I'd been working off that assumption for so long that it shouldn't have come as a shock.

Beside me, Grayson's phone buzzed. "It's Jameson," he said.

My heart skipped a beat, then made up for it. "Answer it," I told Grayson, pulling my hand back from his.

Grayson did as I'd asked. "We're on our way back to the plane," he told Jameson.

He'll want to know what I found. I knew that, knew Jameson. I held up the small metal disk that Jackson Currie had given me. "This is what Toby left with Jackson." Grayson stared at it, then switched Jameson over to a video chat, so he could see it, too.

"What do you think this is?" I asked. The disk was gold and maybe an inch in diameter. It looked like some kind of a coin, but not any I'd seen before, its surface engraved with nine concentric circles on one side and smooth on the other.

"It doesn't look like it's worth much," Jameson commented. "But in this family, that means nothing." The sound of his voice did something to me—something it shouldn't have done. Something it wouldn't have done before I'd read my mother's postcards.

Close your eyes, I could hear Max telling me. *Who's there?*

"We're incoming," Oren announced curtly—to whom, I wasn't sure. "Sweep the plane."

When we arrived at the airstrip, he opened my door, and I got three escorts to the plane. Behind me, Grayson had switched the phone off video, but he was still on the line with Jameson.

My mind was full with images of them both—and with the words my mother had written to Toby.

The night air was cold and getting colder. As I walked toward the jet, a brutal wind picked up, then gave way to sudden and utter stillness. I heard a single, high-pitched beep, and the world exploded. Into fire. Into nothing.

CHAPTER 76

Everything hurt. I couldn't hear. I couldn't see. When blurred images finally began to form, all I saw was fire. Fire and Grayson, standing a hundred feet away from me.

I waited for him to come running.

I waited.

I waited.

He didn't.

And then, there was nothing.

The world around me was dark, and then there was a voice. "Let's play a game."

I couldn't tell if I was standing up or lying down. I couldn't feel my body.

"I have a secret."

If I had eyes, I opened them. Or maybe they were already open? Either way, I did *something*, and the world was flooded with light.

"I'm tired of playing," I told my mom.

"I know, baby."

"I'm so tired," I said.

"I know. But I have a secret, Avery, and you have to play—just one more time, just for me. Okay, baby? You can't let go."

I heard a long and distant beep. Lightning tore through my body. "Clear!" a voice yelled.

"Come on, Avery," my mom whispered. *"I have a secret. . . ."*

Another round of lightning tore through me. "Clear!"

I wanted to stop breathing. I wanted to go where the lightning and the fire and the pain couldn't touch me.

"You have to fight," my mom said. "You have to hang on."

"You're not real," I whispered. *"You're dead.* So either this is a dream, and you're not even here, or I'm . . ."

Dead, too.

CHAPTER 77

I dreamed that I was running through the halls of Hawthorne House. I hit a staircase, and at the bottom, I saw a dead girl. At first, I thought it was Emily Laughlin, but then I got closer—and I realized it was me.

I was standing at the edge of the ocean. Every time a wave crested and came toward me, I thought that it would swallow me whole. I was ready for it to swallow me whole.

But each time, as the darkness beckoned, I heard a voice: Jameson Winchester Hawthorne.

"You son of a bitch." The words cut through the darkness in a way that nothing else had since I'd been here. The voice was Jameson's again, but louder this time, sharper, like the edge of a knife. "She was dying, and you just stood there! And don't tell me it was shock."

I tried to open my eyes. I tried—but I couldn't.

"You would know, Jamie, about standing there and watching someone die."

"*Emily.* It always comes back to Emily with you."

I wanted to tell them that I could hear them, but I couldn't move my mouth. Everything was dark. Everything hurt.

"You know what I think, Gray? I think the whole martyr act was a lie you told yourself. I don't think you stepped back from Avery for my sake. I think you needed an excuse to draw a line so you could stay safe on the other side."

"You don't know what you're talking about."

"You can't let go. You couldn't when Emily was alive, no matter what she did, and you can't now."

"Are you done?" Grayson was yelling now.

"Avery was dying, and you couldn't run toward her."

"What do you want from me, Jamie?"

"You think I didn't fight the same fight? I halfway convinced myself that as long as Avery was just a riddle or a puzzle, as long as I was just playing, I'd be *fine*. Well, joke's on me, because somewhere along the way, I stopped playing."

I can hear you. I can hear every word. I'm right here—

"What do you want from me?"

"Look at her, Gray. Look at her, damn it! *Est unus ex nobis. Nos defendat eius.*"

She is one of us. We protect her. Whatever Grayson said in response was lost to the sound of a crashing wave.

I sat at a chessboard. Across from me was a man I hadn't seen since I was six years old.

Tobias Hawthorne picked up his queen, then set it back down. Instead, he laid three new pieces on the board. A corkscrew. A funnel. A chain.

I stared at them. "I don't know what to do with these."

Silently, he laid a fourth object on the board: a metal disk.

"I don't know what to do with that, either."

"Don't look at me, young lady," Tobias Hawthorne replied. "This is *your* subconscious. All of this—it's a game of your making, not mine."

"What if I don't want to play anymore?" I asked.

He leaned back, picking up his queen once more. "Then stop."

CHAPTER 78

The first thing I was aware of was pressure on my chest. It felt like a cinder block was holding me down. I struggled against the weight of it, and like a switch had been flipped, every nerve in my body began to scream. My eyes flew open.

The first thing I saw was the machine, then the tubes. So many tubes, connected to my body.

I'm in the hospital, I thought, but then the rest of the world came into focus around me, and I realized that this wasn't a hospital room. It was *my* room. At Hawthorne House.

Seconds passed like molasses. It took everything I had not to claw the tubes out of my body. Memory settled in around me. Jameson's voice—and Grayson's. Lightning and fire and—

There was a bomb.

A nearby monitor began sounding some kind of alarm, and the next thing I knew, a woman in a white doctor's coat rushed into the room. When I recognized her, I thought I was dreaming again.

"Dr. Liu?"

"Welcome back, Avery." Max's mother fixed me with a no-nonsense look. "I need you to lie back and breathe."

I was poked and prodded and dosed with pain medication. By the time Dr. Liu let Libby and Max into my room, I was feeling downright loopy.

"I gave her some morphine," I heard Dr. Liu tell Libby. "If she wants to sleep, let her."

Max approached my bed, as tentative as I'd ever seen her.

"Your mom is here," I said.

"Correct," Max replied, taking a seat next to the bed.

"At Hawthorne House."

"Very good," Max said. "Now, tell me what year it is, who's president, and which Hawthorne brother you're going to let fax your brains out first."

"Maxine!" Dr. Liu sounded like *she* was the one with a splitting headache.

"Sorry, Mama," Max said. She turned back to me. "I called her when Alisa brought you back here. Lawyer Lady more or less stole your fine comatose self from the hospital in Oregon, and everyone was pretty faxing mad. We weren't about to let her staff you up with doctors of her choosing. We needed someone we could trust. I might have been disowned, but I'm not stupid. I called. The great Dr. Liu came."

"You were not disowned," Max's mom said sternly.

"I distinctly remember disowning," Max countered. "Agree to disagree."

If you'd told me a few hours ago that Max and her mom would be in the same room, and it wouldn't be painful or awkward or painfully awkward, I wouldn't have believed you.

A few hours ago. My brain latched on to that thought, and I realized the obvious: If there had been time for Alisa to steal me from a hospital, and time for Max to call her mom…

"How long was I out?" I asked.

Max didn't answer, not right away. She looked back at her mom, who nodded. Max opened her mouth, but Libby beat her to speaking. "Seven days."

"A full week?"

Libby's hair was dyed again—not one color, but dozens. I thought about what she'd said about her ninth birthday. About the cupcakes my mom had baked for her, and the rainbow colors she'd clipped into her hair, and I wondered how much of her life Libby had spent trying to get that one perfect moment back.

"They told me you might not wake up." Libby's voice was shaking now.

"I'm okay," I said, but then I realized that I had no idea if that was true. I stole a look at Dr. Liu.

"Your body's been healing nicely," she told me. "The coma was medically induced. We tried to wake you up two days ago, but there was some unexpected swelling in your brain. That's all under control now."

I looked past her toward the doorway. "Do the others know?" I asked. "That I'm awake?" *Do the boys?*

Dr. Liu walked over to my bedside. "Let's take this one step at a time."

CHAPTER 79

Eventually, they let Oren in to see me.

"The bomb was planted inside the plane's engine—forensics suggests it had been there for days and was triggered remotely." Oren had partially healed wounds running down the side of his jaw and across the backs of his hands. "Whoever triggered the explosion must have mistimed things. If you'd been two steps closer, you would have died." His voice got tighter. "Two of my men didn't make it."

Devastating guilt drilled through me, a needle-thin icicle straight to the heart. I felt heavy and numb. "I'm sorry."

Oren didn't tell me not to be. He didn't say that if I hadn't pushed to go to Rockaway Watch, those men would still be alive.

"Wait..." I stared at him. "You said that the bomb was planted days before it exploded? Then the Rooneys"—the reason we'd brought so much security with us—"they weren't the ones who..."

"No," Oren confirmed.

Someone planted that bomb. "It must have been planted sometime after True North." I tried to be logical about this, tried to view it from a distance without thinking about the fire, the lightning, the *pain*. "That man at True North, the professional..." My voice caught in my throat. "Who was he working for?"

Before Oren could answer, I heard the familiar sound of heels on the wood floor. Alisa appeared in the doorway. She stepped across the threshold, and when her eyes landed on me, she reached out to a nearby armoire, her fingers gripping the edge with knuckle-whitening ferocity. "Thank God," she muttered. She closed her eyes, battling for calm, then opened them again. "I appreciate you telling your men to stand down."

That was directed at Oren, not me.

"You have five minutes," he said coldly.

Hurt flashed across Alisa's features, and I remembered what Max had said. Alisa had moved me back here without permission. With my life on the line, she'd acted to save my inheritance.

"Don't look at me like that," Alisa said—to me this time. "It worked, didn't it?"

I was here. I was alive. And I was still a billionaire.

"It cost me dearly." Alisa held my gaze. "It cost me this family. But *it worked*."

I didn't know what to say to that. "What's the status of the police investigation about the bombing?" I asked. "Do they have any idea who..."

"The police made an arrest yesterday." Alisa's tone was brisker now, no-nonsense. Familiar. "The job was a professional one, obviously, but the police traced it back to Skye Hawthorne and..." She had the decency to hesitate, just for a moment. "Ricky Grambs."

That answer shouldn't have been surprising. It shouldn't have mattered to me, but for a split second, I saw myself at four years old. I saw Ricky lifting me up and putting me on his shoulders.

I swallowed. "His name is on my birth certificate. If I die, he and Libby are my heirs." It was the same song in a different key, courtesy of Skye Hawthorne.

"There's something else you should know," Alisa told me quietly. "We got back the DNA test you ordered."

Of course she had. I'd been out for a week. "I know," I said. "Ricky's not my father."

Alisa walked to stand beside my bed. "That's the thing, Avery. He is."

CHAPTER 80

I stared at my birth certificate. At the signature. This made no sense. None. Every single clue had pointed in the same direction. Toby had sought me out after my mother's death. He'd signed my birth certificate. He and my mom had been in love. Tobias Hawthorne had left me his fortune.

I have a secret, my mother had told me, *about the day you were born*.

How was it even remotely possible that Toby wasn't my father?

"Upside, downside, inside, outside, left side, right side." Jameson Hawthorne stood in the doorway. When I saw him, something clicked. It was the feeling of a wave crashing over me—at last. "What's missing?" Jameson asked. He walked toward me, and I tracked every step. He repeated his riddle. "Upside, downside, inside, outside, left side, right side. What's missing?"

He stopped next to my bed, right next to it. "Beside," I whispered.

He stared at me—at my eyes, at the lines of my face, like he was drinking it in. "I have to say, Heiress, I'm not a big fan of comas." Jameson sounded just the same, wry and darkly tempting, but the expression on his face was one I'd never seen before.

He wasn't joking.

I flashed back to something like a dream. *Well, joke's on me, because somewhere along the way, I stopped playing.* Jameson Hawthorne and I had an understanding. No emotions. No mess. This wasn't supposed to be an epic kind of love.

"I came to see you," Jameson told me. "Every day. The least you could have done was wake up while I was here, tragically backlit, unspeakably handsome, and waiting."

Picture yourself standing on a cliff overlooking the ocean. The wind is whipping in your hair. The sun is setting. You long, body and soul, for one thing. One person. You hear footsteps behind you. You turn.

Who's there?

"Every day?" I asked, my voice foreign in my throat. I remembered standing at the edge of the ocean. I remembered a voice. *Jameson Winchester Hawthorne.*

"Every single day, Heiress." Jameson closed his eyes, just for an instant. "But if I'm not the one you want to see..."

"Of course I want to see you." That was true. I could say it. "But you don't have to—" *Tell me I'm special. Tell me I matter.*

"Yes," Jameson cut in, "I do." He sank down beside my bed, bringing his eyes level with mine. "You aren't a prize to be won."

I wasn't hearing this. He wasn't saying this. He *couldn't* be.

"You're not a puzzle or a riddle or a clue." Jameson had laser focus. On me. All on me. "You aren't a mystery to me, Avery, because deep down, we're the same. You might not see that." He gave me a long, searing look. "You might not believe it—yet." He held up his hands, his fingers curled into a loose fist. "But there's no one besides the two of us who would have gone back in the wake of that bomb to look for *this*."

He uncurled his fingers, and I saw a small metal disk in his palm.

Every muscle in my body tightened. Everything in me wanted to reach out to him. "How did you—"

Jameson shrugged, and that shrug, like his smile, was *devastating*. "How could I not?" He stared at me a moment longer, then pressed the disk into my hand. I felt his fingertips on my palm. He left them there for a moment, then trailed them along the inside of my wrist.

I sucked in a breath and looked from Jameson's face to the disk. Concentric circles ringed the metal on one side. The other was smooth.

He was still trailing his fingers down my arm.

"Have you figured out what it is?" I asked, every nerve in my body alive.

"No." Jameson smiled, that crooked, devastating Jameson Hawthorne smile. "I was waiting for you."

Jameson wasn't patient. He didn't *wait*. He lived with his foot on the gas. "You want to figure it out." I stared at him, feeling his stare on me. "Together."

"You don't have to say anything." Jameson stood. I could still feel the ghost of his touch on the inside of my arm. I could see the vein in my wrist and *feel* my heart pumping. "You don't have to kiss me now. You don't have to love me now, Heiress. But when you're ready..." He brought his hand to the side of my face. I leaned into it. His breath went ragged, and then he pulled his hand back and nodded to the disk in my hand. "When you're ready, *if* you're ever ready, if it's going to be me—just flip that disk. Heads, I kiss you." His voice broke slightly. "Tails, you kiss me. And either way, *it means something*."

I stared at the disk in my hand. It was the size of a coin. Every clue we'd followed, every trail that had been left, led to this.

I swallowed and looked back up at Jameson. "Toby wasn't my father," I said, and then I corrected the tense. "He *isn't* my father."

Toby Hawthorne was out there somewhere. He still didn't want to be found.

Beside me, Jameson cocked his head, eyes sparking. "Well then, Heiress. Game on."

CHAPTER 81

I made it through that day. That night. The next day. The next night. And on it went. On the morning that I was cleared to go back to school, I heard a sound on the other side of my fireplace.

Jameson. I made my way to the mantel and closed my hand around the candlestick. With a breath, I pulled it forward.

Jameson wasn't the one standing on the other side.

"Thea?" I said. I was confused. I had no idea what she was doing at Hawthorne House or why she'd come through the passage. My gaze darted toward my door. Oren was in the hall. Even now, with Skye and Ricky in prison, he was staying close.

"Don't say anything," Thea implored me, her voice low. "I need you to come with me. It's Grayson."

"Grayson?" I repeated. He'd been like a ghost in the House since I'd woken up. He either didn't want to see me or couldn't face me. I'd watched him swimming laps every night.

"He's in trouble, Avery." Thea looked like she'd been crying, and that scared me, because Thea Calligaris wasn't a person who cried. She didn't *do* vulnerable.

She didn't do scared.

"What's going on? *Thea.*"

She disappeared back into the passageway. I followed her, and an instant later, hands gripped me from behind. Someone slammed a damp cloth down over my mouth and nose. I couldn't breathe. I couldn't scream.

The smell of the cloth was sickly sweet. Everything started going dark around me, and the last thing I heard was Thea.

"I had to, Avery. They have Rebecca."

CHAPTER 82

I woke up tied to an antique chair. The room around me was packed tight with boxes and knickknacks. The entire place smelled like it had been soaked in gasoline.

Two people stood across from me: Mellie, who looked like she might throw up any second. And Sheffield Grayson.

"Where am I?" I asked, and then the memory of what had happened in the passageway came flooding back. "Where's Thea? And Rebecca?"

"I assure you, your friends are fine." Sheffield Grayson was wearing a suit. He had me tied to a chair in what appeared to be some kind of storage unit, and he was *wearing a suit*.

He has Grayson's eyes.

"I am sorry about all of this," Grayson's father said, flicking a speck off the cuff of his shirt. "The chloroform. The restraints." He paused. "The bomb."

"The bomb?" I repeated. The police had arrested Ricky and Skye weeks ago. They had motive, and there was evidence—there had to be, for an arrest. "I don't understand."

"I know you don't." Grayson's father closed his eyes. "I am not a bad man, Ms. Grambs. I take no joy in... this." He didn't specify what *this* was.

"You kidnapped me," I said hoarsely. "I'm tied to a chair." He didn't reply. "You tried to kill me."

"Injure you. If I'd meant for you to die, my man would have timed the explosion differently, wouldn't he?"

I thought of Oren telling me that if I'd been a few steps closer to the plane when the bomb had detonated, I would have died.

"Why?" I said lowly.

"Why what? The bomb or—" Sheffield Grayson gestured to the bindings on my wrists. "The rest?"

"All of it." My voice shook. *Why kidnap me? Why bring me here? What is he planning to do to me next?*

"Blame your father." Sheffield Grayson broke eye contact then, and for reasons I couldn't quite pinpoint, that sent a chill down my spine. "Your real father. If Tobias Hawthorne the Second weren't such a coward, I wouldn't have had to go to such lengths to lure him out."

My captor's voice was calm, commanding. Like he was the rational one here.

The muscles in my chest tightened, threatening to wring the air from my lungs, but I forced myself to breathe, to stay focused. *Stay alive.* "Toby," I said. "You're after Toby."

"The bomb should have worked." Sheffield began cuffing the sleeves on his dress shirt, a furious motion—and a familiar one. "You were rushed to the hospital. It made worldwide news. I was ready. The trap was set. All that was left to do was wait for that bastard to come to your bedside, the way any self-respecting father would. And then your lawyer had the audacity to have you *moved*."

To Hawthorne House, with all its security.

"So here we are," Sheffield Grayson said, "as unfortunate as that may be."

I tried to read between the lines of what he was saying. It had been clear from Grayson's meeting with his father that the man blamed Toby for Colin's death. My captor must have realized, somehow, that Toby was alive. He'd convinced himself that I was Toby's daughter.

And this entire place smelled like gasoline.

"I'm sorry." Mellie's voice shook. "It wasn't supposed to be like this."

My head pounded. My body was screaming at me to flee, but I couldn't. I had no idea why Mellie would have helped this man kidnap me—or what exactly he planned to do to me now.

"Toby won't come for me," I said. Emotion welled up in my throat, and I bit it back. "He isn't my father." That hurt—more than it should have. "I'm nothing to him."

"I have reason to believe he's in town. He stuck his head out of whatever hole he's hiding in long enough for me to verify that much. You are his daughter. He will come for you."

It was like he wasn't hearing me. "I'm not his daughter." I'd wanted to be. I'd believed that I was.

But I wasn't.

Sheffield Grayson's achingly familiar eyes settled on mine. "I have a DNA test that says otherwise."

I stared at him. What he'd just said made no sense. *Alisa* had done a DNA test. Ricky Grambs *was* my father. That meant, obviously, that Toby wasn't. "I don't understand." I really didn't.

I couldn't.

"Mellie here was quite obliging about providing a sample of your DNA. I'd acquired a sample of Toby's from the Hawthorne

Island investigation years ago." Sheffield Grayson straightened. "The match was definitive. You have his blood." Sheffield gave me a chilling smile. "And you really should pay your help more."

For the first time, I looked at Mellie, really looked at her. She wouldn't meet my eyes. Was she the one who'd knocked me out in the passageway?

Why? Like Eli, had she sold me out for money?

"You can go now, dear," Sheffield Grayson told her. Mellie shuffled toward the door.

She's leaving me here. Panic began slithering up my spine.

"You think he's just going to let you go?" I called after her. "You think he's the kind of man who leaves loose ends?" I didn't know Sheffield Grayson. I didn't even know Mellie, really, but everything in me was saying that I couldn't let her leave me here with him alone. "What do you think Nash would say if he knew what you're doing?"

She hesitated, then kept walking. I was getting frantic—and she was getting farther away. The sound of her footsteps grew fainter.

"And now," Sheffield Grayson told me, in the same calm, commanding voice, "we wait."

CHAPTER 83

Toby wasn't coming. Sooner or later, my captor would realize that. And when he did . . . well, he couldn't just let me go.

"What makes you think Toby's close by?" I tried not to sound scared. I tried not to *be* scared. Pissed was better—much. "How is he even supposed to know that you took me? Or where to come?"

He's not my father. He's not coming.

"I left clues," Sheffield said, inspecting one of his cuff links. "A little game for your father to play. I understand Hawthornes are prone to such things."

"What kind of clues?"

No answer.

"How did you send clues to him if you don't where he is?"

No response.

This was useless. Toby had told me to stop looking for him. He'd been in hiding for decades. I wasn't his daughter.

He wasn't coming.

That was the only thought my brain was capable of producing. It rang in my mind over and over again, until I heard footsteps. They were too heavy to be Mellie's.

"Ah." Sheffield Grayson inclined his head. He walked toward

me, assessing me, then reached a hand out to my face and put two fingers under my chin. He angled it backward. "It's important that you know, Avery: This isn't personal."

I jerked back, but it was useless. I was still bound. I wasn't going anywhere. And the footsteps were getting closer.

Someone was coming for me. It probably just wasn't the person he expected.

"What if you're wrong?" I said, rushing the words. "What if the person who found your *clues* wasn't Toby? What are you going to do if that's Jameson? Xander? *Grayson*?"

The sound of his son's name—his *own* name—gave Sheffield Grayson only the briefest moment of pause. He closed his eyes again for a moment, then opened them, resolute and steeled against whatever unwanted thoughts my questions had raised.

"These were my nephew's things." Sheffield gestured to the items in the storage unit. His voice tightened. "I never could bear to part with them."

The footsteps were almost here. Sheffield Grayson turned toward the entrance to the front of the storage unit. He withdrew a gun from his suit jacket. Finally, the footsteps stopped as a man stepped into view. He'd shaved since the last time I'd seen him, but he was still wearing layers of worn and dirty clothes.

"Harry." That was the wrong name, and I knew it, but I couldn't keep the word from bursting past my lips. *He's here. He came.* Tears welled in my eyes, carving trails down my cheeks as the man I'd known as Harry looked past Sheffield Grayson, past the gun, toward me.

"Horrible girl." Toby's voice was tender. He'd called me a lot of things when we played chess—that was one of them. *Especially when I won.* "Let her go," he told my captor.

Sheffield Grayson smiled, his gun held steady. "Ironic, isn't it? My son carries the last name Hawthorne, and your daughter doesn't. And now..." He walked slowly out of the storage unit toward Toby. "I'm the one holding the match."

I didn't see a match, but he had a gun. This place had been doused in accelerant. If he fired that gun—

"Get in there," Sheffield ordered.

Toby did as he was told. "Avery isn't my daughter." His voice was even.

I'm not. Am I? "He said he has a DNA test," I told Toby, stalling for time, trying to think of a way—any way—out of this, before the whole place went up in flames.

A few feet away from me, Tobias Hawthorne the Second took his eyes off Sheffield Grayson—and the gun—just for a moment. "Queen to rook five," he told me. That was a chess move—one I'd used on him in our last game, as misdirection.

Misdirection. My brain managed to latch on to that. *He's going to distract Sheffield.* I tested the security of the bindings that held me to the chair. They were just as tight as they'd been a minute before, but a surge of adrenaline hit me, and I thought about the fact that mothers had been known to lift cars off their toddlers in crises. This chair was an antique. With enough pressure, could I break the chair's arms?

"I told you." Toby turned his attention back to the man with the gun. "Avery is not my daughter. I don't know what kind of DNA test you think you got, but when Hannah got pregnant, I hadn't seen her for years."

I tried to focus on the chair, not his words, and worked the restraints back to the thinnest part of the wood.

"You came for the girl." Sheffield Grayson sounded different now. Harder. "You're here." He lowered his voice. "You're here, and my nephew is not." That was clearly an accusation—and the man with the gun was judge, jury, and executioner.

"He hated you," Toby shot back.

"He was going to be great," Sheffield said intently. "I was going to make him great."

Toby didn't bat an eye. "The fire was Colin's idea, you know. I kept saying that I wanted to burn everything down, and he dared me to put my money where my mouth was."

"You're a liar."

I jerked my arms upward. Again. And again. I threw the weight of my body into it, and the right arm on the chair gave. The noise it made was loud enough that I expected Sheffield Grayson to whip his gaze toward me, but he was 100 percent focused on Toby.

"Colin dared me to do it," Toby said again. "But it wasn't his fault I took the dare. I was angry. And high. And the house on Hawthorne Island meant something to my father. I was going to make sure that everyone was clear of it. We were supposed to watch it burn *from a distance*."

The second arm on the chair gave, and Toby raised his voice. "We didn't count on the lightning."

Sheffield Grayson stalked toward him. "My nephew is dead. He burned, because of you."

This entire place had been soaked in accelerant. Deep down, I knew why. *He burned, because of you.*

"I am what I am," Toby said. "If you want to kill me, I won't fight it. But let Avery go."

Sheffield Grayson's eyes—*Grayson's eyes*—shifted toward me. "I am truly sorry," he told me. "But I can't leave any witnesses behind. Unlike some people, I don't fancy the idea of disappearing for decades. My family deserves better than that."

"What about Mellie?" I asked, stalling for time. "Or the man you had plant the bomb?"

“You don’t need to worry about that.” Sheffield aimed the gun at Toby. He was still calm, still in control.

He’s going to kill us both. I was going to die here with Toby Hawthorne. My mother’s Toby. *No.* I stood, ready to fight, aware that there was no use in fighting—but what else was I supposed to do?

I launched myself forward. Instantly, a gun fired. The sound of it was deafening.

I expected an explosion. I expected to burn. Instead, as I watched, Sheffield Grayson crumpled to the ground. An instant later, Mellie stepped into view, her eyes wide and unseeing, holding a gun.

CHAPTER 84

"I killed him." Mellie sounded dazed. "I... He was holding a gun. And he was going to... And I..."

"Easy," Toby murmured. He stepped forward and removed the gun from her hand. Mellie let him.

What just happened here? Trying not to look at the body on the ground—at *Grayson's father*—I made my way out of the unit. "I don't understand." That was probably the biggest understatement of my life. "You sold me out, Mellie. You left. Why would you—"

"It wasn't supposed to be like this." Mellie shook her head, and for a few seconds, it seemed like she couldn't stop shaking it. "And we didn't sell you out. This was never about the money."

We? I thought dizzily.

"Who's we?" Toby asked.

In answer, Mellie swallowed and reached a finger up to her eye. I wasn't sure what she was doing at first, but then she removed a contact lens. I walked toward her, and she blinked up at me. The contact she'd removed was colored. Her left eye was still brown, but her right eye was a vibrant blue, with an amber circle around the center. *Just like Eli's.*

"My brother and I agreed that I should be the one to wear contacts," Mellie said, her voice still a little shaky.

"Eli's your brother." My mind raced. "He engineered a threat against me so he could stay close, then he leaked information about Toby to the press. And then you—"

"It wasn't supposed to be like this," Mellie repeated. "We were just trying to flush Toby out of hiding. We just wanted to talk. When Mr. Grayson offered his assistance—"

"You kidnapped me for him."

"No!" Mellie's response was instantaneous. "I mean... *kind of.*" She shook her head again. "After Grayson and Jameson went to see him in Arizona, Sheffield Grayson sent a man to follow them to True North. To watch them." I thought about the professional in the woods. Oren had pulled me out of the tub—and sent one of his men after the interloper. "Eli caught the guy," Mellie continued. "He tackled him, and then... they talked."

"About me?" I paused. "About Toby?"

Mellie didn't answer either question. "We didn't know who the man was working for," she said instead. "Not at first. But we all wanted the same thing."

Toby. "So Eli leaked those pictures," I said, my throat constricting. "And then a few days later, someone blew up my plane."

"That wasn't us! Eli and I never wanted to hurt you. We never wanted to hurt anyone!" Mellie's eyes drifted toward Toby's. "We just needed to talk."

"Why?" I demanded, but Mellie didn't answer me. Now that she'd looked over at Toby, she couldn't stop staring at him.

"Do I know you?" he asked her, his brow furrowing.

Mellie looked down. "You knew my mother."

The world shifted under my feet—suddenly, abruptly. *Sheffield*

Grayson said he had a DNA test linking me to Toby. I sucked in a breath. *But Toby's not my father. It wasn't* my *DNA.*

"This is my mom." Mellie pulled out her phone and showed Toby a picture. "I don't expect you to remember her. Pretty sure she was just another wild night for you that summer."

The summer he "died," I thought. Across from me, Toby looked at the photo, and I remembered Zara saying that Tobias Hawthorne's investigators had talked to at least one of the women that Toby had slept with that summer. *Mellie's mother?*

Across from me, I could see Toby working his way through it, too.

"Sheffield Grayson said you gave him a DNA sample to test," I said, staring at Mellie. "He was certain I was Toby's daughter." I glanced toward Toby, and the muscles in my stomach twisted. "But I'm not. Am I?"

"Not by blood." Toby held my gaze a moment longer, then turned back to Mellie. "You're right. I don't remember your mother."

"I was five," Mellie told him. "Eli was six. Our parents were in a bad place, and suddenly, Mom was pregnant. She didn't know your name. She didn't know the kind of money you came from."

"But you figured it out?" I said. I couldn't stop staring at Mellie. Alisa had told me once that she was one of the ones that Nash had "saved" from unfortunate circumstances. I had no idea what those circumstances were, but it couldn't be coincidence that both she and her brother had ended up in the Hawthornes' employ.

How long had they been planning this?

"You said your mother was pregnant," Toby said quietly. "Did she have the child?"

The child, I thought, my stomach sinking. *His child.* The DNA that Mellie had given Sheffield Grayson, the DNA that had come up as a match for Toby's—it wasn't mine.

"My sister," Mellie replied. "Her name is Evelyn. She goes by Eve."

I saw something—just a hint of emotion—in Toby's eyes. "A palindrome."

"She chose it herself," Mellie replied quietly, "when she was three years old, for that reason. She's nineteen now." Mellie turned to me. "And everything *you* have should be hers."

For the first time, I heard surety burning in Mellie's tone, and I understood that while she hadn't meant for me to be hurt, it was a risk she'd been willing to take, because Toby Hawthorne did have a daughter.

It just wasn't me.

Did the old man know? Did Mellie ever try to tell him?

"What do you want from me?" Toby asked.

"I want Eve taken care of," Mellie said fiercely. "She's a Hawthorne."

My gaze cut to Toby's. "And a Laughlin," I said quietly. I wasn't Mrs. Laughlin's great-granddaughter. I wasn't Rebecca's niece, Emily's niece. Eve was.

She was the one who belonged here.

I swallowed. "Bring her to Hawthorne House." The words chafed against my throat, but I wasn't going to give in to that hurt. "There's plenty of room."

"No." Toby's voice was blade-sharp.

Mellie scrolled furiously through her phone and shoved another picture in his face. "Look at her," she demanded. "She's your *daughter*, and you have no idea what her life has been like."

Toby looked at the photo. Without meaning to, I stepped forward. I looked, too, and the second I saw Mellie's sister's face, I stopped breathing.

Eve was a dead ringer for Emily Laughlin. Strawberry-blonde

hair, like sunlight through amber. Emerald eyes, too big for her face. Heart-shaped lips, a scattering of freckles.

"My daughter isn't coming to Hawthorne House," Toby told Mellie. "If you bring me to her, I will see that she's taken care of. Discreetly."

"What's that supposed to mean?" I asked, finally recovering my voice. Toby was talking about leaving. Like he was just going to walk away. After everything I'd been through, everything that Jameson, Xander, Grayson, and I had done to look for him.

"Do you promise?" Mellie stared at Toby like I wasn't even in the room.

"I promise." Toby's eyes traveled to mine. "But first," he continued softly, "Avery and I need to have a conversation alone."

CHAPTER 85

"You're going to keep her a secret?" I demanded, once we were out of Mellie's earshot. "Eve?"

Toby took my elbow and guided me to the exit. "There's a car outside," he told me. "Key's in the ignition. Take it and drive north."

I stared at him. "That's it?" I said. "That's all you have to say to me?" Eve's face—Emily's—was still fresh in my mind.

Toby reached out and brushed the hair off of my forehead. "In my heart," he said quietly, "you were always mine."

I swallowed. "But biologically, I'm not."

"Biology isn't everything."

I knew in that moment that I'd gotten this much right: Toby *had* sought me out after my mother died. He had been watching me. He had wanted to make sure that I was okay.

"My mom and I had this game," I told him, trying my best not to cry. "We had lots of games, actually—but this one, her favorite, it was about secrets."

He stared off into the distance for a moment. "I made her promise never to tell you—about me, about my family. But if it was just a game, if you guessed…" He looked back at me, and his own eyes were shining. "Damn it, Hannah."

"How the hell was I supposed to guess?" The words burst out of my mouth. I was furious suddenly—at her, at him. "She said that she had a secret about the day I was born."

Toby said nothing.

"You signed my birth certificate." I wanted answers. He owed me that at least.

He reached out to lay a hand against my cheek. "There was a storm that night," he said quietly. "Worst one I'd ever seen—Hawthorne Island included. I shouldn't have been there in the first place. I'd managed to stay away from Hannah for three long years. But something brought me back. I just wanted to *see* her again, even if I couldn't let her see me.

"She was pregnant. Forecasts were calling for a hurricane. And she was alone. I was going to stay away. She was never supposed to know that I was there, but then the power went out—and she went into labor."

With me. I couldn't say that out loud, couldn't say anything, couldn't even tell him that my mother had been capable of making decisions for *herself*.

"The ambulance didn't make it in time," Toby said, his voice growing hoarse. "She needed *someone*."

"You." I managed one word this time—just one.

"I brought you into this world, Avery Kylie Grambs."

There it was. My mother's secret. Toby was there the night I was born. He'd delivered me. I wondered what my mom had felt, seeing him again after years. I wondered if he'd called her *Hannah, O Hannah*, and if she'd tried to make him stay.

"Avery Kylie Grambs." I repeated the last words Toby had said to me. There was something about the way he'd said my full name. "It's an anagram." I swallowed again, and for some reason, whatever force had been holding back my tears gave way. "But you knew that."

Toby didn't deny it. "Your mom had a middle name all picked out. Kylie—like Kaylie but minus a letter."

That hit me hard. I'd never known that I was named after my mother's sister. I'd never known about Kaylie at all.

"Hannah was set on giving you Ricky's last name," Toby continued. "But she didn't like the first name he'd picked out."

Natasha. "Ricky wasn't there." I blinked back tears and stared at Toby. "You were."

"*Something* Kylie Grambs." Toby smiled and gave a little shrug. "I couldn't resist."

He was a Hawthorne. He loved puzzles and riddles and codes. "You chose my name." I didn't phrase it as a question. "You suggested Avery."

"A Very Risky Gamble." Toby looked down. "What I took that night. What Hannah took when she nursed me back to life, knowing what her family would do to her if they found out."

A Very Risky Gamble—the reason Tobias Hawthorne had left me his fortune. Had he recognized his son's fingerprints all over that name? Had he suspected, from the moment he heard it, that I was a link to Toby?

"When the ambulance got there, I disappeared," Toby continued. "I snuck into the hospital one last time to see you both."

"You signed the birth certificate," I said.

"With your father's name, not mine. It was the least he owed her."

"And then you left." I stared at him, trying not to hate him for that.

"I had to."

Something like fury rose up inside me. "No, you didn't." My mom had loved him. She'd spent her entire life loving him, and I'd never even known.

"You have to understand. My father's resources were unlimited. He never stopped looking for me. I had to stay on the move if I wanted to stay dead."

I thought about Tobias Hawthorne, eating at a hole-in-the-wall diner in New Castle, Connecticut. Had it taken him six years to track Toby there?

Had he thought his son would come back?

Had he realized who my mother was?

Had he thought, even for a moment, that I was Toby's?

"What are you going to do now?" I asked, my voice like sandpaper in my throat. "The world knows you're alive. Your father is dead. As far as we know, Sheffield Grayson was the only person who realized the old man had buried the police report about Hawthorne Island. He's the only one who knew—"

"I know what you're thinking, Avery." Toby's eyes hardened. "But I can't come back. I promised myself a long time ago that I would never forget what I did, that I would never move on. Hannah wouldn't let me turn myself in, but exile is what I deserved."

"What about what other people deserve?" I asked vehemently. "Did my mother deserve to die without you there? Did she deserve to spend my entire life in love with a ghost?"

"Hannah deserved the world."

"So why didn't you give it to her?" I asked. "Why was punishing yourself more important than what *she* wanted?"

Why was it more important than what I wanted now?

"I don't expect you to understand," Toby told me gently—more gently than he'd ever spoken to me as Harry.

"I do understand," I said. "You're not staying gone because you have to. You're making a choice, and it's selfish." I thought about Mr. and Mrs. Laughlin, about Rebecca's mother. "What gives you the right to deceive the people who love you? To make that kind of decision for everyone else?"

He didn't answer.

"You have a daughter now," I told him, my voice low.

He looked at me, his expression never wavering. "I have two."

In the span of a heartbeat, fury gave way to devastation. Tobias Hawthorne the Second wasn't my father. He hadn't raised me. I didn't carry a single drop of his blood.

But he'd just called me his daughter.

"I want you to go outside, princess. Get in the car and drive north."

"I can't do that," I said. "Sheffield Grayson is dead! There's a body. The police are going to want to know what happened. And as screwed up as what Mellie did is, she doesn't deserve to go down for murder. If we tell the police what really happened—"

"I know men like Sheffield Grayson." Toby's expression shifted, until it was utterly impossible to read. "He's covered his tracks. No one knows where he is or who he was after. There will be nothing to tie him to this warehouse—nothing to even suggest he was in the state."

"So?" I said.

Toby looked past me, just for a moment. "I know more than I wish I did about what it takes to make something—or some*one*—disappear."

"What about his family?" I asked. *Grayson's family.* "I can't let you—"

"You're not *letting* me do anything." Toby reached out to touch my face. "Horrible girl," he whispered. "Don't you know by now? No one *lets* a Hawthorne do anything."

That was the truth.

"This is wrong," I said again. He couldn't just make that body disappear.

"I have to, Avery." Toby was implacable. "For Eve. The spotlight, the media circus, the rumors, the stalkers, the threats—I can't save you from that, Avery Kylie Grambs. I would if I could, but it's too late. The old man did what he did. He pulled you onto the board. But if I stay in shadows, if I make this disappear, if *I* disappear—then we can save Eve."

It had never been clearer: To Toby, the Hawthorne name, the money—it was a curse. *The tree is poison, don't you see? It poisoned S and Z and me.*

"It's not all bad," I said. "Kidnapping and murder attempts aside, I'm doing fine."

That was a ridiculous statement, but Toby didn't even laugh. "And you will stay fine, as long as I stay dead." He sounded so certain of that. "Go. Get in the car. Drive. If anyone asks you what happened, claim amnesia. I'll take care of the rest."

This was really it. He was really going to walk away from me. He was going to disappear again. "I know about the adoption," I said, desperate to keep him here—to make him stay. "I know your biological mother was the Laughlins' daughter and that she was coerced into the adoption. I know that you blame your parents for keeping secrets, for ruining the three of you. But your sisters—they need you."

Skye was sitting in a jail cell, but she wasn't guilty—this time, at least. Zara was more human than she wanted to admit. And Rebecca? Her mother was still mourning Toby.

"I read the postcards you wrote to my mom," I continued. "I talked to Jackson Currie. I know everything—and I'm telling you: You don't have to stay away anymore."

"You sound just like her." Toby's expression softened. "I never could win an argument with Hannah." He closed his eyes. "Some people are smart. Some people are good." He opened his eyes and put a hand on each of my shoulders. "And some people are both."

I knew, with a strange kind of prescience, that this moment would never leave me. "You're not staying, are you?" I asked. "No matter what I say."

"I can't." Toby pulled me in. I'd never been much of a hugger, but for a moment, I let myself be held.

When Toby finally let me go, I reached into my pocket and pulled out the small metal disk, the one he'd told my mother was valuable. "What is this?"

It was the last question I had for him. The last chance I had of making him stay.

Toby moved like lightning. One second, I held the disk in my hand, and the next, he had it. "Something I'll be taking with me," he said.

"What aren't you telling me?" I asked.

He shook his head. "*Horrible girl*," he whispered, his voice tender.

I thought of my mother, of every word she'd written to him about me, of the way he'd come for me tonight.

You have a daughter, I'd told him.

I have two.

"Am I ever going to see you again?" I asked, my throat closing in on the words.

He leaned forward, pressed a kiss to my forehead, and stepped back. "It would be a very risky gamble."

I opened my mouth to reply, but the door to the warehouse flew inward. Men poured inside. Oren's men.

My head of security stepped between me and Toby Hawthorne and then leveled a deadly look at Tobias Hawthorne's only son. "I think it's time we had a little talk."

CHAPTER 86

I wasn't able to overhear whatever words were exchanged between Oren and Toby. I was shuttled into the SUV, and when Oren took his place in the driver's seat a few minutes later, I noted that he'd left several of his men inside.

I thought about Sheffield Grayson, dead on the floor. About Toby's plan for that body. "Is disposing of corpses part of your job description?" I asked Oren.

He met my eyes in the rearview mirror. "You want a real answer to that?"

I looked out the window. The world blurred as the SUV picked up speed. "Skye and Ricky didn't plant that bomb," I said. I tried to focus on the facts, not the flood of emotions I was barely holding back. "They were framed."

"*This time*," Oren said. "Skye has already tried to have you killed once. Both of them are threats. I suggest we let them cool their heels in prison at least until your emancipation goes through."

Once I was legally an adult, once I could write my own will, Ricky and Skye would stand to gain nothing by my death.

"Rebecca." I lunged forward in my seat suddenly, remembering. "Thea helped Mellie abduct me because someone had Rebecca."

"It's been handled," Oren told me. "They're fine. So are you. The rest of the family is none the wiser." From his tone, you would have thought this was just business as usual. The kidnapping. The body. The cover-up.

"Was it like this for the old man?" I asked. "Or am I just lucky?"

I thought about Toby, sparing Eve from my fate, like inheriting this fortune was less blessing than curse.

"Mr. Hawthorne had a list." Oren took his time with his reply. "It was a different kind of list from yours. He had enemies. Some of them had resources, but by and large, we knew what to expect. Mr. Hawthorne had a way of seeing things coming."

I was starting to think that if I was going to survive being the Hawthorne heiress, I was going to have to start doing the same. I would have to learn to think like the old man.

Twelve birds, one stone.

Back at Hawthorne House, Oren made it clear that he intended to escort me all the way to my room. When we hit the grand staircase, I cleared my throat.

"We'll need to disable the passageway," I told him. "Permanently."

I paused on the staircase, in front of Tobias Hawthorne's portrait. Not for the first time, I stared at the old man. Had he known who Mellie and Eli were? Had he known about Eve? I was certain he would have run a DNA test on me at some point. He knew I wasn't Toby's daughter—not by blood.

But he'd still used me to lure Toby out—the same way Sheffield Grayson had, the same way Mellie and Eli had. *You're not a player,* Nash had told me a small eternity ago. *You're the glass ballerina—or the knife.*

Maybe I was both. Maybe I was a dozen different things, chosen for a dozen different reasons—none of them having a damn thing to do with who I was or what made me special.

I met the portrait's eyes and thought about my dream—about playing chess with the old man. *You didn't choose me. You used me. You're still using me.* But as of this moment?

I was done being used.

CHAPTER 87

An hour later, I went in search of a Hawthorne. "I have something to tell you."

Xander was in his "lab," a hidden room where he built machines that did simple things in complicated ways. "Something to tell me? Is it possible you have me confused with one of my brothers?" he asked. "Because people don't tell me things."

He was tinkering with some kind of miniature catapult mechanism, part of a complicated chain reaction born from the brain of Xander Hawthorne.

"This was your game," I said. "The old man left it to you."

"Or so it appeared." Xander settled a metal ball on the catapult. "At first."

I gave him a look. "What do you mean?"

"Jameson has laser focus. Grayson always finishes what he starts. Even Nash, he might take the scenic route, but he's wired to go from point A to point B." Xander finished tinkering and finally turned to face me. "But me? I'm not wired that way. I start at point A, and somewhere along the way, I end up at the intersection of one hundred and twenty-seven and purple." He shrugged. "It's one of my many charms. My brain likes diversions. I follow the paths that I find. The old man knew that." Xander shrugged. "Did he expect me to start the ball rolling this time? Yes. But where I'd end up?" Xander stepped back from his work and took in the entirety of the Rube Goldberg machine he'd built. "The old man knew damn well that it wasn't going to be point B."

I needed to tell someone what had happened. I'd chosen him because I felt like I owed it to him—like the universe, or maybe his grandfather, owed it to him. And now Xander was seeming an awful lot like someone who didn't want closure.

Someone who didn't need it.

"So where did you end up?" I asked.

Xander leaned forward and triggered the catapult. The metal ball sailed into a funnel, spiraled down a series of ramps, and hit a lever, dumping a bucket of water, releasing a balloon…

Eventually, the entire machine parted, revealing the wall behind it. That wall was covered with pictures—photographs of men with brown skin. The placards beneath the photographs informed me that every one of them had the last name Alexander.

I thought about the game we'd spent the past weeks playing. *Sheffield Grayson. Jake Nash.* Was this the detour that the old man had expected Xander to take?

"Do you want to know what I found?" I asked Xander.

"Sure," he said gamely. "But before I forget: two things." He held up his middle and index fingers. "First, this is Thea's phone number." He handed me a scrap of paper with the number scrawled across it. "I'm supposed to call her and let her know you're alive."

I frowned. "So why give me her number?" I asked.

"Because," Xander replied, "when it comes to Thea, forewarned is forearmed."

I narrowed my eyes. "What's the second thing?" I asked suspiciously.

Xander pressed a button, and the wall slid to reveal a second workshop. “Voilà!”

My eyes widened as I took in the contents of that workshop. “Is that…”

“Life-sized re-creations of the three most lovable droids in the *Star Wars* universe.” Xander grinned. “For Max.”

CHAPTER 88

"You beautiful beaches." Max was beyond pleased with Xander's offering—enough so that it took her a moment to shoot me a reproving look. "I feel obliged to warn you, you're looking a little pale, and the great Dr. Liu is not going to be pleased."

I took that to mean that my doctor would have been really displeased to know what I'd actually been up to in the last twelve hours. "Thank you." I waited until Max looked at me before I continued. "For bringing your mom here."

I knew enough about my best friend to know that it hadn't been an easy call to make.

"Yeah, well…" Max shrugged. "Thank you. For getting blown up."

For giving you a reason to call—and giving her a reason to pick up. "Do you think you'll be headed home soon?"

I didn't want Max to leave, but at the same time, my best friend had her own life to live, and I couldn't help thinking that she'd be safer doing that far away from Hawthorne House. Away from me, from the Hawthorne family, from everything I'd inherited along with Tobias Hawthorne's billions.

Poison tree and all.

When Thea called, I almost didn't pick up. That was why Xander had given me her number. And yet...

"Hello?" I said darkly.

There was a moment of hesitation, and then: "I did some digging and found out who vandalized your locker. It was a freshman. You want the name?"

Silly me. I'd been expecting an apology. "No." I was tempted to leave it there, but I couldn't. "Is Rebecca okay?"

"She's shaken, but fine." Thea's voice was soft, but she spoiled the effect by scoffing audibly. "Fine enough to yell at me for putting you in danger."

"Yeah, well..." I shrugged, even though Thea couldn't see me. "Rebecca's one to talk." That I could joke about this was a true testament to how far Rebecca and I had come.

"I had a choice." Thea's voice shook. She was diabolical and complicated and about a thousand other things, but she wasn't evil. She'd been worried about me. "I had to choose her. Can you understand that, Avery?" Thea didn't wait for my answer. "For me, it's always going to be Rebecca. She doesn't believe that, but no matter how long it takes, I'm going to keep choosing her."

I had never understood what it felt like for one person to be your everything, to look at that person and *know*. I'd never believed myself capable of that. I hadn't wanted to be capable of it.

When Thea and I hung up the phone, I went to see Grayson.

CHAPTER 89

I told Grayson what had happened to his father. I didn't tell him about Eve. The entire time, his face was like stone. "You look like you want to hit something," I told him.

He shook his head.

I made him look at me. "How about swinging a sword?"

Grayson corrected my stance. "Let the blade do the work for you," he reminded me, and in that moment, I was reminded of more.

Of the first day I'd met him. How arrogant he'd been, how sure of himself and his place in the world. I thought about the first time I'd caught him really looking at me, and the way he'd told me that I had an expressive face. I thought about bargains struck and promises made and stolen moments and words spoken in Latin.

But mostly I thought about the ways that the two of us were alike. "I had a dream," I told him. "When I was in the coma. You and Jameson were fighting. About me."

"Avery..." Grayson lowered his sword.

"In my *dream*," I continued, "Jameson was angry that you didn't run toward me. That I was lying there at death's door, and you couldn't move. But, Grayson?" I waited for him to look at me, with silver eyes and the weight of the world on his shoulders. "I'm not angry. I've spent my entire life not running toward anyone. I know what's it like to just stand there—to not be able to do anything else. I know what it's like to lose someone."

I thought about my mom, then Emily.

"I am an expert at not wanting to want things." I held my sword up for a moment longer, then lowered it, the way he'd lowered his. "But I'm starting to realize that the person I need to be, the person I'm becoming—she's not that girl anymore."

I'd been given the world. It was time to stop living scared, time to take the reins.

It was time to take risks.

CHAPTER 90

Ms. Grambs, you understand that if you are emancipated, you will be considered a legal adult. You will be responsible for yourself. You will be held to adult standards. You are literally signing away the rest of your childhood."

In the past six weeks, I'd been shot at, blown up, kidnapped, and paraded around as the living, breathing embodiment of Cinderella stories. To the world, I was a scandal, a mystery, a curiosity, a fantasy.

To Tobias Hawthorne, I'd been a tool.

"I understand," I told the judge. And just like that, it was done.

"Congratulations," Alisa said as we stepped out of the courthouse. Oren's men cleared a path through the paparazzi, and I made my way to the SUV. "You're an adult." Alisa sounded pretty darn satisfied with herself. "You can write your own will."

I leaned back in my seat and thought about how carefully my lawyer had been managing my public image, how much she wanted the world to believe that the firm was calling the shots.

I smiled. "I can do a lot more than that."

Three hours later, I found Jameson on the roof. He was holding a familiar knife in his hands. He faked like he was going to toss it to me, and my heart sped up.

His eyes met mine, and it sped up more.

"I have a lot to tell you." The wind caught my hair, whipping it around my face. "I met Toby, face-to-face. He has a daughter, but it's not me. She looks just like Emily Laughlin."

Jameson's green eyes looked fathomless. "I'm intrigued, Heiress."

I reached into my pocket and pulled out a coin. This felt more dangerous than riding on the back of a motorcycle or speeding down a racetrack or getting shot at in the Black Wood. This wasn't just a rush.

This was a risk—one the old Avery never would have been capable of taking.

My eyes on Jameson's, I uncurled my fingers, revealing the coin in my palm. "Toby took the disk," I said. "We might never know what it was."

Jameson's lips ticked up at the edges. "This is Hawthorne House, Heiress. There will always be another mystery. Just when you think you've found the last hidden passage, the last tunnel, the last secret built into the walls—there will always be one more."

There was an energy in his voice when he spoke about the House. "That's why you love it." I locked my eyes on his. "The House."

He leaned forward. "That's why I love the House."

I held up the coin. "It's not the disk," I said. "But sometimes you have to improvise." My heart was racing. I was vibrating with the same energy I'd heard in his tone.

And like Jameson, I loved it.

"Heads, you kiss me," I said. "Tails, I kiss you. And this time..." My voice cracked. "It means something."

Jameson shot me one of those devastating, crooked Jameson Winchester Hawthorne grins. "What are you saying, Heiress?"

I tossed the coin into the air, and as it turned, I thought about everything that had happened. All of it.

I'd found Toby.

I knew my mother's secret.

I understood, more than ever, why my name had caught the attention of a billionaire who'd only met me once. Maybe that was all there was to it. Or maybe I was one stone meant for twelve birds, most of them still undiscovered.

Like Jameson had said, this was Hawthorne House. There would always be another mystery. Like me, Jameson would always be driven to solve them.

The coin landed. "Tails," I said. "I kiss you." I wrapped my arms around his neck. I pressed my lips to his. And this time, the joke was on me—because I wasn't playing.

This wasn't nothing.

This was the beginning—and I was ready to be bold.

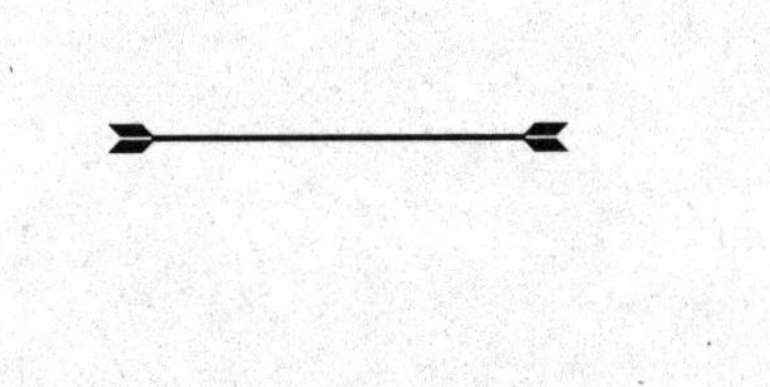

ACKNOWLEDGMENTS

This book was written and revised in the spring and summer of 2020, largely while I was locked down at home with my husband and small children; *The Inheritance Games* came out in September 2020, mid-pandemic. Due to the tireless work and incredible support of my amazing publishing team, the book somehow managed to find its audience during this tumultuous time. More than any other book or series I have written, this one owes an incredible debt of gratitude toward the people without whom it simply could not have happened.

First, I would like to thank my incredible team at Little, Brown Books for Young Readers. What you have done for the Inheritance Games series and for me as an author astounds and humbles me. I have no idea how I got so lucky as to work with a group of people whose enthusiasm, work ethic, generosity, and just all-around brilliance are so far off the charts that the chart isn't even visible anymore. What all of you have done for these books—in unprecedented and incredibly challenging times, no less!—is more amazing than I could possibly say. I get tears in my eyes just thinking of all that this team has put into getting *The Inheritance Games* and *The Hawthorne Legacy* into the hands of readers.

Thank you to my incredible editor, Lisa Yoskowitz, whose brilliant editorial mind is only matched by the kindness and grace she extends to those she works with. Getting to work together again has been a dream come true.

Thank you to Megan Tingley and Jackie Engel; I cannot begin to express what an absolute joy it has been to be published by LBYR under your leadership.

Huge thanks to cover designer Karina Granda and artist Katt Phatt; the covers you have given *The Inheritance Games* and *The Hawthorne Legacy* are nothing short of perfection. I smile literally every time I see them!

To my incredible marketing and publicity teams, thank you, thank you, thank you for helping *The Inheritance Games* and *The Hawthorne Legacy* find so many readers. Thank you to Emilie Polster, who has been an incredible champion for these books from day one, and to Bill Grace, Savannah Kennelly, Christie Michel, Victoria Stapleton, Amber Mercado, and Cheryl Lew, for your tremendous work on *The Hawthorne Legacy*, as well as to Katharine McAnarney and Tanya Farrell, for your help with book one! Huge thanks also go out to the wonderful LBYR sales team: Shawn Foster, Danielle Cantarella, Celeste Risko, Anna Herling, Katie Tucker, Claire Gamble, Naomi Kennedy, and Karen Torres.

I am also incredibly grateful to the production team, who went out of their way to configure our schedule so that I could go on maternity leave with a new baby mid-process. Thank you, Marisa Finkelstein, Barbara Bakowski, Virginia Lawther, and Olivia Davis. Thank you also to Lisa Cahn, Janelle DeLuise, and Hannah Koerner, for helping bring this series to life in audio and overseas.

In addition to my publishing team in the United States, I would also like to thank my wonderful UK publishing team, including Anthea Townsend, Phoebe Williams, Ruth Knowles, Sara Jafari,

Jane Griffiths, Kat McKenna, Rowan Ellis, and everyone else at Penguin Random House UK!

Thank you also to Josh Berman, who is developing *The Inheritance Games* for television. Josh, you were one of the first people to read *The Inheritance Games*, and your belief in this project means the world. To the rest of the team hard at work on this project, including Grainne Godfree, Jeffrey Frost, Jennifer Robinson, Alec Durkheimer, and Sam Lion—thank you!

This is my twenty-second book, and I have been incredibly lucky to have had Curtis Brown as my agency home since I was pretty much a kid myself! Thank you, Elizabeth Harding, for fighting for me for all these years. Holly Frederick, thank you not only for finding these books a wonderful Hollywood home but also for your insightful feedback on the early stages of book one. Thank you, Sarah Perillo, for your incredible work advocating for this series all over the globe. And thank you to the rest of my Curtis Brown team, including Nicole Eisenbraun, Sarah Gerton, Michaela Glover, Madeline Tavis, and Jazmia Young.

Writing is a solitary profession; this year, that solitude was taken up a notch. I am grateful for all the writing friends who made this process less lonely along the way. Thank you to Ally Carter, Rachel Vincent, Emily Lockhart, Sarah Mlynowski, and all of BOB for the tremendous amounts of writerly support, and to the fellow authors who have been incredibly supportive of this series, including Katharine McGee, Karen McManus, Kat Ellis, Dahlia Adler, and so many more.

As is probably obvious by this point, the writing and publishing of a book is a true team effort. For this book, written in one of the hardest and most chaotic periods of my life, I am also hugely indebted to my team at home. Thank you to Avery Eshelman and Ruth Davis, for helping take care of my kids while I wrote, and thank you to my family, for EVERYTHING. Anthony, I could not ask for a better partner. Thank you for all you do; I could not do this without you. To my mom and dad, thank you for always being just a phone call away and for all you have done to help us through this difficult time. And to my children, thank you for the snuggles and fun, but also for understanding that sometimes Mommy has to write!

Finally, thank YOU, dear reader! After all these years and twenty-two books, I am still in awe that the stories I write are read by people like you.

Turn the page for a sneak peek at
the thrilling finale to
the Inheritance Games trilogy

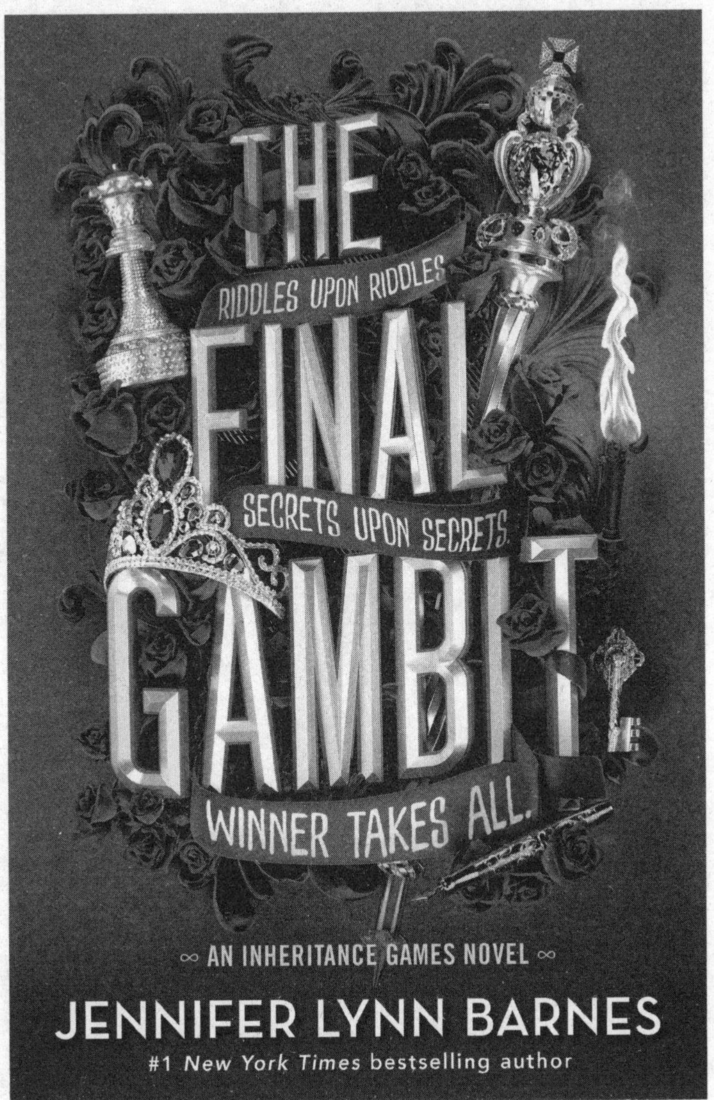

CHAPTER 1

"We need to talk about your eighteenth birthday." Alisa's words echoed through the largest of Hawthorne House's five libraries. Floor-to-ceiling shelves stretched up two stories, encircling us with hardcover and leather-bound tomes, many of them priceless, every single one a reminder of the man who had built this room.

This house.

This dynasty.

I could almost imagine the ghost of Tobias Hawthorne watching me as I knelt and ran my hand over the mahogany floorboards, my fingers searching for irregularities in the seams.

Finding none, I stood and replied to Alisa's statement. "Do we?" I said. "Do we *really*?"

"Legally?" The formidable Alisa Ortega arched an eyebrow at me. "Yes. You may already be emancipated, but when it comes to the terms of your inheritance—"

"Nothing changes when I turn eighteen," I said, scanning the room for my next move. "I won't inherit until I've lived in Hawthorne House for a year."

I knew my lawyer well enough to know *that* was what she really wanted to talk about. My birthday was October eighteenth. I would hit the year mark the first week in November and instantly become the richest teenager on the planet. Until then, I had other things to focus on.

A bet to win. A Hawthorne to best.

"Be that as it may..." Alisa was about as easily deterred as a high-speed train. "As your birthday approaches, there are some things we should discuss."

I snorted. "Forty-six billion of them?"

As Alisa gave me an exasperated look, I concentrated on my mission. Hawthorne House was filled with secret passages. Jameson had bet me that I couldn't find them all. Eyeing the massive tree trunk that served as a desk, I reached for the sheath fixed to the inside of my boot and pulled out my knife to test a natural crack in the desk's surface.

I'd learned the hard way I couldn't afford to go anywhere unarmed.

"Moping check!" Xander "I'm a Living, Breathing Rube Goldberg Machine" Hawthorne poked his head into the library. "Avery, on a scale of one to ten, how much do you need a distraction right now, and how attached are you to your eyebrows?"

Jameson was on the other side of the world. Grayson hadn't called once since he'd left for Harvard. Xander, my self-appointed BHFF—*Best Hawthorne Friend Forever*—considered it his sacred duty to keep my spirits high in his brothers' absence.

"One," I answered. "And ten."

Xander gave a little bow. "Then I bid you adieu." In a flash, he was gone.

Something was definitely exploding in the next ten minutes. Turning back toward Alisa, I drank in the rest of the room: the seemingly endless shelves, the wrought-iron staircases spiraling upward. "Just say what you came here to say, Alisa."

"Yes, Lee-Lee," a deep, honeyed voice drawled from the hall. "Enlighten us." Nash Hawthorne took up position in the doorway, his trademark cowboy hat tipped down.

"Nash." Alisa wore her power suit like armor. "This doesn't concern you."

Nash leaned against the doorframe and lazily crossed his right foot over his left ankle. "Kid tells me to leave, I'll leave." Nash didn't trust Alisa with me. He hadn't for months.

"I'm fine, Nash," I said. "You can go."

"I reckon I can." Nash made no move to push off the doorframe. He was the oldest of the four Hawthorne brothers and used to riding herd on the other three. Over the past year, he'd extended that to me. He and my sister had been "not dating" for months.

"Isn't it not-date night?" I asked. "And doesn't that mean you have somewhere to be?"

Nash removed his cowboy hat and let his steady eyes settle on mine. "Dollars to doughnuts," he said, turning to amble out of the room, "she wants to talk to you about establishing a trust."

I waited until Nash was out of earshot before I turned back to Alisa. "A trust?"

"I merely want you to be aware of your options." Alisa avoided specifics with lawyerly ease. "I'll put together a dossier for you to look over. Now, regarding your birthday, there's also the matter of a party."

"No party," I said immediately. The last thing I wanted was to turn my birthday into a headline-grabbing, hashtag-exploding event.

"Do you have a favorite band? Or singer? We'll need entertainment."

I could feel my eyes narrowing. "No party, Alisa."

"Is there anyone you'd like to see on the guest list?" When Alisa said *anyone*, she wasn't talking about people I knew. She was talking about celebrities, billionaires, socialites, royals....

"No guest list," I said, "because I'm not having a party."

"You really should consider the optics—" Alisa began, and I tuned out. I knew what she was going to say. She'd been saying it for nearly eleven months. *Everyone loves a Cinderella story.*

Well, *this* Cinderella had a bet to win. I studied the wrought-iron staircases. Three spiraled counterclockwise. But the fourth... I walked toward it, then scaled the steps. On the second-story landing, I ran my fingers along the underside of the shelf opposite the stairs. *A release.* I triggered it, and the entire curved shelf arced backward.

Number twelve. I smiled wickedly. *Take that, Jameson Winchester Hawthorne.*

"No party," I called down to Alisa again. And then I disappeared into the wall.

CHAPTER 2

That night, I slid into bed, Egyptian cotton sheets cool and smooth against my skin. As I waited for Jameson's call, my hand drifted toward the nightstand, to a small bronze pin in the shape of a key.

"Pick a hand." Jameson holds out two fists. I tap his right hand, and he uncurls his fingers, presenting me with an empty palm. I try the left—the same. Then he curls my fingers into a fist. I open them, and there, in my palm, sits the pin.

"You solved the keys faster than any of us," Xander reminds me. "It's past time for this!"

"Sorry, kid," Nash drawls. "It's been six months. You're one of us now."

Grayson says nothing, but when I fumble to put the pin on and it drops from my fingers, he catches it before it hits the ground.

That memory wanted to loop into another—*Grayson, me, the wine cellar*—but I wouldn't let it. In the past few months, I'd developed my own methods of distraction. Grabbing my phone, I navigated to a crowd-funding site and did a search for *medical bills* and *rent*. The Hawthorne fortune wasn't mine for another six weeks, but the partners at McNamara, Ortega, and Jones had already seen to it that I had a credit card with virtually no limit.

Keep gift anonymous. I clicked that box again and again. When my phone finally rang, I leaned back and answered. "Hello."

"I need an anagram of the word *naked*." There was a hum of energy to Jameson's voice.

"No, you don't." I rolled over onto my side. "How's Tuscany?"

"The birthplace of the Italian Renaissance? Full of winding roads, hills and valleys, where a morning mist rolls out in the distance, and the forests are littered with leaves so golden red that the entire world feels like it's on fire in the very best way? That Tuscany?"

"Yes," I murmured. "That Tuscany."

"I've seen better."

"Jameson!"

"What do you want to hear about first, Heiress: Siena, Florence, or the vineyards?"

I wanted *all of it*, but there was a reason Jameson was using the standard Hawthorne gap year to travel. "Tell me about the villa." *Did you find anything?*

"Your Tuscan villa was built in the seventeenth century. It's supposedly a farmhouse but looks more like a castle, and it's surrounded by more than a hundred acres of olive orchard. There's a pool, a wood-fired pizza oven, and a massive stone fireplace original to the house."

I could picture it. Vividly—and not just because I had a binder of photos. "And when you checked the fireplace?" I didn't have to ask if he *had* checked the fireplace.

"I found something."

I sat up, my hair falling down my back. "A clue?"

"Probably," Jameson replied. "But to what puzzle?"

My entire body felt electric. "If you don't tell me, I will *end* you, Hawthorne."

"And I," Jameson replied, "would very much enjoy being ended." My traitorous lips threatened a smile. Tasting victory, Jameson gave me my answer. "I found a triangular mirror."

Just like that, my brain was off to the races. Tobias Hawthorne had raised his grandsons on puzzles, riddles, and games. The mirror was probably a clue, but Jameson had been right: There was no telling what game it was meant to be a part of. In any case, it wasn't what he was traveling the world looking for.

"We'll figure out what the disk was." Jameson as good as read my mind. "The world is the board, Heiress. We just have to keep rolling the dice."

Maybe, but this time we weren't following a trail or playing one of the old man's games. We were feeling around in the dark, hoping that there might be answers out there—answers that would tell us why a small coinlike disk engraved with concentric circles was worth a fortune.

Why Tobias Hawthorne's namesake and only son had left that disk for my mother.

Why Toby had snatched it back from me before he'd disappeared, off to play dead again.

Toby and that disk were my last connections to my mother, and they were gone. It hurt to think about that for too long. "I found another entry to the passageways today," I said abruptly.

"Oh, really?" Jameson replied, the verbal equivalent of holding out a hand at the beginning of a waltz. "Which one did you find?"

"Circular library."

On the other end of the phone line, there was a brief but unmistakable silence.

Realization dawned on me. "You didn't know about that one."

Victory was so very sweet. "Would you like me to tell you where it is?" I crooned.

"When I get back," Jameson murmured, "I'll find it myself."

I had no idea when he was coming back, but soon my year at Hawthorne House would be up. I would be free. I could go anywhere, do anything—and *everything*.

"Where are you headed next?" I asked Jameson. If I let myself think too much about *everything*, I would drown in it—in wanting, in longing, in believing we could have it all.

"Santorini," Jameson replied. "But say the word, Heiress, and—"

"Keep going. Keep looking." My voice went hoarse. "Keep telling me everything."

"Everything?" Jameson repeated in a rough, low tone that made me think of what the two of us could be doing if I were there with him.

I rolled over onto my stomach. "The anagram you were looking for? It's *knead*."

CHAPTER 3

Weeks passed in a blur of charity galas and prep school exams, nights talking to Jameson and too much time spent wondering whether Grayson would ever pick up a damn phone.

Focus. Pushing everything from my mind, I took aim. Looking down the barrel of the gun, I breathed in and out and took the shot—then another and another.

The Hawthorne estate had everything, including its own shooting range. I wasn't a gun person. This wasn't my idea of fun. But neither was being defenseless. Forcing my jaw to unclench, I lowered my weapon and took off my ear protection.

Nash surveyed my target. "Nice grouping, kid."

Theoretically, I'd never need a gun—or the knife in my boot. In theory, the Hawthorne estate was impenetrable, and when I went out into the world, I would always have armed security with me. But since being named in Tobias Hawthorne's will, I'd been shot at, nearly blown up, and kidnapped. *Theory* hadn't kept the nightmares away.

Nash teaching me to fight back had. "Your lawyer bring you that trust paperwork yet?" he asked casually.

My lawyer was his ex, and he knew her far too well. "Maybe," I replied, Alisa's explanation ringing in my ears. *Typically, with an heir your age, there would be certain safeguards in place. Since Mr. Hawthorne didn't see fit to erect them, it's an option you should consider yourself.* Per Alisa, if I put the money in a trust, there would be a trustee in charge of safeguarding and growing the fortune on my behalf. Alisa and the partners at McNamara, Ortega, and Jones would, of course, be willing to serve as trustees, with the understanding that I would be denied nothing I requested. *A revocable trust will simply minimize the pressure on you until you're ready to fully take the reins.*

"Remind me again," Nash told me, bending to capture my gaze with his. "What's our rule about fightin' dirty?"

He wasn't nearly as subtle as he thought he was when it came to Alisa Ortega, but I still answered the question. "There's no such thing as fighting dirty," I told Nash, "if you win."

Kim Haynes Photography

JENNIFER LYNN BARNES

is the #1 *New York Times* bestselling author of over twenty novels for young adults, including the Inheritance Games and the Naturals series. She is also a Fulbright Scholar with advanced degrees in psychology, psychiatry, and cognitive science. She received a PhD from Yale University in 2012 and spent many years as a professor of psychology and professional writing. She invites you to follow her on Twitter @jenlynnbarnes and to visit her online at jenniferlynnbarnes.com.

MORE FROM

JENNIFER LYNN BARNES

THE NATURALS

DEBUTANTES

A MYSTERY

THE INHERITANCE GAMES

 LITTLE, BROWN AND COMPANY theNOVL.com

PRAISE FOR

THE INHERITANCE GAMES

A *New York Times*, *USA Today*, and IndieBound Bestseller
A Goodreads Choice Awards Finalist
An Edgar Award Nominee for Best Young Adult Mystery
A *Kirkus Reviews* Best Young Adult Book of the Year
A *Publishers Weekly* Best Book of the Year
A New York Public Library Best Book for Teens
A YALSA Teens' Top Ten Winner
A YALSA Best Fiction for Young Adults Book

"Barnes is a master of puzzles and plot twists. *The Inheritance Games* was the most fun I've had all year." —E. Lockhart, #1 *New York Times* bestselling author of *We Were Liars* and *Again Again*

"A thrilling blend of family secrets, illicit romance, and a high-stakes treasure hunt, set in the mysterious world of Texas billionaires. The nonstop twists kept me guessing until the very last page!" —Katharine McGee, *New York Times* bestselling author of *American Royals*

"Impossible to put down." —Buzzfeed

★ "Part *The Westing Game*, part *We Were Liars*, completely entertaining." —*Kirkus Reviews*, starred review

★ "This strong, *Knives Out*–esque series opener…provides ample enjoyment." —*Publishers Weekly*, starred review

"Perfect for any reader seeking suspense, romance, and glamour.… Fun and fast-paced, fans of Karen M. McManus's *One of Us Is Lying* and Maureen Johnson's *Truly Devious* will find a new home at Hawthorne House." —*SLJ*

"[A] well-characterized mystery that's packed to the brim with twists and tricks." —*Booklist*

ALSO BY JENNIFER LYNN BARNES

THE INHERITANCE GAMES

The Inheritance Games

The Hawthorne Legacy

The Final Gambit

The Brothers Hawthorne

THE NATURALS

The Naturals

Killer Instinct

All In

Bad Blood

Twelve: A Novella

THE DEBUTANTES

Little White Lies

Deadly Little Scandals

The Lovely and the Lost

THE FINAL GAMBIT

∞ AN INHERITANCE GAMES NOVEL ∞

#1 *New York Times* bestselling author

JENNIFER LYNN BARNES

Little, Brown and Company
New York Boston

Little, Brown and Company
Hachette Book Group
1290 Avenue of the Americas, New York, NY 10104
Visit us at LBYR.com

Originally published in hardcover and ebook by Little, Brown and Company in August 2022
First Trade Paperback Edition: July 2023

Little, Brown and Company is a division of Hachette Book Group, Inc.
The Little, Brown name and logo are trademarks of Hachette Book Group, Inc.

The publisher is not responsible for websites (or their content) that are not owned by the publisher.

Little, Brown and Company books may be purchased in bulk for business, educational, or promotional use. For information, please contact your local bookseller or the Hachette Book Group Special Markets Department at special.markets@hbgusa.com.

The Library of Congress has cataloged the hardcover edition as follows:
Names: Barnes, Jennifer (Jennifer Lynn), author.
Title: The final gambit / Jennifer Lynn Barnes.
Description: New York ; Boston : Little, Brown and Company, 2022. |
Series: An inheritance games novel | Audience: Ages 12+. |
Summary: "Eighteen-year-old Avery Grambs is weeks away from inheriting the multibillion-dollar Hawthorne fortune, but first she'll have to survive a dangerous game against an old enemy looking for vengeance."—Provided by publisher.
Identifiers: LCCN 2022017764 | ISBN 9780316370950 (hardcover) |
ISBN 9780316371124 (ebook) | ISBN 9780316466301 (int'l) | ISBN 9780316485050 (Walmart exclusive edition) | ISBN 9780316451338 (B&N exclusive edition)
Subjects: CYAC: Inheritance and succession—Fiction. | Wealth—Fiction. | Puzzles—Fiction. | Secrets—Fiction. | Families—Fiction. | LCGFT: Novels.
Classification: LCC PZ7.B26225 Fin 2022 | DDC [Fic]—dc23
LC record available at https://lccn.loc.gov/2022017764

ISBNs: 978-0-316-37102-5 (pbk.), 978-0-316-37112-4 (ebook)

Printed in the United States of America

LSC-H

Printing 1, 2023

For William

CHAPTER 1

"We need to talk about your eighteenth birthday." Alisa's words echoed through the largest of Hawthorne House's five libraries. Floor-to-ceiling shelves stretched up two stories, encircling us with hardcover and leather-bound tomes, many of them priceless, every single one a reminder of the man who had built this room.

This house.

This dynasty.

I could almost imagine the ghost of Tobias Hawthorne watching me as I knelt and ran my hand over the mahogany floorboards, my fingers searching for irregularities in the seams.

Finding none, I stood and replied to Alisa's statement. "Do we?" I said. "Do we *really*?"

"Legally?" The formidable Alisa Ortega arched an eyebrow at me. "Yes. You may already be emancipated, but when it comes to the terms of your inheritance—"

"Nothing changes when I turn eighteen," I said, scanning the room for my next move. "I won't inherit until I've lived in Hawthorne House for a year."

I knew my lawyer well enough to know *that* was what she really wanted to talk about. My birthday was October eighteenth. I would hit the year mark the first week in November and instantly become the richest teenager on the planet. Until then, I had other things to focus on.

A bet to win. A Hawthorne to best.

"Be that as it may..." Alisa was about as easily deterred as a high-speed train. "As your birthday approaches, there are some things we should discuss."

I snorted. "Forty-six billion of them?"

As Alisa gave me an exasperated look, I concentrated on my mission. Hawthorne House was filled with secret passages. Jameson had bet me that I couldn't find them all. Eyeing the massive tree trunk that served as a desk, I reached for the sheath fixed to the inside of my boot and pulled out my knife to test a natural crack in the desk's surface.

I'd learned the hard way I couldn't afford to go anywhere unarmed.

"Moping check!" Xander "I'm a Living, Breathing Rube Goldberg Machine" Hawthorne poked his head into the library. "Avery, on a scale of one to ten, how much do you need a distraction right now, and how attached are you to your eyebrows?"

Jameson was on the other side of the world. Grayson hadn't called once since he'd left for Harvard. Xander, my self-appointed BHFF—*Best Hawthorne Friend Forever*—considered it his sacred duty to keep my spirits high in his brothers' absence.

"One," I answered. "And ten."

Xander gave a little bow. "Then I bid you adieu." In a flash, he was gone.

Something was definitely exploding in the next ten minutes. Turning back toward Alisa, I drank in the rest of the room: the seemingly endless shelves, the wrought-iron staircases spiraling upward. "Just say what you came here to say, Alisa."

"Yes, Lee-Lee," a deep, honeyed voice drawled from the hall. "Enlighten us." Nash Hawthorne took up position in the doorway, his trademark cowboy hat tipped down.

"Nash." Alisa wore her power suit like armor. "This doesn't concern you."

Nash leaned against the doorframe and lazily crossed his right foot over his left ankle. "Kid tells me to leave, I'll leave." Nash didn't trust Alisa with me. He hadn't for months.

"I'm fine, Nash," I said. "You can go."

"I reckon I can." Nash made no move to push off the doorframe. He was the oldest of the four Hawthorne brothers and used to riding herd on the other three. Over the past year, he'd extended that to me. He and my sister had been "not dating" for months.

"Isn't it not-date night?" I asked. "And doesn't that mean you have somewhere to be?"

Nash removed his cowboy hat and let his steady eyes settle on mine. "Dollars to doughnuts," he said, turning to amble out of the room, "she wants to talk to you about establishing a trust."

I waited until Nash was out of earshot before I turned back to Alisa. "A trust?"

"I merely want you to be aware of your options." Alisa avoided specifics with lawyerly ease. "I'll put together a dossier for you to look over. Now, regarding your birthday, there's also the matter of a party."

"No party," I said immediately. The last thing I wanted was to turn my birthday into a headline-grabbing, hashtag-exploding event.

"Do you have a favorite band? Or singer? We'll need entertainment."

I could feel my eyes narrowing. "No party, Alisa."

"Is there anyone you'd like to see on the guest list?" When Alisa said *anyone*, she wasn't talking about people I knew. She was talking about celebrities, billionaires, socialites, royals. . . .

"No guest list," I said, "because I'm not having a party."

"You really should consider the optics—" Alisa began, and I tuned out. I knew what she was going to say. She'd been saying it for nearly eleven months. *Everyone loves a Cinderella story.*

Well, *this* Cinderella had a bet to win. I studied the wrought-iron staircases. Three spiraled counterclockwise. But the fourth . . . I walked toward it, then scaled the steps. On the second-story landing, I ran my fingers along the underside of the shelf opposite the stairs. *A release.* I triggered it, and the entire curved shelf arced backward.

Number twelve. I smiled wickedly. *Take that, Jameson Winchester Hawthorne.*

"No party," I called down to Alisa again. And then I disappeared into the wall.

CHAPTER 2

That night, I slid into bed, Egyptian cotton sheets cool and smooth against my skin. As I waited for Jameson's call, my hand drifted toward the nightstand, to a small bronze pin in the shape of a key.

"Pick a hand." Jameson holds out two fists. I tap his right hand, and he uncurls his fingers, presenting me with an empty palm. I try the left—the same. Then he curls my fingers into a fist. I open them, and there, in my palm, sits the pin.

"You solved the keys faster than any of us," Xander reminds me. "It's past time for this!"

"Sorry, kid," Nash drawls. "It's been six months. You're one of us now."

Grayson says nothing, but when I fumble to put the pin on and it drops from my fingers, he catches it before it hits the ground.

That memory wanted to loop into another—*Grayson, me, the wine cellar*—but I wouldn't let it. In the past few months, I'd developed my own methods of distraction. Grabbing my phone, I navigated to a crowd-funding site and did a search for *medical bills* and *rent.* The Hawthorne fortune wasn't mine for another six weeks, but the partners at McNamara, Ortega, and Jones had already seen to it that I had a credit card with virtually no limit.

Keep gift anonymous. I clicked that box again and again. When my phone finally rang, I leaned back and answered. "Hello."

"I need an anagram of the word *naked*." There was a hum of energy to Jameson's voice.

"No, you don't." I rolled over onto my side. "How's Tuscany?"

"The birthplace of the Italian Renaissance? Full of winding roads, hills and valleys, where a morning mist rolls out in the distance, and the forests are littered with leaves so golden red that the entire world feels like it's on fire in the very best way? That Tuscany?"

"Yes," I murmured. "That Tuscany."

"I've seen better."

"Jameson!"

"What do you want to hear about first, Heiress: Siena, Florence, or the vineyards?"

I wanted *all of it*, but there was a reason Jameson was using the standard Hawthorne gap year to travel. "Tell me about the villa." *Did you find anything?*

"Your Tuscan villa was built in the seventeenth century. It's supposedly a farmhouse but looks more like a castle, and it's surrounded by more than a hundred acres of olive orchard. There's a pool, a wood-fired pizza oven, and a massive stone fireplace original to the house."

I could picture it. Vividly—and not just because I had a binder of photos. "And when you checked the fireplace?" I didn't have to ask if he *had* checked the fireplace.

"I found something."

I sat up, my hair falling down my back. "A clue?"

"Probably," Jameson replied. "But to what puzzle?"

My entire body felt electric. "If you don't tell me, I will *end* you, Hawthorne."

"And I," Jameson replied, "would very much enjoy being ended." My traitorous lips threatened a smile. Tasting victory, Jameson gave me my answer. "I found a triangular mirror."

Just like that, my brain was off to the races. Tobias Hawthorne had raised his grandsons on puzzles, riddles, and games. The mirror was probably a clue, but Jameson had been right: There was no telling what game it was meant to be a part of. In any case, it wasn't what he was traveling the world looking for.

"We'll figure out what the disk was." Jameson as good as read my mind. "The world is the board, Heiress. We just have to keep rolling the dice."

Maybe, but this time we weren't following a trail or playing one of the old man's games. We were feeling around in the dark, hoping that there might be answers out there—answers that would tell us why a small coinlike disk engraved with concentric circles was worth a fortune.

Why Tobias Hawthorne's namesake and only son had left that disk for my mother.

Why Toby had snatched it back from me before he'd disappeared, off to play dead again.

Toby and that disk were my last connections to my mother, and they were gone. It hurt to think about that for too long. "I found another entry to the passageways today," I said abruptly.

"Oh, really?" Jameson replied, the verbal equivalent of holding out a hand at the beginning of a waltz. "Which one did you find?"

"Circular library."

On the other end of the phone line, there was a brief but unmistakable silence.

Realization dawned on me. "You didn't know about that one."

Victory was so very sweet. "Would you like me to tell you where it is?" I crooned.

"When I get back," Jameson murmured, "I'll find it myself."

I had no idea when he was coming back, but soon my year at Hawthorne House would be up. I would be free. I could go anywhere, do anything—and *everything.*

"Where are you headed next?" I asked Jameson. If I let myself think too much about *everything*, I would drown in it—in wanting, in longing, in believing we could have it all.

"Santorini," Jameson replied. "But say the word, Heiress, and—"

"Keep going. Keep looking." My voice went hoarse. "Keep telling me everything."

"Everything?" Jameson repeated in a rough, low tone that made me think of what the two of us could be doing if I were there with him.

I rolled over onto my stomach. "The anagram you were looking for? It's *knead.*"

CHAPTER 3

Weeks passed in a blur of charity galas and prep school exams, nights talking to Jameson and too much time spent wondering whether Grayson would ever pick up a damn phone.

Focus. Pushing everything from my mind, I took aim. Looking down the barrel of the gun, I breathed in and out and took the shot—then another and another.

The Hawthorne estate had everything, including its own shooting range. I wasn't a gun person. This wasn't my idea of fun. But neither was being defenseless. Forcing my jaw to unclench, I lowered my weapon and took off my ear protection.

Nash surveyed my target. "Nice grouping, kid."

Theoretically, I'd never need a gun—or the knife in my boot. In theory, the Hawthorne estate was impenetrable, and when I went out into the world, I would always have armed security with me. But since being named in Tobias Hawthorne's will, I'd been shot at, nearly blown up, and kidnapped. *Theory* hadn't kept the nightmares away.

Nash teaching me to fight back had. "Your lawyer bring you that trust paperwork yet?" he asked casually.

My lawyer was his ex, and he knew her far too well. "Maybe," I replied, Alisa's explanation ringing in my ears. *Typically, with an heir your age, there would be certain safeguards in place. Since Mr. Hawthorne didn't see fit to erect them, it's an option you should consider yourself.* Per Alisa, if I put the money in a trust, there would be a trustee in charge of safeguarding and growing the fortune on my behalf. Alisa and the partners at McNamara, Ortega, and Jones would, of course, be willing to serve as trustees, with the understanding that I would be denied nothing I requested. *A revocable trust will simply minimize the pressure on you until you're ready to fully take the reins.*

"Remind me again," Nash told me, bending to capture my gaze with his. "What's our rule about fightin' dirty?"

He wasn't nearly as subtle as he thought he was when it came to Alisa Ortega, but I still answered the question. "There's no such thing as fighting dirty," I told Nash, "if you win."

CHAPTER 4

The morning of my eighteenth birthday—and the first day of fall break at the vaunted Heights Country Day School—I woke up to see an unspeakably gorgeous ball gown hanging in my doorway. It was a deep midnight green, floor-length, with a bodice marked by tens of thousands of tiny black jewels in a dark, delicate, mesmerizing pattern.

It was a stop-and-stare dress. A gasp-and-stare-again dress.

The kind one would wear to a headline-grabbing, hashtag-exploding black-tie event. *Damn it, Alisa.* I stalked toward the gown, feeling mutinous—then saw the note dangling from the hanger: *WEAR ME IF YOU DARE.*

That wasn't Alisa's handwriting.

I found Jameson at the edge of the Black Wood. He was wearing a white tuxedo that fit his body far too well and standing next to an honest-to-God hot-air balloon.

Jameson Winchester Hawthorne. I ran like the ball gown wasn't weighing me down, like I didn't have a knife strapped to my thigh.

Jameson caught me, our bodies colliding. "Happy birthday, Heiress."

Some kisses were soft and gentle—and some were like fire.

Eventually, the realization that we had an audience managed to penetrate my brain. Oren was discreet. He wasn't looking *at* us, but my head of security clearly wasn't about to let Jameson Hawthorne fly off with me alone.

Reluctantly, I pulled back. "A hot-air balloon?" I asked Jameson dryly. "Really?"

"I should warn you, Heiress..." Jameson swung himself up onto the edge of the basket, landing in a crouch. "I am dangerously good at birthdays."

Jameson Hawthorne was dangerously good at a lot of things.

He held his hand down to me. I took it, and I didn't even try to pretend that I had grown used to this—all of it, any of it, *him*. In a million years, the life Tobias Hawthorne had left me would still take my breath away.

Oren climbed into the balloon after me and fixed his gaze on the horizon. Jameson cast off the ropes and hit the flame.

We surged upward.

Airborne, with my heart in my throat, I stared down at Hawthorne House. "How do you steer?" I asked Jameson as everything but the two of us and my very discreet bodyguard got smaller and farther away.

"You don't." Jameson's arms curved around my torso. "Sometimes, Heiress, all you can do is recognize which way the wind is blowing and plot a course."

The balloon was just the beginning. Jameson Hawthorne didn't do anything halfway.

A hidden picnic.

A helicopter ride to the Gulf.

Speeding away from the paparazzi.

Slow dancing, barefoot, on the beach.

The ocean. A cliff. A wager. A race. A dare. *I'm going to remember this.* That was my overwhelming feeling on the helicopter ride home. *I'm going to remember it all.* Years from now, I'd still be able to *feel* it. The weight of the ball gown, the wind in my face. Sun-warmed sand on my skin and chocolate-covered strawberries melting on my tongue.

By sundown, we were almost home. It had been the perfect day. No crowds. No celebrities. No..."Party," I said as the helicopter approached the Hawthorne estate, and I took in the view below. The topiary garden and adjacent lawn were lit by thousands of tiny lights—and that wasn't even the worst of it.

"That had better not be a dance floor," I told Jameson darkly.

Jameson took the helicopter in for a landing, threw his head back, and smiled. "You're not going to comment on the Ferris wheel?"

No wonder he'd needed to get me out of the House. "You're a dead man, Hawthorne."

Jameson cut the engine. "Fortunately, Heiress, Hawthorne men have nine lives."

As we disembarked and walked toward the topiary garden, I glanced at Oren and narrowed my eyes. "You knew about this," I accused.

"I may have been presented with a guest list to vet for entrance onto the estate." My head of security's expression was absolutely unreadable...until the party came into full view. Then he *almost* smiled. "I also may have vetoed a few names on that list."

And by *a few*, I realized a moment later, he meant almost all of them.

The dance floor was scattered with rose petals and lit by strings of delicate lights that crisscrossed overhead, softly glowing like fireflies in the night. A string quartet played to the left of the kind of cake I would have expected to see at a royal wedding. The Ferris wheel turned in the distance. Tuxedo-clad waiters carried trays of champagne and hors d'oeuvres.

But there were no guests.

"Do you like?" Libby appeared beside me. She was dressed like something out of a goth fairy tale and grinning from ear to ear. "I wanted black rose petals, but this is nice, too."

"What *is* this?" I breathed.

My sister bumped her shoulder into mine. "We're calling it the introvert's ball."

"There's no one here." I could feel my own smile building.

"Not true," Libby replied cheerfully. "I'm here. Nash turned his nose up at the fancy food and put himself in charge of the grill. Mr. Laughlin's running the Ferris wheel, under Mrs. Laughlin's supervision. Thea and Rebecca are stealing a *super*-stolen moment back behind the ice sculptures. Xander's keeping an eye on your surprise, and here's Zara and Nan!"

I turned just in time to be poked with a cane. Jameson's great-grandmother glowered at me while his aunt looked on, austerely amused.

"You, girl," Nan said, which was basically her version of my name. "The neckline on that dress makes you look like a floozy." She wagged her cane at me, then grunted. "I approve."

"So do I," a voice piped up from my left. "Happy faxing birthday, you beautiful beach."

"Max?" I stared at my best friend, then glanced back at Libby.

"Surprise!"

Beside me, Jameson smirked. "Alisa may have been under the impression that there was going to be a much larger party."

But there wasn't. It was just...*us*.

Max threw an arm around me. "Ask me how college is!"

"How's college?" I asked, still absolutely floored.

Max grinned. "Not nearly as entertaining as Ferris Wheel Leapfrog Death Match."

"Ferris Wheel Leapfrog Death Match?" I repeated. That had Xander written all over it. I knew for a fact the two of them had stayed in touch.

"Who's winning?" Jameson cocked his head to one side.

Max replied, but before I could process what she was saying, I saw movement out of the corner of my eye—or maybe I sensed it. Sensed *him.* Clad entirely in black, wearing a ten-thousand-dollar tuxedo the way other guys wore ratty sweatshirts, Grayson Hawthorne stepped onto the dance floor.

He came home. That thought was accompanied by a memory of the last time I'd seen him: *Grayson, broken. Me, beside him.* Back in the present, Grayson Hawthorne let his eyes linger on mine for just a moment, then swept them over the rest of the party. "Ferris Wheel Leapfrog Death Match," he said calmly. "This never ends well."

CHAPTER 5

The next morning, I woke to the sight of my ball gown strewn over the end of my bed. Jameson was asleep beside me. I pushed back the urge to trail my fingertips across his jawline, to lightly touch the scar that ran down his chest.

I'd asked him a dozen times how he'd gotten that scar, and he'd given me a dozen different answers. In some versions, the culprit was a jagged rock. A steel rod. A windshield.

Someday, I'd get the real answer.

I allowed myself one more moment beside Jameson, then slipped from my bed, picked up my Hawthorne pin, got dressed, and headed downstairs.

Grayson was in the dining room, alone.

"I didn't think you would make it home," I said, somehow managing to take the seat opposite his.

"Technically, it isn't *my* home anymore." Even at low volume, Grayson's voice washed over the room like a tide coming in. "In a very short time, everything in this place will officially be yours." That wasn't a condemnation or a complaint. It was a fact.

"That doesn't mean anything has to change," I said.

"Avery." Piercing pale eyes met mine. "It has to. *You* have to." Before I'd come along, Grayson had been the heir apparent. He was practically an expert in what one *had* to do.

And I was the only one who knew: Beneath that invincible, controlled exterior, he was falling apart. I couldn't say that, couldn't let on I was even thinking it, so I stuck to the topic at hand. "What if I can't do this on my own?" I asked.

"You aren't on your own." Grayson let his eyes linger on mine, then carefully and deliberately broke eye contact. "Every year, on our birthdays," he said, after a moment, "the old man would call us into his study."

I'd heard this before. "*Invest. Cultivate. Create,*" I said. From the time they were kids, each year on their birthdays, the Hawthorne brothers had been given ten thousand dollars to invest. They'd also been told to choose a talent or an interest to cultivate, and no expense had been spared in that cultivation. Finally, Tobias Hawthorne had issued a birthday challenge: something they were to invent, create, perform, or will into being.

"*Invest*—you'll soon have covered. *Cultivate*—you should pick something you want for yourself. Not an item or an experience but a skill." I waited for Grayson to ask me what I was going to choose, but he didn't. Instead, he removed a leather book from the inside of his suit jacket and slid it across the table. "As for your birthday challenge, you'll need to create a plan."

The leather was a deep, rich brown, soft to the touch. The edges of the pages were slightly uneven, as though the book had been bound by hand.

"You'll want to start with a firm grasp of your financials. From there, think about the future and map out your time and financial commitments for the next five years."

I opened the book. The thick off-white pages were blank.

"Write it all down," Grayson instructed. "Then tear it apart and rewrite it. Over and over again until you have a plan that works."

"You know what you would do in my position." I would have bet my entire fortune that somewhere, he had a journal—and a plan—of his own.

Grayson's eyes found their way back to mine. "You aren't me."

I wondered if there was anyone at Harvard—a single person—who knew him even a tenth as well as his brothers and I did. "You promised you would help me." The words escaped before I could stop them. "You said you would teach me everything I needed to know."

I knew better than to remind Grayson Hawthorne of a broken promise. I didn't have the right to ask this of him, to ask anything of him. I was with Jameson. I *loved* Jameson. And, Grayson's entire life, everyone had expected too damn much.

"I'm sorry," I said. "This isn't your problem."

"Don't," Grayson ordered roughly, "look at me like I'm broken."

You are not broken. I'd said those words to him. He hadn't believed me then. He wouldn't now, either. "Alisa wants me to put the money in a trust," I said, because the least I owed him was a subject change.

Grayson responded with an arch of his brow. "Of course she does."

"I haven't agreed to anything yet."

A slight smile pulled at the edges of his lips. "Of course you haven't."

Oren appeared in the doorway before I could reply. "I just got a call from one of my men," he told me. "There's someone at the gates."

A warning sounded in my mind because Oren was perfectly capable of taking care of unwanted visitors himself. *Skye? Or*

Ricky? Grayson's mother and my deadbeat of a father were no longer in prison for an attempt on my life that, remarkably, they *hadn't* orchestrated. That didn't mean they weren't still threats.

"Who is it?" Grayson's expression went blade-sharp.

Oren held my gaze as he answered the question. "She says her name is Eve."

CHAPTER 6

For months, I'd kept the existence of Toby's daughter a secret from everyone but Jameson. Because Toby had asked me to—but not *just* because Toby had asked me to.

"I need to take care of this," I said with a calm that I in no way felt.

"I assume my assistance is not required?" Grayson's tone was cool, but I knew him. I knew he would take my declining help as evidence that I was treating him with kid gloves.

Hawthornes aren't supposed to break, his voice whispered in my memory. *Especially me.*

I didn't have the luxury right now of trying to convince Grayson Hawthorne that he wasn't *weak* or *broken* or *damaged* to me. "I appreciate the offer," I told him, "but I'll be fine."

The last thing Grayson needed was to see the girl at the gates.

As Oren drove me out there, my mind raced. *What is she doing here? What does she want?* I tried to prepare myself, but the moment I saw Toby's daughter outside the gates, a wall of emotion crashed into me. Her amber hair blew in a gentle breeze. Even from behind, even wearing a threadbare white dress smudged with stains, this girl was luminescent.

She's not supposed to be here. Toby had been clear: He couldn't save me from the legacy Tobias Hawthorne had left behind, but he *could* save Eve. From the press. From the threats. *From the poisoned tree,* I thought, stepping out of the SUV.

Eve turned. She moved like a dancer, with equal parts grace and abandon, and the moment her eyes met mine, I stopped breathing.

I'd known that Eve was a dead ringer for Emily Laughlin.

I'd known that.

But seeing her was like looking up to see a tsunami bearing down. She had Emily's strawberry-blond hair, Emily's emerald eyes. The same heart-shaped face, the same lips and delicate dusting of freckles.

Seeing her would kill Grayson. It might hurt Jameson, but it would *kill* Grayson.

I have to get her out of here. That thought pounded through my head, but as I reached the gates, my instincts sent up another warning. I scanned the road.

"Let her in," I told Oren. I didn't see any paparazzi, but experience had taught me the dangers of telescopic lenses, and the last thing Jameson or Grayson needed was to see this girl's face plastered all over every gossip site on the internet.

The gates opened. Eve took a step toward me. "You're Avery." She took a jagged breath. "I'm—"

"I know who you are." The words came out harsher than I'd meant them to—and that was the exact moment I saw blood crusted on her temple. "Oh, hell." I stepped closer. "Are you okay?"

"I'm fine." Eve's fingers wound tightly around the strap of her beat-up messenger bag. "Toby isn't."

No. My mind rebelled. My mom had loved Toby. He'd watched out for me once she was gone. *He has to be okay.* A breath trapped in my chest, I let Oren escort the two of us behind the SUV—away from prying eyes and ears.

"What happened to Toby?" I demanded urgently.

Eve pressed her lips together. "He told me that if anything happened to him, I should come to you. And, look, I'm not naive, okay? I know you probably don't want me here." She said those words like a person used to not being wanted. "But I didn't have anywhere else to go."

When I'd found out about Eve, I'd offered to bring her to Hawthorne House. Toby had vetoed that idea. He hadn't wanted anyone to know about her. *So why would he send her to me?* Every muscle in my jaw and stomach tight, I forced myself to concentrate on the only thing that mattered.

"What happened to Toby?" I said again, my voice low and guttural.

The wind caught Eve's hair. Her pink lips parted. "They took him."

Air whooshed out of my lungs, my ears ringing, my sense of gravity distorted. "Who?" I demanded. "Who took him?"

"I don't know." Eve's arms curved protectively around her torso. "Toby found me months ago. He told me who he was. Who *I* was. We were doing fine, just the two of us, but then last week something happened. Toby saw someone."

"Who?" I asked again, the word torn out of me.

"I don't know. Toby wouldn't tell me. He just said that he had to leave."

Toby does that, I thought, my eyes stinging. *He leaves.* "You said someone took him."

"I'm getting to that," Eve said tersely. "Toby didn't want to take me with him, but I didn't give him a choice. I told him that if he tried to leave me behind, I would go to the press."

Despite a leaked photograph and some tabloid rumors, no media outlet had yet been able to substantiate claims that Toby was alive. "You blackmailed him into taking you with him?"

"If you were me," Eve replied, something almost beseeching in her tone, "you would have done the same." She looked down, impossibly long lashes casting shadows on her face. "Toby and I went off the grid, but someone was tracking us, stalking us like prey. Toby wouldn't tell me who we were running from, but on Monday, he said that we had to split up. The plan was for us to meet back up three days later. I waited. I stayed off the grid, just like he'd taught me. Yesterday, I showed up at our meeting place." She shook her head, her green eyes glistening. "Toby didn't."

"Maybe he had second thoughts," I said, wanting that to be true. "Maybe—"

"No," Eve insisted desperately. "Toby never lied to me. He never broke a promise. He wouldn't—" She cut herself off. "Someone took him. You don't believe me? I can prove it."

Eve pulled her hair away from her face. The dried blood I'd seen was just the tip of the iceberg. The skin around the cut was mottled, a sickening mix of black and blue.

"Someone hit you." Until Oren spoke, I'd almost forgotten he was there. "With the butt of a gun, I'm guessing."

Eve didn't even look at him. Her bright green eyes stayed locked on mine. "Toby didn't show up at our meeting place, but someone else did." She let her hair fall back over the bruise. "They grabbed me from behind and told me that if I knew what was good for me, I would forget all about Toby Hawthorne."

"They used his real name?" I managed to form the question.

Eve nodded. "That's the last thing I remember. They knocked me out. I woke up to find they'd stolen everything I had on me. They even went through my pockets." Her voice shook slightly, and then she steeled herself. "Toby and I had stashed a bag for emergencies: a change of clothes for each of us, a little cash." I wondered if she realized how tightly she was holding that bag now. "I bought a bus ticket, and I came here. To you."

You have a daughter, I'd told Toby when we found out about Eve, and he'd replied, *I have two.* Swallowing back the twisted bramble of emotions inside me, I turned to Oren. "We should call the authorities."

"No." Eve caught my arm. "You can't report a dead man missing, and Toby didn't tell me to go to the police. He told me to come to *you*."

My throat tightened. "Someone attacked you. We can report that."

"And who," Eve bit out, "is going to believe a girl like me?"

I'd grown up poor. I'd been *that girl*—the one nobody expected much from, the one who was treated as less than because I had less.

"Bringing the authorities in could tie our hands," Oren told me. "We should prepare for a ransom demand. In the event that we get no such demand..."

I didn't even want to think about what it meant if the person who'd taken Toby wasn't after money. "If Eve tells you where she was supposed to meet Toby, can you send a team to do recon?" I asked Oren.

"Consider it done," he said—then his gaze shifted abruptly to something or someone behind me. I heard a sound from that direction, a strangled, almost inhuman sound, and I knew, even before I turned around, what I would see there. *Who* I would see there.

"Emily?" Grayson Hawthorne was staring at a ghost.

CHAPTER 7

Grayson Davenport Hawthorne was a person who valued control—of every situation, of every emotion. When I took a step toward him, he stepped back.

"Grayson," I said softly.

There were no words for the way he was staring at Eve—like she was a dream, every hope and every torment, *everything.*

Silvery gray eyes closed. "Avery. You should…" Grayson forced a breath in, out. He straightened and squared his shoulders. "I'm not safe to be around right now, Avery."

It took me a moment to realize that he thought he was hallucinating. *Again.* Breaking down. *Again.*

Tell me again that I'm not broken.

Closing the space between us, I took Grayson by the shoulders. "Hey," I said softly. "*Hey.* Look at me, Gray."

Those light eyes opened.

"That's not Emily." I held his gaze and wouldn't let him look away. "And you aren't hallucinating."

Grayson's eyes flickered over my shoulder. "I see—"

"I know," I said, bringing my hand to the side of his face and forcing his eyes back to mine. "She's real. Her name is Eve." I couldn't be sure he was hearing me, let alone processing what I was saying. "She's Toby's daughter."

"She looks…"

"I know," I said, my hand still on his jaw. "Emily's mom was Toby's biological mother, remember?" Newborn Toby had been adopted into the Hawthorne family in secret. Alice Hawthorne had faked a pregnancy to hide the adoption, passing him off as her own. "That makes Eve a Laughlin by blood," I continued. "There's a family resemblance."

"I thought—" Grayson cut off the words. A Hawthorne did not admit weakness. "You knew." Grayson looked down at me, and I finally let my hand fall away from his face. "You aren't surprised to see her, Avery. You knew."

I heard what he wasn't saying: *That night in the wine cellar—I knew.*

"Toby wanted her existence kept secret," I said, telling myself *that* was why I hadn't told him. "He didn't want this life for Eve."

"Who else knows?" Grayson demanded in that heir-apparent tone, the one that made questions sound perfunctory, like he was doing the person he was questioning a courtesy by asking instead of wresting the answer from their mind himself.

"Just Jameson," I replied.

After a long, torturous moment, Grayson looked past me to Eve, emotion etched in every muscle of his jaw. I wasn't sure how much of his torment was because he thought I considered him weak and how much of it was her. Either way, Grayson didn't hide from his pain this time. He walked toward Eve, letting it come, like a shirtless man stepping out into freezing rain.

Eve stared at him. She must have felt the intensity of the moment—*of him*—but she shook it off. "Look, I don't know what *this* is." She gestured in the vicinity of Grayson's face. "But it has been a really long week. I'm filthy. I'm scared." Her voice broke, and she turned to me. "So are you going to invite me inside and let your security goons figure out what happened to Toby, or are we just going to stand here?"

Grayson blinked, like he was seeing her—*Eve*—for the first time. "You're hurt."

She looked at him again. "I'm pissed."

I swallowed. Eve was right. Every second we spent out here was a second that Oren and his team were focused on safeguarding me instead of finding Toby.

"Come on," I said, the words like rocks in my throat. "Let's go back to the House."

Oren opened the back passenger door of the SUV. Eve climbed in, and as I followed, I wondered if this was what Pandora had felt like the moment she opened the box.

CHAPTER 8

I let Eve use my shower. Given the number of bathrooms in Hawthorne House, I recognized that decision for what it was: I wanted her where I could keep an eye on her.

I neglected to consider the fact that Jameson was still in my bed. Eve didn't seem to notice him on her way to my en suite, but Grayson did—and Jameson definitely noticed Eve. The moment the bathroom door closed behind her, he swung his feet over the side of the bed.

Shirtless. "Tell me everything, Heiress."

I searched his expression for some hint of what he was feeling, but Jameson Hawthorne was the consummate poker player. Seeing Eve had to have provoked some kind of emotion in him. The fact that he was hiding it hit me every bit as hard as the way that Grayson couldn't tear his eyes from the bathroom door.

"I don't know where to start," I said. I couldn't make myself say the words *It's Toby.*

Jameson crossed to me, his strides long. "Tell me what you need, Heiress."

Grayson finally pried his gaze away from the bathroom door. He bent, snatched an undershirt off the floor, and tossed it at his brother's face. "Put on a shirt."

Somehow, the comically disgruntled look that Jameson shot Grayson was *exactly* what I needed. I told the two of them everything that Eve had told me. "Eve wasn't able to give Oren a lot of details," I finished. "He's putting together a team to run recon on the abduction site, but—"

"They're unlikely to find much at this point," Grayson finished.

"Convenient, that," Jameson commented. "What?" he said when Grayson's icy eyes narrowed. "I'm just saying that all we have right now is the story of a stranger who showed up on our doorstep and talked her way inside."

He was right. We didn't know Eve.

"You don't believe her?" Grayson wasn't normally the type to ask questions when the answers were already apparent, so this one came with an undercurrent of friction.

"What can I say?" Jameson shrugged again. "I'm a suspicious bastard."

And Eve looks just like Emily, I thought. Jameson wasn't unaffected by that. Not by a long shot.

"I don't think she's lying," I said. *That wound.*

"You wouldn't," Jameson told me softly. "And neither," he told Grayson in a very different tone, "would you."

That was clearly a reference to Emily. She'd played them both, manipulated them both, but Grayson had loved her to the end.

"You knew." Grayson stalked toward Jameson. "You knew she was out there, Jamie. You knew that Toby had a daughter, and you didn't say a word."

"Are you really going to lecture *me* about secrets, Gray?"

What's he talking about? I'd never said a word to Jameson about the things that his brother had admitted to me in the dark of night.

"At a minimum," Grayson enunciated, his voice soft and deadly, "we owe that girl our protection."

"Because of the way she looks?" Jameson threw down the gauntlet.

"Because she's Toby's daughter," Grayson replied, "and that makes her one of us."

My fingers went to my pin. *Eve's a Hawthorne.* That shouldn't have hurt. It wasn't news. Eve was Toby's daughter—but it was already clear to me that Grayson didn't see her as a cousin. *She isn't related to them by blood. They didn't grow up together.* So when Grayson said that she was one of them, that they owed her protection, all I could think was that he'd once spoken similar words about me.

Est unus ex nobis. Nos defendat eius.

"Can we please just focus on Toby?" I said. Grayson must have heard something in my tone because he stepped back.

Stepped down.

I turned to Jameson. "Pretend for a second that you trust Eve. Pretend she looks nothing like Emily. Pretend she's telling the truth. Other than Oren's search, what's our next move?"

This was what Jameson and I did: questions and answers, looking for what other people missed. If he wouldn't do this with me, if seeing Eve had thrown him off that much…

"Motive," Jameson supplied finally. "If we want to find out who took Toby, we need to know *why* they took him."

Logically, I could think of three broad possibilities. "They want something from him. They want to use him as leverage." I swallowed. "Or they want to hurt him."

They knew his real name. Somehow, they knew how to find him.

"There has to be something we're missing," I said. I needed this to be a puzzle. I needed there to be clues.

"You mentioned that Eve said the person who knocked her out went through her pockets." Jameson had a way of playing with the facts of a situation, turning them over like a coin spun from finger to finger. "So what were they looking for?"

What did Toby have that someone else might want badly enough to kidnap him to get it? What could possibly be worth that kind of risk?

What fits in a pocket? My heart nearly exploded in my chest.

What mystery had Jameson and I spent the last nine months trying to solve?

"The disk," I breathed.

The door to the bathroom opened. Eve stood there, wrapped in a white towel, wet hair trailing down the sides of her neck. She wore a locket and nothing else except the towel. Grayson tried very hard not to look at her.

Jameson looked at me.

"Did you need something?" I asked Eve. Her hair was darker wet, less remarkable. Without it to distract from her face, her eyes looked bigger, her cheekbones higher.

"Bandage," Eve replied. If she was self-conscious about standing there in a towel, she didn't show it. "My cut split open in the shower."

"I'll help you," I volunteered before Grayson could. The sooner I tended to Eve, the sooner I could get back to Jameson and the possibility I'd just breathed into being.

What if the person who took Toby was after the disk? My mind racing, I led Eve back into the bathroom.

"What disk?" she asked behind me. I pulled out a first aid kit and handed it to her. She took it from me, her fingers brushing mine. "When I came into the room, you were talking about what happened to Toby," she said stubbornly. "You mentioned a disk."

I wondered how much else she'd heard and whether she'd meant to eavesdrop. Maybe Jameson was right. Maybe we couldn't trust her.

"It might be nothing," I said, brushing off the question.

"What might be nothing?" Eve pressed. When I didn't answer, she dropped another question like a bomb. "Who's Emily?"

I swallowed. "A girl." That wasn't a lie, but it was so far from the truth that I couldn't leave it there. "She died. The two of you—you're related."

Eve chose a bandage and pushed her wet hair back from her face. I almost offered to help her, but something held me back. "Toby told me he was adopted," she said, fixing the bandage in place. "But he wouldn't tell me anything about his biological family—or the Hawthornes."

She waited, like she expected me to tell her something. When I didn't, she looked down. "I know that you don't trust me," she said. "I wouldn't trust me, either. You have everything, and I have nothing, and I know how that looks."

So did I. From experience, *so did I.*

"I never wanted to come here," Eve continued. "I never wanted to ask you for anything—or them." Her voice strained. "But I want Toby back. I want my *father* back, Avery." Her emerald eyes locked on mine, radiating an intensity that was nearly Hawthorne. "And I will do anything—*anything*—to get what I want, even if that means begging for your help. So please, Avery, if you know something that could help us find Toby, just tell me."

CHAPTER 9

I didn't tell Eve about the disk. I justified it to myself because, for all I knew, there was nothing to tell. Not every mystery was an elaborate puzzle. The answer wasn't always elegant and carefully designed. And even if Toby's abduction did have something to do with the disk, where did that leave us?

Feeling like I owed Eve *something,* I asked Mrs. Laughlin to prepare her a room. Tears overflowed the moment the older woman laid eyes on her great-granddaughter. There was no hiding who Eve was.

No hiding that she belonged here.

Hours later, I was alone in Tobias Hawthorne's study. I told myself that I was doing the right thing, giving Jameson and Grayson space. Seeing Eve had dredged up trauma. They needed to process, and I needed to think.

I triggered the hidden compartment in the old man's desk and reached for the folder that Jameson and I kept inside. Flipping it open, I stared at a drawing I'd made: a small coinlike disk the size of a quarter, engraved with concentric circles. The last time I'd seen this bit of metal, Toby had just snatched it from my hands. I'd asked him what it was. He hadn't answered. All I really knew was what I'd read in a message Toby had once written to my mother: that if she ever needed anything, she should go to Jackson. *You know what I left there*, Toby had written. *You know what it's worth.*

I stared at the drawing. *You know what it's worth*. Coming from the son of a billionaire, that was almost unfathomable. In the months since Toby had left, Jameson and I had scoured books on art and ancient civilizations, on rare coins, lost treasures, and great archeological finds. We'd even researched organizations like the Freemasons and the Knights Templar.

Spreading that research out on the desk, I looked for something, anything we'd missed, but there was no record of the disk anywhere, and Jameson's globe-trotting search of Hawthorne vacation properties hadn't turned up anything meaningful, either.

"Who knows about the disk?" I let myself think out loud. "Who knows what it's worth and that Toby had it?"

Who even knew for certain that Toby was alive, let alone where to find him?

All I had were questions. It felt wrong that Jameson wasn't here asking them with me.

Without meaning to, I reached back into the hidden compartment, to another file, one that billionaire Tobias Hawthorne had assembled on me. *Did the old man know about Eve?* I couldn't shake the feeling that if Tobias Hawthorne *had* known about Toby's daughter, I wouldn't be here. The billionaire had chosen me largely for the effect it would have on his family. He'd used me to force the boys to confront their issues, to pull Toby back onto the board.

It should have been her.

A creak sounded behind me. I turned to see Xander stepping out of the wall. One look at his face told me that my BHFF had seen our visitor.

"I come in peace," he announced gravely. "I come with pie."

"He comes with me." Max stepped into the room behind Xander. "What the ever-faxing elf is going on, Avery?"

Xander set the pie down on the desk. "I brought three forks."

I read meaning into his grim tone. "You're upset."

"About sharing this pie?"

I looked away. "About Eve."

"You knew," Xander told me, more injury than accusation in his tone.

I forced myself to meet his eyes. "I did."

"All those times playing Cookie Golf together, and you didn't think this was worth mentioning?" Xander pulled off a piece of pie crust and brandished it in the air. "This might have escaped your attention, but I happen to excel at keeping secrets! I have a mouth like a steel trap."

Max snorted. "Isn't the expression 'a mind like a steel trap'?"

"My mind is more like a roller coaster inside a labyrinth buried in an M. C. Escher painting that is riding on another roller coaster." Xander shrugged. "But my *mouth* is a steel trap. Just ask me about all the secrets I'm keeping."

"What secrets are you keeping?" Max asked obligingly.

"I can't tell you!" Xander triumphantly dug his fork into the pie.

"So if I'd told you that Toby had a daughter out there who looked exactly like Emily Laughlin, you *wouldn't* have told Rebecca?" I said, referring to Emily's sister and Xander's oldest friend.

"I definitely, one hundred percent, entirely…*would* have told Rebecca," Xander admitted. "In retrospect, good on you for not telling me. Excellent call, shows solid judgment."

My phone rang. I looked down at it, then back up at Xander and Max. "It's Oren." My heart beating in my ears, I answered. "What do we know?"

"Not much. Not yet. I sent a team to the rendezvous point where Eve said she was supposed to meet Toby. There was no physical evidence of an altercation, but with a little digging, we did find record of a nine-one-one call, placed hours before Eve said she showed up."

My hand tightened around the phone. "What kind of nine-one-one call?"

"Shots fired." Oren didn't soften the words. "By the time a patrol unit got there, the scene was clear. They put it down to fireworks or a car backfiring."

"Who called nine-one-one?" I asked. "Did anyone see anything?"

"My team is working on it." Oren paused. "In the meantime, I've assigned one of my men to shadow Eve for the duration of her stay at Hawthorne House."

"Do you think she's a threat?" My hand went reflexively, again, to my Hawthorne pin.

"My job is to treat everyone like a threat," Oren replied. "Right now, what I need is for you to promise that you'll stay put and do nothing." My gaze went to the research spread across the desk. "My team and I will find out everything we can as quickly as we can, Avery. Toby might be the target here, but he also might not be."

I frowned. "What's that supposed to mean?"

"Give us twenty-four hours, and I'll let you know."

Twenty-four hours? I was just supposed to sit here, doing nothing, for twenty-four hours? I hung up the phone.

"Does Oren think Eve is a threat?" Max asked in a dramatic stage-whisper.

Xander made a face. "Note to self: Cancel the welcome festivities."

I thought about Oren telling me to let him handle it, then about Eve swearing that all she wanted was to find Toby. "No," I told

Xander. "Don't cancel anything. I want to get a feel for Eve." I needed to know if we could trust her because if we could, maybe she knew something I didn't. "Got any particular festivities in mind?" I asked.

Xander pressed his hands together. "I believe that our best option for assessing the truth of the mysterious Eve's character is... Chutes and Ladders."

CHAPTER 10

The Hawthorne version of Chutes and Ladders wasn't a board game. Xander promised he would explain further once I got Eve to agree to play. Focused on that task, I made my way to the Versailles wing. At the top of the east staircase, I found Grayson standing statue-still outside the wing, dressed in a silver three-piece suit, his blond hair wet from the pool.

A poolside cocktail party. The memory hit me and wouldn't let go. *Grayson is expertly deflecting every financial inquiry that comes my way. I glance toward the pool. There's a toddler balanced precariously on the edge. She leans forward, topples over, goes under, and doesn't come up. Before I can move or even yell, Grayson is running.*

In one liquid motion, he dives into the pool, fully clothed.

"Where's Jameson?" Grayson's question drew me back to the present.

"Probably somewhere he's not supposed to be," I answered honestly, "making very bad decisions and throwing caution to the wind."

I didn't ask Grayson what he was doing outside the Versailles wing.

"I see that Oren put a man on Eve." Grayson almost managed to sound like he was commenting on the weather, but a comment never felt like just a comment coming from him.

"It's Oren's job to make sure I stay safe." I didn't point out that under other circumstances, Grayson would have considered that his job, too.

Est unus ex nobis. Nos defendat eius.

"Oren shouldn't be worried about *me*." Eve stepped into the hall. Her hair was dry and fell in gentle waves. "Your security team should be focusing everything on Toby." Eve let her vibrant green eyes go from me to Grayson, and I wondered if she recognized the effect she had on him. "What do I have to do to convince you that I am not a threat?"

She was looking at Grayson, but I was the one who answered the question. "How about a game?"

"Hawthorne Chutes and Ladders," Xander boomed, standing in front of a pile of pillows, rope ladders, grappling hooks, suction cups, and nylon rope. "The rules are fairly simple." The list of complicated things that Xander Hawthorne considered to be "fairly simple" was lengthy. "Hawthorne House has three chutes—entrances to the passageways that involve, let's say, a drop," Xander continued.

I smiled. I'd already found all three.

"There are slides built into the walls of your mansion?" Max snorted. "Mother-foxing rich people."

Xander did not take offense. "Some chutes are more advantageous than others. If another player beats you to a chute, that chute is frozen for three minutes, so everyone will need one of these." Xander picked one up a pillow and gave it a gentle, but somehow menacing, swing. "Battles must be waged."

"Hawthorne Chutes and Ladders involves pillow fights?" Max asked in a tone that made me think she was picturing all four Hawthorne brothers swinging pillows at one another. Possibly shirtless.

"Pillow *wars*," Xander corrected. "Once you successfully claim your chute and make it to the ground floor, you exit the House, and it's a race to climb to the roof from the outside."

I surveyed the climbing supplies spread out at our feet. "We get to choose a ladder?"

"One does not," Xander corrected me austerely, "simply *choose* a ladder."

Grayson broke the silence he'd adopted the moment Eve had stepped into the hall. "Our grandfather liked to say that every choice worth anything came with a cost."

Eve assessed him. "And the cost for climbing supplies is..."

Grayson answered her assessing look with one of his own. "A secret."

Xander elaborated. "Each player confesses a secret. The person with the best secret gets to pick their climbing supplies first, and so on and so forth. The person with the least impressive secret goes last." I was starting to see why Xander had chosen this game. "Now," he continued, rubbing his hands together. "Which brave soul wants to go first?"

I eyed Eve, but Grayson intervened. "I'll go." He fixed his silvery eyes straight ahead. I wasn't sure what to expect, but it definitely wasn't him saying, with absolutely no intonation, "I kissed a girl at Harvard."

He...No, I wasn't going to finish that thought. What Grayson Hawthorne did with his lips was none of my business.

"I got a tattoo." Max offered up her own secret with a grin. "It's very nerdy and in a location I will not disclose. My parents can *never* find out."

"Tell me more," Xander said, "about this nerdy tattoo."

Grayson arched a brow at his brother, and I tried to think of something that would make Eve feel like she had to open up.

"Sometimes," I said quietly, "I feel like Tobias Hawthorne made a mistake." Maybe that wasn't a secret. Maybe it was obvious. But the next part was harder to say. "Like he should have chosen someone else."

Eve stared at me.

"The old man didn't make mistakes," Grayson said in one of those tones that dared you to argue—and strongly advised against it.

"My turn." Xander raised his hand. "I figured out who my father is."

"You *what*?" Grayson whipped his head toward his brother. Skye Hawthorne had four sons, each with a different father, none of whom she'd identified. Nash and Grayson had discovered their fathers within the last year. I'd known that Xander was looking for his.

"I don't know if he knows about me." Xander rushed the words. "I haven't made contact. I'm not sure I'm going to, and by the sacred rules of Chutes and Ladders, none of you can *ever* mention this again unless I bring it up first. Eve?"

With the rest of us still focused on Xander, Eve bent and picked up a grappling hook. As I turned to look at her, she trailed her finger along its edge. "Almost twenty-one years ago, my mom got drunk and cheated on her husband, and I was the result." She didn't meet a single person's eyes. "Her husband knew I wasn't his, but they stayed married. I used to think that if I could be good enough—smart enough, sweet enough, *something* enough—the man we all pretended was my father would stop blaming me for being born." She tossed the grappling hook back down. "The worst part was my mom blamed me, too."

Grayson leaned toward her. I wasn't even sure he knew he was doing it.

"As I got older," Eve continued, her voice quiet but raw, "I realized that it didn't matter how perfect I was. I was never going to be good enough because they didn't want me to be *perfect* or *extraordinary*. They wanted me to be invisible." Whatever emotions Eve was feeling were buried too deep to see. "And that is the one thing that I will never be."

Silence.

"What about your siblings?" I asked. Up until now, I'd been so focused on Eve's resemblance to Emily, on the fact that she was Toby's daughter, that I hadn't thought about her other family members—or what they'd done.

"Half-siblings," Eve said with absolutely no intonation.

Technically, the Hawthorne brothers were half-siblings. Technically, Libby and I were. But there was no mistaking Eve's tone: It meant something different to her.

"Eli and Mellie came here under false pretenses," I said. "For you."

"Eli and Mellie never did a damn thing for me," Eve replied, her voice hoarse, her head held high. "Christmas morning when I was five, when they had presents under the tree and I didn't? The family reunions that everyone got to go to but me? Every time I got grounded for existing just a little too loudly? Every time I had to beg a ride home from something because no one bothered to pick me up?" She looked down. "If my *siblings* came to Hawthorne House, it sure as hell wasn't for me. I haven't spoken a word to either of them in two years." Shining emerald eyes made their way back to mine. "Is that personal enough for you?"

I felt a needle's stab of icy guilt. I remembered what it was like coming to Hawthorne House as an outsider, and I thought suddenly about my mom and the way she would have welcomed Toby's daughter with open arms.

About what she would say if she could see me cross-examining her now.

Ballots were passed out. Secrets were ranked. Supplies were chosen.

And then the race was on.

CHAPTER 11

This was what I discovered about Eve during the remainder of Chutes and Ladders: She was competitive, she wasn't afraid of heights, she had a high tolerance for pain, and she definitely recognized the effect she had on Grayson.

She fit here, at Hawthorne House, with the Hawthornes.

That was the thought at the top of my mind as my fingers latched on to the edge of the roof. A hand reached down and closed around my wrist. "You're not first," Jameson told me in a tone that clearly communicated that he knew how I felt about *that*. "But you're not last."

That honor would eventually go to Xander and Max, who had spent far too long pillow fighting each other. I looked past Jameson to the part of the roof that flattened out.

To Grayson and Eve.

"On a scale from boring to brooding," Jameson quipped, "how's he holding up?"

Heaven forbid Jameson Hawthorne get caught openly *caring* about his brother.

"Honestly?" I bit my lip, catching it between my teeth for a moment too long, then pitched my voice low. "I'm worried. Grayson isn't okay, Jameson. I don't think your brother has been okay for a very long time."

Jameson moved toward the edge of the roof—the *very* edge—and looked out at the sprawling estate. "Hawthornes aren't, as a general rule, allowed to be anything else."

He was hurting, too, and when Jameson Hawthorne hurt, he took risks. I knew him, and I knew there was only one way to make him admit to the pain and purge the poison.

"*Tahiti,*" I said.

That was a code word I didn't use lightly. If Jameson or I called *Tahiti,* the other one had to metaphorically strip.

"Your birthday was the second anniversary of Emily's death." Jameson's shoulders and back were taut beneath his shirt. "I almost succeeded in not thinking about it, but now wouldn't be the worst time for you to tell me I didn't kill her."

I stepped up beside him, right on the edge of the roof, heedless of the sixty-foot drop. "What happened to Emily wasn't your fault."

Jameson turned his head toward me. "It also wouldn't be the worst time to tell me that you aren't jealous of Eve standing that close to Grayson."

I'd wanted to know what he was feeling. This was part of it, part of what thinking about Emily did to him.

"I'm not jealous," I said.

Jameson looked me right in the eyes. "*Tahiti.*"

He'd shown me his. "Okay," I said roughly. "Maybe I am, but it's not just about Grayson. Eve is Toby's daughter. I wanted to be. I thought I was. But I'm not, and she is, and now, suddenly, she's here, and she's connected to this place, to all of you—and no, I don't like it, and I feel petty for feeling that way." I stepped back from the edge. "But I'm going to tell her about the disk."

Whether or not I could fully trust Eve, I trusted that we wanted the same thing. I understood better now what it must have meant to her to meet Toby, to be *wanted*.

Before Jameson could question my decision about the disk, Max hauled herself up onto the roof and collapsed. "*Faaaaaaax.*" She drew out the word. "I am never doing that again."

Xander pulled himself up behind her. "How about tomorrow? Same time?"

Their appearance pulled Grayson and Eve toward us.

"So?" Eve said, her expression flecked with vulnerability, her voice tough. "Did I pass your little test?"

In response, I withdrew my drawing of the disk from my pocket and handed it to Eve. "The last time I saw Toby," I said slowly, "he took this disk from me. We don't know what it is, but we know it's worth a fortune."

Eve stared at the drawing, then her eyes found mine. "How do you know that?"

"He left it for my mother. There was a letter." That was as much as I could bring myself to tell her. "Did he ever say anything to you about any of this? Do you have any idea where he was keeping the disk?"

"No." Eve shook her head. "But if someone did take Toby to get this..." Her breath hitched. "What are they going to do to him if he won't give it to them?"

And, I thought, feeling sick, *what will they do to him once they have it?*

CHAPTER 12

That night, the only thing that kept me from nightmares was Jameson's body next to mine. I dreamed about my mom, about Toby, about fire and gold. I woke to the sound of shouting.

"I'm going to throttle him!" There was a grand total of one person who could get a rise out of my sister.

As Jameson began to stir, I slipped out of bed and padded out of my room to the hall. "Another cowboy hat?" I guessed. For the past two months, Nash had been buying cowboy hats for Libby. A veritable rainbow of colors and styles. He liked to leave them where my sister would find them.

"Look at this!" Libby demanded. She held up a cowboy hat. It was black with a bejeweled skull and crossbones in the center and metal spikes down the side.

"It's very you," I told her.

"It's perfect!" Libby said, outraged.

"Face it, Lib," I told her. "You're a couple."

"We're not a couple," Libby insisted. "This isn't my life, Ave. It's yours." She looked down, her hair, dyed black with rainbow tips, falling into her face. "And experience has taught me that I am utterly deficient when it comes to love. So." Libby thrust the cowboy hat at me. "I am not in love with Nash Hawthorne. We are not a couple. We are not dating. And he is definitely not in love with me."

"Avery." Oren announced his presence. I turned to face him, and my pulse jumped.

"What is it?" I asked. *"Toby?"*

"This arrived by courier in the dead of night." Oren held out an envelope with my name written across the front in elegant script. "I screened it—no trace of poison, explosives, or recording devices."

"Is it a ransom demand?" I asked. If it was a ransom demand, I could call Alisa, have her pay it.

Not waiting for a reply, I took the envelope from Oren. It was too heavy to just be a letter. My senses heightened, the world around me falling into slow motion, I opened it.

Inside, I found a single sheet of paper—and a familiar golden disk.

What the hell? I looked up. "Jameson!" He was already on his way to me. *We were wrong.* The words died, trapped in my throat. *The person who kidnapped Toby wasn't after the disk.*

I stared at it, my mind racing.

"Why would Toby's abductor send that to you?" Jameson asked. "Proof of life?"

"Proof that they have him." I didn't want to be making the correction, but this wasn't proof of *life*. "And the fact that they sent it," I continued, steeling myself, "means that either the person who took Toby doesn't know what the disk is worth..."

"Or they don't care." Jameson laid a hand on my shoulder.

Toby's okay. He has to be. He has to. The disk burning my palm like a brand, I closed my fist around it and made myself read the accompanying message. The paper was linen, expensive. Letters had been scripted onto it in a deep blood red.

A
RE
ANCE
A R

"That's it?" Jameson said. "There was nothing else?"

I checked the envelope again. "Nothing." I brought my fingertip to the writing—and the red ink. My stomach twisted. "That *is* ink, isn't it?"

Blood red.

"I don't know," Jameson replied intensely, "but I do know what it says."

I stared at the letters scattered across the page.

A
RE
ANCE
A R

"It's a simple trick," Jameson told me. "One of my grandfather's favorites. You decode the message by inserting the same sequence of letters into every blank. Five letters, in this case."

My heart brutalizing the inside of my rib cage, I tried to focus. What five letters could go after *A* or *RE* and before *ANCE*?

After a few seconds, I saw it. Slowly, painstakingly, my brain ticked off the answer, letter by letter. "*V. E. N.*" I took a sharp breath. "*G. E.*"

Venge. Completed, the message was anything but comforting. "Avenge," I made myself say out loud. "Revenge. Vengeance." Decoded, the last line seemed more like a signature.

My eyes flashed to Jameson's, and he said it for me. "Avenger."

CHAPTER 13

I texted Grayson and Xander. When they met us in the circular library, Eve was with them. Wordlessly, I held up the disk. Hesitantly, Eve took it from me, and the room went silent.

"How much did you say it was worth?" she asked, her voice a jagged whisper.

I shook my head. "We don't know, not exactly—but a lot." It was another four or five seconds before Eve reluctantly handed the disk back to me.

"There was a message?" Grayson asked, and I passed the paper over. "They didn't demand a ransom," he noted, his voice almost too calm.

My chest burned like I'd been holding a breath for far too long, even though I hadn't. "No," I said. "They didn't." The day before, I'd come up with three motives for kidnapping. *The kidnapper wanted something from Toby. The kidnapper wanted to use Toby as leverage.*

Or the kidnapper wanted to hurt him.

One of those options seemed much more likely now.

Xander craned his neck over Grayson's shoulder to get a closer look at the note. He decoded the message as quickly as Jameson had. "Revenge themed. Cheery."

"Revenge for what?" Eve asked desperately.

The obvious answer had occurred to me the moment I'd decoded the message, and it hit me again now with the force of a shovel swung at my gut. "Hawthorne Island," I said. "The fire."

More than two decades earlier, Toby had been a reckless, out-of-control teenager. The fire that the world presumed had taken his life had also taken the lives of three other young people. *David Golding. Colin Anders Wright. Kaylie Rooney.*

"Three victims." Jameson began circling the room like a panther on the prowl. "Three families. How many suspects does that give us in total?"

Eve moved, too, toward Grayson. "What fire?"

Xander popped between them. "The one that Toby accidentally-but-kind-of-on-purpose set. It's a long, tragic story involving daddy issues, inebriated teenagers, premeditated arson, and a freak lightning strike."

"Three victims." I repeated what Jameson had said, but my eyes went to Grayson's. "Three families."

"One yours," Grayson replied. "And one mine."

My mom's sister had died in the fire on Hawthorne Island. Billionaire Tobias Hawthorne had saved his own family's reputation by pinning the blame for the fire on her. Kaylie Rooney's family—my mom's family—was full of criminals. The violent kind.

The kind who hated Hawthornes.

I turned and walked toward the door, my stomach heavy. "I have to make a call."

Out in one of Hawthorne House's massive, winding corridors, I dialed a number that I had only called once before and tried to ignore the memory that threatened to overwhelm me.

If my worthless daughter had taught you the first damn thing about this family, you wouldn't dare have dialed my number. The woman who'd birthed and raised my mother wasn't exactly the maternal type. *If that little bitch hadn't run, I would have put a bullet in her myself.* The last time I'd called, I'd been told to forget my grandmother's name and that, if I was lucky, she and the rest of the Rooney family would forget mine.

Yet there I was, calling again.

She picked up. "You think you're untouchable?"

I took the greeting as evidence that she'd recognized my number, which meant that I didn't need to say anything but "Do you have him?"

"Who the hell do you think you are?" Her rough, throaty voice lashed at me like a whip. "You really think I can't get to you, Miss High and Mighty? You think you're safe in that castle of yours?"

I'd been told that the Rooney family was small-time, that their power paled compared to that of the Hawthorne family—and the Hawthorne heiress. "I think that it would be a mistake to underestimate you." I balled my left hand into a fist as my right hand's grip on the phone went viselike. *"Do. You. Have. Him."*

There was a long, calculating pause. "One of those pretty little Hawthorne grandsons?" she said. "Maybe I do—and maybe he won't be quite so pretty when you get him back."

Unless she was playing me, she'd just tipped her hand. I knew where the Hawthorne grandsons were. But if the Rooneys didn't know that Toby was missing—if they didn't know or believe that he was *alive*—I couldn't afford to let on that she'd guessed wrong.

So I played along. "If you have Jameson, if you lay a finger on him—"

"Tell me, girl, what do they say happens if you lie down with dogs?"

I kept my voice flat. "You wake up with fleas."

"Around here, we have a different saying." Without warning, the other end of the line exploded into vicious barks and growls, five or six dogs at least. "They're hungry, and they're mean, and they have a taste for blood. You think about that before you call this number again."

I hung up, or maybe she did. *The Rooneys don't have Toby.* I tried to concentrate on that.

"You okay there, kid?" Nash Hawthorne had a gentle manner and remarkable timing.

"I'm fine," I said, the words a whisper.

Nash pulled me into his chest, his worn white T-shirt soft against my cheek.

"I've got a knife in my boot," I mumbled into his shirt. "I'm an excellent shot. I know how to fight dirty."

"You sure do, kid." Nash stroked a hand over my hair. "You want to tell me what this is about?"

CHAPTER 14

Back in the library, Nash examined the envelope, the message, and the disk.

"The Rooneys don't have Toby," I announced. "They're ruthless, and if they knew for sure Toby was alive, they would probably be making a real effort to feed his face to a pack of dogs, but I'm almost certain they don't have him."

Xander raised his right hand. "I have a question about faces and dogs."

I shuddered. "You don't want to know."

Grayson took up a perch on the edge of the tree-trunk desk, unbuttoning his suit jacket. "I can likewise clear the Graysons."

Eve gave him a look. "The *Graysons*?"

"My sire and his family," Grayson clarified, his face like stone. "They're related to Colin Anders Wright, who died in the fire. Sheffield Grayson abandoned his wife and daughters some months back."

That was a lie. Sheffield Grayson was dead. Eve's half sister had killed him to save me, and Oren had covered it up. But Eve gave no sign that she knew that, and based on what she'd told us about her siblings, that tracked.

"Rumors place my so-called father somewhere in the Caymans,"

Grayson continued smoothly. "I've been keeping an eye on the rest of the family in his absence."

"Does the Grayson family know about you?" Jameson asked his brother. No banter, no sarcasm. He knew what *family* meant to Grayson.

"I saw no need for them to," came the reply. "But I can assure you that if Sheffield Grayson's wife, sister, or daughters had a hand in this, I would know."

"You hired someone." Jameson's eyes narrowed. "With what money?"

"Invest. Cultivate. Create." Grayson didn't offer any more explanation than that before he stood. "If we've ruled out the families of Colin Anders Wright and Kaylie Rooney, that leaves only the family of the third victim: David Golding."

"I'll have someone look into it." Oren didn't even step out of the shadows to speak.

"Seems like you do that a lot." Eve leveled a gaze in his direction.

"Heiress." Jameson suddenly stopped pacing. He picked up the envelope the message had come in. "This was addressed to *you*."

I heard what he was saying, the possibility he'd seen. "What if Toby isn't the target of revenge?" I said slowly. "What if I am?"

"You have a lot of enemies?" Eve asked me.

"In her position," Grayson murmured, "it's hard not to."

"What if we're looking at this wrong?" When Xander paced, it wasn't in straight lines or in circles. "What if it's not about the message? What if we should be focusing on the code?"

"The game," Jameson translated. "We all recognized that word trick."

"Sure did." Nash hooked his thumbs in the pockets of his worn jeans. "We're looking for someone who knows how the old man played."

"What do you mean *how the old man played*?" Eve asked.

Grayson answered and kept it brief. "Our grandfather liked puzzles, riddles, codes."

For years, Tobias Hawthorne had laid out a challenge for his grandsons every Saturday morning—a game to play, a multi-step puzzle to be solved.

"He liked testing us," Nash drawled. "Making the rules. Watching us dance."

"Nash has granddaddy issues," Xander confided to Eve. "It's a tragic yet engrossing tale of—"

"You don't want to be finishing that sentence, little brother." There wasn't anything explicitly dangerous or threatening in Nash's tone, but Xander was no dummy.

"Sure don't!" he agreed.

My thoughts raced. "If we're looking for someone who knows Tobias Hawthorne's games, someone dangerous and bitter with a grudge against me..."

"Skye." Jameson and Grayson said their mother's name at once. Trying to kill me hadn't worked out too well for her. But given that Sheffield Grayson had framed her for a murder attempt she hadn't committed, *not* trying to kill me hadn't worked out too well for Skye Hawthorne, either.

What if this was her next play?

"We need to confront her," Jameson said immediately. "Talk to her—in person."

"I'm going to have to veto that idea." Nash strolled toward Jameson, his pace unhurried.

"How does that classic proverb go?" Jameson mused. "*You're not the boss of me*? It's something like that. No, wait, I remember! It's *You're not the boss of me, wanker.*"

"Excellent use of British slang," Xander commented.

Jameson shrugged. "I'm a man of the world now."

"Jamie's right." Grayson managed to say that without grimacing. "The only way we'll get anything out of Skye is face-to-face."

No one could hurt Grayson, hurt any of them, like Skye could. "Even if she is behind this," I said, "she'll deny everything."

That was what Skye did. In her mind, she was always the victim, and when it came to her sons, she knew just how to twist the knife.

"What if you show her the disk?" Eve suggested quietly. "If she recognizes it, maybe you can use it to get her talking."

"If Skye had any idea what that disk was worth," I replied, "she definitely wouldn't have sent it to me." Skye Hawthorne had been almost entirely disinherited. No way was she parting with anything valuable.

"So if she makes a play for the disk," Grayson stated archly, "we'll know that she's aware of its value, and ergo, not behind the abduction."

I stared Grayson down. "I'm not letting any of you do this without me."

"Avery." Oren stepped out of the shadows and gave me a look that was part paternal, part military commander. "I strongly advise against any kind of confrontation with Skye Hawthorne."

"I've found duct tape more effective than advice, myself," Nash told Oren conversationally.

"It's settled, then!" Xander said brightly. "Family reunion, Hawthorne style!"

"Uh, Xander?" Max appeared in the doorway, looking rumpled. She held up a phone. "You left this on your nightstand."

Nightstand? I shot Max a look. I'd known that she and Xander were friends, but that was *not* a friendly kind of rumple. "Rebecca texted," Max told Xander, conspicuously ignoring my look. "She's on her way here."

I was distracted enough by the idea of Max and Xander spending the night together that it took a moment for the rest to penetrate. *Rebecca.* Seeing Eve would destroy Emily's sister.

"New plan," Xander announced. "I'm skipping family reunion. The rest of you can report back."

Eve frowned. "Who's Rebecca?"

CHAPTER 15

Oren drove, and Nash sat shotgun. Two additional bodyguards piled into the back of the SUV, which left me in the middle row with Jameson on one side and Grayson on the other.

"Aren't you supposed to be on a flight back to Harvard right about now?" Jameson leaned forward, past me, to shoot his brother a look.

Grayson arched an eyebrow. "Your point?"

"Tell me I'm wrong," Jameson said. "Tell me that you're not staying because of Eve."

"There's a threat," Grayson snapped. "Someone moved against our family. Of course I'm staying."

Jameson reached around me to grab Grayson by his suit. "She's not Emily."

Grayson didn't flinch. He didn't fight back. "I know that."

"Gray."

"I *know* that!" The second time, Grayson's words came out louder, more desperate.

Jameson let go of him.

"Despite what you seem to believe," Grayson bit out, "what you *both* seem to believe, I can take care of myself." Grayson was the Hawthorne who had been raised to lead. The one who was never allowed to need anything or anyone. "And you're right, Jamie—she's *not* Emily. Eve is vulnerable in ways that Emily never was."

The muscles in my chest tightened.

"That must have been a really illuminating game of Chutes and Ladders," Jameson said.

Grayson looked out the window, away from both of us. "I couldn't sleep last night. Neither could Eve." His voice was controlled, his body still. "I found her wandering the halls."

I thought about Grayson kissing a girl at Harvard. Grayson seeing a ghost.

"I asked her if the bruise on her temple was paining her," Grayson continued, the muscles in his jaw visible and hard. "And she told me that some boys would want her to say yes. That some people want to think that girls like her are weak." He went silent for a second or two. "But Eve isn't weak. She hasn't lied to us. She hasn't asked for a damn thing except help finding the one person in this world who sees her for who she is."

I thought of Eve talking about how hard she'd tried as a child to be *perfect*. And then I thought about Grayson. About the impossible standards he held himself to.

"Maybe I'm not the one who needs a reminder that this girl is her own person," Grayson said, his voice taking on a knifelike edge. "But go ahead, Jamie, tell me I'm compromised, tell me that my judgment can't be trusted, that I'm so easily manipulated and fragile."

"Don't," Nash warned Jameson from the front seat.

"I'll be happy to discuss all of your personal shortcomings," Jameson told Grayson. "Alphabetically and in great detail. Let's just get through this first."

This took us to a neighborhood full of McMansions. Once, the sheer size of the lots and the houses that sat on them would have astounded me, but compared to Hawthorne House, these enormous homes seemed absolutely ordinary.

Oren parked on the street, and as he began rattling off our security protocol, all I could think was *How did Skye Hawthorne end up here?*

I hadn't kept track of what happened to her after the DA had dropped the murder and attempted murder charges, but on some level, I had expected to find her in either dire straits or the utter lap of luxury—not suburbia.

We rang the doorbell, and Skye answered the door wearing a loose aquamarine dress and sunglasses. "Well, this is a surprise." She looked at the boys over her sunglasses. "Then again, I drew a change card this morning. The Wheel of Fortune, followed by the Eight of Cups, inverted." She sighed. "And my horoscope did say something about forgiveness."

The muscles in Grayson's jaw tensed. "We're not here to forgive you."

"Forgive *me*? Gray, darling, why would I need anyone's forgiveness?" This, from the woman whose charges had been dropped only because they had arrested her for the wrong attempt on my life. "After all," Skye continued, retreating into the house and graciously allowing us to follow, "I didn't throw *you* out onto the streets, now did I?"

Grayson had forced Skye to leave Hawthorne House—for me. "I made sure you had a place to go," he said stiffly.

"I didn't let *you* rot away in prison," Skye continued dramatically. "I didn't force you to grovel to friends for decent legal counsel. Really! Don't you boys talk to me about forgiveness. I'm not the one who abandoned you."

Nash raised an eyebrow. "Debatable, don't you think?"

"Nash." Skye made a *tsk*ing sound. "Aren't you a bit old to be holding on to childish grudges? You of all people should understand: I wasn't made to be stationary. A woman like me can absolutely die of inertness. Is it really so hard to understand that your mother is also a person?"

She could shred them without even trying. Even Nash, who'd had years to get over Skye's lack of motherly impulses, wasn't immune.

"You're wearing a ring." Jameson cut in with a shrewd observation.

Skye offered him a coy smile. "This little thing?" she said, brandishing what had to be a three-carat diamond on her left ring finger. "I would have invited you boys to the wedding, but it was a small courthouse affair. You know how I detest spectacle, and given how Archie and I met, a courthouse wedding seemed appropriate."

Skye Hawthorne *lived* for spectacle.

"'A courthouse wedding seemed appropriate'," Grayson repeated, digesting her meaning and narrowing his eyes. "You married your defense attorney?"

Skye gave an elegant little shrug. "Archie's children and grandchildren are always after him to retire, but my darling husband will be practicing criminal defense until he dies of old age." In other words: Yes, she'd married her lawyer, and yes, he was significantly older than she was—and quite possibly not long for this world. "Now, if you're not here to beg for my forgiveness..." Skye eyed each of her three sons in turn. "Then why are you here?"

"A package was delivered to Hawthorne House today," Jameson said.

Skye poured herself a glass of sparkling wine. "Oh?"

Jameson withdrew the disk from his pocket. "You wouldn't happen to know what this is, would you?"

For a split second, Skye Hawthorne froze. Her pupils dilated. "Where did you get that?" she asked, moving to take it from him, but like a magician, Jameson made the "coin" disappear.

Skye recognized it. I could see the hunger in her eyes.

"Tell us what that is," Grayson ordered.

Skye looked at him. "Always so serious," she murmured, reaching out to touch his cheek. "And the shadows in those eyes..."

"Skye." Jameson drew her attention away from Grayson. *"Please."*

"Manners, Jamie? From you?" Skye dropped her hand. "Color me shocked, but even so, there's not much I can tell you. I've never seen that before in my life."

I listened closely to her words. She'd never *seen* it. "But you know what it is," I said.

For a moment, Skye let her eyes meet mine, like we were two players shaking hands before a match.

"Sure would be a shame if someone got to your husband," Nash piped up. "Warned him about a few things."

"Archie won't believe a word you say," Skye responded. "He's already defended me against bogus charges once."

"I'd wager I know a thing or two he'd find interesting." Nash leaned back against a wall, waiting.

Skye looked back to Grayson. Of all of them, she still had the tightest hold on him. "I don't know much," she hedged. "I know that coin belonged to my father. I know that the great Tobias Hawthorne cross-examined me for hours when it went missing, describing it again and again. But I wasn't the one who took it."

"Toby was." I said what we were all thinking.

"My little Toby was so angry that summer." Skye's eyes closed, and for a moment, she didn't seem dangerous or manipulative or even coy. "I never really knew why."

The adoption. The secrecy. The lies.

"Ultimately, my darling little brother ran off and took *that* as a parting gift. Based on our father's reaction, Toby chose his revenge very well. To get that kind of response out of someone with my father's means?" Skye opened her eyes again. "It must be *very* precious."

Go to Jackson. Toby's instructions to my mother echoed in my mind. *You know what I left there. You know what it's worth.*

"You don't have Toby." Jameson cut to the chase. "Do you?"

"Are you admitting," Skye said cannily, "that my brother is alive?"

Anything we told her, she might well sell to the press.

"Answer the question," Grayson ordered.

"I don't really *have* any of you anymore, now do I? Not Toby. Not you boys." Skye looked almost mournful, but the glint in her eyes was a little too sharp. "Really, what exactly are you accusing me of, Grayson?" Skye took a drink. "You act like I'm such a monster." Her voice was still high and clear, but intense. For the first time, I could see a resemblance between her and her sons—but especially Jameson. "All of you do, but the only thing that I have ever wanted was to be loved."

I had the sudden sense that this was Skye's truth, as she saw it.

"But the more I needed love, the more I craved it, the more indifferent the world became. My parents. Your fathers. Even you boys." Skye had told Jameson and me once that she left men after she got pregnant as a test: If they really wanted her, they would follow.

But no one ever had.

"We loved you," Nash said in a way that made me think of the little boy he must have been. "You were our mother. How could we not?"

"That's what I told myself, each time I got pregnant." Skye's eyes glistened. "But none of you stayed mine for long. No matter what I did, you were your grandfather's first and mine second." Skye helped herself to another sip, her voice becoming more cavalier. "Daddy never really considered me a player in the grand game, so I did what I could. I gave him heirs." She turned her gaze on me. "And look how that turned out." She gave a little shrug. "So I'm done."

"You really expect us to believe that you're just throwing in the towel?" Jameson asked.

"Darling, I don't particularly care what you believe. But I'd rather rule my own kingdom than settle for scraps of *hers*."

"So you're just stepping back from it all?" I stared at Skye Hawthorne, trying to divine some truth. "Hawthorne House? The money? Your father's legacy?"

"Do you know what the real difference is between millions and billions, Ava?" Skye asked. "Because at a certain point, it's not about the money."

"It's about the power," Grayson said beside me.

Skye raised her glass to him. "You really would have made a wonderful heir."

"So that's it?" Nash asked, looking around the massive foyer. "This is your kingdom now?"

"Why not?" Skye replied airily. "Daddy never saw me as a power player anyway." She gave another elegant little shrug. "Who am I to disappoint?"

CHAPTER 16

The walk down the lengthy driveway was tense.

"Well, I for one found that refreshing," Jameson declared. "Our mother *isn't* the villain this time." He could act like he was bulletproof, like Skye's callousness couldn't touch him, but I knew better. "My favorite part, personally," he continued grandly, "was being blamed for never loving her enough, though I must say the reminder that we were conceived in a vain attempt to get a lock on those sweet, sweet Hawthorne billions never goes astray."

"Shut up." Grayson removed his suit jacket and hung a sharp right.

"Where are you going?" I called after him.

Grayson turned back. "I'd prefer to walk."

"Eighteen miles?" Nash drawled.

"I will assure you—all of you—once again..." Grayson rolled up his shirtsleeves, the motion practiced, emphatic. "I can take care of myself."

"Say that again," Jameson encouraged, "but try to sound even *more* like an automaton this time."

I gave Jameson a look. Grayson was hurting. They both were.

"You're right, Heiress," Jameson said, holding up his hands in defeat. "I'm being horribly unfair to automatons."

"You're spoiling for a fight," Grayson commented, his voice dangerously neutral.

Jameson took a step toward his brother. "An eighteen-mile walk would do."

For several seconds, the two of them engaged in a silent staring contest. Finally, Grayson inclined his head. "Don't expect me to talk to you."

"Wouldn't dream of it," Jameson replied.

"You're both being ridiculous," I said. "The two of you can't walk back to Hawthorne House." I really should have known better by now than to tell a Hawthorne he couldn't do something.

I turned to Nash. "Aren't you going to say anything?" I asked him.

In response, Nash opened the back door of the SUV for me. "I call shotgun."

Alone in the middle row, I spent the drive back to Hawthorne House in silence. Skye had definitely gotten to her sons. Grayson would turn that inward. Jameson would act out. I could only hope they both made it home unscathed. Aching for them, I wondered who had made Skye so desperate to be the center of someone's world that she couldn't even love her own children, for fear they wouldn't love her back enough.

On some level, I knew the answer. *Daddy never really considered me a player in the grand game.* I thought back further, to a poem that Toby had written in code. *The tree is poison, don't you see? It poisoned S and Z and me.*

"Skye loved being pregnant." Nash broke the silence in the SUV, glancing back at me from the front seat. "I ever tell you that?"

I shook my head.

"The old man doted on her. She stayed at Hawthorne House for the entirety of each pregnancy, nested even. And when she had a new baby, it was like magic, those first few days. I remember standing in the doorway, watching her feeding Gray right after they got home from the hospital. All she did was stare at him, softly crooning. Baby Gray was a real quiet little guy, solemn. Jamie was a screamer. Xander wiggled." Nash shook his head. "And every time, those first few days, I thought, *Maybe she'll stay.*"

I swallowed. "But she never did."

"The way Skye tells it, the old man stole us away. Truth is, she's the one who put my brothers in his arms. She *gave* them to him. Problem was never that she didn't love us—she just wanted the rest of it more."

Her father's approval. The Hawthorne fortune. I wondered how many babies Nash had seen his mother give away before he'd decided he didn't want a part of any of it.

"If you had a baby...," I said.

"When I have a baby," came the deep, heart-shattering reply, "she'll be my whole world."

"She?" I repeated.

Nash settled back into his seat. "I can picture Lib with a little girl."

Before I could respond to *that*, Oren got a call. "What have you got?" he asked the moment he answered. "Where?" Oren brought the SUV to a stop outside the gates. "There's been a breach," he told the rest of us. "A sensor was tripped in the tunnels."

Adrenaline flooded my bloodstream. I reached for the knife in my boot—not to draw it, just to remind myself: I wasn't defenseless. Eventually, my brain calmed enough for me to remember the circumstances in which we'd left Hawthorne House.

"I want teams coming in from both sides," Oren was saying.

"Stop." I cut him off. "It's not a security breach." I took a deep breath. "It's Rebecca."

CHAPTER 17

The tunnels that ran beneath the Hawthorne estate had fewer entrances than the secret passageways. Years ago, Tobias Hawthorne had shown those entrances to a young Rebecca Laughlin. The old man had seen a girl living in the shadows of her sick older sister. He'd told Rebecca that she deserved something of her own.

I found her in the tunnel beneath the tennis courts. Guided only by the light on my phone, I made my way toward the place where she stood. The tunnel dead-ended into a concrete wall. Rebecca stood facing it, her red hair wild, her lithe body held stiff.

"Go away, Xander," she said.

I stopped a few feet shy of her. "It's me."

I heard Rebecca take in a shaky breath. "Go away, Avery."

"No."

Rebecca was good at wielding silence as a weapon—or a shield. After Emily's death, she'd isolated herself, wrapped in that silence.

"I have all day," I said.

Rebecca finally turned to look at me. For a beautiful girl, she cried ugly. "I met Eve. We told her the truth about Toby's adoption." She sucked in a gulp of air. "She wants to meet my mom."

Of course she did. Rebecca's mother was Eve's grandmother. "Can your mom handle that?" I asked.

I'd only met Mallory Laughlin a few times, but *stable* wasn't a word I would have used to describe her. As a teenager, she'd given baby Toby up for adoption, unaware that the Hawthornes were the ones who had adopted him. Her baby had been so close, for years, and she hadn't known—not back then. When she'd finally had another child two decades later, Emily had been born with a heart condition.

And now Emily was dead. As far as Mallory knew, Toby was, too.

"*I'm* not handling this," Rebecca told me. "She looks so much like her, Avery." Rebecca sounded beyond angry, beyond gutted, her voice a mosaic of far too many emotions to be contained in one body. "She even sounds like Emily."

Rebecca's entire life growing up had been about her sister. She'd been raised to make herself small.

"Do you need me to tell you that Eve *isn't* Emily?" I asked.

Rebecca swallowed. "Well, she doesn't seem to hate me, so..."

"Hate you?" I asked.

Rebecca sat and pulled her knees tight to her chest. "The last thing Em and I ever did was fight. Do you know how hard she would have made me work to be forgiven for that? For being *right*?" They'd fought about Emily's plans for that night—the plans that had gotten her killed. "Hell," Rebecca said, fingering the ends of her choppy red hair, "she'd hate me for this, too."

I sat down beside her. "Your hair?"

Some of the tightness in Rebecca's muscles gave way, and her entire body shuddered. "Emily liked our hair long."

Our hair. The fact that Rebecca could say that without realizing how screwed up it was, even now, made me want to hit someone on her behalf. "You're your own person, Rebecca," I told her, willing her to believe that. "You always have been."

"What if I'm not good at being my own person?" Rebecca had been different these last few months. She looked different, dressed different, went after what she wanted. She'd let Thea back in. "What if this whole thing is just the universe telling me that I don't *get* to move on? *Ever.*" Rebecca's chin trembled. "Maybe I'm a horrible person for wanting to."

I'd known that seeing Eve would hurt her. I'd known that it would dredge up the past, the same way it had for Jameson—for Grayson. But this was Rebecca, cut to the bone.

"You are not a horrible person," I said, but I wasn't sure that *I* could make her believe that. "Have you told Thea about Eve?" I asked.

Rebecca stood and dug the toe of her beat-up combat boot into the ground. "Why would I?"

"Bex."

"Don't look at me like that, Avery."

She was hurting. This wasn't going to *stop* hurting any time soon. "What can I do?" I asked.

"Nothing," Rebecca said, and I could hear her breaking. "Because now I have to go and figure out how to tell my mother that she has a grandchild who looks exactly like the daughter she would have chosen to keep, if the universe had given her a choice between Emily and me."

Rebecca was here. She was alive. She was a good daughter. But her mother could still look right at her and sobbingly say that all her babies died.

"Do you want me to go with you to tell your mom?" I asked.

Rebecca shook her head, the choppy ends of her hair catching in a draft. "I'm better at wanting things now than I used to be, Avery." She straightened, an invisible line of steel running down her spine. "But I don't get to want you with me for this."

CHAPTER 18

I stayed in the tunnels after Rebecca was gone, debating, then wound my way back toward Hawthorne House and exited up a hidden staircase into the Great Room. Once I had cell phone reception again, I pulled the trigger and made the call.

"To what do I owe this rather dubious honor?" Thea Calligaris had perfected the art of the verbal smirk.

"Hello to you, too, Thea."

"Let me guess," she said pertly. "You're in desperate need of fashion assistance? Or maybe one of the Hawthornes is having a meltdown?" I didn't reply, and she amended her guess. "More than one?"

A year ago, I never would have imagined the two of us as anything even remotely resembling friends, but we'd grown on each other—more or less. "I need to tell you something."

"Well," Thea replied coyly, "I don't have all day. In case you missed the memo, my time is *very* valuable." Over the summer, Thea had gone viral. Somewhere between Saint Bart's and the Maldives, she'd become an Influencer with a capital *I*. Then she'd come back, to Rebecca.

No matter how long it takes, Thea had told me once. *I'm going to keep choosing her.*

I told her everything.

"When you say this girl looks exactly like—"

"I mean *exactly*," I reiterated.

"And Rebecca—"

Rebecca was going to kill me for this. "They just met. Eve wants to meet Bex's mom."

For a full three seconds, Thea was uncharacteristically silent. "This is messed up, even by Hawthorne and Hawthorne-adjacent standards."

"Are *you* okay?" I asked. Emily had been Thea's best friend.

"I don't do vulnerable," Thea retorted. "It clashes with my bitch aesthetic." She paused. "Bex didn't want you to tell me, did she?"

"Not exactly."

I could practically *hear* Thea shrugging that off—or trying to. "Just out of curiosity," she said lightly, "exactly how many Hawthornes *are* having meltdowns right now?"

"Thea."

"It's called schadenfreude, Avery. Though really, the Germans should come up with a word that more precisely captures the emotion of getting petty satisfaction out of knowing that the world's most arrogant bastards have itty-bitty feelings, too." Thea wasn't as cold as she liked to pretend to be, but I knew better than to call her on it where Hawthornes were concerned.

"Are you going to call Rebecca?" I asked instead.

"And let her avoid my call?" Thea replied tartly. There was a beat. "Of course I am." She'd let Rebecca go once. She wasn't going to again. "Now, if that's everything, I have an empire to build and a girl to chase."

"Take care of her, Thea," I said.

"I will."

CHAPTER 19

Oren waited until I was off the phone with Thea to make his presence known. He stepped into view, and I forced my brain to focus.

"Anything yet?" I asked him.

"No luck tracing the courier service, but the team I sent to the rendezvous point where Toby was supposed to meet Eve reported in again."

The memory of two words rang in my mind: *shots fired*. "Did you figure out who placed the nine-one-one call?" I asked, holding on to my calm the way a person dangling over a forty-foot drop holds on to whatever they can reach.

"The call was placed from a neighboring warehouse. My men tracked down the owner. He has no idea who placed the call, but he did have something for us."

Something. The way Oren said that made my stomach feel like it had been lined with lead. "What?"

"Another envelope." Oren waited for me to process before he continued. "Sent last night via courier, untraceable. The warehouse owner was paid cash to give it to anyone who came asking about a nine-one-one call. Payment came with the package, so it's likewise untraceable." Oren held out the envelope. "Before you open it—"

I wrenched it out of his hands. Inside, there was a picture of Toby, his face bruised and swollen, holding a newspaper with yesterday's date. *Proof of life.* I swallowed and turned the picture over. There was nothing on the back, nothing else in the envelope.

As of yesterday, he was alive. "No ransom demand?" I choked out.

"None."

I looked back at Toby's bruises, his swollen face. "Were you able to find out anything about the family of David Golding?" I asked, trying to get a grip on myself.

"Currently out of the country," Oren replied. "And their financials are clear."

"What now?" I asked. "Do we know where Eli and Mellie are? What about Ricky? Is Constantine Calligaris still in Greece?" I hated how frantic I sounded and the way my mind was jumping from possibility to possibility with no segue: Eve's half-siblings, my father, Zara's recently estranged husband, *who else?*

"I've been tracking all four of the individuals you just mentioned for more than six months," Oren reported. "None were within two hundred miles of the location of interest when Toby was taken, and I have no reason to suspect any kind of involvement from any of them." Oren paused. "I also did some checking into Eve."

I thought about Eve slicing herself open for that game of Chutes and Ladders, about what Grayson had said about her in the car. "And?" I asked quietly.

"Her story checks out," Oren told me. "She moved out the day she hit eighteen, went no contact with her entire family, siblings included. That was two years ago. She had a waitress job that she showed up to regularly until she and Toby went dark last week. From age eighteen until she met Toby a couple of months ago, she was living hand to mouth with what seemed to be some truly awful roommates. Digging deeper and going back a few more years, I found a record of an incident at her high school involving Eve and an apparently beloved male teacher. *He said, she said.*" Oren's expression hardened. "She has reason to distrust authority."

And who, Eve had asked me, *is going to believe a girl like me?*

"What else?" I asked Oren. "What aren't you telling me?" I knew him well enough to know that there was *something.*

"Nothing regarding Eve." Oren stared at me for a long moment, then reached into his shirt pocket and handed me a square of paper. "This is a list of members of your security team and our close associates who have been approached with job offers in the past three weeks."

I did a quick count. *Thirteen.* This couldn't be normal. "Approached by whom?" I asked.

"Private security firms, mostly," Oren replied. "Far too many of them for comfort. There's no common denominator in ownership between the different companies, but something like this doesn't just happen unless someone is *making* it happen."

Someone who wanted holes in my security. "You think this is related to Toby's abduction?" I asked.

"I don't know." Oren clipped the words. "My men are loyal and well-paid, so the attempts failed, but I don't like this, Avery—any of it." He gave me a look. "Your friend Max is scheduled to return to college tomorrow morning. I would like to send a security detail back with her, but she seems...*resistant* to the idea."

I swallowed. "You think that Max is in danger?"

"She could be." Oren's voice was steady. *He* was steady. "I would be negligent at this point to assume that you weren't the target of a concentrated and multipronged assault. Maybe you are. Maybe you aren't. But until we know otherwise, I have no choice but to proceed like there's a major threat—and that means assuming that anyone close to you could be the next target."

CHAPTER 20

I wasn't sure which was going to be harder: convincing Max to let Oren assign a bodyguard to her or showing that picture of Toby to Eve. I ended up going in search of Max first and found her *and* Eve in the bowling alley with Xander, who had a bowling ball in each hand.

"I call this move *the helicopter*," he intoned, lifting his arms to the side.

Even in the darkest of times, Xander was Xander. "You're going to drop one of those on your foot," I said.

"That's okay," Xander responded cheerfully. "I have two feet!"

"Did Skye know anything about the disk?" Eve brushed past Xander and Max. "Is she involved?"

"No to the second question," I said. "And the first doesn't matter right now." I swallowed, my plan of confronting the Max situation first evaporating. "This does." I handed Eve the picture of Toby and looked away.

I couldn't watch, but not watching didn't help. I could *feel* Eve beside me, staring at the picture. Her breathing was audible and uneven. She *felt* this, the way I did.

"Get rid of it." Eve dropped the photograph. Her voice rose. *"Get it out of here."*

I bent to pick up the photo, but Xander ditched the bowling balls and beat me to it. He took out his phone. As I watched, he turned it to flashlight mode and ran it behind the photo.

"What are you doing?" Max asked.

I was the one who answered. "He's looking to see if there's a message embedded in the paper's grain." If some parts of the page were denser than others, the light wouldn't penetrate as well. I hadn't *wanted* to look that closely at the photograph, at Toby's face, but now that Xander had turned on flashlight mode, my brain shifted gears. *What if there's more to this message?*

"We're going to need a black light," I said. "And a heat source." If we were dealing with someone familiar with Tobias Hawthorne's games, then invisible ink was a definite possibility.

"On it!" Xander said. He handed me the photo, then bounded out of the room.

"What are you doing?" Eve asked me, her words coming out hollow.

I was scanning the photo, looking past Toby's injuries this time. "The newspaper," I said suddenly, forcefully. "The one Toby's holding." I took out my own phone and took a photo of the photo, so I could zoom in. "The front-page article." Adrenaline flooded my bloodstream. "Some of the letters are blacked out. See this word? You can tell from context that it should be *crisis*, but the first *I* is blacked out. Same for the *A* in this word. Then *L*, *W*. Another *A*."

Sliding over to the bowling computer, I hit the button to enter a new player and typed in the five letters I'd already read off, then kept going. In total, there were eighteen letters blacked out in the article.

D. I typed the last one, then went back and added spacing. I hit

Enter, and the message flashed across the scoring screen overhead. ***I ALWAYS WIN IN THE END.***

I'd known that someone was playing with us, with me. But this made it so much clearer that Toby's abductor wasn't just playing *with* me. They were playing *against* me.

When Xander came back carrying a black light in one hand and a Tiffany lamp in the other, he took one look at the words on the screen and set them down. "A bold choice of name," he said. He gave me a hopeful look. "Yours?"

"No." I refused to give in to the darkness that wanted to come and instead turned to Max. "I'm going to need you to agree to take a bodyguard back with you tomorrow."

Max opened her mouth, probably to object, but Xander poked her shoulder. "What if we can get you someone dark and mysterious with a tragic backstory and a soft spot for puppies?" he said in a wheedling tone.

After a long moment, Max poked him back. "Sold."

When things settled down even a little, she and I were going to be having a long talk about poking, nightstands, and her *friendship* with Xander Hawthorne. But for now...

I turned to Oren, a new fear hitting me far too late. "What about Jameson and Grayson? They're still not home." If anyone close to me could be a target, then—

"I have a man on each of them," Oren replied. "Last I heard, the boys were still together, and things were getting ugly. Hawthorne ugly," he clarified. "No external threats."

Given their emotional states after that conversation with Skye, *Hawthorne ugly* was probably the best we could hope for.

They're safe. For now. Feeling claustrophobic, I turned back to the words on the screen. ***I ALWAYS WIN IN THE END.***

"Single first-person pronoun," I said, because it was easier to dissect the message than to wonder what *winning* looked like to the person who had Toby. "That suggests we're dealing with an individual, not a group. And the words *in the end*, those seem to imply that there might have been losses along the way." I breathed, and I thought, and I willed myself to see more than that in the words. "What else?"

Two and a half hours later, Jameson and Grayson still weren't home, and I was spinning my wheels. I'd been over and over the message, and then the photo itself again and the envelope, in case there was something else there. But nothing I did seemed to matter.

Avenge. Revenge. Vengeance. Avenger. I always win in the end.

"I hate this," Eve said, her voice quiet and reedy. "I *hate* feeling helpless."

I did, too.

Xander looked from Eve to me. "Are you two brooding?" he asked. "Because, Avery, I am, as ever, your BHFF, and you *know* the penalty for brooding!"

"I am not playing Xander Tag," I told him.

"What's Xander Tag?" Max asked.

"What *isn't* Xander Tag?" Xander replied philosophically.

"Is this all a joke to you?" Eve asked sharply.

"No," Xander said, his voice suddenly serious. "But sometimes a person's brain starts cycling. No matter what you do, the same thoughts just keep repeating, over and over. You get stuck in a loop, and when you're inside that loop, you can't see past it. You'll keep coming up with the same possibilities, to no end, because the answers you need—they're outside the loop. Distractions aren't just distractions. Sometimes they can break you out of the loop, and once you're out, once your brain stops cycling—"

"You see the things you missed before." Eve stared at Xander for a moment. "Okay," she said finally. "Bring on the distractions, Xander Hawthorne."

"That," I warned her, "is a very dangerous thing to say."

"Pay no attention to Avery!" Xander instructed. "She's just a little gun-shy from The Incident."

Max snorted. "What incident?"

"That doesn't matter," Xander said, "and in my defense, I didn't expect the zoo to send an *actual* tiger. Now..." He tapped his chin. "What are we in the mood for? The Floor Is Magma? Sculpture Wars? Jell-O Assassins?"

"I'm sorry." Eve's voice was stilted. She turned toward the door. "I can't do this."

"Wait!" Xander called after her. "What are your thoughts on fondue?"

CHAPTER 21

In Hawthorne House, *fondue* involved twelve fondue pots accompanied by three full-sized chocolate fountains. Mrs. Laughlin had it all set up in the chef's kitchen within the hour.

Distractions aren't just distractions, I reminded myself. *Sometimes, you need them to break the loop.*

"In terms of cheese fondue," Xander orated, "we've got your gruyère-based, your gouda-based, your beer cheddar, your fontina, your chällerhocker—"

"Okay," Max cut in. "Now you're just making up words."

"Am I?" Xander said in his most dashing voice. "For dipping, we've got your baguettes, your sourdough, breadsticks, croutons, bacon, prosciutto, salami, sopressata, apples, pears, and various vegetables, grilled or raw. Then there's the dessert fondues! For the purists among us, dark chocolate, milk chocolate, and white chocolate fountains. More inventive dessert combinations are in the pots. I *highly* recommend the salted caramel double chocolate."

Surveying the vast array of options for dessert dippers, Max picked up a strawberry in one hand and a graham cracker in the other.

"Hit me," Xander yelled, jogging backward. "I'm going wide!"

Max tossed the graham cracker. Xander caught it in his mouth. Grinning, Max dipped the strawberry in one of the dessert pots, took a bite, then moaned. "Fax me, this is good."

Break the loop, I thought, so I began to make my way through the spread myself, dying with every bite. Beside me, Eve slowly started to do the same.

With a mouth full of bacon, Xander picked up a spare fondue fork and brandished it like a sword. "En garde!"

Max armed herself. The result was chaos. The kind of chaos that ended with Max and Xander both drenched from the fountains and Eve taking a dark chocolate banana to the chest.

"I beg your chocolatey pardon," Xander said. Max whapped him with a breadstick.

Eve looked down at the mess that was her shirt. "This was my only top."

I glanced at Max. *You and I will be talking very soon.* Then I turned to Eve. "Come on," I said. "I'll get you a new shirt."

"*This* is your closet?" Eve was stunned. Racks, cabinets, and shelves stretched twelve feet overhead, all of them full.

"I know," I told her, remembering how I'd felt when they'd brought the clothes in. "You should see the closet in the bedroom that used to be Skye's. It's nineteen hundred square feet, two stories tall, and has its own champagne bar."

Eve stared at the clothes.

"Help yourself," I told her, but she didn't move.

"Really," I said. "Take whatever you want."

She reached for a pale green shirt but froze when she felt the fabric. I wasn't a fashion person, but the incredible softness of expensive clothes, the *feel* of them—that was what still got me, too.

"Toby didn't want me to be a part of this." Eve just kept looking at that shirt. "The mansion. The food. The clothes." She took a breath, the sharp intake of air audible. "He hated this place. *Hated* it. And when I asked why, all he would say was that the Hawthorne family wasn't what they appeared to be, that this family had secrets." She finally pulled the green shirt off the hanger. "Dark secrets. Maybe even dangerous ones."

I thought about all the Hawthorne secrets I'd learned since coming here—not just the truth about Toby's adoption or his role in the fire on Hawthorne Island, but everything else, too.

Nan killed her husband. Zara cheated on both of hers. Skye named her sons after their fathers, and at least one of them was a dangerous man. Tobias Hawthorne bribed Nash's dad to stay away. Jameson watched Emily Laughlin die.

And that wasn't even taking into account the secrets I'd had a hand in creating since I got here. I'd allowed Grayson to cover up his mother's involvement in an attempt on my life and pin all the blame on Libby's abusive ex. I'd looked the other way when Toby and Oren had decided that Sheffield Grayson's body needed to disappear.

Across from me, Eve was still waiting for me to say something.

"I'll let you get dressed," I told her.

Back in my bedroom, I found myself wondering what other Hawthorne secrets I still didn't know. I went back to the photo of Toby, and this time, I let myself look directly at his eyes. *Is this about you or me or this family? How many enemies do we have?*

A knock broke into my thoughts. I opened my door to find Mr. Laughlin standing there—and Oren, along with Eve's guard, positioned down the hall.

"Pardon the interruption, Avery. I've got something for you." The old groundskeeper had a cart with him, filled with long rolls of paper.

Another special delivery? My heart rate ticked up. "Did these come by courier service?"

"I dug these out for you myself." As gruff as Mr. Laughlin's manner was, there was something almost gentle in his moss-colored eyes. "You just had a birthday. Each year following *his* birthday, Mr. Hawthorne had plans drawn up for the next expansion on the House."

Tobias Hawthorne had never finished Hawthorne House. He'd added on every year.

"These are the blueprints." Mr. Laughlin nodded to the cart as he wheeled it into the room. "One set for each year since we broke ground on the House. Thought you might want to see them if you're planning an addition of your own."

"Me?" I said. "Add on to Hawthorne House?"

Eve stepped into the room, wearing the green silk shirt, and for a moment she stared at the blueprints the way she'd stared at the clothes in my closet. Then a figure appeared in the doorway.

Jameson. His face and body were drenched in mud. His shirt was torn, his shoulder bleeding.

Mr. Laughlin put an arm around Eve's shoulder. "Come on, missy. We should go."

CHAPTER 22

"You're bleeding," I told Jameson.

He showed his teeth in a wicked smile. "I'm also dangerously close to getting mud on . . . everything."

There was mud on his face, in his hair. His clothes were drenched in it, his shirt clinging to his abdomen, letting me see every line of the muscles underneath.

"Before you ask," Jameson murmured. "I'm fine, and so is Gray."

I wondered if Grayson Hawthorne had even a fleck of mud on him.

"Oren said things got Hawthorne ugly." I gave Jameson a look.

He shrugged. "Skye has a way of messing with our heads." Jameson did not elaborate on the mud, the blood, or what exactly he and Grayson had gotten up to. "At the end of the day, we all learned what we needed to know. Skye's not involved in the kidnapping."

I'd learned a lot more than that since. The words tumbling out, I told Jameson everything: the picture of Toby, the message the kidnapper had hidden in it, Eve's comment about dark and dangerous secrets, what Oren had told me about the attempts to hire my security team away.

The more I talked, the closer Jameson moved toward me, the closer I needed to be to him.

"No matter what I do," I said, our bodies brushing, "I don't feel like I'm getting anywhere."

"Maybe that's the point, Heiress."

I recognized the tone in his voice, knew it as well as I knew each of his scars. "What are you thinking, Hawthorne?"

"This second message changes things." Jameson's arms curved around me. I could feel mud soaking into my shirt, feel the heat of his body from underneath his. "We were wrong."

"About what?" I asked.

"The person we're dealing with—they're not playing a Hawthorne game. In the old man's games, the clues are always sequential. One clue leads you to the next, if only you can solve it."

"But this time," I said, picking up his train of thought, "the first message didn't lead us anywhere. The second message just came."

Jameson reached one hand up to touch my face, smearing my jawline with mud. "Ergo, the clues in this game aren't sequential. Working one isn't going to magically lead you to the next, Heiress, no matter what you do. Either Toby's captor just wants you scared, in which case, these are vague warnings with no greater design."

I stared at him. "Or?" He'd said *either.*

"Or," Jameson murmured, "it's all part of the same riddle: one answer, multiple clues."

His hip bones pressed lightly into my stomach. "A riddle," I repeated, my voice rough. "Who took Toby—and why?"

Avenge. Revenge. Vengeance. Avenger. I always win in the end.

"An incomplete riddle," Jameson elaborated. "Delivered piece by piece. Or a story—and we're at the mercy of the storyteller."

The person doling out hints, clues that went nowhere in

isolation. "We don't have what we need to solve this," I said, hating what I was saying and how defeated I sounded saying it. "Do we?"

"Not yet."

I wanted to scream, but I looked up at him instead. I saw a jagged cut on the underside of his jaw and reached for his chin. "This looks bad."

"On the contrary, Heiress, bleeding is a devastatingly good look for me."

Xander wasn't the only Hawthorne who specialized in distractions.

Needing this and not liking the look of that cut on his jaw, I allowed myself to be distracted. "Let's make this a game," I told Jameson. "I bet that you can't shower and wash off all that mud before I find what we need from the first aid kit."

"I have a better idea." Jameson lowered his lips to mine. My neck arched. More mud on my face, my clothes. "I bet," he countered, "that *you* can't wash all this mud off before I..."

"Before you what?" I murmured.

Jameson Winchester Hawthorne smiled. "Guess."

CHAPTER 23

"Your move."

I'm back in the park, playing chess opposite Harry. Toby. *The second I think the name, his face changes. The beard is gone, his face bruised and swollen.*

"Who did this to you?" I ask, my voice echoing and echoing until I can barely hear myself think. "Toby, you have to tell me."

If only I can get him to tell me, I'll know.

"Your move." Toby thunks the black knight into a new position on the board.

I look down, but suddenly, I can't see any of the pieces. There's only shadows and fog where each of them should be.

"Your move, Avery Kylie Grambs."

I whip my head up because it's not Toby's voice that says the words this time.

Tobias Hawthorne stares back at me from across the table. "The thing about strategy," he says, "is that you always have to be thinking seven moves ahead." He leans across the table.

The next thing I know, he has me by the neck.

"Some people kill two birds with one stone," he says, strangling me. "I kill twelve."

I woke up frozen, locked in my own body, my heart in my throat, unable to breathe. *Just a dream.* I managed to suck in oxygen and roll sideways off my bed, landing in a crouch. *Breathe. Breathe. Breathe.* I didn't know what time it was, but it was still dark outside. I looked up at the bed.

Jameson wasn't there. That happened sometimes when his brain wouldn't stop. The only question tonight was *stop what?*

Trying to shake off the last remnants of the dream, I strapped on my knife then went to look for him, making my way to Tobias Hawthorne's study.

The study was empty. No Jameson. I found myself staring at the wall of trophies the Hawthorne grandsons had won—and not just trophies. Books they'd published, patents they'd been granted. Proof that Tobias Hawthorne had made his grandsons extraordinary.

He'd made them in his own image.

The dead billionaire *had* always thought seven moves ahead, always killed twelve birds with one stone. How many times had the boys told me that? Still, I couldn't help feeling like my subconscious had just served up a warning—and not about Tobias Hawthorne.

Someone else was out there, strategizing, thinking seven steps ahead. A storyteller telling a story—and making moves all the while.

I always win in the end.

Frustration building inside me, I pushed open the balcony doors. I let the night air hit my face, breathed it in. Down below, Grayson was in the pool, swimming in the dead of night, the pool lit just enough that I could make out his form. The moment I saw him, memory took me.

A crystal glass sits on the table in front of him. His hands lay on either side of the glass, the muscles in them tensed, like he might push off at any moment. I didn't let myself sink into the memory, but another slice of it hit me anyway as I watched Grayson swimming down below.

"You saved that little girl," I say.

"Immaterial." Haunted silver eyes meet mine. "She was easy to save."

Another outdoor light turned on below. *The motion sensor by the pool.* My hand went to my knife, and I was on the verge of calling out for security when I saw the person who had tripped the sensor.

Eve was wearing a nightgown, one of mine that I didn't remember her taking. It hit her mid-thigh. A breeze caught the material the second before Grayson saw her. From this distance, I couldn't make out the expressions on their faces. I couldn't hear what either of them said.

But I saw Grayson pull himself from the pool.

"Avery."

I turned. "Jameson. I woke up, and you weren't there."

"Hawthorne insomnia. I had a lot on my mind." Jameson pushed past me and looked down. I took that as permission to look again, too. To see Grayson placing an arm around Eve. *He's wet. She doesn't care.*

"How long would you have stood here, watching them, if I hadn't come?" Jameson asked, an odd tone in his voice.

"I already told you, I'm worried about Grayson." My mouth felt like cotton.

"Heiress." Jameson turned back to me. "That's not what I meant."

A ball rose in my throat. "You're going to have to be more specific."

Slowly, deliberately, Jameson pushed me up against the wall. He waited, as he always did, for my nod, then obliterated the space between us. His lips crushed mine. My legs wrapped around him as his body pinned mine to the wall.

Jameson Winchester Hawthorne.

"That was very...specific," I said, trying to catch my breath. He was still holding on to me, and I couldn't pretend that I didn't know why he'd needed to kiss me like that. "I'm with you, Jameson," I said. "I want to be with *you*."

Then why do you care how Grayson looks at her? The question was alive in the air between us, but Jameson didn't ask it.

"It was always going to be Grayson," he said, letting go of me.

"No," I insisted. I reached for him, pulled him back.

"For Emily," Jameson told me. "It was always going to be Grayson. She and I—we were too much alike."

"You are *nothing* like Emily," I said fiercely. Emily had used them, both of them. She'd played them against each other.

"You didn't know her," Jameson told me. "You didn't know me back then."

"I know you now."

He looked at me with an expression that made me ache. "I know about the wine cellar, Heiress."

My heart stilled in my chest, my throat closing in around a breath I couldn't expel. I pictured Grayson on his knees in front of me. "What is it you think you know?"

"Gray was in a bad place." Jameson's tone was a perfect match for that expression on his face—cavernous and full of *something*. "You went down to check on him. And..."

"And what, Jameson?" I stared at him, trying to anchor myself to this moment, but unable to completely banish memories I had no right to hold.

"And the next day, Grayson couldn't look at you. Or me. He left for Harvard three days early."

Comprehension washed over me. "No," I insisted. "Whatever you're thinking, Jameson—I would *never* do that to you."

"I know that, Heiress."

"Do you?" I asked, because his voice had gone hoarse. He wasn't acting like he knew.

"It's not *you* who I don't trust."

"Grayson wouldn't—"

"It's not my brother, either." Jameson gave me a look, dark and twisted, full of longing. "Trustworthiness has never really been *my* thing, Heiress."

That sounded like something Jameson would have said when we first met. "Don't say that," I told him. "Don't talk about yourself that way."

"Gray has always been so perfect," Jameson said. "It's inhuman how good he was at just about everything. If we were competing—at anything, really—and I wanted to win, I couldn't do it by being better. I had to be *worse*. I had to cross lines that he wouldn't, take risks—the bigger and more unfathomable to him the better."

I thought about Skye and the way she'd told me once that Jameson Winchester Hawthorne was *hungry*.

"I never learned how to be good or honorable, Heiress." Jameson placed a hand on either side of my face, pushed his fingers back into my hair. "I learned how to be bad in the most strategic ways. But now? With you?" He shook his head. "I want to be better than that. *I do*. I don't ever want for you—for us, for *this*—to become a game." He trailed his thumb down my jawline, his fingers lightly skimming my cheekbone. "So if you decide you're not sure about this, Heiress, about me—"

"I *am* sure," I told him, capturing his hands in mine. I pressed his knuckles to my mouth and realized they were swollen. "I am, Jameson."

"You have to be." There was an urgency to Jameson's words, a *need*. "Because I'm terrible at hurting, Heiress. And if what we have now—if *everything* we have now—starts to feel like another competition between Grayson and me, like a game? I don't trust myself not to play."

CHAPTER 24

The next morning, I awoke to an empty bed and someone rapping on my door.

"I'm coming in," Alisa called. She tried to open the door, but Oren stopped her from the hallway.

"I could be naked in here," I grumbled loudly, hastily throwing on designer sweatpants before telling Oren to let her in.

"And you could count on my discretion if you were," Alisa replied briskly. "Attorney-client privilege."

"Was that an actual joke?" I asked. In response, Alisa placed a leather satchel on my dresser. "If that's more paperwork for me to look over," I told her, "I don't want it."

I had enough on my plate right now without thinking about the trust paperwork—or the journal Grayson had given me, its pages still blank.

"That's not paperwork." Alisa didn't clarify what the bag *was*. Instead, she fixed me with what I had termed the Alisa Look. "You should have called me. The moment someone showed up claiming to be Toby Hawthorne's daughter, you should have called."

I glanced at Oren, wondering if he'd changed his mind and told her about Eve. "Why?" I asked Alisa. "The will is through probate. Eve isn't a legal threat."

"This isn't just about the will. That threatening note you received—"

Notes, plural. I glanced at Oren, and he gave a slight shake of his head—he wasn't the one who had tipped her off to any of this.

Alisa rolled her eyes at the two of us. "This is the part where you tell me—erroneously—that you have everything under control."

"I advised against calling you," Oren told her point-blank. "This was a security issue, not a legal one."

"Really, Oren?" For a split second, Alisa looked hurt, then she converted that to extreme professional annoyance. "Let's address the elephant in the room, shall we?" she said. "Yes, I took a chance when Avery was in that coma, but if I hadn't moved her back to Hawthorne House when I did, she wouldn't *have* a security team. The terms of the will were ironclad. Do you understand that, Oren? If I hadn't done what I did, Avery wouldn't be entitled to live at Hawthorne House with all its fancy security. You wouldn't be able to pay your men." Alisa stared at him, hard. "She would be out there with *nothing*, so, yes, I took a calculated risk, and thank God I did." She turned to me. "Since I am the *only* one in this room who can claim to make the good, smart decision under fire—when things start going up in flames, *you damn well pick up the phone*."

I winced.

"As it was," Alisa muttered, "I had to hear about this from Nash."

That startled a response out of me. "Nash called you?"

"He can't even stand to be in the same room with me," Alisa said softly, "but he called. Because *he* knows I am good at my job." She walked toward me, her heels clicking against the wood floor. "I can't help you if you won't let me, Avery, not with this and not with everything you're about to have on your plate."

The money. She was talking about my inheritance—and the trust.

"What happened, Alisa?" Oren crossed his arms over his chest.

"What makes you think something happened?" Alisa asked coolly.

"Instinct," my head of security replied. "And the fact that someone has been trying to chip away at Avery's security team."

I could practically see Alisa filing that piece of information away. "I've become aware of a smear campaign," she said, giving Oren tit for tat. "Gossip websites, mostly. Nothing you need to concern yourself with, Avery, but one of my connections in the press has informed me that the going rate for pictures of you with any of the Hawthornes has inexplicably tripled. Meanwhile, at least three companies that Tobias Hawthorne owned a significant stake in are experiencing... turbulence."

Oren's eyes narrowed. "What kind of turbulence?"

"CEO turnover, sudden scandal, FDA investigations..."

Avenge. Revenge. Vengeance. Avenger. I always win in the end.

"On the business end of things, what are we looking for?" Oren asked Alisa.

"Wealth. Power. Connections." Alisa set her jaw. "I'm on it."

She was on it. Oren was on it. But we weren't any closer to an answer or to getting Toby back, and there was nothing I could do about it. *An incomplete riddle. A story—and we're at the mercy of the storyteller.*

"I'll let you know as soon as I find something," Alisa said. "In the meantime, we need to keep Eve happy, away from the press, and under surveillance until the firm can assess the best course of action. I suspect a modest settlement, in exchange for an NDA, may be in order." In full-on lawyer mode, Alisa didn't even pause before moving on to the next item on her agenda. "If, at any point, a ransom needs to be arranged, the firm can handle that as well."

Was that where this was headed? The end of this story, once the riddle was complete? Was Toby's captor just waiting until he had me where he wanted me to make demands?

"I'll have my team keep you in the loop," Oren told Alisa briskly.

My lawyer nodded like she expected nothing less, but I got the sense that Oren letting her back in mattered to her. "I suppose the only business that remains is *that*." Alisa nodded toward the leather satchel she'd placed on my dresser. "When I updated the partners on the current situation, I was given this bag and its contents to pass along to you, Avery."

"What is it?" I asked, walking toward my dresser.

"I don't know." Alisa sounded perturbed. "Mr. Hawthorne's instructions were that it was to remain secure and unopened, unless certain conditions were met, in which case it was to be delivered promptly to you."

I stared at the bag. Tobias Hawthorne had left me his fortune, but the only message I'd ever received from him was a grand total of two words: *I'm sorry.* I reached out to touch the leather bag. "What conditions?"

Alisa cleared her throat. "We were to deliver this to you in the event that you ever met Evelyn Shane."

I remembered vaguely that *Eve* was short for *Evelyn*—but then another realization took over. *The old man knew about Eve.* That revelation hit me like splinters to my lungs. I'd assumed that the dead billionaire hadn't known about Toby's *actual* daughter. At some point, I'd started believing, deep down, that I'd only been chosen to inherit because Tobias Hawthorne hadn't realized there was someone out there who suited his purposes better than I did.

A stone that killed at least as many birds. A more elegant glass ballerina. A sharper knife.

But he knew about Eve all along.

CHAPTER 25

Alisa left. Oren took up position in the hall, and all I could do was stare at the bag. Even without opening it, I knew in my gut what I would find inside. *A game.*

The old man had left me a game.

I wanted to call Jameson, but everything he'd said the night before lingered, ghostlike in my mind. I didn't know how long I stood there staring at my last bequest from Tobias Hawthorne before Libby poked her head into my room.

"Cupcake pancakes?" My sister held out a plate, piled high with her latest concoction, then followed the direction of my gaze. "New laptop bag?" she guessed.

"No," I said. I took the pancakes from Libby and told her about the leather satchel.

"Are you going to . . . open it?" my sister prodded innocently.

I wanted to see what was in that bag. I wanted—*so badly*—to play a game that actually *went* somewhere. But opening the satchel without Jameson here felt like admitting that there was something wrong.

Libby handed me a fork, and my gaze caught on the inside of her left wrist. A few months ago, she'd gotten a tattoo, a single word inked from wrist bone to wrist bone, just under the heel of her hand. *SURVIVOR*.

"Still thinking about what you want for the other wrist?" I asked.

Libby looked down at her arm. "Maybe, for my next tattoo, I should go with... *open the bag, Avery!*" The enthusiasm in her voice reminded me of the moment when we'd first found out that I'd been named in Tobias Hawthorne's will.

"How about *love*?" I suggested.

Libby narrowed her eyes. "If this is about me and Nash..."

"It's not," I said. "It's just about you, Lib. You're the most loving person I know." Enough of the people she'd loved had hurt her that, these days, it seemed like she saw her giant heart as a point of weakness, but it wasn't one. "You took me in," I reminded her, "when I had no one."

Libby stared at both of her wrists. "Just open the darn bag."

I hesitated again, then got annoyed with myself. This was *my* game. For once, I wasn't a part of the puzzle, a tool. I was a player.

So, play.

I reached for the bag. The leather was supple. I let my fingers explore the bag's strap. It would have been just like the old man to leave a message etched in the leather. When I found nothing, I unclasped the flap and flipped it open.

In the main pouch, I found four things: a handheld steamer, a flashlight, a beach towel, and a mesh bag filled with magnetic letters. On the surface, that collection of objects seemed random, but I knew better. There was always a method to the old man's madness. At the beginning of each Saturday-morning challenge for the boys, the billionaire had laid out a series of objects. *A fishing hook, a price tag, a glass ballerina, a knife.* By the end of the game, all of those objects would have served a purpose.

Sequential. The old man's games are always sequential. I just have to figure out where to start.

I searched the side pouches and was rewarded with two more objects: a USB drive and a circular piece of blue-green glass. The latter was the size of a dinner plate, as thick as two stacked quarters, and just translucent enough that I could see through it. As I held up the glass and peered through it, my mind went to a piece of red acetate that Tobias Hawthorne had left taped to the inside cover of a book.

"This could serve as a decoder," I told Libby. "If we can find something written in the same blue-green shade as the glass..." My head swam with the possibilities. Was this the way it was for the Hawthorne boys after so many years of playing the old man's games? Did every clue call to mind one they'd solved before?

Libby darted to my desk and grabbed my laptop. "Here. Try the USB."

I plugged it in, feeling like I was on the verge of something. A single file popped up: **AVERYKYLIEGRAMBS.MP3**. I stared at my name, mentally rearranging the letters. *A very risky gamble.* I clicked on the file. After a brief delay, I was hit with a blast of sound, undecipherable, verging on white noise.

I pushed down the urge to cover my ears.

"Should we turn it down?" Libby asked.

"No." I hit Pause, then pulled the audio track back to the start. Bracing myself, I turned the volume *up*. This time, when I hit Play, I didn't just hear noise. I heard a voice, but there was no way I could make out actual words. It was like the file had been corrupted. I felt like I was listening to someone who couldn't get a full sound out of their mouth.

I played the full clip six, seven, eight times—but repeating it didn't help. Playing it at different speeds didn't help. I downloaded an app that let me play it backward. Nothing.

I didn't have what I needed to make sense of the USB. *Yet.*

"There has to be something here," I told my sister. "A clue that starts things off. We might not be able to make out the audio file now, but if we follow the trail the old man left, the game might tell us how to restore the audio."

Libby gave me a wide-eyed look. "You sound exactly like them. The way you just said *the old man*, it's like you knew him."

In some ways, I felt like I did. At the very least, I knew how Hawthornes thought, so this time, I didn't just trail my fingers over the leather of the satchel. I gave the entire bag a thorough inspection, looking for anything I'd missed, then went through the objects one by one.

I started with the steamer, plugging it into the wall. I released the compartment that would hold water. After verifying that it was empty, I added water, half expecting some kind of message to appear on the sides when I did.

Nothing.

I clicked the compartment back into place and waited until the ready light came on. Holding the steamer away from my body, I gave it a try. "It works," I said.

"Should we try it on that bag, which probably costs ten thousand dollars and undoubtedly should not be steamed?" Libby asked.

We did, to no effect—at least, none related to the puzzle. I turned my attention to the flashlight next, turning it on and off, then checking the battery chamber to ensure that it contained nothing but batteries. I unfolded the beach towel and stood up so I could get an eagle's-eye view of the design.

Black-and-white chevron, no unexpected breaks in the pattern.

"That just leaves this," I told Libby, picking up the mesh bag. I opened it, spilling dozens of magnetic letters onto the floor. "Maybe it spells out the first clue?"

I began by sorting the letters: consonants in one pile, vowels in another. I hit a 7 and started a third pile for numbers.

"Forty-five pieces in total," I told my sister once I was done. "Twelve numbers, five vowels, twenty-eight consonants." Moving as I spoke, I pulled out the five vowels—one each of *A*, *E*, *I*, *O*, and *U*. That didn't strike me as a coincidence, so I started pulling out consonants, too—one of each letter, until I had the whole alphabet represented, with seven letters left behind.

"These are the extras," I told Libby. "One *B*, three *P*'s, and three *Q*'s." I did the same thing for the numbers, pulling out each digit from one to nine and turning my attention to the leftovers. "Three *fours*," I said. I stared at what I had. "*B*, *P*, *P*, *P*, *Q*, *Q*, *Q*, four, four, four."

I repeated that a few times. A phrase came into my head: *Mind your P's and Q's.* I lingered on it for a moment, then dismissed it. What wasn't I seeing?

"I'm not exactly a rocket scientist," Libby hedged, "but I don't think you're going to get words out of those letters."

No vowels. I considered starting over again, playing with the letters in a different way, but couldn't bring myself to do it. "There's three of each," I said. "Except for the *B*."

I picked up the *B* and rubbed my thumb over its surface. What wasn't I seeing? *P*, *P*, *P*, *Q*, *Q*, *Q*, *4*, *4*, *4—but only one B*. I closed my eyes. Tobias Hawthorne had designed this puzzle for me. He must have had reason to believe not just that it could be solved, but that *I* could solve it. I thought about the file folder the billionaire had kept on me. Pictures of me doing everything from working at a diner to playing chess.

I thought of my dream.

And then I saw it—first in my mind's eye, and once my eyelids flew open, right in front of me. *P*, *Q*, *4*. I pulled those three down, then repeated the process. *P*, *Q*, *4*. When I saw what I had left, my heart jumped into my throat, pounding like I was standing at the edge of a waterfall.

"*P*, *Q*, *B*, four," I told Libby breathlessly.

"Cream cheese frosting and black velvet corsets!" Libby replied. "We are just saying random combinations of things now, right?"

I shook my head. "The code—it's not words," I explained. "These are chess notations—descriptive, not algebraic."

After my mother had died, long before I'd ever heard the name Hawthorne, I'd played chess in the park with a man who I'd known as Harry. *Toby Hawthorne.* His father had known that—known that I played, known who I played with.

"It's a way of keeping track of your moves and your opponent's," I told Libby, a rush of energy thrumming through my veins. "This one—P-Q4—is short for pawn to Queen four. It's a common opening move, which is often countered by black making the same move—pawn to Queen four. Then the white pawn goes to Queen's Bishop four."

P-QB4.

"So," Libby said sagely, "chess."

"Chess," I repeated. "The move—it's called the Queen's Gambit. Whoever's playing white puts that second pawn in a position to be sacrificed, which is why it's considered a gambit."

"Why would you sacrifice a piece?" Libby asked.

I thought about billionaire Tobias Hawthorne, about Toby, about Jameson, Grayson, Xander, and Nash. "To take control of the board," I said.

It was tempting to read more meaning into that, but I couldn't linger. I had the first clue now. It would lead me to another. I started walking.

"Where are you going?" Libby called after me. "And do you want me to have Jameson meet us there? Or Max?"

"The game room." I made it to the door before I answered the second half of that question, my stomach twisting. "And yes to Max."

CHAPTER 26

Built-in shelves lined the walls, all of them overflowing with games.

"Do you think the Hawthornes have played all of them?" Max asked Libby and me.

There were hundreds of boxes on those shelves, maybe a thousand. "Every single one," I said. There was nothing more Hawthorne than winning.

If what we have now—if everything *we have now—starts to feel like another competition between Grayson and me, like a game? I don't trust myself not to play.*

I slammed that door in my mind. "We're looking for chess sets," I said, focusing on that. "There is probably more than one. And while we're looking..." I shot my best friend a pointed look. "Max can catch us up on the Xander situation."

Better her romantic drama taking center stage than mine.

"Everything involving Xander is a situation," Max hedged. "He specializes in situations!"

I scanned the boxes on the closest shelf, checking for chess sets. "True." I waited, knowing that she would break.

"It's...*new.*" Max squatted to stare at the lower shelves. "Like, really new. And you know I hate labels."

"You love labels," I told her, skimming my fingers across game after game. "You literally own multiple label makers."

Chess set! Victorious, I pulled the box from the shelf and kept looking.

"The situation—Xander, me. It's...*fun.* Are relationships supposed to be fun?"

I thought about hot-air balloons and helicopters and dancing barefoot on the beach.

"I mean, I've never actually been friends with a guy first," Max continued. "Like, even in fiction, *friends to lovers*? Never my thing. I'm more *star-crossed tragedy, supernatural soul mates, enemies to lovers.* Epic, you know?"

"You don't get much more epic than Hawthornes," Libby told her, and then, as if she'd caught herself, she straightened, turned her attention back to the shelf, and pulled out chess set number two.

"Do you know what Xander did when I had my first college test?" Max was rambling now. "Before things even got romantic? He sent me a book bouquet."

"What's a book bouquet?" Libby replied.

"*Exactly!*" Max said. "*Mother-faxing exactly.*"

"You like him," I translated. "A lot."

"Let's just say I am definitely reconsidering my favorite tropes." Max popped up to standing, a wooden box held in her hand. "Number three."

Ultimately, there were six. I scoured the boxes, looking for anything scribbled onto cardboard, etched into metal, or carved into wood. *Nothing.* I verified that no pieces were missing, then reached into my leather satchel and pulled out the flashlight. As far as I could tell, it was just a normal flashlight, but I'd been Hawthorne-adjacent long enough to know that there were dozens of kinds of invisible ink. That thought in mind, I shined the light on each of the six chessboards. After that, I inspected the individual pieces. *Nothing.*

Frustrated, I looked up—and saw Grayson in the doorway, backlit. In my mind, I could still see him putting an arm around Eve. *He's wet. She doesn't care.*

I stood.

"Xander's looking for you," Grayson told Max dryly. "I suggested he text, but he claims that's cheating."

Max turned to me. "Xander's my ride to the airport."

I hated this. "Are you sure you have to go?" I asked, dread heavy in the pit of my stomach.

"Do you want me to fail out of college, thereby ruining my chances at grad-school-slash-med-school-slash-law-school?"

I let out a long huff of air. "Oren assigned someone to go with you?"

"I have been assured that my new bodyguard is exceptionally broody with hidden layers." Max hugged me. "Call me. Constantly. And you!" she said as she turned and walked past Grayson. "Watch where you're aiming those cheekbones, buddy."

And just like that, my best friend was gone.

Grayson stayed in the doorway, like there was an invisible line just over the threshold. "What's all of this?" he asked, looking at the mess spread out in front of me.

Your grandfather left me a game. I didn't tell Grayson that. I couldn't. I needed to find Jameson and tell *him* first.

Libby took my silence as her cue to exit, squeezing past Grayson as she did.

"I talked to Eve last night." Grayson must have decided not to push me on the chess sets. "She's struggling."

So was I. So was Jameson. So was *he*.

"I think it would help her," Grayson said, "to see Toby's old wing."

I remembered Eve's comment about Hawthorne secrets. If there was one place in Hawthorne House rife with secrets, it was the deserted wing that Tobias Hawthorne had kept bricked up for years.

"I know that Toby means something to you, Avery." Grayson stepped toward me, across that invisible line into the room. "I can imagine that letting Eve see his wing might feel like an intrusion on something that was just yours until now."

I looked away and sat back down among the chess pieces. "It's fine."

Grayson moved forward again and crouched beside me, his forearms braced against his knees, his suit jacket falling open. "I know you, Avery. And I know what it feels like to have a stranger show up at Hawthorne House and threaten the very ground beneath your feet."

I'd been that stranger for him.

Pushing back against what felt like a lifetime of memories, I focused on Grayson in the here and now. "I'll make you a deal," I said. Jameson was wagers; Grayson was deals. "I'll show Eve Toby's wing if you tell me how you're doing. How you're *really* doing."

I expected him to look away, but he didn't. Silvery gray eyes stayed locked on mine, never blinking, never wavering. "Everything hurts." Only Grayson Hawthorne could say that and still sound utterly bulletproof. "It hurts all the time, Avery, but I know the man I was raised to be."

CHAPTER 27

I told Grayson that he could take Eve to Toby's wing, and he informed me that that wasn't the deal. I'd said that *I* would show Eve Toby's wing. I deeply suspected he was headed for the pool.

Packing up the satchel and taking it with me, I held up my end of the bargain.

Eve's pace slowed as Toby's wing came into view. There was still rubble visible from the brick wall that the old man had erected decades ago.

"Tobias Hawthorne closed off this wing the summer that Toby disappeared," I told Eve. "When we found out that Toby was still alive, we came here looking for clues."

"What did you find?" Eve asked, something like awe in her tone as we stepped through the remains of bricks and into Toby's foyer.

"Several things." I couldn't blame Eve for wanting to know. "For starters, this." I knelt to trigger the release on one of the marble tiles. Beneath, there was a metal compartment, empty but for a poem engraved on the metal.

"'A Poison Tree,'" I said. "An eighteenth-century poem written by a poet named William Blake."

Eve dropped to her knees. She trailed her hand over the poem, reading it silently without so much as taking or expelling a breath.

"Long story short," I said, "teenaged Toby seemed to identify with the feeling of wrath—and what it cost to hide it."

Eve didn't respond. She just stayed there, her fingers on the poem, her eyes unblinking. It was like I'd ceased to exist for her, like the entire world had.

It was at least a minute before she looked up. "I'm sorry," she said, her voice wavering. "It's just, what you just said about Toby identifying with this poem—you could have been describing me. I didn't even know he liked poetry." She stood and turned three-sixty, taking in the rest of the wing. "What else?"

"The title of the poem led us to a legal text on Toby's bookshelf," I said, the air thick with memories. "In a section on the fruit of the poisonous tree doctrine, we found a coded message that Toby left behind before he ran away—another poem, one he wrote himself."

"What did it say?" Eve asked, her tone almost urgent. "Toby's poem?"

I'd been over the words often enough that I knew them by heart. "*Secrets, lies, all I despise. The tree is poison, don't you see? It poisoned S and Z and me. The evidence I stole is in the darkest hole. Light shall reveal all, I writ upon the . . .*"

I trailed off, the way the poem had. I expected Eve to finish it for me, to fill in the word that both Jameson and I had known went at the end. *Wall.*

But she didn't. "What does he mean, the evidence he stole?" Eve's voice rang through Toby's empty suite. "Evidence of what?"

"His adoption, I'm guessing," I said. "He kept a journal on his walls, written in invisible ink. There are still some black lights in this room from when we read them. I'll turn them on and kill the lights."

Eve reached out to stop me before I could. "Could I do this part alone?"

I hadn't been expecting that, and my knee-jerk reaction was *no.*

"I know you have just as much right to be here as I do, Avery—or more. It's your house, right? But I just..." Eve shook her head, then looked down. "I don't look like my mom." She fingered the ends of her hair. "When I was a kid, she kept my hair short—these ugly, uneven bowl cuts she'd do herself. She said it was because she didn't want to have to mess with it, but when I got older, when I started taking care of my hair myself and grew it out, she let it slip that she'd kept it short because no one else in our family had hair like mine." Eve took a breath. "No one had eyes like mine. Or a single one of my features. No one thought the way I did or liked the things I liked or felt things the same way." She swallowed. "I moved out the day I hit eighteen. They probably would have kicked me out if I hadn't. A few months later, I convinced myself that maybe I had family out there. I did one of those mail-in DNA tests. But...no matches."

No one even remotely Hawthorne-adjacent would have handed over their DNA to one of those databases. "Toby found you," I reminded Eve gently.

She nodded. "He doesn't really look like me, either. And he's a hard person to get to know. But *that poem...*"

I didn't make her say anything else. "I get it," I told her. "It's fine."

On my way out the door, I thought about my mom and all the ways we were alike. She'd given me my resilience. My smile. The color of my hair. The tendency to guard my heart—and the ability, once those guards were down, to love fiercely, deeply, unapologetically.

Unafraid.

CHAPTER 28

I found Jameson on the climbing wall. He was at the top, where the angles became treacherous, his body held to the wall through sheer force of will.

"Your grandfather left me a game," I said. My voice wasn't loud, but it carried.

Without a moment's hesitation, Jameson dropped from the wall.

He was too high up. In my mind, I saw him landing wrong. I *heard* bones shattering. But just like the first time I'd met him, he landed in a crouch.

When he stood up, he gave no signs of being worse for wear.

"I hate it when you do that," I told him.

Jameson smirked. "It's possible that I was deprived of maternal attention as a child unless I was bleeding."

"Skye noticed if you were bleeding?" I asked.

Jameson gave a little shrug. "Some of the time." He hesitated, just for a fraction of a second, then stepped forward. "I'm sorry about last night, Heiress. You didn't even call *Tahiti*."

"You don't have to apologize," I told him. "Just ask me about the game your grandfather designed to be delivered to me if and when Eve and I ever met."

"He knew about her?" Jameson tried to wrap his mind around that. "The plot thickens. How far through the game are you?"

"Solved the first clue," I said. "Now I'm looking for a chess set."

"There are six in the game room," Jameson replied automatically. "That's how many it takes to play Hawthorne chess."

Hawthorne chess. Why was I not surprised? "I found all six. Do you know if there's a seventh somewhere else?"

"I don't *know* of one." Jameson gave me a look: part trouble, part challenge. "But do you still have that binder Alisa made for you, detailing your inheritance?"

I found an entry in the binder's index: *Chess set, royal.* I flipped to the page indicated and read, tearing through the description as fast as I could. The set was valued at nearly half a million dollars. The pieces were made of white gold, encrusted with black and white diamonds—nearly ten thousand of them. The pictures were breathtaking.

There was only one place *this* chess set could be.

"Oren," I called out to the hallway, knowing he'd be somewhere within earshot. "I need you to take us to the vault."

The last time I'd been to the Hawthorne vault, I'd jokingly asked Oren if it contained the crown jewels, and his very serious response had been *To what country?*

"If what you're looking for isn't here," Oren told Jameson and me as we surveyed the steel drawers lining the walls, "some pieces are kept in an even more secure location off-site."

Jameson and I got to work gingerly opening drawer after drawer. I managed not to gawk at anything until I came to a scepter made of shining gold interwoven with another lighter metal. *White gold? Platinum?* I had no idea, but it wasn't the materials that caught my eye. It was the design of the scepter. The metalwork was impossibly intricate. The effect was delicate, but dangerous. *Beauty and power.*

"Long live the Queen," Jameson murmured.

"The Queen's Gambit," I said, my mind racing. Maybe we weren't looking for a chess set.

But before I could follow that thought any further, Jameson opened another drawer and spoke again. "Heiress." There was something different in his tone this time.

I looked at the drawer he'd opened. *So this is what ten thousand diamonds looks like.* Each chess piece was magnificent; the board looked like a jewel-encrusted table. According to the binder, forty master artisans had spent more than five thousand hours bringing this chess set to life—and it looked it.

"You want to do the honors, Heiress?"

This was my game. A familiar, electric feeling coming over me, I examined each piece, starting with the white pawns and working my way up to the king. Then I did the same thing with the black pieces, glittering with black diamonds.

The bottom of the black queen had a seam. If I hadn't been looking for it, I wouldn't have seen it. "I need a magnifying glass," I told Jameson.

"How about a jeweler's loupe?" he countered. "There has to be one around here somewhere."

Eventually, he found one: a small lens with no handle, just a cylindrical rim. Using the loupe to look at the bottom of the black queen told me that what I'd seen as a seam was actually a gap, like someone had cut a paper-thin line into the bottom of the piece. And peeking through that gap, I saw something.

"Were there any other jeweler's tools with the loupe?" I asked Jameson.

Even the smallest file he brought me couldn't fully fit into the gap, but I managed to wedge the tip through—and it caught on something.

"Tweezers?" Jameson offered, his shoulder brushing mine.

File. Tweezers. Loupe.

File. Tweezers. Loupe.

Sweat was pouring down my temples by the time I finally managed to lock the tweezers onto the edge of something. *A strip of black paper.*

"I don't want to tear it," I told Jameson.

His green eyes met mine. "You won't."

Slowly, painstakingly, I pulled the strip out. It was no bigger than a fortune tucked inside a fortune cookie. Golden ink marked the page—with handwriting I recognized all too well.

The only message Tobias Hawthorne had ever left me before was that he was sorry. Now, to that, I could add two more words.

I turned to Jameson and read them out loud: *"Don't breathe."*

CHAPTER 29

A person stopped breathing when they were awestruck or terrified. When they were hiding and any sound could give them away. When the world around them was on fire, the air thick with smoke.

Jameson and I scoured every single smoke detector in Hawthorne House.

"You're smiling," I told him, disgruntled when the last one turned up nothing.

"I like a challenge." Jameson gave me a look that reminded me that I'd *been* a challenge for him. "And maybe I'm feeling nostalgic for Saturday mornings. Say what you will about my childhood, but it was never boring."

I thought back to the balcony. "You didn't mind being set against your brothers?" I asked. *Against Grayson?* "Being forced to compete?"

"Saturday mornings were different," Jameson said. "The puzzles, the thrill, the old man's attention. We *lived* for those games. Maybe not Nash, but Xander and Grayson and me. Hell, Gray even let loose sometimes because the games didn't reward perfection. He and I used to team up against Nash, at least until the end. Everything else our grandfather did—everything he gave us, everything expected of us—was about molding the next generation of Hawthornes to be something extraordinary. But Saturday mornings, those games—they were about showing us that we already *were*."

Extraordinary, I thought. *And a part of something.* That was the siren call of Tobias Hawthorne's games.

"Do you think that's why your grandfather left me this game?" I asked.

The billionaire had set my game to start if and only if I met Eve. Had he known that I would start questioning his almighty judgment in choosing me the moment she showed up? Had he wanted to show me what I was capable of?

That I was extraordinary?

"I think," Jameson murmured, relishing the words, "that my grandfather left three games when he died, Heiress. And the first two both told us something about why he chose you."

Don't breathe. We didn't solve the clue that night. The next day was Monday. Oren cleared me to go to school so long as he stuck to my side. I could have called out sick and stayed home, but I didn't. My game had proven an effective distraction, but Toby was still in danger, and nothing could keep my mind off that for long.

I went to school because I wanted the paparazzi—that my opponent had so kindly set on me like dogs—to take a picture of me with my head held high.

I wanted the person who had taken Toby to realize that I wasn't down.

I wanted him to make his next damn move.

I spent my free mods in the Archive—prep school for *library*. I was almost done with the calculus homework I'd ignored over the long weekend when Rebecca came in. Oren allowed her past.

“You told Thea.” Rebecca stalked toward me.

“Is that such a bad thing?” I asked—from a safe distance.

“She is *relentless*,” Rebecca muttered.

Proving the point, Thea appeared in the doorway behind her. “I was under the impression that you *liked* relentless.” Only Thea could make that sound flirty in these circumstances.

Rebecca grudgingly met her girlfriend’s eyes. “I kind of do.”

“Then you’re going to *love* this part,” Thea told her. “Because it’s the part where you stop fighting this, stop fighting me, stop running away from this conversation, and let go.”

“I’m fine, Thea.”

“You’re not,” Thea told her achingly. “And you don’t have to be, Bex. It’s not your job to be *fine* anymore.”

Rebecca’s breath hitched.

I knew when my presence wasn’t necessary. “I’m going to go,” I said, and neither one of them even seemed to hear me. In the hallway, I was informed by an office aid that the headmaster’s office was looking for me.

The headmaster’s office? I thought. *Not the headmaster?*

On the way there, I made conversation with Oren. “Think someone tipped the school off about my knife?” I wondered how seriously private schools took their weapons policies when it came to students who were on the verge of inheriting billions. But when Oren and I got to the office, the secretary greeted me with a sunny smile.

“Avery.” She held out a package—not an envelope, but a box. My name was scripted on the top in familiar, elegant writing. “This was delivered for you.”

CHAPTER 30

Oren commandeered the package. It was hours before I got it back—and by the time I did, I was safely ensconced inside the walls of Hawthorne House, and Eve, Libby, and all the Hawthorne brothers had joined me in the circular library.

"No note this time," Oren reported. "Just this."

I stared at what looked to be a jewelry box: square, a little bigger than my hand, possibly antique. The wood was a dark cherry color. A thin line of gold rimmed the edges. I went to open the lid, then realized the box was locked.

"Combination lock." Oren nodded toward the front edge of the box, where there were six dials, grouped in pairs. "Added recently, I would guess. I was tempted to force it open, but given the circumstances, preserving the integrity of the jewelry box seemed like a priority."

After two envelopes, the fact that Toby's abductor had sent a package this time felt like an escalation. I didn't want to think about what I might find inside that jewelry box. The first envelope had contained the disk, the second, a picture of a beaten Toby. As far as proof went, as far as a reminder of the stakes, a reminder of who held the power here...

How long until the kidnapper starts sending pieces?

"The combination might be just a combination." Jameson stared at the box like he could see through it—into it. "But there's also the possibility that the numbers themselves are a clue."

"The package was sent to the school?" Grayson's gaze was sharp. "And it made it all the way to the headmaster's office? Whoever sent it knows how to get around Country Day security protocols."

That seemed like a message in and of itself: The person who'd sent this wanted me to know that they could get to me.

"It would be best," Oren stated calmly, "if you planned to stay home from school for a few days, Avery."

"You, too, Xan," Nash added.

"And just let someone make us run and hide?" I looked from Oren to Nash, furious. "No. I'm not going to do that."

"Tell you what, kid." Nash cocked his head to the side. "We'll spar for it. You and me. Winner makes the rules, and loser doesn't whine about it."

"Nash." Libby gave him a reproachful look.

"If you don't like that, Lib, you ain't gonna love my thoughts about *your* safety."

"Oren and Nash are right, Heiress." Jameson's hand found its way to mine. "It's not worth the risk."

I was fairly certain Jameson Hawthorne had never said those words before in his life.

"Can you all just stop arguing?" Eve demanded, her voice high and terse. "We have to open it. Right now. We have to get inside that box as quickly as humanly possible and—"

"Evie," Grayson murmured. "We need to be careful."

Evie?

"For once," Jameson declared, "I agree with Gray. Caution isn't the worst idea here."

That wasn't like Jameson, either.

Xander turned to Oren. "How certain are we that this box won't explode the second we open it?"

"Very," Oren replied.

I made myself ask the next question—*the* question—even though I didn't want to. "Any idea what's inside?"

"From the looks of the X-rays," Oren replied, "a phone."

Just a phone. Relief rolled over me slowly, like feeling coming back to a limb that had gone numb. "A phone," I said out loud. Did that mean Toby's captor was planning to call?

What happens if I don't answer?

I didn't let myself linger on that question. Instead, I turned my attention back to the boys. "You're Hawthornes. Who knows how to crack a combination lock?"

The answer was all of them. Within ten minutes, they had the combination: *fifteen, eleven, thirty-two.* Once it clicked open, Oren took the box, inspected its contents, and turned the whole thing back over to me.

The inside of the box was lined with deep red velvet. A cell phone sat nestled in the fabric. I picked the phone up and turned it over, looking for anything out of the ordinary, then I turned my attention to the touch screen. I tried the same combination that had opened the box as a passcode. *Fifteen. Eleven. Thirty-two.*

"I'm in," I said. I clicked through the icons on the phone one by one. The photo roll was empty. The weather app was set to local weather. There were no notes, no text messages, no locations saved in the map function. Under the clock app, I found a timer counting down.

12 HOURS, 45 MIN, 11 SEC...

I looked up at the others, feeling each tick of the timer in the pit of my stomach. Eve said what I was thinking. "What happens when it hits zero?"

My stomach clenching, I thought of Toby, of what I *hadn't* found in this box. Jameson stepped in front of me, green eyes steady on mine. "Forget the timer for now, Heiress. Go back to the main screen."

I did and, fury building, checked out the rest of the phone. There was no music loaded onto it. The internet browser's home screen was a search engine—nothing special there. I clicked on the calendar. There was an event set to begin on Tuesday at six in the morning. *When the timer hits zero,* I realized.

All the calendar entry said was *Niv.* I turned the phone so the others could read it.

"Niv?" Xander said, wrinkling his forehead. "A name, maybe? Or the last two letters could be a roman numeral."

"N-four." Grayson took out his own phone and executed a search. "The first two things that come up when I search the letter and the numeral are a federal form and a drug called phentermine hydrochloride—an appetite suppressant, apparently."

I rolled that over in my mind but couldn't make sense of it. "What kind of federal form?"

"A financial one," Eve replied, reading over Grayson's shoulder. "Securities and Exchange Commission. It looks like it might have something to do with investment companies?"

Investment. There could be something there.

"What else?" Nash threw the words out. "There's *always* something else."

This wasn't a Hawthorne game, not exactly, but the tricks were the same. I clicked on the icon for email, but that just brought up a prompt with instructions for setting up that function. Finally, I navigated to the phone's call log. *Empty.* I clicked over to voicemail messages. *None.* One more click took me to the phone's contacts.

There was exactly one number stored on this phone. The name it was stored under was CALL ME.

I sucked in a breath.

"Let me do it," Jameson said. "I can't protect you from everything, Heiress, but I can protect you from this."

Jameson wasn't the Hawthorne I usually associated with protection.

"No," I told him. The package had been sent to *me*. I couldn't let anyone do this for me—not even him. I hit Call before anyone could stop me and set it to speakerphone. My lungs refused to breathe until the second someone picked up.

"Avery Kylie Grambs." The voice that answered was male, deep and smooth with an intonation that sounded almost aristocratic.

"Who is this?" I asked, the words coming out tight.

"You can call me Luke."

Luke. The name reverberated through my mind. The person on the other end of the line didn't sound particularly young, but it was impossible to place his age. All I knew was that I'd never spoken to him before. If I had, I would have recognized that voice.

"Where's Toby?" I demanded. In response, I received only a chuckle. "What do you want?" No answer. "At least tell me that you still have him." *That he's still okay.*

"I have many things," the voice said.

Holding the phone so tightly that my hand started to throb, I clung to my last shreds of control. *Be smart, Avery. Get him talking.* "What do you want?" I asked again, more calmly this time.

"Curious, are you?" Luke played with the words like a cat playing with a mouse. "Fine word, *curious*," he continued, his voice like velvet. "It can mean that you're eager to learn or know something, but also, *strange* or *unusual*. Yes, I think that description fits you very well."

"So this is about me?" I asked through gritted teeth. "You want me curious?"

"I'm just an old man," came the reply, "with a fondness for riddles."

Old. How old? I didn't have time to dwell on that question—or the fact that he'd referred to himself in the same way that Tobias Hawthorne's grandsons referred to the dead billionaire.

"I don't know what kind of sick game you're playing," I said harshly.

"Or maybe you know exactly what kind of sick game I'm playing."

I could practically hear his lips curving into a knife-sharp smile.

"You have the box," he said. "You have the phone. You'll figure the next part out."

"What next part?"

"Tick tock," the old man replied. "The timer's counting down to our next call. You won't like what happens to your Toby if you don't have an answer for me by then."

CHAPTER 31

What did we learn? I tried to concentrate on that, not the threat, not the timer counting down.

Toby's captor had referred to himself as old.

He'd called me by my full name.

He played with words—and with people. "He likes riddles," I said out loud. "And games."

I knew someone who fit that description, but billionaire Tobias Hawthorne was dead. He'd been dead for a year.

"What precisely are we supposed to figure out?" Grayson asked crisply.

I looked reflexively toward Jameson. "There must be something to find or decode," I said, "just like there was in the earlier deliveries."

"The next part of the same riddle," Jameson murmured, our minds in sync.

Eve looked between the two of us. "What riddle?"

"*The* riddle," Jameson said. "Who is he? Why is he doing this? The first two clues were straightforward enough to decode. He's upped his ante with this installment."

"We must be missing something," I said. "A detail about the box or the package or—"

"I recorded the phone call." Xander held up his phone. "In case there's a clue in something he said. Beyond that . . ."

"We have the combination," Jameson finished. "And the calendar entry."

"Niv," I said out loud. Moving on instinct, I checked the box for hidden compartments. There weren't any. There was nothing else on the phone, nothing that popped out when we listened to my exchange with Toby's captor a second time. Or a third.

"Can your team trace the call?" I asked Oren, trying to think ahead, trying to come at this problem from all sides. "We have the number."

"I can try," Oren replied evenly, "but unless our opponent is far less intelligent than he appears, the number is unregistered, and the call was routed through the internet, not a phone tower, with the signal split across a thousand IP addresses, bouncing all over the world."

My throat tightened. "Could the police help pin it down?"

"We can't call the police," Eve whispered. "He could *kill* Toby."

"Discreet inquiries could potentially be made to a trusted police contact without providing details," Oren said. "Unfortunately, my three most trusted contacts have been recently transferred."

There was no way that was a coincidence. Attacks on my business interests. Attempts to chip away at my security team. Paparazzi set on my every move. Police contacts transferred. I thought about what Alisa had said we were looking for. *Wealth. Power. Connections.*

"Play the recording again," I told Xander.

My BHFF did as I asked, and this time, as the conversation

ended, Jameson looked to Grayson. "He said that Avery could *call* him Luke. Not that his name *was* Luke."

"Does that matter?" I asked.

Grayson held Jameson's gaze. "It could."

Eve started to say something, but the sound of a ringing phone silenced her. It wasn't the burner phone. It was mine. My eyes darted to the caller ID. *Thea.*

I answered. "I'm kind of busy right now, Thea."

"In that case, do you want the bad news first or the really bad news?"

"Is Rebecca—"

"Someone got a picture of Eve standing outside the gates of Hawthorne House. It just went live."

I winced. "Was that the bad news or—"

"It went live," Thea continued, "on the internet's biggest gossip site, alongside a picture of Emily and an exposé on rumors that Emily Laughlin was killed by Grayson and Jameson Hawthorne."

CHAPTER 32

I texted Alisa first. Handling scandals like this was part of her job. Breaking the news to the boys and Eve was harder. Forcing my mouth to say the words felt like breaking my ankle. *A moment of wrongness. A sick* crunch. *The shock.* Then the shock wore off.

"This is bullshit," Nash bit out. He took a breath, then turned discerning eyes on his brothers. "Jamie? Gray?"

"I'm fine." Grayson's face was like stone.

"And in keeping with my general superiority in our sibling relationship," Jameson added with a sardonic smile that was just a little too sharp, "I am better than fine."

This was Luke's doing. It had to be.

Eve pulled the gossip site up on her phone. She stared at it. Her own picture. Emily's.

I flashed back to that moment in Toby's wing when she'd told me that she didn't look like anyone in her family.

"Why does it say you killed her?" Eve asked, her voice reedy. She didn't look up from her phone, but I knew who she was addressing that question to.

"Because," Grayson replied, his voice blade-edged, "we did."

"Like hell you did," Nash swore. He looked around at the rest of us. "What's the rule about fightin' dirty?" he asked. No one answered. "Gray? Jamie?" He swiveled his gaze to me.

"There's no such thing as fighting dirty," I said lowly, "if you win." I wanted to win. I wanted to get Toby back. I wanted to take the bastard who had kidnapped him—the bastard who had just done this to Jameson and Grayson and Eve—*down.*

"Fighting dirty?" Eve asked, finally looking up from the website. "Is that what you call this? My face is going to be everywhere."

This was exactly what Toby *hadn't* wanted.

"Glitter cannon," Xander said.

I shot him a look. This really wasn't the time for levity—or sparkles.

"This right here is a glitter cannon," Xander reiterated. "Detonate one in the middle of a game, and it makes a huge mess. The kind that gets everywhere, sticks to everything."

Grayson's expression hardened. "And runs down the clock while you clean it up."

"While you *try* to clean it up," Libby said gently. She'd been quiet in all of this, but my sister had empathy in spades, and she didn't have to know Grayson or Jameson or even Eve as well as I did to know how hard they'd been hit.

"Some things don't clean easy," Nash agreed in a slow, steady drawl, his eyes finding Libby's like it was the most natural thing in the world. "You'll think you've finally got it all. Everything's fine. And then five years later..."

"There's still glitter in Grayson's bathroom," Xander finished. I got the feeling that wasn't a metaphor.

"Luke did this," I said. "He set this up. He detonated the blast. He wants us distracted." *He wants to run down the clock. He wants us to lose.*

Tick tock.

Eve turned her phone off and tossed it roughly onto the desk. "Screw the glitter," she said. "I don't want to figure out what happens to Toby if that timer hits zero."

None of us did.

Xander played the conversation with Luke back again, and we got to work.

CHAPTER 33

6 HOURS, 17 MIN, 9 SEC...

It was getting to the point where I didn't even need to look at the time. I just knew. We weren't getting anywhere. I tried to clear my head, but fresh air didn't help. Giving money anonymously to people who needed it didn't help.

When I went back inside, I arrived in the circular library just in time to hear Xander's phone go off. He was the only person I knew who used the first twelve digits of pi as a ringtone. After an uncharacteristically muted conversation, he brought the phone to me.

"Max," he mouthed.

I took the phone. "Let me guess," I said, holding it to my ear. "You've seen the news?"

"What makes you think that?" Max responded. "I was just calling to catch you up on my bodyguard situation. Piotr stubbornly refuses to choose a theme song, but otherwise, our bodyguard-and-bodyguard-ee relationship is working out quite well."

Leave it to Max to make light of needing security. *Because of me.* I couldn't help feeling responsible, any more than I could help feeling like Eve had been outed to the world only because she'd made the poor choice of coming to *me* for help.

My name was the one on the envelopes, the one on the box. I was the one in Luke's sights, but anyone close to me could end up in the crosshairs.

"I'm sorry," I told Max.

"I know," my best friend replied. "But don't worry. I'll choose a theme song for him." She paused. "Xander said something about... a cannon?"

The whole story burst out, like water demolishing a broken dam: the package delivery, the box, the phone, the call with "Luke"—and his ultimatum.

"You sound like a person who needs to think out loud," Max opined. "Proceed."

I did. I just kept talking and talking, hoping my brain would find something different to say this time. I got to the event in the calendar and said, "We thought *Niv* might be a reference to an SEC form, N-four. We've spent hours trying to track down Tobias Hawthorne's filings. I guess *Niv* could be a name, or initials, but—"

"Niv," Max repeated. "Spelled *N-I-V*?"

"Yes."

"N-I-V," she repeated. "As in *New International Version*?"

I tilted my head to the side. "New international version of what?"

"The B-I-B-L-E—and now, I am officially going to have Sunday school songs running on a loop all night."

"The Bible," I repeated, and suddenly, it clicked. "Luke."

"My second-favorite Gospel," Max noted. "I'll always be a John girl at heart."

I barely heard her. My brain was going too fast, images flashing through my mind, slices of memory piling up one after the other. "The numbers."

The combination might be just a combination, Jameson had said. *But there's also the possibility that the numbers themselves are a clue.*

"What numbers?" Max asked.

My heart beat viciously against my rib cage. "Fifteen, eleven, thirty-two."

"Are you faxing kidding me?" Max was delighted. "Am I about to solve a Hawthorne riddle?"

"Max!"

"The book of Luke," she said, "chapter fifteen, verses eleven through thirty-two. It's a parable."

"Which one?" I asked.

"The parable of the prodigal son."

CHAPTER 34

None of us slept more than three hours that night. We read every version of Luke 15:11–32 that we could find, every interpretation of it, every reference to it.

Nine seconds left on the timer. Eight. I watched it count down. Eve was sitting beside me, her feet curled under her body. Libby was on my other side. The boys were standing. Xander had the recorder ready.

Three. Two. One—

The phone rang. I answered it and set it to speaker so everyone could hear. "Hello."

"Well, Avery Kylie Grambs?"

The use of my full name did not go unnoticed. "Luke, chapter fifteen, verses eleven through thirty-two." I kept my voice calm, even.

"What about Luke, chapter fifteen, verses eleven through thirty-two?"

I didn't want to perform for him. "I solved your puzzle. Let me talk to Toby."

"Very well."

There was silence, and then I heard Toby's voice. "Avery. Don't—"

The rest of that sentence was cut off. My stomach sank. I felt fury snaking its way through my body. "What did you do to him?"

"Tell me about Luke, chapter fifteen, verses eleven through thirty-two."

He has Toby. I have to play this his way. All I could do was hope my adversary would eventually tip his hand. "The prodigal son demanded his inheritance early," I said, trying not to let any of the emotions I was feeling into my voice. "He abandoned his family and squandered the fortune he'd been given. But despite all of this, his father embraced him upon his return."

"A wasteful youth," the man said, "wandering the world—ungrateful. A benevolent father, ready to welcome him home. But if memory serves correctly, there were three characters in that story, and you've only mentioned two."

"The brother." Eve came to stand beside me and spoke before I could. "He stayed and worked alongside his father for years for no reward."

There was silence on the other end of the phone line. And then, the slash of a verbal knife: "I will talk only to the heiress. The one Tobias Hawthorne *chose*."

Eve shrank in on herself, like she'd been struck, her eyes wet, her expression like stone. On the other end of the line, there was silence.

Had he hung up?

Panicked, my grip on the phone tightened. "I'm here!"

"Avery Kylie Grambs, there are three characters in the parable of the prodigal son, are there not?"

Breath left my lungs. "The son who left," I said, sounding calmer than I felt. "The son who stayed. And the father."

"Why don't you ruminate on that?" There was another long pause, and then: "I'll be in touch."

CHAPTER 35

Ruminating looked like this: Libby went to make coffee, because when things got bad, she took care of other people. Grayson stood, straightened his suit jacket, and turned his back on the rest of us. Jameson began pacing like a panther on the prowl. Nash took off his cowboy hat and stared at it, an ominous expression on his face. Xander darted out of the room, and Eve lowered her head into her hands.

"I shouldn't have said anything," she said hoarsely. "But after he cut Toby off—"

"I understand," I told her. "And it wouldn't have mattered if you'd stayed silent. We would have ended up in the exact same place."

"Not *exactly*." Jameson came to a stop directly in front of me. "Think about what he said after Eve interrupted—and the way he referred to you."

"As *the heiress*," I replied, and then I remembered the rest of it. "The one Tobias Hawthorne chose." I swallowed. "The prodigal son is a story about inheritance and forgiveness."

"Everyone who thinks that Toby was kidnapped as part of a giant *forgiveness* plot," Nash said, his drawl doing nothing to soften the words, "raise your hand."

All our hands remained down. "We already know this is about revenge," I said harshly. "We know it's about winning. This is just another piece of the same damn riddle that we aren't meant to solve."

Now I was the one who couldn't stand still. Rage didn't simmer. It burned.

"He wants us driving ourselves crazy, going over and over it," I said, striding toward the massive tree trunk desk and bracing my hands against it, *hard.* "He wants us *ruminating.* And what's even the point?" I was so close to punching the wood. "He's not done yet, and he's not going to give us what we need to solve this until he wants it solved."

I'll be in touch. Our adversary was like a cat that had a mouse by the tail. He was batting at me, then letting me go, creating the illusion that maybe, if I was very clever, I could slip his grasp, when he wasn't the least afraid I would.

"We have to try," Eve said with quiet desperation.

"Eve's right." Grayson turned back toward us—toward her. "Just because our opponent *thinks* this is beyond our capabilities to figure out doesn't mean that it is."

Jameson placed his hands next to mine on the desk. "The other two clues were vague. This one, less so. Even partial riddles can sometimes be solved."

As futile as it felt, as angry as I was, they were right. We had to try. For Toby, we had to.

"I'm back!" Xander burst into the room. "And I have props!" He thrust his hand out. In his palm, there were three chess pieces: a king, a knight, and a bishop.

Jameson reached for the chess pieces, but Xander smacked his hand away. "The father." Xander brandished the king and set it down on the desk. "The prodigal son." He plunked down the knight. "And the son who stayed."

"The bishop as the son who kept faith," I commented as Xander placed the final piece on the desk. "Nice touch." I stared at the three pieces. *A wasteful youth, wandering the world—ungrateful.* The memory of that voice stuck to me like oil. *A benevolent father, ready to welcome him home.*

I picked up the knight. "*Prodigal* means wastrel. We all know what teenage Toby was like. He slept and drank his way across the country, was responsible for a fire that killed three people, and allowed his family to think he was dead for decades."

"And through all of that," Jameson mused, picking up the king, "our grandfather wanted nothing more than to welcome his prodigal son home."

Toby, the prodigal. Tobias, the father.

"That just leaves the other son," Grayson said, walking over to join us as the desk. Nash circled up, too, leaving only a muted Eve on the outskirts. "The one who toiled faithfully," Grayson continued, "and was given nothing."

He managed to say those words like they held no meaning to him, but this part of the story had to hit close to home for him—for all of them. "We already talked to Skye," I said, picking up the bishop, the faithful son. "But Skye isn't Toby's only sibling."

I hated to even say it because I hadn't seen Tobias Hawthorne's older daughter as an enemy in months.

"It's not Zara," Jameson said with the kind of intensity I associated with him and only him. "She's Hawthorne enough to pull it off, if she wanted to, but unless we believe that the man on that phone call was an actor—a front—we *know* who the third player in this story is."

Avenge. Revenge. Vengeance. Avenger.

I always win in the end.

The three characters in the story of the prodigal son.

Each piece of the riddle told us something about our opponent. "If Toby is supposed to be the unworthy prodigal," I said, my entire body wound tight, "and Tobias Hawthorne is the father who forgave him, the only role left for Toby's abductor is the other son."

Another son. My body went utterly still as that possibility sank in.

Xander raised his hand. "Anyone else wondering if we have a secret uncle out there no one knows about? Because at this point, *secret uncle* just kind of feels like it belongs on the Hawthorne bingo card."

"I don't buy it." Nash's voice was steady, sure, unhurried. "The old man wasn't exactly scrupulous, but he *was* faithful—and damn possessive of anyone or anything he considered his. Besides, we don't have to go lookin' for *secret* uncles."

I registered his meaning at the exact same time that Jameson did. "That wasn't Constantine on the phone," he said. "But—"

"Constantine Calligaris wasn't Zara's first husband," I finished. Tobias Hawthorne might have had only one son, but he'd had more than one *son-in-law.*

"No one ever talks about the first guy," Xander offered. "Ever."

A son, cut from the family, ignored, forgotten. I looked to Oren. "Where's Zara?"

That question was loaded, given their history, but my head of security answered like the professional he was. "She wakes up early in the mornings to tend the roses."

"I'll go." Grayson wasn't asking permission or volunteering.

Eve finally joined the rest of us at the desk. She looked up at Grayson, tear tracks on her face. "I'll go with you, Gray."

He was going to take her up on the offer. I could tell that just by looking at him, but I didn't object. I didn't let myself say a single word.

But Jameson surprised me. "No. You go with Grayson, Heiress."

I had no idea what to read into that—if he still didn't trust Eve, if he didn't trust Grayson around Eve, or if he was just trying to fight his demons, set aside a lifelong rivalry, and trust me.

CHAPTER 36

Grayson and I found Zara in the greenhouse. She wore white gardening gloves that fit her hands like a second skin and held a pair of shears so sharp they probably could have cut through bone.

"To what do I owe this pleasure?" Zara angled her head toward us, the look in her eyes coolly advertising the fact that she was a Hawthorne and, by definition, missed nothing. "Out with it, both of you. You want something."

"We just want to talk," Grayson said evenly.

Zara ran her finger lightly over a thorn. "No Hawthorne has ever just wanted to talk."

Grayson didn't argue that point. "Your brother Toby has been abducted," he said, with that uncanny ability to say things that *mattered* as if they were simply facts. "There's been no demand for ransom, but we've received several communications from his kidnapper."

"Is Toby alright?" Zara took a step toward Oren. "John—is my brother alright?"

He gently met her gaze and gave her what he could. "He's alive."

"And you haven't found him yet?" Zara demanded. Her tone was pure ice. I could see the exact moment she remembered who she was talking to and realized that if *Oren* couldn't find Toby, there was a very good chance he couldn't be found.

"We think there might be a family connection between Toby and the person who took him," I said.

Zara's expression wavered, like ripples across the water. "If you came here to make accusations, I suggest you stop beating around the bush and make them."

"We're not here to accuse you of anything," Grayson said with absolute, unerring calm. "We need to ask you about your first husband."

"Christopher?" Zara arched a brow. "I assure you, you don't."

"Toby's abductor has been sending clues," I said, rushing the words. "The most recent involves the biblical story of the prodigal son."

"We're looking," Grayson stated, "for someone who viewed Tobias Hawthorne as a father and felt as though he got a raw deal. Tell us about Christopher."

"He was everything that was expected of me." Zara lifted the shears to clip a white rose. *Off with its head.* "Wealthy family, politically connected, charming."

Wealth, Alisa had said. *Power. Connections.*

Zara set the white rose in a black basket, then clipped three more. "When I filed for divorce, Chris went to my father and played the dutiful son, fully expecting the old man to talk some sense into me."

It was Grayson's turn now to arch a brow. "How thoroughly was he destroyed?"

Zara smiled. "I assure you, the divorce was civil." In other words:

utterly. "But it hardly matters. Christopher died in a boating accident not long after everything was finalized."

No, I thought, a visceral, knee-jerk reaction. *Not another dead end*. "What about his family?" I asked, unwilling to let this go.

"He was an only child, and his parents are likewise deceased."

I felt like the mouse I'd imagined earlier, like I'd been made to think I had a chance when I never really had. But I couldn't give up. "Is it possible that your father had another son?" I asked, going back to that possibility. "Besides Toby?"

"A pretermitted heir who *didn't* come crawling out of the woodwork after the will was read?" Zara responded archly. "With billions at stake? Hardly likely."

"Then what are we missing?" I asked, more desperation in my tone than I wanted to admit.

Zara considered the question. "My father liked to say that our minds have a way of tricking us into choosing between two options when there are really seven. The Hawthorne gift has always been seeing all seven."

"Identify the assumptions implicit in your own logic," Grayson said, clearly citing a dictate he'd been taught, "then negate them."

I thought about that. What assumptions had we made? *That Toby is the prodigal son, Tobias the father.* It was the obvious interpretation, given Toby's history, but that was the thing about riddles. The answer *wasn't* obvious.

And on that first phone call, Toby's captor had referred to himself as an *old man*.

"What happens if we take Toby out of the story?" I asked Grayson. "If your grandfather *isn't* the father in the parable?" My heart drummed in my chest. "What if he's one of the sons?"

Grayson looked to his aunt. "Did the old man ever talk to you about his family? His parents?"

"My father liked to say that he didn't have a family, that he came from nothing."

"That was what he *liked* to say," Grayson confirmed.

In my mind, all I could picture were the three chess pieces. If Tobias Hawthorne was the bishop or the knight...who the hell was the king?

CHAPTER 37

"We need to find Nan," Jameson said immediately, once Grayson and I had reported back. "She's probably the only person alive who could tell us if the old man had family that Zara doesn't know about."

"Finding Nan," Xander explained to Eve, in what appeared to be an attempt to cheer her up, "is a bit like a game of Where's Waldo, except Waldo likes to jab people with her cane."

"She has favorite places in the House," I said. *The piano room. The card room.*

"It's Tuesday morning," Nash commented wryly.

"The chapel." Jameson looked at each of his brothers. "I'll go." He turned to me. "Feel like a walk?"

The Hawthorne chapel—located beyond the hedge maze and due west of the tennis courts—wasn't large, but it was breathtaking. The stone arches, hand-carved pews, and elaborate stained-glass windows looked like they'd been the work of dozens of artisans.

We found Nan resting in a pew. "Don't let in a draft," she barked without so much as turning around to see who she was barking at.

Jameson shut the chapel door, and we joined her in the pew. Nan's head was bowed, her eyes closed, but somehow, she seemed to know exactly who had joined her. "Shameless boy," she scolded Jameson. "And you, girl! Forget about our weekly poker game yesterday, did you?"

I winced. "Sorry. I've been distracted." That was an understatement.

Nan opened her eyes for the sole purpose of narrowing them at me. "But now that you *want* to talk, it doesn't matter if I'm in the middle of something?"

"We can wait until you're finished praying," I said, properly chastened—or at least trying to look that way.

"Praying?" Nan grumbled. "More like giving our Maker a piece of my mind."

"My grandfather built this chapel so Nan would have someplace to yell at God," Jameson informed me.

Nan harrumphed. "The old coot threatened to build me a mausoleum instead. Tobias never thought I'd outlive him."

That was probably as close to an opening as we were going to get. "Did your son-in-law have any family of his own?" I asked. "Parents?"

"As opposed to what, girl? Springing forth fully formed from the head of Zeus?" Nan snorted. "Tobias always did have a God complex."

"You loved him," Jameson said gently.

A breath caught in Nan's throat. "Like my own child." She closed her eyes for a second or two, then opened them and continued. "He had parents, I suppose. From what I remember, Tobias said they had him older and didn't much know what to do with a boy like him." Nan gave Jameson a look. "Hawthorne children can be trying."

"So he was a late-in-life baby," I summarized. "Did they have any other children?"

"After having Tobias, I doubt they would have dared."

"What about older siblings?" Jameson asked.

One father, two sons...

"None of those, either. By the time Tobias met my Alice, he was well and truly alone. Father died of a heart attack when Tobias was a teenager. Mother only outlasted the father by about a year."

"What about mentors?" Jameson asked. I could practically see him playing out a dozen different scenarios in his mind. "Father figures? Friends?"

"Tobias Hawthorne was never in the business of making friends. He was in the business of making money. He was a single-minded bastard, wily and brutal." Nan's voice shook. "But he was good to my Alice. To me."

"Family first," Jameson said softly beside me.

"No man has ever built an empire without doing a thing or two they aren't proud of, but Tobias didn't let that follow him home. His hands weren't always clean, but he never once raised them—not to Alice or their children or you boys."

"You would have killed him if he had," Jameson said affectionately.

"The mouth on you," Nan chided.

His hands weren't always clean. That single phrase sent me back to the first message we'd received from Toby's kidnapper. At the time, it had seemed likely that the target of revenge was either Toby or me. But what if it was Tobias Hawthorne himself?

What if this—all of it—had always been about the old man? *What if I'm just the one* he *chose? What if Toby is just* his *lost son?* The possibility took hold of my mind, gripped it like fingernails digging into flesh.

“What did your son-in-law do?” I asked. “Why weren’t his hands clean?”

Nan offered no reply to that question.

Jameson reached out and took her hand. “If I told you that someone wanted revenge against the Hawthorne family—”

Nan patted the side of his face. “I’d tell that person to get in line.”

CHAPTER 38

Identify your assumptions. Question them. Negate them. As I stepped out of the chapel, I felt like a shell over my brain had been cracked wide open, and now possibilities were streaming in from every side.

What would I have done from the very beginning if I'd assumed that Toby had been taken as revenge for something that his father had done? I thought about Eve talking about Hawthorne secrets—*dark secrets, maybe even dangerous ones*—and then about Nan and her talk of empires and dirty hands.

What had Tobias Hawthorne done on his way to the top? Once he'd amassed all that money and all that power, what had he used it to do? *And to whom?*

My brain sorting through possible next moves at warp speed, I turned to Oren. "You tracked threats against Tobias Hawthorne, back when you were his head of security. He had a List, like mine."

List, capital L, threats. People who required watching.

"Mr. Hawthorne had a List," Oren confirmed. "But it was a bit different than yours."

My List was heavy on strangers. From the moment I'd been

named Tobias Hawthorne's heir, I'd been thrust into the kind of worldwide spotlight that automatically came with online death threats and would-be stalkers, people who wanted to be me and people who wanted to hurt me.

It was always worse right after a new story broke. *Like now.*

"Would my grandfather's List happen to be a list of people he screwed over?" Jameson asked Oren.

He saw what I did: If Toby's captor was telling a story about envy, revenge, and triumphing over an old enemy, Tobias Hawthorne's List was a hell of a place to start.

Jameson and I caught the others up to speed, and Oren had the List delivered to the solarium. The room had glass walls and a glass ceiling, so no matter where you stood, you could feel the sun on your skin. After our near all-nighter, the seven of us were going to need all the help staying awake that we could get.

Especially because this was going to take a while.

Tobias Hawthorne hadn't just had a list of names. He'd had file folders like the one he'd assembled on me, but for hundreds of people. Hundreds of *threats.*

"You tracked all these people?" I asked Oren, staring at the stack and stacks of files.

"It wasn't a matter of actively tracking so much as knowing what they looked like, knowing their names, keeping an eye out." Oren's expression was smooth, unreadable, *professional.* "The files were Mr. Hawthorne's doing, not mine. I was only allowed to look at them if the person started popping up."

Right now, we didn't have a face. We didn't have a name, so I focused on what we did have. "We're looking for an older man," I told the others quietly. "Someone who was bested and betrayed by Tobias Hawthorne." I wanted there to be more than that for us to go on. "There might be a family connection or a family-like connection or maybe even just a story focused on three people."

"Three *men*," Eve said, seeming to have recovered her voice, her grit, and her poise. "In the parable, they're all *men*. And this guy took Toby, not Zara or Skye. He took the *son*."

She'd clearly been thinking about this. I stole a look at Grayson, and the way he was looking at Eve made me think that she hadn't been *thinking* alone.

"Well," Xander said, in an attempt at cheer. "That's not nothing to go on!"

I turned my attention back to the folders—stacks and stacks of them that left a heavy feeling in my stomach. "Whoever this man is," I said, "whatever his history with Tobias Hawthorne, whatever he lost—he's wealthy, powerful, and connected now."

CHAPTER 39

By the time we'd each made it through three or four folders, even the sunlight streaming in from all sides couldn't banish the dark pall that had settled over the room.

This was what I'd known before reading the files: Tobias Hawthorne had filed his first patents in the late sixties and early seventies. At least one had turned out to be valuable, and he'd used the profits from that to fund the land acquisitions that had made him a major player in Texas oil. He'd eventually sold his oil company for upward of a hundred million dollars, and after that, he'd diversified with a Midas touch for turning millions to billions.

All of that was public information. The information in these files told the parts of the story that the myth of Tobias Hawthorne glossed over. *Hostile takeovers. Competitors run out of business. Lawsuits filed for the sole purpose of bankrupting the other party.* The ruthless billionaire had a habit of zeroing in on a market opportunity and moving into that space with no mercy, buying up patents and smaller corporations, hiring the best and the brightest and using them to destroy the competition—only to pivot to a new industry, a new challenge.

He paid his employees well, but when the wind changed or the profits dried up, he laid them off without mercy.

Tobias Hawthorne was never in the business of making friends. I'd asked Nan exactly what her son-in-law had done that he wasn't proud of. The answer was all around us, and it was impossible to ignore the details in any of the files just because they didn't match what we were looking for.

I stared down at the folder in my hand: *Seaton, Tyler.* It appeared that Mr. Seaton, a brilliant biomedical engineer, had been caught up in one of Tobias Hawthorne's pivots after seven years of loyal—and lucrative—service. Seaton was downsized. Like all Hawthorne employees, he'd been given a generous severance package, including an extension of his company insurance. But eventually, that extension had run out, and a noncompete clause in the fine print of his contract had made it nearly impossible for him to find other employment.

And insurance.

Swallowing, I forced myself to stare at the pictures in this file folder. Pictures of a little girl. *Mariah Seaton.* She'd been diagnosed with cancer at age nine, just before her father lost his job.

She was dead by twelve.

Feeling sick to my stomach, I forced myself to continue paging through the file. The final sheet contained financial information about a transaction—a generous donation the Hawthorne Foundation had made to St. Jude Children's Research Hospital.

This was Tobias Hawthorne, billionaire, balancing his ledger. *That's not balance.*

"Did you know about this?" Grayson said, his voice low, his silver eyes targeting Nash.

"Which 'this' might we be talkin' about, little brother?"

"How about buying patents from a grieving widow for one one-hundredth of what they were worth?" Grayson threw down the file, then picked up another one. "Or posing as an angel investor when what he really wanted was to incrementally acquire enough of the company to be able to shut it down to clear the way for *another* of his investments?"

"I'll take *boilerplate contracts that give him control of his employees' IP* for two thousand, Alex." Jameson paused. "Whether that IP was created on the clock or not."

Across the room, Xander swallowed. "You really don't want to read about his foray into pharmaceuticals."

"Did you know?" Grayson asked Nash again. "Is that why you always had one foot out the door? Why you couldn't stand to be under the old man's roof?"

"Why you save people," Libby said quietly. She wasn't looking at Nash. She was looking at her wrists.

"I knew who he was." Nash didn't say more than that, but I could see tension beneath the rough stubble on his jaw. He angled his head down, the rim of his cowboy hat obscuring his face.

"Do you remember the bag of glass?" Jameson asked his brothers suddenly, an ache in his tone. "It was the puzzle with the knife. We had to break a glass ballerina to find three diamonds inside. The prompt was *Tell me what's real*, and Nash won because the rest of us focused on the diamonds—"

"And I handed the old man a real bag of shattered glass," Nash finished. There was something in his voice that made Libby stop looking at her wrists and walk to put one hand silently on his arm.

"The shattered glass," Grayson said, a wave of tension rippling through his body. "That lecture he gave us about how, to do what he had done, sacrifices had to be made. Things got broken. And if you didn't clean up the shards…"

Xander finished the sentence, his Adam's apple bobbing, "People got hurt."

CHAPTER 40

Thirty-six hours passed—no word from Toby's captor, an ever-growing hoard of paparazzi outside the gates, and too much time spent in the solarium with files on Tobias Hawthorne's enemies. His many, many enemies.

I finished the files in my stack. Each of the four Hawthorne brothers finished theirs. So did Libby. So did Eve. Nothing matched. Nothing fit. But I didn't want to admit that we'd hit another wall. I didn't want to feel cornered or outmatched or like everyone around me had taken repeated shots to the gut for *nothing*.

So I kept going back to the solarium, rereading files the others had already gone through, even though I knew the Hawthornes hadn't missed a damn thing. That these files were burned into them now.

The moment Jameson had finished his stack, he'd disappeared into the walls. The only reason I knew he hadn't taken off for parts unknown halfway around the world was that the bed was warm beside me when I woke in the morning. Grayson took to the pool, pushing himself past the point of human endurance again and again, and after Nash had finished, he'd dodged the press at the gates, snuck out to a bar, and came back at two in the morning with a split lip and a trembling puppy tucked into his shirt. Xander was barely eating. Eve seemed to think that she didn't need sleep and that if she could just memorize every detail of every file, an answer would present itself.

I understood. The two of us didn't talk about Toby, about the silence from his captor, but it fueled us on.

I'll be in touch.

I reached for another file—one of the few I hadn't made it through myself yet—and opened it. *Empty.* "Have you read this one?" I asked Eve, my heart whamming against my rib cage with sudden, startling force. "There's nothing here."

Eve looked up from the file she'd been scouring for the past twenty minutes. The desperate hope in *her* eyes flickered and died when she saw which file I was referring to. "Isaiah Alexander? There was a page in there before. Just one. Short file. Another disgruntled employee, fired from a Hawthorne lab. *PhD, rising star*—and now the guy has nothing."

No wealth. No power. No connections. *Not what we're looking for.*

"So where's the page?" I asked, the question gnawing at me.

"Does it matter?" Eve said, her tone dismissive, annoyance marring her striking features. "Maybe it got mixed in with another file."

"Maybe," I said. I closed the file, and my gaze caught on the tab. *Alexander, Isaiah.* Eve had said the name, but I hadn't processed it—not until now.

Grayson's father was Sheffield *Grayson.* Nash's father was named Jake *Nash.* And Xander's name was short for *Alexander.*

I found my BHFF in his lab. It was a hidden room filled with the most random assortment of items imaginable. Some people did found art, turning everyday objects into artistic commentary. Xander was more of a found *engineer.* As far as Hawthorne-brother coping mechanisms went, it was probably the healthiest one in the House.

"I need to talk to you about something," I said.

"Can it be about off-label uses for medieval weaponry?" Xander requested. "Because I have some ideas."

That was concerning on many levels, and it was so Xander that I wanted to cry or hug him or do anything except hold up that file and make him talk to me about something he'd made it very clear during Chutes and Ladders that he didn't want to talk about.

"Is this your father?" I said gently. "Isaiah Alexander?"

Xander turned to look at me. Then, as if coming to a very serious decision, he lifted his hand and pressed one finger to the end of my nose. "Boop."

"You're not going to distract me," I told him, the exasperation I might have normally felt replaced by something more tender and painful. "Come on, Xan. I'm your BHHFF. Talk to me."

"Double boop." Xander pressed my nose again. "What's the extra *H* for?"

"Honorary," I told him. "You guys made me an honorary Hawthorne, and that makes me your Best Honorary Hawthorne Friend Forever. So *talk*."

"Triple boo—" Xander started to say, but I ducked before he could touch my nose. I straightened, caught his hand gently in mine, and squeezed.

This was *Xander*, so there wasn't a hint of accusation in my voice when I asked my next question. "Did you take the page that was in this file?"

Xander gave an emphatic shake of his head. "I didn't even know Isaiah was on the List. I can probably tell you what his file says, though. I kind of spent the past several months making a file of my own."

This time, I didn't push down the urge to hug him. Hard. "Eve said he was a PhD who got fired from a Hawthorne lab," I said, once I'd pulled back.

"That about covers it," Xander replied, his cheery tone a copy of a copy of the real thing. "Except for timing. It's possible that Isaiah was fired around the time I was conceived. Maybe because I was conceived? I mean, maybe not! But maybe?"

Poor Xander. I thought about what he'd said in Chutes and Ladders. "Is that why you haven't contacted him?"

"I can't just call him." Xander gave me a plaintive look. "What if he hates me?"

"No one could possibly hate you, Xander," I told him, my heart twisting.

"Avery, people have hated me my whole life." There was something in his tone that made me think that very few people understood what it was like to be Xander Hawthorne.

"Not anyone who knows you," I said fiercely.

Xander smiled, and something about it made me want to cry. "Do you think it's okay," he said, sounding younger than I'd ever heard him, "that I loved playing those Saturday morning games? Loved growing up here? Loved the great and terrible Tobias Hawthorne?"

I couldn't answer that for him—for any of them. I couldn't make these past few days hurt less. But there was one thing I could say. "You didn't love the great and terrible Tobias Hawthorne. You loved the old man."

"I was the only one who knew that he was dying." Xander turned to pick up what looked like a tuning fork, but he didn't make a single move to add it to whatever contraption he was building. "He kept it a secret from everyone else for weeks. He wanted me with him at the end, and do you know what he said to me—the very last thing?"

"What?" I asked quietly.

"By the time this is over, you'll know what kind of man I was—and what kind of man you want to be."

CHAPTER 41

I headed back to the solarium empty-handed, having hit yet another dead end. *I'll be in touch.* That sinister promise echoed in my mind as I rounded the corner and saw Eve's guard. I nodded to him, glanced briefly back at Oren, then pushed opened the solarium door.

Inside, Eve was sitting with a file laid out on the ground in front of her and a phone in her hand. *Taking pictures.*

"What are you doing?" I asked, startled.

Eve looked up. "What do you think I'm doing?" Her voice broke. "I need sleep. I know I need sleep, but I can't stop. And I can't take these files out of this room, so I thought..." She shook her head, her eyes tearing, amber hair falling into her face. "Never mind. It's dumb."

"It's not dumb," I told her. "And you do need sleep."

We all did.

I checked Jameson's wing before I returned to my own. He wasn't in either. I remembered what it had been like when I'd discovered that my mom wasn't who I'd thought she was. I'd felt like I was mourning her death all over again, and the only thing that had helped was Libby reminding me of the kind of person my mom had been, proving to me that I *had* known her in every way that mattered.

But what could I say to Jameson or Xander or any of them about Tobias Hawthorne? That he really *was* brilliant? Strategic? That he'd had some small shreds of conscience? That he'd cared for his family, even if he'd disinherited all of them for a stranger?

By the time this is over, you'll know what kind of man I was—and what kind of man you want to be. I thought about the billionaire's last words to Xander. By the time *what* was over? By the time Xander had found his father? By the time all the games that Tobias Hawthorne had planned before his death had been played?

That thought drew my gaze to the leather satchel on my dresser. For two days, I'd been consumed with Toby's captor's sick riddle and the hope, however thin, that we were getting closer to solving it. But the truth was that all the *ruminating* we'd done had gotten us nowhere. It had probably been *designed* to lead us nowhere—until the riddle was complete.

I'll be in touch.

I hated this. I needed a win. I needed a distraction. *By the time this is over, you'll know what kind of man I was.* Slowly, I walked over to my dresser, thought about Tobias Hawthorne and those files, and picked up the satchel.

Moving methodically, I laid out the objects I hadn't yet used. *The steamer. The flashlight. The beach towel. The glass circle.* I said the last clue Jameson and I had uncovered out loud. *"Don't breathe."*

I cleared my mind. After a moment, my gaze locked on the towel, then on the blue-green circle. *That color. A towel. Don't breathe.*

With sudden, visceral clarity, I knew what I had to do.

A person stopped breathing when they were terrified, surprised, awed, trying to be quiet, surrounded by smoke—or underwater.

CHAPTER 42

A motion-sensor light came on as I stepped onto the patio. In my mind, in the span of a single heartbeat, I saw the pool the way it looked in daytime, with light reflecting off the water, the tiles on the bottom making it look as breathtakingly blue-green as the Mediterranean.

The same shade as the piece of glass I carried in my right hand. I held the beach towel in my left. Clearly, this was going to require getting wet.

At night, the water was darker, shadowy. I heard Grayson swimming before I saw him and felt the exact moment he became aware of my presence.

Grayson Davenport Hawthorne's hand slapped the edge of the pool. He pulled himself upright. "Avery." His voice was quiet, but in the still of the night, it carried. "You shouldn't be here." *With me* went unsaid. "You should be asleep."

Grayson and his *oughts* and *shoulds*. *Hawthornes aren't supposed to break.* His voice spoke deep in my memory. *Especially me.*

I shook off the memory as much as I could. "Is there a light out here?" I asked. I didn't want to have to deal with things going dark every time I stood too still—and I couldn't bring myself to look at Grayson, look at his light, piercing eyes, the way I had that night.

"There's a control panel under the portico."

I managed to find it and turn the pool lights on but ended up accidentally turning a fountain on, too. Water sprayed upward in a magnificent arc as the pool light cycled through colors: pink, purple, blue, green, violet. It felt like watching fireworks. Like magic.

But I hadn't come down here for magic. One touch turned off the fountain. Another stopped the cycle of colors in the light.

"What are you doing?" Grayson asked me, and I knew that he was asking why I was *here*, with him.

"Did Jameson tell you about the bag your grandfather left me?" I asked.

Grayson pushed off the wall, treading water as he measured his response. "Jamie doesn't tell me everything." The silences in Grayson's sentences always spoke volumes. "In fairness, there's quite a bit that I don't tell him."

That was the closest he'd ever come to mentioning that night in the wine cellar, the things he'd confessed to me.

I held up the glass circle. "This was one of several items in a bag that your grandfather instructed be delivered to me if Eve and I ever met. There was also—"

"What did you say?" Without warning, Grayson pulled himself out of the water. It was October and cool enough at night that he had to be freezing, but he did a very good impression of someone utterly incapable of feeling cold.

"When I met Eve, it triggered one of your grandfather's games."

"The old man knew?" Grayson was standing so still that if the pool light hadn't been on, he would have disappeared into the darkness. "My grandfather knew about Eve? He knew that Toby had a daughter?"

I swallowed. "Yes."

Every muscle in Grayson's body had gone tight. "He knew," he repeated savagely. "And he left her there? He knew, and he didn't say a damn word to any of us?" Grayson strode toward me—then past me. He braced himself against the portico wall, his palms flat, the muscles in his back so tense that it looked like his shoulder blades might split the skin.

"Grayson?" I didn't say more than that. I wasn't sure what else to say.

"I used to tell myself that the old man loved us," Grayson stated with all the precision of a surgeon slicing through good flesh to get to bad. "That if he held us to impossible standards, it was for the noble purpose of forging his heirs into what we needed to be. And if the great Tobias Hawthorne was harder on me than on my brothers, I told myself that it was because I needed to be more. I believed that he taught me about honor and duty because *he* was honorable, because he felt the weight of *his* duty and wanted to prepare me for it."

Grayson slammed his hand down onto the wall hard enough for the rough surface to tear into his palm.

"But the things he did? The dirty little secrets in those file folders? Knowing about Eve and letting her be raised by people who treated her as less than? Pretending that our family owed Toby's daughter nothing? There's nothing *honorable* about that." Grayson shook. *"Any of it."*

I thought about Grayson never allowing himself to break because he knew the man he'd been raised to be. I thought about Jameson saying that Grayson had always been so *perfect*. "We don't know how long your grandfather knew about Eve," I said. "If it was a recent discovery, if he knew that she looked like Emily, maybe he thought it would be too painful—"

"Maybe he thought I was too weak." Grayson turned to face me. "That's what you're saying, Avery, as hard as you try to make it mean something else."

I took a step toward him. "Grief doesn't make you weak, Grayson."

"Love does." Grayson's voice went brutally low. "I was supposed to be the one who was above it all. Emotion. Vulnerability."

"Why you?" I asked. "Why not Nash? He's the oldest. Why not Jameson or Xan—"

"Because it was supposed to be me." Grayson took in a ragged breath. I could practically see him fighting to slam the cage door closed on his emotions once more. "My whole life, Avery, it was supposed to be me. That was why I had to be better, why I had to sacrifice and be honorable and put family first, why I could *never* lose control—because the old man wasn't going to be around forever, and *I* was the one who was supposed to take the reins once he was gone."

It was supposed to be Grayson. I thought. *Not me.* A year on, and part of Grayson still couldn't let go of that, even knowing that the old man had never really intended to leave him the fortune.

"And I understood, Avery—*I did*—why the old man might have looked at this family, looked at *me*, and decided that we were unworthy of *his* legacy." Grayson's voice shook. "I understood why he thought I wasn't good enough—and you were. But if the great Tobias Hawthorne *wasn't* honorable? If he never met a line he wouldn't cross for his own selfish gain? If 'family first' was just some bullshit lie he fed to me? Then why?" Grayson brought his eyes to mine. "What's the point, Avery, of any of this?"

"I don't know." My voice sounded just as raw as his. Hesitantly, I raised the glass circle again. "But maybe there's more to it, a piece of the puzzle that we don't know. . . ."

"More games." Grayson slammed his hand against the wall again. "The old bastard has been dead a year, and he's still pulling strings."

My right hand holding the blue-green glass, I dropped the towel with my left and reached for him.

"Don't," Grayson breathed. He turned to walk past me. "I told you once before, Avery: I'm broken. I won't break you, too. Go back to bed. Forget about that piece of glass and whatever else was in that bag. Stop playing the old man's games."

"Grayson—"

"Just stop."

That felt final in a way that nothing else between us ever had. I didn't say anything. I didn't go after him. And when the way he'd told me to stop rang in my mind, I thought about Jameson, who never stopped.

About the person I was with Jameson.

I walked over to the water. I took off my pants and my shirt, laid the glass gingerly on the side of the pool, and dove in.

CHAPTER 43

I barreled through the water with my eyes open. The blue-green mosaic at the bottom of the pool beckoned me, illuminated by the lights I'd turned on. I swam closer, then ran my hand over the tiles, taking everything in: *that* color, the smoothness, the variation in the cut and size of the tiny tiles, the way they'd been laid, almost in a swirl.

I kicked off the bottom, and when I broke the surface, I paddled to the side. Taking the glass circle in one hand, I pulled myself along the edge to the shallow end with the other. Standing, I submerged the glass, then went under myself. *Don't breathe.*

Filtered through the glass, the blue-green tiles disappeared. Beneath them, I could see a simpler design: squares, some of them light, some dark. *A chessboard.*

There was always a moment in these games when I was hit with the almost physical realization that nothing Tobias Hawthorne had ever done had been without layers of purpose. All those additions to Hawthorne House, and how many of them contained one of his tricks just waiting for the right game?

Traps upon traps, Jameson had told me once. *And riddles upon riddles.*

I came back up for air, the image of the chessboard burned into my mind. I thought about Grayson telling me not to play, about Jameson, who should have been playing alongside me. And then I cleared my mind of all of that. I thought about the clues that had preceded this one: the Queen's Gambit, leading to the royal chess set to *Don't breathe*. I went down again, held up the glass again, and mentally populated the squares with pieces.

I played out the Queen's Gambit in my mind. *P-Q4. P-Q4. P-QB4.*

Refusing to blink, I memorized the locations of the squares involved in those moves, then came up for air. Setting the glass back on the side of the pool, I pulled myself out, the night air a brutal shock to my system.

P-Q4, I thought. With single-minded purpose, I dove for the bottom. No matter how I pushed or prodded at the mosaic of tiles that made up the first square, nothing happened. I swam to the second—still nothing, then went up for air again, swam to the side again, pulled myself out again, shivering, shaking, *ready*.

I drew in air, then dove again. *P-QB4*. The location of the last move in the Queen's Gambit. This time, when I pushed against the tiles, one turned, hitting the next and the next, like some kind of clockwork marvel.

I watched the chain reaction go, piece by piece, afraid to even blink, terrified that whatever this was, it would only last a moment. A final tile turned, and the entire section—the square I'd seen through the glass—popped up. My lungs starting to burn, I wedged my fingers underneath. They brushed something.

Almost. Almost.

My body was telling me to go to the surface—*screaming* at me to go to the surface—but I shoved my fingers under the tile again. This time, I managed to pull a flat package out, an instant before the compartment began to close.

I pushed off, kicked, then exploded past the surface of the water. I gasped and couldn't stop gasping, sucking in the night air again and again. I swam for the side of the pool. This time, when my hand reached for the edge, another hand grabbed mine.

Jameson pulled me out of the water. *"Don't breathe,"* he murmured.

I didn't ask him where he'd been or even if he was okay. I just held up the package I'd retrieved from the bottom of the pool.

Jameson bent to pick up the beach towel and wrapped it around me. "Well done, Heiress." His lips brushed mine, and the world felt charged, brimming with anticipation and the thrill of the chase. This was the way he and I were supposed to be: no running, no hiding, no recriminations, no regrets.

Just *us*, questions and answers and what we could do when we were together.

I went to open the package and found it vacuum sealed. Jameson held out a knife. I recognized it. *The* knife—from the shattered glass game.

Taking it from him, I sliced the package open. Inside, there was a fireproof pouch. I unzipped it and found a faded photograph. Three figures—all women—stood in front of an enormous stone church.

"Do you recognize them?" I asked Jameson.

He shook his head, and I turned the photograph over. On the back, written in Tobias Hawthorne's familiar scrawl, was a place and a date. *Margaux, France, December 19, 1973.*

I'd been playing the billionaire's games long enough for my brain to latch immediately onto the date. *12/19/1973*. And then there was the location. "Margaux?" I said out loud. "Pronounced like Margo?"

That could mean we were looking for a person with that name—but in a Hawthorne game, it could also mean so many other things.

CHAPTER 44

Jameson got me into a hot shower, and my mind raced. Decoding a clue required separating meaning from distraction. There were four elements here: the photograph; the name *Margaux*; the location in France; and the date, which could have been an actual date or could have been a number in need of decoding.

In all likelihood, some combination of those four elements was meaningful, and the rest were just distractions, but which were which?

"Three women." Jameson hung a towel, warm from the towel heater, over the shower's glass door. "A church in the background. If we scan the photograph, we could try a reverse image search—"

"—which would only help," I filled in, the water white-hot against my chilled skin, "if a copy of this exact photograph exists online." Still, it was worth a try. "We should try to locate the church, figure out its name," I murmured, steam growing thicker in the air around me. "And we can talk to Zara and Nan. See if they recognize any of these women."

"Or the name Margaux," Jameson added. Through the steam on the glass door, he was a blur of color: long, lean, familiar in ways that made me ache.

I turned off the rain shower spray. I wrapped my towel around my body and stepped out onto the bathroom rug. Jameson met my eyes, his face moonlit through the window, his hair a mess my fingers wanted to touch. "There's also the date to consider," he murmured. "And the rest of the objects in the bag."

"A steamer, a flashlight, a USB," I rattled off. "We could try the steamer and the flashlight on the photograph—and the pouch it came in."

"Three objects left." Jameson's mouth ticked upward at the ends. "And three already used. That puts us halfway through, and my grandfather would say that's a good point to step back. Go back to the beginning. Consider the framing and your charge."

I felt my own lips parting and tilting up at the ends. "There were no instructions given. No question, no prompt."

"No question, no prompt." Jameson's voice was low and silky. "But we know the trigger. You met Eve." Jameson chewed on that for a moment, then turned. His green eyes looked like they were focused on something no one but him could see, as if a multitude of possibilities suddenly stretched out before him like constellations in the sky. "The start of the game was triggered when you met Eve, which means this game might tell us something about you or something about Eve, something about why my grandfather chose you instead of Eve, or…"

Jameson turned again, caught up in a web of his own thoughts. It was like everything else had ceased to exist, even me.

"*Or*," he repeated, like that was the answer. "I didn't see it at the beginning," he said, his voice low and struck through with electric energy. "But now that it seems like the old man might be at the center of the current onslaught?" Jameson's gaze snapped back to the real world. "What if…"

Jameson and I lived for those two words. *What if?* I *felt* them now. "You think there could be a connection," I said, "between the game your grandfather left me and everything else?"

Toby's abduction. The old man with a fondness for riddles. Someone coming at me from all sides.

My question grounded Jameson, and his gaze leapt to mine. "I think that this game was delivered to you because Eve showed up here. And the *only* reason that Eve came here was because there was trouble. No trouble, no Eve. If Toby hadn't been abducted, she wouldn't be here. My grandfather always thought seven steps ahead. He saw dozens of permutations in how things could play out, planned for every eventuality, strategized for each and every possible future."

Sometimes, when the boys talked about the old man, they made him sound more than mortal. But there were limits to what a person could foresee, limits to even the most brilliant mind's strategy.

Jameson caught my chin in his hand and tilted my head gently backward, angling it up toward him. "Think about it, Heiress. What if the information we need to find out who took Toby is really in *this* game?"

My throat tightened, my entire body feeling the shot of hope with physical force. "Do you really think it could be?" I asked, my voice breaking.

Shadows fell across Jameson's eyes. "Maybe not. Maybe I'm stretching. Maybe I'm just seeing what I want to see, seeing him the way I want to see him."

I thought about the files, about Jameson disappearing into the walls of Hawthorne House. "I'm here," I told him softly. "I am right here with you, Jameson Hawthorne." *Stop running.*

He shuddered. "Say *Tahiti*, Heiress."

I brought my hand to the side of his neck. *"Tahiti."*

"Do you want to know the worst part? Because the worst part

isn't knowing what my grandfather would do—and has done—to win. It's knowing in my gut and in my bones, with every fiber of my being, *why.* It's knowing that everything he's done in the name of winning, I would have done, too."

Jameson Winchester Hawthorne is hungry. That was what Skye had told me during my first few weeks at Hawthorne House. Grayson was dutiful and Xander was brilliant, but Jameson had been the old man's favorite because Tobias Hawthorne had been born *hungry,* too.

It hurt me to see them as alike. "Don't say that, Jameson."

"It was all just strategy to him," Jameson said. "He saw connections that other people missed. Everyone else played chess in two dimensions, but Tobias Hawthorne saw the third, and when he recognized a winning move, he took it."

There's nothing more Hawthorne than winning.

"Just because you *could* do it," I told Jameson fiercely, "doesn't mean you would have."

"Before you, Heiress? I *absolutely* would have." His voice was intense. "I can't even hate him now. He's a part of me. He's in me." Jameson's fingers lightly touched my hair, then curled into it. "But mostly, I can't hate him, Avery Kylie Grambs, because he brought me you."

He needed me to kiss him, and I needed it, too. When Jameson finally pulled away—*just one centimeter, then two*—my lips ached for his. He brought his mouth to my ear. "Now, back to the game."

CHAPTER 45

We worked until almost dawn, slept briefly, woke intertwined. We talked to Nan and Zara, played with the numbers, identified the church, which wasn't even in France, let alone in Margaux. We went back to the unused objects in the bag: a steamer, a flashlight, the USB.

By midmorning, we were stuck in a loop.

As if he'd divined the need for something to snap us out of it, Xander texted Jameson's phone. Jameson held it out for me to see. *911.*

"An emergency?" I asked.

"More like a summons," Jameson told me. "Come on." We made it as far as the hallway before we ran into Nash, who was leaving Libby's room in the clothes he'd worn the day before, holding a small, wiggling ball of chaos and brown fur.

"I really hope you didn't try to give that incredibly adorable puppy to my sister," I told him.

"He didn't." Libby padded into the hallway wearing an I EAT MORNING PEOPLE shirt and black pajama pants. "He knows better. That is a Hawthorne dog." Libby reached out to stroke the puppy's ear. "Nash found her in an alley. Some drunk assholes were poking at her with a stick." Knowing Nash as I did, I doubted that had turned out well for the drunk assholes. "He saved her," Libby continued, letting her hand drop. "That's what he does."

"I don't know, darlin'," Nash said, giving the pup a scratch, his eyes on my sister. "I was in pretty rough shape. Maybe she saved me."

I thought about little Nash watching Skye with his baby brothers, watching her give them away. And then I thought about Libby taking me in.

"You get Xander's nine-one-one?" Jameson asked his brother.

"Sure did," Nash drawled.

"Nine-one-one?" Libby frowned. "Is Xander okay?"

"He needs us," Nash told my sister, allowing the puppy to lick his chin. "We each only get one a year. A text like that comes in, it doesn't matter where you are or what you're doing. You drop everything and go."

"Xander just hasn't told us where to go yet," Jameson added.

Right on cue, Jameson's phone buzzed; Nash's, too. A series of texts came through in quick succession. Jameson angled his phone toward me so that I could see.

Xander had sent four photographs, each containing a little drawing. The first was a heart with the word *CARE* written in the middle of it. I scrolled to the second picture and frowned. "Is that a monkey riding a bicycle?"

Libby moved toward Nash and took his phone from his pocket. There was something intimate about the action—the way he let her, the way she knew he would. "The monkey appears to be saying *EEEEEE!*" Libby commented

Nash looked at the picture. "Could be a lemur," he opined.

I shook my head and looked at the third picture: Xander had drawn a tree. The fourth picture was an elephant jumping on a pogo stick, also saying *EEEEEE!*

I looked at Jameson. "Do you have any idea what this means?"

"As previously established, nine-one-one means Xander is calling us in," Jameson said. "By Hawthorne rules, this summons cannot be ignored. As for the pictures... work it out for yourself, Heiress."

I looked at the pictures again. The *care* heart. The animals yelling *Eeee.*

"Tree's an oak, if that helps," Nash told me. The puppy barked.

Care. Eee. Oak. Eee. I thought—and then I put it all together. "You've got to be kidding me," I told Jameson.

"What?" Libby asked.

Jameson smirked. "Hawthornes never kid about karaoke."

CHAPTER 46

Five minutes later, we were in the Hawthorne theater. Not to be confused with the Hawthorne *movie* theater, this one had a stage, a red velvet curtain, stadium and box seating—the whole shebang.

Xander stood on the stage, holding a microphone. A screen had been set up behind him, and there must have been a projector somewhere because "911!" danced on the screen.

"I need this," Xander said into the microphone. "You need this. We all need this. Nash, I've cued up the Taylor Swift for you. Jameson, get ready to break out those dance moves because this stage is calling your name, and we all know that your hips are utterly incapable of falsehood. And as for Grayson..." Xander paused. "Where *is* Gray?"

"Grayson Hawthorne skipping out on karaoke?" Libby said. "I'm shocked, I tell you. *Shocked.*"

"Gray has a voice so deep and smooth that you will shed literal tears as he sings something so old school that you will come to believe he spent the 1950s wearing the most dapper of suits and hanging out with his bestie, Frank Sinatra," Xander swore. He swung his gaze to his brothers. "But Gray's not here."

Jameson glanced at me. "You don't ignore a nine-one-one text," he told me. "No matter what."

"Where *is* Grayson?" Nash asked. And that was when I heard it—a sound halfway between a crash and the shattering of wood.

Jameson jogged out to the hallway. There was another crash. "Music room," he told us.

Xander jumped off the stage. "My duet will have to wait!"

"Who were you going to duet with?" Libby asked.

"Myself!" Xander yelled as he ran for the door, but Nash caught him.

"Hold on there, Xan. Let Jamie go." Nash looked toward me. "You go, too, kid."

I wasn't sure what Nash thought was going on here—or why he seemed so sure that Jameson and I were the ones Grayson needed.

"In the meantime," Nash told Xander, "give me the mic."

As Jameson and I made our way down the corridor, the sound of achingly beautiful violin music began drifting into the hall. The music room door was open, and when I stepped through it, I saw Grayson poised in front of open bay windows, wearing a suit without the jacket, his shirt unbuttoned, a violin pressed to his chin. His posture was perfect, each movement smooth.

The floor in front of him was covered with shards of wood.

I couldn't remember how many ultra-expensive violins Tobias Hawthorne had purchased in pursuit of *cultivating* his grandson's musical ability, but it looked like Grayson had destroyed at least one.

The song reached a final note, so high and sweet it was almost unbearable. Then there was silence as Grayson lowered the violin, took a step away from the windows, and then raised the instrument again—over his head.

Jameson caught his brother's forearm. "Don't." For a moment, the two of them grappled, sorrow and fury. "*Gray.* You're not hurting anyone but yourself." That had no effect, so Jameson went for the jugular. "You're scaring Avery. And you missed Xander's nine-one-one."

I wasn't scared. I could never be scared of Grayson—but I could ache for him.

Grayson slowly lowered the violin. "I apologize," he told me, his voice almost too calm. "It's your property I've been destroying."

I didn't care about my *property.* "You play beautifully," I told Grayson, pushing back the urge to cry.

"Beauty was expected," Grayson replied. "Technique without artistry is worthless." He looked down at the remains of the violin he'd destroyed. "Beauty is a lie."

"Remind me to mock you for saying that later," Jameson told him.

"Leave me," Grayson ordered, turning his back on us.

"If I'd known we were having a party," Jameson half sang, "I would have ordered food."

"A party?" I asked.

"A pity party." Jameson smirked. "I see you dressed for the occasion, Gray."

"You're right." Grayson walked toward the door. "This is self-indulgent. Thoroughly beneath me."

Jameson reached out to trip him, and then it was on. I understood now why Nash had sent Jameson. Sometimes Grayson Davenport Hawthorne needed a fight—and Jameson was only too happy to oblige.

"Let it all out," Jameson said, ramming his head into Grayson's stomach. "Poor baby."

Tobias Hawthorne hadn't just expected *beauty.* The four Hawthorne grandsons were also damn near lethal.

Grayson flipped Jameson onto his back, then went in for the kill. I knew Jameson well enough to realize that he'd just *let* himself be pinned.

Every muscle in Grayson's body was tight. "I thought that *we* failed *him*," he said, his voice low. "I thought we weren't enough. *I* wasn't enough, wasn't worthy. But you tell me, Jamie: What the hell is there for us to be worthy *of*?"

"He played to win," Jameson gritted out beneath his brother. "Always. You can't tell me that comes as a surprise."

"You're right." Grayson didn't loosen his grip. "He was ruthless. He raised us to be the same. Especially me."

Jameson locked his eyes onto his brother's. "To hell with what he wants. What do you want, Gray? Because we both know that you haven't let yourself want anything in a very long time."

The two of them were sucked into a staring contest: silvery gray eyes and deep green ones, one set narrowed and one wide open.

Grayson looked away first, but he didn't remove his forearm from Jameson's neck. "I want to get Toby back. For Eve." There was a pause, and then Grayson's head turned toward mine, the light reflecting off his blond hair in a near-halo. "For you, Avery."

I closed my eyes, just for a moment. "Jameson thinks—we both think—that there might be a connection between Toby's kidnapping and the game your grandfather left me. That it might tell us something."

Grayson angled his gaze back toward his brother's, then dropped his hold and abruptly stood.

I continued, "I know you didn't want to play—"

"I will," Grayson said, the words cutting through the air. He reached a hand down to Jameson and pulled him to his feet, leaving the two of them standing just inches apart. "I'll play, and I'll win," Grayson said, with the force of absolute law, "because we are who we are."

"We always will be," Jameson said. No matter how close I got to the Hawthorne brothers, there would always be things they shared that I could barely fathom.

"Here, Heiress." Jameson broke eye contact with his brother, removed the photograph from his pocket, and handed it to me. "You're the one who found this clue. You're the one who should explain it."

It felt significant: Jameson bringing me closer to Grayson instead of pushing me away.

I held the picture out, and Grayson's fingers brushed mine as he took it.

"We don't know who those three women are," I said. "There's a date on the back. And a caption. We can take you through what we've already done."

"That won't be necessary." Grayson's gaze was sharp. "What else was in the bag that our grandfather left you?"

I went to get it, and when I came back, Grayson and Jameson were standing farther apart. Both of them were breathing heavily, and the expressions on their faces made me wonder what had passed between them while I was gone.

"Here," I said, ignoring the tension in the room. I laid out the remaining three objects in the game, naming them as I did. "A steamer, a flashlight, a USB drive."

Grayson set the photograph down next to them. After what felt like a small eternity, he flipped the photograph over to read the caption once more.

"The date gives us numbers," Jameson said. "A code or—"

"Not a code," Grayson murmured, picking up the steamer. "A vintage." His gaze found its way slowly and inexorably to mine. "We need to go down to the wine cellar."

CHAPTER 47

As I pulled open the door to the wine cellar, so much of that night came back to me: the cocktail party, the way Grayson had deftly deflected every person who *just wanted a minute* of my time to tell me about *a unique financial opportunity*, the little girl in the pool, Grayson diving in to save her.

I could remember the way he'd looked climbing out of the water, dripping wet in an Armani suit. Grayson hadn't even asked for a towel. He'd acted like he wasn't even wet. I remembered people talking to him, the little girl being returned to her parents. I remembered the brief glimpse I caught of his face—his *eyes*—right before he disappeared down these stairs.

I'd known that he wasn't okay, but I'd had no idea why.

Focus on the game. I tried to stay in the moment—here, now, with both of them. Jameson went first down the spiraling stone steps. I was a step behind him, walking where he walked, not daring to look back over my shoulder at Grayson.

Just find the next clue. I let that be my beacon, my focus, but the moment we hit the bottom of the stone staircase, the landing came into view: a tasting room with an antique table made of the darkest cherry wood. Chairs sat on either side of the table, their arms carved so that the ends became lions: one set watchful, one set roaring.

And just like that, I was taken back.

The lines of Grayson's body are like architecture: his shoulders even, his neck straight, though his head and eyes are cast down. A crystal glass sits on the table in front of him. His hands lay on either side of the glass, the muscles in them tensed, like he might push off at any moment.

"You shouldn't be here." Grayson doesn't pull his eyes from the glass—or the amber liquid he's been drinking.

"And it's your job to tell me what I should and shouldn't do?" I retort. The question feels dangerous. Just being here does, for reasons I can't even begin to explain.

"Did someone say something to you?" I ask. "At the party—did someone upset you?"

"I do not upset easily," Grayson says, the words sharp. He still hasn't looked away from the glass, and I can't shake the feeling that I'm not supposed to be seeing this.

That no one is supposed to see Grayson Hawthorne like this.

"The child's grandfather." Grayson's tone is modulated, but I can see the tension in his neck, like the words want to come roaring out of him, ripping their way from his throat. "Do you know what he told me?" Grayson lifts his glass and drains what remains—every last drop. "He said that the old man would have been proud of me."

And there it is, the thing that has Grayson down here drinking alone. I cross to sit in the chair opposite his. "You saved that little girl."

"Immaterial." Haunted silver eyes meet mine. "She was easy to save." He picks up the bottle, pours exactly two fingers into the glass, those icy eyes of his watchful. There's tension in his fingers, his wrists, his neck, his jaw. "The true measure of a man is how many impossible things he accomplishes before breakfast."

I understand suddenly that Grayson is gutted because he doesn't believe that Tobias Hawthorne was or would be proud of him—not for saving that girl or anything else.

"Being worthy," he continues, "requires being bold." He lifts the glass to his mouth again and drinks.

"You are worthy, Grayson," I tell him, reaching for his hands and holding them in mine.

Grayson doesn't pull back. His fingers curl into fists beneath my hands. "I saved that girl. I didn't save Emily." That's a statement of fact, a truth carved into his soul. "I didn't save you." He looks up at me. "A bomb went off, and you were lying on the ground, and I just stood there."

His voice vibrates with intensity. Beneath my touch, I can feel his body doing the same.

"It's okay. I'm fine," I say, but it's clear he doesn't hear it—won't hear it. "Look at me, Grayson. I am right here. I am fine. We are fine."

"Hawthornes aren't supposed to break." His chest rises and falls. "Especially me."

I stand and make my way to his side of the table without ever letting go of his hands. "You're not broken."

"I am." The words are swift and brutal. "I always will be."

"Look at me," I say, but he won't. I bend down toward him. "Look at me, Grayson. You are not broken."

His eyes catch on mine. Our chests rise and fall in unison now.

"Emily was in my head." There's something hushed and barely restrained in his voice. "I heard her after the bomb went off, like she was right there. Like she was real."

This is a confession. I'm standing, and he's sitting, back straight, head bowed.

"For weeks, I hallucinated her voice. For weeks, she whispered to me." Grayson looks up at me. "Tell me again that I'm not broken."

I don't think. I just take his head in my hands. "You loved her, and you lost her," I start to say.

"I failed her, and she will haunt me until the day I die." Grayson's eyes close. "I'm supposed to be stronger than this. I wanted to be stronger than this. For you."

Those last two words nearly undo me. "You don't have to be anything for me, Grayson." I wait until he opens his eyes, until he's looking at me. "This," I say. "You. It's enough."

He drops from the chair to his knees, his eyes closing again, the enormity of this moment all around us. I kneel, wrap my arms around him.

"You're enough," I say again.

"It will never be enough."

The memory was everywhere. I could feel Grayson curling in on himself, into me. I could feel his shudder. And then he'd told me to go, and I'd fled because deep down, I knew what he meant when he said that it would never be enough. He meant *us*. What we were—and what we weren't. What had shattered in those weeks when Emily had been whispering in his ear.

What might have been.

What *could* have been.

What couldn't be, now.

The next day, Grayson had left for Harvard without even saying good-bye. And now he was back, right there behind me, and we were doing this.

Grayson, Jameson, and me.

"This way." Grayson nodded to a clear glass door to our right. When he opened it, a burst of cold air hit my face. Stepping through the doorway, I let out a long, slow breath, half expecting to see it, wispy and white in the chilly air.

"This place is enormous." I stayed in the present through sheer force of will. *No more flashbacks. No more what-ifs.* I focused on the game. That was what was needed. What I needed and what both of them needed from me.

"There are technically *five* cellars, all interconnected," Jameson narrated. "This one's for white wine. Through there is red. If you keep wrapping around, you'll hit scotch, bourbon, and whiskey."

There had to be a fortune down here in alcohol alone. *Think about that. Nothing but that.*

"We're looking for a red wine." Grayson's voice cut into my thoughts. "A Bordeaux."

Jameson reached for my hand. I took it, and he stepped away, allowing his fingers to trail down mine—an invitation to follow as he wound into the next room. I did.

Grayson pushed past me, past Jameson, snaking his way through aisle after aisle, scanning rack after rack. Finally, he stopped. "Chateau Margaux," he said, pulling a bottle out of the closest rack. "Nineteen seventy-three."

The caption on the photograph. Margaux. 1973.

"You want to guess what the steamer's for?" Jameson asked me.

A bottle of wine. A steamer. I took the Chateaux Margaux from Grayson, turning it over in my hand. Slowly, the answer took hold. "The label," I said. "If we try to tear it off, it might rip. But steam will loosen the adhesive...."

Grayson held the steamer out to me. "You do the honors."

CHAPTER 48

On the back of the label of the lone bottle of Chateau Margaux 1973 in Tobias Hawthorne's collection, there was a drawing. A pencil sketch of a dangling, tear-drop crystal.

"Jewelry?" Grayson ventured a guess, but I'd already been in the vault.

"No," I said slowly, picturing the crystal in the drawing and thinking back. *Where have I seen something like that before?* "I think we're looking for a chandelier."

There were eighteen crystal chandeliers in Hawthorne House. We found the one we were looking for in the Tea Room.

"Are we going up?" I asked, craning my neck at the twenty-foot ceilings. "Or is that thing coming down?"

Jameson strolled over to a wall panel. He hit a button, and the chandelier slowly lowered to eye level. "For dusting purposes," he told me.

Even the thought of trying to dust this monstrosity gave me palpitations. There had to be at least a thousand crystals on the chandelier. One wrong move, and they could all shatter.

"What now?" I breathed.

"Now," Jameson told me, "we take it one by one."

Examining the individual crystals took time. Every few minutes, I brushed against Jameson or Grayson, or one of them brushed against me.

"This one," Grayson said suddenly. "Look at the irregularities."

Jameson was on top of him in a heartbeat. "Etching?" he asked.

Instead of responding to his brother, Grayson turned and handed the crystal to me. I stared at it, but if there was a message or clue contained in this crystal, I couldn't make it out with my naked eye.

We could use a jeweler's loupe, I thought. *Or—*

"The flashlight," I breathed. I reached inside the leather satchel. Locking my hand around the flashlight, I took a quick breath. I held out the crystal, then shined the light through. The irregularities caused the light to refract just so. At first, the result was incomprehensible, but then I flipped the crystal over and tried again.

This time, the flashlight's beam refracted to form a message. As I stared at the light projected onto the floor, there was no missing the words—the warning.

DON'T TRUST ANYONE.

CHAPTER 49

A chill hit the base of my neck, like the feeling of being watched from behind or standing knee-deep in long grass and hearing the rattle of a snake. My grip tightening around the crystal, I couldn't look away.

DON'T TRUST ANYONE.

"What is that supposed to mean?" I said, my stomach lined with dread as I finally looked to Jameson and Grayson in quick succession. "Is it a clue?"

We still had one object left in the bag. This wasn't over. Maybe the letters of this warning could be rearranged, or the first letter in every word made out initials, or—

"Can I see the crystal?" Jameson asked. I gave it to him, and he slowly rotated it under the flashlight's beam until he found what he was looking for. "There, at the top. Three letters, too small and faint to make out without the light."

"*Fin*?" Grayson said, an edge to the question.

"*Fin.*" Jameson placed the crystal back in my hand, then brought his dark green eyes to mine. "As in *finished*, Heiress. The end. This isn't a clue. This is *it*."

My game. Quite possibly the last bequest of Tobias Hawthorne.

And this was it? *Don't trust anyone.* "But what about the USB?" I said. The game couldn't be over. This couldn't be all that Tobias Hawthorne had left us with.

"Misdirection?" Jameson tossed out. "Or maybe the old man left you a game *and* a USB. Either way, this started with the delivery of the bag, and it ends here."

Setting my jaw, I righted the crystal in the flashlight's beam, and the words reappeared on the floor. *DON'T TRUST ANYONE.*

After everything, that was all the billionaire had for me? *My grandfather always thought seven steps ahead,* I could hear Jameson saying. *He saw dozens of permutations in how things could play out, planned for every eventuality, strategized for each and every possible future.*

What kind of strategy was this? Was I supposed to think that Toby's captor was closer than he appeared? That his reach was long, and anyone could be in his pocket? Was I supposed to question *everyone* around me?

Take a step back, I thought. *Go back to the beginning. Consider the framing and your charge.* I stopped. I breathed. And I thought. *Eve.* This game had been triggered when we met. Jameson had theorized that his grandfather had foreseen something about the trouble that had brought Eve here, but what if it was simpler than that?

Much, much simpler.

"This game started because Eve and I met." I said the words out loud, each leaving my mouth with the force of a shot, though I barely spoke over a whisper. "She was the trigger."

My thoughts jumped to the night before. To the solarium, the files, and Eve with her phone. "What if 'Don't trust anyone,'" I said slowly, "really means 'Don't trust her'?"

Until I said the words, I hadn't realized how much I'd let my guard down.

"If the old man had intended for you to be wary only of Eve, the message wouldn't have said *don't trust anyone*. It would have said *don't trust her*." Grayson spoke like someone who couldn't possibly be anything less than correct, let alone *wrong*.

But I thought about Eve asking to be left alone in Toby's wing. The way she'd looked at the clothes in my closet. How quickly she'd gotten Grayson on her side.

If Eve hadn't looked so much like Emily, would he be defending her now?

"*Anyone* includes Eve by definition," I pointed out. "It has to. If she's a threat—"

"*She. Is. Not. A. Threat.*" Grayson's vocal cords tensed against his throat. In my mind's eye, I could still see him on his knees in front of me.

"You don't want her to be one," I said, careful not to let myself feel too much.

"Do *you*, Heiress?" Jameson asked suddenly, his eyes searching mine. "Do you want her to be a threat? Because Gray's right. The message wasn't 'Don't trust her.'"

Jameson was the one who'd mistrusted Eve from the start! *I'm not jealous. That's not what this is.* "Last night," I said, my voice hitching, "I caught Eve taking pictures of the files in the solarium. She had an excuse. It sounded plausible. But we don't know her."

You don't know her, Grayson.

"And your grandfather never brought her here," I continued. "*Why?*" I brought my eyes back toward Jameson, willing him to latch on to the question. "What did he know about Eve that we don't?"

"Avery." Oren saying my name from the doorway was the only warning I got.

Eve walked into the Tea Room, her hair damp, wearing the

white dress she'd worn the day she arrived. "He knew about me?" She looked from me to Grayson, a portrait of devastation. "Tobias Hawthorne knew about me?"

I was a good poker player, in large part because I could spot a bluff, and this—her chin trembling, her voice hardening, the aching look in her eyes, the set of her mouth, like she wouldn't *let* her lips turn down—didn't feel like a bluff.

But a voice in the back of my head said three words. *Don't trust anyone.*

The next thing I knew, Eve was walking toward me. Oren moved to stand between us, and Eve's eyes angled upward, like she was taking a moment to steel herself. *Trying not to cry.*

She held out her phone. "Take it," Eve spat out. "Passcode three eight four five."

I didn't move.

"Go ahead," Eve told me, and this time, her voice sounded deeper, rougher. "Look at the photos. Look at anything you want, Avery."

I felt a stab of guilt, and I glanced at Jameson. He was watching me intently. I didn't let myself react—at all—when Grayson came to stand beside Eve.

Looking down, wondering if I'd made a mistake, I plugged the passcode Eve had given me into her phone. It unlocked the screen, and I navigated to her photo roll. She hadn't deleted the one I'd seen her taking, and this time, I identified which file she'd photographed.

"Sheffield Grayson." I brought my eyes back up to Eve's, but she wouldn't even look at me.

"I'm sorry," she told Grayson, her voice quiet. "But he's the wealthiest person in any of those files. He has motive. He has means. I know you said it wasn't him, but—"

"*Evie.*" Grayson gave her a look, the kind of Grayson Hawthorne look that burned itself into your memory because it said everything he wouldn't. "It's not him."

Sheffield Grayson was dead, but Eve didn't know that. And she was right: He *had* come after Toby. *Just not now.*

"If it's not Sheffield Grayson," Eve said, her voice cracking, "then we have *nothing.*"

I knew that feeling: the desperation, the fury, the frustration, the sudden loss of hope. But I still looked back down at Eve's phone and scrolled backward through her photo reel. *Don't trust anyone.* There were three more photos of Sheffield Grayson's file and a few of Toby's room, and that was it. If she'd taken photos of any other files—or anything else—they'd been deleted. I scrolled back further and found a picture of Eve and Toby. He looked like he was trying to swat the camera away, but he was smiling—and so was she.

There were more pictures of the two of them, going back months. Just like she'd said.

If the old man had intended for you to be wary only of Eve, the message wouldn't have said don't trust anyone. *It would have said* don't trust her.

Doubt shot through me, but I pulled up her call log. There were a lot of incoming calls, but she hadn't picked up a single one. She hadn't placed any, either. I went to her texts and quickly realized why she'd been getting so many calls. *The story. The press.* When I'd been in a similar situation, I'd had to get a new phone. I kept clicking through texts, needing to know if there was more, and then I came to one that said simply: *We have to meet.*

I looked up. "Who's this from?" I asked, angling the phone toward her.

"Mallory Laughlin," Eve shot back. "She left voicemails, too. You can verify the number." She looked down. "I guess she's seen the pictures of me. Rebecca must have given her my number. I turned my phone off once the story broke so I could concentrate on Toby, but look at all the good that did." Eve drew in a ragged breath. "I am done with this sick bastard's twisted little games." Her chin came up, and her emerald eyes went diamond hard. "And I am not going to stay where I'm not wanted. *I can't.*"

I could feel this entire situation getting away from me, like sand slipping through my fingers.

"Don't go," Grayson told Eve, the words soft. And then he turned to me, and that softness fell away. "Tell her not to go." This was the tone he'd used with me right after I'd inherited, the one made for warnings and threats. "I mean it, Avery." Grayson looked at me. I expected his eyes to be icy or blazing, but they were neither. "I have never asked for anything from you."

It was palpable in his voice: the many, many things he had never asked for.

I could feel Jameson watching me, and I had no idea what he wanted or expected me to do. All I knew was that if Eve left, if she walked out of Hawthorne House and past the gates, into the line of fire, and something happened to her, Grayson Hawthorne would never forgive me.

"Don't go," I told Eve. "I'm sorry."

I was, and I wasn't. Because those words just wouldn't leave me alone: *Don't trust anyone.*

"I want to meet Mallory." Eve lifted her chin. "She's my grandmother. And at least *she* didn't know about me."

"I'll take you to see her," Grayson said quietly, but Eve shook her head.

"Either Avery takes me," she said, equal parts challenge and injury in her tone, "or I walk."

CHAPTER 50

Oren wasn't happy about me leaving Hawthorne House, but when it became clear that I wasn't going to be dissuaded, he ordered security teams to all three SUVs. When we departed, a trio of identical vehicles pulled out past the gates, leaving the paparazzi hoarde with no way of knowing which one Eve and I were in.

Xander was the only Hawthorne with us. He'd come for Rebecca's sake, not Eve's, and Eve had allowed it. We'd left Grayson and Jameson behind.

"What's she like?" Eve asked Xander, once we were clear of the paparazzi. "My grandmother?"

"Rebecca's mom was always...intense." Xander's response pulled my attention away from the heavily tinted window. "She used to be a surgeon, but once Emily was born and they found out about her heart, Mallory quit to devote herself to managing Em's condition full-time."

"And then Emily died," Eve said softly. "And..."

"Kablooey." Xander made an exploding motion with his fingers. "Bex's mom started drinking. Her dad goes on these monthlong business trips."

"And now I'm here." Eve looked at her hands: her fingers were thin, her nails uneven. "So this is going to go really well," she muttered.

That was probably an understatement. I texted Thea to give her a heads-up. No response. I pulled up her social media and found myself staring at the last four photos she'd posted. Three of them were black-and-white self-portraits. In one, Thea stared directly at the camera, wearing heavy mascara, her face streaked black with tears. In the second, she was curled into a ball, her hands fisted, almost no clothing visible on her body. In the third, Thea was flipping off the camera with both hands.

Beside me, Eve looked at my phone. "I think I might like those even better than poetry." That sounded like the truth. Everything she said did. That was the problem.

I focused on Thea's fourth picture, the most recently uploaded, the only color photo in this set. There were two people in the picture, both laughing, their arms around each other: Thea Calligaris and Emily Laughlin. That picture was the only one with a caption: *She was MY best friend, and YOU don't know what you're talking about.*

I goggled at the enormous number of responses the picture had, then glanced at Xander. "Thea's doing damage control." I couldn't fight the gossip sites, but she could.

Xander angled his phone to me. "She posted a video, too." He hit Play.

"You may have heard certain...rumors." Thea's voice was coy. "About her." The picture of Thea and Emily flashed across the screen. "And them." A picture of all four Hawthorne brothers. "And her." The picture of Eve. "This. Is. A. Mess." Thea moved her body with each word, a captivating dance that made all of this seem less calculated. "But," she continued, "they're *my* mess. And those rumors about Grayson and Jameson Hawthorne and my dead best friend? They aren't true." Thea leaned toward the camera, until her face took up the whole screen. "And I know they're not true because I'm the one who started them."

The video ended abruptly, and Xander leaned his head back against the seat. "She is by far the most magnificent and terrifying individual I have ever fake dated."

Eve gave him a look. "You fake date a lot?"

She seemed so normal. I hadn't found anything on her phone. But I had to keep my guard up.

Didn't I?

CHAPTER 51

Rebecca answered the door before we even had a chance to knock. "My mom's right through there," she told Eve quietly. Taking a deep breath, Eve walked past Rebecca.

"On a scale of one to pi," Xander murmured, "how bad is it?"

Rebecca pulled her hand from his and laid three fingers on his palm. Her normally creamy skin was red and chapped around her nailbeds and knuckles.

Three, on a scale of one to pi. Given the value of pi, that definitely wasn't good.

Rebecca led Xander and me from the small entryway into the living room, where Eve and her mother were. The first thing I noticed were the snow globes sitting on a shelf. They looked like they had been polished until they gleamed. In fact, everything that I could see looked freshly cleaned, like it had been scrubbed and scrubbed again.

Rebecca's hands. I wondered if the cleaning had been her idea—or her mother's.

"Rebecca, this was supposed to be a family affair." Mallory Laughlin didn't take her eyes off Eve, even once Xander and I came into view.

Rebecca looked down, ruby-red hair falling into her face. She always looked like the kind of person an artist would want to paint. Even partially obscured, there was something fairy-tale beautiful about the pain on her face.

Eve reached out to take her grandmother's hand. "I'm the one who asked Avery to come with me. Toby... he considers her family, too."

Ouch. If Eve had meant that as a guilt trip, it was both brutal and effective.

"That's ridiculous." Mallory sat, and when Eve did the same, Mallory leaned toward her, drinking in her presence like a woman gulping down sand in a desert mirage. "Why would my son pay that girl any attention when you're right here?" She lifted a hand to the side of Eve's face. "When you're so perfect."

Beside me, Rebecca sucked a breath in around her teeth.

"I know I look like your daughter," Eve murmured. "This must be difficult."

"You look like me." Rebecca's mom smiled. "Emily did, too. I remember when she was born. I looked at her, and all I could think was that she *was* me. Emily was mine, and nobody was ever going to take her away from me. I told myself that she would never want for anything."

"I'm sorry for your loss," Eve said quietly.

"Don't be sorry," Mallory replied, a sob in her voice. "You've come back to me now."

"Mom." Rebecca cut in without ever looking up from the floor. "We talked about this."

"And I've told you that I don't need you or anyone else to infantilize me." Mallory's reply was sharp enough to slice through glass. "The world is like that, you know." The woman oriented back toward Eve, sounding more maternal. "You have to learn to take what you want—and never, ever let someone take what you don't want to give." Mallory laid a hand on Eve's cheek. "You're strong. Like me. Like Emily was."

This time, there was no audible response from Rebecca. I bumped my shoulder gently against hers, a silent, deliberate *I'm here.* I wondered if Xander felt as useless as I did standing there, watching her oldest scars seeping.

"Can I ask you something?" Eve said to Mallory.

Mallory smiled. "Anything, sweet girl."

"You're my grandmother. Is your husband here? Is he my grandfather?"

Mallory's reply was controlled. "We don't need to talk about that."

"All I've ever wanted is to know where I come from," Eve told her. "Please?"

Mallory stared at her for the longest time. "Could you call me Mom?" she asked softly. I saw Rebecca shake her head—not at her mother or at Eve or at anyone. She was just shaking it because this was not a good idea.

"Tell me about Toby's father?" Eve asked. "Please, Mom?"

Mallory's eyes closed, and I wondered what dead places inside of her had seized with life when Eve had uttered that one little word.

"Eve," I said sharply, but Rebecca's mother spoke over me.

"He was older. Very attractive. Very mysterious. We used to sneak around the estate, up to the House, even. I had free rein of it all in those days, but I was forbidden to bring guests. Mr. Hawthorne valued his privacy. He would have lost his mind if he'd known what I was getting up to, what we did in his hallowed halls." Mallory opened her eyes. "Teenage girls and the forbidden."

"What was his name?" Rebecca asked, taking a step toward her mother.

"This really doesn't concern you, Rebecca," Mallory snapped.

"What *was* his name?" Eve co-opted Rebecca's question. Maybe it was supposed to be a kindness, but it felt cruel because *she* got an answer.

"Liam," Mallory whispered. "His name was Liam."

Eve leaned forward. "What happened to him? Your Liam?"

Mallory stiffened like a marionette whose strings were suddenly pulled tight. "He left." Her voice was calm—too calm. "Liam left."

Eve took both of Mallory's hands in hers. "Why did he leave?"

"He just did."

The doorbell rang, and Oren strode to the door. I followed him to the foyer. As his hand closed over the knob, he gave an order, doubtless to one of his men outside.

"Close in." Oren glanced over his shoulder at me. "Stay put, Avery."

"Why is Avery staying put?" Xander asked, coming into the foyer beside me. Rebecca took one step to follow him, then hesitated, frozen in her own personal purgatory, caught between us and the words being murmured between Eve and her mother.

My brain got to the answer to Xander's question before Oren could articulate it. "This is the first time I've left the estate since the last package was delivered," I noted. "You're expecting another delivery."

In reply, my head of security answered the door with his gun drawn.

"Hello to you, too," Thea said dryly.

"Don't mind Oren." Xander greeted her. "He mistook you for a threat of the less passive-aggressive variety."

The sound of Thea's voice shattered the ice that had frozen Rebecca's feet to the ground. "Thea. I wanted to call, but my mom took my phone."

"And someone turned mine off," Thea said. She looked from Rebecca to me. "While I was in the shower, someone came into my house, into my bedroom, turned off my phone, and left *this* beside it, with handwritten instructions to bring it here."

Thea held out an envelope. It was a deep golden color, shining and reflective.

"Someone broke into your house?" I asked, my voice hushed.

"Into your bedroom?" Rebecca was beside Thea in a heartbeat.

Oren took possession of the envelope. He'd set a trap for the courier *here*, but the message had been delivered elsewhere—to Thea.

Did you see her photos? That video? I asked Toby's captor silently. *Is this what she gets, for helping me?*

"I had a guard on your house," Oren told Thea. "He didn't report anything unusual."

I stared at the envelope in Oren's hand, at my full name written across the front. *Avery Kylie Grambs.* Something in me snapped, and I snatched the envelope, turning it over to see a wax seal holding it closed.

The design of the seal took my breath away. *Rings of concentric circles.*

"It's like the disk," I said, the words catching in my throat.

"Don't open it," Oren told me. "I need to make sure—"

The rest of his words were lost to the roar in my mind. My fingers tore into the envelope, like my body had been set to autopilot at full throttle. Once I'd broken the seal, the envelope unfolded, revealing a message written on the interior in shining silver script.

363-1982.

That was it. Just those seven digits. *A phone number?* There was no area code, but—

"Avery!" Rebecca yelped, and I realized the paper I was holding had caught fire.

Flames devoured the message. I dropped it, and seconds later, the envelope and the numbers were nothing but ashes. "How…" I started to say.

Xander came to stand beside me. "I could rig an envelope to do that." He paused. "Honestly? I *have* rigged an envelope to do that."

"I told you to wait, Avery." Oren gave me what I could only describe as a Dad Look. I was clearly on very thin ice with him.

"What did the message say?" Rebecca asked me.

Xander produced a pen and a sheet of paper shaped like a scone, seemingly out of nowhere. "Write down everything you remember," he told me.

I closed my eyes, picturing the number—and then wrote: *363-1982.*

I turned the paper around so that Xander could see it. "Nineteen eighty-two." Xander latched on to the numbers after the dash. "Could be a year. The three-hundred-and-sixty-third day of which was December twenty-ninth."

December 29, 1982.

"Looks like a phone number to me," Thea scoffed.

"That was my first thought, too," I murmured. "But no area code."

"Was there anything that could indicate location?" Xander asked. "If we could derive an area code, that would give us a number to call."

A number to call. A date to check. And who knew how many other possibilities there were? It could be a cipher, coordinates, a bank account…

"I recommend we return to Hawthorne House immediately,"

Oren cut in. His expression was downright stony. "That is, if you're still interested in letting me do my job, Avery."

"I'm sorry," I said. I trusted Oren with my life, and I owed him better than making his job harder than it had to be. "I saw the seal on the envelope, and something in me snapped."

Rings of concentric circles. When Toby was taken, I'd thought that the disk might have something to do with why, but when his captor had sent it back, I'd assumed that I was wrong.

But what if I wasn't?

What if the disk had always been part of the riddle?

"The number could be a misdirection," Xander said, bouncing lightly on the balls of his feet. "The seal might *be* the message."

"Out!"

I turned back toward the living room. Mallory Laughlin was stalking toward us.

"I want all of you out of my house!"

Our presence here had never been welcome, and now there'd been *fire*.

"Ma'am." Oren held up a hand. "I'm recommending that we *all* return to Hawthorne House."

"What?" Thea asked, her honey-brown eyes narrowing.

Oren flicked his gaze toward her. "You should plan for an extended stay. Call it a slumber party."

"You think Thea's in danger." Rebecca looked around the room. "You think we all are."

"Breaking and entering is an escalation." Oren's tone was measured. "We're dealing with an individual who has proved that he is willing to go through intermediaries to get to Avery. He used Thea to send a message this time—and not just in the literal sense."

I can get to anyone. You can't protect them. That was the message.

"This is ridiculous," Rebecca's mom spat. "I won't be accompanying you anywhere, Mr. Oren, and neither will my daughters."

"Daughter," Rebecca said quietly. I felt my heart twist in my chest.

Oren was not dissuaded. "I'm afraid that even if you weren't already at risk, this visit would put you on our villain's radar. As much as you don't want to hear it, Ms. Laughlin—"

"It's *doctor*, actually," Rebecca's mother snapped. "And I don't care about the risk. The world can't take any more from me than it already has."

I moved closer to Rebecca, whose arms were wrapped around her middle, like all she could do was stand there and just keep taking the blows.

"That isn't true," Thea said quietly.

"Thea." Rebecca's voice was strangled. "Don't."

Mallory Laughlin spared a fond look for Thea. "Such a nice girl." She turned to Rebecca. "I don't know why you have to be so nasty to your sister's friends."

"I am not," Thea said, steel in her voice, "a nice girl."

"You need to come with us," Eve told Mallory. "I need to know you're safe."

"*Oh.*" Mallory's expression softened. There was something tragic about the moment the tension gave way, like it was the only thing that had kept her from crumbling. "You need a mother," she told Eve. The tenderness in her voice was almost painful.

"Come to Hawthorne House," Eve said again. "For me?"

"For you," Mallory agreed, not even sparing a look for Rebecca. "But I'm not setting a foot in the mansion. All these years, Tobias Hawthorne let me think my boy was dead. He never told me that I had a granddaughter. It was bad enough that he stole my baby, bad enough that those boys killed my Emily—*I am not stepping foot in the House.*"

"You can stay at Wayback Cottage," Oren said soothingly. "With your parents."

"I'll stay with you," Rebecca said quietly.

"No," her mother snapped. "You love Hawthornes so much, Rebecca? Stay with them."

CHAPTER 52

Oren called in one of the decoy SUVs to bring Mallory, Rebecca, and Thea back to the estate. Eve opted to ride with them instead of Xander and me, and when the second SUV pulled up to the House, neither she nor Mallory were in it.

"Eve said to tell you she's staying at the cottage." Rebecca looked down. "With my mom."

I am not going to stay where I'm not wanted, I could hear Eve saying. *I can't.* I felt another stab of guilt, then wondered if that was the point.

"She said she'll try to figure out what the number means herself," Thea added. "Just not here."

If Eve was trustworthy, I'd hurt her. Badly. But if she wasn't...

I turned to Oren. "You still have a man on Eve?"

"One for her," my head of security confirmed, "one for Mallory, six securing the gates, four more guarding the immediate perimeter here, and three besides me in the House."

That should have made me feel safer, but all I could think was *don't trust anyone.*

Alisa was waiting for me in the foyer. Oren must have known, but he hadn't warned me.

Before I could say a thing, a small barking blur rounded the corner.

An instant later, Libby followed, giving chase. "House too big!" she huffed. "Puppy too fast! I hate cardio!"

"Have you named her yet?" Xander called as the puppy closed in on us.

Libby stopped running and bent over, her hands on her knees. "I told you to name her, Xander. She's—"

"A Hawthorne dog," Xander finished. "As you wish." He picked the puppy up and snuggled her to his chest. "We shall call you Tiramisu," he declared.

"This is Nash's doing, I presume?" Alisa reached out to stroke the puppy's ear. "Fair warning," she told the pup softly, "Nash Hawthorne has never loved anything he didn't leave."

Libby stared at Alisa for a moment, then pushed her sweaty hair out of her kohl-rimmed eyes. "Would you look at that," she said in a deadpan. "It's time for my cardio."

As my sister stalked off, I narrowed my eyes at Alisa. "Was that really necessary?"

"We have bigger problems right now." Alisa held out her phone. There was a news article on the screen.

"People Are Getting Very Nervous": Hawthorne Heiress on Verge of Taking the Reins.

Apparently, *Market Watch* did not have a high opinion of my capabilities. All ventures in which Tobias Hawthorne had been a major investor were being flagged with caution.

"The onslaught continues," I muttered. "I don't have time for this."

"And you won't have to be the one to deal with things like this," Alisa replied, "if you establish a trust."

Don't trust anyone. Suddenly, I heard that warning in a different way. Had Tobias Hawthorne meant it to have a double meaning?

The closer I got to the year mark, the harder Alisa pushed, and the closer she and her firm got to losing the reins.

"Leave her alone, Alisa."

I looked up to see Jameson striding toward us. He was wearing a crisp white dress shirt, cuffed to his forearms. "A trust isn't necessary. Avery can make do with financial advisors."

"Financial advisors won't calm anyone's nerves about the idea of an eighteen-year-old calling the shots with one of the world's biggest fortunes." Alisa offered Jameson a closed-lipped, *the defense rests* kind of smile. "Perception matters." She turned back to me. "And to that end, there's something else you should see."

She took her phone from me, toggled to a new page, then passed it back to me. This time, I found myself looking down at the celebrity gossip site that had broken the story about Emily and Eve.

Switching Hawthornes? Hawthorne Heiress and Her Swinging New Lifestyle.

Beneath that *lovely* headline, there was a series of pictures. *Jameson in his tuxedo and me in my ball gown, dancing on the beach. A still frame taken from an interview I'd done months ago with Grayson—when he'd kissed me.* The last picture was of me with Xander, standing on the porch at Rebecca's house less than an hour earlier.

I hadn't realized the paparazzi had caught us there. *Then again, maybe it wasn't the paparazzi.* It was getting harder not to feel like our adversary was everywhere.

"Let's look at the positives here," Xander suggested. "I look dashing in that photo."

"There's no reason for Avery to see something like this," Jameson said forcefully.

Jameson Winchester Hawthorne in protective mode was a thing to behold.

"Perception matters," Alisa reiterated.

"Right now," I replied, handing her phone back to her, "other things matter more. Tell me you've found something, Alisa. Who's pulling the strings?"

She'd said that she was on it days ago—and then I hadn't heard a word.

"Do you know how many people there are out there with a net worth of at least two hundred million dollars?" Alisa said calmly. "About thirty thousand. There are eight hundred billionaires in the United States alone, and this wouldn't take billions."

"It would take connections."

I looked up to the stairs—and Grayson. He walked down them to join us but stopped short of looking at me. He was wearing all black, but not a suit.

"Whatever you have," Grayson told Alisa, "send it to me." Finally—*finally*—his eyes made their way to mine. "Where's Eve?"

I felt like he'd struck me.

"The cottage." Rebecca answered. "With my mom and grandpa."

"If we find anything," I said, trying not to let Grayson's cutting look cut me, "we'll call her."

"Find anything..." Jameson's eyes laser-locked on mine. "About what?"

"The person who took Toby is getting more aggressive," Oren said.

"More aggressive how?" Alisa pressed.

Xander held Tiramisu up to his face and spoke in the puppy's voice. "Don't worry. The fire was very small."

"What fire?" Jameson demanded, and he closed the space between us taking my hand. "Tell us, Heiress."

"Another envelope. The message caught fire when it hit the air. Seven numbers."

Jameson's thumb traced the heel of my hand. "Well then, Heiress. Game on."

CHAPTER 53

We had two potential clues: the seal and the number. Given that we were no closer to identifying the disk than Jameson and I had been for months, I opted to concentrate on the number.

Divide and conquer wasn't a Hawthorne family motto, but it might as well have been. Grayson took financials: bank records, investment accounts, transactions. Xander, Thea, and Rebecca took the date angle: *December 29, 1982*. That left a myriad of possibilities for Jameson and me, among them the phone number. If we really were missing an area code, then filling in the blank would accomplish two things: First, it would give us a number to try calling. Second, it would give us a location.

A hint to where Toby was being held? Or another piece of the riddle?

"There are more than three hundred area codes in the United States," Jameson said from memory.

"I'll print out a list," I told him, but what I really wanted to say was *Are we okay?*

Thirty minutes into making phone calls—each area code, followed by *363-1982*—I hadn't had a single call go through. Taking a break, I plugged the number into an internet search and skimmed the results. *A court case involving discriminatory housing practices. A baseball card valued at over two thousand dollars. A hymn from the 1982 Hymnal in the Episcopal Church.*

A phone rang. I looked up. Thea held up her phone. "Blocked number," she said, and because she was Thea Calligaris and didn't know the meaning of the words *hesitation* or *second-guess*, she answered.

Two seconds later, she passed the phone to me. I pressed it to my ear. "Hello?"

"Who am I?" a voice—*that* voice—said.

That question didn't just *get* under my skin; it had been living there for days, and I wondered if he'd called Thea's phone for the sole purpose of reminding me that he'd gotten to her.

"You tell me," I replied. He wasn't going to get a rise out of me. Not now.

"I already did." His voice was as smooth as ever, his cadence distinct.

Jameson grabbed the list with the area codes, then scrawled a message on it. *ASK ABOUT THE DISK.*

"The disk," I said. "You knew what it was." I paused to allow for a response that never came. "When you sent it back to me as proof that you had Toby, you knew what it was worth."

"Intimately."

"And you want me to guess? What it is, what all of this means?"

"Guessing," Toby's captor said silkily, "is for those too weak in mind or spirit to *know*."

That sounded like something Tobias Hawthorne would have said.

"I had a program installed on your little friend's cell phone. I've been tracking you, listening to you. You're there, in his inner sanctum, aren't you?"

Tobias Hawthorne's study. That was what he meant by inner sanctum. He *knew* where we were. The phone in my hand felt dirty, threatening. I wanted to hurl it out a window, but I didn't.

"Why does it matter where I am?" I asked.

"I tire of waiting." Somehow, that sounded more threatening than any words I'd ever heard this man speak. *"Look up."*

The line went dead. I handed the phone to Oren. "He had someone install a program to let him spy on us." So why had he given it up?

Because he wants me to know that he's everywhere.

Oren dropped the phone and stamped his heel down on it, hard. Thea's outraged squeal was drowned out by the cacophony of thoughts in my head.

"*Look up.*" I repeated the words. My eyes traveled toward Jameson's. "He asked me if I was in your grandfather's inner sanctum, but I think he knew the answer. And he told me to *look up.*"

I angled my head toward the ceiling. It was high, with mahogany beams and custom moldings. If *look up* had been part of one of Tobias Hawthorne's riddles, I would have been fetching a ladder right now, but we weren't dealing with Tobias Hawthorne.

"He's been listening to us," I said, feeling that like oil on my skin. "But even if he hacked Thea's camera, he wouldn't have been able to see me. So where would someone picture me in this room if they didn't know where I was sitting?"

I walked toward Tobias Hawthorne's desk. I knew he'd spent hours sitting there, working, strategizing. Putting myself in his position, I took a seat behind the desk. I looked down at it, like I was working, and then I looked up. When that didn't work, I thought about the way that neither Jameson nor Xander could think sitting down. Standing, I walked to the other side of the desk. *Look up.*

I did and found myself staring at the wall of trophies and medals that the Hawthorne grandsons had won: national championships in everything from motocross to swimming to pinball; trophies for surfing, for fencing, for riding bulls. These were the talents that Tobias Hawthorne's grandsons had cultivated. These were the kind of results he'd expected.

There were other things on the wall, too: comic books written by Hawthornes; a coffee table book of Grayson's photographs; some patents, most of them in Xander's name.

The patents, I realized with a start. Each certificate had a number on it. *And each number*, I thought, the world around me suddenly crisp and in hyperfocus, *has seven digits*.

CHAPTER 54

We looked up US Patent number 3631982. It was a utility patent issued in 1972. There were two patent holders: Tobias Hawthorne and a man named Vincent Blake.

Who am I? the man on the phone had said. And when I'd told him to tell me, he'd said that he already had.

"Vincent Blake," I said, turning to the boys. "Did your grandfather ever mention him?

"No," Jameson replied, energy and intensity rolling off him like a storm rolling in. "Gray? Xan?"

"We all know the old man had secrets." Grayson's voice was tight.

"I got nothing," Xander admitted. He wedged himself in front of me to get a better look at the computer screen, then scrolled through the patent information and stopped on a drawing for the design. "It's a mechanism for drilling oil wells."

That rang a bell. "That's how your grandfather made his money—at least at first."

"Not with this patent," Xander scoffed. "Look. Right here!" He pointed at the drawing, at some detail I couldn't even make out. "I'm not exactly an expert at petroleum engineering, but even I can see that right there is what one would call a fatal flaw. The design is supposed to be more efficient than prior technology, but . . ." Xander shrugged. "Details, details, boring things—long story short is that this patent is worthless."

"But that's not the only patent the old man filed in nineteen seventy-two." Grayson's voice was like ice.

"What was the other patent?" I asked.

A few minutes later, Xander had it pulled up. "The goal of this mechanism is the same," he said, looking at the design, "and you can see some elements of the same general framework—but this one *works*."

"Why would anyone file two patents in the same year with such similar designs?" I asked.

"Utility patents cover the creation of new or improved technologies." Jameson came to stand behind me, his body brushing mine. "Breaking a patent isn't easy, but it can be done if you can weasel your way around the claims to uniqueness made by the prior patent. You have to break each claim individually."

"Which this patent does," Xander added. "Think of it like a logic puzzle. This design changes just enough that the infringement case isn't there—and *then* it adds the new piece, which forms the basis of *its* claims. And it's that new piece that made this patent valuable."

This patent had only one holder: Tobias Hawthorne. My mind raced. "Your grandfather filed a bad patent with a man named Vincent Blake. He then immediately filed a better and non-infringing patent by himself, one that made the first completely worthless."

"And made our grandfather millions," Grayson added. "Before that, he was working on oil rigs and playing inventor at night. And afterward . . ."

He became Tobias Hawthorne.

"Vincent Blake." My chest tightened around my racing heart. "That's who we're dealing with. That's who has Toby. And this is why he wants revenge."

"A patent?"

I looked up to see Eve. "I texted her," Grayson told me, preempting any suspicions I might have had about her sudden appearance.

"All of this," Eve continued, emotion palpable in her tone, "because of a *patent*?"

Who am I? Vincent Blake had asked me. But that wasn't the end of this. It couldn't be. I'd thought the riddle was who took Toby—and why. But what if there was a third element, a third question?

What does he want?

"We need to know who we're dealing with." Grayson sounded nothing like the shattered boy from the wine cellar. He sounded more than capable of *dealing with* threats.

"You've really never heard of this guy?" Thea asked. "He's rich and powerful and hates your family's guts, and you've never even heard his name?"

"You know as well as I do," Grayson replied, "that there are different kinds of rich."

Jameson tossed me his phone, and I skimmed the information he'd pulled up on Vincent Blake. "He's from Texas," I noted. This state suddenly felt much smaller. "Net worth just under half a billion dollars."

"Old oil money." Jameson met Grayson's gaze. "Blake's father hit liquid gold in the Texas oil boom of the nineteen thirties. By the late nineteen fifties, a young Vincent had inherited it all. He spent two more decades in oil, then pivoted to ranching."

That didn't tell us anything about what the man was *really* capable of—or what he wanted. "He must be in his eighties now," I said, trying to stick to the facts.

"Older than the old man," Grayson stated, his tone balanced on a knife's edge between icy and cool.

"Try adding your grandfather's name to the search terms," I told Jameson.

Besides the patent, we got one other hit: a magazine profile from the eighties. Like most coverage of Tobias Hawthorne's meteoric rise, it mentioned that his first job had been working on an oil rig. The difference was that this article also mentioned the name of the man who had owned that rig.

"So Blake was his boss," Jameson spitballed. "Picture this: Vincent Blake owns the whole damn company. It's the late sixties, early seventies, and our grandfather is nothing but a grunt."

"A grunt with big ideas," Xander added, tapping his fingers rapidly against his thigh.

"Maybe Tobias takes one of those ideas to the boss," I suggested. "The gutsy move pays off, and they end up collaborating on the design for a new kind of drilling technology."

"At which point," Grayson continued with deadly calm, "our grandfather double-crosses a rich and powerful man to claim a fortune in intellectual property for himself."

"And said powerful man doesn't sue him into oblivion?" Xander was dubious. "Just because the second patent doesn't infringe the first doesn't mean that a wealthy man couldn't have buried a nobody from nowhere in legal fees."

"So why didn't he?" I asked, my body buzzing with the adrenaline that always accompanied finding the kind of answer that raised a thousand more questions.

We knew who had Toby.

We knew what this was about.

But there were still details that ate at me, pulling at the edges of my mind. The disk. The *three* characters in the story. *What's his endgame here? What does he want?*

"Someone must know more about Blake's connection to your grandfather." Eve looked at each of the Hawthorne brothers in turn.

I thought through our next move. Tobias Hawthorne had married Alice in 1974—just two years after the patent was filed. And when Jameson had asked Nan about friends and mentors, her response had been that Tobias Hawthorne had never been in the business of making friends.

She hadn't said a word about mentors.

CHAPTER 55

This time, I went to see Nan alone. "Vincent Blake." I placed the metallic disk on the dining room table, where Nan was having tea.

She snorted in my general direction. "That supposed to be a bribe?"

Either Nan had no more idea what the disk was than we did, or she was bluffing. "Tobias Hawthorne worked for a man named Vincent Blake in the early seventies. It might have been before he and Alice started dating—"

"It wasn't," Nan grunted. "Long courtship. The fool insisted he wanted to make something of himself before he gave my Alice his ring."

Nan was there. She remembers.

"Tobias and Vincent Blake collaborated on a patent," I said, trying to tune out the incessant pounding of my heart. "And then your son-in-law cheated Blake out of a development that was worth millions."

"Did he now?" For a moment, it seemed like that was all Nan was going to say, then she scowled. "Vincent Blake was rich and fancied himself more powerful than God. He took a liking to Tobias, brought him into the fold."

"But?" I prompted.

"Not everyone was happy about it. Mr. Blake liked to pit his protégés against each other. His son was too young to be a factor back then, but Mr. Blake had made it very clear to his nephews that being family didn't get you a free pass. Power had to be earned. It had to be *won*."

"Won," I repeated. I thought of that first phone call with Blake. *I'm just an old man with a fondness for riddles.* All this time, we'd thought that Toby's captor was playing one of Tobias Hawthorne's games. But what if Tobias Hawthorne had taken his cue from Vincent Blake? What if, before he'd been the orchestrator of those Saturday morning games, he'd been a player?

"What happened?" I pressed Nan. "If Tobias was in Blake's inner circle, why double-cross him?"

"Those nephews I mentioned? They wanted to send a message. Mark their territory. Put Tobias in his place."

"What did they do?" I asked.

"There was no Mrs. Blake in those days," Nan grunted. "She passed away when their little boy was born, and the child couldn't have been more than fifteen when Mr. Blake started inviting Tobias over for dinner. Eventually, Tobias started bringing my Alice along. Mr. Blake took a liking to her, too, but he was of a certain type." She gave me a look. "The type who believed that boys would be boys."

"Did he..." I couldn't even finish the sentence. "Did they..."

"If you're thinking the worst, the answer is *no.* But if you're thinking that the nephews came at Tobias through Alice, that they harassed her, manhandled her, and one went so far as to pin her down, force his lips to hers—*well, then.*"

Nan had strongly implied on more than one occasion that she'd killed her first husband, a man who'd broken her fingers for playing the piano a little too well. I deeply suspected she would have castrated Vincent Blake's nephews if she'd had even half a chance.

"And Blake didn't do anything?" I asked.

Nan didn't reply, and I remembered how she'd characterized the man: as the type who believed that boys would be boys. "And that's when your son-in-law decided to get out," I guessed, the picture becoming clearer.

"Tobias stopped dreaming of working for Blake and set his sights on becoming him. A better version. A better *man*."

"So he filed two patents," I said. "One that they'd worked on together and then a different one—a better one. Why didn't Blake sue him?"

"Because Tobias beat him, fair and square. Oh, it was a little underhanded, maybe, and a betrayal, certainly, but Vincent Blake appreciated someone who could play the game."

A rich and powerful man had let a young Tobias Hawthorne go, and in return, Tobias Hawthorne had eclipsed him—billions to his millions.

"Is Blake dangerous?" I asked.

"Men like Vincent Blake and Tobias—they're always dangerous," Nan replied.

"Why didn't you tell Jameson and me this earlier?"

"It was more than forty-five years ago," Nan scoffed. "Do you know how many enemies this family has made since then?"

I thought about that. "Your son-in-law had a list of threats. Blake wasn't on it."

"Then Tobias must not have considered Blake a threat—that, or he thought the threat was neutralized."

“Why would Blake take Toby?” I asked. “Why now?”

“Because my son-in-law isn’t here anymore to hold him at bay.” Nan took my hand and held it tight. The expression on her face grew tender. “You’re the one playing the piano now, girl. Men like Vincent Blake—they’ll break every one of those fingers of yours if you let them.”

CHAPTER 56

As I made my way back to the others, I thought about the fact that Vincent Blake had addressed every one of his missives to *me*. And he'd made it clear on the phone that he wouldn't speak to anyone but "the heiress."

You're the one playing the piano now, girl.... Nan's words were still echoing in my mind when I stepped into the foyer and heard a hushed conversation, bouncing off the walls of the Great Room.

"Don't do this." That was Thea, her voice low and intense. "Don't fold in on yourself."

"I'm not." *Rebecca.*

"Don't be *sad*, Bex."

Rebecca read meaning in that emphasis. "Be angry."

"Hate your mom, hate Emily and Eve, hate me if you have to, but don't you dare disappear."

The second he saw me, Jameson crossed the foyer. "Anything?"

I swallowed. "Vincent Blake brought your grandfather into his inner circle. Treated him like family—or his version of family, anyway."

"The prodigal son." Jameson's eyes lit on mine.

"Eve?" That was Grayson—and he was yelling. I scanned the

foyer. *Oren, Xander, Thea and Rebecca stepping in from the Great Room. But no Eve.*

Grayson burst into view. "Eve's gone. She left a note. She's going after Blake."

"What about her guard?" I asked Oren.

Grayson was the one who answered. "She went to the bathroom, gave him the slip."

"Should we be worried?" Xander threw that question out there.

Men like Vincent Blake and Tobias, I could hear Nan warning me, *they're always dangerous.*

"I'm going after her." Grayson viciously cuffed his sleeves, like he was preparing for a fight.

"Grayson, stop," I said urgently. "Think." Eve bolting made no sense. Did she think she could just show up on Vincent Blake's door and demand Toby back?

Jameson stepped between Grayson and me. He held my gaze for a second or two, then turned to his brother. "Stand down, Gray."

Grayson looked like someone who didn't know the meaning of the words. He was stone: unmovable, the muscles in his jaw rock hard. "I can't fail her again, Jamie."

Again. My heart twisted. Jameson placed a hand on his brother's shoulder. "I invoke *On Spake.*"

Grayson swore. "I don't have time—"

"*Make. Time.*" Jameson leaned forward and said something—I couldn't hear what—directly into Grayson's ear. *On Spake* was a Hawthorne rite; it meant that Grayson couldn't speak until Jameson was done.

As Jameson finished whispering furiously in his ear, Grayson stood very still. I waited for him to call for a fight, to exercise his right to respond to what Jameson had said in a physical way. But instead, Grayson Davenport Hawthorne parted with two and only two words. "I waive."

"Waive what?" Rebecca asked.

Thea snorted derisively. "Hawthornes."

"Heiress?" Jameson turned back to me. "I need to speak to you. Alone."

CHAPTER 57

Jameson led me to the third floor, to a hobby room filled with model trains. There were dozens of them and twice as many tracks set up on glass tables. Jameson pressed a button on the side of one of the trains. At his touch, the wall behind us split in two, revealing a hidden room the size and shape of an old-fashioned phone booth. Its walls were made entirely out of gemstone slabs—a shining, metallic black for half the room and iridescent white for the other.

"Obsidian," Jameson told me. "And agate crystal."

"What are we doing here, Jameson?" I asked. "What do you need to tell me?"

It felt like we were on the verge of something. *A secret? A confession?* Jameson nodded toward the gemstone room. I stepped inside. The ceiling overhead glimmered in a rainbow of colors—more gems.

I realized too late that Jameson hadn't followed me into the room.

The wall behind me closed. It took me a second to process what had just happened. *Jameson trapped me in here.* "What are you doing?" I banged on the wall. "Jameson!" My phone rang. "Let me out of here," I demanded the second I hit Answer.

"I will," Jameson promised on the other end of the line. "When we get back."

We. Suddenly, I understood why Grayson had waived his right to fight, post–*On Spake*. "You promised him you'd go after Eve together."

Jameson didn't tell me I was wrong.

"What if she's dangerous?" I asked. "Even if all she wants is to get Toby back, can you honestly say that she wouldn't trade you or Grayson to get him? We barely know her, and your grandfather's message said—"

"Heiress, have you ever known me to shy away from danger?"

My fingers curled into a fist. Jameson Winchester Hawthorne lived for danger. "If you don't let me out of here, Hawthorne, I will—"

"Do you want to know how I got my scar?" Jameson's voice was softer than I'd ever heard it. I knew immediately what scar he was talking about.

"I want you to open the door," I said.

"I went back." He let those words linger. "To the place where Emily died—*I went back.*"

Emily's heart had given out after cliff jumping. "Jameson..."

"I jumped from dangerously high up, the way she did. Nothing happened the first time. Or the second. But the third..."

I could picture the scar in my mind, running the full length of Jameson's torso. How many times had I dragged my fingers along its edges, feeling the smooth skin of his stomach on either side?

"There was a fallen tree, submerged in the water. I could only see one branch. I had no idea what was underneath. I thought I'd cleared the whole thing, but I was wrong."

I pictured Jameson barreling down from the top of a cliff, hitting the water. I pictured a jagged branch catching his flesh, barely slowing him down.

"I didn't feel pain, not at first. I saw blood in the water—and *then* I felt it. Like my skin was on fire. I made my way to the shore, my body screaming. Somehow, I managed to pull myself to my feet. The old man was standing there. He didn't bat an eye at the blood, didn't ask me if I was okay, didn't yell. All he said, looking my bleeding body up and down, was *Got that out of your system, did you?*"

I leaned against the wall of my gemstone cage. "Why are you telling me this now?"

I could hear the sound of his footstep on the end of the line. "Because Gray is going to keep jumping until it hurts. He's always been the solid one, Heiress. The one who never trembles, never backs down, never doubts. And now, he's lost his mooring, and I have to be the strong one."

"Take me with you," I told Jameson.

"Just this once," he said, an aching tone in his voice, "let *me* be the one who protects you, Avery."

He'd used my actual name. "I don't need you to protect me. You can't just leave me here, Jameson!"

"Can't. Shouldn't. Have to. This is my family's mess, Heiress." For once, there was nothing wicked in Jameson's tone, no innuendo. "It's up to us to clean it up."

"And what about Eve?" I asked. "You know what your grandfather said. *Don't trust anyone.* Grayson isn't thinking straight, but you—"

"I'm thinking more clearly than I ever have. I don't trust Eve." His voice was low and aching. "The only person I trust with all that I am and all that could be, Heiress, is you."

And just like that, Jameson Winchester Hawthorne hung up the phone.

CHAPTER 58

I was going to throttle Jameson. The two of us were races and wagers and dares, not this.

I tried calling Oren, but it went to voicemail. Libby didn't pick up, either, which probably meant her phone wasn't charged. I tried Xander, then Rebecca. I was halfway to calling Thea before I remembered her phone had been destroyed. Trying to calm myself, I took out my knife, plotted murder, then gave away ten thousand dollars to strangers struggling to pay rent.

Finally, I texted Max. *Jameson locked me in the world's most expensive dungeon,* I wrote. *He's got some asinine idea about protecting me.*

Max's reply didn't take long. *THAT GREEN-EYED BASTARD.*

I grinned despite myself and typed back: *You cursed.*

Max replied in rapid-fire: *Would you prefer "smirking, paternalistic ship-head who can shove his mother-faxing paternalism up his mother-faxing asp"?*

I snorted, then finally calmed down enough to take in the three-hundred-and-sixty-degree view of the gemstone room. *Two walls made of obsidian,* I thought. *Two walls made of white agate.* Probing the walls didn't lead me to an exit switch but did reveal that the gemstones had been formed into bricks, and if you pressed at the top or bottom of any of those bricks, they rotated. Rotating a black brick turned it white. Rotating a white brick turned it black.

I thought about all the times I'd seen Xander fiddling with a handheld puzzle, then craned my neck, taking in every detail of the walls, the ceiling, the floor. Jameson hadn't locked me in a dungeon.

He'd locked me in an *escape room.*

Three hours in, I still hadn't hit on the right pattern, and with each passing minute, I wondered if Jameson and Grayson had caught up to Eve. Warnings of all kinds swirled in my mind.

Don't trust anyone.

Anyone close to you could be the next target.

I tire of waiting.

In my darkest moments, I thought about how Eve had sworn that she would do anything—*anything*—to get Toby back.

Don't think about her. Or them. Or any of it. I stared at the glittering room around me—the opulence, the beauty—and tried not to feel like the walls were closing in. "Glittering," I muttered. "Opulence. What about diamonds?"

I'd already tried dozens of designs: *the letter H; a chessboard, a key...*

Now I tried a black diamond on each of the white walls, a white diamond on each of the black ones. *Nothing.* Frustrated, I swept my hand over one of the diamonds, wiping it away.

Click.

My eyes went wide at the sound. *Two black diamonds, one white one, nothing on the other obsidian wall.* With a second click, a panel on the floor popped up. I squatted to get a better look. *Not a panel. A trapdoor.* "Finally!"

No thinking, no hesitation, I dropped down into darkness. I grabbed my phone and switched on the flashlight, then followed the twists and turns of the winding passageway until I hit a ladder. I climbed it and came to a ceiling—and another trapdoor.

Laying my palms flat against it, I pushed until it gave, then pulled myself up into a bedroom, though not one I'd seen before. A beat-up six-string guitar leaned against the wall in front of me; a king-sized bed made of what looked to be repurposed driftwood sat to my left. I turned around to see Nash perched on a metal stool next to a large wooden workbench that seemed to be doubling as a dresser.

He was blocking the door.

I walked toward him. "I'm leaving," I said, my temper simmering. "Don't try to stop me. I'm going after Jameson and Grayson."

"That right?" Nash didn't move from the stool. "I taught you to fight because I trust you to *think*, kid." He stood, his expression mild. "That trust misplaced?" Nash gave me a second to chew on that question, then stepped aside, clearing the way to the door.

Damn it, Nash. I blew out a long breath. "No."

I thought past my fury and worry and the dark, looping thoughts. I was three hours behind, and it wasn't like Oren would have let Jameson and Grayson run off alone.

"If you want to borrow some duct tape when the knuckleheads get back," Nash drawled, "I could be persuaded."

"Thanks, Nash." A little calmer, I stepped into the hall and saw Oren. "Jameson, Grayson, and Eve," I said immediately, an edge in my voice. "What's their status?"

"Safe and accounted for," Oren reported. "Eve made it to the Blake compound but wasn't allowed admittance. The boys got there shortly thereafter and talked her down. They're all on their way back now."

Relief hit, clearing the way for my annoyance to surge. "You let Jameson lock me up!"

"You were safe." Oren's lips twitched. "Secured."

"Behold!" boomed a voice from the other side of Oren. "The heroes ride into battle! Avery will be liberated!"

I looked past Oren to see Xander, Thea, and Rebecca incoming. Xander was holding an enormous metal shield that looked like it had been lifted straight off the arm of a medieval knight.

"I swear to all that is good and holy," Thea said under her breath, "if you say one more word about LARPing right now, Xander—"

I stepped around Oren. "I appreciate the 'rescue,' Xan, but you couldn't answer your phone?" I looked to Rebecca. "You, either?"

"Sorry," Rebecca said. "My phone was on silent. We were blowing off some steam." Her green eyes slid to Thea's. "Playing pool."

I glanced at Thea. Her sweater was ripped at the shoulder, her hair markedly less than perfect. The two of them might have been in the billiards room or arcade, but there was no way in hell they'd been *playing pool*. But at least Rebecca didn't look like a shell of herself anymore.

"What's your excuse?" I asked Xander.

He held his shield to the side. "Step into my office."

I rolled my eyes but joined him.

Xander used the shield to block us off from Oren, then led me around the corner. "I went down the rabbit hole of doing a deep dive on Vincent Blake's holdings, current and past," Xander admitted. "Blake was the sole funder of the VB Innovation Lab." Xander paused, steeling himself. "I recognized the name. VB is where Isaiah Alexander worked right after he was fired."

Xander's father worked for Vincent Blake. That thought was like a domino in my mind, knocking down another and another. *There are three characters in the parable of the prodigal son, are there not?*

The king, the knight, and the bishop. The son who'd stayed faithful.

"Does Isaiah Alexander still work for Blake?" I asked Xander, my mind whirring.

"No," Xander said emphatically. "Not for fifteen years. And I know what you're thinking, Avery, but there's no way Isaiah had any involvement in Toby's abduction. He's a mechanic who owns his own garage, and the other mechanic who works for him is out on maternity leave, so he's been pulling double shifts for weeks." Xander swallowed. "But still…he might know something that could give us the upper hand. Or know someone who knows something. Or know someone who knows someone who knows—"

Thea placed a hand helpfully over Xander's mouth.

The file. The domino chain in my mind hit its conclusion, and I sucked in a breath. *Isaiah Alexander's file was empty, and Xander didn't take the page.*

What were the chances that the missing page had mentioned Vincent Blake?

Eve took it. That might have been a leap. It might not have been fair. I couldn't even tell anymore.

My entire body buzzing, I stepped around Xander's shield and looked to Oren, who—not surprisingly—had followed us around the corner. "Jameson, Grayson, and Eve are on their way back here?" I asked, clipping the words. "They're secured, under the watchful eyes of your men, and will be for the next three hours?"

Oren's eyes narrowed with suspicion. "What are you going to do if I say yes?"

That gives us three hours. I looked to Xander. "I think we need to talk to Isaiah. But if you're not ready—"

"I was born ready!" Xander brandished his shield. He smiled a very Xander Hawthorne smile, then let his bravado falter. "But before we go, group hug?"

CHAPTER 59

An hour later, we were parked outside a small-town mechanic shop with a large security team in tow, having given the paparazzi the slip on the highway. There was only one man working inside the shop. He was under a car when we walked in.

"You'll have to wait." Isaiah Alexander's voice was neither low nor high.

I hoped, for Xander's sake, that he really wasn't involved in any of this.

"Need a hand?" Xander offered. When some people got nervous, they clammed up. Xander babbled. "I'm pretty good with mechanical things, unless or maybe especially if they're flammable."

That got a chuckle. "Spoken like someone with too much time on their hands." Isaiah Alexander rolled out from underneath the car and stood. He was tall like Xander but broader through the shoulders. His skin was a darker brown, but their eyes were the same.

"You looking for a job?" he asked Xander, like wayward teenagers showed up here all the time with a trio of teenage girls and several bodyguards in tow.

"I'm Xander." Xander swallowed. "Hawthorne."

"I know who you are," Isaiah said, his tone no-nonsense but somehow gentle. "Looking for a job?"

"Maybe." Xander shifted his weight from foot to foot and then resumed nervous babbling. "I should probably warn you that I've dismantled four and a half Porsches past the point of no return in the last two years. But in my defense, they had it coming, and I needed the parts."

Isaiah took that in stride. "Like to build things, do you?"

The question—and the slight upward curve of his lips—almost undid me, so I couldn't imagine how hard it hit Xander.

"You're not surprised to see me." Xander sounded stunned—this from a person who could *literally* stun himself and proceed without missing a beat. "I thought you would be," he blurted out. "Surprised. Or that you wouldn't know who I was. I prepared a mental flowchart that geared my reaction toward your exact level of surprise and knowledge."

Isaiah Alexander looked at his son, his expression steady. "Was it three-dimensional?"

"My mental flowchart?" Xander threw his hands up in the air. "Of course it was three-dimensional! Who makes two-dimensional flowcharts?"

"Nerds?" Thea suggested, and then she stage-whispered, "Ask me who makes three-dimensional flowcharts, Xander."

"Thea." Rebecca nudged her.

"I'm helping," Thea insisted, and sure enough, Xander seemed to steady a little.

"You knew about me?" he asked Isaiah, quiet but more intense than I'd ever seen him.

Isaiah met Xander's eyes. "Since before you were born."

Then why weren't you there? I thought with a ferocity that stole my breath. My own father had been mostly absent, but this was *Xander*, king of distractions and chaos, BHFF, who'd known about this man for *months* but had only come here for me.

I couldn't bear the idea of him getting hurt.

"Do you want me to go?" Xander asked Isaiah hesitantly.

"Would I have asked you if you wanted a job," Isaiah replied, "if I did?"

Xander blinked. Repeatedly. "I came here because we need to talk to you about Vincent Blake," he said, like that was the one thing he *could* say of the thousands pounding through his brain.

Isaiah cocked an eyebrow. "Sounds like a want more than a need to me."

"That's what people say about second lunch," Xander replied, reverting to babble mode, "and it's a dirty lie."

"On the lunch bit," Isaiah told him, "we agree." Then he turned, eyeing a nearby car. "I worked for Blake for just over two years, beginning shortly after you were born."

Xander took a deep breath. "Right after you worked for my grandfather?"

Isaiah seemed to steel himself at the mention of Tobias Hawthorne. "The entire time I worked for Hawthorne, competitors tried to steal me away. Each time, your grandfather would sweeten my contract. I was twenty-two, a prodigy, on the top of the world—and then I wasn't." Isaiah popped the hood of the car. "After Hawthorne fired me, the offers dried up pretty damn quick. I went from young, rash, and flying high with a mid-six-figure salary to untouchable overnight."

"Because of Skye," Xander bit out.

Isaiah looked up from the engine to pin Xander with a look. "I made my own decisions where your mother was concerned, Xander."

"And the old man punished you for them," Xander replied, like a kid pushing on a bruise to see how much it hurt.

"It wasn't a punishment." Isaiah returned his attention to the car. "It was strategy. I was a twenty-two-year-old who'd been so flush with cash that I'd never imagined it would stop coming. I'd blown through most of what I'd made, so once I was fired and blacklisted, I conveniently didn't have the resources to put up much of a fight for custody."

It wasn't about Skye. I realized with a start what Isaiah Alexander was saying. *Tobias Hawthorne fired Isaiah because of Xander.* Not because the old man had been unhappy about his youngest grandson's conception but because he'd refused to share him.

"So you just gave up on your son?" Rebecca asked Isaiah sharply. She wasn't a person who knew how to fight for herself, but she'd fight for Xander every time.

"I managed to scrape together enough for a third-rate lawyer to file suit when Xander was born. The court ordered a paternity test. But wouldn't you know, it came back negative."

So said the man with Xander's eyes. Xander's smile. The man who heard the word "flowchart" and asked if Xander built them in three dimensions.

"Skye named me Alexander." Xander wasn't, by nature, a quiet person, but his voice was barely audible now. "They faked the DNA test."

"I couldn't prove it," Isaiah told him. "I couldn't get near you." He tweaked something, then slammed the hood of the car. "And I couldn't get a job. Enter Vincent Blake."

"I don't want to talk about Vincent Blake," Xander said with enough intensity that I half expected him to start yelling. Instead, his voice dropped to a whisper. "You're saying that you *wanted* me?"

I thought about how badly I'd wanted Toby to be my father

instead of Ricky Grambs, about Rebecca growing up invisible and Eve moving out the day she turned eighteen. I thought about Libby, whose mother had taught her she deserved a partner that degraded and controlled her, about Jameson's *hunger* and Grayson's punishing perfection, both of them competing for approval that was always just out of reach.

I thought about Xander and how scared he'd been to come here. *You're saying that you* wanted *me?* The question echoed all around us.

Isaiah responded: "Still do."

Xander bolted. One second, he was there, and the next, he was out the door.

"We'll go after him," Rebecca told me, taking Thea with her. "You ask whatever you need to, Avery, because Xander can't. He shouldn't have to."

The door slammed behind Rebecca and Thea, and I looked up at Isaiah Alexander. *Your son is amazing,* I thought. *You can't ever hurt him.* But I forced myself to focus on the reason we'd come here and the questions Xander couldn't ask. "So after you were fired and blacklisted, Vincent Blake just came out of nowhere and offered you a job?"

Isaiah assessed me for so long that I felt about four years old and five inches tall. But whatever he saw in my face earned me an answer. "Blake came to me at my lowest point, told me that he wasn't scared of Tobias Hawthorne, and if I wasn't, either, we could do great things together. He offered me a position as the head of his new innovation lab. I had free rein to invent whatever I wanted, as long as I did it in his name. I had money again. I had freedom."

"So why did you quit?" I asked. That was a guess, but my gut said it was a good one.

"I started noticing things I wasn't supposed to notice," Isaiah said calmly. "The pattern's there if you look for it. People who stand in Vincent Blake's way—they aren't standing for long. Accidents were had. People disappeared. Nothing anyone could prove. Nothing that could be tied to Blake, but once I saw the pattern, I couldn't unsee it. I knew who I was working for."

We'd come here in part to find out what Vincent Blake was capable of. And now I knew.

"So I quit," Isaiah said. "I took the money I'd earned—and saved this time—and I bought this place so I'd never have to work for another Vincent Blake or Tobias Hawthorne again."

What had happened to Isaiah wasn't right. None of this was right.

Rebecca and Thea reappeared. Xander wasn't with them. "There's a doughnut shop down the street," Rebecca told me, out of breath. "We have a twelve-jelly-and-cream situation."

I looked back at Isaiah.

"Sounds like you're needed," he said, calmly returning his attention to the car he'd been working on. "I'll be here."

CHAPTER 60

Rebecca and Thea led me to a doughnut shop, then waited outside. I found Xander sitting at a table by himself, stacking doughnuts one on top of the other. By my count, there were five.

"Behold!" Xander declared. "The Leaning Tower of Bavarian Cream-a!"

"Where are the other seven doughnuts?" I asked him, taking his cue and not pushing this too much too soon.

Xander shook his head. "I have so many regrets."

"You literally just picked up another doughnut," I pointed out.

"I couldn't possibly regret *this* doughnut," Xander stated emphatically.

I softened my voice. "You just found out that the Hawthorne family faked a paternity test to keep your father, who *wanted* you, out of your life. It's okay to be angry or devastated or..."

"I don't super excel at anger, and devastation is really more for people who slow down long enough to let their brains focus on the sadness. My expertise falls more squarely in the Venn diagram overlap between unbridled enthusiasm and infinite—"

"Xander." I reached across the table and laid my hand on top of his. For a moment, he just sat there, looking down at our hands.

"You know I love you, Avery, but I don't want to talk to you about this." Xander removed his hand from underneath mine. "I don't want to have to explain to you what I don't want to explain to you. I just want to finish this doughnut and eat his four best doughnut-y friends and congratulate myself for probably not vomiting."

I didn't say another word. I just sat there with him until Oren appeared in my peripheral vision. He inclined his head to the right. Xander and I had been spotted—by a local, I was guessing, but when it came to the Hawthorne family and the Hawthorne heiress nothing stayed *local* for long.

We went back to Isaiah's garage. "Do you want us to wait outside?" I asked Xander.

"No. I just want you to give me that little metal disk," Xander replied. "I'm assuming you have it on you?"

I did, and I handed it to him because right now, I would have done anything Xander wanted.

He pushed open the door and walked slowly back to the car Isaiah was working on. "I need to ask you two things. First, what are your thoughts on Rube Goldberg machines?"

"Never made one." Isaiah met Xander's gaze. "But I tend to think they should have catapults."

Xander nodded, like that was an acceptable answer. "Second, have you ever seen something like this before?" He held the disk out to Isaiah, the two of them towering over everyone else present.

Isaiah took the disk from Xander. "Where the hell did you kids get this?"

"You do know what it is," Xander said, his eyes lighting up. "Some kind of artifact?"

"Artifact?" Isaiah shook his head, handing the disk back to Xander, who handed it to me. "No. *That* is Mr. Blake's calling card. He always called it the family seal."

I thought about the wax seal on the envelope of the last message, bearing the same symbol.

"I think he had, what, five of those coins?" Isaiah continued. "If you had one of the seals, it meant you had Blake's blessing to play in his empire as you wished—until you displeased him. If that happened, you were stripped of the seal and the status and power that came with it. It's how Blake kept his family on a very short string. Every person with a drop of his blood or his dead wife's fought tooth and nail to have one of the seals."

I considered the implications. "Only family?"

"Only family," Isaiah confirmed. "Nephews, great-nephews, cousins once removed."

"What about Blake's son?" I asked. Nan had mentioned a son.

"I heard there was a son," Isaiah replied. "But he took off years before I came into the picture."

The prodigal son, I thought suddenly, and adrenaline rushed into my veins.

"What do you mean when you say Vincent Blake's son *took off*?" I asked Isaiah.

"I meant what I said." Isaiah fixed me with a look. "The son took off at some point and didn't come back. It's part of what made the seals so valuable. There was no direct heir to the family fortune. Rumor had it, when Blake dies, anyone holding one of *those*—" Isaiah nodded toward the disk. "Gets a stake."

Isaiah had said that there were five seals. That meant the disk I was holding in my hand was worth somewhere in the neighborhood of a hundred million dollars. I thought of Toby and the instructions he'd left my mother about going to Jackson if she needed anything. *You know what I left there*, he'd written. *You know what it's worth.*

"More than twenty years ago, Toby Hawthorne stole this from his father." I stared at the seal, at the layers of concentric rings. "But why did Tobias Hawthorne have one of the Blake family seals? There's no way Blake was planning to leave one-fifth of his fortune to a billionaire who betrayed him."

Isaiah gave a shrug, but there was something hard about it, like he refused to give Tobias Hawthorne or Vincent Blake any space in his mind. "I've told you what I know," he said. "And I should be getting back to work." His gaze went to Xander. "Unless…"

For a moment, I heard the same uncertainty in his tone that I'd heard in Xander's when I asked him about his father's file.

"I do want to talk," Xander said, rushing the words. "I do, I mean, if you do."

"Okay, then," Isaiah said.

The rest of us were almost out the door when Rebecca stopped and turned around. "What was the name of Vincent Blake's son?" she asked, an odd tone in her voice.

"It's been a long time," Isaiah said, but then he glanced back at Xander and sighed. "Just let me think for a minute.… Will." Isaiah snapped his fingers. "The son's name was Will Blake."

Will Blake. For a split second, I wasn't standing there in Isaiah's shop. I was in Toby's wing of Hawthorne House, reading a poem inscribed on metal.

William Blake. "A Poison Tree."

CHAPTER 61

What if Toby hadn't chosen that poem just for the emotions it conveyed? What if the secrets and lies he'd written about himself went beyond his hidden adoption?

Why did Tobias Hawthorne have that seal?

Rebecca, Thea, and I gave Xander time with his father. The rest of us waited in the SUV. I had Oren pull around the block so that if the paparazzi showed up at the doughnut shop, they'd focus on my SUVs, not Isaiah's garage. While we waited, my mind raced. *William Blake. The Blake family seal. Revenge. Avenge. Vengeance. Avenger.*

When Xander climbed into the SUV, he didn't say a word about his father. "Hit me with all those thinky thoughts," he told me.

I studied him for a moment. His brown eyes were steady and bright, so I obliged. "What Vincent Blake is doing now—kidnapping Toby, playing games with me—I don't think any of that is really about a patent filed fifty years ago." The patent number had told us who we were dealing with. We'd *assumed* that it also gave us motive, but we were wrong. "I think this is about Vincent Blake's son."

"The prodigal son," Xander murmured. "Will Blake."

A wasteful youth. Vincent Blake's distinctive voice rang in my mind. *Wandering the world—ungrateful. A benevolent father, ready to welcome him home. But if memory serves correctly, there were three characters in that story…*

Everything pointed to the third person in this story being Tobias Hawthorne—and if that was the case, maybe Xander had it wrong. "What if Will isn't the prodigal?" I said. "On the phone, Blake emphasized that there were three characters in the parable of the prodigal son. The father—"

"Vincent Blake," Thea filled in.

I nodded. "The son who betrayed his family, took the money, and ran—what if that's not Vincent Blake's *actual* son? What if it's a man he'd brought into the family fold? Young Tobias Hawthorne. Nan said that Blake's son was younger at the time, fifteen when your grandfather would have been…" I did the math. "Twenty-four."

"At fifteen, Vincent Blake's son might not have been old enough to have one of those seals," Xander said, thinking out loud, "but he was plenty old to witness the betrayal."

My entire body felt alive and alert, horrified and entranced. "Witness the betrayal," I echoed, "and wonder why his father let some nobody from nowhere get away with screwing him out of millions?"

That put Will Blake in the position of the son who had stayed—the good son, upset that the prodigal's betrayal was rewarded instead of punished.

There are three characters in the parable of the prodigal son, are there not?

Avenge. Revenge. Vengeance. Avenger.

I always win in the end.

"The question is," Xander said, "why did Toby leave a poem by a poet named *William Blake* hidden in his wing, way back when?"

"And what are the chances," I added, one thought leaping to the forefront of my mind, "that Will *did* have one of the Blake family seals with him when he disappeared?"

If the seal in Tobias Hawthorne's possession had belonged to Vincent Blake's son…

It felt like we were barreling toward the edge of a cliff.

"How long ago did Will Blake go missing?" Rebecca wasn't looking at any of us. Light from the window hit her hair. Her tone was throaty and intense.

I got out my phone and did a search. And then another. Eventually, I was sure: The last time that Vincent Blake had been publicly photographed with his son, Will had been in his early twenties. "Forty years ago?" I estimated. "Plus or minus. Rebecca—"

"Will is one nickname for William," Rebecca said, sucking every last molecule of oxygen out of the car. "But another one is Liam."

CHAPTER 62

Mallory Laughlin hadn't revealed much about the man who'd gotten her pregnant. She'd said that he was older, very charming. She'd said that his name was *Liam*. And when Eve had asked what had happened to Liam, all she would say was that he had left.

If Liam was Will Blake...

If he'd sought out a sixteen-year-old girl living on the Hawthorne estate...

If he got that girl pregnant...

And if Will really hadn't been seen for more than forty years... *plus or minus*...

Questions piled up in my head. Did Toby know or suspect that Will Blake was his biological father? Did Vincent Blake know that Toby was his grandson? *Is that why he took him?* And if the seal that Toby had stolen from his father really did belong to Vincent Blake's son—how had it come to be in Tobias Hawthorne's possession in the first place?

What happened to Will Blake?

If we'd been barreling toward the edge of the cliff before, I was in the free fall now.

The moment we arrived back at Hawthorne House and I burst out of the SUV, Jameson was there. He stopped, inches from me, intensity radiating off his body. Everything we'd learned was about to come pouring out of my mouth when he spoke.

"What the hell is wrong with you, Heiress?"

I stared at him, disbelief giving way to anger that bubbled up in me and exploded out. "What's wrong with *me*? You're the one who locked me in the world's most bejeweled escape room!"

"To keep you safe," Jameson emphasized. "Vincent Blake is powerful, and he's connected, and he's going to keep coming for *you*, Avery, because you're the one holding the keys to this kingdom. And I don't know if he wants what you have, or if he wants to burn it down, but either way, how am I supposed to keep you safe if you won't let me?"

I knew that Jameson loved me—and that pissed me off because our love wasn't supposed to be like this. "You're not supposed to *keep* me anything!" I burst out. He tried to look away, but I wouldn't let him. "Ask me what we found."

He didn't.

"Just ask me, Jameson."

I could see him wanting to, warring with himself. "Promise me first."

"Promise you what?" I asked.

"That you'll be more careful. That I won't come home to find you gone again."

I wasn't sure how to say this to make him believe it, so I put both my hands flat on his chest and stared into green eyes that I knew better than anyone else's. "I'm not going to stay locked up here, and it is not your place to lock me up. I don't need your protection."

"This is what you want!" Jameson sounded like the words had been ripped out of him. Breathing heavily, he curled his fingers around mine. "It's what you've always wanted. An arrogant, duty-bound asshole who tries to be honorable and would die to protect the girl he loves."

I froze. Logically, I knew that my heart was still beating. I was still breathing. But it didn't feel like it. I could see the others in my peripheral vision, but I couldn't move, couldn't ask Jameson to lower his voice, couldn't focus on anything but the green of his eyes, the lines of his face.

"I'm not Grayson," he told me, ravaged by the words.

"I don't want you to be," I said, pleading—for what, I wasn't even sure.

"Yes, you do," Jameson insisted quietly. "And it doesn't even matter because I'm not putting on a show here, Heiress. I'm not playing at being overprotective or pretending that, for once in my life, I want to do the right thing." He brought his hands to the side of my face, then the back of my neck, and I felt his touch through every square inch of my body. "I love you. I *would* die to protect you. I would make you hate me to keep you safe because *damn it, Avery*—some things are too precious to gamble."

Jameson Winchester Hawthorne loved me. He *loved* me, and I loved him. But I didn't know how to make him believe that when I said I didn't want him to be Grayson, I meant it.

"This is who I want to be," Jameson said, his voice hoarse, "for you."

I wished suddenly that neither one of us was standing on the lawn of Hawthorne House. That it was my birthday again or that the year mark had passed and we were halfway around the world, seeing everything, doing everything, having it all. I wished that Toby had never been taken, that Vincent Blake didn't exist, that Eve had never come here—

Eve, I thought suddenly, and then I realized something that I should have realized much sooner. If Vincent Blake's son was Toby's father, that made Eve the man's great-granddaughter.

Eve and Vincent Blake are family. The words exploded in my mind like shrapnel. I thought about Eve telling me about doing a mail-in DNA test, about the way that she'd first earned my trust because I'd thought I understood what Toby meant to her, how it must have felt for her to finally be wanted, to finally have *family* who wanted her.

But what if that family *wasn't* Toby?

What if someone else had found her first?

I thought back to showing her Toby's wing, to the moment when I'd mentioned "A Poison Tree" and said the poet's name: William Blake. Eve had dropped to her knees, reading the poem over and over again. *She recognized the name.*

"Heiress." Jameson was still looking at me, and I knew, just from the way he let his thumbs skim lightly over my cheekbones, that he knew my mind had taken flight. He didn't blame me for it. He didn't ask me for anything else. All he said was "Tell me."

So I did.

And then he told me that Eve was at Wayback Cottage—with Grayson.

CHAPTER 63

Oren and two of his men drove Jameson and me to Wayback Cottage. Rebecca didn't come with us, didn't *want* to come with us. Thea and Xander stayed with her.

I rang the bell—again and again until Mrs. Laughlin answered.

"Grayson and Eve," I said, trying to sound calmer than I felt. "Are they here?"

Mrs. Laughlin pinned me with a look that had probably been used on generations of Hawthorne children. "They're in the kitchen with my daughter."

I made my way there, Jameson on my heels, Oren directly to my left, his men only steps behind him. We found Eve sitting across a worn wooden table from Mallory. Grayson stood behind Eve like a wayward angel keeping watch.

Eve swiveled her gaze toward us, and I wondered if I was imagining the canny look in her eyes, imagining her assessing the situation, assessing me, before speaking. "Any updates?"

One, I thought. *I know that you're related to Vincent Blake.*

"I tried to get to Toby," Eve continued intently, "but I couldn't. *Someone* brought me back."

That someone was standing so close to her now.

"Grayson," I said. "I need to talk to you."

Eve turned to look at him. There was something delicate about the way her hair fell off her shoulder, something almost mesmerizing about the way she lifted her eyes to his.

"Grayson," I said again, my voice urgent and low.

Jameson didn't give me the opportunity to say his brother's name a third time. "Avery found out something that you need to know. Outside, Gray. Now."

Grayson walked toward us. Eve came, too. "What did you find out?" she asked.

"What is it you're hoping I'll find out—or hoping I won't?" I hadn't meant to say that out loud, but now that I had, I marked her reaction.

"What is that supposed to mean?" Eve snapped, something like hurt flickering over her face.

Was that an act? *This whole time—has it all been an act?* My gaze landed on the chain around her neck, and I flashed back to the moment she'd stepped out of my bathroom wearing nothing but a towel and a locket. Why would Eve, who'd insisted she'd spent her whole life with no one, wear a locket?

What was inside?

A small metal disk. Isaiah had said that there were five, that Vincent Blake gave them exclusively to family—and Eve was family.

"Open your locket," I said sharply. "Show me what's inside."

Eve stood very still. I moved, reaching for it—but Grayson caught my hand. He gave me a look like a shard of ice. "What are you doing, Avery?"

"Vincent Blake had a son," I said. I hadn't wanted to do this here, in front of Mallory and Mrs. Laughlin, but so be it. "His name was Will. I think he was Toby's father. And *this*?" I withdrew the Blake family seal, the one that had been in Toby's possession when he disappeared. "It was almost certainly Will's. Blake gave them to family members who held his favor." I could feel Eve watching me. Her face was blank—so carefully blank. "Isn't that right, Eve?"

"You have no right," Mallory Laughlin snapped shrilly, "to come in here and say any of this. *Any of it.*" She looked past me to Mrs. Laughlin. "Are you going to just stand there and let her do this?" she demanded, her voice going up an octave. "This is your home!"

"I think it would be best," Mrs. Laughlin told me stiffly, "if you left."

I'd spent a year making inroads with her and the rest of the staff. I'd gone from being an outsider and an enemy to being accepted. I didn't want to lose that, but I couldn't back down.

"He called himself Liam," I said quietly, my gaze going to Mallory's. "He didn't tell you who he really was—or why he was here."

Mrs. Laughlin took a step toward me. "You need to go."

"Will Blake sought out your daughter," I said, turning back toward the woman who'd served as a steward of the Hawthorne estate for most of her life. "He would have been in his twenties. She was only sixteen. She snuck him onto the estate—up to Hawthorne House, even." I didn't stop. "It was probably his idea."

A pained expression forced Mrs. Laughlin's eyes closed. "Stop this," she begged me. "Please."

"I don't know what happened," I said, "but I do know that Will Blake hasn't been seen since. And for some reason, you and your husband let the Hawthornes adopt your grandson and pass him off as their own flesh and blood, even to the baby's mother."

A high-pitched mewling sound escaped Mallory's throat.

"You were trying to protect them, weren't you?" I asked Mrs. Laughlin softly. "Your daughter *and* Toby. You were trying to protect them from Vincent Blake."

"What is she talking about?" Eve glided back toward Mallory, then ducked down, angling her head so that her eyes were looking directly into Mallory's. "You have to tell me the truth," she continued. "All of it. Your Liam . . . he didn't *leave*, did he?"

I saw then what she was doing—what she had been doing. "That's why you're here," I realized. "What did Vincent Blake offer you if you brought him answers?"

"That's enough," Grayson told me sharply.

"It really, really isn't," Jameson replied, blazing by my side.

"You know what this necklace means to me, Grayson," Eve said, her fist covering the locket. "You know why I wear it. *You know, Grayson.*"

"*Don't trust anyone,*" I said, my tone a match for hers. "That was the old man's message. His final message, Gray. Because if Eve's here, Vincent Blake might not be far behind."

Eve turned her body into Grayson's, her every movement a study in grace and fury. "Who cares about Tobias Hawthorne's final message?" she asked, her voice shattering at the end of that question. "He didn't want me, Grayson. He chose Avery. I was *never* going to be enough for him. You know what that's like, Gray. Better than anyone—you know."

I could feel him slipping through my fingers, but I couldn't stop fighting. "You pushed us to ask Skye about the seal," I said, staring Eve down. "You've been asking around about deep, dark Hawthorne family secrets. You pressed and pressed for answers on Toby's father—"

A single tear rolled down Eve's cheek.

"*Avery.*" Grayson's tone was one I recognized. This was the boy who'd been raised as the heir apparent. The one who didn't have to dirty his hands to put an adversary in their place.

Am I the enemy again, Gray?

"Eve has done nothing to you." Grayson's voice cut into me like a surgeon's knife. "Even if what you're saying about Toby's parentage is true, Eve is not to blame for her family."

"Then get her to open the locket," I said, my mouth dry.

Eve walked toward me. When she got within three feet, Oren shifted. "That's close enough."

Without a word to him, or to anyone, Eve opened her locket. Inside, there was a picture of a little girl. *Eve*, I realized. Her hair was cut short and uneven, her little cheeks gaunt. "No one ever cherished her. No one ever would have put her picture in a locket." Eve met my gaze, and though she looked vulnerable, I thought I saw something else underneath that vulnerability. "So I wear this as a reminder: Even if no one else loves you, you can. Even if no one else ever puts you first, *you can*."

She was standing there admitting that she was going to put herself first, but it was like Grayson couldn't see that. "Enough," he ordered. "This isn't you, Avery."

"Maybe, Gray," Jameson countered, "you don't know her as well as you think."

"Out!" Mrs. Laughlin boomed. "All of you, out!"

Not one of us moved, and the older woman's eyes narrowed.

"This is my house. Mr. Hawthorne's will granted us lifelong, rent-free tenancy." Mrs. Laughlin looked at her daughter, then at Eve, and finally she turned back to me. "You can fire me, but you can't evict me, and you *will* leave my home."

"Lottie," Oren said quietly.

"Don't you *Lottie* me, John Oren." Mrs. Laughlin glared at him. "You take your girl, you take the boys—and you get out."

CHAPTER 64

"What is wrong with you?" Grayson exploded as soon as we were outside.

"Did you hear a word I said in there?" I asked, my heart breaking like cracking glass, bit by jagged bit. "Did you hear what *she* said? She's going to put herself first, Grayson. She *hates* your grandfather. We aren't her family. *Blake* is."

Grayson stopped walking toward the SUV. He went stiff, attending to the cuffs of his dress shirt and brushing an imaginary speck off the lapel of his suit. "Clearly," he said, his tone almost regal, "I was wrong about you."

I felt like he'd just thrown ice-cold water in my face. Like he'd hit me.

And then I watched Grayson Hawthorne walk away.

A guy who thinks he knows everything, I could hear myself saying what felt like a lifetime ago.

A girl with a razor-sharp tongue.

I could hear Grayson telling me that I had an expressive face, telling Jameson that I was one of them, in Latin, so I wouldn't understand it. I could feel Grayson correcting my grip on a longsword, see him catching my Hawthorne pin before it could hit the ground. I saw him sliding a hand-bound journal across the dining room table to me.

"Oren can post men to watch the cottage." Jameson spoke beside me. He knew how much I was hurting but did me the courtesy of pretending he didn't. "If Eve is a threat, we can keep her contained."

I turned to look at him. "You know that this isn't about Grayson and me," I said, forcing the image of Grayson walking away out of my mind. "Tell me you know that, Jameson."

"I know," he replied, "that I love you, and despite all odds, you love me." Jameson's smile was smaller but no less crooked than usual. "I also know that Gray's the better man. He always has been. The better son, the better grandson, the better Hawthorne. I think that's why I wanted so badly for Emily to choose me. For once, I wanted to be the one. But it was always him, Heiress. I was a game to her. She loved *him*."

"No." I shook my head. "She didn't. You don't treat people you love like that."

"*You* don't," Jameson replied. "You're honorable, Avery Kylie Grambs. Once you were with me, you were *with me*. You love me, scars and all. I know that, Heiress. *I do*." Jameson said those words, and he meant them. He believed them. "Is it so awful," he continued, "that I want to be a better man for you?"

I thought about our fight. "*Better* is being my friend and my partner and realizing that you don't get to make decisions for me. *Better* is the way you make me see myself as a person who's capable of anything. I would jump out of a plane with you, Jameson, snowboard down the side of a volcano with you, bet everything that I have on *you*—on us, against the world. You don't get to run off and take risks and expect me to stay behind in a gilded cage of your making. That isn't who you are, and it's *not* what I want." I didn't know how to say this so that he would really hear me. "You," I told him, taking a step closer, "have always made me bold. You're the one who pushes me out of my comfort zone. You don't get to box me back in now."

Jameson looked at me like he was trying to memorize every detail of my face. "I moved on from Emily," he said. "Gray didn't. And I know in my soul that if he had, he could have loved you. He would have. With everything you are, Heiress, what other choice would he have had?"

"It was always going to be you," I told Jameson. He needed to hear it. I needed to say it, even though *always* painted over so much.

In response, Jameson gave me another crooked smile. "It's times like this, Heiress, that I wish I'd fallen in love with a girl who wasn't quite so good at bluffing."

Jameson left, the way Grayson had.

"Let's get you back up to the House," Oren said. He didn't offer any commentary on what had just happened.

I didn't let myself think about Jameson or Grayson. I thought about the rest of it instead, about Vincent Blake's missing son and *vengeance* and the games that Blake was never going to stop playing with me. The stories in the tabloids, the paparazzi, financial assaults from every side, trying to chip away at my security team, and the entire time, taunting me that he had Toby.

Clue after clue.

Riddle after riddle.

I was sick of it. When I got back to the House, I went to get the phone Blake had sent me. I called the only number I had for him, and when he didn't answer, I started placing other calls from my real phone—to every person who had received a coveted invitation to the owner's suite of *my* NFL team, to every player in Texas society who had tried to cozy up to me at a charity gala, every person who'd wanted my buy-in for a *financial opportunity*.

Money attracted money. Power attracted power. And I was done waiting for the next clue.

It took some time, but I found someone who had Vincent Blake's cell phone number and was willing to give it to me, no questions asked. My heart beat with the force of punch after punch in my chest as I dialed the number.

When Blake answered, I didn't bother with pretense. "I know about Eve. I know about your son."

"Do you?"

Questions and riddles and games. *No more.* "What do you *want*?" I asked. I wondered if he could hear my anger—and every ounce of emotion buried underneath.

I wondered if that made him think he was winning.

"What do I want, Avery Kylie Grambs?" Vincent Blake sounded amused. "Guess."

"I'm done guessing."

Silence greeted me on the other end of the line—but he was still there. He didn't hang up. And I wasn't going to be the one to break the silence first.

"Isn't it obvious?" Blake said at long last. "I want the truth that Tobias Hawthorne hid from me all these years. I want to know what happened to my son. And I want you, Avery Kylie Grambs, to dig up the past and bring me his body."

CHAPTER 65

Vincent Blake believed his son was dead. He believed the body was *here*. I thought about the Blake family seal, the fact that Toby had stolen it, his father's reaction when he had.

You know what I left there, Toby had written my mother long ago. *You know what it's worth.* A teenage Toby had stolen the seal—and left a hidden copy of "A Poison Tree" by William Blake for his father to find.

"He wanted you to know that he knew the truth." It felt right somehow to be addressing Tobias Hawthorne. This was his legacy.

All of it.

"What did you do," I whispered, "when you found Vincent Blake's son on your property?"

When he'd realized that a man had come at him through a sixteen-year-old girl. That girl might have fancied herself in love, but Tobias Hawthorne wouldn't have seen it that way. Will Blake was in his twenties. Mallory was only sixteen.

And unlike Vincent Blake, Tobias Hawthorne didn't believe that *boys would be boys*.

What happened to him? I could hear Eve asking. *Your Liam.* And all Mallory Laughlin had said was *Liam left*.

Why did he leave?

He just did.

I started walking and ended up in Toby's old wing, reading the lines of "A Poison Tree" and the diary that Toby had kept in invisible ink on his walls. I understood young Toby's anger now, in a way I hadn't before. *He knew something.*

About his father.

About the reason the adoption was kept secret.

About Will Blake and the decision to hide a dangerous man's only grandchild in plain sight. I thought about Toby's poem, the one we'd decoded months ago.

Secrets, lies,
All I despise.
The tree is poison,
Don't you see?
It poisoned S and Z and me.
The evidence I stole
Is in the darkest hole.
Light shall reveal all
I writ upon the...

"*Wall*," I finished now, the way I had then. But this time my brain was seeing all of it through a new lens. If Toby had known what the seal was when he stole it, that meant he knew who Will Blake was, who Vincent Blake was. And if Toby knew that...

What else had he known?

The evidence I stole

Is in the darkest hole.

When I'd recited this poem for Eve, she'd asked me, *Evidence of what?* She'd been looking for answers, for proof. *For a body,* I thought. *Or more realistically at this point, for bones.* But Eve hadn't found any of it yet. If she had, Blake wouldn't have laid this task before me.

I want the truth that Tobias Hawthorne hid from me all these years. I want to know what happened to my son.

Hawthorne House was full of dark places: hidden compartments, secret passages, buried tunnels. Maybe all Toby had ever found was the seal. *Or maybe he found human remains.* That thought was insidious because some part of me had suspected, deep down, that that was what we were looking for, before Vincent Blake had ever told me as much.

His son had come here. He'd targeted a child under Tobias Hawthorne's protection. In his *home.*

Where would a man like Tobias Hawthorne hide a body?

Oren had disposed of Sheffield Grayson's body—how, I wasn't sure. But Vincent Blake's son had disappeared long before Oren had come to work for the old man. Back then, the Hawthorne fortune was new and considerably smaller. Tobias Hawthorne probably hadn't even had security.

Back then, Hawthorne House was just another mansion.

Tobias Hawthorne added onto it every year. That thought wound its way through my mind; my heart pumped it through my veins.

And suddenly, I knew where to start.

I pulled out the blueprints that Mr. Laughlin had given me. Each one detailed an addition that Tobias Hawthorne had made to Hawthorne House over the decades since it was built. *The garage. The spa. The movie theater. The bowling alley.* I unrolled sheet after sheet, plan after plan. *The rock-climbing wall. The tennis court.* I found plans for a gazebo, an outdoor kitchen, a greenhouse, and so much more.

Think, I told myself. There were layers of purpose in everything

Tobias Hawthorne had ever done—everything he'd *built*. I thought about the compartment at the bottom of the swimming pool, about the secret passages in the House, the tunnels beneath the estate, all of it.

There were a thousand places that Tobias Hawthorne could have hidden his darkest secret. If I came at this randomly, I'd get nowhere. I had to be logical. Systematic.

Lay the plans out in chronological order, I thought.

Only a handful of blueprints were marked with years, but each set showed how the proposed addition would be integrated with the House or surrounding property. I needed to find the earliest plan—the one in which the House was the smallest, the simplest—and work forward from there.

I went through page after page until I found it: the original Hawthorne House. Slowly, painstakingly, I put the rest of the blueprints in order. By dawn, I'd made it halfway through, but that was enough. Based on the few sets that had dates on them, I could calculate years for the rest.

I'd been focused on the wrong question in Toby's wing. *Not where Tobias Hawthorne would have hidden a body—but when?* I knew the year that Toby had been born, but not the month. That let me narrow it down to two sets of plans.

The year before Toby's birth, Tobias Hawthorne had erected the greenhouse.

The year of Toby's birth had been the chapel.

I thought about Jameson saying that his grandfather had built the chapel for Nan to yell at God—and then I thought about Nan's response. *The old coot threatened to build me a mausoleum instead.*

What if that hadn't been a threat? What if Tobias Hawthorne had just decided it was too obvious?

Where would a man like Tobias Hawthorne hide a body?

CHAPTER 66

Stepping through the stone arches of the chapel, I scanned the room: the delicately carved pews, the elaborate stained-glass windows, an altar made of pure white marble. This early in the day, light streamed in from the east, bathing the room in color from the stained glass. I studied each panel, looking for something.

A clue.

Nothing. I went through the pews. There were only six of them. The woodwork was captivating, but if it held any secrets—hidden compartments, a button, instructions—I couldn't find them.

That left me with the altar. It came up to my chest and was a little over six feet long and maybe three feet deep. On the top of the altar, there was a candelabra; a gleaming, golden Bible; and a silver cross. I carefully examined each one, and then I knelt to look at the script carved into the front of the altar.

A quote. I ran my fingers over the inscription and read it out loud. *"So we fix our eyes not on what is seen, but on what is unseen, since what is seen is temporary, but what is unseen is eternal."*

That sounded biblical. It was too early to call Max, so I typed the quote into the phone and it gave me a Bible verse: *2 Corinthians 4:18*.

I thought about Blake using a different Bible verse as a combination on a lock. How many of *his* games had a young Tobias Hawthorne played?

"Fix our eyes not on what is seen," I said out loud, *"but on what is unseen."* I stared at the altar. *What is unseen?*

Kneeling in front of the altar, I ran my fingers along it: up and down, left and right, top to bottom. I made my way around to the back, where I found a slight gap between the marble and the floor. I bent to look, but I couldn't see anything, so I slid my fingers into the gap.

Almost immediately, I felt a series of raised circles. My first instinct was to push one, but I didn't want to be rash, so I kept exploring until I had a full count. There were three rows of raised circles, with six in each row.

Eighteen, total. *2 Corinthians 4:18,* I thought. Did that mean that I needed to press four of the eighteen raised circles? And if so, which four?

Frustrated, I stood. With Tobias Hawthorne, nothing was ever easy. I walked around the altar again, taking in its size. The billionaire had wanted to build a mausoleum, but he hadn't. He'd built this chapel, and I couldn't help but notice that if this giant slab of marble was hollow, there would be room for a body inside.

I can do this. I stared at the verse inscribed on what I suspected was Will Blake's tomb. *"So we fix our eyes not on what is seen,"* I read out loud again, *"but on what is unseen, since what is seen is temporary, but what is unseen is eternal."*

Unseen.

What did it mean to fix your eyes on something that was unseen? I had no way of looking at the raised circles. I couldn't see them. I'd had to feel them. *With my fingers*, I thought, and suddenly, just like that, I knew what this inscription meant—not in a biblical sense, but to Tobias Hawthorne.

I knew exactly how I was supposed to see what was unseen.

I took out my phone, and I looked up how numbers were written in Braille. *Four. One. Eight.*

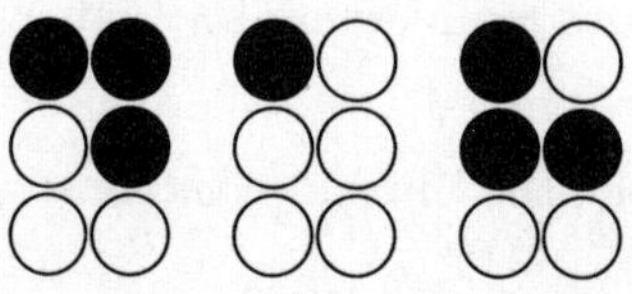

Crouching back down behind the altar, I slid my fingers under the marble and pressed only the raised circles indicated. *Four. One. Eight.*

I heard a creak, and my eyes darted to the top of the altar. A slab of marble had separated from the rest. *Unlocked.*

I moved the candelabra, the Bible, and the cross to the floor. The slab that had released was maybe two inches thick and too heavy for me to move myself.

I looked to Oren, who was standing guard as always. "I need your help," I told him.

He stared at me, long and hard, then cursed under his breath and came to help me. We slid the marble slab, and it didn't take much movement to realize that my instincts had been right. The inside of the altar *had* been hollowed out. There was a space big enough for a body.

But there were no remains. Instead, I found a shroud, the kind that might have once draped a skeleton or a corpse. *By the time the chapel and this altar were finished, would there have been anything left but bones?* I didn't smell death. Stretching to reach in and move the shroud, I saw that the marble inside this makeshift crypt had been defaced with familiar handwriting.

Toby's.

I wondered how long it had taken him to angrily carve six words into the marble. I wondered if this was where he'd found the Blake family seal. I wondered what else he'd found here.

I KNOW WHAT YOU DID, FATHER.

Those were the words he'd left behind—the words that Tobias Hawthorne would have found, once Toby ran away, if he'd checked to see if this secret remained.

And then I saw one last thing in what must have once been Will Blake's tomb.

A USB drive.

CHAPTER 67

I locked my hand around the USB. As I pulled it out, my mind raced. The drive definitely hadn't been sitting in a tomb for twenty years. It looked new.

"You know, Avery, I want to be surprised that you got here first, but I'm not." *Eve.* I whipped my head up to see her standing in the chapel doorway beneath a stone arch. "Some people just have that magic touch," she continued softly. She walked toward me, toward the altar. "What did you find in there?"

She sounded hesitant, vulnerable, but the second Oren stepped into her path, the matching expression on her face flickered like a light bulb a second before it burns out.

"There was supposed to be human remains in there," Eve said calmly. *Too* calmly. "But there weren't, were there?" She cocked her head to the side, her hair falling in gentle amber waves as her gaze landed on the USB in my hand. "I'm going to need you to give me that."

"Are you out of your mind?" I asked. I didn't notice her hands moving until it was too late.

She's got a gun. Eve held her weapon the way that Nash had taught me to hold mine. *Her gun is pointed straight at me.* That thought shouldn't have computed, but I had a knife in my boot. I'd spent all that time training. So when my body should have been panicking, an unnatural calm settled over me instead.

Oren drew his sidearm. "Put the weapon down," he ordered.

It was like Eve didn't even hear him, like the only person in this room she could see or hear was me.

"Where did you even get a gun?" I was stalling for time, assessing the situation. "There's no way you made it onto the estate with one that first morning." Even as I said the words, I thought about Eve bolting the moment she'd "discovered" Vincent Blake's name.

"Put the gun down!" Oren repeated. "I guarantee you that I can get a shot off before you can, and I don't miss."

Eve took a step forward, utterly, beautifully unafraid. "Are you really going to let your bodyguard shoot me, Avery?"

This was a different Eve. Gone were the layers of self-protection, the vulnerability, the raw emotion—all of it.

"You helped Blake abduct Toby, didn't you?" I said, certainty washing over me like a wave of heat.

"I wouldn't have had to," Eve replied, her tone smooth and hard, "if Toby had opened up. If he'd just agreed to bring me here. *But he wouldn't.*"

"This is the last time that I'm going to tell you to put the gun down!" Oren boomed.

"I'm still Toby's daughter," Eve said, adopting a familiar, wide-eyed expression, her gun unwavering. "And honestly, Avery, how do you think Gray will feel if Oren shoots me? What do you think will happen if that beautiful, broken boy walks in here to find me bleeding out on the floor?"

At her mention of Grayson, I instinctively looked for him, but he wasn't there. My body shaking with pent-up rage, I turned to Oren. "Put the gun down," I told him.

My head of security stepped directly in front of me. "She puts hers down first."

A haughty expression on her face, Eve lowered her weapon. Oren was on her in an instant, taking her to the ground, pinning her down.

Eve looked up at me from the chapel floor and smiled. "You want Toby back, and I want whatever you found in that tomb."

She'd called it a tomb. She'd said earlier that there were supposed to be remains in there. I wondered how she'd come to that conclusion, and then I remembered where I'd left her—and with whom. "Mallory," I said.

"She admitted that Liam didn't leave. I believe her exact words were *There was so much blood.*" Eve's gaze went to the altar. "So where's the body?"

"Is that really all you care about?" I asked her. From the very beginning, she'd told me that there was only one thing that mattered to her. I was starting to think that wasn't a lie—it was just that her single-minded purpose had nothing to do with Toby.

It had never been about Toby.

"*Caring* is a recipe for getting hurt, and I haven't let anyone hurt me in a very long time." Eve smiled again, like she was the one who had the upper hand, not the one pinned to the ground. "In all fairness, I did warn you, Avery. I told you that if I were you, I wouldn't trust me, either. I told you that I am a person who will do anything—*anything*—to get what I want. I told you that *invisible* is the one thing that I will never be."

"And Toby," I said, staring at her, sick understanding coming over me, "wanted you to hide."

"Blake wants me by his side," Eve said, zeal in her voice. "I just have to prove myself first."

"You don't have one of the seals yet, do you?" I asked. I thought about Nan saying that Vincent Blake didn't give anyone—not even family—a free ride.

"I'm going to get one," Eve told me, her voice burning with the fury of purpose. "Give me that USB, and maybe you can get what you want, too." She paused, then hit a nail right through my heart. "*Toby.*"

I hated even hearing her say his name. "How could you do this?" I said, thinking of the picture Blake had sent, the bruises on his face—and then of the pictures of Toby and Eve on Eve's camera roll. "He trusted you."

"It's easy to make people trust you," Eve commented softly, "if you let them see you bleed." I thought about the bruises she'd shown up here sporting and wondered if she'd *told* someone to hit her. "You can spend your whole life trying not to hurt," Eve continued, her voice high and clear, "but making people hurt *for* you? That's real power."

I thought of Toby telling me that he had two daughters.

"Give me the USB," Eve said again, her eyes still blazing, "and you won't ever have to see me again, Avery. I'll earn my seal, and you can have this place and those boys all to yourself. Win-win."

She was delusional. Oren had her pinned. She'd come at me *with a gun*. She was in no position to negotiate. "I'm not giving you anything," I said.

A flash of movement. I whipped my head toward the chapel door. Grayson stood there, backlit, his eyes locked on Oren, who was still restraining Eve.

"Let her go," Grayson ordered.

"She's a threat." Oren clipped the words. "She pulled a gun on Avery. The only place I am *letting* her go is far, far away from all of you."

"Grayson." I felt sick. "This isn't what it looks like—"

"Help me," Eve begged him. "Get the USB that Avery has. Don't let them take this from me, too."

Grayson stared at her a moment longer, then walked slowly toward me. He took the USB from my hand. I just stood there. Feeling like my insides had been hollowed out, I watched as he turned back to Eve. "I can't let you have this," Grayson said softly.

"Grayson—" Eve and I said his name in unison.

"I heard."

Eve was unabashed. "Whatever you heard, you *know* that I am not the villain here, Grayson. Your grandfather—he owed me better. He owed you better, and you and your family owe Avery *nothing*."

Grayson's eyes met mine. "I owe her more than she realizes."

A dam broke inside me, and all of the hurt I hadn't let myself feel came flooding out, and with it, everything else I felt—and had ever felt—for Grayson Hawthorne.

"You're as bad as your grandfather was," Eve tried. "Look at me, Grayson. *Look at me.*"

He did.

"If you let Oren kick me out of here or call the police, if you try to force me to go back to Vincent Blake empty-handed, I swear to you, I will find a cliff to jump off of." There was something fierce and mad and savage in Eve's voice—something that sold that threat completely. "Emily's blood is on your hands. Do you really want mine there, too?"

Grayson stared at her. I could see him reliving the moment he'd found Emily. I could see the effect that Eve's specific threat—a *cliff*—had on him. I could see Grayson Davenport Hawthorne drowning, fighting the undertow in vain. And then I saw him stop fighting and let the memories and the grief and the truth wash over him.

And then Grayson took a breath. "You're a big girl," he told Eve. "You make your own choices. Whatever you do after Oren sends you packing—that's on you."

I wondered if he really meant that. If he believed it.

"This is your chance," Eve said, fighting Oren's grip. "This is redemption, Grayson. I'm yours, and you could be mine. It's your fault Emily's dead. You could have stopped her—"

Grayson took a single step toward her. "I shouldn't have had to." He looked down at the USB in his hand. "And this would be useless to you."

"You can't know that." Eve was a wild thing now, fighting Oren with everything she had.

"Assuming this USB is my grandfather's handiwork," Grayson told her, "you would need a decoder to make sense of any of the files. A Hawthorne never leaves any knowledge of value unprotected."

"So I'll break the encryption," Eve said dismissively.

Grayson arched an eyebrow at her. "Not without a second drive."

A second drive.

"You can't do this to me, Grayson. We're the same, you and I." There was something in the way Eve said that, something in her voice that made me think she believed it.

Grayson didn't blink. "Not anymore."

An instant later, Oren's men came crashing through the door.

Oren turned to me. "How do you want to handle this, Avery?"

Eve had pointed a gun at me. That, at least, was a crime. Lying to us wasn't. Manipulating us wasn't. I couldn't prove anything else. And she wasn't the *real* enemy here.

The real threat.

"Have your men escort Eve off the estate," I told Oren. "We'll deal directly with Vincent Blake from now on."

Eve didn't make them drag her. "You haven't won," she told me. "He'll keep coming—and sooner or later, all of you will wish to God that this had ended with me."

CHAPTER 68

Oren left Grayson and me alone in the chapel.

"I owe you an apology."

I met Grayson Hawthorne's eyes, as light and piercing as they'd been the first time I saw him. "You don't owe me anything," I said—not out of compassion but because it hurt to let myself think about how much I'd expected from him.

"Yes. I do." After a long moment, Grayson looked away. "I," he said, like that one word cost him everything, "have been punishing myself for so long. Not just for Emily's death—for every weakness, every miscalculation, *every*—" He cut off, like his windpipe had closed suddenly around the words. I watched as he forced a jagged breath into his lungs. "No matter what I was or what I did—it was never enough. The old man was always there, pushing for better, for more."

I'd thought once that he had bulletproof confidence. That he was arrogant and incapable of second-guessing himself and utterly sure of his own power.

"And then," Grayson said, "the old man was gone. And then… there was you."

"Grayson." His name caught in my throat.

Grayson just looked at me, his light eyes shadowed. "Sometimes, you have an idea of a person—about who they are, about what you'd be like together. But sometimes that's all it is: an idea. And for so long, I have been afraid that I loved the *idea* of Emily more than I will ever be capable of loving anyone real."

That was a confession and self-condemnation and a curse. "That's not true, Grayson."

He looked at me like the act of doing so was painful and sweet. "It was never just the idea of you, Avery."

I tried not to feel like the ground was suddenly moving underneath my feet. "You *hated* the idea of me."

"But not you." The words were just as sweet, just as painful. "Never you."

Something gave inside me. "Grayson."

"I know," he said roughly.

I shook my head. "You're still so convinced that you know everything."

"I know that Jamie loves you." Grayson looked at me the way you look at art in a glass case, like he wanted to reach out to touch me but couldn't. "And I've seen the way that you look at him, the way the two of you are together. You're in love with my brother, Avery." He paused. "Tell me you're not."

I couldn't do that. He knew I couldn't. "I am in love with your brother," I said, because it was true. Jameson was part of me now—part of who I'd spent the past year becoming. I'd changed. If I hadn't, maybe things could have been different, but there was no going back.

I was who I was *because* of Jameson. I hadn't been lying when I'd told him that I didn't want him to be anyone else.

So why was this so hard?

"I wanted Eve to be different," Grayson told me. "I wanted her to be you."

"Don't say that," I whispered.

He looked at me one last time. "There are so many things that I will never say."

He was getting ready to walk away, and I had to let him—but I couldn't. "Promise me you won't leave again," I told Grayson. "You can go back to Harvard. You can go wherever you want, do whatever you want—just promise me that you won't shut us out again." I lifted my hand to my Hawthorne pin. I knew he had one of his own. I knew that, but I took mine off and pinned it on him anyway. "*Est unus ex nobis.* You said that to Jameson once, do you remember? *She is one of us.* Well, it goes both ways, Gray."

Grayson closed his eyes, and I was hit with the feeling that I would never forget the way he looked standing there in the light from the stained-glass windows. Without his armor. Without pretense. Raw.

"*Scio,*" Grayson told me. *I know.*

I looked down at the USB in his hand.

"I have the other one," I told him. "It was the one object in the leather satchel that we never used, remember?"

Grayson's eyes opened. He stepped out of the light. "Are you going to call my brothers?" he asked me. "Or shall I?"

CHAPTER 69

Xander plugged the first USB into his computer, dragged the audio file onto the desktop, then removed the USB and exchanged it for the USB from the tomb. He dragged the second file to his desktop, too.

"Play the first one," Jameson instructed.

Xander did. Garbled, undecipherable speech filled the air, a blast of white noise.

"And the second?" Nash prompted. For as long as I'd known him, he'd resisted dancing to the old man's tune. But he was here. He was doing this.

The lone file on the second USB was also an audio clip. It was just as messed up as the first.

"What happens if you play them together?" I asked. Grayson had said that to make sense of one file, you needed a decoder. In isolation, the clips were nothing but noise. But if you had both USBs, both files...

Xander opened an audio editing app and dumped the files in. He lined them up, then hit a sequence of buttons that caused them to play.

Combined, the result wasn't garbled. "Hello, Avery," a man's voice said, and I felt the change in the air around me, in all of *them*. "We're strangers, you and I. I imagine that's something you've thought about quite a bit."

Tobias Hawthorne. The one and only time I'd met him, I was six years old. But he was omnipresent in this place. Hawthorne House bore his mark. Every room. Every detail.

The boys bore it, too.

"All great lives should have at least one grand mystery, Avery. I won't apologize for being yours." Tobias Hawthorne was a man who didn't apologize for much. "If you've spent late nights and early mornings asking yourself *Why me?* Well, my dear, you are not the only one. What is the human condition, if not *Why me?*"

I could feel the shift in each of the Hawthorne brothers as they listened to Tobias Hawthorne's words and the cadence of his speech.

"As a young man, I believed myself destined for greatness. I fought for it, I *thought* my way to the top, I cheated, I lied, I made the world bend to my will." There was a pause, and then: "I got lucky. I can admit that now. I'm dying, and not slowly, either. *Why me?* Why is this body giving out? Why am I the one sitting in a palace of my own making when there are others out there with minds like mine? I got lucky. Right place, right time, right ideas, right mind." He let out an audible breath. "If only that were it.

"If you are playing this message, then things have become as dire as I projected. Eve is there, and certain events have led you to finding the tomb that once housed this family's greatest secret. How much, I wonder, have you put together for yourself, Avery?"

Every time he said my name, I felt like he was here in this room. Like he could see me. Like he had been watching me from the moment I'd stepped through Hawthorne House's grand front door.

"But then," he continued, an odd sort of smile in his voice, "you're not alone, are you? Hello, boys."

I felt Jameson shift, his arm brushing mine.

"If you boys are indeed there with Avery, then at least one thing has worked out as I intended. You know quite well that she is not your enemy. Perhaps, if I have chosen as well as I think I have, she has reached a place inside of you that I never could. Dare I even say made you whole?"

"Turn it off," Nash said, but none of us listened. I wasn't even sure he meant it.

"I hope you enjoyed the game I left you. Whether your mother and aunt have found and played theirs, I cannot say. The odds I've calculated suggest it could go either way, which is why, Xander, I left you with the charge I did. I trust that you have looked for Toby. And Avery, I believe in my heart of hearts that Toby has found you."

Each word the dead man said made this entire situation feel that much eerier. How much of what had happened since he'd died had he foreseen? Not just foreseen, but planned, moving us all around like pawns?

"If you are listening to this, then there is a high likelihood that Vincent Blake has revealed himself as a clear and present threat. I'd hoped to outlive the bastard. For years, he and I have had an armistice of sorts. He considered himself magnanimous at first, to let me go. Later, once he began to resent my growing fortune, my power, my status—well, those things kept him in check.

"*I* kept him in check."

There was another pause, and it felt sharper somehow this time, honed.

"But now I am gone, and if Blake knows what I suspect you now know, God help you all. If Eve is there, if Blake knows or even suspects what I have kept from him all these years, then he is coming.

For the fortune. For my legacy. For you, Avery Kylie Grambs. And for that, I do apologize."

I thought of the letter that Tobias Hawthorne had left me. The only explanation I'd been given, back at the start. *I'm sorry.*

"But better you than them." Tobias Hawthorne paused. "Yes, Avery. I really am that much of a bastard. I really did paint a target on your forehead. Even without the truth surfacing, I saw the probabilities for what they were. Once I was no longer there to hold him at bay, Blake was always going to make his move. *Hunting season*, he might call it—playing the game, destroying all opponents, taking what was mine. And that, my dear, is why it is now *yours*."

I'd known that I was a tool. I'd known he'd chosen me for what he could use me to do. But I hadn't realized, hadn't ever even suspected, that Tobias Hawthorne had named me his heir because I was disposable.

"I met your mother, you know." The billionaire didn't stop. He never stopped. "Once when I believed her to be merely a waitress and once after I had deduced that she was Hannah Rooney, my only son's great love. I thought to use her to get to Toby. I tried my hand at working her—cajoling, threatening, bribing, manipulating. And do you know what your mother told me, Avery? She told me that she knew who Vincent Blake was, knew what had happened to his son, knew where Toby had hidden the Blake family seal, and that if I came near her—or you—again, she would bring the whole house of cards tumbling down."

I tried to picture my mom threatening a man like Tobias Hawthorne.

"Did you know about the seal?" Tobias asked, his tone almost conversational. "Did you know this family's darkest secret? I think not, but I am a man who has made an empire by always, *always* questioning my own assumptions. I excel at nothing if not contingencies. So here we are, Avery Kylie Grambs. The little girl with the funny little name. A skeleton key for so many little locks.

"I had six weeks from my diagnosis until now. Another two, I wager, until my deathbed. Enough time to put the final pieces in place. Enough time to draw up one last game with so very many layers. *Why you*, Avery? To draw the boys in one last time? To bequeath to them a mystery befitting Hawthornes, the puzzle of a lifetime? To bring them back together through you? *Yes.*" He said the word *yes* like a man who relished saying it. "To pull Toby out of the shadows? To do in death what I was unable to do in life and force him back onto the board? *Yes.*"

The sound of my own body was suddenly overwhelming. The beating of my heart. Each breath I somehow managed to draw. The rush of blood in my ears.

"And," Tobias Hawthorne continued with an air of finality, "to my great shame, to pull Blake's attention and focus—and the attention and focus of all of my enemies, of whom there are doubtlessly many—to you."

Yes. He didn't say it this time, but I thought it, and then I thought about Nan telling me that I was the one playing the piano now—and men like Vincent Blake, they'd break every single one of my fingers if they could.

"Call it misdirection," the dead billionaire said. "I needed someone to draw fire, and who better than Hannah Rooney's daughter, on the off chance that she *had* told you my secret? You'd hardly have motive to reveal it once the money was yours."

Traps upon traps. And riddles upon riddles. The words that Jameson had spoken to me long ago came back to me—followed by something Xander had said. *Even if you* thought *that you'd manipulated our grandfather into this, I guarantee that he'd be the one manipulating you.*

"But take as your consolation this, my very risky gamble: I have watched you. I have come to know you. As you draw fire away from those that I hold most dear, know that I believe there is at least a sliver of a chance that you will survive the hits you take. You may be tested by the flames, but you need not burn.

"If you are listening to this, Blake is coming." Tobias Hawthorne's tone was intense now. "He will box you in. He will hold you down. He will have no mercy. But he will also underestimate you. You're young. You're female. You're nobody—*use that.* My greatest adversary—and yours now—is an honor-bound man. Best him, and he'll honor the win."

Something in Tobias Hawthorne's tone made those words sound not just like advice but also like *good-bye.*

"My boys." Hawthorne sounded like he was smiling again, a crooked smile like Jameson's, a hard one like Grayson's. "If you are indeed listening to this, judge me as harshly as you like. I've made my deals with so very many devils. Find me wanting. Hate me if you must. Let your anger light a fire that the world will never extinguish.

"Nash. Grayson. Jameson. Xander." He said their names one at a time. "You were the clay, and I was the sculptor, and it has been the joy and honor of my life to make you better men than I will ever be. Men who may curse my name but will never forget it."

My hand found its way to Jameson's, and he held on to me for dear life.

"On your marks, boys," Tobias Hawthorne said on the recording. "Get set. *Go.*"

CHAPTER 70

Silence had never sounded this loud. I'd never seen the Hawthorne brothers so still—all of them, like they'd been stung with a paralyzing venom. As big an impact as hearing the truth from Tobias Hawthorne's mouth had on me, he wasn't the formative influence of *my* life.

I forced myself to speak because they couldn't. "You always did say that the old man liked to kill ten birds with one stone."

Jameson brought his eyes up from the ground to me, then let out a rough, pained chuckle. "Twelve."

Twelve birds, one stone. I'd been warned. From the moment I'd received a ring holding a hundred keys—from before that, even—I'd been warned by each of the Hawthorne brothers in turn.

Traps upon traps. And riddles upon riddles.

Even if you thought *that you'd manipulated our grandfather into this, I guarantee that he'd be the one manipulating you.*

This family—we destroy everything we touch.

You're not a player, kid. You're the glass ballerina—or the knife.

And then there was the message that Tobias Hawthorne had left me himself, back at the very beginning. *I'm sorry.*

"We did exactly what he thought we would." Xander snapped out of it and began to move—wild gestures, weight on the balls of his feet. "All of us. From the beginning."

"That sonofabitch." Nash let out a long whistle, then leaned back against the wall. "How dangerous do we think Vincent Blake is?" The question sounded casual and calm, but I could imagine Nash strolling up to a rabid bull with that exact expression on his face.

"Dangerous enough to require a decoy." Grayson's calm was a different sort than Nash's—icy and controlled. "We're dealing with a family whose fortune, though significantly smaller, goes back a lot further than ours. There's no telling what people or institutions Blake has in his pocket."

"The old man took the four of us off the board." Jameson swore. "He raised us to fight but never intended this fight for us."

I thought about Skye saying that her father had never considered her a player in the grand game, then about a letter that Tobias Hawthorne had left his daughters. There was a part where he'd said that not one of them would see his fortune. *There are things I have done that I am not proud of, legacies that you should not have to bear.*

The truth had been there, right in front of us, for months. Tobias Hawthorne had left me his fortune so that if and when his enemies descended after his death, they would descend on *me*. He'd picked his target carefully, placed me as a cog in a complicated machine.

Twelve birds, one stone.

If you are listening to this, Blake is coming. He will box you in. He will hold you down. He will have no mercy. I could feel something inside me hardening. Tobias Hawthorne hadn't foreseen exactly *how* Vincent Blake would come at me. Hawthorne hadn't known that Toby would be caught in Blake's plot, but he'd damn well known what the man was capable of. And his only consolation to me had been that he thought there was a *sliver* of a chance that I could survive.

I wanted to despise Tobias Hawthorne—or at least judge him—but all I could think was the other words he'd left me. *You may be tested by the flames, but you need not burn.*

"Where are you going?" Jameson called after me.

I didn't look back over my shoulder, couldn't quite bring myself to look at any of them. "To make a call."

Vincent Blake answered on the fifth ring, a power play in and of itself. "Presumptuous little thing, aren't you?"

You're young. You're female. You're nobody—use that.

"Eve is gone," I said, banishing any hint of emotion from my tone. "You don't have anyone on the inside now."

"You seem very sure of that, little girl." Blake was amused, like my attempt at playing this game was nothing to him but that—an amusement.

He wants me to believe that he has someone else inside Hawthorne House. Staying silent even a moment too long would have been seen as weakness, so I spoke. "You want the truth about what happened to your son. You want his remains found and returned to you." My breathing wanted to go shallow, but I was a better bluffer than that. "What, besides Toby, will you give me if I deliver what you want?"

I didn't know where whatever remained of William Blake was. But a person could only play the cards they'd been dealt. Blake thought that I had something he wanted. Without Eve here, I might be his only way of getting it.

I needed an advantage. I needed leverage. Maybe this was it.

"What will I give you?" Blake's amusement deepened into

something darker, twisted. "What, besides Toby, do I have that you want? I am so very glad you asked."

The line went dead. He'd hung up on me. I stared down at my phone.

A moment later, Oren stepped into my peripheral view. "There's a courier at the gate."

CHAPTER 71

There was no point in cross-examining the person who delivered the package. We knew who it was from. We knew what he wanted.

"Everything okay?" Libby asked me when Oren's man appeared in the foyer with the package. I shook my head. *Whatever this is—it's definitely not okay.*

Oren completed his initial security screen, then handed both the contents and the packaging over to me: one gift box large enough to hold a sweater; inside it, thirteen letter-sized envelopes; inside each envelope, a clear, thin, rectangular sheet of plastic with an abstract black-and-white design inked onto it. Looking at any one sheet in isolation was like doing one of those inkblot tests.

"Stack them," Jameson suggested. I wasn't sure when he'd come into the room, but he wasn't alone. All four of the Hawthorne brothers circled around me. Libby hung back, but only slightly.

I laid sheet on top of sheet, the designs combining to form a single picture—but it wasn't that easy. Of course it wasn't. There were four ways that each sheet could go—*up or down, front or back.*

I felt the sheets with my fingertips, locating the side on which the ink had been printed. Moving with lightning speed, I began matching the sheets in the lower left corner, using the patterns to guide me.

One, two, three, four—no, that one's the wrong way. I kept going, one sheet on top of another on top of another, until a picture emerged. A black-and-white photograph.

And in that photograph, Alisa Ortega lay on a dirt floor, her head lolled to one side, her eyes closed.

"She's alive," Jameson said beside me. "Unconscious. But she doesn't look..."

Dead, I finished for him. *What, besides Toby, do I have that you want?* I could hear Vincent Blake saying. *I am so very glad you asked.*

"Lee-Lee." Nash didn't sound calm, not this time.

I swallowed. "Is there any chance she's in on it?" I asked, hating myself for even giving life to the question, for letting Blake get to me that much.

"*None*," Nash said, biting out the word with almost inhuman ferocity.

I looked to Jameson and Grayson. "Your grandfather said *don't trust anyone*, not just *don't trust her.* He at least considered it possible that Blake would be able to get to someone else in my inner circle." I looked back down at Alisa's seemingly unconscious body. "And right now, Alisa and her firm have a lot to lose if I don't agree to a trust."

The power behind the fortune. The ability to move mountains and make men.

"You can trust Alisa," Nash said roughly. "She's loyal to the old man, always has been." Libby came closer and laid a hand on his back, and he turned his head to look at her. "This ain't what you think, Lib. I don't have feelings for her, but just because things don't work out with a person doesn't mean they stop mattering."

"No one ever stops mattering," Libby said, like the words were a revelation, "to you."

"Nash is right. There's no way Alisa is in on it," Jameson said. "Vincent Blake took her, just like he took Toby."

Because she works for me.

"The bastard can't do this," Grayson swore with a powerful intensity I hadn't seen from him in months. "We'll *destroy* him."

You can't. That was why Tobias Hawthorne had disinherited them, why he'd drawn Blake's focus to me—and the people I cared about. Oren had assigned a bodyguard to Max. He'd brought Thea and Rebecca here. He'd shut down avenue after avenue of using other people to get to me—but Alisa hadn't been on lockdown.

She'd been out there playing games of her own.

With shaking hands, I called her number. Again. And again. She didn't pick up. "Alisa always picks up," I said out loud. I forced my eyes to Oren's. "*Now* can we call the police?"

Toby was a dead man. You couldn't report a dead man missing. But Alisa was very much alive, and we had the picture as proof of foul play.

"Blake will have someone—maybe multiple someones—high up in all the local police departments."

"And I don't?" I said.

"You did," Oren told me, past tense, and I remembered what he'd said about the rash of recent transfers.

"What about the FBI?" I asked. "I don't care if the case is federal or not—Tobias Hawthorne had people, and they're my people now. Right?"

No one replied, because whoever Tobias Hawthorne may or may not have had in his pocket, there was no one in mine. Not without Alisa there to pull the strings.

Check. I could practically see the board, see the moving pieces, see the way that Vincent Blake was boxing me in.

"Lee-Lee wouldn't want us to go to the authorities." Nash seemed to have trouble finding his voice. It came out in a slow, deep rumble. "The optics."

"You don't care about optics," I told him.

Nash took off his cowboy hat, his eyes shadowed. "I care about a lot of things, kid."

"What do we have to do," Libby asked fiercely, "to get Alisa back?"

I was the one who answered the question. "Find a body—or what's left of one after forty years."

Nash's eyes narrowed. "This had better be one hell of an explanation."

CHAPTER 72

The moment I finished explaining, Nash strode off ominously. Libby went with him. Strategizing our next move, I asked Xander where Rebecca and Thea were.

"The cottage." Xander was rarely this solemn. "Bex was ignoring her mom's calls, but then her grandma called, after Eve..."

After Eve got the truth out of Mallory, I finished silently. Forcing my mind to focus on that truth and what it meant for us now, I led the boys to my room and showed them the blueprints.

"These are in chronological order," I said. "I used that chronology to find the construction project erected in the wake of Toby's conception: the chapel. The altar was made of stone and hollow inside." I swallowed. "A tomb—but no body hidden in it, just the USB, which your grandfather must have hidden there shortly before his death, and a message scratched into the stone by Toby way back when."

"Not that you need another nickname," Xander commented, "but I'm liking *Sherlock*. What did the message say?"

I looked past Xander to Jameson and... Grayson wasn't there. I wasn't sure when we'd lost him. I didn't let myself wonder why.

"*I know what you did, Father.*" I answered Xander's question. "I'm taking that to mean that at some point after Toby found out he was adopted and before he ran away at nineteen..."

"He found out about *Liam*," Jameson finished.

I thought about all the messages Toby had left his father: "A Poison Tree," hidden under a floor tile; a poem of his own making, coded into a book of law; the words inside the altar.

The now-empty altar.

"Toby found the body." Saying it out loud made it seem real. "It was probably just bones by then. He stole the seal, moved the remains, left a series of hidden messages for the old man, and went on a self-destructive tear across the country that ended in the fire on Hawthorne Island."

I thought about Toby, about his collision course with my mother and the ways their love might have been different if Toby hadn't been broken by the horrific secrets he carried.

The real Hawthorne legacy.

I saw now why Toby was determined to stay away from Hawthorne House. I could understand why he'd wanted to protect my mother—his *Hannah, the same backward as forward*—and later, once she was dead and I'd already been pulled into this mess, why he had needed to at least try to protect *Eve* from everything that came along with the Hawthorne fortune.

From the truth and the poisonous tree. From Blake.

"*The evidence I stole*," I said out loud, staring down at the blueprints, "*is in the darkest hole....*"

"The tunnels?" Jameson was behind me—right behind me. I felt his suggestion as much as heard it.

"That's one possibility," I said, and then I pulled four sets of blueprints. "The others are these—the additions made to Hawthorne House during the time span in which Toby must have discovered and moved the remains. He could have taken advantage of the construction somehow."

Toby had been sixteen when he'd discovered that he was adopted, nineteen when he'd left Hawthorne House forever. I pictured crews breaking ground on each of those additions. *The evidence I stole is in the darkest hole....*

"This one," Jameson said urgently, kneeling over the plans. "Heiress, look."

I saw what he saw. "The hedge maze."

Jameson and I made our way to the maze. Xander went for reinforcements. "Start at the outside and work our way in?" Jameson asked me. "Or go to the center of the maze and spiral out?"

It felt right somehow that it was just the two of us. Jameson Winchester Hawthorne and me.

The hedges were eight feet tall, and the maze covered an area nearly as large as the House. It would take days for us to search it all. Maybe weeks. Maybe longer. Wherever Toby had hidden the body, his father either hadn't found it or had chosen not to risk moving it again.

I pictured men planting these hedges.

I pictured nineteen-year-old Toby, in the dead of night, somehow finding a way to bury the bones of the man responsible for half his DNA.

"Start at the center," I told Jameson, my voice echoing in the space all around us, "and spiral out."

I knew the path that would take us to the heart of the maze. I'd been there before, more than once—with Grayson.

"I don't suppose you know where he went, do you, Heiress?" Jameson had a way of making every question sound a little wicked and a little sharp—but I knew, *I knew* what he was really asking.

What he was always trying not to ask himself when it came to Grayson and me.

"I don't know where Grayson is," I told Jameson, and then I hung a left, and the muscles in my throat tightened. "But I do know that he's going to be okay. He confronted Eve. I think he finally let go of Emily, finally forgave himself for being human."

Right turn. Left turn. Left again. Straight. We were almost to the center now.

"And now that Gray is okay," Jameson said close behind me, "now that he's so delightfully *human* and ready to move on from Emily..."

I hit the center of the maze and turned around to face Jameson. "Don't finish that question."

I knew what he was going to ask. I knew he wasn't wrong to ask. But still, it stung. And the only way that he was ever going to stop asking—himself, me, Grayson—was if I gave him the full, unvarnished truth.

The truth I hadn't let myself think too often or too clearly.

"You were right before when you called my bluff," I told Jameson. "I can't say that it was always going to be you."

He walked past me toward the hidden compartment in the ground where the Hawthornes kept their longswords. I heard him opening the compartment, heard him searching.

Because Jameson Winchester Hawthorne was always searching for something. He couldn't stop. He would never stop.

And I didn't want to, either. "I can't say that it was always going to be you, Jameson, because I don't believe in destiny or fate—I believe in choice." I knelt next to him and let my fingers explore the compartment. "You chose me, Jameson, and I chose to open up to you, to all of the possibilities of *us*, in a way that I had never opened up to anyone before."

Max had told me once to picture myself standing on a cliff overlooking the ocean. I felt like I was standing there now, because love wasn't just a choice—it was dozens, hundreds, thousands of choices.

Every day was a choice.

I moved on from the compartment that held the swords, running my hands over the ground at the center of the maze, looking, searching still. "Letting you in," I told Jameson, the two of us crouched feet apart, "becoming *us*—it changed me. You taught me to *want*."

How to want things.

How to want *him*.

"You made me hungry," I told Jameson, "for everything. I want the world now." I held his gaze in a way that *dared* him to look away. "And I want it with you."

Jameson made his way to me—just as my fingers hit something, buried in the grass, wedged into the soil.

Something small and round and metal. *Not the Blake family seal. Just a coin. But the size, the shape*...

Jameson brought his hands to my face. His thumb lightly skimmed my lips. And I said the two words guaranteed to take that spark in his eyes and set it on fire.

"Dig here."

CHAPTER 73

My arms were aching by the time the ground caved in, revealing a chamber below—part of the tunnels, but not a part I'd ever seen.

Before I could say a word, Jameson leapt into the darkness.

I lowered myself down more cautiously, landing beside him in a crouch. I stood, shining the light from my phone. The chamber was small—and empty.

No body.

I scanned the walls and saw a torch. Latching my fingers around the torch, I tried to pull it from the wall, to no avail. I let my fingers explore the metal sconce that held the torch in place. "There's a hinge back here," I said. "Or something like it. I think it rotates"

Jameson placed his hand over mine, and together we twisted the torch sideways. There was a scraping sound and then a hiss, and the torch burst into flame.

Jameson didn't let go, and neither did I.

We pulled the flaming torch from the sconce, and as the flame came close to the wall's surface, words lit up in Toby's writing.

"*I was never a Hawthorne*," I read out loud. Jameson let his hand fall to his side, until I was the only one holding the torch. Slowly,

I walked the perimeter of the room. The flame revealed words on each wall.

I was never a Hawthorne.

I will never be a Blake.

So what does that make me?

I saw the message on the final wall, and my heart contracted. *Complicit.*

"Try the floor," Jameson told me.

I brought the torch low, careful of the flame, and one final message lit up. *Try again, Father.*

The body wasn't here.

It had never been here.

A light shone down from up above. *Mr. Laughlin.* He helped us out of the chamber, silent the whole time, his expression absolutely unreadable, right up to the point that I tried to step from the center back into the maze, and he moved to stand right in front of me.

Blocking me.

"I heard about Alisa." The groundskeeper's voice was always gruff, but the visible sorrow in his eyes was new. "The kind of man who would take a woman—he's no man at all." He paused. "Nash came to me," he said haltingly. "He asked me for help, and that boy wouldn't even let you help tie his shoes as a toddler."

"You know where Will Blake's remains are," I said, giving voice to the realization as it dawned on me. "That's why Nash went to you and asked you for help."

Mr. Laughlin forced himself to look at me. "Some things are best left buried."

I wasn't about to accept that. I *couldn't.* Anger snaked through me, burning in my veins. At Vincent Blake and Tobias Hawthorne and this man who was supposed to work for me but would always put the Hawthorne family first.

"I'll raze this entire thing to the ground," I swore. Some situations required a scalpel, but this? *Bring on the chain saws.* "I'll hire men to tear this maze apart. I'll bring out cadaver dogs. I will burn it all down to get Alisa back."

Mr. Laughlin's body trembled. "You have no right."

"Grandpa."

He turned, and Rebecca stepped into view. Thea and Xander followed, but Mr. Laughlin barely noticed them. "This isn't right," he told Rebecca. "I made promises—to myself, to your mother, to Mr. Hawthorne."

If I'd had any doubts that the groundskeeper knew where the body was, that statement erased them. "Vincent Blake has Toby, too," I said. "Not just Alisa. Don't you want your grandson back?"

"Don't you talk to me about my grandson." Mr. Laughlin was breathing heavily now.

Rebecca laid a calming hand on his arm. "It wasn't Mr. Hawthorne who killed Liam," she said quietly. "Was it?"

Mr. Laughlin shuddered. "Go back to the cottage, Rebecca."

"*No.*"

"You used to be such a good girl," Mr. Laughlin grunted.

"I used to make myself small." Rebecca's was a subtle kind of steel. "But here with you—I didn't have to. I used to live for the few weeks we spent here each summer. I'd help you. Do you remember? I liked working with my hands, getting them dirty." She shook her head. "I was never allowed to get dirty at home."

Back when Emily was young and medically vulnerable, Rebecca's home had probably been entirely sterile.

"Please go back to the cottage." Mr. Laughlin's tone and mannerisms were a perfect match for his granddaughter's: quiet, understated steel. Until that moment, I'd never seen the resemblance between the two of them. "Thea, take her back."

"I loved working with you," Rebecca told her grandfather, the sun catching her ruby-red hair. "But there was one part of the maze that you always insisted on doing yourself."

My stomach twisted. *Rebecca knows where to dig.*

"Emily looked like your mother," Mr. Laughlin said roughly. "But you have her mind, Rebecca. She was brilliant. Is still." He choked on the next words. *"My little girl."*

"It wasn't Mr. Hawthorne who killed Vincent Blake's son," Rebecca said softly. "Was it?" There was no answer. "Eve's gone. Mom lost it when she couldn't find her. She said—"

"Whatever your mother said," Mr. Laughlin cut in harshly, "you forget it, Rebecca." He looked from her to the horizon. "That's how this works. We've all done our share of forgetting."

For more than forty years, this secret had festered. It had affected all of them—two families, three generations, one poisonous tree.

"Your daughter was only sixteen." I started with what I knew. "Will Blake was a grown man. He came here with something to prove."

"He used your daughter." Xander took over for me. "To spy on our grandfather."

"Will used and manipulated your sixteen-year-old daughter. He got her pregnant," Jameson continued, cutting straight to the heart of the matter.

"I've given my life to the Hawthorne family. I don't owe any of you this." Mr. Laughlin's voice wasn't just harsh now. It was vibrating with fury.

I felt for him. I did. But this wasn't theoretical. It wasn't a game. This might well be life or death.

"Show us the part of the maze he wouldn't let you work on," I told Rebecca.

She took a step, and Mr. Laughlin grabbed her arm. Hard.

“Let her go,” Thea said, raising her voice.

Rebecca caught Thea’s gaze, just for a moment, then turned back to her grandfather. “Mom’s distraught. She started rambling. She told me that Liam was angry when he found out about the baby. He was going to leave her, so she stole something from the House, from Mr. Hawthorne’s office. She told Liam that she had something he could use against Tobias Hawthorne, just so he would meet with her again. But when he came, when she went to give him what she’d taken, it wasn’t in her bag.”

I pictured them someplace isolated. The Black Wood, maybe.

“Tobias.” At first that was all Mr. Laughlin managed—the dead billionaire’s name. “He was spying on them. He followed Mal that day. He didn’t know why she’d stolen from him, but he was damn set on finding out.”

“What he found,” Jameson concluded, “was Vincent Blake’s adult son taking advantage of a teenage girl under his protection.”

I thought about the reason that Tobias Hawthorne had turned on Blake in the first place. *Boys will be boys.*

“That little bastard Liam got angry when Mal couldn’t give him what she’d promised. He went cold, told her that she was nothing. When he went to leave, she tried to stop him, and that monster raised a hand to my little girl.”

I got the very real sense that if Will Blake rose from the dead right now, Mr. Laughlin would put him six feet under all over again.

“The second Liam got rough, Mr. Hawthorne stepped out from wherever he’d been hiding to issue some very pointed threats. Mal was sixteen. There were laws.” Mr. Laughlin let out a breath, and it was a ragged, ugly sound. “The man should have slunk away like the rat he was, but Mal—she didn’t want Liam to go. She threatened him, too, said that she would go to his father and tell him about the baby.”

"Will needed to keep his father's favor to keep his seal," I said, thinking about Vincent Blake's *short string* for his family. "More than that, if he'd come here to prove something to Blake, to impress him—the idea of doing the opposite?"

I swallowed.

"Liam snapped and lunged for her again. Mal—she fought back." Mr. Laughlin's eyes closed. "I came in just as Mr. Hawthorne was pulling that man off my daughter. He got that bastard under control, had his arms pinned behind his back, and then—" Mr. Laughlin forced his eyes open and looked toward Rebecca. "Then my little girl picked up a brick. She went at him too quick for me to stop her. And not just once.... She hit him over and over again."

"It was self-defense," Jameson said.

Mr. Laughlin looked down, then forced his gaze to mine, like he needed me, of everyone here, to understand. "No. It wasn't."

I wondered how many times Mallory had hit her Liam before they stopped her. I wondered *if* they had stopped her.

"I got a hold of her," Mr. Laughlin said, his voice heavy. "She just kept saying that she thought he loved her. She thought—" There were no tears in his eyes, but a sob racked his chest. "Mr. Hawthorne told me to go. He told me to take Mal and get her out of there."

"Was Liam dead?" I asked, my mouth almost painfully dry.

There wasn't a hint of remorse in the groundskeeper's face. "Not yet."

Will Blake had been breathing when Mr. Laughlin left him alone with Tobias Hawthorne.

"Your daughter had just attacked Vincent Blake's son." Jameson was wired to find hidden truths, to turn everything into a puzzle, then solve it. "Back then, our family wasn't wealthy enough or powerful enough to protect her. Not yet."

"Do you even know what happened after you left?" Rebecca asked after a long and painful silence.

"My understanding is that he needed medical attention." Mr. Laughlin looked at each of us in turn. "Shame he didn't get it."

I pictured Tobias Hawthorne standing there and watching a man die. Letting him die.

"And afterward?" Xander said, uncharacteristically muted.

"I never asked," Mr. Laughlin said stiffly. "And Mr. Hawthorne never told me."

My mind raced—through the years, navigating through everything we knew. "But when Toby moved the body..." I started to say.

Mr. Laughlin locked his gaze back on the horizon. "I knew he'd buried something. Once Toby ran off and Mr. Hawthorne started asking questions, I figured out pretty quick what that something was."

And you never said a word, I thought.

"Show them the spot if you have to, Rebecca." Mr. Laughlin gently pushed his granddaughter's hair away from her face. "But if Vincent Blake asks what happened, you protect your mother. You tell him that it was me."

CHAPTER 74

We found the remains.

I brought out my phone, ready to place the call to Blake, but before I could pull the trigger, it rang. I glanced at caller ID and stopped breathing.

"Alisa?" I forced my lungs to start working again. "Are you—"

"Going to kill Grayson Hawthorne?" Alisa said evenly. "Yes. Yes, I am."

Just hearing her voice—and the absolute normality of her tone—sent a shock wave of relief through me. It was like I'd been carrying extra weight and pressure in every cell in my body, and suddenly, all that tension was gone.

And then I processed *what* Alisa had said.

"Grayson?" I repeated, my heart seizing in my chest.

"He's the reason Blake let me go. A trade."

I should have known when he hadn't come with us to find the body. *Grayson Hawthorne and his grand gestures.* Frustration, fear, and something almost painfully tender threatened to bring tears to my eyes.

"Your brother's playing sacrificial lamb," I told Jameson, trying to let that first emotion mute the rest. Xander heard my terse statement, too, and Nash appeared behind them.

"Alisa?" he said.

"She's fine," I reported. *And this time, we'll take care of her.* "Oren, can you have someone bring her in?"

Oren gave a curt nod, but the expression in his eyes betrayed how glad he was that she was okay. "Give me the phone, and I'll coordinate a pickup."

I passed the phone to him.

"This doesn't change anything," Jameson told me. "Blake still has the upper hand."

He had *Grayson*. There was a terrifying symmetry to that. Tobias Hawthorne had stolen Vincent Blake's grandson—and now he had Tobias Hawthorne's.

He has Toby. He has Grayson. And I have his son's remains. All I had to do was give Vincent Blake what he wanted, and this would be over.

Or at least, that was what Blake wanted me to believe.

But Tobias Hawthorne's final message hadn't just cautioned me that Blake would be coming for the truth, for proof. No, Tobias Hawthorne had told me that Blake would be coming for me, that he would box me in, hold me down, have no mercy. Tobias Hawthorne had been expecting a full-on assault on his empire. Assuming he'd projected correctly, Vincent Blake wasn't just after the truth.

He is coming. For the fortune. For my legacy. For you, Avery Kylie Grambs.

But Tobias Hawthorne—manipulative, Machiavellian man that he was—had also thought that I had a sliver of a chance. I just had to outplay Blake.

Take as your consolation this, my very risky gamble: I have watched you. I have come to know you. The words pumped through my body like blood, my heart beating out a brutal, uncompromising rhythm. Tobias Hawthorne had believed that Blake would underestimate me.

On the phone, he'd called me *little girl*.

What did that mean? *That he expects me to react, not act. That he thinks I'll never look ahead.*

I forced myself to stop, to slow down, to think. All around me, the others were fighting loudly about next moves. But I shut out the sound of Jameson's voice, of Nash's and Xander's, Oren's, everyone's. And eventually, I circled back to the Queen's Gambit. I thought about how it required ceding control of the board. It required a loss.

And it worked best when your opponent thought it was a rookie error, rather than strategy.

A plan took shape in my mind. It ossified. And I made a call.

CHAPTER 75

"What did you just do?" Jameson looked at me the way he had the night he'd told me that I was their grandfather's last puzzle, like after all this time, there were still things about me, about what I was capable of, that could surprise him.

Like he wanted to know them all.

"I called the authorities and reported that human remains had been found at Hawthorne House." That much had probably been obvious if they'd overheard me. What Jameson was really asking me was *why*.

"Far be it from me to state the obvious," Thea cut in, "but wasn't the point of digging *that* up to make a trade?"

I could feel Jameson reading me, feel his brain sorting through the possibilities in mine.

"I have another call to make," I said.

"To Blake?" Rebecca asked.

"No," Jameson answered for me.

"I don't have time to explain," I told all of them.

"You're playing him." Jameson didn't phrase that as a question.

"Blake said to bring him the body, and it will be returned to him. Eventually. And when it is, I won't have broken any laws."

It was easier thinking of this like chess. Trying to see my opponent's moves coming before he made them. Baiting the moves I wanted, blocking attacks before they happened.

Xander's eyes widened. "You think that if you'd taken him the remains, he would have held the illegality of that move over you?"

"I can't afford to hand him any more leverage."

"Because, of course, this is all about you." Thea's voice was dangerously pleasant—never a good sign.

"Thea," Rebecca said quietly. "Let it go."

"No. This is your *family*, Bex. And no matter how hard you try, no matter how angry you manage to get—that's always going to matter to you." Thea lifted a hand to the side of Rebecca's face. "I saw you back there with your mom."

Rebecca looked like she wanted to get lost in Thea's eyes, but she didn't let herself. "I always thought there was something wrong with me," she said, her voice breaking. "Emily was my mom's world, and I was a shadow, and I thought it was *me*."

"But now you know," Thea said softly, "it was never you."

Mallory's trauma was Rebecca's trauma—probably was Emily's, too.

"I am done living in the shadows, Thea," Rebecca said. She turned to me. "Bring on the light. Tell the world the truth. Do it."

That wasn't my plan—not exactly. There was one move that would let me protect the people who needed protecting. One sequence, if I could execute it.

If Blake didn't see it coming.

Reporting the body was just step one. Step two was controlling the narrative.

"Avery." Landon answered my call on the third ring. "Correct me if I'm wrong, but our working relationship came to an end quite some time ago."

I'd had other publicists and media consultants since, but for what I was planning, I needed the best. "I need to talk to you about a dead body and the story of the century."

Silence—enough of it that I wondered if she'd hung up on me. Then Landon offered up two words, her British accent crisp. "I'm listening."

I threw Tobias Hawthorne under the bus. Thoroughly and without mercy. Dead men didn't get to be picky about their reputations, and that went double for dead men who'd used me the way he had.

Tobias Hawthorne had killed a man forty years ago—and covered it up. That was the story I was telling, and it was one hell of a story.

"Where are you going?" Jameson called after me once I'd hung up with Landon.

"The vault," I replied. "There's something I need before I go to confront Vincent Blake."

Jameson ran to catch up with me. He made it past me, then turned back just as I took a step that put his body far too close to mine.

"And what do you need out of the vault?" Jameson asked.

"If I tell you," I said, "are you going to try to lock me up again?"

Jameson lifted a hand to the side of my neck. "Is it risky?"

I didn't look away. "Extremely."

"Good." His green eyes intense, he let his thumb trace the edge of my jaw. "To best Blake, it will have to be."

Some words were just words, and others were like fire. I felt it catching inside of me, spreading, as searing as any kiss. *We're back.*

"And once you've bested him," Jameson continued, "because you *will*..." There was no feeling in the world like being *seen* by Jameson Hawthorne. "I'm going to need an anagram for the word *everything*."

CHAPTER 76

After the vault, I made it as far as the foyer before chaos descended on me in the form of one very pissed-off Alisa Ortega. "What have you done?"

"Welcome back," Oren told her dryly.

"What I had to do," I answered.

Alisa took what was probably supposed to be a calming breath. "You didn't wait for me to get here because you *knew* I'd tell you that calling the police was a bad idea."

"You would have told me that calling the police on *Blake* was a bad idea," I countered. "So I didn't call them on Blake."

"We have local PD at the gate," Oren informed me. "Given the circumstances, my men can't refuse them entrance. I suspect the DPS Special Agents aren't long behind."

Alisa kneaded her temples. "I can fix this."

"It's not yours to fix," I told her.

"You have no idea what you're doing."

"No," I replied, staring her down. "*You* have no idea what I'm doing. There's a difference." I didn't have the time or inclination to explain everything to her. Landon had promised me a two-hour head start, but that was it. Any delay past that and we might lose our opportunity to control the narrative.

If I waited too long, Vincent Blake would have too much time to regroup.

"I'm glad you're okay," I told Alisa. "You've done a lot for me since the will was read. I know that. But the truth is that Tobias Hawthorne's fortune will be in my hands very soon." I didn't like playing it this way, but I didn't have a choice. "The only question you have to ask yourself is whether you still want to have a job when that happens."

Even I wasn't sure if I was bluffing. There was no way I could do this on my own, and even though I'd doubted her, I trusted Alisa more than I would trust anyone else I could hire next. On the other hand, she was in the habit of treating me like a kid—the same wide-eyed, overwhelmed, never-had-two-nickels-to-rub-together kid I'd been when I'd gotten here.

To take on Vincent Blake, I had to grow up.

"You'd drown without me," Alisa told me. "And take an empire down with you."

"So don't make me do this without you," I responded.

Fixing her gaze on me with almost frightening precision, Alisa gave a slight nod of her head. Oren cleared his throat.

I turned to face him. "Is this the part where you start talking about duct tape?"

He cocked an eyebrow at me. "Is this the part where you threaten my job?"

On the day that Tobias Hawthorne's will had been read, I'd tried to tell Oren I didn't need security. He'd calmly replied that I would need security for the rest of my life. It had never been a question of *whether* he would protect me.

"This isn't just a job to you," I told Oren, because I felt like I owed him that much. "It never has been."

He'd told me months ago that he owed Tobias Hawthorne his life. The old man had given Oren a purpose, dragged him out of a very dark place. His last request to my head of security had been that Oren protect me.

"I thought he'd done something noble," Oren said quietly, "asking me to take care of you."

Oren was my constant shadow. He'd heard Tobias Hawthorne's message. He knew what my purpose was—and that had to have shed new light on his.

"Your boss asked you to run my security. Taking care of me..." My voice hitched. "That was all you."

Oren gave me the briefest of smiles, then he allowed himself to fall back into bodyguard mode. "What's the plan, boss?"

I retrieved the Blake family seal from my pocket. "This." I let it fall into my palm and closed my fingers around it. "We're going to Blake's ranch. I'm going to use this to get past the gates. And I'm going in alone."

"I have a professional obligation to tell you that I don't like this plan."

I gave Oren a sympathetic look. "Would you like it more if I told you that I'll be doing a press conference right outside his gates so that the whole world knows I'm inside?"

Vincent Blake couldn't touch me with the paparazzi watching.

"You going to put a stop to this, Oren?" Nash ambled toward us, clearly having overheard our exchange. "Because if you don't, I will."

As if drawn by the chaos, Xander chose that moment to pop in, too.

"This doesn't concern you," I told Nash.

"Nice try, kid." Nash's tone never advertised the fact that he was pulling rank, but no matter how casual the delivery, it was always one hundred percent clear when that was what he was doing. "This ain't happening."

Nash didn't care that I was eighteen, that I owned the House, that I wasn't actually his sister, or that I would put up one hell of a fight if he tried to stop me.

"You can't protect the four of us forever," I told him.

"I can damn well try. You don't want to test me on this one, darlin'."

I glanced at Jameson, who was well-acquainted with the pitfalls of *testing* Nash. Jameson met my gaze, then glanced at Xander.

"Flying leopard?" Jameson murmured.

"Hidden mongoose!" Xander replied, and an instant later, they were crashing into Nash in a truly impressive synchronized flying tackle.

In a one-on-one fight, Nash could take either one of them. But it was hard to get the upper hand when you had one brother on your torso and another pinning your legs and feet.

"We should go," I told Oren. Nash was cursing up a storm behind us. Xander began serenading him with a brotherly limerick.

"Oren!" Nash hollered.

My head of security didn't so much as hint at any amusement he might have felt. "Sorry, Nash. I know better than to get in the middle of a Hawthorne brawl."

"Alisa—" Nash started to say, but I interjected.

"I want you with me," I told my lawyer. "You'll wait with Oren, right outside."

Nash must have smelled defeat because he stopped trying to dislodge Xander from his feet. "Kid?" he called. "You sure as hell better play dirty."

CHAPTER 77

Vincent Blake's ranch was about a two-and-a-half-hour drive north, stretching for miles along the Texas/Oklahoma border. Taking the helicopter cut our travel time down to forty-five minutes, plus transit on the ground. Landon had done her part, so the press arrived shortly after I did.

"Earlier today," I told them in a speech that I had rehearsed, "the remains of a man that we believe to be William Blake were found on the grounds of the Hawthorne estate."

I stuck to my script. Landon had timed the leak about the body perfectly—the story she'd planted was already up, but it was the footage of what I was saying now that would define it. I sold the story: Will Blake had physically assaulted an underage female, and Tobias Hawthorne had intervened to protect her. Law enforcement was investigating, but based on what we'd been able to piece together ourselves, we expected the autopsy to reveal that Blake had died from blunt-force trauma to the head.

Tobias Hawthorne had dealt those blows.

That last bit might not have been true, but it was sensational. It was *a story*. And I was here now to pay my respects to the deceased's family, on behalf of myself and the remaining Hawthornes.

I didn't take questions. Instead, I turned and walked toward the boundary of Vincent Blake's property. I knew from my research that Legacy Ranch was more than a quarter of a million acres—nearly four hundred square miles.

I stopped under an enormous brick arch, part of an equally enormous wall. The archway was big enough for a bus to fit underneath. As I approached, a black truck barreled toward me from inside the compound, down a long dirt road.

Beyond this wall, there were more than eighty thousand acres of active farmland, more than a thousand productive oil wells, the world's largest privately owned collection of quarter horses, and a truly substantial number of cattle.

And somewhere, beyond this wall, on these acres, there was a house.

"You're about to trespass on private property." The men who exited the black truck were dressed like ranch hands, but they moved like soldiers.

Hoping I hadn't miscalculated—because if I had, the entire world was witnessing that miscalculation—I replied to the man who had spoken. "Even if I have one of these?"

I opened my fingers just far enough for them to see the seal.

Less than a minute later, I was in the cab of the truck, barreling toward the unknown.

It was a full ten minutes before the house came into view. The driver, who was definitely armed, hadn't said a word to me.

I looked down at the seal resting in my palm. "You haven't asked where I got it."

He didn't take his eyes off the road. "When someone has one of those, you don't ask."

If Hawthorne House looked like a castle, Vincent Blake's home called to mind a fortress. It was made of dark stone, its square lines interrupted only by two giant round columns rising into turrets. A wrought-iron balcony lined the front perimeter on the second floor. I half expected a drawbridge, but instead there was a wraparound porch.

Eve stood on that porch, her amber hair blowing in the wind.

Blake's security followed me as I walked toward her. When I stepped up onto the porch, Eve turned, a strategic move designed to force me into following.

"This all would have been so much easier," she said, "if you'd just given me what I asked for."

CHAPTER 78

Eve didn't lead me into the house. She led me around back. A man stood there. He had suntanned skin and silver hair shorn to the scalp. I knew he had to be in his eighties, but he looked closer to sixty-five—and like he could run a marathon.

He was holding a shotgun.

As I watched, he took aim at the sky. The sound of the shot was earsplitting and echoed through the countryside as a bird plummeted to the ground. Vincent Blake said something—I couldn't hear what—and the largest bloodhound I'd ever seen took off after the kill.

Blake lowered his weapon. Slowly, he turned to face me. "Around here," he called, in that smooth, borderline-aristocratic voice I recognized all too well from the phone, "we cook what we shoot."

He held out the gun, and someone rushed to take it from him. Then Blake strode toward us. He settled down on a cement wall near a massive firepit, and Eve led me right up to it—and him.

"Where are Grayson and Toby?" That was the only greeting this man was going to get out of me.

"Enjoying my hospitality." Blake eyed the large box I carried in my hands. Wordlessly, I opened it. I'd stopped in the vault to retrieve the royal chess set. Once I'd been granted admission to Blake's lands, I'd had Oren surreptitiously hand it to me.

Now I set it in front of Blake, an offering of sorts.

He picked up one of the pieces, examining the multitude of shining black diamonds, the artistry of the design, then snorted and tossed the piece back down. "Tobias always was the showy type." Blake held out his right hand, and someone placed a bowie knife in it.

My heart leapt into my throat, but all the king of this kingdom did was withdraw a small piece of wood from his pocket.

"A set you carve yourself," he told me, "plays just the same."

That's not a carving knife. I didn't let him intimidate me into saying that out loud. Instead, I leaned forward to place the seal I'd flashed to gain entrance beside him on the wall. "I believe this is yours," I told him. Then I nodded to the chess set I'd brought. "And we'll call that a gift."

"I didn't ask you to bring me a gift, Avery Kylie Grambs."

I met his iron-hard gaze. "You didn't ask for anything. You *told* me to bring you your son, and you'll get him." By now, Blake doubtlessly would have heard the reports that Landon had leaked. There was a good chance that he'd watched my press conference. "Once the investigation is complete," I continued, "the authorities will release his remains to you. For what it's worth, I'm sorry for your loss."

"I don't lose, Avery Kylie Grambs." Blake's knife flashed in the sun as he scraped it along the wood. "My son, on the other hand, appears to have lost quite a bit."

"Your son," I said, "impregnated an underage girl, then got physical with her when she had the audacity to be devastated at the realization that he'd just been using her to get close enough to make a move against Tobias Hawthorne."

"Hmmmm." Blake made a humming sound that felt far more

threatening than it should have. "Will was fifteen when Tobias and I parted ways. The boy was irate that we'd been double-crossed. I had to disabuse him of the notion that *we* had been anything. What happened was between young Tobias and me."

"Tobias bested you." That was my first thrust in this little verbal sword match of ours.

Blake didn't even feel it. "And look how well that turned out for him."

I wasn't sure if that was a reference to the fact that the only person who had ever bested Vincent Blake had turned out to be one of the most formidable minds in a generation—or a self-satisfied prediction that all of Tobias Hawthorne's achievements would be nothing in the end.

The billionaire was dead, his fortune ripe for the taking.

"Your son hated him." I tried again, with a different type of attack. "And he was desperate to prove himself to you."

Blake didn't deny it. Instead, he brought the bowie knife away from the wood and tested its sharpness against the pad of his thumb. "Tobias should have let me handle Will. He knew the kind of hell there would be to pay for bringing harm to *my* son. Choices, young lady, have consequences."

"And how would you have handled what your son did to Mallory Laughlin?"

"That's neither here nor there."

"And boys will be boys," I shot back. "Right?"

Blake studied me for a moment, then laid the knife on his leg. "I understand you have some friends at the gate."

"The entire world knows I'm here," I said. "They know what happened to your son."

"Do they?" Eve said, a challenge in her tone. The story I was telling—she must have heard enough from Mallory to question it.

"That's enough, Eve." Blake's voice was clipped, and Eve swallowed as her great-grandfather looked between the two of us. "I shouldn't have sent a little girl to do a man's job."

Little girl. On the phone earlier, he'd referred to me that way, too. Tobias Hawthorne had been right. I was young. I was female. And this man *would* underestimate me.

"If I'd brought you your son's remains," I said, "you would have blackmailed me for breaking the law."

"Blackmailed you into what, I wonder?" Blake meant that *I* should wonder.

I knew that it was to my advantage for him to think he had the upper hand, so I had to tread carefully now. "If Grayson and Toby don't leave here with me, I'll give another interview on the way out."

It was dangerous to threaten a man like Vincent Blake. I knew that. I also knew that I needed him to believe that *this* was my play. My only play.

"An interview?" That got me another little hum. "Will you tell them about Sheffield Grayson?"

I'd anticipated that he would counter my move, but I hadn't foreseen how, and suddenly, I couldn't hold my pulse steady anymore. I couldn't keep my face completely blank.

"Eve may have failed at her primary task," Blake said, "but she's a Blake—and we play to win. I'm still considering whether she's earned this." He brandished a golden disk identical to the one I'd placed on the wall. "But the information she brought me when she returned was... quite impressive."

Information. About what happened to Grayson's father. I thought about the file, the pictures on Eve's phone.

"I read between the lines," Eve said, her lips curving up. "Grayson's father is missing, and based on what I was able to put together, he *went* missing shortly after someone orchestrated an attempt on your life. Sheffield Grayson had motive to be that someone. I didn't have proof, of course, but then..." Eve gave a little shrug. "I called Mellie."

Eve's sister was the one who had shot Sheffield Grayson. She'd killed him to save Toby and me. "The sister who never did a damn thing for you?" I asked, my throat bone-dry.

"Half sister." The correction told me that Eve hadn't lied about her feelings for her siblings. "It was a very touching reunion, especially when I told her that I *forgive* her." Eve's lips twisted. "That I was there for her. Mellie is wracked with guilt, you know. About what she did. About what *you* covered up."

I'd been ushered out of the storage facility when Sheffield Grayson's blood was still fresh on the ground. "I didn't cover up anything."

Blake brought his blade back to the wood and began carving again—slow, smooth motions. "John Oren did."

I'd come here with a plan, but I hadn't planned for this. I'd thought that by calling the police about Will Blake's remains, I would sap his father of much-needed leverage. I hadn't foreseen that Vincent Blake had leverage in reserve.

"It seems," the man commented mildly, "that I have the advantage on you once again."

He'd never doubted it.

"What do you want?" I asked. I let him see my very real distress, but inside, the logical part of my brain took over. The part that liked puzzles. The part that saw the world in layers.

The part that had come here with a plan.

"Anything I want from you," Blake said simply, "I'll take."

"I'll play you for it," I told him, improvising and letting my brain adjust, adding a new layer, one more thing that had to go right. "Chess. If I win, you forget about Sheffield Grayson and see to it that Eve and Mellie do the same."

Blake seemed amused, but I could see something much darker than amusement glinting in his eyes. "And if you lose?"

I had a trump card, but I couldn't play it—not yet. Not if I wanted even a sliver of a chance that I'd walk away today with the kind of win I needed.

"A favor," I said, my heart brutalizing my rib cage. "Very soon, I'll have control of the Hawthorne fortune. Billions. A favor from someone in my position has to be worth something."

Vincent Blake didn't seem overly tempted by my offer. Of course he didn't, because he already had a plan to come for Tobias Hawthorne's fortune on his own.

After a moment, however, amusement won out. "A game seems fitting, but I'm not going to play you, little girl. I will, however, let *her* play you." He jerked his head toward Eve, then tilted his head to the side, considering. "And Toby."

"Toby?" I croaked. I hated the way I sounded—the way I felt. I couldn't let my emotions take control. I had to think. I had to modify my plan—again.

"My grandson has asked about you," Blake told me. "You could say I have a knack for recognizing pressure points."

Vincent Blake had kidnapped Toby to get at me, to win Eve entrance to Hawthorne House. I realized, in that moment, that Blake had also doubtlessly leveraged me against Toby.

"Eve," he said, his voice carrying the weight of an order that no living person would dare disobey, "why don't you fetch your father?"

CHAPTER 79

Toby's bruises were healing, and he needed to shave. Those were my first two thoughts, followed immediately by a dozen others about him and my mom and the last time I'd seen him, each thought accompanied by a wave of emotion that threatened to take me down.

"You shouldn't be here." Toby kept a handle on whatever emotions he was feeling, but the intensity in his eyes told me he was holding on to that composure by a thread.

"I know," I replied, and I hoped my tone made him realize that I wasn't just saying I knew I shouldn't be here. *I know who Blake is. I know what he's capable of. I know what I'm doing.*

For this to work, Toby didn't have to trust me, but I did need him to stay out of my way.

"You're going to play a game," Vincent Blake told Toby. "All three of you—a tournament of sorts, consisting of three matches." Blake lifted a single finger and gestured from Toby to Eve. "My grandson and his daughter." A second finger came up. "My grandson and the girl who is *not* his daughter."

Toby and me. *Ouch.*

"And..." Blake raised a third and final finger. "Avery and Eve against each other." The man gave us a few seconds to process that, then continued. "As for incentive...well, these things must have stakes."

Something about the way he said *stakes* sent a shiver down my spine.

"Win both of your matches and you can go," Blake told Toby. "Disappear however you like. You'll never hear from me again, and I'll allow the world to continue to believe that you are dead. Lose one of your matches and you're still free to go, but not as a dead man. You'll confirm for the world that Toby Hawthorne is alive and never go off the grid again."

Toby didn't blanch. I wasn't sure if Blake had expected him to.

"Lose both of your matches," the older man continued with a tilt to his lips that I did not trust, "and you won't be coming back to life as Toby Hawthorne. You'll agree to stay here of your own free will as Toby Blake."

"No!" I objected. "Toby, you—"

Toby cut me off with the slightest shift in his expression—a warning. "What are their terms?" he asked his grandfather.

Blake drank in Toby's response, pleased, and then turned to Eve. "Win one of your matches," he told her, "and you can have this." He brandished a Blake family seal at Eve. "Lose both, and you'll be at the service of whoever I give it to in your stead." There was something deeply disconcerting about the way he said *service*. "Win both of your matches," Blake finished silkily, "and I'll give you all five."

All five seals. An electric current swept through the premises. Isaiah had said that anyone holding a seal when Vincent Blake died was entitled to one-fifth of his fortune, and that meant Blake had just promised Eve that if she could beat Toby *and* me, he'd give her everything.

All the power. All the money. All of it.

"And as for you, Tobias Hawthorne's *very risky gamble*..." Vincent Blake smiled. "Lose both, and I'll take that favor you offered—a blank check, if you will, to be cashed at a time of my choosing."

Toby caught my gaze. *No.* He didn't make the objection out loud. After a moment, I looked away. There wasn't a warning he could issue that would be news to me. Owing Vincent Blake a favor was a very bad idea.

"Win at least one game," Blake continued, "and I'll release Grayson Hawthorne to you, with a guarantee that I won't make a guest of anyone under your protection again."

Guest was one way of phrasing it—but as far as incentives went, it was enticing. Too enticing. *If he's willing to keep his hands off my loved ones, he must have other buttons to push. Other forms of leverage.*

Another plan to take everything from me.

"Win both games," Blake promised, "and I'll also swear secrecy on the matter of Sheffield Grayson."

Toby flinched. Clearly, he hadn't known about that bit of leverage his biological grandfather had been holding in reserve.

"Are these terms acceptable to you?" Blake asked Toby and only Toby, like Eve and I were foregone conclusions.

Toby gritted his teeth. "Yes."

"*Yes*," Eve said, alive in a way that made all other versions of her seem faded and incomplete.

And as for me...

Blake will honor his word. If I won both matches, the truth about Grayson's father would stay buried. The people I loved would be safe. Blake would still be coming for me. He'd find a way of destroying me and all I held dear, but he'd be limited in how he could do that.

"I agree to your terms," I said, even though he'd never given me the option to do anything else.

Blake turned to the glittering, five-hundred-thousand-dollar chess set I'd gifted him. "Well then. Shall we begin?"

CHAPTER 80

Toby and Eve went first. I'd played against Toby often enough to know that he could have ended it within the first twelve moves if he'd wanted to.

He let her win.

Blake must have concluded the same thing because once the board had been reset for my match against Toby, the older man picked up his bowie knife. "Throw this game, too," he told Toby contemplatively, "and I'll ask Eve to give me her arm and use this to open a vein."

If Eve was disturbed by the implication that her great-grandfather would slice her open, she didn't show it. Instead, she held tight to the seal she'd been given and kept her eyes on the board.

I took my position and met Toby's eyes. It had been more than a year since we'd played, but the second I moved my first pawn, it was like no time had passed at all. Harry and I were right back in the park.

"Your move, princess." Toby wasn't pulling his punches, but he did his best to put me at ease, to remind me that even if he played his hardest, I'd beaten him before.

"Not a princess." I echoed my line in our script back at him and slid my bishop across the board. "Your move, *old man*."

Toby narrowed his eyes slightly. "Don't get cocky."

"Fine words from a Hawthorne," I retorted.

"I mean it, Avery. Don't get cocky."

He sees something I don't.

"Eve," Vincent Blake said pleasantly. "Your arm?"

Her chin steady, Eve held it out to him. Blake rested the edge of his blade against her skin. "Play," he told Toby. "And no more hints to the girl."

There was a beat—a single second—and then Toby did as he'd been instructed. I scanned the board, then saw why he'd cautioned me against getting cocky. It took three moves, but then: "Check," Toby gritted out.

I took in the board, all of it at once. I had three possible next moves, and I played all of them out. Two led to Toby getting checkmate within the next five moves. That meant I was stuck with the third. I knew how Toby would counter it, and from there I had four or five options. I let my brain race, let the possibilities slowly untangle themselves.

I tried not to think too much about the fact that if Toby beat me, the cover-up of Sheffield Grayson's death would be exposed. Either that, or I'd have to give Blake something much more significant than a favor to keep it quiet.

The man would own me.

No. I could do this. There was a way. *My move. His. My move. His.* Again and again, faster and faster, we played.

Then, finally, a breath whooshed out of my chest. "Check."

I knew the exact moment that Toby saw the trap I had laid. "Horrible girl," he whispered roughly, and the tenderness in his eyes when he said it almost took me down.

His move. Mine. His move. Mine.

And then, finally—*finally*... "Checkmate," I said.

Vincent Blake kept the bowie knife on Eve's arm a moment longer, then slowly lowered it. His grandson had lost, and as the realization of what that meant fell over me, my insides twisted.

Toby had lost both matches. He was Blake's.

CHAPTER 81

"I expect better next time," Vincent Blake told Toby. "You're a Blake now, and Blakes don't lose to little girls."

I caught Toby's gaze. "I'm sorry," I said quietly, urgently.

"Don't be." Toby reached out to cup my face. "I see so much of your mother in you."

That felt far too much like good-bye. From the moment Eve had arrived at the gates of Hawthorne House, I had been determined to *get him back*. And now—

"Will I . . ." The words stopped, like the question was gumming up my throat. "Can I see you?" I asked.

You have a daughter, I could hear myself saying.

I have two.

Blake didn't give Toby the chance to reply. He shifted his attention to Eve. She basked in it, like he was the sun and she had the type of skin that didn't burn. For the first time, instead of looking at her and seeing Emily, I saw something very different.

An intensity that was Toby's. *Blake's.*

"If I win this game . . . ," she said, steel and wonder in her tone.

"It's yours," Blake confirmed. "All of it. But before we begin . . ."

Blake lifted a finger, and a member of his security team rushed over. "Could you fetch our other guest for Ms. Grambs?"

Grayson. I didn't let myself fully believe that he was okay until I saw him, and then I let myself think about what I'd won—not just his freedom, but a promise that no one I cared about would find themselves a *guest* here again.

"Avery." Grayson's blue-gray eyes—his irises icy and light against the inky black of his pupils—locked on to mine. "I had a plan."

"Reckless self-sacrifice?" I retorted. "Yeah, I got that." I pulled him close and spoke directly into his ear. "I told you, Grayson, we're *family.*"

I let go of him. The board was set up a final time. Eve was white. I was black. With tens of thousands of diamonds glittering between us, we faced off in a game of greatest stakes.

Based on Eve's level of play against Toby, I hadn't anticipated the challenge I soon found myself facing. It was like she'd watched my game against her father, internalized a dozen new strategies, and learned how I saw the board.

She's playing to win. I was desperate to save Oren, and I had no idea how much of a crime *I* had committed by not reporting Sheffield Grayson's death. But Eve? She was playing for the keys to the kingdom—for wealth and power beyond imagining.

For acceptance from someone she was desperate to be accepted by.

The rest of the room faded away until I couldn't hear anything but the sounds of my own body and couldn't see anything but the board. It took longer than I'd anticipated, but finally, I saw my opening.

I could have her in check in three moves, checkmate in five.

Just like that, I could walk away from here with Grayson, knowing that Vincent Blake had that many fewer ways of coming at me.

But he'll still come.

The assaults on my financial interests, the paparazzi, playing games and boxing me in. *He'll just keep coming.* That thought grew louder in my mind, pushing my focus from my match against Eve to the bigger picture.

For me, *this* wasn't the ultimate game.

I could win, and I would still walk out of here no better off than when Tobias Hawthorne had died. It would still be hunting season. A man who Tobias Hawthorne had so feared that he had left a virtual stranger his fortune would still be gunning for me.

Even without violence, even with our physical safety guaranteed, Vincent Blake would still find a way of destroying anyone, everyone, and everything that stood in his way.

This win right now against Eve—it wouldn't be enough.

I had to play the long game. I had to look past the board, play ten moves ahead, not five, think in three dimensions, not two. If I beat Eve, Vincent Blake would send me on my way, and he'd do so knowing that I was more than he'd given me credit for. He'd adjust his expectations in the future.

You're young. Tobias Hawthorne's voice rang in my mind. *You're female. You're nobody—use that.* If I gave Vincent Blake an excuse to continue underestimating me, he would.

I'd come here with a plan in mind. The tournament hadn't been a part of that plan—but I could use it.

Playing chess wasn't just about anticipating your opponent's moves. It was about planting those moves in their mind—baiting them. After listening to the recording the old man had left for us, Xander had marveled at the fact that Tobias Hawthorne had foreseen exactly what we would all do after his death, but Hawthorne hadn't just foreseen it.

He'd manipulated it. Manipulated us.

If I wanted to beat Blake, I had to do the same. So I didn't take the opening Eve had given me. I didn't beat her in five moves.

I let her beat me in ten.

I saw the exact moment when Eve realized that Vincent Blake's empire was in her grasp—and the moment, right afterward, when Toby's eyes flashed. Did he suspect I'd thrown the game?

Did my *real* opponent?

"Well done, Eve." Blake offered her a small, self-satisfied smile, and Eve glowed, the smile on her face luminescent. Blake turned to me—and Grayson. "The two of you may leave."

His men closed in on us, and I didn't have to fake my panic. "Wait!" I said, sounding desperate—and feeling that desperation, because even though this had been a calculated risk, I had no way of knowing that I hadn't miscalculated. "Give me another chance!"

"Have some dignity, child." Blake stood and turned his back on me as his hunting dog returned to his side and dropped a dead duck at his feet. "No one likes a sore loser."

"You could still have a favor," I shouted as Blake's security began to remove me from the premises. "One last game. Me against you."

"I don't need a favor from you, girl."

That's okay, I tried to tell myself. *There's another option.* An option I'd come prepared for. An option I'd planned for. The gift of the chess set, the fact that I had Alisa waiting for me outside—I'd always known what my gambit was going to be.

What it was going to *have* to be.

"Not a favor, then," I said, trying to hold on to the panic and the desperation so he wouldn't see the deep sense of calm rising up inside me. "What about the rest of it?"

Grayson cut a sharp look in my direction. "Avery."

Vincent Blake held up his hand, and his men all took a silent step back. "The rest of what, exactly?"

"The Hawthorne fortune." I let the words come out in a rush. "My lawyer has been after me to sign these papers for weeks. Tobias Hawthorne didn't tie my inheritance up in a trust. The fine people at McNamara, Ortega, and Jones are nervous about a teenager taking the reins, so Alisa drew up paperwork that would put everything in a trust until I turn thirty."

"Avery." Toby's voice was low and full of warning. Part of me wanted to believe he was just helping me sell the in-over-my-head act, but he was probably offering a genuine word of caution.

I was risking too much.

"If you play me," I told Blake, nodding toward the chessboard, "and you win, I'll sign the papers and make *you* the trustee."

Coming here, I'd been counting on Blake's ego to make him think that he could beat me, but there had always been the chance that he would realize I'd suggested chess specifically because I stood a good chance at winning. But now?

He'd seen me play.

He'd seen me lose.

He thought I was making this offer on impulse *because* I had lost.

And still, he looked at me with sharp eyes and the most suspicious of smiles. "Now, why would you do a thing like that?"

"I don't want anyone finding out about Sheffield Grayson," I bit out. "And I've read the paperwork! With a trust, the money would still belong to me. I just wouldn't control it. You would have to promise me that you would okay any purchases I wanted to make, that you'd let me spend as much money as I wanted, whenever I wanted. But everything I can't spend? You'd be the one making the decisions about how it's invested."

Do you know what the real difference is between millions and billions? Skye Hawthorne had asked, what felt like a small eternity ago. *Because at a certain point, it's not about the money.*

It was about the power.

Vincent Blake didn't want or need Tobias Hawthorne's fortune to *spend* it.

"All of this, for double or nothing?" Blake asked pointedly. Like Tobias Hawthorne, the man across from me thought seven steps ahead. He knew I had another card up my sleeve.

But hopefully just one.

"No," I admitted. "If you win, you get control of everything free and clear until I'm thirty or you're six feet under. But if I win, you make sure that any nasty rumors about Sheffield Grayson stay buried, *and* you give me your word that this ends here."

This was the plan. This had always been the plan. *My greatest adversary—and yours now—is an honor-bound man,* Tobias Hawthorne had told me. *Best him, and he'll honor the win.*

"If I win," I continued, "the armistice you had with Tobias Hawthorne—you extend that to me. End of hunting season." I gave him a hard look, which I deeply suspected he found amusing. "You let me go, the way you let a young Tobias Hawthorne go, way back when."

I willed him to see me as impulsive, to see this as me scrambling because I'd lost. *I'm young. I'm female. I'm nobody. And you just saw Eve beat me at chess.*

"How am I to know you'll keep up your end of the deal?" my adversary queried.

It took everything in me not to allow even a shadow of victory to pulse through me. "If you accept the wager," I said, all wide eyes and bravado, "we'll make two calls: one to your lawyer and one to mine."

CHAPTER 82

"What the hell are you doing?" Alisa hissed.

The two of us were—purportedly—alone, but even with no one visibly listening, I didn't want to explain anything that could tip my hand to Blake. "What I have to," I said, hoping Alisa would read so much more in my tone.

I have a plan.

I can do this.

You have to trust me.

Alisa stared at me like I'd grown horns. "You absolutely do not have to do this."

I wasn't going to win this argument, so I didn't even try. I just waited for her to realize that I wasn't backing down.

When she did, Alisa swore under her breath and looked away. "Do you know why Nash and I broke off our engagement?" she asked in a tone that was far too calm for both the words she'd spoken and our current situation. "He was so determined that his grandfather wasn't going to pull his strings—or mine. He expected me to walk away from all things Hawthorne, too."

"And you couldn't." I wasn't sure where she was going with this.

"Nash was raised to be extraordinary," Alisa said. "But he wasn't the only one the old man had a hand in raising, so yes, I stayed." Alisa clipped the words, refusing to allow them more importance than she had to. "I did what Nash *should* have done. It cost me everything, but before Mr. Hawthorne passed, he stipulated to my father and the other partners that I would be the one who took the lead with you." She looked down. "I can just hear what the old man would say about the mess I've made of my job. First, I let myself get kidnapped, and now this."

The mess that she thought I was making right now.

"Or maybe," I told her in a tone that somehow captured her attention, "you've done exactly what he raised you to do—exactly what he *chose you* to do."

I willed her to read meaning into my emphasis. *He didn't just choose you. He chose me, too, Alisa—and maybe I'm doing exactly what he chose me for.*

Slowly, the expression in her deep brown eyes shifted. She knew that I was telling her to believe that I'd been chosen for a reason. That *this* was the reason.

This was our play.

"Do you have any idea how risky this is?" Alisa asked me.

"It always has been," I replied, "from the moment Tobias Hawthorne changed his will."

This was his very risky gamble—and mine.

CHAPTER 83

Blake let me play white, which meant that the first move was mine. I went with the Queen's Gambit. It wasn't until a dozen moves later that Vincent Blake realized my instincts went beyond classic maneuvers. Four moves after that, he took my bishop, allowing me to execute a sequence that ended with me taking his queen.

Slowly, move by move and counterattack by counterattack, Vincent Blake realized that we were much more evenly matched than he'd anticipated.

"I see now," he told me, "what you're doing."

He saw what I had *done*. The young woman he was playing against now wasn't the one who'd lost to Eve. I'd hustled him, and he knew it—far too late.

In four moves, I thought, my heartbeat brutal and incessant in my chest, *I'll have him*.

After two, he realized I had him trapped. He stood, tipping his king, conceding the match. White gold clattered as the piece hit the jewel-encrusted board, the black-diamond king glittering in the sun.

Vincent Blake was a dangerous man, a wealthy man, a formidable opponent—and he had underestimated me.

"You can keep the chess set," I told him.

For a moment, I felt Blake fighting with himself. The lawyers had been there to ensure my end of the bargain—not his. *I promise I won't slowly and strategically destroy you* wasn't a legally enforceable term. I'd bet everything on the only real assurance Tobias Hawthorne had given me.

That if I bested Blake, he'd honor the win.

"What just happened here?" Eve demanded.

Vincent Blake offered me one last hard look, and then he rocked back on his heels. "She won."

CHAPTER 84

Vincent Blake would honor our wager, but he never wanted to see me on his property again. "Escort Avery, Grayson, and Ms. Ortega back to the gate," he ordered his men. "See that the press is dispersed before they get there."

A hand locked around my forearm, suggesting exactly what kind of "escort" I could expect. But the next thing I knew, the man who'd grabbed me was on the ground, and Toby was standing over him. "I'll escort them," he said.

Blake's men looked to their boss.

Vincent Blake gave Toby a foreboding smile. "As you wish, Tobias Blake."

The name was a razor-sharp reminder: I might have won my wager, but Toby had lost his. With a hand on my back, he led me away, back around the house.

We'd nearly made it to the driveway when a voice spoke behind us. "Stop."

I wanted to ignore Eve, but I couldn't. Slowly, I turned to face her, aware that Grayson was exercising ironclad control over any impulse he might have felt to do the same.

"You let me win," Eve said. That was an accusation, furious and low. Her gaze slipped to Toby's. "Did you throw our game, too?" she asked him, her voice shaking. When Toby didn't reply, Eve turned back to me. "Did he?" she demanded.

"Does it matter?" I asked. "You got what you wanted."

Eve had won all five seals. She was now the sole heir to Blake's empire.

"I wanted," Eve whispered, her voice quiet but brutally fierce, "for once in my life, to prove to someone that I was good enough." Her eyes betrayed her, going to Grayson, but he didn't turn around. "I wanted Blake to *see* me," Eve continued, her gaze coming back to mine, "but now the only thing he is ever going to see when he looks at me is *you*."

I'd used Eve to best Blake, and she was right—he would never forget that.

"I saw you, Eve." Grayson's voice was emotionless, his body still. "You could have been one of us."

Eve's expression wavered, and for the barest moment, I was reminded of the little girl in the locket. Then the person in front of me straightened, a haughty look settling over her features like a porcelain mask. "The girl you knew," she told Grayson, "was a lie."

If she thought that would get a rise out of Grayson Davenport Hawthorne, she was wrong.

"Get them out of here." Eve whipped her head toward Toby. "*Now.*"

"Eve—" Toby started to say.

"I said *go*." A spark of victory, hard and cruel, glinted in her emerald eyes. "You'll be back."

That felt like an arrow aimed at my heart. *Toby doesn't have a choice.*

Without flinching, he escorted me away from his daughter and didn't speak until he, Alisa, Grayson, and I had made it to the truck.

"What you did back there with Blake was very risky," Toby told me—half censure, half praise.

I shrugged. "You're the one who chose my name." *Avery Kylie Grambs. A very risky gamble.* Toby had helped bring me into the world. He'd named me. He'd come to me when my mother died. He'd saved me when I needed saving.

And now I was losing him all over again.

"What happens now?" I asked him, my eyes beginning to sting, my throat tight.

"I become Tobias Blake." Toby had known the truth about his lineage for two decades. If he'd wanted this life, he would have been living it already.

I thought of the words he'd written in the chamber under the hedge maze. *I was never a Hawthorne. I will never be a Blake.*

"You don't have to do this," I told him. "You could run. You managed to evade Tobias Hawthorne for years. You could do the same thing with Blake now."

"And give that man justification to renege on his deal with you?" Alisa cut in. "Invalidate one wager in a set and he could easily argue that you've invalidated them all."

"I'm not running this time," Toby said intently. I followed his gaze to Eve, who was standing on the porch again, her amber hair blowing in the wind, looking for all the world like some kind of unearthly, conquering queen.

"You're staying for *her*." I hadn't meant that to sound like an accusation of betrayal.

"I'm staying for both of you," Toby replied, and for a moment, I could see the two of us, hear the last conversation we'd had.

You have a daughter.

I have two.

"She helped Blake kidnap you," I said roughly. "She used me—used all of us."

"And when I was her age," Toby replied, opening the passenger door of the truck and gesturing for me to get in, "I killed your mother's sister."

I wanted to object, to say that he hadn't lit the fire, even if he'd doused the house in gasoline, but he didn't give me the chance.

"Hannah thought I was redeemable." Even after all these years, Toby couldn't reference my mom without emotion overtaking him. "Do you really think she'd want me to walk away from Eve?"

I felt a sob caught somewhere. "You could have told me," I said, my voice scraping against my throat. "About Blake. About the body. About why you were so damn set on staying in the shadows."

Toby lifted a hand to the side of my face, brushing my hair back from my temple. "There are a lot of things I would do differently if I could live this life all over again."

I thought about what I'd said to Jameson about destiny and fate and *choice*. I knew why Tobias Hawthorne had chosen me. I knew that this had never been about *me*. But unlike Toby, I had no regrets. I would have done it—all of it—all over again.

Tobias Hawthorne's game hadn't made me extraordinary. It had shown me that I already was.

"Will I ever see you again?" I asked Toby, my voice breaking.

"Blake isn't going to keep me under lock and key." Toby waited for Alisa and Grayson to climb in after me, then closed the passenger door and rounded to the other side of the truck. When he spoke again, it was from the driver's seat. "And Texas really isn't that big—especially at the top."

Money. Power. Status. My path and Vincent Blake's would probably cross again—and so would mine and Toby's. Mine and Eve's.

"Here." Toby placed a small wooden cube in my hand as he started up the truck. "I made you something, horrible girl."

The endearment nearly undid me. "What is it?"

"Blake didn't give me much to entertain myself with—just wood and a knife."

"And you didn't use the knife?" Grayson asked beside me. His tone made it very clear the kind of *uses* he would have approved of.

"Would you have," Toby countered, "if you thought your captor could get to Avery?"

Toby had protected me. He'd made something for me.

You have a daughter.

I have two.

I looked down at the wooden cube in my hand, thinking about my mom, about this man, about the decades and tragedies and small moments that had led all of us to right now.

"Watch out for her," Toby told Grayson when the border of Blake's property came into sight. "Take care of each other." The press had been cleared out, but Oren and his men were still there waiting—and so was Jameson Winchester Hawthorne.

Grayson saw his brother standing there, and he answered on behalf of both of them. "We will."

CHAPTER 85

"The knight returns with the damsel in distress," Jameson declared as I made my way toward him. He glanced toward Grayson. "You're the damsel."

"I figured," Grayson deadpanned.

"What are you doing here?" I asked Jameson, but the truth was, I didn't care why he'd come—only that he was here. I'd won—after everything, *I had won*—and Jameson was the only person on the planet capable of fully understanding exactly how it had felt the moment I'd realized that my plan was going to work.

The rush. The thrill. The adrenaline-soaked awe.

The moment victory had been within my grasp had been like standing at the edge of the world's most powerful waterfall, the roar of the moment blocking out everything else.

It was like jumping off a cliff and finding out you could fly.

It was like Jameson and me and Jameson-and-me, and I wanted to live it all over again with him.

"I thought you could use a ride home," Jameson told me. I looked past him, expecting to see the McLaren or one of the Bugattis or the Aston Martin Valkyrie, but instead, my gaze landed on a helicopter—smaller than the one Oren had flown here.

"Pretty sure you aren't allowed to land a helicopter there," Grayson told his brother.

"You know what they say about permission and forgiveness," Jameson replied, then he focused back on me with a familiar look—equal parts *I dare you* and *I'll never let you go.* "Want to learn to fly?"

That night, I turned the cube Toby had given me over in my hands. My finger caught on an edge, and I realized that it was made of interlocking pieces. Working slowly, I solved the puzzle, disassembling the cube and laying the pieces out in front of me.

On each one, he'd carved a word.

I

See

So

Much

Of

Your

Mother

In

You

And that, even more than the moment I'd defeated Blake, was when I knew.

The next morning, before anyone else was awake, I went to the Great Room and lit a fire in the massive fireplace. I could have done this in my own room—or in any of the other dozen fireplaces in Hawthorne House—but it felt right to return to the room where the will had been read. I could almost see ghosts here: all of us, in that moment.

Me, thinking how life-changing inheriting a few thousand dollars would be.

The Hawthornes, learning the old man had left their fortune to me.

The flames flickered higher and higher in the fireplace, and I looked down at the papers in my hand: the trust paperwork Alisa had drawn up.

"What are you doing?" Libby padded toward me, wearing house shoes shaped like coffins and stifling a yawn.

I held up the papers. "If I sign this, it will tie my assets up in a trust—at least for a little while."

All that money. All that power.

Libby looked from me to the fireplace. "Well," she said as chipper as anyone wearing her *other* I EAT MORNING PEOPLE shirt had ever sounded, "what are you waiting for?"

I looked down at the trust paperwork, up at the fireplace—and tossed it all in. As the flames licked at the pages, devouring the legalese and, with it, the option to foist the power and responsibility I'd been given off on anyone else, I felt something in me begin to loosen, like the petals of a tulip opening to the slightest bloom.

I could do this.

I would do this.

If the past year had been any kind of test—I was ready.

I started taking the leather notebook Grayson had given me everywhere. I didn't have a year to make my plans. I had days. And yes, there were financial advisors and a legal team and a status quo that I could lean into if I wanted to buy myself time, but that wasn't what I wanted.

That wasn't the plan.

Deep down, I knew what I wanted to do. What I needed to do. And all of the lawyers and financial advisors and power players in the state of Texas—they weren't going to like it.

CHAPTER 86

On the biggest night of my life, I stood in front of a full-length mirror wearing a deep red ball gown fit for a queen. The color was unbearably rich, darker than a ruby but just as luminescent. Golden thread and delicate jewels combined to form understated vines that twisted and turned their way up the full skirt. The bodice was plain, custom fit to my body, with airy, translucent red sleeves that kissed my wrists.

Around my neck, I wore a single teardrop diamond.

Five hours and twelve minutes to go. Anticipation built inside me. Soon, my year at Hawthorne House would be up.

Nothing would ever be the same again.

"Regretting letting Xander talk you into this party?"

I turned from my mirror to the doorway, where Jameson stood wearing his white tuxedo—with a red vest this time, the same deep color as my dress. His jacket was unbuttoned, the black bow tie around his neck a little crooked and a little loose.

"It's hard to regret Hawthornes in tuxedos," I told him, a smile pulling at my lips as I walked to join him. "And tonight is going to be my kind of affair."

We were calling it the Countdown Party. *Like New Year's Eve,*

Xander had said, making his pitch for the festivities, *but at midnight, you're a billionaire!*

Jameson held out a hand, palm up. I took it, our fingers intertwining, the tip of my index finger grazing a small scar on the inside of his.

"Where to first, Heiress?"

I grinned. Unlike the introvert's ball, tonight was of my design, a rotating party where we would be spending one hour each in five different locations in Hawthorne House, counting our way down to midnight. The guest list was small—the usual suspects minus Max, who was stuck at college and would be joining via video call near the end of the party. "The sculpture garden."

Jameson's green eyes made a study of my face. "And what will we be doing in the sculpture garden?" he asked, an appropriate amount of suspicion in his tone.

I smiled. "Guess."

"The name of the game is Hide and Go Soak." Wearing a brilliant-blue tuxedo that looked like it belonged on the red carpet, and holding what had to be the world's biggest water gun, Xander was truly in his element. "The objective: utter aqua domination."

Five minutes later, I ducked behind a bronze sculpture of Theseus and the Minotaur. Libby was already back there, squatting on the ground, her vintage 1950s dress bunched up around her thighs.

"How are you feeling?" Libby asked me, keeping her voice low. "Big night."

I peeked out around the Minotaur's haunches, then retreated again. "Right now, I'm feeling *hunted.*" I grinned. "How are you?"

"Ready." Libby looked down at the water balloons she held in each hand—and at her twin tattoos: *SURVIVOR* on one wrist, and on the other... *TRUST.*

Footsteps. I braced myself just as Nash scaled Theseus and landed between Libby and me, holding what appeared to be a *melted* water gun. "Jamie and Gray have joined forces. Xander has a blowtorch. This is never good." Nash looked to me. "You're still armed. Good. Steady and calm, kid. No mercy."

Libby leaned around Nash to catch my eyes. "Remember," she told me, her eyes dancing, "there's no such thing as fighting dirty if you win."

I turned my water gun on Nash right as she creamed him with a water balloon.

At eight, the party moved indoors to the climbing wall. Jameson sidled up to me. "Soaking wet in a ball gown," he murmured. "This could be a challenge."

I wrung out my hair and flicked water his way. "I'm up for it."

At nine, we made our way to the bowling alley. At ten, we headed for the pottery—as in, a room with potting wheels and a kiln.

By the time eleven o'clock rolled around and we made our way down the labyrinthine halls of Hawthorne House to the arcade, our gowns and tuxes had been soaked, ripped, and spattered with clay. I was exhausted, sore, and filled with an exhilaration that defied description.

This was it.

This was *the* night.

This was everything.

This was *us.*

In the arcade, four private chefs met us, each with a signature dish to present. *Slow-braised beef soup served with pork buns so tender they should be illegal. Lobster risotto.* The first two courses nearly undid me, and that was before I bit into a sushi roll that looked like a work of art just as the final chef set our dessert on fire.

I looked to Oren. He was the one who'd cleared the private chefs to come here tonight. "You have to try this," I told him. "All of it."

I watched as Oren gave in and tasted a pork bun, and then I felt someone else watching me. Grayson was wearing a silver tuxedo with sharp, angular lines, no bow tie, the shirt buttoned all the way up.

I thought he might keep his distance, but he strode over to me, his expression assessing. "You have a plan," he commented, his voice low and smooth and sure.

My heart rate ticked up. I didn't just have a plan. I had *A Plan*. "I wrote it down," I told Grayson. "And then I rewrote it, again and again."

He was the Hawthorne I'd thought of the most as I was doing it, the one whose reaction I could least predict.

"I'm glad," Grayson told me, the words slow and deliberate, "that it was you." He took a step back, clearing the way for Jameson to slide in next to me.

"Have you decided yet," Jameson asked me, "what room you're going to add on to Hawthorne House this year?"

I wondered if he could feel my anticipation, if he had any idea what we were counting down *to*. "I've made a lot of decisions," I said.

Alisa hadn't arrived yet, but she would be here soon.

"If you're planning to build a death-defying obstacle course on the south side of the Black Wood," Xander said, bouncing up, high off a Skee-Ball victory, "count me in! I have a lead on where we can get a reasonably priced two-story-tall teeter-totter."

I grinned. "What would you do," I asked Jameson, "if you were adding on a room?"

Jameson pulled my body back against his. "Indoor skydiving

complex, accessible from a secret passage at the base of the climbing wall. Four stories tall, looks just like another turret from the outside."

"Please." Thea sauntered over holding a pool cue. She was wearing a long silver dress that left wide strips of bronze skin on display and was slit to the thigh. "The correct answer is obviously *ballroom*."

"The foyer is as big as a ballroom," I pointed out. "Pretty sure it's been used that way for decades."

"And yet," Thea countered, "it remains *not a ballroom*." She turned back toward the pool table, where she and Rebecca were facing off against Libby and Nash. Bex leaned over the table, lining up what looked to be an impossible shot, her green velvet tuxedo pulling against her chest, her dark red hair combed to one side and falling into her face

The world had accepted my account of Will Blake's death. The blame was laid squarely at the feet of Tobias Hawthorne. But once Toby had appeared, miraculously alive, and announced that he was changing his name to Tobias Blake, it hadn't taken the press long to piece together that he was Will's son—or to start speculating about who Toby's biological mother was.

Rebecca had made it clear that she still didn't regret stepping into the light.

She sank the shot, and Thea strolled back toward her, shooting Nash a gloating look. "Still feeling cocky, cowboy?"

"Always," Nash drawled.

"That," Libby said, her eyes catching his, "is an understatement."

Nash smirked. "Thirsty?" he asked my sister.

Libby poked him in the chest. "There's a cowboy hat in the refrigerator, isn't there?"

She looked down at her wrists, then stalked over to the

refrigerator and pulled out a pink soda and a black velvet cowboy hat. "I'll wear this hat," she told Nash, "if *you* paint your nails black."

Nash gave her what could only be described as a *cowboy smile*. "Fingers or toes?"

A yip behind me had me turning toward the doorway. Alisa stood there holding a very wiggly puppy. "I found her in the gallery," she informed me dryly. "Barking at a Monet."

Xander took the puppy and held her up, crooning at her. "No eating Monets," he baby-talked. "Bad Tiramisu." He gave her the world's biggest, goofiest smile. "Bad dog. Just for that . . . you have to cuddle Grayson."

Xander dumped the puppy on his brother.

"Are you ready for this?" Alisa asked beside me as Grayson let the puppy lick his nose and challenged his brothers to a round of hold-the-puppy pinball.

"As ready as I'm ever going to be."

Thirty minutes to go. Twenty. Ten. No amount of winning or losing at pool, air hockey, or foosball, no amount of puppy pinball or trying to beat the high score on a dozen different arcade games could distract me from the way the clock was ticking down.

Three minutes.

"The trick to a good poker face," Jameson murmured, "isn't keeping your face blank. It's thinking about something other than your cards—the same something the whole time." Jameson Winchester Hawthorne offered me a hand, and for the second time that night, I took it. He pulled me in for a slow dance, the kind that required no music. "You've got your poker face on now, Heiress."

I thought about flying around a racetrack, standing on the edge of the roof, riding on the back of his motorcycle, dancing barefoot on the beach. "Gen H verity," I said.

Jameson arched a brow. "As in generational truth for people far older than us?"

"It's your anagram," I told him, "for *everything*."

My phone rang before he could reply, a video call from Max. I answered.

"Am I in time for the countdown?" she asked, yelling over what appeared to be very loud music.

"Do you have your champagne?" I asked.

She brandished a flute. Right on cue, Alisa appeared beside me, holding a tray of the same. I took a glass and met her eyes. *It's almost time.*

"Piotr," Max said darkly, "absolutely refuses to have a glass on duty. He did, however, pick a bodyguard theme song. I threatened him with show tunes."

"That's my girl!" Xander bellowed.

"Woman," Max corrected.

"That's my woman! In a completely not possessive and absolutely unpatriarchal kind of way!"

Max lifted her glass to toast him. "Elf yeah."

"It's time." Jameson said. I leaned into him as the others crowded around. "Ten... nine... eight..."

Jameson, Grayson, Xander, and Nash.

Libby, Thea, and Rebecca.

Me.

Alisa held a glass of champagne but stood back from the group. She was the only one who knew what was about to happen.

"Three..."

"...two..."

"...one."

"Happy New Year!" Xander yelled. The next thing I knew,

confetti was flying everywhere. I had no idea where Xander had gotten confetti, but he continued to produce it, seemingly out of nowhere.

"Happy new life," Jameson corrected. He kissed me like it was New Year's Eve, and I savored it.

I'd survived a year in Hawthorne House. I had fulfilled the conditions of Tobias Hawthorne's will. I was a billionaire. One of the richest, most powerful people on the planet.

And I had *A Plan*.

"Shall I?" Alisa asked me. Nash's eyes narrowed. He knew her—and that meant he knew quite well when she was up to something.

"Do it," I told Alisa.

She turned the flat-screen television on and to a twenty-four-hour financial channel. It took a minute or two, but then the *BREAKING NEWS* beacon flashed across the screen.

"Precisely what kind of breaking news?" Grayson asked me.

I let the reporter answer for me. "We've just received word that Hawthorne heiress Avery Grambs has officially inherited the billions left to her by the late Tobias Hawthorne. After estate taxes and taking into account appreciation over the past year, the current value of the inheritance is estimated to be upward of thirty billion dollars. Ms. Grambs has announced—"

The reporter cut off, the words dying in his throat.

For the second time in my life, I felt every pair of eyes in a room turn to me. There was an eerie symmetry between this moment and the moment right before Mr. Ortega had read the final terms of Tobias Hawthorne's will.

"Ms. Grambs has announced," the reporter tried again, his voice strangled, "that as of midnight, she has signed paperwork transferring ninety-four percent of her inheritance into a charitable trust to be distributed in its entirety in the next five years."

It was done. It was legal. I couldn't have undone it even if I'd wanted to.

Thea was the first one to break the silence. "What the hell?"

Nash turned to his ex-fiancée. "You helped her give away all that money?"

Alisa raised her chin. "The partners at the firm didn't even know."

Nash let out a low chuckle. "You are so getting fired."

Alisa smiled—not the tight, professional smile she normally used, but a real one. "Job security isn't everything." She shrugged. "And as it so happens, I've accepted a new position at a charitable trust."

I couldn't quite bring myself to look at Jameson. Or Grayson. Or even Xander or Nash. I hadn't asked for their permission. I wasn't going to be asking for forgiveness, either. Instead, I thrust my chin out, the way Alisa had. "You'll all be receiving your invitations to join the board of the Hannah the Same Backward as Forward Foundation soon."

Silence.

This time, it was Grayson who broke it. "You want us to help you give it away?"

I met his eyes. "I want you to help me find the best ideas and the best people to determine how to give it all away."

Libby frowned. "What about the Hawthorne Foundation?" In addition to Tobias Hawthorne's fortune, I'd also inherited control of his charitable enterprise.

"Zara's agreed to stay on for a few years while I'm otherwise occupied," I answered. The Hawthorne Foundation had its own charter, which laid out the minimum and maximum percentage of its assets that could be given away each year. I couldn't empty it out—but I could make sure that my foundation had different rules.

That my inheritance wouldn't stay *earmarked* for charity for long.

Grinning, I handed Libby a sheet of paper.

"What's this?" she asked.

"It's account information for about a dozen different websites I signed you up for," I told her. "Mutual aid, mostly, and microloans to women entrepreneurs in the developing world. The new foundation will be handling official charitable giving, but we both know what it's like to need help and have nowhere to go. I've set aside ten million a year for you—for that."

Before she could reply, I tossed something to Nash. He caught it, then examined what I'd tossed him. *Keys.*

"What's this?" he drawled, his accent thick with amusement at this entire turn of events.

"Those," I told him, "are the keys to my sister's new cupcake truck."

Libby stared at me, her eyes round, her lips making an O. "I can't accept this, Ave."

"I know." I smirked. "That's why I gave the keys to Nash."

Before I could say anything else, Jameson stepped in front of me. "You're giving it away," he said, his expression as much of a mystery to me as it had been the day we met. "Almost everything the old man left to you, everything he chose you *for*—"

"I'm keeping Hawthorne House," I told him. "And more than enough money to maintain it. I might even keep a vacation home or two—after I've seen them all."

After *we* had seen them all.

"If Tobias Hawthorne were here," Thea declared, "he would *lose it.*"

All that money. All that power. Dispersed, where no one person would ever control it again.

"I guess that's what happens," Jameson said, his eyes never leaving mine as his lips curled upward, "when you take a very risky gamble."

ONE YEAR LATER...

"I'm here today with Avery Grambs. Heiress. Philanthropist. World changer—and at only nineteen years old. Avery, tell us, what is it like to be in your position at such a young age?"

I'd prepared for this question and for every question the interviewer might ask. She was the only one I'd granted an interview to in the past year, a media maven whose name was synonymous with savvy and success—and, more importantly, a humanitarian herself.

"Fun?" I answered, and she chuckled. "I don't mean to sound cavalier," I said, projecting the sincerity I felt. "I am fully aware that I am pretty much the luckiest person on the planet."

Landon had told me that the art to an interview like this one—intimate, much anticipated, with an interviewer who was almost as much of a draw as I was—was to make it sound like a conversation, to make the audience feel like we were just two women talking. Honest. Open.

"And the thing is," I continued, the awe in my voice echoing through the room in Hawthorne House where the interview was taking place, "it never really becomes normal. You don't just get used to it."

Here in this room, which the staff had taken to calling the

Nook, it was easy to feel awed. The Nook was small by Hawthorne House standards, but every aspect of it, from the repurposed wood floors to the ridiculously comfortable reading chairs, bore my mark.

"You can go anywhere," the interviewer said, quietly matching the awe in my voice. "Do anything."

"And I have," I said. Built-in shelves lined the Nook's walls. Every place I went, I found a keepsake—a reminder of the adventures I'd had there. Art, a book in the local language, a stone from the ground, something that had spoken to me.

"You've gone everywhere, done everything..." The interviewer smiled knowingly. "With Jameson Hawthorne."

Jameson Winchester Hawthorne.

"You're smiling," she told me.

"You would, too," I told her, "if you knew Jameson." He was exactly what he'd always been—a thrill chaser, a sensation seeker, a risk taker—and he was so much more.

"How did he react when he found out that you were giving so much of the family's fortune away?"

"He was shocked at first," I admitted. "But after that, it became a game—to all of them."

"All the Hawthornes?"

I tried *not* to smile too big this time. "All the boys."

"The boys, as in the Hawthorne brothers. Half the world is in love with them—now more than ever."

That wasn't a question, so I didn't answer.

"You said that after the shock of your decision wore off, giving away the money became a game to the Hawthorne brothers?"

Everything's a game, Avery Grambs. The only thing we get to decide in this life is if we play to win. "We're in a race against the clock to find the right causes and the right organizations to give the money to," I explained.

"You set up your foundation with the stipulation that all of the money had to be gone in five years. Why?"

That was more of a softball question than she realized. "Big changes require big actions," I said. "Hoarding the money and doling it out slowly over time never felt like the right call."

"So *you* put out a call—for experts."

"Experts," I confirmed. "Academics, people with boots on the ground—and even just people with big ideas. We had open applications for spots on the board, and there are more than a hundred of us working at the foundation now. Our team includes everyone from Nobel Prize and MacArthur genius award winners to humanitarian leaders, medical professionals, domestic abuse survivors, incarcerated persons, and a full dozen activists under the age of eighteen. Together, we work to generate and evaluate action plans."

"And review proposals." The interviewer kept the same thoughtful tone. "Anyone can submit a proposal to the Hannah the Same Backward as Forward Foundation."

"Anyone," I confirmed. "We want the best ideas and the best people. You can be anyone, from anywhere. You can feel like you're no one. We want to hear from you."

"Where did you get the name for the foundation?"

I thought of Toby, of my mom. "That," I told the whole world watching, "is a mystery."

"And speaking of mysteries..." The shift in tone told me that we were about to get serious. "Why?"

The interviewer let that question hang in the air, then continued. "Why, having been left one of the largest fortunes in the world, would you give almost all of it away? Are you a saint?"

I snorted, which probably wasn't a good look with millions watching, but I couldn't help it. "If I were a saint," I said, "do you really think I would have kept *two billion dollars* for myself?" I shook my head, my hair escaping from behind my shoulders as I did. "Do you understand how much money that is?"

I wasn't being combative, and I hoped my tone made that clear.

"I could spend a hundred million dollars a year," I explained, "every year for the rest of my life, and there's still a good chance that I would have more money when I died than I have right now."

Money made money—and the more of it you had, the higher the rate of return.

"And frankly," I said, "I *can't* spend a hundred million dollars a year. Literally can't! So, no, I'm not a saint. If you really think about it, I'm pretty selfish."

"Selfish," she repeated. "Giving away twenty-eight billion dollars? Ninety-four percent of all your assets, and you think people should be asking why you're not doing more?"

"Why not?" I said. "Someone told me once that fortunes like this one—at a certain point, it's not about the money, because you couldn't spend billions if you tried. It's about the power." I looked down. "And I just don't think anyone should have power like that, certainly not me."

I wondered if Vincent Blake was watching—or Eve, or any of the other high rollers I'd met since inheriting.

"And the Hawthorne family was really okay with that?" The interviewer asked. She wasn't combative, either. Just curious and deeply empathetic. "The boys? Grayson Hawthorne has dropped out of Harvard. Jameson Hawthorne has had brushes with the law on at least three continents in the past six months. It was recently reported that Xander Hawthorne is working as a mechanic."

Xander was working with Isaiah—both at his shop and on several pieces of new technology that they were *very* excited about. Grayson had dropped out of Harvard to turn the full force of his mind to the project of giving the money away. And the only reason Jameson had been arrested—or *almost* arrested—so many times was that he couldn't turn down dares.

Specifically, mine.

The only reason *I* hadn't made similar headlines was that I was better at not getting caught.

"You forgot Nash," I said easily. "He's tending bar and working as a cupcake taster on the weekends."

I was smiling now, emanating the kind of contentedness—not to mention amusement—that a person couldn't fake. The Hawthorne brothers weren't, as she'd suggested, going off the rails. They were—all of them—exactly where they were supposed to be.

They'd been sculpted by Tobias Hawthorne, formed and forged by the billionaire's hands. They were extraordinary, and for the first time in their lives, they weren't living under the weight of his expectations.

The interviewer caught my smile and shifted subjects—slightly. "Do you have any comments on rumors of Nash Hawthorne's engagement to your sister?"

"I don't pay much attention to rumors," I managed to say with a straight face.

"What's next for you, Avery? As you pointed out, you still have an incredibly massive fortune. Any plans?"

"Travel," I answered immediately. On the walls all around us, there were at least thirty souvenirs—but there were still so many places I hadn't been.

Places where Jameson hadn't yet taken an inadvisable dare.

Places we could fly.

"And," I continued, "after a gap year or two, I'll be enrolling as an actuarial science major at UConn."

"Actuarial science?" Her eyebrows skyrocketed. "At UConn."

“Statistical risk assessment,” I said. There were people out there who built models and algorithms, whose advice my financial advisors took. I had a lot to learn before I could start managing the risks all on my own.

And besides, the moment I’d said UConn, Jameson had started talking about Yale. *Do you think their secret societies could use a Hawthorne?*

“Okay, travel. College. What else?” The interviewer grinned. She was enjoying herself now. “You must have plans for something fun. This has been the ultimate Cinderella story. Give us just a taste of the kind of extravagance that most people can only dream of.”

The people watching were probably expecting me to talk about yachts or jewels or private planes—private islands, even. But I had other plans. “Actually,” I said, well aware of my tone changing as excitement bubbled up inside me, “I do have one fun idea.”

It was the reason I’d agreed to this interview. Subtly, I dipped my hand down to the side of my chair, where I’d tucked a golden card etched with a very complicated design.

“I already told you that it would be difficult for me to spend all the money that two billion dollars makes in a year,” I said, “but what I didn’t tell you is that I have no intention of growing my fortune. Each year, after I balance my expense sheet, take stock of any changes in my net worth, and calculate the difference, I’m earmarking the rest to be given away.”

“More charity?”

“I’m sure there will be a lot more charity work in my future, but this is for fun.” There wasn’t much I wanted to buy. I wanted experiences. I wanted to keep adding on to Hawthorne House, to maintain it and make sure the staff stayed employed. I wanted to make sure that no one I loved ever wanted for anything.

And I wanted *this.*

"Tobias Hawthorne wasn't a good man," I said seriously, "but he had a human side. He loved puzzles and riddles and games. Every Saturday morning, he would present his grandsons with a challenge—clues to decipher, connections to make, a complicated multistage puzzle to solve. The game would take the boys all over Hawthorne House."

I could picture them as children as easily as I could picture them now. *Jameson. Grayson. Xander. Nash.* Tobias Hawthorne had been a real piece of work. He'd played to win, crossed lines that should never be crossed, expected perfection.

But the games? The ones the boys had played growing up, the ones *I* had played? Those games hadn't *made* us extraordinary.

They'd showed us that we already were.

"If there's one thing that the Hawthornes have taught me," I said, "it's that I like a challenge. I like to *play*."

As Jameson had said once, there would always be more mysteries to solve, but I knew in my core that we'd played the old man's last game.

So now I was planning one of my own. "Every year, I'll be hosting a contest with substantial, life-changing prize money. Some years, the game will be open to the general public. Others . . . well, maybe you'll find yourself on the receiving end of the world's most exclusive invitation."

This wasn't the most responsible way to spend money, but once I'd had the idea, I couldn't shake it, and once I'd mentioned it to Jameson, there was no turning back.

"This game." The interviewer's eyes were alight. "These puzzles. They'll be of your making?"

I smiled. "I'll have help." Not just the boys. Alisa had sometimes joined in Tobias Hawthorne's games growing up. Oren was running logistics for me. Rebecca and Thea, in combined force, were downright *diabolical* in their contributions to what I had been calling *The Grandest Game.*

"When will the first game start?" the woman across from me asked.

That was the question I'd been waiting for. I held up the gold card in my hand and brandished it at the camera—design out.

"The game," I said, my voice ripe with promise, "starts right now."

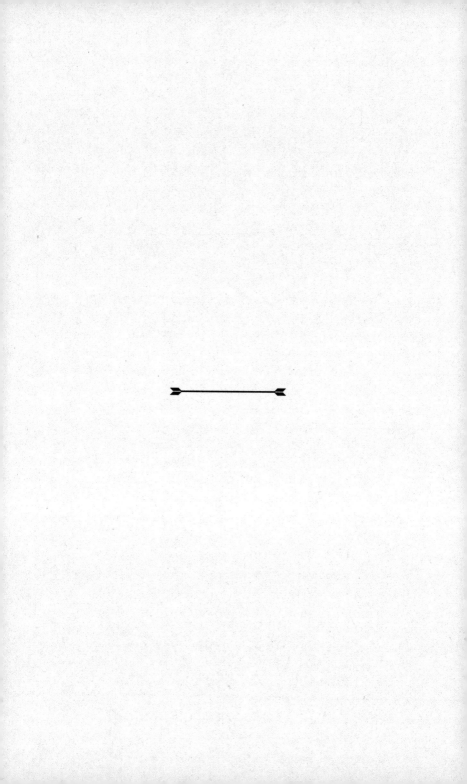

ACKNOWLEDGMENTS

When I wrote *The Inheritance Games* and *The Hawthorne Legacy*, I didn't know for certain whether they would find a big enough audience to justify the publication of a third book. I had hoped and planned—SO MUCH PLANNING—to be able to share the twists and turns that I knew awaited Avery, but *The Final Gambit* only exists because of the incredible support the first two books have received from my publishing team, booksellers, librarians, and readers. I am truly grateful to everyone who made this book possible.

My editor, Lisa Yoskowitz, has been a tireless advocate for these books from the moment she first read *The Inheritance Games*. It's hard to describe how valuable her editorial insights have been. So many of my favorite parts of *The Final Gambit* are the direct result of Lisa's incredible instincts for what a story needs and her ability to inspire me to do everything I can to take the characters, plot, and world to the next level. Further, as grateful as I am for our creative collaboration, I am just as grateful for the grace, understanding, and support Lisa offers at every stage of the publishing process. I wrote this book during the first year of my new baby's life, in the middle of a pandemic, while dealing with spotty childcare. Lisa, I could not have done it without you!

My agent, Elizabeth Harding, has been a champion for my books since I was barely more than a teenager myself. Eighteen years and twenty-three books later, I am so thankful for everything she has done and continues to do for me and for my books. Elizabeth, working with you is a joy.

I owe an enormous debt of gratitude to my amazing team at Little, Brown Books for Young Readers. I am in absolute awe of the creativity, vision, and work that has gone into getting this series into so many hands! Thank you to cover designer Karina Granda and artist Katt Phatt for creating the gorgeous cover for *The Final Gambit*. You have so perfectly captured this book, and the end result is nothing short of stunning! Another big thank-you goes out to production superstar Marisa Finkelstein, who helped work magic with our schedule to give me as much time with the book as I needed. Marisa, I appreciate all the work you did to make sure the book was what it needed to be when it needed to be—and under a tight schedule, no less!

Thank you also to Megan Tingley and Jackie Engel for their incredible support of this series; to Shawn Foster, Danielle Cantarella, Celeste Risko, Anna Herling, Katie Tucker, Claire Gamble, Leah CollinsLipsett, and Karen Torres for putting this book in front of readers *everywhere*; to Victoria Stapleton, Christie Michel, and Amber Mercado for everything they've done to connect libraries and young readers to the series; to Cheryl Lew, Savannah Kennelly, Emilie Polster, and Bill Grace for making and keeping these books so visible for so long; to Virginia Lawther, Olivia Davis, Jody Corbett, Barbara Bakowski, Su Wu, and Erin Slonaker for their help in getting *The Final Gambit* reader-ready; to Caitlyn Averett for her help at every stage of the process; to Lisa Cahn and Christie

Moreau for their work on the audiobooks for the series; and to Janelle DeLuise and Hannah Koerner for finding such a wonderful UK home for the series! Thank you also to my UK publishing team at Penguin Random House, especially Anthea Townsend, Phoebe Williams, Jane Griffiths, and Kat McKenna.

My incredible team at Curtis Brown has done more for the Inheritance Games series than I ever could have imagined possible! Huge thanks to Sarah Perillo for helping to bring the Inheritance Games series to readers all over the world and to Holly Frederick for working her magic on the television front! I am also incredibly grateful for the help of Mahalaleel M. Clinton, Michaela Glover, and Maddie Tavis.

I have wanted to be an author since I was five years old, and one of the most incredible things about living this dream has been becoming a part of an incredible community of young-adult authors. Thank you to Ally Carter, Maureen Johnson, E. Lockhart, and Karen M. McManus for being lovely conversation partners at the virtual events that helped launch this series. Rachel Vincent is always there when I need to talk out a part of the book I can't quite figure out, and I'm incredibly grateful for our weekly writing days! Thank you also to all my other writing friends; it's been a long time since I've seen many of you in person, but you are all the reason that the community I've found in writing feels like home.

Finally, thank you to my family. For years, while I was balancing a demanding day job, writing, and being a mom to three young kids, people would ask, *How do you do it all?* And the answer has always been *I'm not doing it all alone; I have so much help and support.* Thank you to my parents for being the best parents a person could possibly ask for. They are my biggest fans, an incredible source of support, and the ones who will get in a car and drive two hours to watch my kids and bring me food when there just aren't enough hours in the day. My dad, Bill Barnes, also helped proofread this book, and both my parents helped me create the world the Hawthornes inhabit by answering tons of questions on a whole range of topics!

Thank you to my husband, Anthony, who is a partner in every sense of the word. I cannot imagine a better husband or father, and I am so grateful for everything you do. Finally, thank you to my three small children, the oldest of whom was five when I started writing this book, for the cuddles, learning to sometimes entertain yourselves, and bringing so much joy to my life.

TURN THE PAGE TO DISCOVER WHAT'S NEXT FOR THE HAWTHORNE BROTHERS IN THIS SNEAK PEEK OF

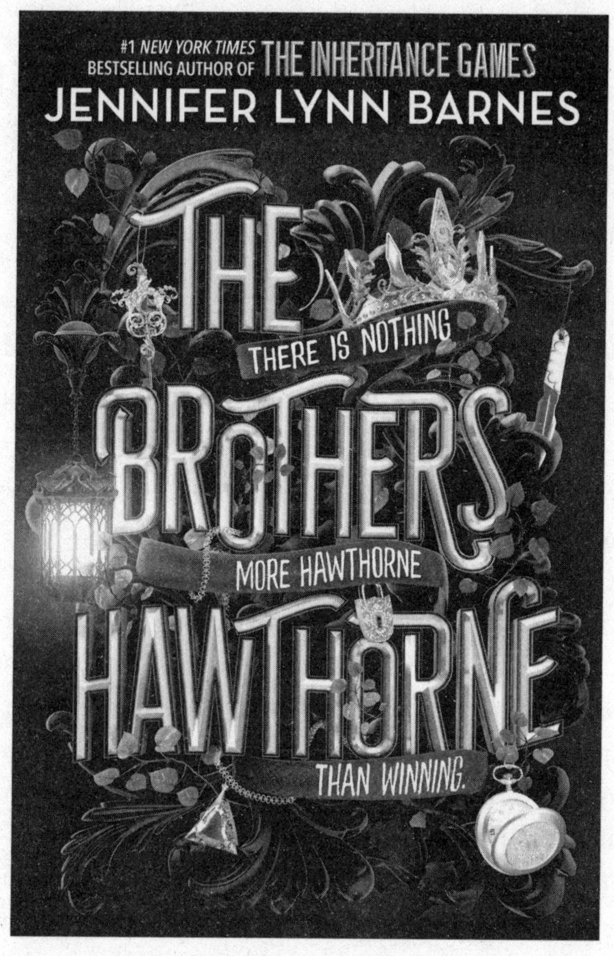

CHAPTER 1

GRAYSON

Faster. Grayson Hawthorne was power and control. His form was flawless. He'd long ago perfected the art of visualizing his opponent, *feeling* each strike, channeling his body's momentum into every block, every attack.

But you could always be faster.

After his tenth time through the sequence, Grayson stopped, sweat dripping down his bare chest. Keeping his breathing even and controlled, he knelt in front of what remained of their childhood tree house, unrolled his pack, and surveyed his choices: three daggers, two with ornate hilts and one understated and smooth. It was this last blade that Grayson picked up.

Knife in hand, Grayson straightened, his arms by his side. Mind, clear. Body, free of tension. *Begin.* There were many styles of knife fighting, and the year he was thirteen, Grayson had studied them all. Of course, billionaire Tobias Hawthorne's grandsons had never merely *studied* anything. Once they'd chosen a focus, they were expected to live it, breathe it, master it.

And this was what Grayson had learned that year: Stance was everything. You didn't move the blade. You moved, and the blade moved. Faster. *Faster.* It had to feel natural. It had to *be* natural. The moment your muscles tensed, the moment you stopped breathing, the moment you broke your stance instead of flowing from one to the next, you lost.

And Hawthornes didn't lose.

"When I told you to get a hobby, this isn't what I meant."

Grayson ignored Xander's presence for as long as it took to finish the sequence—and throw the dagger with exacting precision at a low-hanging branch six feet away. "Hawthornes don't have hobbies," he told his little brother, walking to retrieve the blade. "We have specialties. Expertise."

"*Anything worth doing is worth doing well,*" Xander quoted, wiggling his eyebrows—one of which had only just started to grow back after an experiment gone wrong. "*And anything done well can be done better.*"

Why would a Hawthorne settle for better, a voice whispered in the back of Grayson's mind, *when they could be the best?*

Grayson closed his hand around the dagger's hilt and pulled. "I should be getting back to work."

"You are a man obsessed," Xander declared.

Grayson secured the dagger in its holder, then rolled the pack back up, tying it closed. "I have twenty-eight billion reasons to be obsessed."

Avery had set an impossible task for herself—and for them. Five years to give away more than twenty-eight billion dollars. That was the majority of the Hawthorne fortune. They'd spent the past seven months just assembling the foundation's board and advisory committee.

"We have five more months to nail down the first three billion in donations," Grayson stated crisply, "and I promised Avery I would be there with her every step of the way."

Promises mattered to Grayson Hawthorne—and so did Avery Kylie Grambs. The girl who had inherited their grandfather's fortune. The stranger who had become one of them.

"Speaking as someone with friends, a girlfriend, and a small army of robots, I just think you could do with a little more balance in your life," Xander opined. "An *actual* hobby? Down time?"

Grayson gave him a look. "You've filed at least three patents since school let out for the summer last month, Xan."

Xander shrugged. "They're recreational patents."

Grayson snorted, then assessed his brother. "How *is* Isaiah?" he asked softly.

Growing up, none of the Hawthorne brothers had known their fathers' identities—until Grayson had discovered that his was Sheffield *Grayson*. Nash's was a man named Jake *Nash*. And Xander's was Isaiah *Alexander*. Of the three men, only Isaiah actually deserved to be called a father. He and Xander had filed those "recreational patents" together.

"We're supposed to be talking about you," Xander said stubbornly.

"I should get back to work," Grayson reiterated, adopting a tone that was very effective at putting everyone *except* his brothers in their place. "And despite what Avery and Jameson seem to believe, I don't need a babysitter."

"You don't need a babysitter," Xander agreed cheerfully, "and I am definitely not writing a book entitled *The Care and Feeding of Your Broody Twenty-Year-Old Brother.*"

Grayson's eyes narrowed to slits.

"I can assure you," Xander said with great solemnity, "it doesn't have pictures."

Before Grayson could summon an appropriate threat in response, his phone buzzed. Assuming it was the figures he'd requested, Grayson picked the phone up, only to discover a text from Nash. He looked back at Xander and knew instantly that his youngest brother had received the same message.

Grayson was the one who read the fateful missive out loud: "Nine-one-one."

CHAPTER 2

JAMESON

The roar of the falls. The mist in the air. The feel of the back of Avery's body against the front of his. Jameson Winchester Hawthorne was *hungry*—for this, for her, for everything, all of it, *more*.

Iguazú Falls was the world's largest waterfall system. The walkway they were standing on took them right up to the edge of an incredible drop-off. Staring out at the falls, Jameson felt the lure of *more*. He eyed the railing. "Do you dare me?" he murmured into the back of Avery's head.

She reached back to touch his jaw. "Absolutely not."

Jameson's lips curved—a teasing smile, a wicked one. "You're probably right, Heiress."

She turned her head to the side and met his gaze. "Probably?"

Jameson looked back at the falls. *Unstoppable. Off limits. Deadly.* "Probably."

They were staying in a villa built on stilts and surrounded by jungle, no one around for miles but the two of them, Avery's security team, and the jaguars roaring in the distance.

Jameson felt Avery's approach before he heard it.

"Heads or tails?" She leaned against the railing, brandishing a bronze-and-silver coin. Her brown hair was falling out of its ponytail, her long-sleeved shirt still damp from the falls.

Jameson brought his hand to her hair tie, then worked it slowly and gently down—and off. *Heads or tails* was an invitation. A challenge. *You kiss me, or I kiss you.* "Dealer's choice, Heiress."

"If I'm the dealer..." Avery placed a palm flat on his chest, her eyes daring him to do something about that wet shirt of hers. "We're going to need cards."

The things we could do, Jameson thought, *with a deck of cards.* But before he could voice some of the more tantalizing possibilities, the satellite phone buzzed. Only five people had the number: his brothers, her sister, and her lawyer. Jameson groaned.

The text was from Nash. Nine seconds later, when the satellite phone rang, Jameson answered. "Delightful timing, as always, Gray."

"I take it you received Nash's message?"

"We've been summoned," Jameson intoned. "You planning to play hooky again?"

Each Hawthorne brother got a single nine-one-one a year. The code didn't mean *emergency* so much as *I want you all here,* but if one brother texted, the others came, no questions asked. Ignoring a nine-one-one led to... consequences.

"If you say *one word* about leather pants," Grayson bit out. "I will—"

"Did you say *leather pants*?" Jameson was enjoying this way too much. "You're breaking up, Gray. Are you asking me to send you a picture of the incredibly tight leather pants you had to wear the one time you ignored a nine-one-one?"

"Do not send me a picture—"

"A video?" Jameson asked loudly. "You want a video of yourself singing karaoke in the leather pants?"

Avery plucked the phone from his hands. She knew as well as Jameson did that there would be no ignoring Nash's summons, and she had a bad habit of *not* tormenting his brothers.

"It's me, Grayson." Avery examined Nash's text herself. "We'll see you in London."

TURN THE PAGE TO START ANOTHER UNPUTDOWNABLE SERIES FROM JENNIFER LYNN BARNES!

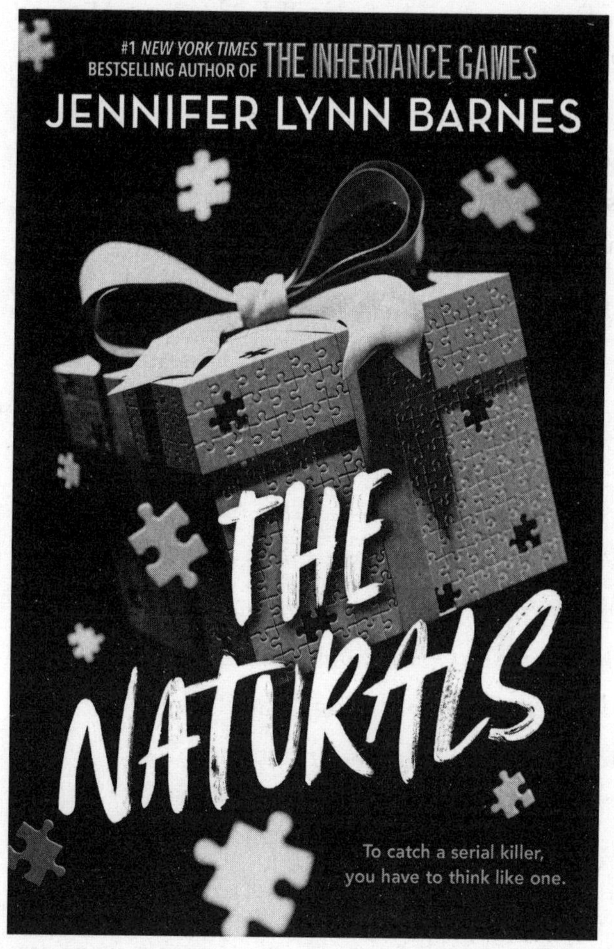

YOU

You've chosen and chosen well. Maybe this one will be the one who stops you. Maybe she'll be different. Maybe she'll be enough.

The only thing that is certain is that she's special.

You think it's her eyes—not the color: an icy, see-through blue. Not the lashes, or the shape, or the way she doesn't need eyeliner to give them the appearance of a cat's.

No, it's what's behind those icy blues that brings the audience out in droves. You feel it, every time you look at her. The certainty. The knowing. That otherworldly glint she uses to convince people that she's the real deal.

Maybe she is.

Maybe she really can see things. Maybe she knows things. Maybe she's everything she claims to be and more. But watching her, counting her breaths, you smile, because deep down, you know that she isn't going to stop you.

You don't really want her to stop you.

She's fragile.

Perfect.

Marked.

And the one thing this so-called psychic won't see coming is you.

CHAPTER 1

The hours were bad. The tips were worse, and the majority of my coworkers definitely left something to be desired, but *c'est la vie*, *que será será*, insert foreign language cliché of your choice here. It was a summer job, and that kept Nonna off my back. It also prevented my various aunts, uncles, and kitchen-sink cousins from feeling like they had to offer me temporary employment in their restaurant/butcher shop/legal practice/boutique. Given the size of my father's very large, very extended (and very Italian) family, the possibilities were endless, but it was always a variation on the same theme.

My dad lived half a world away. My mother was missing, presumed dead. I was everyone's problem and nobody's.

Teenager, presumed troubled.

"Order up!"

With practiced ease, I grabbed a plate of pancakes (side

of bacon) with my left hand and a two-handed breakfast burrito (jalapeños on the side) with my right. If the SATs didn't go well in the fall, I had a real future ahead of me in the crappy diner industry.

"Pancakes with a side of bacon. Breakfast burrito, jalapeños on the side." I slid the plates onto the table. "Anything else I can get for you gentlemen?"

Before either of them opened their mouths, I knew exactly what these two were going to say. The guy on the left was going to ask for extra butter. And the guy on the right? He was going to need another glass of water before he could even *think* about those jalapeños.

Ten-to-one odds, he didn't even like them.

Guys who actually liked jalapeños didn't order them on the side. Mr. Breakfast Burrito just didn't want people to think he was a wuss—only the word he would have used wasn't *wuss*.

Whoa there, Cassie, I told myself sternly. *Let's keep it PG.*

As a general rule, I didn't curse much, but I had a bad habit of picking up on other people's quirks. Put me in a room with a bunch of English people, and I'd walk out with a British accent. It wasn't intentional—I'd just spent a lot of time over the years getting inside other people's heads.

Occupational hazard. Not mine. My mother's.

"Could I get a few more of these butter packets?" the guy on the left asked.

I nodded—and waited.

"More water," the guy on the right grunted. He puffed out his chest and ogled my boobs.

I forced a smile. "I'll be right back with that water." I managed to keep from adding *pervert* to the end of that sentence, but only just.

I was still holding out hope that a guy in his late twenties who pretended to like spicy food and made a point of staring at his teenage waitress's chest like he was training for the Ogling Olympics might be equally showy when it came to leaving tips.

Then again, I thought as I went for refills, *he might turn out to be the kind of guy who stiffs the little bitty waitress just to prove he can.*

Absentmindedly, I turned the details of the situation over in my mind: the way that Mr. Breakfast Burrito was dressed; his likely occupation; the fact that his friend, who'd ordered the pancakes, was wearing a much more expensive watch.

He'll fight to grab the check, then tip like crap.

I hoped I was wrong—but was fairly certain that I wasn't.

Other kids spent their preschool years singing their way through the ABCs. I grew up learning a different alphabet. Behavior, personality, environment—my mother called them the BPEs, and they were the tricks of her trade. Thinking that way wasn't the kind of thing you could just turn off—not even once you were old enough to understand that when your mother told people she was psychic, she was *lying*, and when she took their money, it was *fraud*.

Even now that she was gone, I couldn't keep from figuring people out, any more than I could give up breathing, blinking, or counting down the days until I turned eighteen.

"Table for one?" A low, amused voice jostled me back into reality. The voice's owner looked like the type of boy who would have been more at home in a country club than a diner. His skin was perfect, his hair artfully mussed. Even though he phrased his words like they were a question, they weren't—not really.

"Sure," I said, grabbing a menu. "Right this way."

A closer observation told me that Country Club was about my age. A smirk played across his perfect features, and he walked with the swagger of high school nobility. Just looking at him made me feel like a serf.

"This okay?" I asked, leading him to a table near the window.

"This is fine," he said, slipping into the chair. Casually, he surveyed the room with bulletproof confidence. "You get a lot of traffic in here on weekends?"

"Sure," I replied. I was starting to wonder if I'd lost the ability to speak in complex sentences. From the look on the boy's face, he probably was, too. "I'll give you a minute to look over the menu."

He didn't respond, and I spent my minute bringing Pancakes and Breakfast Burrito their checks, plural. I figured that if I split it in half, I might end up with half a decent tip.

"I'll be your cashier whenever you're ready," I said, fake smile firmly in place.

I turned back toward the kitchen and caught the boy by the window watching me. It wasn't an *I'm ready to order* stare. I wasn't sure what it was, actually—but every bone in my body told me it was *something*. The niggling sensation that there was a key detail that I was missing about this whole situation—about *him*—wouldn't go away. Boys like that didn't usually eat in places like this.

They didn't stare at girls like me.

Self-conscious and wary, I crossed the room.

"Did you decide what you'd like?" I asked. There was no getting out of taking his order, so I let my hair fall in my face, obscuring his view of it.

"Three eggs," he said, hazel eyes fixed on what he could see of mine. "Side of pancakes. Side of ham."

I didn't need to write the order down, but I suddenly found myself wishing for a pen, just so I'd have something to hold on to. "What kind of eggs?" I asked.

"You tell me." The boy's words caught me off guard.

"Excuse me?"

"Guess," he said.

I stared at him through the wisps of hair still covering my face. "You want me to guess how you want your eggs cooked?"

He smiled. "Why not?"

And just like that, the gauntlet was thrown.

"Not scrambled," I said, thinking out loud. Scrambled eggs were too average, too common, and this was a guy who liked to be a little bit different. Not too different, though, which ruled out poached—at least in a place like this. Sunny-side up would have been too messy for him; over hard wouldn't be messy enough.

"Over easy." I was as sure of the conclusion as I was of the color of his eyes. He smiled and closed his menu.

"Are you going to tell me if I was right?" I asked—not because I needed confirmation, but because I wanted to see how he would respond.

The boy shrugged. "Now, where would the fun be in that?"

I wanted to stay there, staring, until I figured him out, but I didn't. I put his order in. I delivered his food. The lunch rush snuck up on me, and by the time I went back to check on him, the boy by the window was gone. He hadn't even waited for his check—he'd just left twenty dollars on the table. I had just about decided that he could make me play guessing games to his heart's content for a twelve-dollar tip when I noticed the bill wasn't the only thing he'd left.

There was also a business card.

I picked it up. Stark white. Black letters. Evenly spaced. There was a seal in the upper left-hand corner, but relatively little text: a name, a job title, a phone number. Across the top of the card, there were four words, four little words that knocked the wind out of me as effectively as a jab to the chest.

I pocketed the card—and the tip. I went back to the kitchen. I caught my breath. And then I looked at it again.

Tanner Briggs. The name.

Special Agent. Job title.

Federal Bureau of Investigation.

Four words, but I stared at them so hard that my vision blurred and I could only make out three letters.

What in the world had I done to attract the attention of the FBI?

Kim Haynes Photography

JENNIFER LYNN BARNES

is the #1 *New York Times* bestselling author of more than twenty acclaimed young-adult novels, including the Inheritance Games trilogy, *The Brothers Hawthorne*, *Little White Lies*, *Deadly Little Scandals*, *The Lovely and the Lost*, and the Naturals series: *The Naturals*, *Killer Instinct*, *All In*, *Bad Blood*, and the novella *Twelve*. Jen is also a Fulbright Scholar with advanced degrees in psychology, psychiatry, and cognitive science. She received her PhD from Yale University in 2012 and was a professor of psychology and professional writing at the University of Oklahoma for many years. She invites you to find her online at jenniferlynnbarnes.com or follow her on Twitter @jenlynnbarnes.

MORE FROM

JENNIFER LYNN BARNES

THE NATURALS

DEBUTANTES

A MYSTERY

THE INHERITANCE GAMES

NOVL  LITTLE, BROWN AND COMPANY theNOVL.com